MURPHY'S LAWLESS

A TERRAN REPUBLIC NOVEL

CHARLES E. GANNON

&

GRIFFIN BARBER, KACEY EZELL, KEVIN IKENBERRY, CHRIS KENNEDY, MIKE MASSA, AND MARK WANDREY

BEYOND TERRA PRESS
VIRGINIA BEACH, VA

Chris Kennedy/Beyond Terra Press
2052 Bierce Dr.
Virginia Beach, VA 23454
http://chriskennedypublishing.com/

Cover Design by J Caleb Design.

Ordering Information:
Quantity sales. Special discounts are available on quantity purchases by corporations, associations, and others. For details, contact the "Special Sales Department" at the address above.

Murphy's Lawless/Charles E. Gannon -- 1st ed.
ISBN: 978-1648551062

Dedication

This book is dedicated to many people, because it took a whole lot of people to make it a reality.

Firstly, thanks to Chris Kennedy, who said "yes" to this project before I could finish telling him about it (really). Further thanks to Kevin Ikenberry, and then Mark Wandrey, who did the same soon after. As did those now-scattered members of the Lost Signals Crewe that convened and conspired with me at World Fantasy Con in Baltimore a few months later: Griffin Barber, Kacey Ezell, and Mike Massa.

Another huge thank you goes to Toni Weiskopf without whose blessings and support this project would never have made it onto the runway, let alone take wing and soar. Not a lot of publishers (whether traditional or start-up indies) can boast the inspired mix of personal kindness and professional craftiness that discerned this project as a win-win. Most would simply have seen it as a threat to exclusivity regarding a successful IP and would have killed it in its notional crib. Instead, at every step of the way, Toni's encouragement and material support has been unwavering.

Thanks also to my agent, Eleanor Wood of Spectrum Literary Agency, who generously gave of her time and peerless professional counsel as we came up with the basic contractual and governing documents that helped ensure this was not just a successful, but well-grounded, endeavor in today's extremely volatile marketplace.

And never last nor least, to my family: none of this would be possible if it wasn't for you.

But when all is said and done, it is you readers and fans of the series who made this unique project a stellar success (literally and figuratively). Without you, we wouldn't be here, doing what we love, and expanding a universe that has begun to take on a life of its own. So, all our thanks for coming along for the ride…which has only just begun!

November, 1993: Mogadishu

Chapter One

MOGADISHU

The Blackhawk banked, giving Murphy his last glimpse of Somalia. It was a mostly brown and tan expanse except for two dark epicenters of activity. The smaller of the two was home to the runways and tarmac above which they were rapidly rising. Around it was a gridwork of tents. Around those were angular defenses backed by outward-facing, Matchbox-sized vehicles and tiny figures. That was the American base in-theater. Other, smaller compounds were scattered around the city, more ragged but roughly analogous.

However, even the least orderly of those compounds were punctiliously arranged marvels compared to the far larger smudge at their approximate center, the smudge that marred the otherwise unexceptioned desert waste palette: Mogadishu—a sprawling, chaotic jumble of low, sunbaked buildings, tin-roofed shacks, and every other conceivable kind of rudimentary shelter. At the lowest end of the survival spectrum, he saw blue plastic hurricane tarps unevenly lashed to the sheared and crumbling walls of long abandoned colonial ruins, desperate havens from the punishing sun.

"Good riddance," breathed Melissa "Missy" Katano as she leaned sharply inboard, her nostrils pinched tight. You couldn't smell Mogadishu from up here, but it seemed that she wasn't willing to lean any closer than necessary to the source of the superheated stink.

She must have seen Murphy's small smile. "What? You like it here?"

He hadn't seen that question coming, so didn't have an answer ready. However, it was Murphy's good fortune that Dr. Hampson was there to lean over and observe in an almost fatherly tone, "Well sometimes, no matter how unpleasant a place might be, we don't want to leave all of it—or what we experienced there—behind."

The one SEAL on the chopper, who was going home after having had his tour extended twice, glanced over at the unexpected interjection by the doctor. He glanced briefly at Murphy, then turned his gaze back out the other open door, eyes fixed upon the broad, blue expanse of the Indian Ocean and the thin sprinkling of fishing boats upon it.

Murphy managed not to frown. Doc Hampson meant well, but every once in a while, his deep civilian roots showed through. Like in this case. Sent in-country to look at the head wounds of a congresswoman's son, he had done something that few military doctors were likely to do: stop by to take a quick look at a much less urgent case that was puzzling the base's medicos.

It was the case of one Rodger Y. Murphy, US Army, a hotshot young major who had experienced some mild unsteadiness in the wake of being a few meters too close to an improvised explosive device. He hadn't been close enough to be significantly roughed up by it. There were no concussion or open wounds, even though there were plenty of contusions on hands, knees, and back where the shockwave had rolled him in the dust along Mogadishu's Maxud Harbi Street. The young medicos were trying to figure out why the young major still had lingering difficulties when he tried to type a report or clean a weapon.

But Dr. Hampson looked at him for all of three minutes, leaned back, and pronounced the diagnosis that was also a life sentence. "Multiple sclerosis," Hampson had said frankly. "No question about it. Well, not much question, but if you conduct the standard battery, I think that's what you're going to find."

Which, of course, the medicos had no reason to suspect. What with shock trauma in a combat zone and no history of the disease, it was a million-to-one that Major Murphy was suffering the onset of an unlooked-for disease instead of after-effects of the trauma. Doctors with five times their experience would have been just as likely to misdiagnose.

Then again, there weren't a whole lot of doctors of Robert Hampson's caliber. Not in the whole world, and not when it came down to brain and neurological diagnosis and treatment. After Hampson had trundled out of the ward with his perennial good humor, the young medicos had clustered near Murphy's end of the ward, trading muttered reports about what they knew of the specialist. To hear them talk, he was either the elect of God or a deity himself when it came to nerves or the brain.

The doc was also a good guy—sometimes too good, Murphy reflected as the heavily built man leaned back into his seat, eclipsing a small, spare soldier seated on his other side. Hampson's reflex had been pure civvy: jumping into a conversation to help out a startled or rattled pal. But here, in this chopper, it wasn't a civilian world. It was a world of fighters and the people who worked with them. People who took care of themselves.

Of all of them, Katano was the closest to civilian, but she'd been in-country so long—trying to keep all the allies working on the same page, and supply and logistics flowing without completely ditching protocol—that she had almost as hard an edge as the soldiers and airmen and sailors she dealt with.

The rest of the compartment was filled with other weary faces that were just waiting out another ride in a shuddering Blackhawk. The SEAL officer was the size of a bear, but his young face was already seamed by lines that most people wouldn't acquire until well into their thirties. Next to him was a blue-eyed, sunburned guy wearing a flight suit, a pilot's wings, and a hastily reattached captain's patch. Another guy, about the same age, was sitting just beyond the flight engineer/chief, wearing a hundred-yard stare instead of a rank patch, his face faintly dark with deep-driven grit except for a raccoon mask of paleness around his eyes. Definitely a cav officer who'd spent a lot of time driving around looking for UN-baiting bandits and bad guys—who were often the same thing.

Their collective stillness was offset by the middle-aged man on Murphy's side of the fuselage, wearing well-worn tactical gear and clothes to match. No signs of rank or service branch. Defense contractor rep? Smuggler? Private security? Spook?

No, Murphy revised, not a spook: way too jumpy, even for an analyst thrown into the field.

The fellow leaned forward and shouted over the rotors toward the cockpit. "Hey, how much longer?"

The pilot glanced at her copilot, whose hands were already more firmly locked on the controls. "Who wants to know?" the pilot shouted back.

"An American citizen," the guy answered loudly, a little more testy.

"Well then, John Q. Public, it's like your momma said when you were in the back of that hot station wagon: we'll get there when we get there." She turned to face the plexiglass cockpit.

John Q. Public sputtered, striving for a retort as the passenger beside him—another guy in sanitized tactical dress—shook his head and tilted a slow, almost sleepy smile at him. "Not worth it, friend."

Mr. Citizen glanced at the man—whose eyes hardened slightly—then shrugged and slumped back in his seat.

The still-smiling fellow turned toward Murphy. Almost every pair of eyes in this damned country measured you, assessed you, but these were different. His assessment seemed professional. Like an interrogator's. Or a cop's.

What he said didn't give any clues about his origins. "You look like you're going back to the world."

"So do you."

"That's 'cause I am." The man's smile widened before it faded. "For now." And he waited.

Murphy kept the frown off his face. Kept the annoyance off, too. Annoyance at himself for no longer being able to instantly access the stockpile of bullshit responses, empty remarks, and harmless comebacks that he'd picked up ever since ROTC, fourteen years and several lifetimes ago. The MS—the ever-present fear of it—had taken that from him, too.

And the guy saw it. A slight frown, the kind when a person encounters a conversational twist they didn't expect, a break or a flaw they hadn't foreseen. His eyes simultaneously became slightly more wary but also slightly more compassionate. And in that instant, Murphy saw what he hated to see most of all: a shift to pity.

Damn it: no. "I'm just glad to be going—"

The Blackhawk shifted; not a thermal, a small, sharp banking maneuver. "Hold on," the pilot shouted over her shoulder.

"Trouble?" asked the copilot in way too calm a voice.

"Not sure. Dye in the water. Ours. Near that raft."

Her copilot glanced over. "We've got orders—"

"Can't ignore the dye. SOP."

"But the VIP—"

"Enough." The pilot's voice was sharper. "My bird, my call." She craned her neck.

The copilot did as well. "Yeah, that's one of ours down there in the—"

"That's one of our *uniforms*," the pilot emphasized. "Doesn't tell us who's wearing it. Zipper," she called back at her crew chief, "get eyes-on while I come around. Too many boats out here. We've gotta watch for—"

"Launch plume!" yelled Zipper. "Eight o'clo—!"

He never finished; the pilot's sharp evasive maneuver threw him back from the door into the passenger compartment.

"Lieutenant, eyes on the other side. I need to know if—"

"Captain," shouted the copilot—too loud and too panicked to be anything but a complete newb. "Bigger plume. Coming up from the trawler at our—"

The threat warning system began to wail. The Blackhawk's engines screamed as the pilot pulled it into what felt like a counter-banking maneuver so steep that Murphy would have sworn they were going backward—

A flash. A blast that blew his ability to hear right out of his head. Pieces of the craft spraying up and out from where the copilot's seat should have been. Some of the eyes around him were wide, others narrowed and alert as the Blackhawk seemed to both roll and pitch forward, as if the tail was coming over the nose…

Chest hard against his straps, the guy with the raccoon mask sighed. "Ah, shit—"

And then there was nothing.

August, 2125
55 Tauri B 3
(“R’Bak”)

Chapter Two

NEAR 55 TAURI B 3

The small rotational habitat—four pods cycling around a central docking hub—was hit by three missiles. It came apart in a ruin of components that recalled a pair of bolos tearing free from a splintering discus, the rotational tethers hurling away transport pods like bullets from a sling.

Richard Downing was unable to suppress a sharp flinch, whereas, alongside him, his "nephew" Trevor Corcoran didn't even react. The young-ish captain was a SEAL and had seen far worse, and far more, during the invasion of Earth. But his lack of reaction was diagnostic of a deeper change, a partial detachment from his own humanity. For which, Downing admitted bitterly, he himself was at least partially responsible.

The view in Downing's holographic visor changed. The station was now a tiny, discorporating smudge of debris, black against the surface of the planet near which the battle was being fought. If you could even call it a fight. The local craft, interlopers from the main world in 55 Tauri's primary system, were attempting to flee but being unerringly slaughtered before they could make any significant progress. The closest of them—a long truss-work keel with engines at one end, a hab-ring at the other, and cargo and docking frames in between—was swarmed by motes that, had the view not been coming from one of those same drones, would otherwise have been invisible.

Dully gleaming bursts of ellipses marked where the enemy ship's point defense fire batteries were releasing streams of projectiles at the small attack platforms. Futile: the swarming drones' ability to crowd gees rapidly and along very different vectors made nonsense of maneuver projections and intercept algorithms. In reply, the teardrop-shaped harriers swung in wide arcs, their micro-second megawatt-level UV laser bursts carving and shearing away the struts and modules of the fleeing ship. Occasional explosions and tongues of flame marked where they found rarities such as oxygenated fuel or missile racks.

Trevor grunted. "Got to hand it to the Dornaani; they sure can put on a show. Considerate enough to make sure that the visors are synced with their lasers' wavelength." He shared the calm observation as one of the crew modules attached to the stricken ship's ring habitat sparked as it was rent, and then sent out a weak rush of flame and a litter of writhing stick figures.

"I am glad you appreciate the proximal viewpoint," added a voice from behind.

Downing removed his visor, turned, stared at their fellow traveler and captain of the alien ship to which they owed their continued existence. "How much longer, do you think, Alnduul?"

The Dornaani's two large, pupilless eyes nictated twice, rapidly as he thought. "Not more than three minutes. We have taken care to interdict the enemy craft on vectors that would have brought them out from behind the local obstructions blocking line-of-sight communications to their home system. The remainder are collected at the center of the lee of the combined masses of this system's sun and the planet below."

"And scratch one more," added Trevor. "That transport, or whatever it is, just vaporized. A hit on its drives. Damn, those drones are fast. And how do you Dornaani pack so much punch in those short focal-length lasers?"

"You know I will not answer that question, Captain."

"Never hurts to try. And here comes the local cavalry to clean up what's left."

Downing put his visor back on.

A new perspective, closer to the planet: a hazy mix of greens, blues, and a wide equatorial belt of dusty ochre. In the foreground, the spindly craft of their allies were bearing down upon the last enemy ships. With the exception of one or two craft designed for planetary interface, they didn't have fuselages at all. All struts and tanks and modules, they were held together by spiderweb frames: partly gridwork, partly geodesic cradles. Not sturdy, but fast and spare—and loaded with missiles. Which they released in coveys toward the comparatively sluggish enemy hulls.

The comms crackled slightly on the sender's side, then a woman's voice was in their earbuds. "Lee to *Olsloov*."

Alnduul nodded to Downing, who replied, "*Olsloov* Actual. Go, Captain Lee."

"Please switch to secure five."

"Done, Captain. What's troubling you, that you don't want our allies—well, co-combatants—on the channel?"

"Sirs, this is—this is wrong. We're not breaking off to assess, as per the opord you and the locals agreed upon."

Downing frowned. He did not know a great deal about Captain Mara Lee, other than that she was USAF and, so to speak, a woman out of time. Far out of her time. They had reanimated her from cold sleep because their new allies' leader was not just a woman, but furnished with what sounded like a hereditary title: Matriarch. And in their first broken exchanges, that leader intimated that she would prefer another female as the liaison to her people. So, they had reanimated Mara "Bruce" Lee: USAF helicopter pilot who had last flown—and last lived—133 years ago, like the rest of the Lost Soldiers being towed along (so to speak) behind *Olsloov*.

Downing nodded even though she had no visual of him; since she had to keep communicating through the radio of a local ship, the locals couldn't be prevented from hearing if they wanted to. "Details please, Captain."

"Sir, I have asked when the flight leader intends to inform the enemy ships to cut thrust, stand down, and prepare to be boarded."

"And?"

"And he has not replied."

Trevor glanced over. "Don't like the sound of that."

Lee sounded like she was speaking through clenched teeth. "Neither do I, sir. This is…wait, what the—?"

The comm channel terminated with a sharp snap, replaced by the hiss of static. Downing glanced quickly at Alnduul.

The Dornaani's mouth flattened. "Transmission terminated at the source."

Downing glanced quickly at the tactical holotank; all the aqua-colored motes—friendly forces—were still there.

Alnduul murmured, "Changing visual feed."

Eyes refocusing on the visor, Downing saw their allies' ships angling in toward the enemy craft. Their weaker lasers, still picked out by the spectrum-scanning Dornaani visors, played over the fleeing ships. The beams tore rents in fuel tanks and caused small, dense, wildly spinning clouds of debris to jet out from the sides of cargo and crew modules.

Silent, the two humans and the Dornaani watched the ruthless and efficient slaughter unfold until the last of the orange motes denoting enemy craft had vanished.

Downing wet dry lips before commenting, "Well, I suspect that whoever cut off Captain Lee's comm channel no longer has anything to hide. Can we raise her?"

Alnduul waved a hand of falling fingers at one of his bridge crew, who manipulated her control surfaces. She stared at them a moment, her gills closing slowly. "No reply."

Trevor cleared his throat. "Richard, I think I know why."

As Downing re-centered his attention on the scene in the visor, Mara Lee's voice arose from the bridge's sound system as an amplified whisper. "*Olsloov*, send pulse to confirm you receive me."

Alnduul nodded at his crewperson, exchanged glances with Downing. "The captain was not to use our secure comm bud except in case of emergency."

"I think Trevor is watching that emergency unfold," Downing answered, swallowing.

In the visor, their allies' ships had begun to counter-boost, slowing their approach to the debris field. In it, a number of escape pods were flashing their location. Space-suited individuals were waving glove-mounted lights.

Mara Lee's voice, back as an even fainter, huskier whisper, reported. "This ship is still weapons-free, sir. So are the others, from what I hear. And now—oh, shit!" Her voice became a muffled, pressure-hose hiss. "*Shit! SHIT!*"

The allied ships' own, more modest point defense fire systems began sending short bursts of two or three rounds at the blinking lights that marked the locations of the survivors. And, one by one, those lights went out.

All of them.

Fifteen minutes later, their allies restored normal comm channels. Mara Lee was breathing heavily as she reported.

"Killed every one of them. Every. Single. Fucking. One of them. They straight-up lied to us, sirs."

"Yes," Downing answered, "they obviously did. And it will make our next conversation with them quite difficult."

"You think so?" Mara Lee caught herself, then added, "Sir."

"Yes, I do 'think so,' Captain, and you will watch your tone." Downing waved at *Olsloov*'s comms operator, who signaled that they were now connected on their secret link. "Captain, are you receiving through the Dornaani comm bud?"

"I hear you, sir. Loud and clear." Lee had to keep her replies consistent with the communication on the main link, or their "allies" would realize she was receiving a transmission they could not hear.

"Good. Put a stopper in that rage so you can see the bigger picture. Vengeance may be part of their motive, but that doesn't explain what they just did."

"Waiting on your next send, sir," Mara muttered bitterly.

"They just lost the opportunity to interrogate the survivors, as well as collect salvage they could have used from the ships they gutted." He switched to the normal comm channel. "Have our allies offered any explanation for their departure from the opord?"

"Haven't heard any yet, sir."

Downing went back to the Dornaani channel. "Here is what I suspect. They killed the survivors so that *we* couldn't talk to them. Our allies have been hiding in this system for centuries, so they are genuinely in fear for their existence. But if they are interested in keeping parts of their own past hidden, particularly from before they went into hiding, allowing survivors to talk is a risk they might not be willing to take. At this moment, they still have absolute control over the narrative of who, what, and why they are here." He went back to the normal channel. "We'll see what explanations they offer when we meet them later today."

"Roger that, sir. Although it's hard to imagine any need, any level of caution, that would explain what I just saw. Sir."

"I agree. Downing out."

Alnduul's eyelids cycled slowly, somberly. "It is indeed difficult to understand why they would need such absolute measures. They could have simply restricted your access to the survivors."

Trevor pulled off his visor. "Yeah, but you're forgetting something, Alnduul."

"And what is that, Captain?"

"In this system, everyone is a descendent of the Ktor."

Alnduul's mouth tucked in. "Yes. There is that."

To use one of Mara Lee's most colorful profanities, from the moment *Olsloov* had shifted into the 55 Tauri B system, it had been one "shit show" after another.

Emerging slightly above the ecliptic, the Dornaani had scanned for the classic signs of a space-faring civilization—pinpoint radiant energy sources, broadcast or microwave activity, small objects on unusual vectors or maintaining usefully close and regular orbits—and found nothing.

Nothing nearby, that is. The primary system—an F 7 main sequence star with three planets—was a riot of just such activity and emissions. Most of it was centered on the third planet, but there were also noticeable signatures clustered near planet two. There were also plentiful thermal blooms along trajectories that were consistent with either high-energy transits or Hohmann transfers between the various planets and their satellites and, by conjecture, space stations. However, as expected and as they had encountered elsewhere since entering what was nominally Ktor space, there were no high-power broadcast or radar emissions. To use those, or a Faster Than Light drive (a misnomer that everyone used, anyhow), was to invite the retributive attention of the Ktoran Sphere, from which they had been exiled.

The readings emanating from the high-energy transit vehicles were consistent with nuclear thermal rockets. The plenitude of artificial objects in space indicated a highly industrialized population, probably in the billions. Which made the comparative silence of this secondary system all the more puzzling. *Olsloov* approached the apparently biogenic third planet for a better look.

Within the hour, a handful of small objects were detected maneuvering in the vicinity of, or in orbit around, that planet. However, the planet itself showed no radiant energy sources nor even the weakest of radio signals. Surprisingly, those signatures came from asteroids .7 AU distant from the green world, out beyond the fourth orbit of the K 3 main sequence secondary star. The signatures were unusual in the type and degree of spectral diffusion they evinced, and if it had not been for the extremely advanced nature of *Olsloov*'s sensors, would have probably been completely overlooked.

The reason for the strange emissions was quick in coming. The asteroids shared an unusual characteristic: a very slow roll around their long axis. Their surfaces were also unusually dark, as if any reflective points had been dulled to a matte finish. Trevor's frown had signaled doubt even as he asked the question: could that be a result of natural phenomena?

Alnduul answered that while nothing was impossible, the selective kind of abrasion that would be required to create such a non-reflective surface had never been observed in nature. Rather than pass these mile-long objects, (and thereby risk putting *Olsloov* between the two points of local activity) it was decided to make for the longish asteroids and get a better sample of the very weak, brief radio bursts that were emanating from them and/or nearby.

The explanations came quickly. The heavily encrypted bursts were handily decoded by the Dornaani computers, which identified the underlying language in a moment: a devolved form of Ktoran as it had been spoken at least 1,400 years ago.

Hardly surprising. Since *Olsloov* had begun fleeing from both human and Dornaani pursuers as it also searched for missing friends—Caine Riordan and the self-styled Crewe that had followed him into distant space—Ktoran linguistic roots had been the norm in every system with a human population. What made this one unusual—and useful—was its size and level of technological sophistication. If peaceful contact could be established, then *Olsloov*'s almost completely depleted consumables could be restored and the mission to find Caine and company could continue.

The only real debate was over whether the locals had also inherited their Ktoran ancestors' cultural (and arguably, encoded) predilections for aggression and domination. However, caution was counterweighted by desperate need.

In the end, the green world's lack of development was taken as a moderately hopeful sign. It was difficult to foresee how or why a culture that had inherited the Ktoran reflex toward conquest would have left such an obvious prize uncolonized and unutilized. Instead, the population of the primary system appeared to be avoiding contact with the third planet, choosing instead to observe from near space and create asteroid habitats at some remove. The only logical conjecture was that the Ktoran instincts toward dominion had either diminished or had been actively rejected and replaced with a more compassionate and conscientious value system.

Made hopeful by having seen other systems which had made such a choice, Downing and Alnduul agreed that, given their rapidly dwindling supplies, they had to risk making contact. And here, at the binary system's furthest inhabited edge, was the best and safest place to do so. Using the Dornaani computer to translate their words into the local Ktoran patois, a greeting was sent using the only sure means of reaching the locals: broadcast.

That was the moment at which the shit show did not merely begin, but exploded into full-blown chaos.

All radio emanations from the asteroids ended instantly. Previously undetected small craft activated drives and sped out of the green world's Trojan Point asteroids toward the outer system. The ships that had been observed around the planet itself reacted promptly, crowding gees on what were clearly intercept courses. The perplexing, even contradictory activity became clear only when one of the few ships not giving chase rose toward the ecliptic, high enough to send a quick, high-energy broadcast burst back toward the primary system. The Dornaani computer promptly decoded it and spat out the translation: "Investigating local anomaly; stand by for details. Confirm lascom coordinates for subsequent comms."

Downing prided himself on being hard to confuse, disorient, or surprise: qualities that had served him well in the SAS before medicaling out. But he spent a full minute experiencing all three. It took that long to figure out that the "local anomaly" was not *Olsloov* or its radio message; it was the small craft which were clearly fleeing the inner system. Which meant that the asteroid habitats were not facilities owned and manned by persons from the primary system, but were, instead, hiding from its forces. And *Olsloov*'s broadcast signal had spooked them into fleeing for home.

The realizations tumbled out quickly after that. Those asteroid habitats were very large, and as scans continued to pick up low energy signatures scattered throughout the outer system, it became clear that these space dwellers had led a secret existence for a very long time. But how?

It was Trevor who saw the reason: the primary and secondary system achieved perihelion only once every eighty-eight years. Even for a nuclear thermal rocket, the median distance between them—26 AU—would be a long, expensive trip. And if, as now seemed the case, the local culture had retained a great deal of the Ktor's impulse toward aggression and absolute control, then they might very well choose not to found a permanent colony on the world, lest it break away and become a rival. So they probably made the trip only when the systems neared perihelion, the peak of which was approximately six years off.

All of which meant that *Olsloov*'s one message had put the entire population of the second system at imminent risk of subjugation or extermination.

After that, there was not enough time to examine any one of the cascading decisions too long. Swift action was necessary if the damage was to be contained and controlled. Identification and offers of help were sent to the asteroid habitats. *Olsloov*'s impressive comms and electronic countermeasures suite initiated full-bandwidth jamming of the ships from the primary system. Dornaani drones were launched toward the green world, crowding gees so high that Downing was startled; their acceleration and duration outstripped anything human technical intelligence analysts had imagined possible, let alone possessed by another species.

The foresight of that move was not long in being felt. Shortly after the interloping vessels were jammed, several of them began altering course to get out of the shadow of the combined mass and interference of the planet and the system's star. The only logical reason: to initiate line-of-sight communications to the main system and report.

No one slept for forty-eight hours. The locals—who, according to the Dornaani translator, called themselves the "Dogs"—agreed to a hastily arranged and incompletely defined alliance. Their Matriarch asked for a liaison, so Mara Lee was pulled out of suspended animation, briefed in a rush, and sent straight into twelve hours of virtual language training. With a ten-to-one time compression, she was hustled out to join the Dogs with the equivalent of one hundred twenty hours of "old Ktoran" language instruction and an overview of the kind of culture she might encounter. Downing marveled at her resilience and mission focus, and he experienced more than one pang of regret that they were going to have to leave her behind with about one hundred other Lost Soldiers. Their cryocells had begun to fail at an alarming rate, which augured a need to reanimate untold numbers of them before arriving at their final destination. A sober assessment of the shipped consumables dictated the only reasonable solution: unload as many as possible to ensure there was enough to feed those who remained.

During those early, tense hours, the interlopers from the primary's main world of Kulsis had split into two groups. One was pursuing the Dogs' vessels that had been hiding in the third planet's Trojan point asteroids. Apparently, the Kulsians had arrived earlier than ever before, so the Dogs hadn't all returned to their out-system hiding spots yet.

The other enemy formation was pushing out-system at what seemed to be maximum gees to examine the source of the first, unexpected transmission and the general area at which the Dog craft had aimed their lascoms. Within twenty-four hours, they would arrive at the asteroid habitats.

Subsequent events and decisions were something of a blur. The preemptively launched Dornaani drones intercepted and eliminated the Kulsian ships that had attempted to establish line-of-sight communication back to their home system. The Dog ships fleeing from the Trojan Point asteroids began slowing, altering course; their pursuers kept after them. *Olsloov* pushed six gee constant to intercept the other Kulsian formation, disabled every ship without slowing or taking damage. A swarm of local craft from the asteroid habitats followed in its wake to finish that hurried job as the Dornaani ship released more drones and, its full complement in acceleration couches, arrowed in-system to finish the final act of the drama.

Which had now just concluded. The drones that had eliminated the ships attempting to send to Kulsis and the second flurry launched by *Olsloov* bracketed the second formation; it had been drawn into the interlocking net of Dornaani remote weapon platforms by chasing the Dog ships from the Trojan points. The most difficult part of the operation was to ensure maximum containment before initiating the chaos of battle. After twelve hours, that had been accomplished and the fastest of the Dog ships from out-system—Mara's among them—arrived just in time for the slaughter to begin.

What no one had foreseen was that the Dogs had determined that it was not to be a slaughter, but a mass execution. Or as Trevor put it as they shrugged off the spacesuits they had worn to travel to the ship carrying the Dogs' Matriarch, "They may be generations removed from the Ktor, but they are still just as cut-throat."

Downing nodded, glanced at the glass-shard glints marking the debris field where the Kulsian ships had died *en masse.* "'Dead men tell no tales.'"

Trevor nodded back. "Yup. Now, there's just one last question we need to get answered."

Downing sighed. "Whether the Lost Soldiers we leave behind will fall into the same category."

Alnduul was waiting for them outside the airlock. "Was your meeting with the Matriarch successful?"

Downing shrugged. "I'll let you decide. Let's go someplace where we can speak privately."

Chapter Three

NEAR 55 TAURI B 3

Once Alnduul was seated—although it looked more like he was straddling a forward-leaning saddle—Downing rattled off the most important facts. "All spaceside Kulsian assets have been eliminated, including their recently-deployed satellites. Your drones destroyed the two planetside comm arrays capable of reaching the primary system. Which they call Jrar, I'm told. We have also established handshake and security protocols for data-sharing with the Dogs."

Trevor shook his head. "I'm still not sure about giving them so many schematics, Richard. If the Ktor ever come here and see old Terran weapons and vehicles in our new friends' hands, that could cause the post-war pot to boil over and scald Earth. Far worse, this time."

Alnduul joined his hands, fingers steepled each to their opposite. "Among your own people, it would be a small minority who would remember military equipment made in your 1960s and all but forgotten a hundred years later...and before either of you gentlemen were even born. We do not know many details about the Ktor, but I am fairly sure that they do not make a habit of memorizing such data. Particularly none of those who would venture among the exiles they've sent out here into the Scatters. Such knowledge would be solely the domain of scholars. If them."

"And you're sure you've sanitized the schematics? Not just the language, but the units of measurement?"

Alnduul effected a human nod: after almost half a dozen years, it was still painful to watch him try. "As we speak, every element of the devices the Dogs will be replicating is being converted in every detail. Should anyone ever see them or the schematics from which they were produced, there will be nothing that suggests Terran origin."

For a moment, Trevor looked sheepish. "Yeah, and I'm a fine one to be asking opsec questions."

"Why?"

"Because I let it slip that we have cryocell technology." He shook his head. "It never occurred to me the Dogs wouldn't have it."

Downing nodded. "Completely understandable, lad. The Ktor who came here certainly must have used cryogenic suspension. Their exiles—er, Exodates—are restricted to slower-than-light drives, so they couldn't have survived the multi-generational trip without it."

Trevor squinted at the tabletop. "Gotta wonder how they lost the technology."

"That is an unusual, even suspicious discovery," Alnduul agreed with slightly pinched eyelids. "However, any inquiry would alert the Dogs to your knowledge of their origins."

Trevor screwed up his face. "Do you really think they'd be upset that our arch-enemies are the same people who kicked them off their home worlds? We have an axiom for that scenario: 'the enemy of my enemy is my friend.'"

Alnduul's eyelids tightened further. "That may obtain on Earth, but it might not here."

Trevor appeared at pains to remain deferential. "It's pretty much a human constant, Alnduul."

"So it would seem. Yet, as you say, we do not know the events that led to their exile here. Nor can we be certain that various politically significant factions—both here and in the main system of Jrar—do not aspire to rejoin the Ktoran Sphere, or at least, elect to follow its teachings and tactics, and so, share the same presumptions and prejudices.

"Which is why," Alnduul continued, looking at both of them, "we must carefully consider the circumstances in which we leave Major Murphy and his detachment. If the Dogs have reason to be suspicious or dismissive of us as allies—or as effective protectors of our friends—then the moment we depart, they may attempt to put Major Murphy in a subordinate, or at least difficult, position."

"Or out an airlock." Trevor's face was as glum as his tone.

Downing frowned but nodded. "Not out of the realm of possibility. The Hardliner faction we just encountered seems predisposed to 'absolute' solutions."

Trevor matched his nod. "They were the ones responsible for most of the mass executions that Lee witnessed, if I read those comm transcripts correctly."

"You did. They are," Alnduul answered. "I suspect that, overall, their faction is more observant of Ktor cultural rituals and attitudes. From what you have conveyed, the Matriarch's supporters seem more…welcoming?"

Downing winced. "I don't know that I'd use so cheery a term as that. I'd say 'open-minded.' From what I can tell, she was suitably impressed by Captain Lee. Not just her fighting spirit, but her composure and balance when the Hardliners broke from the plan. Diplomatically, that was a potentially disastrous moment."

Alnduul's gills had widened, were stiff. "And how is Captain Lee, herself? She sounded…shaken."

Before Richard could answer, Trevor jumped in. "I don't think Lee gets shaken, Alnduul. At least not where anyone else can see it. But she's furious, and I think a little desperate."

"It is certainly reasonable that she would be furious over witnessing such senseless killing."

Trevor shook his head. "That's not what she's furious about. She just woke up and discovered everyone she's ever known is dead, including her kids. Then she's pitched right into a space battle alongside people who she doesn't know, and now, realizes she can't trust." He shrugged. "After all that, most soldiers I know would be too rattled, too shell-shocked, to be effective. Not her. But I've seen the look in her eyes before, just like I've seen the sudden jerks and starts every time she moves her head. Too much more craziness and even she could unravel."

Alnduul nodded, looked back toward Downing. "Then should we awaken the one you have selected to be their commanding officer, Major Murphy?"

Richard managed not to blink. "You mean, now?"

"Yes."

"Why?"

Alnduul's fingers rose and flopped: a shrug. "Companionship and comfort for Captain Lee."

Oh, bloody hell. "No, precisely the wrong move," Downing snapped, glancing at Trevor and hoping to get off the topic quickly enough. "Captain Corcoran's father—and I—did something like that, once. Just before we met you at Convocation. It was not…helpful."

Alnduul nodded. "Yes, I am aware. When you awakened Caine Riordan, you awakened another sleeper, Captain Opal Patrone, who became his bodyguard. I reasoned you did that to ensure that neither one of them awakened from the past alone." Downing struggled to maintain an expressionless face as Alnduul turned his gaze upon Trevor's grim one. "But…was that not helpful, that they had each other for commiseration, for solace?"

Trevor's eyes remained focused on Alnlduul; they had become carefully blank.

As Alnduul's gills rippled in perturbation, maybe confusion, Downing had to resist the impulse to drag the Dornaani out of the room before he could do any more damage. *Bloody alien git, you've put your foot in it, now.* Apparently, Alnduul had never understood the painful triangle that had grown up out of that dual reanimation. Trevor falling for Opal, Opal for Caine, and Caine's affections already fixed on someone else—although initial memory loss prevented him from immediately recalling whom.

But Alnduul did not read the present human social dynamics any more accurately than he had read those earlier ones. He pressed on. "Is it not helpful if there is a chance that the two might become emotionally, even romantically, attached to each other?"

"No," Trevor said in a calm, quiet, almost dangerous tone. "It is not a good idea. What you're proposing would compromise the relationship between a CO and his subordinate officer. Wrong in more ways than I can explain to you. And if they are the only two Lost Soldiers awake, or in contact with each other, you are dramatically increasingly the likelihood of that happening."

"Besides," Downing added hastily, "for human companionship to have been of any real benefit to Captain Lee, it would have had to have been available right now, in the immediate aftermath. Or before. No, it's best we stick with the timetable we agreed upon." Which had been buggered from the start. Lee's skills had been needed so quickly that the optimal procedure—awakening and debriefing Murphy first, and then the cadre, and so on, down the ranks—had been promptly dumped in the tip. Which, of course, mucked up every step that was to have followed.

Just like every other operation Downing had ever been on.

PART ONE:

MURPHY

Chapter Four

NEAR *SPIN ONE*

Murphy awoke with a start.

Gray, utilitarian walls and lighting—although the lights were unusual, somehow. The air was canned: no doubt about it. And he was not lying, but reclining.

Careful now; maybe you've been captured—

"Take it easy, Major. You are safe and among friends."

English accent. Measured, the way medical personnel talk to people who may or may not be screwed up. Murphy struggled to rise up on his elbows. He felt slightly weak, had a momentary wash of vertigo, then the world righted.

Two men were seated at the end and to either side of where he lay, which from his angle looked like a cross between a sick bay bed and a gurney. Labels were in English. They were both in what looked kind of like flight suits, but more bulky and more substantial. There were no markings on either.

Not enough information to make any assumptions either way—which wouldn't have been safe or wise to do anyway. So he said, "Murphy. Rodger Y.; Major, US Army. Serial number 984—"

The two men—both tall, but one much older than the other—smiled. The older and thinner one waved a hand. "Yes. We know. In fact, my companion here—let's call him Mr. Nephew—is still a reservist in your military. Different branch, however."

Mr. Nephew reminded Murphy of the SEAL in the chopper, but whereas that guy was a bear, this one was more a tiger: a little taller and leaner. But Murphy's intended query—an attempt to sniff out if he really was affiliated with the US military—died in his throat as memory rose up. "The Blackhawk. What—?"

Mr. Nephew nodded. "Went down in the Indian Ocean. November 17, 1993. Copilot and crew chief were KIA, although the copilot's body was never found. The pilot and passengers survived."

Murphy frowned. "How? And why? Hell, the second missile wasn't an RPG round; it was homing on us and made a contact hit. The front half of the chopper should have been gone—and me with it."

"As best we can tell, the second missile's warhead was defective. Went off late and weak. Damage to the cockpit—and the copilot—was essentially from the impact. That's why the pilot and everyone else close survived."

Murphy did not even nod. No falling into the trap of routine or casual exchanges. Hell, his training was to not communicate at all. But if these guys were working for hajis—No; something was off, but not something as simple as that. If this was theater, a bid to get him to believe himself in safe hands, then it was all at once way too good and way too amateurish.

The two guys, particularly the big one, emitted service vibe as strong as he'd ever felt. And not service as pogues; these guys had been in the shit. And that was damn near impossible to fake. Just like the accents: they were too damned good. The older one was speaking in that kind of controlled cant of the Brits—King's English, he'd heard it called—and the other had just enough of a twang that Murphy guessed he was from the mid-Atlantic states, probably Virginia or Maryland, possibly Delaware.

But if these guys were impostors trying to inveigle his trust, then why were they such amateurs about uniforms? Their weird flight suits weren't in anyone's inventory, and they just looked wrong. Flight suits were fitted out with the kinds of loops and fasteners that you'd need in a plane; fatigues for ground pounders had buttons not zippers, more pockets in different places, and more places to hang or attach gear. Their suits had both—sorta—but also a number of flaps that didn't make sense, as well as what looked like sealable collars and cuffs.

And why no rank patches, no national or service branch insignias? Okay, so maybe they were playing the "intel neutral" game, but still, that was usually done by covering things up or removing velcroed patches. These suits looked like they had never had either affixed.

So how was it they were so good at the vibe and the language, and so bad at the costuming? It didn't make any sense. Unless they weren't trying to put on an act, which made even less sense. And was a whole lot more creepy, if true.

And another thing— "You read out the whole date of the attack on us, year and all. Why?" He paused, ditching the prohibition against talking; it was more important to learn what was going on. "So, are we being recorded? Is this a—a sanitized debrief? Who are you guys with?"

Mr. Nephew smiled slightly, shook his head. "We are not being recorded, although come to think of it, that might have been a good idea. And if anyone is providing debrief information, it's not you conveying it to us: it's we who have to convey it to you."

"Huh? What the hell do you mean?"

The tiger-guy's smile widened. "I'll let my colleague—Mr. Nuncle—explain."

"Major Murphy, we mentioned the precise date of your crash because you've been unconscious for a while."

"Then why am I still in the same fatigues?" He could even smell the same heat-brewed body odor, but he wasn't going to mention that. Come to think of it, he could also smell a faint salt-water tang as well… "Wait a minute, you didn't even bother to change my clothes when you fished me out of the ocean?"

Mr. Nuncle held up a helpless hand. "We most certainly would have. But we were not the ones who recovered you."

There was something in the older guy's voice and the younger guy's reaction that spiked Murphy's wariness meter. For the first time, they grew slightly tense—just a moment, and just a shade of it—but it had been there. "Okay, what aren't you telling me?" *Wait: the date.* "This has something to do with the date of the crash."

The older guy frowned sadly; his face got longer and a little older looking. "You are to be congratulated on your conjecture, Major Murphy. Our recounting of the date is indeed central to what you must learn about what has happened to you."

Murphy responded to the sudden chill of fear by heading straight at its source. "Then spit it out: why is the date so important?"

Mr. Nephew's eyes did not blink as they sought his. "Because it's not that date anymore. Not even close."

Murphy kept pushing toward the center of the growing terror. "Stop the theatrics. What's the date?"

"August. 2125."

Murphy shunted his burgeoning terror into outraged facetiousness. "Okay, guys. I don't know who you are, or who put you up to this, but this is a pretty shitty joke. I mean, maybe if we hadn't lost someone on the chopper, it would be okay, but it's lousy to build a practical joke on the copilot's grave, because that's pretty much what you're doing here."

"You're right," Tiger-Nephew said with a slow nod. "That would be a shitty joke. But this isn't a joke."

Murphy had been watching their eyes. They were somber, even sad. They didn't check their performances against each other, nor were they so rigidly focused on the act that it caused an unnatural sense of timing or predetermined intent. Unless, that is, it wasn't an act— "No," Murphy rebutted, surging forward, "this is all bullshit. Weirdest damn strategy for producing POW disorientation I've ever heard of, but it isn't going to work. It's too freaking ridiculous."

Mr. Nuncle sighed, rose. "We presumed you would have that reaction. We'd probably have the same one, put in your place. That is why we're going to let you spend as long as you need with someone from your time. He even served in your theater of operations—Somalia—albeit a few years later."

The heavy bulkhead door slid aside—just like in old reruns of *Star Trek*—and a new guy walked in, saluting the two already in the room. He wore a uniform Murphy recognized. Pararescue jumper. Lieutenant. A little younger than Murphy. He saluted as he introduced himself. "Ike Franklin, Major

Murphy. Nice to meet you, sir. Wish it was under better—well, sane—circumstances."

Time to blow their cover, whatever game they might be playing. "Nice try. Uniform is a complete match. Accent is perfect. You guys have done your homework well. Or are you working for some rogue cell? Is that it?"

The new guy sighed. "I get it, Major, I really do. Those of us who had higher clearances wondered the same thing when we were awakened: was this some elaborate mind game to disorient us, get us to drop classified information? And you know what we figured out?"

Murphy shook his head, swallowed. The guy who called himself Franklin seemed so natural, so genuine, that Murphy's worst fears—no matter how irrational—were growing. "No. What did you figure out?"

"That none of us knew anything important enough to warrant all of this." The guy in the pararescue fatigues waved a broad hand to take in the whole compartment. "Tell me, Major. Just what do you know that would make an enemy willing to put on this kind of crazy show? I'm familiar with the info that is dished out at your rank, probably heard a lot of the same material since I served roughly during those years. I heard it because we might have to make snap decisions having to do with wounded personnel with sensitive intel. So I know most of the same sensitive data points about nukes, particularly small ones. I'm also guessing we both know a bit about comm protocols that probably never made it online, at least not where Netscape could find it."

Murphy blinked. There was something about the casualness with which he said, "Netscape"…

"But at the end of the day, you know how it goes: the services are full of folks from O3 to O5 who have a gambling habit, a drug habit, a sex habit, or alimony payments to beat the band. Those are the folks who are spilling the semi-secrets, not us—and for pennies on the dollar, compared to what it would cost to set up something like this."

Murphy struggled to find something to say, some brash counterpoint to which he could affix his flagging defiance and courage—but nothing showed up. His well of snappy comebacks was dry.

Mr. Nuncle rose, followed a moment later by Mr. Nephew, who said, "Sorry, Major. I really am. I've known several people who've had to grapple with this kind of one-way trip into the future. It's never easy, and the longer the time they've been gone, the harder it is. And you—well, you've been gone a very long time." He nodded and departed right behind Mr. Nuncle.

Murphy swallowed again, realized he was shaking slightly.

Franklin slid into the chair Mr. Nuncle had vacated and folded his hands. "Listen—"

"NO. *You* listen." Murphy clasped his hands to keep them still. "I don't buy this. Any of it. There's no way I could be in the future. That I could have—what? Slept through more than a century? That kind of technology—no one has, or had, it. Not even close."

Franklin shrugged. "You're right about that. But like the others said, our people weren't the ones who recovered you."

"So who did?"

Franklin leaned back and sighed. "You're not going to like or believe the answer, not at first."

"Of course I won't, because this is all bullshit. But tell me anyway—just for the entertainment value."

"Okay. You were abducted by aliens."

"By—?" And before he could stop himself, Murphy was laughing. Hysterically. Too loud and too wild, even to his own ears. Because if this wasn't an increasingly improbable charade…

"By aliens," Franklin repeated. "The same ones who grabbed me."

Murphy didn't immediately realize that he had stopped laughing, as if someone had turned off a switch. "What do you mean?"

"I mean just what I said, Major. Me and a buddy—Special Forces—we were as good as dead near the Ethiopian border in Somalia. Surrounded. No water, and not half a mag left between us. Then everything goes quiet. A few minutes later, a guy in shades and a suit walks up toward us and gives us the spiel a lot of us heard, 'You can come with me or you can die right here.' Not much of a choice. And we didn't know that going with him meant a one-way ride into the future. And even farther."

"Even farther?"

"Really? You haven't guessed by now? That we are nowhere near Earth?"

Murphy suppressed a shudder. "Go ahead: it's a good story. Lie to me some more."

Franklin shook his head, frustrated but smiling. "Major, you're one tough nut. Gonna be a real asset when you come around."

"Don't count on it."

Franklin's shrug was larger this time. "Suit yourself. The universe has got plenty of time. We're the ones who are playing beat the clock."

"And what does that mean?"

"It means that there's a reason you're being awakened at this place and at this time. It's because we're at war. Have been for a few years, now."

"At war with whom?"

"Well, as it turns out, with the same people who snatched us from Earth."

"Yeah, sure. So, tell me: are we fighting the greens or the grays?"

Franklin frowned. "Far as I know, there aren't any 'greens.' And the grays—if that's what they are—are on our side. Kinda."

Murphy was shaking inside but steeled himself to keep plunging forward, to get this impostor to finally show his hand, to reveal a crack in his act, a flaw in the story. "Okay. So why don't you tell me about the enemies who abducted me and the war and all the rest."

"That'll take a while."

"Well, according to you, I've got nothing but time."

Franklin smiled. "True, that." Then he leaned back and started to talk.

Murphy held up his hand. "Stop."

Franklin halted mid-word and squinted appraisingly at Murphy. "You look…uh, ill. Major."

"Nope," Murphy lied. "It's just a lot to take in."

Franklin smiled sympathetically. "Don't I know it."

Well, maybe you do and maybe you don't, Murphy retorted silently. But it sure did sound like he did. Franklin had answered every question not only with ease, but the kind of casual side commentary that you just didn't get in a constructed scenario. Frankly, not even the best spies on TV shows or in films demonstrated the unaffected, almost lazy inventiveness that Ike did. Which meant that it might not be invented. Which would mean that what he was saying was the truth.

Murphy once again had to clamp down the rising nausea. For a brief moment, he envied the contents of his stomach; at least they could escape. For Murphy, there was no leaving himself behind, no way to find the ejection seat if this was his new reality, slightly more than one hundred thirty years further along the timeline from the moment when he'd lost consciousness in the Blackhawk heading down toward the Indian Ocean. Which brought up an interesting glitch in the story of his "abduction," one that might prove to be the loose thread that would undo Franklin's tapestry of lies. "Wait a minute. You said that the abductors—the Kuh-torr—?"

"K-tor," Franklin corrected with a nod, eliding the syllables until they almost ran together.

"Yeah—you said that they gave you a choice. They spoke to you. Why not us?"

Franklin nodded—a casually confident gesture which made Murphy's hopeful stomach plummet. "That happened sometimes. For instance, some of the other abductees were on subs when their ticket was about to be punched. The Ktor intervened, but there wasn't the time for any chitchat. For them, like you, all they knew was that one moment they were expecting to be dead, the next they woke up safe and sound." Franklin's expression hardened. "Well, comparatively speaking. Not much safe about this new life. Not for us, anyhow."

"Not for us." No special emphasis, nor any theatrical de-emphasis. Just a conversational tone, a phrase like any other. *Jesus Christ, he's telling the truth. He really is.*

Murphy managed to turn his head before he threw up.

Franklin offered a second face towel. Murphy waved it away.

"Another glass of water?" the pararescue asked.

"No, thanks." Murphy coughed. "I'm good." Which was probably the biggest lie he'd ever told.

How the hell could he—or anyone—be "good" when their entire life was wiped away in an eyeblink? It was kind of the reverse of dying. Dying meant that you dropped out of everybody else's story, that you ceased to be. Which was terrifying. But this way, it was everybody else who dropped out of *your* story—leaving you as alone as any human had ever been. Family, friends, dreams went flitting past his mind's eye—and were gone, like vapor. Like they'd never existed. The nausea threatened again, but he choked it back down.

"We can stop now," Franklin said quietly, shifting in his chair as if he meant to get up in the direction of the hatch—if you could really call it that.

Murphy didn't respond. Did he want to stop? First, he'd wanted to disprove it all. Just now, he'd wanted to escape it. But the second after the desire to escape had passed, he knew—without even thinking—that there was nothing left but to go forward. *Yeah, but forward into what—?*

To hear Franklin tell it, he was now in a world which, about half a century after he left it, had slid into a crazy patchwork quilt of decline. Not what all the doomsday predictors had foreseen, either. Yeah, climate impact played a role, but before it could really roll out the huge effects that everyone had been talking about, simple human issues trumped them.

And even there, it wasn't what had been expected. It wasn't anything as simple as global overpopulation or famine. Because although the globe was more interconnected than ever, that didn't mean that a disaster in one region or at any given economic level turned into equally awful disasters in all the others. Instead, the bow wave of the crisis struck at coastal cities—well, megalopoli. Places like Manila and Rio and Lagos and Mumbai, where the services fell so far behind the urban influx, chaos, and crime, that cargo ships ultimately started avoiding them, urged along by Lloyds' refusal to insure any docking there.

That was the tipping point. Once cut off from sea-borne goods and supplies, the local population almost immediately became exponentially greater than those cities' carrying capacities. Unrest became revolt. Hunger became starvation. And crime lords became war lords.

Economies toppled. Refugees fled to the countryside, hoping to find a way to feed themselves. Others, paradoxically, collapsed upon the cities, the lure of jobs and services stronger than the fear of, or belief in, the decaying conditions there. Cities in the interior were swamped, drowned in the same wave of human desperation.

Currencies collapsed, followed by the governments that backed them. Coups pitted military juntas against crime syndicates that were almost as powerful as they were, and often came from the same backgrounds. Clean water, already in short supply, became the new currency in many places, along with canned food, medicines, and bullets.

And what had the rest of the world done? Less and less. Most of the Western powers that had the money and power to possibly—*possibly*—make a difference were also decried as opportunistic recolonizers. Voting publics in the West fretted and fought among themselves about what steps to take—but even if they had been able to make any productive plans, the situation deteriorated too rapidly for it to matter.

The other great powers? Russia was still attempting to sort out its own maelstrom of conflicting sociopolitical currents: capitalism, cronyism, communism, and crime. China saw the chaos as an opportunity to realize its global ambitions, attempted to intervene, and found itself mired in regional and tribal wars and even campaigns of genocide, old hatreds given new life by the struggle to survive. Ultimately, the PRC spent billions—right before their own very different demographic problems crushed them: the number of dependent-aged persons rose to make up seventy percent of the population. The Party's solutions were logical, ruthless, and led to large-scale "disaffection."

Meanwhile, the smaller but stable nations of the Developed World responded the only way they could: duck and hunker down, particularly those who had large and unstable neighbors.

And so, the globe did not plunge into complete darkness, but rather, along the predictable fault lines of developed infrastructure and geographical separation. Countries with functional economies and at great remove from the disintegrating states of South America, Asia, and particularly Africa, watched—first in horror, then in mute numbness—as almost a third of the globe's population sank into disarray, despair, and a desperate struggle for survival. And as if making good on apocalyptic prophesy, famine and death were quickly joined by war and pestilence, which only led to a greater hardening of borders.

Franklin had referred to the entire period as the Megadeath, which sounded like the name of a thrash metal band to Murphy. But it turned out that the name was not inspired by a dark poetic response to the unfolding tragedy, but by actuarial statistics. Specifically that, during the peak years of the crisis, the daily fatalities exceeded the normal average value by one million. Or about a third of a billion every year.

Ultimately, the Megadeath burned itself out. Nations restructured, began to rebuild, but the world was never quite the same. The greater powers lived with the inchoate but lingering guilt of not having done more, and the new nations nursed the grim conviction that they had been abandoned in their hour of need. Neither was completely true, yet neither was completely groundless, either.

As rebuilding began reenergizing economies and nations, cybernetic implants moved out of the realm of enhancements for the wealthy into main market. But numerous waves of hacking and targeted EMP attacks resulted in widespread avoidance. And just as that panic was dying out, the resurgent space programs of various countries collectively discovered and confirmed an object heading straight for Earth. They dubbed the interloper from the Kuiper Belt the Doomsday Rock, which was intercepted and diverted just in time to save Earth from being blasted back to the Bronze Age. Or worse.

It was, however, a galvanizing moment. Space research budgets mounted, and as access to space became habitation in space and ultimately communities in space, the competition between nations increasingly moved off Earth. One or two small wars flared and were quelled, and just after the turn of the 22nd century, a successful interstellar field effect system—the Wasserman Drive—was invented. Colonization of green worlds—a surprising, even suspicious, number of them—commenced with unusual drive and fervor.

But that lasted for just a little over a decade—because that was the point at which ruins were discovered on Delta Pavonis Three, only seven years ago. The events that followed were difficult for Murphy to keep straight: Earth tried to form a confederation; exosapients contacted humanity; what should have been a friendly meeting went sour; Earth was invaded; but with some ill-defined assistance, it threw back the occupiers and turned the tables on them in their own systems.

And just after all that was finally winding down, a mission was sent to one of those enemy's worlds: Turkh'saar. There were humans there, which should have been impossible. But there they were, anyhow—and all of them from the twentieth century. The abductees of which Franklin spoke. The so-called Lost Soldiers. Of which he was one.

And therefore, so was Murphy.

He hung his head. "I'm going to need a little time to…to take it all in."

Franklin rose. "Sure." On the seat of the other chair, he left behind what looked like a pane of glass acting like a computer screen. "We've patched the OS so that it will be easy for you to use. Anything you want to know, it'll be right there." He started toward the bulkhead door, turned back. "Need anything else?"

"Yeah." Murphy tried to grin, knew it must look feeble. "A time machine to go back home."

Franklin sighed. "You and me both, Major. You and me both." He left.

Murphy let out a long shuddering sigh and lay back on the gurney/bed. He was tired—exhausted, all of a sudden—but he didn't want to go to sleep.

Because if he did, he'd have to wake up and realize—all over again—that this was not a nightmare; it was his new reality.

Chapter Five

NEAR *SPIN ONE*

Waking up wasn't as bad as Murphy had anticipated, probably because he had kept at the dataslate for almost fourteen straight hours, hammering away at the history he'd missed, the technology that had arisen. He had drilled the new reality so deep and hard into his consciousness that awakening to it was not accompanied by a shock, but a deep and gnawing sense of just how much more he had to catch up on.

So, when Messrs. Nephew and Nuncle dropped in after breakfast, he was washed, fed, and marginally informed. And had enough of his wits about him to stand and ask, "Sirs, as I understand it, at least one of you is in the US armed forces, and I'm guessing that both of you rank me." He started to raise his hand into a salute.

Mr. Nuncle waved it down. "We're a little less strict about that, now, Major."

"Regulations have become more, er, casual, sir?"

"Not intentionally. However, when you are in space, you quite frequently need your hands to steady yourself. So, the protocol for salutes changed. We'll send some guidelines, if you are interested."

"I am, sirs. I was also wondering if I could perhaps call you by your real names?"

Nuncle found the same seat he'd occupied the prior day. "I would like that, Major, but I'm afraid that would not be wise. Not for us, and not for you. Please, sit down."

Murphy complied.

"You are correct that we outrank you, but that is all we are going to say on the matter. Indeed, the limited amount of information we can convey will surely be a frustration to us both."

Murphy nodded. "I suspected that. Sir. When I tried to find information on the abductees—the Lost Soldiers—I ran into a solid wall of 'access denied.' In the rare event that I was able to open a file, the material that remained was barely equal to the amount that was redacted."

Mr. Nephew smiled crookedly. "That sounds about right." His smile fell away. "We're here to give you what information we can and also to answer the questions we're allowed to."

"Very well. May I start?"

"By all means."

"*Who* won't allow you to answer all my questions?"

Nephew grinned. "That would be us. Our circumstances and official status are, well, ambiguous."

"You mean, you're renegades?"

Nuncle scratched his head. "To be perfectly frank, we're not really sure. For a number of reasons, we had to strike out on our own before we could make a full report. On several crucial matters."

"Sounds like you were one step ahead of the headsman," Murphy said with a grin.

"Could have gotten the axe," Nuncle agreed. "Or could have gotten a medal. Or both. But probably in that unfortunate order. And since we are all quite fond of keeping our heads attached to our bodies, we decided that it would be prudent to show high personal initiative and undertake our current rescue operations."

"Wait. You're trying to rescue someone, even though you're on the run?"

"Yes, that is correct. And unfortunately, that is all we may tell you."

"Why?"

Nephew leaned forward, hands clasped. "Because if the enemy gets hold of you, you can't reveal what you don't know."

Murphy hoped he didn't grow as suddenly pale as he felt he might. "Understood, sir. SOP. But, assuming the enemy are these Ktor, why would they care what I know?"

"The Ktor, or their proxies, would be very interested just to learn that there are humans from Earth running around in their space."

Murphy swallowed. "We're in their space? Right now?"

Nuncle nodded. "Have been for some weeks. And we wouldn't be here at all if there was any other way to effect the rescue. But now we have reached a crossroads, so to speak."

Murphy just nodded.

Nuncle looked uncomfortable. "I cannot divulge the size of our unit, nor its full complement. However, suffice it to say that our carrying capacity—both in terms of lading and consumables—is heavily overtaxed. That is why we had to stop in this system: 55 Tauri. We detected signs of habitation and had no choice but to risk contact. We needed to refuel and take on comestibles."

Murphy glanced at Nephew. "But he said we're in enemy space."

Nephew sighed and leaned back. "I did. We are. But the Ktorans are not unified. Hell, we didn't realize just how ununified they are until we started moving through what they call the Scatters: where we are now."

"The Scatters?" Murphy echoed.

"Yeah. A stretch of space they haven't bothered to colonize. Or, to put it another way, that they decided was off limits because the competition it would have sparked among the older planets—or 'Houses'—would probably have turned into a civilization-wrecking free-for-all. So out here, it's just the descendants of their exiles."

"They have so many exiles that they leave a whole, uh, interstellar outback for them to flee to?"

Nuncle nodded. "Sounds mad, doesn't it? But that is the situation. The great powers of the Sphere have wars that escalate to the point where they are likely to get completely out of hand: nukes and planetary bombardments and the like. So, they have what you might call a pressure release valve. Any power that knows it will lose, and therefore has no reason *not* to employ maximum destructive force, is offered a choice: be exterminated or be exiled. Those who choose the latter—the

Exodatcs—are allowed to flee into the Scatters, where they are ostensibly free to develop how and where they will, with two provisos: no FTL drives and no long-range radio comms."

"And if they ignore those restrictions?"

"Then the Sphere allows the equivalent of young-Turk bounty hunters to visit retribution upon the violators. We have seen such planets, or rather, what is left of them." Nuncle seemed to grow a little more pale than he usually was. "Not a pretty sight. Barely habitable, sometimes."

"And the person or persons you're rescuing, they're someplace in these, uh—these Scatters?"

Nephew shrugged. "Might be. Might be further. That's one of the reasons we have to travel lighter. Getting there faster means a better chance of getting there in time."

Murphy looked from one to the other. "Why do I get the feeling that the conversation is moving around to the part that concerns me? Personally."

Nuncle managed to smile and be crestfallen at the same time. "And that is just the kind of insight we knew you'd have, and why you are just the man for the mission that has to be undertaken."

Oh, shit. "I see."

It was as if they had both heard his silent *"Oh, shit."* "Yes," Nuncle said with a nod. "I'm afraid you are about to get the dirty end of the stick, Major. Here's the situation:

"We can't abandon much of our equipment. We are too likely to need it for either fighting through to the rescue point or once we get there. The only thing we have too much of is, well, bodies in cold sleep. They take up space, draw power, and if we find ourselves in a situation where we needed to reanimate all of them, we'd be out of food within days.

"We discovered that there are friendly communities in this companion system, all of whom live in space, on concealed habitats. They go into hiding whenever the malign forces from the main system put in their occasional but largely predictable appearance. We, however, were not aware of that when we intercepted their very subtle communications and announced ourselves."

Murphy grimaced. "Let me guess: by announcing yourselves to them, you also announced yourself to the malign forces from the main system."

Nephew nodded. "Yep. We blew their centuries-old cover in a single afternoon. So, we had to make it right. Which meant locating and taking out all the spaceside opposition and any ground-based communication sites the OpFor had for sending word back to the main system."

Murphy stared at him. "But that means their HQ back home has got to be realizing that its task force to this system has gone off the grid. Entirely. They're gonna want to know what happened, and how."

Nuncle nodded vigorously. "Precisely. And that is where you—and others—come in."

Why am I not surprised? "Sir, I don't mean to be uncooperative, but I'm not part of your formation."

Nephew's expression was like he was pulling a long splinter out of his foot. "Actually, Major, you are. This came up when the awakened Lost Soldiers were exfilled from Turkh'saar. Technically, the missing were never mustered out of their different services. Besides, beyond fixing the problem we caused for the friendlies here in 55 Tauri B, there's also this: we can't take all of the Lost Soldiers with us. Not anymore. We've run the logistics. In fact, you know the person who cranked those numbers. Missy Katano."

Murphy started. "From Mogadishu? Yes, I knew her. Well, I knew *of* her. She was the grease that made the wheels turn in logistics. She was on the chopper. So, she made it?"

"As we told you, only the crew chief and the copilot were lost. The rest of you were—salvaged—by the Ktor. And don't ask me how. Not all their methods are a mystery, but in your case and a few others, we have no idea how they got people out of sinking wrecks before they drowned." He shook his head. "Anyhow, we have to leave approximately one hundred of the Lost Soldiers behind, along with their gear and a small number of vehicles. Just enough for you to fulfill your first objectives."

The operational nitty-gritty was shit to hear, too, but at least this kind of shit was familiar to Murphy: new superiors setting impossible objectives. "And what is that first objective, sirs?"

"Objective*s*, Major Murphy," Nuncle stressed. "They must be pursued concurrently. Firstly, once you are landed on this system's habitable planet, you must commandeer indigenous equipment. This is both because there is no certainty of resupply and because there must be a minimal Terran—er, Earth-force footprint. The only way to do that is to blend in with the locals: use their equipment, learn their languages, adopt their ways. Where practicable and ethical."

"And the other objective? Sir?"

Nephew was sitting ramrod straight in his chair now. "As we said, we eliminated all the spaceside comm platforms that could reach back to the main system. And we took out the ground installations that we knew of which had a similar capability. But the OpFor still has units on the ground. Creating a long-range transmitter isn't rocket science. It isn't easy, but we can be sure that some of the OpFor knows how to do it and is taking the necessary steps."

Murphy rubbed the bridge of his nose. "And I'm supposed to locate and eliminate them with a hundred men, sirs?"

Nuncle shook his head. "The spaceside locals have means of introducing you favorably to R'Bak's locals, the ones that the opposition forces raid and then 'cull' when they arrive. You won't lack allies."

Well, it was nice that at least *one* bit of good news had popped up. "Sirs, I'd like to go back a moment. You mentioned that there is 'no certainty of resupply.' Could you expand upon that, please?"

Nuncle looked at Nephew, who sighed and rested his hands on his knees. "Major, it is our intent to come back this way. We're confident you will succeed in your further objectives: to establish a secure operating base for yourselves and for us to retire to for resupply, should our rescue efforts prove to require multiple journeys beyond the Scatters.

"Unfortunately, it is just as possible that we will not return. That we will run into the Ktor. Or their proxies. Or any one of a thousand different anomalies that are a death sentence when you are operating in uncharted space. So, yes, unfortunately, there is no guarantee of resupply. But I promise you this: we mean to come back and either evacuate you or reinforce your position."

"If any of us are still here and breathing," Murphy added.

Nephew just nodded. "That's the op, Major."

Murphy didn't feel like he might puke, but he certainly wanted to spit in disgust. "I understand, sir. Sounds like I have a lot to accomplish."

Nuncle got that hangdog look that always seemed to precede some dire addition from him. "You do indeed, Major. And I'm afraid there's one further challenge of which you must be apprised."

Of course there is. "Yes, sir?"

"Your men for this mission—the Lost Soldiers we've chosen—are not necessarily the most coherent force."

Great. "I'm not sure I understand what you mean by that, sir."

"Major, our rescue mission will be almost constantly in space. When traveling in that unforgiving environment, you need individuals who are team players, self-starters, and not easily distracted from their task. In short, in space or new exoplanetary environments, there are often crises that arise quickly and without warning. The soldiers best able to survive are the ones who are most dedicated to their profession, to their job."

Better still. "Sir, does this mean I'm getting a bunch of…of discipline cases?"

"Not entirely, Major. Some have demonstrated phobias that would paralyze them in space—claustrophobia and agoraphobia are two such, despite being direct opposites. There are individuals who do not handle contact with alien life forms well. There are others who have expressed religious difficulties operating alongside intelligent beings that are not human. And yes, you are also drawing the con-artists, black marketeers, and barracks lawyers."

Total perfection. "Sounds like I'll have to whip them into shape before they'll be ready for duty. Sirs."

Nephew nodded. "True, but you won't have to do it alone. The other survivors from the crash are going to be your cadre, minus Missy and Dr. Hampson. That gives you a number of excellent officers who are, variously, specialists who can oversee air, space, armor, even ground and spec ops."

It was a pretty narrow ray of hope—but a ray, nonetheless. "Any reason why all of us crash survivors are being selected?"

"Three reasons, Major. First, since all of you were taken during one of the last abductions, you have the best understanding of truly modern warfare. You're going to need that. Secondly, once again, being from the late 20th century, the abductors were able to get data on all of you, mostly from the civilian sector. Consequently, if we took you on the rescue mission and ran into the Ktor, any of you who were captured or unrecoverable could possibly be ID'd by them. And then the Ktor would have all the grounds they need for declaring war. Hell, they'd almost have to, given their own cultural standards and expectations. And third, all of you are among the very best at what you do."

"No insolence intended, sir, but how the heck do you know that?"

Nephew smiled. "Like I said, the late-stage abductors were able to get various records pertaining to the people they grabbed. And with help from the exosapients you'd call 'grays,' we were finally able to access and decode the records on the Lost Soldiers. At least, those whose cryocells we still possess." He leaned back. "We may be giving you a challenging bunch of troops, Major, but you are going to have an outstanding cadre with which to whip them into shape and get the job done."

Murphy discovered that his eyes were drifting to the floor. He didn't want to say anything else, but he had to. They had to know. "Sirs, I am not sure my records were updated by the Ktor in time to reflect this, but…I was diagnosed with MS right before the chopper went down. Not quite twenty-four hours earlier. That's the reason I was being shipped stateside, to confirm the diagnosis and take me off the line. So my condition could not endanger others."

Nuncle nodded soberly. "Yes, Major Murphy. We know. We also know that we do not exist in a perfect world. Neither you in terms of your personal health, nor us in terms of our operational imperatives. Under any other circumstances, we would have kept you in stasis until and unless we could access a cure.

"But you may be interested to learn that the Blackhawk's pilot, whom we awoke before you, conducted joint operations with the locals against the OpFor. She gained their trust, made several friends among them. Through a few carefully tailored and coached questions, she was able to determine that neither the spaceside nor dirtside locals have any record of MS or its symptoms among their population. And those records go back almost two millennia.

"This is particularly interesting in light of the fact that the habitable planet in this companion system—R'Bak—is an object of contention precisely because it is a source of various flora with powerful and highly unusual therapeutic properties."

"And you think one of those plants is going to prove to be a miracle cure for MS? That's a pretty long shot, don't you think, sir?"

Nuncle nodded sadly. "I agree. On the other hand, it is, as you Yanks say, the only shot you've got. But that's the compassionate side of the equation of putting you in charge. The practical side is that you are very early in the course of the disease and have an outstanding record, along with outstanding recommendations from your superiors and your subordinates, right down to scuttlebutt from E1s and E2s." He stood, Nephew following a moment later.

Murphy rose also. "One last thing, sirs. I understand what our mission is. But I don't know why we are doing it, what's at stake."

"That is part of what we need to keep close, Major."

Murphy cleared his throat. "Permission to speak freely, sirs."

Both nodded.

"Listen, if you expect me to get people to keep fighting toward an objective, light years from a home they may never see again, I have to be able to tell them *something*. I have to be able to tell them why it matters. Otherwise, they are going to walk away thinking you're just ditching them to lighten your load. That they are just garbage you're off-loading and that you're just shining us on with a bullshit mission, a fiction meant to convince us that we're not just being left here to die. Which won't work, sirs."

Nephew and Nuncle looked at each other. Nephew squared his shoulders as he turned toward Murphy again. "Okay. Then you can tell them this. The Ktor are derived from *homo sapiens*. They can pass unnoticed amongst us. They tricked other races into invading and almost conquering Earth. They want to take us over, to make us a part of their Sphere and grab our DNA to help boost their fading, overtaxed genelines." He leaned forward slightly. "And you can add this, if you want. They killed my father, gutted my sister so that she's on permanent life support, and have tried—or succeeded in—destroying almost everything else that I love. And they'll do the same to you, to all the Lost Soldiers, and every good and beautiful thing you remember on planet Earth." He leaned back and his voice became quiet again. "Is that cause enough, Major?"

Murphy swallowed. "Sir, yes, sir." Then: "Where do I start?"

Chapter Six

NEAR *SPIN ONE*

Murphy approached the airlock. Although he was finally getting accustomed to moving in zero gee, he had hoped to return to the pseudo-gravity of a rotating environment before starting his final test. However, his Dog trainer had explained why that would have been a very bad idea.

Murphy admitted it was just common sense, once you thought about it. If some poor unsuspecting slob exited the airlock of a rotating structure, said unsuspecting slob carried its momentum. Said slob might not notice it right away, but he would…the moment he tried using the back-mounted maneuver pack. On which Murphy had to qualify today.

Worse still was that moment when the outer hatch opened and you found yourself perched at the edge of a starfield that was wheeling past at a puke-worthy clip. Hard enough for an experienced Dog to handle that kind of dizzying disorientation, but for a complete neophyte like Murphy? Disaster, probably of the sort that would require medical treatment. Or possibly, last rites. Murphy secretly doubted the Dogs bothered to memorialize individuals. Probably just reduced their dead to distilled water and basic proteins before discharging whatever remained into hard vacuum.

"Your tether, Major Murphy."

He turned at the voice, even though it came from his helmet's speakers. Behind him, his zero-gee maneuver trainer was miming the actions of fastening his safety line to a mooring ring. They had another term for the action, but Murphy was Airborne and for that part of the process, he was going to stick with the term he'd learned at Fort Benning, local equivalents be damned.

He attached the tether's C-clip, locked it off, and announced, "Hooked up." He punctuated that with an erect thumb—which drew a blank stare.

The trainer sounded like someone trying very hard not to be bored. "Move slowly. Keep an eye on your helmet gauges. If you are in doubt, remember that your training suit is skinless; you can see all the systems and visually confirm their operation. The only exception is the maneuver unit and life-support supply on your back." The trainer waited, then sighed. "Visor, Major Murphy."

Damn. Murphy pulled down the dark, polarized filter from its retracted position atop his helmet. Its tabs clicked into the neck ring's receptacles.

The trainer nodded and pressed the outer hatch release.

It opened slowly, revealing a widening sliver of ink-black space. At first, Murphy couldn't even make out any stars. Then, just as he did, a space-suited figure floated into view—and it clearly was not a Dog. Not only was this person wearing a bare-bones training suit like his own, but they had their hands spread out as far as they could, apparently to stop themselves when they reached the side of the training station. But the desperate tension in the arms and shoulders reminded him of a little kid grasping for the edge of a pool after having been thrown into the deep end.

So, that was Captain Mara "Bruce" Lee.

He had hoped to meet her here since the Dogs hadn't yet taken the time to train her for "vacuum ops." They had kept her busy and quartered near their leadership, which had prevented her from making private, face-to-face reports to Nuncle and Nephew. It had also kept her from meeting her new CO, Major Rodger Y. Murphy. All chance? Maybe, maybe not.

But now Lee was heading planetside, and the Dogs had yet to bring her up to speed on vacc-ops. Murphy had bet that their hosts, in order to finish training such distasteful lesser beings all at once, would push their sessions together. And sure enough, here she was.

A gentle push with his toes sent Murphy out into space, past the station's hull—and into a sudden chill of realization: in just another second, he'd have no way to stop himself. If he didn't grab the edge of the hatch…

But he did, just as Lee—the body in the suit was definitely gravity born-and-bred—reached out a hand to help stabilize him. Her next motion eliminated any lingering uncertainty regarding her identity: as she cocked her head quizzically, she gave a thumbs-up.

Murphy returned the gesture, scanned the area. Another space-suited figure was approaching casually. However, the moment he noticed that Murphy had emerged, puffs started jetting out of his maneuver pack. So, two minutes, maybe three. Certainly no more. Murphy touched the emergency comms jack located just behind his left ear.

Lee nodded and in five seconds they'd plugged into each other's helmets.

"Major Murphy, I presume?" Her voice was a husky alto.

"Captain Lee. Glad we've got a minute or two—barely—to talk. How are you holding up? I've heard the audio feed from the battle."

"I'm ready for duty, sir. I will be—"

"Lee, there's no time for the formalities. Really, how are you?"

A pause. "Not sure, sir. Lot to get used to. What I lost back on Earth. This new world. Allies that are barely co-combatants. Assuming they don't turn into adversaries."

"And assuming the people who brought us here were really saving us from politicos determined to pull the plugs on our cryocells."

Lee's reply was immediate. "Sir, my gut tells me those two guys are on the level. Despite all that Nuncle and Nephew skullduggery."

"So they used that codename crap on you, too?"

She shrugged. "'You can't reveal what you don't know.' Their answer to almost every question I asked."

"What about your time with the Dogs? Any revelations yet?"

"Just that there are two different kinds. The big asteroid habitats? They call those the Spins. The folks from them are the SpinDogs. Then there are prospectors, miners, salvage-monkeys, scattered in small communities all over the outer system. They're the RockHounds."

"That's useful data, but what can you tell me *about* them?"

Lee sighed. "That's a work in progress, sir, and slow going. Haven't met any RockHounds. But I can tell you that the SpinDogs are definitely not all alike. The ones who I'm with now, the Matriarch's Family, seem to be the best of the bunch. For some values of 'best.'"

"Such as?"

"They're not as ruthless. Actually seem to care about each other. Have a larger sense of community."

"In what way?"

She glanced at the approaching SpinDog. "Some Families are worried about the fate of everyone up here, SpinDogs and RockHounds alike. But the rest of the Families? Not so much. Some, not at all."

"I've seen evidence of that. I hear you're heading down to the planet soon, to train them on helicopters."

"Correct, sir."

"Keep me apprised. The Dornaani are leaving some satellites for us. I don't know the details, but their sat comms are absolutely secure and private. Or so I'm told."

"Good to know, sir." Another glance toward the trainer. "Look, this guy who'll be qualifying you on the maneuver pack. His name is Jarat. There's something hinky about him."

"Thirty seconds, Lee; give me specifics."

"Nothing obvious, sir. But he wasn't just assessing my vacc skills; he was sizing me up."

"I take it you don't mean sexually."

"Correct, sir. Jarat's attention was all business. Measuring my strengths and weaknesses. Character. Guts. That kind of thing."

"So he's gathering intel. Training, particularly under hazardous conditions, is a good opportunity for that."

Lee shrugged. "In their shoes, wouldn't you do the same?"

"Might try to be a little more friendly—or at least a little less creepy—about it."

"No debate, there, sir. Uh, oh, teacher's on the headset. Gotta go. Major: you turned your radio off by accident. I just talked you through turning it back on."

"Got it, Captain."

But Mara Lee had already yanked out her jack and was turning to face Jarat as he slowed to meet them next to the airlock hatch.

If Jarat suspected that the radio snafu was just a cover story, and that Murphy and Lee had managed a quick confab, he gave no sign of it. Then again, if Jarat actually was an intel operative, he'd almost certainly be able to conceal his reactions.

"So," Jarat began, "do you feel familiar enough with the suit and maneuver pack to proceed with the final exercise, Major Murphy?"

Murphy looked down at the training suit. Either the SpinDogs had achieved major miracles in thin, lightweight protective materials, or he was going to pick up more than a few rads today. The lack of an outer covering, which allowed the trainee to observe the suit's various systems in operation, also made all the hoses and wiring and filters and heat exchangers look naked, vulnerable. Which made Murphy a little nervous.

"Major Murphy, did you hear my question?"

"I did. I'm ready to go."

"Very well, Major. Learning to use the maneuver pack is arguably the most important part of your training. It is also the most dangerous. Turn slowly, as you have been taught."

Murphy swung his arm gently to the side; he began to rotate slowly in that direction.

Jarat nodded, inspected both the maneuver pack and life-support unit on his back. "You seem to have adequately mounted and connected both systems. Restabilize."

Murphy counter-swung his other arm, but in smaller increments, correcting until he was motionless.

"Now run a standard check of the maneuver pack's controls."

Murphy did.

Jarat might have shrugged before he unclipped the tether from Murphy's suit.

Murphy started: space suddenly felt much larger than it had a moment ago.

"We shall start with a simple ten-second burst, Major."

Murphy almost started again. "Ten seconds? Isn't that a lot more than—?"

"It is necessary to show you what can occur if you depress the thrust trigger for too long. You will remember to use short bursts, afterward. But on this occasion, you will maintain thrust for ten seconds. You will maintain constant vector…er, 'hold a straight course,' until you terminate the burst. You will then drift for ten seconds, tumble and initiate a precise ten second counter-burst. That will bring you to a stop."

"Figured that much," Murphy muttered.

"You will then fire two half-second bursts to commence your return along a reciprocal vector. It will be slow, but this is to teach you that in space it is more important to perform actions correctly than to complete them quickly. Are you ready?"

"As ready as I'm ever going to be," Murphy admitted.

"Then you may commence."

Murphy released the safety on the compressed gas jets. He braced himself for rapid acceleration as he squeezed the activation trigger.

Murphy had expected a sudden jolt, but the system was quite smooth, and the rate of acceleration seemed fairly modest—until he saw the velocity meter in his helmet, positioned just above his left eye. He watched the remaining seconds of thrust tick past on the recalibrated and Anglicized clock over his right eye. Six seconds remaining. Five, four, three…

Darkness. The primary life-support pump wheezed to a stop a moment after the gas thrusters cut out.

Damn it. Murphy toggled the radio with his chin. "Jarat, I've lost power in the suit. Thrusters are offline. Hell, *everything's* offline." Silence. "Jarat?"

That was when Murphy remembered that the suit's systems all drew power from a single source. So, his radio was dead, too. Real suits had battery backups, but not training shells. Which meant he was heading downrange, totally dark, and at a velocity of…of…

Rising fear prevented him from making that calculation, but eight seconds of constant acceleration would reduce him to an undetectable speck pretty quickly. He felt panic coming up through the fear—

He swatted it down, the way he had plenty of times in the Mog and before. Yes, the blackness yawned before him, and yes, he was desperate to get eyes on the training station, to gauge how far off he was. But the quickest way to get the measure of that was also the worst. A sideways turn was fast, but later, he'd have to correct that rotation before he could initiate any attempt to return to the station—and now, wasted effort or seconds could be the difference between life and death. So, Murphy decided to go with the more difficult, but ultimately, more economical maneuver.

Making sure to keep all his motions in one axis so that he didn't add any side-vector momentum, Murphy swung his hands forward and down. Sure enough, just like in the lessons he'd learned and practiced just this morning, he started into a lazy forward tumble: 'ass over teakettle,' as his grandfather would have said. The motion was initially more disorienting than a sideways turn, but once he adjusted, it gave him an upside-down look at the training station about every fourteen seconds.

The good news was that he could still make it out clearly. The bad news was that in another two or three minutes, he wouldn't. The strange news was that there was no visible activity near it. In fact, he could still see Jarat, waiting alongside the airlock.

What the hell? By now, Jarat should have realized that something was wrong. Of course, Murphy allowed, with his clock dead and suppressed fear stretching each second into an eternity, he might have an exaggerated sense of just how long ago he'd lost power. But surely Jarat must have at least realized that Murphy's radio was dead, and that a rescue was needed…

Unless…

Unless Jarat was not a trainer, and not even a surreptitious observer, but an assassin. If there was ever a plausibly deniable means of getting rid of one Major Rodger Murphy, this had to be it: a training accident on the riskiest vacc-ops qualification exercise. An unfortunate short in the suit's power system when the neophyte was untethered for his first free space movement away from the station. Without the skills to correct his course, send or receive messages, or any thrust to effect a return, he would be out of range before his trainer "realized" that assistance was needed. At least, that's the story Jarat would peddle, and who'd be able to prove otherwise?

As he started to counter his tumble—very slowly, so as not to impart force along any other vector—Murphy allowed that it was a relief to be able to keep eyes on the station, now. But his fate was sealed because he had no way to generate thrust.

Or did he?

He checked his suit: no impediment to manipulating the straps. Same with the various exposed systems, which suddenly went from looking like fragile bits of ugly machinery to a glittering array of lifesaving devices.

Murphy manually adjusted the choke that regulated the flow of air from the life-support unit. Without power, the rate at which it entered his suit couldn't be fine-tuned, but the pressure in the air reservoir sent it rushing in. When he felt pressure starting to increase in his ears and along his body, he twisted the choke closed; that cut off the air flow. Then he rotated the intake valve into the closed position, thereby sealing the only opening in his suit.

Moving slowly, Murphy worked at loosening the strap releases until he was able to slip off the life-support unit without moving his shoulders or upper arms. He double-checked the lanyard that connected the unit to the suit harness, guided it off his back and around to his front. The rear of the life-support unit was now facing the dwindling station. Last step, now.

Using small arm movements, he repositioned himself so he could look over his left shoulder and see the station, and over his right, see the darkness into which he was disappearing. Then he used his left hand to reposition and brace the unit so that the air flow connector was also facing the blackness, while his right hand gripped the air flow choke…and briefly loosened it.

Air gushed out. Murphy closed the choke again, assessed. The burst of air had come out almost directly counter to his current trajectory. He had definitely reduced the rate at which he was moving away from the station but not by much, and his vector had altered a bit.

He repeated the action: opened the valve, closed it, reassessed. The range to the station was opening even more slowly, but he was also a bit more off course.

But Rodger Murphy smiled. Because at this rate, he would ultimately cancel his forward motion and begin returning. Very slowly, very crookedly, probably far off course. But he didn't have to rendezvous with the station. All he had to do was get close enough so that even casual observers couldn't miss him: a drifting speck that wasn't going to conveniently get swept under the endless black carpet of deep space.

So, before too long, someone—maybe Jarat himself—was going to realize that they had no choice but to rescue him if they wanted to cover up the botched attempt on his life. Soon enough, he'd be safely back on the station.

Surrounded by people who wanted him dead.

Chapter Seven

SPIN ONE

Still in the liner he'd had to wear beneath the training suit, Murphy reached *Olsloov*'s docking collar just as the hatch opened and Nuncle's voice invited, "Please enter, Major. First compartment on your right."

Murphy followed the instructions, resisted the impulse to walk deeper into the alien ship, see if he could get a glimpse of one of the Dornaani. Instead, he walked toward the dilating iris valve to his right. "Ready for that briefing, sirs," he announced as he entered.

Nephew and Nuncle were seated at a very human-looking table. Still, Dornaani compartments were weird. The room didn't really have corners, at least not the sharp, right angle variety: just a curving spot where walls and floor (or ceiling) joined. It felt a little like being inside a big, boxy egg.

Nuncle smiled, waved him toward the empty chair opposite. Once Murphy was seated, the Englishman folded his hands, began in a sympathetic tone, "We are aware that this has been a terrible shock, Major, and that we've thrown a great deal of information at you. And on top of it all, you had a close call just an hour ago. So if, all things considered, you'd like to put off this briefing another day or two—"

"I'm good, sir." Seeing doubt, Murphy leaned forward. "Let me see if I can boil the situation down to the basics."

Nephew smiled. "Go ahead."

Murphy leaned back. "So, by the numbers. One: we're stuck here.

"Two: if the enemy sends a signal back to Kulsis, we're dead.

"Three: to stop them from signaling, we have to initiate ground ops to keep them from building a makeshift transmitter.

"Four: we can't get to the ground without the SpinDogs' help, so we need to establish a workable *modus vivendi*."

"A what?" Nephew grinned, seemed surprised.

"Look, I was gonna be a lawyer, once, yeah?"

Nephew, still smiling, nodded. "Please: go on."

Murphy picked up where he had left off. "Five: you're not leaving enough of us 'Lost Soldiers' behind to do the job on our own, and you aren't leaving enough of the right kind of equipment.

"Six: even if we did have the gear, we know squat about what's down there. And the SpinDogs don't have much info about the area where the OpFor is building the transmitter.

"Seven: that means we need the cooperation of the locals to mount the operation and get the necessary gear.

"Eight: we do that by recruiting the indigs, and with their help, grab an equipment cache the last bunch of bad guys left behind about eighty years ago. And in the bargain, we show the indigs that together, we can win.

"Nine: we parlay that alliance, and infusion of modern gear, into strikes to seize other caches. That enables us to equip a large enough force to attack and destroy the transmitter.

"Ten: and if we actually get that far, *then* we think about other plans." Murphy leaned back. "Does that about sum it up?"

Downing's mouth was not smiling, but his eyes were. "More or less," he muttered.

Murphy nodded. "Good. Where do we start?"

Nephew waved a hand at the universe in general. "We thought we'd leave that up to you. At least for this first session. You're the guy who's going to have to come up with the plans and wrangle the locals. So, what do you need to know more about?"

Everything. But instead, Murphy answered, "Do the Dogs have dirtside informers?"

"Firstly, it's important to make a distinction between the SpinDogs and the RockHounds. The SpinDogs have contact with R'Bak, the planet. The RockHounds, being scattered throughout the system, have no planetary interface that we know of. So only the SpinDogs have planetside HUMINT assets. In fact, they have a class of people who are liaisons to select communities up near the poles. The locals who interact with those liaisons are known as Skydreamers, in their own towns. In most places, it's considered legend."

Murphy frowned. "So, the SpinDogs travel down there routinely?"

"Apparently."

"For what purpose? Can't be volatiles; it costs less and is easier to harvest them spaceside."

Nuncle's eyebrows raised; he clearly had not expected a space-savvy reply. "We believe they have an annual need for various consumables, which increases as the two stars near perihelion."

"Because that's when the Kulsians arrive and the Dogs have to go into hiding."

Nephew nodded. "Yep. They've got to stockpile for almost a decade of zero access to R'Bak while the Kulsians are crawling all over the surface. And of course, the more the SpinDog population grows, the more they need." He saw the perplexity that was evidently showing in Murphy's face. "Yeah, you might expect that a civilization that's been living in deep space habitats for centuries might have achieved self-sufficiency. But a one hundred percent closed bioloop is a lot easier to imagine than create. So even if they're able to produce their own life support, potable water, and basic foodstuffs, they're going to have deficits and gaps."

Murphy nodded. "Okay, so there are liaisons. And they could recruit informers. But they'd only be useful if they had a means of exchanging information routinely."

Nephew smiled. "Looks like you're going to have people listening for, and triangulating on, planetary radio transmissions."

Murphy shrugged. "How else would informers be of any use to the Dogs?"

Nuncle nodded. "I quite agree. Now, I believe you have met the rest of your cadre?"

"I have, sirs."

"And are you comfortable with them?"

Murphy nodded cautiously. "Harry Trapper and Bo Moorehouse are solid, sir. Not sure about Bowden, yet. He's got ghosts—or maybe a skeleton—in his closet, haunting him. Can you provide any insight on that?

"We know there was an incident, but the Dornaani were never able to pull up details."

"Redacted?"

Nuncle shrugged. "Or deemed unimportant. Or some other reason. No way to say. What about Chalmers?"

"Got to be honest, sirs, I'm not a fan." Murphy kept his voice neutral. "You've seen his record?"

"We have. Regrettable. But there's no arguing that he was effective in his roles as investigator and interrogator. And he's the only Lost Soldier we're leaving with you who has any experience in intelligence or counterintelligence."

Yeah, sure, but that may have been because he had leverage back in Somalia—underworld contacts and dirt—that he won't have here. But Murphy simply nodded and replied, "No arguing that, sirs. And the rest of my detachment, when are they scheduled for reanimation?"

"Within the week, Major. And they may not come around quite as quickly; some of the cryocells are of more rudimentary designs than others. Their occupants take two, or even three days to get fully back to normal."

The words "rudimentary design" sparked Murphy's next question. "Sirs, one of the linchpins of our alliance with the SpinDogs is the part I understand the least. Specifically, how can they replicate our technology so quickly and in such volume? I mean, it's surprising enough that they are already cranking out our weapons and ammo, but whole helicopters? In just three or four weeks? How is that even possible?"

Nephew shrugged. "Necessity is the mother of invention, Major. The Dogs have had to live in space to hide from the Kulsians, because if 'Skypeople' were anything other than a baseless and discounted legend on R'Bak, they'd have been hunted down and exterminated."

Nuncle nodded. "Our new allies have not been entirely forthcoming, but from what we know, they were expelled from R'Bak centuries ago. Their early days required that they find some means of expanding more quickly than their initial population could achieve. So, they developed robots that can be automatically reprogrammed and reconfigured to produce a wide variety of parts. Others can assemble an equally wide variety of devices. And they've had centuries to refine that technology."

Murphy shook his head. "Still hard to believe, but I guess we'll see it in action."

Nuncle's voice became quieter. "*You* will see it in action, Major. I'm afraid we'll be on our way by then." He stood and put out his hand. "As you come up with more questions, we'll answer as best we can."

Murphy nodded, stood, shook both their hands, exited, and as he found himself back in the oddly smooth corridors of *Olsloov*, he suddenly felt further from home than the 152 light years that separated him from Earth.

Alnduul emerged from a previously undetectable door in the small compartment's bulkhead. His voice sounded both surprised and uncertain. "Do you really intend to 'answer him best as you can?' Is that wise?"

Downing sighed. "'As best we can' includes an unspoken but invariable strategic caveat: 'as best as the situation allows.' Murphy is a professional. He branched to intelligence for two years as a first lieutenant. He understands."

"You sure about that, Richard?" Trevor's voice was sharp, not jocular.

Richard glared at his notional nephew. The sudden, reactive spurt of anger was a bow wave before the rising tide of guilt over what he had concealed in the past from his "nephew" and from others. "And what would you have me tell him? 'Well, Murphy, if we *did* share everything with you, why, you'd just be more likely to get yourself killed, you poor sod. Because you're over your head, here. In fact, a trained operative would take one leery look and bunk off if they were assigned to oversee this...this shit show. Staying here with a force of just over a hundred, eternally at the mercy of a mob of twitchy space dwellers? Who are the only thing standing between his command and a bigger mob of planet-rapers? Ah, but buck up, Murphy; better luck and times are sure to be just around the corner, hey?'"

Trevor stared at his uncle. If the Englishman's tortured outburst had moved him, he didn't show it. "Yeah," he said, "that's *exactly* what I'd tell him. The damn truth."

Downing's guilt was washed away by genuine anger. "Yes, I suppose you just might. Probably congratulate yourself, too, sitting on that lofty dais of moral superiority. So lofty that you'd never have to see the results. Murphy would be paralyzed by uncertainty, or he'd double- and triple-guess himself at every step. Or he'd inadvertently reveal just how much he knew about the SpinDogs and they'd deem him an unacceptable security risk. However it played out, he'd be headed into the gutter, along with the poor blighters shackled to him.

"Fortunately, I'm just corrupt, duplicitous, and professional enough to tell him what he *needs* to know rather than everything we know or suspect. It's a distinction you might do well to keep in mind in case I get cashiered by Dame Fate, Captain. Because God help those depending upon you if you haven't yet awakened to reality."

Trevor's eyes were wide—not in anger, but surprise. "Listen, Richard, you know I—"

"Right now, we have one job: to figure out what we can tell Murphy and what we can't in order to maximize his chances of living long enough to improve his odds of survival. Agreed?"

"Agreed," murmured both Alnduul and Trevor.

Downing stared at his hands. "This is a bloody awful list to make—all the things we *can't* tell him—but I think we can agree on item one: the SpinDogs' actual replication capabilities."

Trevor frowned. "You mean that each Family has their own, in concealed locations?"

"That, too, but also their total capacity."

Trevor looked dubious. "I've got to say that I think those estimates are…inflated."

Alnduul's eyes shuttered slightly. "I'm somewhat familiar with the logistical signatures of replication facilities. The ones *Olsloov*'s sensors have detected in this system are much greater than what would be required for their claimed production capability. Exponentially greater."

Trevor shook his head. "But eventually, he needs to be told that. I understand that he's not a trained operator, and that if he lets that knowledge slip while he's still vulnerable, the Hardliners might jettison him from the nearest airlock."

Downing nodded. "Which is one of the most important reasons we can't tell him everything. But I take your point: we need to find some way to make sure Murphy will have access to the rest of our intelligence when he comes to have need of it."

Alnduul raised two, long walking-stick fingers that he started trailing like streamers in a gentle breeze: affirmation and assent. "I believe I have a solution for that."

Downing felt an eyebrow rising. "Which is?"

Alnduul's mouth half-rotated. "You would find the details quite dull, I'm sure." His tone said that he knew otherwise.

Downing smiled back. *He may be a clueless alien git at times…but he certainly can be a crafty one, too.*

Chapter Eight

SPIN ONE

Murphy checked his watch; he was already running late. He had to hit the CP, grab his dataslate, and get an update from his staff officer. From there, he had to track down Bowden and finally read him in on the mission to derail the completion of the enemy transmitter on R'Bak, and then head double-quick to the ops center the SpinDogs had set up to monitor Captain Lee's mission up near the poles. Which had apparently gone sideways. By the end of the day, Murphy expected he'd have a headache, but at least he wasn't starting with one.

It was, in fact, the first day since emerging from the Dornaani virtual language training that he really felt like himself. The headaches were gone, but two irksome after-effects persisted. The first was that the world now seemed to be moving much too slowly, the way it does when you get out of a car that comes to a sudden stop after driving half a day at a hundred miles an hour. Not a surprising sensation, since virtuality's event stream ran at ten times normal speed. Well, not *speed* exactly. It was more like the way time works in a dream; events occur, resolve, and you move on without any break. But whereas the human dreamstate is intermittent and free-floating, virtuality was unrelenting and focused.

And it was that nonstop mental exertion which probably gave rise to the second after-effect. Now, if he was between tasks and his mind started to wander, he didn't just get drowsy; he was catching himself in mid-fall from his chair, already half-asleep.

Mara Lee had reported similar sensations, evidently, but he had no way to compare notes with her. She'd been dirtside well over a week and had almost completed training the first SpinDog chopper pilot, who would also become the liaison to subsequent student rotations. Assuming the ominous overnight report from R'Bak did not signify that one or both of them had been lost.

Getting more pilots ready for the new Hueys couldn't happen fast enough, actually. The satraps were little more than the Kulsians' lackeys during the stars' shared periastron—called the Searing—and had made definitive progress on their transmitter. Definitive in the sense that they had collected too many resources and expended too much effort for the site to be a decoy or a feint. In short, the Lost Soldiers now had a confirmed target. It also meant that a countdown clock was running to take it out before it was operational.

But before he could mount that attack, Murphy had to get local support and intelligence. And unfortunately, Lee's training base was thousands of kilometers away from the target zone. Besides, contacting and recruiting indigenous peoples was not in her job description. That fell to Harry Tapper and Marco Rodriguez, who'd have to be inserted directly into the area of operations. Establishing contact, turning that into trust, and then into an alliance was the necessary edge of the wedge to gather the forces needed. But the question of whether ground forces would be the primary tool or more in a supporting role was becoming more uncertain every day. Which was why Murphy needed to bring Bowden into the discussion and planning team before dropping by the SpinDogs' ops center.

His one-man staff, Captain Makarov, rose as Murphy speed-walked into the CP. "What's the word, Mak?"

"Mak"—clearly, he was still not fond of that nickname—frowned. "What's the wo—? Ah, a colloquialism. Nothing unusual to report, Major."

Murphy nodded approval and gestured for Makarov to resume his seat or at least relax. The Russian remained standing; if he relaxed, the American couldn't detect it. Typical for Makarov: he was stiff and wasn't comfortable engaging in the banter, which was one of the few commonalities among all the Lost Soldiers. Whether that was because the Russian captain was a product of the 1980s Soviet military or because he wasn't really a soldier, Murphy had yet to determine.

Pyotr Ivanovitch Makarov had been an interpreter in Afghanistan but had not come up the ranks in the Red Army. Rather, like many individuals who had rare but necessary specialties, he had been pulled out of his doctorate program in linguistics at Moscow University. Whereas many in his field had the cognitive ability to analyze languages, many lacked a natural ear for them. Makarov had both.

He was recruited aggressively (as only the Soviets could) and was given the rank of captain out of necessity. It was the minimum ante for him to be able to carry out his routine duties in the rarefied circles in which he was to work: liaison to the Russian Embassy in Kabul, staff at general headquarters, occasional consultant to intelligence. During his first few months in-country, the closest he'd come to combat was hearing a couple of car bombs go off in the distance. Ironically, his first op outside the wire was also the one which brought him so close to the edge of death that he was among those dragooned by a Ktor.

Murphy snagged his data slate, a folder containing the most recent recon images from the Dornaani satellites, and a full new water bulb. Even in space, the mantra was *hydrate, hydrate, hydrate*.

"Sir," began Makarov after a loud swallow, "there *is* a message for you."

"What is it, Mak?"

"The SpinDog ops center sent a reminder. You are wanted there in thirty minutes."

Thirty minutes? What the— "Why did they move the time up, Captain?"

"Sir, they did not."

"They told me to be there at local dawn, R'Bak time zone three."

"That is correct, sir." Makarov swallowed again. "However, they anticipated that the major may have forgotten that R'Bak has an 18-hour day."

Oh, for the love of— "Okay, Mak. Let them know I'll be there."

"Very good, sir. But before you go, there is one other matter that—"

"It's gonna have to wait, Mak." Murphy paused, *Always take a second or two to build rapport.* "But...what's the *basic* issue?"

"Consumption of stores, sir. It seems excessive. Also, I suspect there is some falsification in current requisitions."

Murphy rolled his eyes. "Hoarding for resale? There's a black market starting up already?"

"I think so, Major."

"Then look into it, Captain Makarov. You've got the chops—um, skills for the job. Let me know when you have something to report."

Makarov snapped as straight as a ruler. "Yes, sir."

Murphy waved a quick combination farewell and salute and got moving toward the refectory; he was just glad Mak hadn't called him "your Excellency."

"Mind if I sit here?"

Kevin Bowden looked up from his lunch, seriously annoyed that individual meals were served on a rigid, and widely distributed, schedule. His eyes took in the unwelcome visitor in front of him, then all the empty tables in the refectory that served the section of the habitat in which the Lost Soldiers were billeted. He shrugged. "Fine with me, sir," he finally said. "The answer's 'no,' though."

Major Murphy raised an eyebrow as he sat. "Not sure what you mean."

Right. Bowden pointed with his spoon toward Murphy's folder-filled hands. "You're not here for lunch. That means you're here to recruit me for a mission, just like you did everyone else who was in the Mogadishu chopper wreck. The answer's 'no.'"

Murphy's tone cooled. "How do you know what the answer is when I haven't even asked the question?"

"Because I'm done. I've done enough for my country." Bowden looked back down at his food and shoveled in another mouthful. *Hell, more than enough.*

"I need you for this. You're the only one who can do it."

"*What?*" Bowden exclaimed, loud enough to cause everyone nearby to glance over at the pair of humans. "*You've got more kids for me to kill?*"

"Easy, Lieutenant," Murphy said, making a calming motion with his hands. "This is not a combat op. You're the only tactical aviation guy we've got from around our time frame, and that's the skillset I need to look at a mission in the CONOPS stage."

Bowden's eyes narrowed. "Just look at something?"

"For now, I just need you to look. There are no missions being planned."

"'No missions being planned *yet*,' you mean."

Murphy shrugged. "Lieutenant, you and I know that, given our current situation, there's no guaranteeing you won't have to get back into a cockpit again. And I'm not going to insult your intelligence and make myself a liar by saying otherwise. But at this point, what I need is your knowledge and expert assessment. And only that."

Bowden sighed as he let his shoulders slump. "Guess I could look at something for you. It's not like I have a whole lot else to do here. Don't appear to be going home any time soon."

Murphy's smile was small, brittle, and shadowed by more than a little regret. "Thanks," he said. "Meet me in three hours in docking bay 2A."

Bowden, appetite suddenly gone, shrugged. "I could go now, sir."

Murphy was already moving away. "Wish I could. Got to get back to our hosts' ops center."

"Captain Lee's mission?"

"Why do you ask?"

Bowden shrugged. "Because you were at the comms early this morning. Or so I was told. That's right after the SpinDogs stood up a full staff for their ops center in the middle of the night. Generally not good signs."

"How'd you hear about all that?"

"Scuttlebutt is just as lively amongst officers as enlisted, sir."

"Ain't that the truth. See you in three hours."

Bowden looked after him, pushed the tray away. Yep, his appetite was completely gone.

Murphy paged the door into the ops center, was admitted quickly.

The hatch sealed just as quickly behind him. Two of the SpinDog security types had their trademark angular submachine guns pointed at his gut.

Murphy decided that he was losing the ability to be shocked by anything. "Anyone care to tell me what's going on here?"

"I was hoping you would answer that exact question," said a SpinDog that Murphy had seen at one of the meetings with Nuncle and Nephew. Bramath. From a "breedline" that was under the umbrella of Family Kormak. A junior nephew of its Primus, if memory served.

"All I heard last night was that there was a mechanical failure. Your team here was not very forthcoming with more information. I was told I'd be contacted as soon as there was any news." Murphy stared at the two unwavering muzzles. "Wasn't told that would be done at gunpoint."

"That was before we had reason to believe that you may be duping us."

"Duping you? How?"

"By presenting yourself as our allies when you may be working for the Kulsians."

Okay, I guess I can *still be shocked.* "What?"

"How else would you explain the attack that has destroyed one of the polar towns where Family Otlethes' liaisons visit, and which has taken various hostages?"

"Taken by whom?"

Bramath's smile was not friendly. "That is what we are waiting for you to tell us."

Somehow, Murphy forgot about the two submachine guns; he was too busy trying to get his head around the suppositions behind Bramath's accusation. "So, let me see if I understand this. Despite the huge losses we inflicted on your enemies not quite three weeks ago, you believe that we are actually on the Kulsian's side?"

"Perhaps you are only pretending to be outsiders. Perhaps you are working for a single faction, or just one of the Overlords, whose own units were not present at the battle," Bramath suggested. "An attempt to lessen his rivals' power in this system so that he might have more exclusive access to the high-value exoflora during the coming Harvesting."

"Really?" Murphy folded his arms. "So why wouldn't this treacherous Overlord use all the superior technology demonstrated during the battle here to eliminate his opposition back on Kulsis? Because it seems certain that none of his peers could have stood against it."

Bramath was silent but no longer smiling. Several of the others in the ops center, particularly the observers from Matriarch Kelrevis's own family, were watching him, waiting for a reply that never came.

Murphy shrugged and continued. "And if we're the agents of this Overlord, then how the heck did we know about your existence in this system? Because we'd have had to *already know you were here* in order to orchestrate everything that happened."

Even the pair holding the machine guns were glancing toward Bramath, now.

"I could keep asking questions—there are plenty more to ask—but I'll let you reply to those first."

Bramath's brow was lowering. "You take great chances with your—"

The comms specialist gestured sharply. "Scion Bramath, there is communication from R'Bak!"

"A ransom demand? A parley?"

"No, Scion. From Healer Naliryiz of Family Otlethes."

"Is she, too, a captive?" Bramath did not sound entirely displeased.

"No, Scion. She has the troglody—she has Captain Lee standing by."

Bramath glared briefly at Murphy before questioning the comms officer. "Does Lee intend to make demands?"

"No, to coordinate rescue attempts."

Murphy unfolded his arms. "Let me speak to her."

"Why? So, you can exchange coded information?"

Murphy shook his head. "Bramath, can you really—?"

"Silence! This could all be part of an act, a means to lure even more of us to our death. Perhaps with the cooperation of some in Family Otlethes." The silence in the ops center became simultaneously tomb-like and tense.

Okay; so, I'm up against paranoia, not rational thought. "Look, that's why you have me at gunpoint, right? To use me as hostage, as leverage, to prevent…well, whatever it is you think you're preventing. So, if by speaking to Captain Lee I activate some treacherous scheme, I'll be its first casualty, won't I?"

Bramath considered. "Yes."

"Well, I'm not suicidal, and it sounds like we need to arrange a rescue."

One of the individuals from Family Otlethes stood. "Bramath, allow him to speak."

"And why should I trust *you*?"

"Because you did not allow any of our Family to carry guns here, either. We, too, are your hostages, it seems."

Bramath frowned, stepped back from the console, drew his sidearm: another almost box-like weapon. "You may speak to your captain, Major Murphy. But should your conversation become questionable—"

Murphy almost rolled his eyes. "Yes. I understand why you have your pistol out, Bramath." He reached for a headset. "Captain Lee, this is Major Murphy. Status and sitrep."

A grainy image of Lee, looking somewhat worse for wear, appeared in a small screen located just under Murphy's equally small camera/mic combination. She said that she and her student were alive and well, their Huey was not, nor was the town to which they'd traveled. Evidently a group of Kulsian raiders had wandered unusually far north in their depredations, an event which she unironically described as "Murphy's Law in action"—which caused trigger fingers to tighten in the ops center. Fortunately, her next sentence included a statement of the axiom: "Yesterday, anything that could go wrong did, and at the worst possible time and place."

Trigger fingers relaxed; so did Murphy's belly muscles.

However, as Lee started her appeal for additional units to aid in a rescue, Bramath shook his head. Remaining quiet and outside the range of the pickup, he warned, "You will send no additional personnel, Major. The hostages are SpinDogs; they are our affair."

Murphy kept his face and voice as neutral as he could when he responded to Lee. "I understand your position, Captain, but the rest of the task force isn't ready to deploy planetside yet. And if it was, it is far too early for us to show our hand."

Her reaction, her eyes in particular, gave him a sense of what it might be like to crisped by a very large laser. "Fine," she said. "Then given the *strategic imperative* of our mission here, I request permission to take command and do it my damn self!"

Murphy returned her glare; her tone warranted that sternness, at least, but more importantly, he had to keep her from suspecting that there was something hinky happening on his end. He kept his tone crisp. "A moment, Captain Lee."

Bramath reached over and cut the comm feed. "What do you mean, a moment? There is nothing to discuss. Order her to remain as she is."

Murphy looked sideways at Bramath. "Let's say that this raid is exactly what it appears to be: extremely bad luck. Murphy's Law, as you heard her say. Then when I prohibit her from joining a rescue, I am also prohibiting the use of the helicopter they have available." Murphy glanced at the crew present from Family Otlethes. "How do you think the hostages' Family will feel knowing that you prevented their own personnel from using the helicopter, which is probably the only way they can hope to effect the rescue?"

Bramath did not turn toward the persons Murphy had glanced at; the Scion could probably feel their eyes boring into his back. He nodded but raised his weapon slightly higher. "Careful, Major." He reactivated the comm feed.

As soon as Lee's face appeared, Murphy said, "Agreed. We can provide assistance, but you should send your student instead, Bruce. Your abilities are far more strategically important than—"

"Ending the call. Enemy could triangulate and locate." Lee cut the connection before Murphy had a chance to say more. He suppressed the urge to nod; she'd made the right decision, the one he had hoped she'd make: to take the initiative and mount the rescue.

Bramath was frowning mightily. "That was less than completely reassuring, Major."

Murphy shrugged. "I did what I could. Now what?"

"Now we wait."

Murphy sighed. "Then I have just one favor to ask."

"What would that be?"

"If I don't leave here alive, I'd appreciate it if you'd contact Lieutenant Bowden and tell him I'm not going to make our meeting after all." Murphy sighed. "Now, in the meantime, can I at least have a seat while you're deciding whether or not to shoot me?"

It took Bramath two hours of close consultation with the senior members of Family Otlethes and then his own uncle, Primus Kormak, for the hapless Scion to decide in the negative.

Chapter Nine

SPIN ONE

Kevin Bowden walked into docking bay 2-A, exactly three hours later, to find Major Murphy talking to two of the SpinDogs—who sure didn't *look* like aliens—standing next to one of their interface craft. Murphy nodded to the two humanoids, and they went back to working on something on its nose.

"What do you think?" Murphy asked as he walked up, nodding toward the craft. He seemed calm, but the armpits of his duty uniform were as wet and black as if he'd been working half a day in the tropical sun.

Bowden managed not to raise an eyebrow, instead he went over to the interface craft and started walking around it slowly, picking out details. "Looks like a cheap version of the space shuttle with ducted-thrust nacelles, built by the lowest bidder." He looked again and saw where some of the pieces had been hammered to make them fit in place. "In Russia." He took a few steps to one side to get a better look at the forward section of the craft. "Looks like it's seen a lot of use. Wouldn't be surprised if they bounced the nose off an asteroid or two. I'm not talking little ones, either."

He shrugged and walked back. "Looks like a work vehicle that's been ridden hard and put away wet plenty of times. Why?"

"We're going to turn that craft—and two others just like it—into fighter/bombers, just like your old Hornet."

Bowden laughed for at least 20 seconds, finally stopping when his stomach started hurting. "Thanks, Major," he said when he caught his breath. "I haven't had a laugh like that since…" His voice trailed off as his thoughts came up short against the event that split his life into two parts: everything that had come before, and everything since *that day*. "I haven't laughed like that in a long time," he finished after a few seconds. He smiled. "Seriously, though, what's it for?"

"Exactly what I said. We're going to turn it into an attack craft for a mission we have coming up, while giving it enough air-to-air capability to get it there and back safely."

"That thing is a beast," Bowden said, walking up to one of the wings and slapping it. The sound it made told him it wasn't made of the same metal as his beloved Hornet. "It'll never be a fighter. Maybe a bomber. It's ugly enough, just like the old A-6E Intruders that used to be in my air wing."

"You may not know this," Murphy said, "but the SpinDogs have never thought about fighting in atmosphere before, and this is their craft with the best in-atmo performance. All they were ever worried about was getting in and out fast, so it's got plenty of power, but no real armament."

"Reminds me of an F-4 Phantom," Bowden said. "You know? The plane that proved even a refrigerator will fly if given enough thrust?" He paused and then added, "That's why you brought me here, isn't it? You want *me* to turn this into a fighter/attack craft." He narrowed his eyes. "You probably want me to fly it, too, and then you want me to carry out whatever mission you've got in mind for it."

"Well, of course I want you to turn it into a bomber. You're the guy with the aviation engineering background. You're also a Navy Test Pilot School graduate, and you were an applicant for the astronaut program—"

"Yeah, and now look at me," Bowden said, his voice heavy with sarcasm. "Now I'm a 'real' astronaut."

"I'm not here to debate your qualifications. I'm here—"

"How *do* you know all that about me, anyway?"

Murphy's jaw tightened, and his eyes hardened; he clearly did not like being interrupted. "I probably know everything there is to know about you." His jaw relaxed a little. "Our liberators found extensive records on all of us. They knew more about me than I think I knew myself."

"Then you know why I'm not going to fly this thing."

Murphy nodded. "I do. Although it took digging in general records, not your personnel file. Nothing ever was entered there about your last flight in Africa. I also know that event happened hundreds of years ago, and it wasn't your fault."

"Doesn't matter whose fault it was," Bowden said. "I can still see that child…and it *feels* like it was just yesterday. To me, anyway."

"I understand. It seems like just yesterday to me, as well, and I'm hoping to use your experience to make sure we don't have it happen here, too. There are civilians in the vicinity of the target and killing them will…will only piss off their leaders that much more." Murphy's voice was as hard and carefully controlled as his face.

Bowden nodded and turned away so the major wouldn't see the moisture in his eyes. "What—" His voice caught, then he said more normally, "Tell me about the target and its environment."

"The target is an intersystem transmitter and antenna complex located in the foothills of the planet below us. Our leading plan is a ground operation: recruit indigs, grab cached enemy equipment, and take it out.

"But we can't depend on just one plan. The transmitter *must* be destroyed, or the locals are going to announce our presence here and call in the Kulsians to wipe us out. I'd rather that didn't happen as I'd like to still be here when our ride home gets back."

Bowden nodded. "Okay, so probably an antenna and a building. Both can be taken out with the appropriate application of high explosives. What's so hard about it?"

"There's a town nearby that we absolutely *cannot* drop bombs on. Also, we don't know how well it will be defended. We know they're activating secret weapons caches as fast as they can, but we don't know what's in them. They have armored vehicles—even though most are beat-to-shit hand-me-downs—so we have to assume they have triple-A and probably some sort of handheld IR SAMs, even if they're early generation ones. They may also have air support. You'll have to take that into account, too."

"What kind?"

"Blimps."

"*Blimps?*" Bowden asked incredulously. He pointed to the interface craft. "Even with that thing, blimps aren't air support; they're obstacles."

"Either way, they have to be dealt with."

"True," Bowden replied as he considered flying through a landscape littered with giant, moving airships. That might be…complicated. "Okay, get me the info on the target complex and the environment around it, and I'll do some back-of-the-napkin weaponeering on it."

Bowden spread out the imagery on one of the refectory tables and pointed at the target area. "For this being the equivalent of a third world country, this is still going to be a bitch, based on the target, what they're defending it with, and what we have to attack it." He scratched his head. "They're using the terrain well, too, which makes it hard to get at."

When Murphy only nodded, Bowden continued, "The target is this massive dish and the arm holding the transmitter and receiver hanging over it. The complex is a lot like Arecibo back home, but—due to the level of local technology—probably isn't quite as sophisticated.

"It looks like the main collecting dish is a spherical array about 300 meters across, so it's similar in scale to Arecibo. The receiver and transmitter complex are on a platform suspended above the dish by four cables anchored in the mountains surrounding it. There is also a control building about a hundred meters off to the side. Based on the latest pictures, they're almost done building it, although it's impossible to know whether their electronics and control systems are installed, let alone online." He shrugged. "If I was going to hit it, I wouldn't wait for it all to get set up; it may go operational as soon as everything's built and in place."

Murphy nodded. "That's the plan."

"Okay, so in order to take out the target, we either need to drop the antenna arm by cutting the lines holding it in place, destroy the control building, or, better yet, both."

"Why both?"

"The control building is an obvious and easy target," Bowden said. "However, it's also more easily replaceable than a giant antenna arm suspended 150 meters above the dish. We also don't know if they have other, hidden control stations the system may tie into."

"Their tech level is pretty low. The fact that they have one is pretty surprising."

"And yet they do." Bowden smiled. "Do you want to bet our continued existence on the fact that they don't have another control station?"

"Not if I don't have to."

"Me either, which is why we also drop the antenna into the dish, making a big-ass mess of both, and setting the project back several years."

"Why don't we just go with that, then? Focus all our efforts into dropping the antenna?"

"Because that's pretty much a pinpoint target. You'd have to have your bombs—or whatever you're using—hit close enough to where these cables are anchored to snap the wire or cause the retention mechanism to fail. It'd be easy if your guys were flying Hornets with a bunch of precision-guided munitions; they could easily drop the antenna. But with the interface craft and weapons you'll be using? Good luck. You're better off pounding the control station and taking a swing at the antenna. You may get lucky, but if you don't, you've at least covered your ass to some extent."

"And bombing the dish? It's huge. That would seem to be a pretty easy target."

"It would. You could poke a bunch of holes into it pretty easily, and then next week you'd have to do it all again, as the panels are probably fairly easy to replace. And the next week, and the next week…"

"So that's not an option."

"Well, at some point, they may run out of replacement panels, but it really isn't a viable solution. It's like bombing a runway. You put craters into it making it unusable, but then they come out with a dump truck of dirt and a bulldozer, and they make the runway operational again in a few hours. Better to bomb the airplanes on the ramp, instead; go for the stuff that can't be easily replaced, rather than hitting what can."

"Leaving us with the control room and cables." Murphy shrugged. "Okay, I get it, the target's hard."

"No, the target is *damn* hard, based on the placement." Bowden pulled out a new image that showed the dish and the area in which it was located. "The antenna is located here, in this valley, surrounded on three sides by what appears to be pretty impassable mountains."

Murphy nodded. "I've talked with the locals. Aside from some goat paths the local indigs may know about, there aren't many ways into the area that we've been able to find."

Bowden sighed. "Figured as much, which is why we're looking at doing it with the interface craft." He sighed again. "Okay, so the target is surrounded by mountains on three sides, making bombing runs difficult, and on the fourth side by this town, which pretty much blocks off anyone trying to get to it on the ground. It would be easy if you had an airwing from back home. They could just orbit way overhead and plink away with some Walleyes or Mavericks…hell, even generic LGBs would work."

"None of which we have."

Bowden smiled and realized that viewing the attack clinically—as a problem-solving exercise—made it easier for him to not dwell on his last flight. "No, we don't," he said with a sigh. "And your guys can't orbit overhead and do high-performance dives on it; the three craft we have for the mission aren't able to support those kinds of maneuvers. You could get them to augur into the target if you've got any kamikazes in your group of Lost Soldiers…"

"I won't order, and we can't afford, that kind of mission. Also, the SpinDogs would be annoyed if we didn't return their craft when we were done with them. They're old and crappy, sure, but the SpinDogs don't have a lot of them and can't throw away three of them without a *really* good reason."

"I figured as much. So the easy way is out." Bowden shrugged. "I guess the next option is a Skipper attack."

"A Skipper attack? Is that a Navy thing for killing their commanding officer?"

Bowden chuckled. "You really are a funny guy. Being around you is good for my morale."

"Glad to hear it. But still, I don't get it."

"No, an Army ground-pounder probably wouldn't," Bowden said with a smile. "A Skipper is a kind of bomb the Intruder guys used to use. It was good for blowing up targets that had serious close-in defenses, like all of the soldiers defending the building and antenna."

"They're just guys with guns and—maybe—handheld missiles. Are they really as big of a threat as that, once you get past any SAMs?"

Bowden looked at him intensely. "More planes have been brought down by guns than missiles. And whoever you find to fly this may not be your stereotypical fighter jock. There are a *lot* of people with guns near the target. You can subscribe to the 'Big Sky, Little Airplane' theory all you want, but with that many troops, someone's going to get lucky and hit those big-ass interface craft of yours. And 'get past any SAMs' is a lot easier to say than it is to do. If they've got IR-guided missiles, your guys will be lucky to get out of there alive. Even first-generation SAMs can hit a slow, non-maneuvering target."

"So what's a Skipper, and how's it going to help us?"

"It's a laser-guided, rocket-propelled bomb. The rocket on the back gives it some stand-off distance, while the laser receiver on the front makes it into a precision weapon. Back home, they had a range of about fifteen klicks. It'll be interesting to see what we can do here."

"Interesting? 'We?' Sounds like you're 'in' for this mission."

"It's an interesting problem," Bowden said, "and I'm happy to put my experience into solving it. It helps me not think of…other things." *Please, God, don't try to make me do it. I can't. I won't.* He shook his head. "I'm *not* flying it." He looked suspiciously at Murphy. "Who *are* the people flying this mission? You never did say."

"No, I didn't." Murphy gave him a sharp nod, with perhaps a hint of regret in his eyes, as if he knew something Bowden didn't. "It looks like the crews will end up having SpinDogs as pilots and Lost Soldiers as weapons officers. They refused to let me have three interface craft to operate on my own. Although the SpinDogs haven't wanted to participate in the planetside action, they are going to pilot the three craft. All of the weapons, however, will be operated by Lost Soldiers."

"And which Lost Soldiers are these?" Bowden asked with the same suspicious look. "I don't see a lot of Hornet, Intruder, or even Viking pilots running around here. In fact, I only see one—me—and I'm not doing it."

Murphy frowned. "I'm not telling you what to do at the moment, *Lieutenant*. But you sure as hell aren't telling *me* what I won't do, either. We're walking this forward, and we'll see where it takes us."

Bowden didn't like that open-ended statement, but Murphy's tone was at least as much one of regret as firmness. Which made it acceptable—barely—to not get into a show-down. *Not yet, anyway.* Murphy stared at Bowden for a minute as if challenging him to dispute it further.

When Bowden finally looked down, Murphy added in a grudging tone, "I've got a Phantom pilot, a Phantom radar intercept officer, and a Thud driver."

Bowden shrugged. They'd do. *Even if they weren't the best candidates for the job, they were still better than having* him *fly the mission.* "Well, the RIO probably had some experience operating weapons and systems similar to the ones the SpinDogs will have to piece together for this mission," Bowden said, trying to upsell his experience, "and the others will have done bombing runs before. They're also going to be used to the concepts of how to perform a multi-plane strike, flying in formation, and anti-aircraft fire avoidance." He nodded. "I'm sure they'll be able to complete the mission."

Chapter Ten

SPIN ONE

Time to go. Murphy looked around his now almost naked stateroom and then shouldered the SpinDog version of a duffle bag; synthetic, light, entirely too flimsy looking. But beggars couldn't be choosers, and he and the rest of the Lost Soldiers had arrived with, literally, just the clothes on their back. And guns. Which were going to start becoming the more important portion of their scant belongings all too soon. He left his quarters.

Bowden was at the boarding tube with Makarov. Murphy half-grinned at the lieutenant. "Well, here to say farewell, or to make sure I'm really leaving?"

Bowden quirked a smile. "Sorta both."

Murphy's grin became complete as he considered the lieutenant's double-barreled truth. Bowden had plenty of good reasons not to like him, just as Murphy didn't have any choice but to rely on Bowden's expertise for an op sure to give the aviator nonstop nightmare flashbacks. Two guys doing their job. Hating it for different reasons. Well, that much about military life hadn't changed a bit. "Makarov, you look anxious. Or eager. I can't tell which. You have any updates before I head out?"

Makarov nodded. "Yes, Major. Construction of the improvised meteoritic assault capsules is nearing completion and they should be at waypoint zero in three days. Training for Lieutenant Tapper and Sergeant Rodriguez is also progressing on schedule. No unusual difficulties. And virtual language training for the rest of the detachment has been completed."

"And the black market?"

Makarov flushed. "Those inquiries are proving…frustrating, sir. I have a suspect—one of the individuals who was on your helicopter, actually—but no conclusive evidence. I continue to observe and gather reports."

"You keep at it, Mak."

"Yes, sir. Shall I send updates to you while you are off *Spin One*?"

"No. The only comms I'm going to get while I'm on Outpost are highest priority; fast encrypted lascom bursts, twice a day. The SpinDogs don't like unnecessary sends, particularly not when they're aimed anywhere in the vicinity of R'Bak." He explained in response to the two men's puzzled stare: "Paranoia working overtime, I'm afraid. Despite the Dornaani sweeps, some of the SpinDogs are convinced there might be unspotted, deep-space Kulsian spysats capable of detecting the lascom's vector and tracking it back here." He shook his staff officer's hand, turned to Bowden. "Still trying to figure out why you're standing there, Lieutenant."

"Like I said, to make sure you really leave. Give you a helping shove, if needed."

Murphy laughed. "Sounds about right." He put out his hand.

Bowden took it uncertainly, pulled his back quickly, looked out the narrow, extremely thick view port next to the boarding tube. "So, they're really leaving us behind."

Murphy followed his eyes to where *Olsloov* was maneuvering away from its berth. He nodded. "They really are."

Bowden shook his head. "That close to aliens…and I never got to see one." He glanced at Murphy. "I'll bet you got a glimpse, though. C'mon," he pushed when Murphy shook his head, "not even you?"

"Actually, I suspect I was the Lost Soldier least likely to get a glimpse."

Bowden nodded. "Sure. Because if anything goes sideways while we're alone in this system, you're going to be the one who gets the deluxe SpinDog interrogation experience."

Murphy tried to smile, wasn't sure he managed it. "I guess. Either way, I received the same chaperoning you did. Every time I stepped aboard *Olsloov*, Melissa Katano was there to greet, and shepherd, me."

Bowden nodded. "Yeah, and great conversation along the way. 'How are you feeling? Settling in? Any requests?' But she never shared any info on where *Olsloov* is going next or about who Nephew and Nuncle really are." He paused. "Or if they're actually going to come back."

Murphy nodded. "Ms. Katano did her job well." And she certainly had; not one Lost Soldier ever saw more of *Olsloov* than the short, dull route from the boarding area to the cargo bay that had been refitted as a mass virtual reality training facility. "I'll see you soon, Lieutenant."

"Yeah. Hurry back."

Murphy shook his head at the sardonic tone. "And you take care, Makarov. This guy next to you wouldn't be half bad at running the show, if you needed him to."

Bowden looked like his breakfast might be coming back up.

"*Spaseebo*, Major," said the Russian. "And *udachi*."

Murphy nodded, turned with a wave, and thought, *Yeah, because I* will *need all the luck I can get*.

Bowden kept staring at the latest recon imagery of the transmitter site, trying to will a tactical revelation into sudden existence. *Yeah, like* that *ever works*.

Bowden sighed, tried to forget the stats and numbers and visualize a better attack plan to achieve the mission he'd been given. Three aircraft. Two targets to be destroyed. By equipment that had never been field-tested. Deployed on craft that hadn't been built to carry them, much less release them. Probably while taking ground fire, which definitely included guns and might include missiles, as well.

He sighed, and his face fell forward into his hands. It didn't seem possible, and it certainly wasn't probable they'd get both targets. Even if all three went after the control station—and *only* the control station—the odds they'd hit it were far less than he'd have liked. And even if they destroyed it, that didn't ensure success, because the locals might have another station. But hitting the cables and dropping the antenna complex—

which *would* ensure success—was every bit as hard as he'd told Murphy it would be.

"What's wrong?" a deep voice asked.

Bowden looked up to find one of the other survivors of the UH-60 Blackhawk crash he'd been in. Although Bowden didn't know the man, he had the look of a SEAL—immense shoulders and solid torso. Bowden had seen him around since he'd been pulled out of cold sleep; the Blackhawk survivors had all been defrosted early on, ostensibly because they were all ranking officers and had the best preparation for dealing with the advanced electronics of this new century. But, despite participating in a lot of the same initial training, Bowden hadn't let himself get close to the SEAL. Or any of the other Lost Soldiers, for that matter.

The SEAL also had the penetrating gaze that everyone in his trade had, but at the moment, it had softened.

"I'm sorry?" Bowden asked.

"I asked what was wrong," the big man said. He nodded to the imagery. "Something I can help with?"

"Working on a target for an airstrike," Bowden said. "Unfortunately, I'm just not sure I can pull it off with what I have available."

The man chuckled. "I know exactly what you mean." He shrugged. "Anything I can help with?"

"You're a SEAL, right?"

"Yeah, Lieutenant Harold Tapper, Navy SEAL, at your service." He held out his hand, which Bowden took.

"Lieutenant Kevin Bowden, Hornet pilot and strike planner for the most idiotic attack ever attempted."

"I don't know about that. I've been on some pretty stupid ones in my time, both back home and now the one I've been planning here. In a few days, I go dirtside to link up with some indigs and convince them to work with us. Then, along with them and a few other Lost Soldiers, we're going to seize a modern mechanized column using nothing but infantry." He smiled. "Want to trade?"

Bowden swallowed. "Uh, no. I'm not sure, but your mission may be even more fucked up than mine. Good luck with that."

"I've got a few minutes, and I could use something else to think about for a bit. What have you got?"

Bowden showed him the target and told him what he was planning.

Tapper chuckled when he was finished. "Well, that's a bitch in its own right, but I'd still trade you if you wanted."

"No thanks." Bowden looked down at the imagery. "Got any ideas?"

"The only way you're going to do that is with a ground designate."

"I wanted to do that, but I don't think we can get people in place."

"A mule's not that heavy, and the terrain will support it…I think. That's what I would do, anyway."

"A mule?"

"The ground designate equipment—Modular Universal Laser Equipment, or MULE—to be exact. It's the handheld laser we used back home to lase a high-value target for you brown shoes to drop bombs on. If you could get a couple of them in close—or some other sort of handheld laser—you wouldn't have to worry about keeping your laser on target once you dropped. That would at least take care of some of the targeting problems you're going to have while avoiding potential triple-A, and it would help with hitting your point targets."

"You think we can get a couple close enough?"

"Maybe over here." Tapper pointed to a maze of canyons and crevices that could be seen at the base of the high terrain to the east of the target. "If you can't get through there, though, the ground designate option is out. And that's certainly going to make the mission a lot harder." He smiled. "That's the best I can do for you." The big SEAL rubbed his forehead then shrugged as he stood. "Maybe some of the local indigs can help with it. Sorry, but I have to get back to prepping for the drop into my own very special clusterfuck."

Bowden chuckled. "No worries. Thanks for taking a look." He held out his hand. "Good luck with your mission."

"Thanks. I head to the orbital FOB tomorrow, then off to the insertion point. I'll take all the luck I can get. Good luck with yours." He turned and walked over to the corner table Bowden had seen him sitting at before.

Bowden sat and looked back through the imagery again with an eye toward ground-based lasing. He'd originally given up on it due to the terrain, but if Tapper thought it was possible to get someone in there, maybe it was. *If* they could build a couple of handheld lasers, and *if* they could get them into the target area, then it would be a *lot* easier to cut the cables to the antenna complex. It might not make the mission's success probable—there was too much untried tech for that—but it just might make it possible.

"You want to make a what?" Lotho Ferenc asked. The SpinDog pilot was Bowden's liaison for setting up the mission and would be the lead pilot for the strike. Based on his attitude, it didn't appear that his participation had been by choice.

"I want to make a laser-guided, rocket-propelled bomb."

"I understand the need to drop bombs on the antenna, but why laser-guided and rocket-propelled? That seems like a lot of extra work. Just fly over the antenna, release a large load of bombs, and fly back home. No more antenna."

Bowden cocked his head at the SpinDog. "Have you ever actually *dropped* a bomb?"

"No, but it cannot be that hard. Fly over the target. Push the button. Bombs fall. How is that so difficult?"

"When people are shooting at you, it's a lot harder than that. You have to maneuver to keep from getting shot, but still be flying in a manner that the bombs come off the aircraft going in the right direction to hit the target."

"Just fly higher," the SpinDog said with a smile. "Their rifles can only shoot so high."

"I would agree with you...but not only does that make accuracy a lot harder as the winds the bombs fly through will be different at every level, it also puts you into their missile envelope. I don't know how many missiles they have, but Murphy thinks they have them, and your aircraft is a great big, lumbering target. If you fly high, you're going to get shot down."

Ferenc frowned. "Very well; fly lower."

"So now you're back to people shooting at you with guns. The first time you see all those tracers reaching up for you, and you realize how many bullets there are that you *can't* see, you're going to be yanking the plane around so they don't hit you. And that's going to throw your bombs all over the place."

Ferenc shrugged. "It can't be done, then. Why are you wasting my time?"

Bowden smiled. "It *can* be done, but we need a laser-guided, rocket-propelled bomb to do it. Because it's rocket-propelled, we can launch it from about fifteen kilometers away, so we don't have to fly through the triple-A—"

"The what?"

Bowden had to work hard to stifle the sigh. *Remember, they've never done this before.* The fact that Ferenc seemed to not want to listen to any advice, though, had Bowden ready to scream. He smiled again, instead. "Triple-A is Anti-Aircraft Artillery. Basically, every gun they have that can be pointed into the air, whether it was originally made to shoot at aircraft or not."

"Their guns. Okay. I understand."

Bowden nodded. *Finally. Progress.* "A rocket-propelled bomb can be launched from outside the area where they can shoot at you—which is a good thing, trust me—and the fact that it will be laser-guided means that it will still be accurate enough to hit the targets we're aiming for." *I hope.*

Ferenc squinted at the bomb two of the SpinDogs had trundled up in a dolly. "Where do you attach the laser to it? Do you mount it on the side?"

This time Bowden did sigh, although he tried to keep it to himself. "You don't put it on here." He slapped the side of the bomb, and Ferenc jumped back as if it would detonate. "The laser goes on the aircraft or—better yet—is carried by someone on the ground. You put a laser *receiver* on the nose of the bomb and give it steerable wings. Then, when the bomb senses returning laser energy, it flies to the source of it and blows up. Target destroyed."

The SpinDog counted on his fingers. "So, we will need a laser on the aircraft, a laser receiver on the bomb, steerable fins on the bomb, and a rocket motor for the bomb." He paused for a second. "They will not like interrupting normal production to make these four items."

Bowden chuckled. "It's not four items. It's three of the aircraft lasers—one for each aircraft—and at least twenty of the laser receivers, wing packages, and rocket motors. Plus, the twenty bombs to strap them onto, of course. And the two handheld lasers we'll need."

"There are only two targets—the control station and the antenna cable." Bowden opened his mouth, and Ferenc added, "Sorry, *two* cables need to be cut. So, three bombs. One aircraft can carry three bombs, so all you need are three bombs, and one aircraft laser. Simple, and it will disrupt production less."

"If only things worked like that," Bowden said. "Let me introduce you to a little thing we call Murphy's Law. Murphy says that anything that can go wrong, will. Nowhere is this more true than in aircraft operations. You can almost count on the fact that if we try to launch two planes, one will break, so you need an extra. We have two targets, so we need three aircraft to be outfitted and ready to go."

"But cannot one aircraft launch bombs at both targets? The craft is big enough to carry bombs for both targets."

"Yes, but it is unlikely they'd be able to guide both of them to separate targets on the same bombing run."

"Well—"

"No," Bowden said. "You never make two runs on the same target. Never. By the time you come around again, everyone in the world with a gun is firing at you. Only. One. Run. Ever. And, since we have two targets, we need two handheld lasers on the ground to identify them, and two aircraft to hit them. And, since we need two *working* aircraft to hit them, we need a total of *three* aircraft armed and ready to go. "

It was Ferenc's turn to sigh. "I will see what I can do. Why do we need twenty bombs, though? Is this more guidance from your Major Murphy?"

"Yes. Well, no, but yes." Bowden shook his head, trying to decide how best to explain it so the SpinDog would understand. "We are using untested technology. Some of the bombs won't work. Some may not see the laser spot or guide on it. Some may not blow up. The aircraft will each hold four of the bombs; I want each of them to have four, just in case."

"But that's—"

"I'm aware that's only twelve and I said twenty. I want eight extra bombs for them to run tests with to make sure they work. There's nothing worse than flying into an enemy's triple-A envelope only to find out your weapons don't work, and it was all for nothing. I won't be there if that happens, but you will, and I doubt you would like to have risked your life for nothing."

Ferenc sighed again. "I will do my best, but I don't know…"

"Wait!" Bowden called as the SpinDog started to walk away. "We haven't talked about Sidewinders yet!"

Chapter Eleven

"OUTPOST"

Murphy leaned back, having just jabbed a period at the end of his most recent log entry. The change in posture once again brought his eyes level with the op-center's forward observation screen. The view from Outpost's bow was mesmerizing: a slowly falling starfield on endless loop, repeating every seventy seconds.

He forced himself to look back down before the Zen-trance of the cycling image put him to sleep. Which would not have surprised anyone in the operations center. Murphy had been standing oversight on final approach and insertion for twenty hours straight, and at a certain point, stim tabs lost their efficacy.

However, just because the others in the op-center would be unsurprised did not mean they would be understanding. Rather, they were likely to see grogginess as yet another confirmation of their perception of him, and, by extension, the rest of the Lost Soldiers. Namely, that they were undisciplined, imprecise, ill-trained, dim-witted, and clumsy.

It was hard to argue the last point, at least as long as they were spaceside. Even in the long, hollow asteroids where Murphy's men were now billeted, they remained awkward, still acclimating to the .75-gee equivalent. There was also their lack of adaptation to the Coriolis effect. Specifically, their planet-trained eyes had not yet learned to predict the seemingly curved trajectories of free flying or moving objects in a rotating environment. Nor had they learned to anticipate the potential for disorientation when they turned their heads perpendicular to the direction of the spin. So the SpinDogs were not simply fabricating an unflattering characterization when they labeled their guests "awkward:" the Terrans were broader, heavier, and stumbled around like inebriated gorillas. Among the most prejudiced locals, the Hardliners, the term "Terran" was being supplanted by "Trog." Murphy considered the odds to be about fifty percent that it would become the most common label for his people.

Unless, of course, the Lost Soldiers decisively proved their claimed superiority in a planetary environment. Which they were about to do, and which was why Murphy had been in Outpost's op-center for the past twenty hours. Officially, he was a coordinator of the first joint Terran-SpinDog mission to the surface of R'Bak. But more essentially, he was the guardian angel for the two Lost Soldiers assigned to it. Their relations with the SpinDogs were still evolving and not all of their hosts were happy with it. Not happy at all.

He checked his G-Shock; only fourteen minutes to orbital insertion. Time enough to make sure that the mission log entry he'd just completed made some kind of sense when read in the context of all the ones he'd written before. He flipped open the green-covered, ring-bound notebook he'd dragged with him all the way from Fort Benning, and stared at the last three entries:

Day 023	*Olsloov* departs.
Day 024	Mission dropship commences op with tug boost toward R'Bak along retrograde orbital track.
Day 028	Dropship lascom confirms all parameters are nominal; mission on track.

Murphy read his last entry. In minutes, he would know what fateful emendation he would have to make to that final clause: "mission on track."

But the actions that would determine the change he would have to make were out of his hands, as they were for everyone else in Outpost. That would be decided in real time by the crew of the dropship and the joint ops team, now almost thirty million kilometers behind them.

"Behind"? Murphy frowned at himself: in space, nothing was ever really "behind" or "in front" of you, any more than the terms up and down had any real utility. But it was hard getting used to the strange terms that prevailed when trying to establish spatial relationships independent of gravity or fixed objects. Still, no better time than the present…

So: "behind." Murphy pinched the bridge of his nose, tried to visualize the actual positions of the objects in question. Outpost shared R'Bak's orbit around the secondary star, which they called Shex. However, Outpost preceded R'Bak in that orbital track, maintaining a constant distance of about 22 million kilometers—which was also .15 AU (astral units). Or, more important when calculating the comms delay, 75 light-seconds. And because it was "ahead" of R'Bak in the same orbit (anything up to 180 degrees in the lead was deemed "ahead"), Outpost was "spinward" of the planet. Conversely, any object following up to 180 degrees "behind" R'Bak was deemed to be "trailing" it.

So, in the shorthand of everyone from the 22nd century—aliens included—R'Bak and the dropship carrying the ops team were presently .15 AU to the "trailing" of Outpost. Murphy pinched the bridge of his nose again. When he had enough time to write the terms down or think them through, they all made sense. But then the locals started rattling them off in their high-speed jabber, often adding two positional coordinates that could either be oriented to the system's ecliptic *or* to the observer's own location and attitude. That was when Rodger Y. Murphy conceded defeat and simply resolved to wear an expression of calm focus instead of slack-jawed confusion.

Which was pretty much the same expression he had worn the first time he saw Outpost from the bridge of the spindly RockHound "packet" that brought him out from the largest of the habitats: *Spin One*.

Like the "spins," Outpost was an oblong asteroid. But whereas the spins revolved around their long axes, like huge stony logs rolling slowly in place, Outpost was tumbling ass-over-eyeballs. So, where the spins' centripetally-generated "gees" held your feet down upon their long inner walls, at

Outpost, the maximum gees were felt at its ends. Murphy had come to envision it as living and working inside the rubber caps of a high-school twirler's baton, the soles of his feet racing past the faces in the watching crowd.

Shortly after arriving, he'd made the mistake of commenting that these features made Outpost seem like a pretty awkward choice for a facility so proximal to R'Bak. When the ops support staff from the Hardliner families had drifted away hiding (but not really) sneers of contempt, a comparatively tolerant Expansionist technician had explained that Major Murphy could not be more mistaken in his assessment.

Firstly, Outpost was the closest semi-stable object from which they could watch R'Bak. Murphy accepted this as proof that the mantra of 20th century real-estate agents was universal: location, location, location! Specifically, Outpost had started its existence as part of the swarm of planetoids that any planet captured in both the spinward and trailing equilibrium points of its orbit. Murphy had actually heard of those, they were called LaGrangian points. Unfortunately, that infobite did not impress the technician in the slightest. In retrospect, Murphy supposed trying to impress her with his space knowledge was the equivalent of her proudly pointing out how, when trees grow close together in a big bunch, that's called a *forest*!

However, Outpost was, in every way, an outlier from the asteroids in R'Bak's spinward LaGrangian—or Trojan—point. Not only had it fallen thirty million kilometers behind that cluster, but its end-over-end tumble was both uncommon and unusually "clean." By which she meant that its motion was all along the vector Murphy thought of as pitch; there was almost none of what he called roll or yaw. The terms the locals' used to describe these vectors of motion made no sense to him and did not seem to have transliterations; they were not inherited from the cant of mariners, and the technician gave no clue as to their origins.

Considered together, she concluded, this made Outpost an extremely fortuitous find for the SpinDogs. Murphy frowned, expressed concern that the rock's unusual tumble might attract unwanted attention.

The technician's lips strained into an indulgent smile. Even if the space-faring monsters from the Jrar system began to suspect the existence of space dwellers somewhere among the planets and asteroids of Shex, a freakish rock like Outpost would be the *last* place they'd check. Just over 800 meters long, and with a spin rate that provided barely sufficient gee-forces to a small portion of its opposed poles, it could not support a viable long-duration community. Consequently, the raiders' first searches would be for something more like the spins themselves: long, large asteroids in slow, stable rolls. But the only reason the invaders from Kulsis would ever search at all was if they detected movement, artifacts, or emissions that did not originate with them. Which was why the present mission to R'Bak had been launched in the first place: to ensure that the SpinDogs and RockHounds remained undiscovered and unsuspected.

One of the more Hardline overseers—the ops command group had been carefully drawn from across the SpinDogs' and RockHounds' strange political spectrum—glanced sharply in Murphy's direction but did not make eye contact. "Drop time is on track: two minutes."

Murphy resisted the impulse to chew on his lip or cuticle or both. "Two minutes" actually meant "forty-five seconds until their capsules are released and then seventy-five seconds for word to reach us." Meaning that in just a little over half a minute now, the first part of this insanely ambitious—not to say risky—plan would begin. And by the time that word reached him, the outcome would already belong not to the present, but to history. As would the ops team if things went wrong.

And me, too, maybe. Murphy reached for his water bulb in the low gravity, affected a bored, roving stare as he sipped. But behind his (hopefully) duty-dulled eyes, he assessed the faces in the ops center. *Which of them might have orders to cut their Family's losses if the insertion fails?* It was no secret that many of the leading Families among the SpinDogs had felt it better to go to ground—hide hard and deep—rather than try to go planetside in an attempt to silence the remaining interlopers from the Jrar system.

There were a lot of flaws with their "hide and do nothing" strategy, of course. If the thugs, failed rent-a-cops, and contractor wannabes now on R'Bak made like E.T. and phoned home, there'd be little to zero chance of the SpinDogs and RockHounds remaining undetected. But if one or more Families had a contingency for that, had maybe decided to sell out the others in order to become spaceside satraps who swore service to the overlords on Kulsis, well, in that case…

Murphy finished scanning the room as he returned the water bulb to its holder. He wasn't sure what signs of incipient treachery he'd hoped to detect. None of them wore facial hair, so any unrevealed villains among them didn't have greasy mustachios to twirl. Still, it stood to reason that if one or more Families had a contingency plan for mission failure, it probably involved either a cover-up or selling out directly to the Kulsians. Either way, that put every Terran in the system at risk, Dornaani promises of return and reward—or retribution—notwithstanding. For the SpinDogs and RockHounds, alien promises and threats were a distant maybe; a visit from the bloodthirsty and ruthless Kulsians was an already-established, in-your-face fact.

But how could he be sure if such contingency plans even existed? Or if there was only *one* such plan? Or which of the faces in the ops center would be the expediters? *Hell, I'm an infantry officer, not James-friggin-Bond. I can't tell who they are—*

But…but maybe I don't have to.

Murphy stood into the one-third gee, looked at his watch for theatrical purposes. "In the event that the mission is a failure, I will need your collective cooperation on comms."

The most stone-hearted Hardliner didn't keep all the contempt out of his voice. "You mean, to inform the rest of your men of their comrades' tragic sacrifice in a timely fashion?"

"No, in order to ensure that the Dornaani microsat net does not self-destruct."

All around the ops center, hooded eyes opened wide. An overseer from one of the Expansionist Families stood. "What do you mean?"

Murphy checked his watch again. "There is little time to explain. Briefly: in addition to me, my cadre were all given failsafe implants. If we die, the implant ceases to signal. When it stops, the net self-destructs."

"We have detected no such signals during—"

Murphy rode over the top of that and other nascent objections. "Since the signal frequency and interval are not known to anyone—even us—but are preprogrammed into the Dornaani satellites and control elements, there is no way to know if we would have seconds or days before the next failsafe check. In order to maintain the tactical advantages—" *to put it lightly* "—conferred by the microsat network, I will need to act with all haste. Please stand ready to re-task your lascom links to the coordinates I shall provide. If it becomes necessary."

Murphy sat. The ops center was silent for a long moment, and then a distempered buzz of murmurs and whispers rose up. He could guess the content: that the Terran major was lying; that he was *not* lying; that he was bluffing; that this duplicity was expected; that it was wholly unanticipated; that even Dornaani technology was not capable of sustaining such a subtle failsafe system over such extraordinary distances; that if the microsat net were lost, the SpinDogs and RockHounds would be blind to events on R'Bak just when they needed to see them more than ever.

But Murphy didn't care which they believed, because at the base of it all, they would realize that any contingency plans to disappear the rest of the Lost Soldiers or present them as a bloody gift to the captains of Kulsis, now had to be paused. For a few days, at the very least. Maybe permanently. And that would give Murphy time enough to pull another plan or ploy out of his ass.

He hoped.

It wasn't pure fabrication; the Dornaani *had* rigged their microsats with a failsafe. It just wasn't arranged along the lines that Murphy had drawn for his suddenly sullen and mistrustful audience.

The now fury-faced Hardliner looked up again. "Signal received from the dropship; capsules have been deployed. Now entering upper atmosphere. Telemetry and instrumentation nominal."

Murphy held in a sigh of relief, thought it might burst out of his gut or lungs. So, in order to maintain an expression of calm, almost bored composure, he reached out for the logbook and scanned down for his last entry:

> Day 028 Dropship confirmed all parameters are nominal; mission on track.

He erased the concluding words, and wrote instead:

> Day 028 Dropship confirmed all parameters are nominal; orbital insertion confirmed.

He leaned back again, fought against the downward drag of his suddenly heavy eyelids, and wondered how long it would be before the op team would be able to make contact.

If they survive the drop, that is.

PART TWO:

TAPPER

Chapter Twelve

R'BAK

Damn. I've heard of getting the shakes during a drop, but this is ridiculous.

The insertion capsule was shuddering violently as it slowed, plunging deeper into the gravity well of the new planet. Despite all the precautions, both his limited equipment and body were rattling uncomfortably against the improvised padding and alloy bracing, creating a rapid thrumming. The little cone-shaped ship had stubby wings, but the thin atmosphere at high altitude denied them purchase. Dynamic forces snapped the vehicle back and forth across several degrees of pitch and yaw every second, resembling a ride inside the paint mixer of his father's hardware store. The very worst of the uncomfortable oscillations made his vision gray out. Harry tried to relax, deliberately inhaling through his mouth and exhaling through his nose, as the rapid vibration created an ever louder metallic banging which was growing alarming. He had no idea if this was normal or not.

It was his first space drop.

Lieutenant Harold Tapper, formerly of the United States Navy, fought to clear his vision as he scanned the scant handful of monochromatic screens facing his acceleration cradle. A red peanut light began to blink as the adjacent display flashed a block of alternating black and gray text. The accompanying warning siren was mostly drowned out by the hammering sounds made by the tortured hull of the ship. His blurring eyesight made the mostly incomprehensible alien script useless, not that it would have made any difference during the meteoric insertion via a scratch-built pod. Regardless, he was pretty sure the alarm wasn't a good sign.

Unfortunately for Harry, his automated single person craft was lean on comfort and instruments, sharing those qualities with his last ride on the UH-60 Blackhawk which had ferried him out of Mogadishu almost one hundred and fifty years ago. Of course, that helicopter had been built in a proper factory. This *thing* had exposed fasteners and there were parts simply *glued* together. On the other hand, there wasn't a window from which to see his surroundings. If he wanted a better view, he'd have to wait until this sorry excuse for a spaceship came apart around him. Which was, come to think of it, the last thing he remembered from that Blackhawk ride.

An especially severe bit of turbulence rattled his teeth together for a moment. Some things never changed. He was still a passenger, entirely at the mercy of a product from the lowest bidder and the whim of the gods.

Harry felt a change as the automated systems won out against the high-altitude winds, orienting his craft on the drop zone far below. Abruptly, the ride calmed. Even better, Harry's earpiece pinged an alert as the networked systems aboard the other two aeroshells automatically re-established contact.

"Seeker Six, this is Five," Rodriguez said, reporting in. Sergeant First Class Marco Rodriguez was the only other Terran on this trip. "Hey, boss, everything okay over there? This ride is fucking number ten, like a Saigon boom-boom gi—"

"Five, this is Six," Harry replied, stepping on the Green Beret's transmission, using their new shared language instead of his mother tongue. "No English. Ktoran only. I'm good. How about you, over?"

"Well, there ain't no red lights flashing anymore," Rodriguez replied, using the language they shared with the third member of their team. "Now all I need is to wake up from this dream and find myself in the land of the Big PX."

"Copy that, Marco. Break, Four, this is Six, come in."

"I hear you, Lieutenant," an accented tenor voice answered him in perfect English, no doubt making a point to the primitives from Earth. Volo Zobulakos' English was better than Harry's High Ktor, despite the forced learning program many of the Terrans had endured during their brief time awake on the Dornaani cruiser. He continued in the clipped syllables of his own language. "Passing thirty-five thousand meters. All systems nominal. Tracking directly for the principal LZ. Parachute deployment in two hundred and twenty seconds."

Harry acknowledged the transmission and ran through his sparsely populated landing checklist. Despite having nothing to do but wait for nearly four minutes, Harry compulsively scanned the inside of his capsule for the hundredth time. The stealthy re-entry vehicles were the product of the space-faring civilization to which Volo belonged. In fact, his entire people, nicknamed the SpinDogs, were now entirely based off-planet and had been for hundreds of years. Technologically, they were far, far ahead of the re-usable space shuttles which had been the state of art in America when Harry had deployed to Operation RESTORE HOPE in Somalia. However, this disposable and stealthy one-man capsule wasn't the way he'd expected to be inserted. Harry had seen myriad craft in use around the SpinDogs' habitats. From the single person scooters used to prospect in the asteroid clusters to large intra-system shuttlecraft, the SpinDogs had plenty of options for delivering the little team. However, the small, space-based civilization was paranoid to the point of making the average Explosive Ordinance Demolition tech seem careless.

Rather than risk the detection and possible destruction of the dropship *Hidden Knife*, they'd eschewed a landing and chosen the simpler option of dropping individual personnel capsules in the vicinity of the target. If the mission succeeded, they could recover and recycle the aeroshells at leisure. If the mission failed, the SpinDogs were out three unpowered craft, two Lost Soldiers, and one very expendable scion of an upstart House.

Harry expected that the Terrans didn't count, of course.

He watched the shiny digital altimeter count down as they fell toward the surface, just like a normal parachute jump. Instead of the old-school HALO method all SEALs practiced, back when there had been SEALs, this was something Major

Murphy had dubbed an "OILO," or Orbital Insertion Low Opening operation. It seemed unlikely any of the Kulsian raiders which had survived the strike against their orbital assets and planetary comm would be maintaining a radar net, but the clandestine drop also reduced the likelihood of visual detection. Much like the spec ops mission profiles back on Earth, Harry's little team would survive by using discretion and craft, not brute firepower.

That was a good thing because his current mission wasn't even half-baked. Harry still wasn't convinced this was the best Earth's supposed allies and keepers of some high and mighty interstellar compact, the Dornaani, could do. Dump six dozen archaic humans on an enemy-occupied planet in order to secure a fallback point for a larger-scale mission which was itself just shy of being a forlorn hope? Entrust opening negotiations to an unproven local and a pair of junior military personnel? Convince your new allies to risk everything for strangers?

And yet, here he was, hurtling downward like so much cargo.

Harry looked intently at one of the few manual controls in the vehicle. The big red lever located between his knees was labeled in blocky Ktor script, but next to it some helpful wag among his English-speaking comrades had taped a label, "Manual Deployment. Not For Use Underwater. Activate Only In Atmosphere!" The next panel over included an electronic warfare warning menu which would warn of potentially hostile radar. Mercifully, it remained blank. That suggested the close approach of the drop ship had gone unnoticed.

Something was going right, anyway. So much for Murphy's Law.

At which point a second red light began to blink as the previously blank EW alert flashed. The capsule abruptly turned, loading so many gees on Harry he didn't have time to register surprise, let alone make a last radio call, before blacking out.

He came to an unknown time later, but the ride was back to being smooth. The radio comms weren't.

"—ome in! Seeker Six, come in!"

"This is Six. What the hell, over?" Harry replied muzzily.

"Parachute deployment in thirty seconds!" Volo said urgently.

Harry shook his head and yawned, then looked at the instruments. Crap, they were very nearly on the surface! There was no time to be surprised; he needed to work the problem. The shortness of the landing checklist didn't make his situation any less dire.

"Ten seconds!" Volo said, unnecessarily warning both Terrans. "Prepare for manual deployment."

If Marco Rodriguez was anything like Harry, he was watching the altimeter with growing apprehension. An impatient SpinDog technician had carefully repeated the instructions to an audience he doubtless regarded as incapable of using tools more sophisticated than rocks and sharp sticks. In theory, each craft would use a flicker laser to sense the minimum height-over-ground required for deployment of the chute to guarantee a safe landing. If he didn't feel the automated systems deploy the capsule's drogue and parachute combination, he'd have less than two seconds to mechanically initiate that critical step. Harry placed both hands on the pebbly surface of the L-shaped lever and took a deep breath. He watched his displays intently, counting down internally.

In three, two, o—

He was interrupted by the audible *pop* of the drogue ribbon launching over his head. One of his screens flashed the corresponding message, as the drogue gave his capsule a single, hard jerk, pressing him heavily into his couch. After dramatically slowing the freefall to a speed the twin parachutes could withstand, the drogue detached. A second, mushier jerk announced the canopies' successful opening.

The capsule had barely steadied underneath the green and brown parachutes before the capsule crashed to a painful stop. The scant padding on the seat might have prevented any serious injury, but Harry still ached all over. But like the pain caused by a misaligned crotch strap during a regular jump, this was a good sort of pain to have. The parachute had worked, and the capsule was down. The cone shaped vehicle came to rest on its side, however. Getting out was going to require a bit of scrambling.

"Four, Five, this is Six," he said, trusting the hands-free microphone on his helmet while hanging sideways in his straps. "Sound off."

"Five on the ground. Mind the first step, it's a doozy," Rodriguez said jauntily.

"I've opened the hatch already, Lieutenant," Volo answered. "It's daylight, and we must cover the ships immediately."

"Copy," Harry said, releasing his chest strap. He fell heavily against one of the instrument panels, painfully bruising his arm. He suppressed a heartfelt curse.

"Popping the hatch."

He reached for the door lever, now inconveniently located over his head. After a pause, the capsule verified his intent, requiring a second yank before it obediently ejected the hatch outward with a percussive *bang*. Instantly, a cold wind filled his capsule, making him shiver. He poked his head outside and surveyed a bleak and rocky landscape which was partially obscured by the capsule's billowing parachute.

After donning a hooded parka from a storage cabinet underneath his feet, he withdrew his personal equipment and weapon. Then, with an athleticism he didn't feel, Harry used an inner handhold to swing outside. On either side of his aeroshell, the terrain rose several meters in elevation, forming a shallow canyon. His 'chute was tangled in some stunted gray-green trees that bordered the drop zone. Knee-high, rust-colored spiky grass poked up in between the fist-sized stones covering much of the ground. The breeze smelled wet and musty, but the ground appeared dry. A football field distant, Harry could make out another capsule, and began trotting over. It was supposed to be dusk on R'Bak, but the overcast diffused the light. Out of reflex, he checked his wristwatch, which rode alongside a new gadget doubling as a short-range radio and compass. Both were still set to SpinDog station time, adopted during the mission prep. He supposed he could check with Volo. It didn't matter yet. Experience had taught the SEAL exactly what time it was.

The local hour is half past "your ass is in a sling." My team is untested and outnumbered, the local population is mostly hostile, the wildlife carnivorous, and, in two years, the local star is going to approach its binary twin, boiling the oceans and scorching the land. Oh, and your extract off-planet depends entirely on mission success, so don't screw up.

Welcome to R'Bak.

Chapter Thirteen

R'BAK

Harry couldn't even hear the noise of the Mog, anymore. Just Sara's voice and stateside sounds low in the background. He tried to get his ear closer to the phone without being aware of it in his hand.

I'm sorry for everything. I'm sorry I was such an asshole.

I'm sorry, too.

I miss you terribly. I can't wait to come back home.

I miss you, too.

Look, I was thinking, when I get back, we can take a trip up the coast. Monterey, Morro Bay...

That sounds nice, but I wish we could do it now. I wish we'd done it before.

Me, too.

God, I love you, baby.

I love you, too. I know you have to go. Goodb—

No, don't hang up yet. How are the kids?

Missing you. We all miss the daddy-man. But you have to go now. Because duty calls. And it always will. You have things to do. Important things.

No, wait! Sara! Wait!

I'll love you forever...

Sara!

He started awake, his hands still shaking. He'd been dreaming. Dreaming about Sara. Her touch, her beautiful eyes, even her slightly crooked smile. He'd screwed it up, and it was no one's fault but his. It had been time and past time to hang it up and fix things at home. The Teams could take care of themselves for a while. The pain in his throat interrupted his dream and, as he returned to full consciousness, a raging thirst asserted itself, driving all other concerns to the distant background.

His eyes felt like sandpaper. Harry blinked, trying to ease the discomfort. He turned his head, feeling a pillow crinkle under his neck, and the ambient light began to grow.

"Welcome back, Lieutenant," a warm tenor voice said.

It came from his right side, so he looked that way. First, he saw a small, opaque observation window. As his vision cleared, Harry noted the room included a few television-style monitors and the familiar shapes of medical equipment wrapped in curved beige plastic. He'd been in his share of hospital rooms, usually to check on a teammate who'd earned a bad luck medal. His eyes slowly tracked further, taking in a pair of flight-suited men standing at *his* bedside.

So, this time, he was the star of the show. Well, shit.

"Helicopter…shot…down?" he managed. "Hospital?"

"Yes," the taller of the two men replied, picking up a wired remote and pressing the button to slowly raise Harry's bed to a sitting position. As it smoothly whined upwards, the plain-faced attendant continued. "Your helo was shot down off Somalia. Nearly all of the crew and passengers were recovered. Can you hold this?"

He proffered a white plastic cup, and Harry leaned forward, carefully grasping it with both hands. He noticed in passing that rather than one of those embarrassing ass-less hospital smocks, he was fully dressed. In fact, his shirt sleeve was the same, familiar desert tricolor camo he'd worn in the Mog, right down to the modified pocket he'd asked Sara to sew onto the upper sleeve. After a long sip of cool water from the convenient straw, he leaned back and exhaled.

"Thanks, I really needed that," he croaked, looking at the speaker. The stranger looked vaguely familiar, though the bulky flight suit didn't match any American pattern he recognized. The gold oak leaves on the collar points were familiar, as was the Midwestern American accent. "Commander…"

"It's major, actually." The sandy haired man smiled. "Rodger Murphy. You and I were on the same Blackhawk.

They woke me up a short while ago. We've got a bit of a system now, so if you let me give you some background, we can skip past the first ten or so questions. Okay?"

Harry looked at him suspiciously, then gave the room another once over. There were English labels here and there, but otherwise there was no information. No charts, no hospital PA system, not even a call button. Just a coat of gray paint, newly applied, by the smell.

"We?"

"Yes, we," Murphy replied with a smile and held up one hand. His shorter companion rolled his eyes and passed the major a small blue piece of paper. "I can tell from the squint in your eyes you're already figuring out this isn't a regular hospital room, and this isn't a normal recovery. I've been helping wake up paranoid, pissed off, and otherwise uncooperative military personnel for a week or so. Let me give you a basic data dump, then we can proceed to the more interesting questions. Ready?"

This definitely wasn't normal procedure for bringing someone out of deep sedation or a medically induced coma, Harry realized. This Major Murphy, or whatever his name really was, had it right. Harry surreptitiously flexed his arms and legs. No pain, no restraints.

Murphy's smile broadened and he held up his hand again. The second man placed another blue chit, grimacing.

"Of course, you could continue like this," Murphy said, as the second man scowled and folded his arms. "Captain Makarov has made a series of rather unwise wagers and you're making me plenty of drink chits, those being one of the few forms of currency we have at the moment. And to your unspoken questions: no, you're not restrained. Yes, you're medically recovered. Shall we proceed?"

Harry nodded warily, looking at both men. Drink chits? This was not your average reassuring medical speech. Were these guys the opposition? Could the Aideed militia even shop him out to…whoever these guys belonged too?

Harry took another pull on the straw to hide his confusion, but nodded assent. Murphy deferred to the shorter man with a "c'mon" gesture.

"Your *vertolet,* how you say, *'copter,* was shot down November 17, 1993," Makarov said with a heavy Slavic accent. Russian? It was a bit more slurred, sounding a bit like their guys who spent too long in the 'Stans. A Kazakh, maybe? And what the hell was he doing here?

Makarov made direct eye contact with Harry. "We still don't know who responsible, but the *'copter* carrying you and Major Murphy took two missiles. Crash was pretty spectacular. Killed copilot and crew chief. You were severely injured. You've received highly advanced medical treatment, but now only need the usual rest, healthy diet, and exercise. In fact, you're medically approved for duty. Clear so far?"

How long have I been here? Where's Sara?

"Have you informed my wife?" Harry asked, overcome with a sudden sense of urgency. Sara would be losing her mind. In fact, he was surprised she wasn't here right now, knowing how pushy she could be, especially where family was concerned. Singularly unimpressed with military protocol, she'd fight her way to his bedside if she had to. "How long have I been out? Where are we—Frankfurt? San Antonio?"

The expressions on both men changed to something a doctor might wear on the cusp of delivering a fatal prognosis.

Harry began to feel something akin to panic, though he steeled his emotions. What had happened to Sara? The creepy feeling he always got in combat was prickling up his spine.

"Who are you guys?" he demanded. "Who you with? Is this an Agency op? Why the hell am I in my field uniform in a hospital and who the fuck is the Russki?"

Murphy took over, with an apologetic glance at Makarov. "This is where it gets…weird, I'm afraid. Your recovery took a long time. A very long time. The US didn't recover the survivors. The people who saved your life used an advanced cryogenic technique which preserved your uniform, your equipment, everything. There's no easy way to say this, so I'll just say it. The shoot down was a hundred and thirty-eight years ago. Today's date, Earth-style, is September 9, 2125."

Harry just stared at him. Then, involuntarily, started to laugh. It came out of nowhere, and he couldn't help it. This was the setup for every crappy sci-fi movie he'd ever heard of. He continued for a bit, looking at the men at his bedside. He expected them to get angry. Murphy just looked sad. Makarov managed a stolid indifference.

"What, no more betting?" Harry said sarcastically. "Come on, who do you work for? This is a set up. Time travel isn't real. Cryogenic tech isn't real. If you tried to pull a Disney on me, my brain would be torn apart by ice crystals, just like Walt's. Stop wasting my time and tell me what you want; otherwise, all you get is Tapper, Harold R., Lieutenant, US Navy. 620-11-2129."

"Like Major said, we've been doing this for long time," Makarov answered, moving toward the window. "Is easier to show than tell." He touched a light switch on the window frame, and it blinked into transparency.

Stars were slowly drifting past. Stars against a deep, perfect black. There was a wall of gray and brown rock filling a third of the field of view. As he watched, it slowly moved, no, rotated. Craters and lines were visible. The moon? After a few more moments, he discerned he was looking at one end of a rocky cylinder, immense in size. A construct, reminiscent of NASA's old Spacelab, was slowly emerging from a shadowed opening at one end of the cylinder. Harry struggled to get a sense for scale. He recognized a human figure in a bulky looking, helmeted coverall, sitting astride a girder that made up part of the vehicle, if that's what it was. It was a space-suited person, Harry belatedly realized. The entire scene snapped into focus. The rotating cylinder was more than a couple klicks long and half as thick. The decidedly non-aerodynamic ship carefully emerging had an industrial look, covered in a mixture of silver and white panels, some pristine and some stained and scratched. Piping and cableways snaked through trestles.

A solar panel array, recognizable anywhere, slowly swept into view. It was tended by a tiny, delta winged craft, colored white and black. Though it was much further away, Harry realized this ship was the size of a 747 wide-body jet. Harry watched them slowly swing past the window. Then the limb of a planet swam into view, by degrees. It was banded in swirling clouds like Jupiter, but it wasn't from the Solar System, unless Jupiter had changed colors to include purple and yellow.

He was *on* a space station.

No. Impossible. His head began to swim, and he shook it hard, before looking back toward the two men.

"This overview is what you SEALs like to call the mission summary—first, you're aboard a spaceship, the Dornaani cruiser *Olsloov*," Murphy said, carefully pronouncing the unfamiliar word. *Alls-sluv.* "The Dornaani are an allied, non-Terran species who are very advanced. We're docked next to a space habitat, that moon-looking thing you see out the window. It's run by another branch of humanity, refugees really. Also, there's an interstellar war on, and you were recovered from a stolen cache of cryogenically suspended humans, mostly men and mostly military, kidnapped out of conflict zones on Earth starting about two hundred years ago, ending in the early two thousands. The folks who did it are another alien species, the Ktor, and they were using us to do some dirty work they could blame on Earth. The only way we get to go home is to work together, kick Ktor ass, and win this war. The details will take days to absorb. What do you think so far?"

Harry returned to looking out the window. The solar array had rotated out of sight and the swirling surface of the gas giant now spanned the view.

"T-trick," Harry said, almost stuttering the word. "Some kind of trick. That's some kind of special effects. One of those new rear-projection big screen televisions. You're trying to fool me—"

"Well, we're taught American SEALs are stubborn, selected for it, in fact," Makarov said, shrugging. "So, reaction is no surprise. Next step we use for tough cases is suit them up for EVA. So far, weightlessness and new planet convince everyone. We need to do this, or can we save some time?"

Harry was staring at the sharply drawn shadow creeping up the curved sweep of the hull plating outside.

This can't be real.

This can't be real.

THIS ISN'T REAL.

His thinking brain was trying to pick out flaws in the computer-generated simulation. Meanwhile, his hindbrain was desperately trying to control his rising gorge.

His efforts at rationalization failed first by a narrow margin, and then he vomited over the side of his bed, splashing the shoes of both men.

"Ha!" Harry heard Makarov exclaim, just before Harry's gut convulsed a second time. "I predict correctly. Give last chit back, Major."

Harry had taken over a table in the corner of the refectory serving this quadrant of the habitat. The Lost Soldiers, as the Terrans called themselves, ate together. What their mostly human hosts who ran the station, the SpinDogs, thought about it was a mystery since the two groups didn't readily mix.

During the mandatory orientation and safety training arranged by the SpinDogs, Harry and a company's worth of the Lost Soldiers had trooped for hours through myriad passageways, engineering spaces, and general-use compartments and had still only visited a fraction of the station. The visit for his motley group had been comprehensive, equipping Harry with an appreciation for the engineering feat represented by the SpinDogs' cylindrical asteroid, which had been cored out and converted into a difficult-to-detect space habitat. Each end of the station housed heavy equipment, docking bays, and power generation, leaving the multi-decked center section to house living quarters, light industrial work, hydroponics, and the like. This was the beating heart of the habitat. Even one such deck was several times larger than the biggest aircraft carrier ever built by his country, and yet the degree to which the SpinDogs maximized the productivity of every available cubic meter pushed home the point that their growth had outstripped their capacity. The addition of less than a hundred Terrans to a population of almost one hundred thousand was still a strain, more so because of Major Murphy's insistence his team be housed together, isolated from the general population.

Of course, all of that followed a week of acclimatization to the new reality. The world Harry had known was beyond reach, and the new Earth was almost as unknowable. Current reports painted an Earth very different from the 1990s. Borders had been redrawn, and he barely recognized what passed for political parties. The newly woken soldiers were mostly American, but there were enough Poles, Afghanis, Vietnamese, and Russians to give their group an international feel. Of course, that diversity seemed modest once told there were at least five intelligent species in contact with humanity. The combat videos of the alien invasion of Earth revealed giant roach-like insects and bipedal anteater-werewolf hybrids. Bizarrely, negotiations were now underway to convert both of those alien races into allies while Earth entered a fight against the mostly human group which had kidnapped the Lost Soldiers out of their own time.

And of course, the worst reality of all: Harry couldn't stop thinking about his irredeemable failure, the loss of his family. The number one thing he had finally sworn to do, to be present for Sara and the kids, was now forever beyond his reach.

The former SEAL heard the soft footsteps of a person approaching his makeshift workspace and a sudden, powerful wave of irritation surged, blanketing his self-pity. Every six hours, he had to pack his work into a plastic crate while the space was used for its original purpose. A glance at his venerable Casio G-Shock confirmed he should have plenty of time left. With an hour to go until the next meal, he expected to be left alone unless there was an emergency, and he hadn't heard any of the alarms they'd memorized as the result of frequent drills.

"Harry, do you have a moment?" asked a now-familiar voice.

A glance over his shoulder confirmed his new boss, if that's what he was, was approaching, an insulated stainless-steel mug in hand.

"No problem, sir," Harry replied, smiling as genuinely as he could. He felt the anger rekindling itself in the wake of his initial irritation, and shoved it back down, hard. The guy in charge was entitled to interrupt whenever he felt like it, especially since he wasn't here by choice, either. Harry twisted in his seat, lifting a stack of z-folded printouts, old-style notebooks, and a variety of maps from the bench across from him.

"I've told all of you to call me Rodger, or Roj, if you prefer," Murphy replied with a smile as he slid onto the bench. "While we're a military outfit, we're all professionals, and I'm not enough of a little tin god to insist on unctuous military protocol."

"Okay, Roj," Harry replied, wrinkling his brow unconsciously.

"How goes your mission prep?"

"Well…"

"Let me guess," Murphy replied, raising one hand. "You're underwhelmed with your choice of teammates. You're questioning the limitations on unit size. You keep asking yourself how this can possibly be the best option. Am I getting close?"

"Spot on," Harry said, schooling his face into neutrality. "Look, you're asking, right? This is actually a lot more complicated than the mission summary you gave me when I woke up. Let's pretend our people are successful getting over the loss of their families and everything they knew. I won't even mention the crap equipment we have to use. Let's assume I accept the restrictions the fu—our hosts are imposing on us. Bottom line, damn near everything depends on planetside locals we haven't yet met. And we'll be operating across some pretty crappy terrain, almost entirely on foot, for the first several phases."

Harry pushed aside more papers, this time on top of the table. He exposed a featureless, black-screened device he'd been given. He'd gotten over the vast differences from the IBM PC he'd last used in the 20th century and rapidly mastered the finger movements needed to control the legal document-sized, touch-operated screen.

"Here's what I mean."

A touch from a single thick finger illuminated the screen to reveal a grid of multicolored icons. He tapped a symbol shaped like a simplified, yet old-fashioned Mercator map projection. The planetary surface which blinked into existence showed the familiar swirl of clouds and blue ocean that might have been mistaken for Earth at a casual glance. However, there were only three main continents, two of which covered the poles. The equatorial region was mostly large islands, and those showed the light browns and sandy yellow colors of the deep desert. Harry used two fingers to orient the map on a point north of the equator, and then zoomed the view. He turned the datapad on its built-in stand so they both could see an area which included a mix of terrain ranging from grassy plains to rocky, channeled hills to outright desert.

"We insert via a high-risk orbital drop and land up to fifty klicks from the objective in order to avoid detection by the Kulsians, who have an established intelligence network, including aerial patrols." As Harry talked, he couldn't avoid thinking about how absurd the situation was, even as he pointed to each feature on the map. "After a long foot infil, I link up with tribes the SpinDogs *think* will be receptive to our plan. Once we've found the right bunch, I get to convince them, however I'm going to manage it, that they should work with us and allow me to train them. After which our merry band of hunter-gatherers plus yours truly perform local ops in order to gather more tribes to our forces. Then—and we still haven't reached the good part—our combined force preps for an assault landing with one—that's *one*—shuttle to deliver the rest of the Lost Soldiers and we seize a modern mechanized column intact using nothing but infantry. If I'm anything but perfectly successful, I'm stuck on a planet where the opposition is entrenched and more than a bit pissed that unknown forces—which would be me—have killed dozens, maybe hundreds, of their people and sparked an insurgency. To top it off, the planet is turning into a goddamn oven in two years, inhabitable nowhere but at the poles—which are thousands of klicks from where I'm going to land. Forlorn hope—hell—it would be simpler and kinder to just eat a goddamned bullet!"

As he finished, Harry abruptly realized he'd almost yelled the last couple sentences. Raising his voice to a man, who, if he wasn't exactly his commanding officer, was certainly sufficiently in charge to have Harry tossed out an airlock.

"Got it out of your system?" Murphy asked, smiling thinly.

"I'm sorry, but—yeah. Sorry." Harry took a drink, ignoring the flat taste of water re-filtered countless times. It gave him something to do besides look at his boss.

"In case you haven't figured it out yet," Murphy said, his eyes cold, "this *is* a forlorn hope. I didn't ask for this. *None of us asked for this*. Yet here we are. The facts of the case are not in dispute and the hard truths I've previously explained to each member of this team still stand. The world we knew is literally history. The family you were lucky enough to have in 1993 is gone. Somewhere on Earth you may have adult great-grandchildren, but you're not a memory to them. Hell, you aren't even a book report for some great-great-grandkid's school assignment. The people, and hell, even the *culture*, we knew are as dead as they believed you to be after you were declared missing. We're all in the same boat, and time has fucking well moved on. Are you clear?"

"Yes, sir," Harry said miserably, rubbing his forehead hard enough to draw the skin white across his brow.

"Are you fucking clear?" Murphy asked again, almost hissing.

There was a long pause.

"Yeah. I'm clear," Harry replied again, this time looking the other man in the face.

"Then you will stop feeling sorry for yourself," Murphy replied more normally. He drummed his fingers on the tabletop for a few moments. "We've all lost everything. Maybe we can get back and maybe we can't. All that's left is hope and each other. Some of the Lost are so broken that they can't cope, not now and maybe never. When we picked who we were bringing out of cryo-suspension, I thought you could hack it. Was I wrong?"

"I can hack it," Harry said, instantly. Being able to endure anything was the closest thing to a SEAL religion there was. Or had been, anyway.

"So, we get to figure out how to do the impossible," Murphy said, warming to the topic. "The SpinDogs won't risk everything by landing in force. Their support for large-scale surface operations and directly confronting the Kulsians is contingent on a demonstration of our superior warfighting skills. A *successful* demonstration."

There was an uncomfortable silence. Harry felt guilty, not as much for losing his cool, even momentarily, but because he wasn't living up to his image of himself.

"You ever heard of Murphy's Law?" the major asked.

"Practically live by it, in the Teams," Harry answered automatically. Everyone who spent enough time in the military knew that whatever could go wrong, would go wrong. A deep understanding that the universe was waiting to trip you up had spawned several other sayings among those who took up the profession of arms.

"Two is one, one is none" and *"tracers work both ways"* as well as the ever popular *"fifteen minutes prior to fifteen minutes prior"* mantra intended to promote punctuality—and many others—were the half-humorous watchwords by which modern soldiers lived. All were intended to counter the reality of Murphy's Law.

Harry suddenly and belatedly made the connection to his new boss' surname.

"Glad to hear it," Murphy said decisively. "We're going to break that law. We're going to plan ahead for things to go wrong in order to make sure they end up right. That starts with you. You are going to come up with a plan making Murphy's Law a problem for the other guy. We're going to be a sharp, unexpected stick in the opposition's tender spots. Now, have you settled on who's going with you?"

"This is going to be a variation on an exchange training mission, so whoever goes with me should have worked with indigs before," Harry answered, using the abbreviated form of "indigenous" to refer to the local population. "This isn't a job for junior cadre. Rodriguez is the best candidate. He also has the best Ktor language rating of the available senior enlisted."

Most of the Lost Soldiers had spent days in the Dornaani cruiser's virtual reality bay, receiving accelerated Ktor language training at ten-to-one time compression. The unpleasant experience had left them with persistent migraines for a few days. However, they were all now conversant, though not perfectly fluent, with the dominant language of the system.

In addition to his language score, Rodriguez's folio called out several missions in the sixties with the Cambodians, the South Vietnamese, and the Hmong. On the personal side, it highlighted his readiness to rebel against authority figures, his womanizing, and the resulting children in Saigon, Manila, and elsewhere, which struck him as a bit odd, until Murphy explained something of the Ktoran preoccupation with genetics. He was also suspected of having fragged a newly promoted Army officer after that man's decisions had led to the death of Rodriguez's best friend in-country.

Speaking of which, Harry had initially been shocked at the detail in the personnel folders of the men from which he could choose. There was a lot more there than the basics of a military service record. It was a cross section of their life, including family details, bank statements, and school transcripts. It was probably more information than the subjects had even assembled for themselves. Which meant…

Might as well get it all out on the table.

Harry tapped the personnel folders he'd reviewed for this operation. "Roj, I'm betting the British spook you mentioned is your source of information on everyone, including me."

"No bet."

"Then you know why I was on the helicopter." Harry made it a statement, not a question.

"I know, Harry," Murphy answered, nodding. "And, frankly, I can't see the conditions we're under are going to help. If you haven't figured it out, the group *Olsloov* left behind were the last to be roused from cold sleep for one reason or another. We weren't woken by the Ktor, and we weren't initially revived by our own allies. The files the Dornaani recovered were remarkably complete. Your decorations, correspondence, counseling records, everything. Bottom line: your last CO could afford to send you back stateside because he had options. I don't. What's more, you and I are from very nearly the last batch of Terrans the Ktor kidnapped. We share the same military and cultural context, which means a lot. And, like you said, if you screw this up, you're gonna be stuck down there. Seems like pretty good motivation, if you ask me."

Harry watched as the senior man took another pull from his mug. It trembled very slightly as he sat it down, and Murphy grimaced.

"As long as you're down there, check to see if they have anything better than this dishwater tea."

"I'm hoping for some coffee, Roj," Harry said, extending an olive branch.

"Hell, if they have real coffee, I'll come retrieve you myself."

Chapter Fourteen

R'BAK

Volo squinted at the horizon, trying to match the outline of the rolling hills with the terrain relief on the expedition map. Ignoring the pack straps cutting into his shoulders, he glanced down at the plastic-coated map to confirm the bearing of the three peaks dominating the view to the east during their march. Although he'd begun the second morning of their hike with a precise location fix, courtesy of the just-emplaced Dornaani stealth-sats, he needed two, or preferably three, of the very small satellites to be in line-of-sight at the same time. Another such intermittent conjunction would occur this night, so navigation wasn't the top issue. His little group's location was the current problem.

The automated evasion by their drop capsules had placed them far away from the usual range of their trading partners on the surface. This meant much more travel on foot and an associated delay. It also meant considerably more discomfort.

Before turning to face his companions, he carefully groomed his expression into neutrality, erasing any sign of the discomfort his tailored boots or borrowed Terran backpack were inflicting. His brother Stabilo, the most recent Zobulakos to have landed on R'Bak, had cautioned Volo to rigorously condition himself in the high-gee pod of *Second Spin*. At the time, Volo believed his brother's outlandish claims about conditions on the surface were exaggerations designed to deter the youngest of their family, or even plant the seed of failure in Volo's mind, leaving the way open for Stabilo to remain the favored son. The unexpected arrival of the Dornaani cruiser and its cargo of rootstock humans had radically accelerated the schedule for

Volo's first visit to the surface, and, while his wind was good, the soreness of his feet and joints was distracting at best, and potentially a dangerous weakness at worst. Such was not the way of their family, where personal strength vied with utility and efficiency as the most prized qualities.

"We're proceeding as planned," Volo said, looking over his shoulder to the next man. The over-muscled Terran officer had paused several steps behind him, endlessly looking to both sides. "I updated the satlink with your situation report. We should get a reply tonight."

"Sounds good," Tapper replied, nodding but otherwise showing no expression. Establishing some rapport with the archaic humans was important to Volo's mission, but the larger man, the officer, had been difficult to approach. Volo watched him scratch his neck, and, unbidden, his own dirty collar began to itch almost unbearably. Instead of giving in to the weakness, he turned to continue the march, suppressing the desire to scratch. Volo despised Tapper's casual acceptance of the sweat and dirt coating them both. It was a reflection of the Terran's barbarous people, who, by their own admission, mostly still scrabbled on the surface of their homeworld.

Volo's father, the Arko Primus of the entire habitat, regarded these humans as a potential resource even more valuable than the centuries-old space wreckage the SpinDogs used as their principle source of refined alloys. Finding a rich hulk was the sort of event that could guarantee the succession of a favored heir. These Terrans, and their patrons, the Dornaani, might change everything, and the success of this mission would leapfrog Volo ahead of all his siblings. Better, the Terrans were terribly naive and had accepted everything the Primus had told them. Of course, most of the facts about the millennium-old conflict between Kulsis and R'Bak were not in dispute.

The two halves of the binary star system had been sought out by three separate waves of Ktoran outcasts. Volo's people, the SpinDogs, had been part of the second wave, and were surprised to find both systems already inhabited. The greatest power was on Kulsis, the habitable planet of the main system. Fortunately, there had been no sign that the modest Kulsian presence in space was poised for journeys to the companion system, so the second wave settled on R'Bak. Although the details were sketchy, the later generations of those settlers were split by disputes, one of which led to a sizeable group being sent off-planet: the ancestors of the SpinDogs. Given the unpleasant relations with their dirtside cousins, Volo's forebears elected to build their communities in secret locations. This protection against local aggression was ultimately what spared them from the out-system depredations that began about a century later. And so, the small SpinDog civilization remained hidden, sheltering on asteroids scattered among the uninhabitable planets of the ecliptic, biding its time.

Volo suppressed a smile. What the Terrans didn't know was that the recent death of the Matriarch was an opportunity for his family, and for Volo personally. That these Terran visitors felt partially responsible was a useful lever he would use to steer their behavior. Once he linked up with the tribe which had previously traded with the SpinDogs, he could exploit the good relationship built by his father and siblings on previous excursions to the surface to sway the Sarmatchani toward the Terran's plan. The natural suspicion the tribesmen had for his people was nothing compared to their visceral hate for the Kulsians and their satraps. Their instinctive distrust of the Terrans would help Volo establish and maintain control.

Volo paused again at the top of yet another hill and wiped his sweaty face. He looked around skeptically, but the terrain they'd been traversing offered little of interest. He glanced over his shoulder again. Both Terrans were ascending stolidly, apparently unaffected by the absurdly high gravity and the increasing heat.

Whether these visitors could actually defeat the Kulsians or not remained to be seen. A win would interrupt the cycle of destruction wrought by the Kulsians' "harvest" and the surface turmoil caused by the weather effects of the two stars at periastron. A loss could still mean a chance to directly ally with the Dornaani, if they ever returned—and if all the Terrans had conveniently died, of course. Either way, Volo would squeeze every opportunity from his temporary position of advantage and become the one to succeed his father.

The sand shifted under Harry's boots, making each stride that much more difficult as he followed several meters behind Volo. Despite his muscular frame and what he'd been promised was a gravity slightly lower than Earth's, the weight of the pack was an uncomfortable irritant and his back was really starting to ache. The well-worn Vietnam-era ALICE ruck was not the most ergonomic bit of kit Harry had used, carrying most of the weight too low on his spine, but more American equipment from that era was available than any other. Rodriguez had accepted his gear without comment, but the last time Harry had seen some of this stuff, it had been gathering dust on the shelves of an Army surplus store.

Out of long habit, he'd slung his equally dated M-14 rifle so he could keep one hand on the grip, patrol fashion. Harry watched ahead as the SpinDog followed the narrow game trail winding through the swaying, hip- to shoulder-high yellow saw grass.

Over the course of the day, the earlier sparse forest had largely thinned as the little party hiked further west. Occasional bare trunks of dead trees poked up here and there from the tall, dry grass. Some past violent weather event had shaped the sand into a series of rolling hills, each rising as much as fifty meters high, and, while the trail they followed mostly wound between successive ridges, they inevitably spent a lot of time going up and down.

Apart from looking straight ahead or down toward his boots, Volo seemed unconcerned with their surroundings.

Harry paused for a moment to look over his shoulder. An equal distance behind, Rodriguez had also stopped, scanning their back trail, which reassured Harry nearly as much as Volo's casual manner irritated him. After a short interval, Rodriguez turned and continued, and Harry caught his eye while making the hand signal for a rally point. After receiving a nod in return, Harry lengthened his stride to close the gap to the lead member of their little group.

"Volo, we'll take a water break," Harry told their guide, who was stopped, consulting a partially folded plastic map. If Volo was unhappy to be using the same weapon that Harry carried, instead of the boxy carbines Harry had seen on *Second Spin*, he wasn't showing it. The nonchalant way Volo had slung his M-14 backwards, muzzle-down from one shoulder, allowed the SpinDog to use both hands. It also increased the time needed to deploy the weapon.

Harry bit back a caustic remark and watched Volo as he looked up the ascending slope of the track, then to the horizon ahead, and back to the map, consulting some spidery hand-written notes on the margin, as he'd periodically done throughout their march. He certainly wasn't in any hurry.

"How much further to the rendezvous coordinates?" Harry prompted. "I'd like to stop while there's enough light to make camp."

"It's dusk already," the slightly built young man replied, looking at his wristcom to double-check some reading. He didn't like what he saw and shook his head. "Midday tomorrow, perhaps the following day. The automated evasion response during our drop pushed our landing further north and east than we'd hoped. This morning, I had a solid microsat position, but now I must estimate. We're in the harvest fief claimed by the J'Stull, satraps to Kulsis, but they rarely venture this far from their cities. We seek a branch of the Sarmatchani who are distant kin to the group we trade with at the poles. They'll be found in this direction."

"So as long as it's still these Sarmatchani we link up with, it's all good then," Rodriguez said as he strode up, making the statement a question.

Harry looked at the NCO, wondering how the man was dealing with the impossibility of this situation. Rodriguez absentmindedly worked a bright orange plastic toothpick in his jaws as his eyes continued to look restlessly opposite the direction Harry was facing. His rifle moved to match his eyes, dipping now and again as the experienced sergeant kept the muzzle from flagging his teammates. "If they're expecting company, I mean?"

"The Sarmatchani are tribal and don't recognize a formal central authority," Volo replied. "They agree on little but their enmity for the satraps of Kulsis. They are good fighters, and the local Sarmatchani know every track around every hill in their territory. They may be watching already."

"If they see us, why don't they come meet us?" Harry asked, tilting his canteen up and swigging some warm water.

"It's their way," Volo answered calmly, folding the map closed. "We can't precisely schedule our visits, but we do land at regular intervals, when it's safe to trade. They watch for the J'Stull and guard their territory fiercely against competing clans. They will see us."

The SpinDogs land at regular intervals?

"Wait a minute," Harry said, fighting the instant and familiar surge of anger. "Your people routinely land on the surface? Why the hell did we do that crazy insertion then?"

With every word, Harry felt the heat of his rage begin to fill the channels and runnels lying under his otherwise calm exterior. Like a pusher who recognized every weakness in the addict, the rage soothed Harry's fear of the consequences if he gave in. It reminded him of every time he'd been let down or betrayed, cut, or stung. And here was another indig, withholding information while demanding everything. Harry struggled to keep his tone even because he wouldn't yield to the temptation. He couldn't. Control was his friend; rage his enemy.

"You've been instructed," Volo answered, pale eyes narrowing as he omitted the obvious qualifier *"you ignorant savage,"* "The Second Exodate, *my people*, must conceal our very existence, lest we share the fate of all on R'Bak. The raiders from Kulsis have sent their advance parties, as they have done each time our stars draw close to one another, making travel possible. So extra caution would have been required, regardless. And then, uninvited, your people arrived and sent incautious signals, drawing unwanted attention at just the time when discretion was most important."

Harry's rage didn't like the youngster's tone. The SpinDogs had briefed their network on-planet, and Harry knew they'd landed before. But routine landings had never been mentioned. What else had his so-called allies left out? He tried to think of the most constructive reply while suppressing the adrenaline which always accompanied his familiar, unbidden fury. He squeezed the wooden pistol grip of his rifle to hide his anger and stared at Volo, who insolently returned his glare. Harry noted Rodriguez's concerned glance and flicked his offhand that way.

Deal with this.

"Look, Volo, we're sorry about this whole mess, but we didn't know you SpinDogs were in the system," Rodriguez said placatingly. "And afterwards, we even tried to help out, save your queen—"

"She was no queen. *She was a Matriarch.* And she perished!"

"—and besides, the boss and I were still asleep when it happened," the sergeant finished his attempt at smoothing things over. "You didn't ask for this, and we didn't ask for this. But it is what it is."

"Yes, I know about you Sleepers," Volo replied, firmly jamming the map into a thigh pouch. Harry could tell he was only partially mollified. "We used a similar suspension technique to bridge the distance from our parent system. Though much of our history is lost, we SpinDogs remember how the other Ktor cast us out hundreds of years ago. Ktor technology is now far ahead of our own, and the Kulsians have a fleet whose size is possible because of their planetary control—which is the reason we must remain unseen. With your ship gone, we cannot directly challenge them in space."

Harry took a deep breath. He dismissed his anger by careful stages, which finally and sullenly retreated beyond immediate thought. He flexed one hand and nodded thanks to Rodriguez, who returned it before turning around and resuming his scan.

"Your people and mine have agreed to work together," Harry said, fully back in control.

Harry had worked with indigenous personnel several times during the course of many deployments. Panama, Kuwait, Somalia; it was always the same. Each one was so sure they had all the answers. They just wanted the Americans to fix their problems, give them funding and tech, and of course do it all for free, and then go away. But he had to work with these people, so he'd swallow his anger. Like he always did.

Almost always.

"Out of respect for your situation, we've agreed to proceed carefully and prove we can accomplish what we claim," he finished.

"Uh, sir?" Rodriguez called from behind them.

"Before conveniently departing, *your* ship destroyed the raiders' craft, their satellites, and their orbital habitat," Volo said angrily, putting both hands on his hips. "Those who were on this planet and survived your attack know something is badly wrong. They have undoubtedly already changed their operational pattern while they await more of their comrades, who may arrive at any time. Even now, they warn their loyal satraps, seeking to turn every hand against those who have struck this blow. Against this change we must still protect the secret of our race. Thus, the space drop and this, admittedly, slow route to our rendezvous."

He gestured ahead.

"That is why we took the time to cover the descent pods with parachutes," he added tartly. "That is why the LZ was so distant from our previous landing points, just in case we'd been detected before. Now, if you are sufficiently reassured, Lieutenant," he said, turning to continue the march, "we should press on."

"Hey!" Rodriguez said a little more loudly. "You officers want to take a look at this and maybe argue later?"

Harry glanced up immediately. One of the dead trees scattered about stood close to the track, extending a few meters above the waving grass. As he watched, a pair of dark eyes blinked, and the motion served to reveal a small gray form, the outline of which blended into the bark. The middle of the creature seemed to pulse, and a soft hooting sound carried around the immediate area. Small teeth projected from the seam of its jaw, no bigger than the last joint of Harry's little finger.

"Well, that's hardly an emergency," Harry said, eyeing the meter-sized creature. "We'll just skirt around to one side."

But then he noticed Volo's reaction, and stopped. A moment earlier he'd been angry and determined, but now the SpinDog had frozen.

"Quiet!" Volo whispered. He began to slowly reach for the slung weapon with one trembling hand, before he stopped and let his arm gradually descend to his side. "It's not alone."

Harry scanned both sides of the track, but the grass concealed possible dangers.

"It's not very large," he said softly. "Is it venomous?"

"No," Volo answered. "That's a juvenile, forced into sentry duty by the adults. They get much bi—"

The creature hooted again, and this time, deeper calls sounded all around the three humans. Perhaps ten meters away, a much larger version of the sentry's head, reminiscent of a Terran bat, slowly rose from the grass until it was nearly at shoulder level with Harry. Two dark eyes sparkled with intelligence above membranous slits which pulsed slowly. Furred ears projected from each side of the head, swiveling in concert to orient on the humans. Four paired tusks nearly as long as Harry's forearm hung from the bottom of the skull. Stained the same color as the grass, the tusks moved rhythmically as the creature chewed a mouthful of foliage. The hooting calls were repeated, more strident this time, and Harry was able to see they were emitted from the nasal slits, while the jaws ceaselessly ground together.

Harry instantly raised his rifle, flicking the safety off. His peripheral vision showed movement all around, and Harry could feel his sergeant switching his aim between targets as more of the creatures loomed into view on both sides.

"Aw, crap," Rodriguez said in a strained voice. "You seeing this?"

"Don't shoot!" Volo said, keeping his voice low and slowly stepping closer to Harry and laying a hand on top of his rifle. "They have no fear of men. There are dozens we can't see, and they are dangerous when roused; even larger predators leave these alone. Don't look in their eyes; it's a challenge. Don't make sudden movements. No loud noises—they will attack whoever makes the loudest sound. We don't want to provoke them."

"Boss?" Rodriguez said in a strained voice. "Make the call, Harry."

The nearest animal shuffled onto the track. It was massively built, and the nightmare head was perched above the hunched shoulders of a hyena. The gray fur was shaggy, dappled with darker spots down the flanks. The forelimbs had digits tipped with a shiny, keratinlike substance. Since Harry was looking downwards, he had a good view as the creature's knuckles took the weight of the muscular forequarters, splaying a little and sinking into the sandy track.

Heavy. Third of a ton, maybe more.

The troop leader used one paw to pound the ground, accompanied by a particularly loud hoot. Harry was confident he could shoot it several times before it closed the distance, but he had no idea what passed for a nervous system on this planet, nor did he know how large the troop was. Worse, the antique he was carrying held only twenty rounds of standard ball ammo, and if there was something less attractive than trying for a magazine change while wrestling with a tusked gorilla, it wasn't obvious at the moment. For a second, Harry thought wistfully of the CAR727 and the hundred round magazine he had carried in Somalia. It was probably somewhere on the now-departed *Olsloov*. The Ktor had evidently been insistent about ammunition commonality and using the largest caliber rifle they had in numbers, which was the M-14. At least he'd been able to snag two of the squad support variants—the M14E3—for himself and Rodriguez.

On the other hand, Volo might know what he was talking about. Harry struggled for a moment and then decided. At some point, he had to trust him. Exhaling, he kept his eyes down, but maintained his weapon at the low ready.

"Okay, now what?" he asked Volo, murmuring softly.

"They're migrating, with young," Volo replied, still keeping his voice low. "It makes them aggressive. We very slowly back away from the pack leader. Stay together, move quietly, and don't make any quick or threatening motions."

"What the hell is a threatening motion to an alien baboon-bat?" Harry heard Rodriguez mutter. However, the noncom also looked down and slowly backed away as all three retraced their steps.

One animal, larger than the sentry but still much smaller than the troop master, shuffled forward, hooting and raising its upper body off the ground before slapping the turf with loud thuds. The display was probably calculated only to intimidate. However, the newcomer was stirring the passions of the increasingly loud troop and more animals knuckle-walked into direct line-of-sight, slapping the ground and hooting. The sentry began shaking the tree, and the dry limbs clattered together.

Harry resigned himself to opening fire. He'd try for head and neck shots and hope for the best. But, before he could do so, the troop master moved forward with unexpected agility. Two quick steps brought him to his target and a blow from one massive forearm drove the smaller, louder animal into the ground. The tusks of the larger beast clacked together as it bellowed a crashing challenge or command. The rest of the pack was suddenly quiescent, scuttling back into the grass and out of view. Just as suddenly as it had attacked the upstart, the lead animal appeared to calm. The giant remained watchfully poised on one forelimb, which rested on the back of the downed smaller animal, but it used the other to rip a clump of vegetation from the ground. It stuffed the morsel into its neck-mouth and resumed the important business of eating, all the while observing the humans.

Maintaining control, check. I hear you, big guy.

Harry continued to step slowly away, while the pack leader remained in the center of the track, quietly watching the humans disappear back up the darkening track.

"Sitting around a campfire on an alien planet might be the weirdest thing I've ever done on an op, *sir*," Rodriguez said, in English. "But it ain't the alien planet that bugs the shit out of me, it's the damn fire. Breaks every rule I've ever heard of, *sir*."

Harry raised his eyebrows. *When your experienced NCO starts "sirring" you in the field, he isn't being polite, he's communicating something. Pointedly.*

The two men had gone for a short walk around their perimeter, getting oriented and accustomed to the differences in the appearance of nearby terrain as darkness enveloped their site. Both were professionals and knew without the need for discussion that getting a feel for their immediate surroundings at night would prevent false alarms and provide a corresponding advantage in a true crisis. The blackness wasn't absolute. R'Bak's tiny moons and the brilliant night constellations were still shining through the light cloud cover. Harry looked up and considered the empty sky with a pang of homesickness.

Helluva lot darker than the high desert in California, or Saudi for that matter.

He shrugged it off.

Mission first. Whine later.

Both men were trying to preserve their night vision by keeping their backs oriented towards the fire which Volo was occasionally poking with a handy stick. Rodriguez's unspoken question deserved an answer.

"Always show your enemies what they expect to see," Harry explained. "Out here, anyone skipping a fire is trying to hide. Someone who's trying to hide is someone who might be dangerous. Anyone who sees this fire will figure we're just another party of hide-hunters and not particularly interesting."

Rodriguez answered with a noncommittal grunt, navigating around a cluster of thick-stemmed, thorny plants which they had learned to avoid.

"Last night, we were still close to the drop capsules," Harry said, patiently, ignoring the sudden flare of aggravation at the NCO's non-answer. "Volo says we're firmly in tribal territory now, and a fire makes us easier for the Sarmatchani to find, which is the entire point of the exercise.

"You say so."

"Hold up, Marco," Harry ordered, trying to draw the sergeant out. "If you've got a feeling, tell me. I read about your ops. Your old team was more than half South Vietnamese. You've worked with more indigs than I have, and more closely. Do you think we can trust these people?"

"Yeah, I ran a bunch of ops into Indian Country in sixty-six, sixty-seven and again last year…" Rodriguez stopped suddenly, no doubt realizing that he was referring to a time more than a century past. Then he picked up the thread again. "Anyhow, they all went pretty well and SOG always composed the team with more ARVNs than Americans," he continued, pronouncing the abbreviation for the soldiers from the Army of Republic of Vietnam as a single word: *Ar-vin*.

Harry knew about the ARVNs and he knew about SOG. The work of the early special operators from the Military Assistance Command-Vietnam, Studies and Observation Group or MACV-SOG was—had been—legend inside SOCOM.

"The brass wanted to use the lowest number of Americans they could get away with. So last op, we get inserted by an ARVN Huey, not one from AirCav. And that's the op where ST UTAH never came back."

"And?" Harry prompted after a long pause. "What happened, exactly?"

"This time, the whole Viet Cong army was waiting," Rodriguez said, looking straight ahead. "We got rolled up even before the sound of the helo faded. We tried to di-di out of there, fought like hell, but half of us were blown away in the first two minutes. We got trapped in this little draw in the stinking jungle, not even a hundred yards from the insert LZ. Leaves, twigs, and shit raining down over our heads from all the fire going through the trees, covering the dead and wounded, sticking to the blood and the open holes showing through their gear."

Rodriguez paused again. Without looking directly at his teammate, Harry could sense that NCO was reliving the scene again, as fresh as the moment that it happened. He let the sergeant resume when he was ready.

"Bao, the last ARVN, was on the radio, trying to yell for a dust-off over the noise. Behind me, Steve was screaming, trying to stuff his guts back in, knowing he was gonna die lying in the dirt of the A-Shau valley. Then the shooting stops, all at once. You could hear the damn birds chirping. Some freaky dude in shades and a suit just appears, standing right there in the mud with us, offers us a way out but we had to decide right then. Next thing I know, I wake up on a goddamned spaceship, and two weeks later I'm looking at a strange sky that don't have no real moon in it, and all my men are gone. The files I got from the English spook say the two other guys extracted from UTAH got wasted fighting for the Ktor on the planet before this one. Same logs say the intel weenies back at the puzzle palace in Da Nang figured one of the ARVN air crew shopped our team to the VC a couple days before the op. 'Course, no way to know for sure. I'm here, now."

No way to know for sure: isn't that *the truth.*

Harry was looking up at the night sky. At some point during Rodriguez's story, Harry slipped back onto the Blackhawk for the ride out of Mog. The breeze of the slipstream, still hot despite the altitude and the speed of the helo. Electronic alarms suddenly blaring, the sound of the straining engine and the shaking, bucking airframe. The white face of the crew chief. An instant to think of Sara. The kids. An explosion. Then a kaleidoscope of sea-sky-sea—blackness.

Rodriguez turned to face Harry. The red light of the campfire several meters away danced across his face.

"Thing is, these teams of locals, soldiers, and spooks and shit only work good so long as everyone on the op has as much on the table as everybody else," he said before hawking and spitting downwind. "That alien dude over there, he looks like us, talks kinda like us, and maybe we can trust him. Maybe not. His ass seems to be on the line, same as ours. You and I want to go home. No way to know what he wants."

"I see it the same, Marco," Harry replied, holding out his hand for the sergeant, who took it firmly. "The way I figure it, it's you and me. The op is to get back to Earth."

"Roger that, El-Tee," Rodriguez said. "Back to Earth. So, yeah, I can put up with a campfire during an op. Or anything else. But who you gonna trust?"

"We can take turns keeping watch," Harry said to Volo, who was still sitting next to the small fire. "In case something happens."

"There's no need, Lieutenant," the SpinDog replied, preoccupied. He gently poked a dried branch into the flames and withdrew it before it caught. He repeated the motion. "Most animals on this planet won't willingly approach a fire. It's an ingrained behavior due to the Searing. As for the Sarmatchani, they will contact us or not."

"There are only three of us, and we will take turns staying awake," Harry said more firmly. "This isn't a negotiation. I'll go first and wake you up in two hours. When your two hours are up, you wake up Rodriguez. We repeat till morning and pick up the rotation tomorrow night. Got it?"

"As you wish." Volo never looked up from the fire.

Harry frowned, although he was glad to skip the expected argument. He watched the younger man stare into the flames.

"It's just a fire," Harry said, wondering about Volo's apparent fascination.

"I've never seen deliberately set fire before," he answered absently, holding his hands out, palms towards the dancing flames. "In person, that is. It's beautiful. And warm."

"How have you never seen a fire?" Harry asked, so startled his irritation was totally forgotten. He looked at Rodriguez, who had crossed his arms and turned to face outwards. "It's pretty basic. Everyone's seen a fire."

"*Intelligent* people don't allow fires in space habitats," Volo answered with a contemptuous look. "We conduct safety drills, but actual fire would be deadly in our habitats. Then there's the matter of fuel. Even if I could gather enough material from the farm compartment, it would be too wet to set alight easily, assuming I survived the wrath of the Chief of Hydroponics."

Harry had been genuinely curious, with no intention of setting Volo off, but now he had again aggravated his only connection to the locals, critical to the success of his mission. Before he could articulate a neutral response, Rodriguez spoke up.

"Makes sense," the sergeant said over his shoulder. Harry looked up and caught the NCO making little "take it easy" hand motions. "Didn't your brothers tell you what to expect?"

"The last person my father sent was my brother, Stabilo," Volo said, shrugging. "He told me about the gravity, of course. He talked about the richness of the land, where water and food were unrationed. He briefed me on the tribes we seek. We trade some simple tech and orbital survey information in exchange for samples of useful botanicals, other biological samples and information about the R'Baku satraps who've pledged fealty to Kulsis."

"Why haven't you allied with them outright?" Harry asked. "Couldn't you wipe the satraps off the planet and be ready for Kulsis yourself?"

"We are too few to control a planet while building the industrial base needed for orbital shipyards and munitions factories, all in the time available in a single cycle of the Searing," Volo replied, briefly looking up. "The raiders from Kulsis still have space superiority. They could strike the planet and find our hidden stations in the asteroid clusters, and that would be the end. If your friends can help us seize the weapons and vehicle caches the Kulsians have seeded on the surface, we can interrupt the pattern that's kept us in hiding since our arrival. If we stop the cycle for even a single Searing, we would have a chance. We could finally control our own planet."

"You mean control along with the Sarmatchani, of course," Harry said wryly. "We need the tribesmen, and we need their willing help, Volo."

"Indeed," Volo said moodily, stirring the coals. He seemed to have completely missed Harry's semi-sarcastic remark. "Stabilo informed me he left on excellent terms with the local tribes and said they'd welcome our return."

"Is that so, Sky Man?" a new voice boomed from just beyond the firelight, opposite the side where both Harry and Rodriguez sat. Harry elected to slowly rise to his feet. After a beat, Volo began to stand, but a lance, its metal head gleaming orange and silver in the firelight, was abruptly laid across the SpinDog's shoulder. Footsteps crunched and a party of tall, hooded persons came into view. Volo sank back down, turning carefully to avoid the edge of lance head and still see behind him.

"You claim blood-ties with Stabilo the Liar?" the lance owner asked, stepping even closer. With an impatient shake, the tall man discarded the hooded robe which had obscured his face. Harry first noticed a magnificent graying mane and beard, only partially controlled with what appeared to be braids and fabric bands dyed some dark color. The man's face was lean and weathered, like shiny, tough leather. The protuberant nose and sharp cheekbones gave him the cast of a wolf. Bright, dark eyes peered out from under his beetled brow, meeting Harry's own, and they shone with intelligence and intent.

Harry held the newcomer's eyes and nodded toward Volo before he continued giving the man the once over, noting the fine white scars that crisscrossed the calloused hand holding the lance. With an effortless twitch, the shaft of the lance snapped vertical, coming to rest on a dark metal ferule. Several other robed figures stepped closer, all armed. Most carried lances and wore long knives, almost the length of short swords. Two cradled wooden-stocked firearms whose bores appeared wider than the width of Harry's thumb. None of them appeared particularly pleased to see the visitors.

"My name is Volo of the House Zobulakos," the SpinDog announced haughtily. Harry watched as his slender ally found his feet and made a show of brushing imaginary dust from his shoulder where the lance had rested.

Volo was defiant even in the face of drawn weapons; Harry had to give him points for style.

"I am here representing the esteemed friend to all Sarmatchani, my father, Arko Primus Heraklis Zobulakos. This is a mission of great importance. What honorless prole names my brother a liar and interferes with the will of the Primus? Tell me, that I might inform your chief of this insolence."

Harry tensed as two of the newcomers surged forward in angry reaction to the word “honorless,” but the tall man interposed his lance, barring their way.

“Father!” the shorter one objected, throwing back her hood, revealing a sharp featured young woman. She’d drawn her blade and balefully eyed the SpinDog. “Let me teach this arrogant weakling about honor!”

“Nay, Stella,” the broad-shouldered man said grimly. “Even my daughter must cleave to the law. This is a clan matter. And as to the stripling’s question…

“I, hight Yannis al-Caoimhip ex-huscarlo, Patrisero of the Herdbane, First among the Sarmatchani,” he went on, fixing his eyes first on Volo and then each of the Terrans. “I name Stabilo of the Sky People a liar, a cheat, and a coward. I call his people to account. Blood or treasure. At dawn tomorrow either will suffice.”

Harry didn’t say a word but heard a deep sigh from Rodriguez. These were the allies he’d been sent to find, all right. Just like every other joint operation with indigs, it was SNAFU.

Murphy’s Law was still in effect.

Chapter Fifteen

R'BAK

I'm not too sure about this.

"Are you sure about this?" Rodriguez asked in English, standing a pace behind Harry. "I'm not particularly bad with a knife, but that boy looks like he's been to school."

Opposite them, waiting patiently in the wan pre-dawn light, was a broad-chested young man, perhaps twenty years old or so, if Harry was any judge. He'd been the male half of the two young people flanking the clan chief the night before, and his resemblance to the man in charge was unmistakable. An inch or two taller than Harry's own six feet, the younger man stood confidently, having shed his rifle and pack. Unlike Harry's camos, he wore simple trousers and a long-sleeved shirt, both of a grayish leather. The material was gathered below the knees and elbows with broad leather wraps, and his dark brown, shoulder-length hair was likewise bound. Behind him stood his sister, the one who'd indicated a desire to show Volo his own guts the previous night. As Harry watched, she passed a long, gleaming knife to her brother. The wooden handled weapon was shaped like a patcha skinning knife, and the drop point looked unsharpened above the tip, suggesting it was a slashing weapon.

The four of them were surrounded by the rest of the tribe, which stood inside a circle bounded by four large, wooden carts. The length of a prairie schooner, they were built with surprising skill, using a variety of metals for reinforcement and decoration. More than eighty meters away, a few of the younger members watched the clan's massive beasts of burden crop the short grass and roots in the ground. The animals were a peculiar cross between reptile and mammal. They resembled Earth's Komodo dragons, had those extinct beasts been covered in a scaled hide colored with alternating bands of tan and olive or stood shoulder high to a man, massing a couple of tons each. The creatures sported neck fringes they erected and shook when upset or aggressive, which seemed to be most of the time. They frequently whistled and bugled at their handlers, usually when the packs were loaded or when animals spotted a bit of choice forage. According to the chief, the whinnies, as they were called, would also eat anything and were sensitive to the smell of blood. Despite their objections, the youngsters along on the expedition didn't get to watch the impending duel, but had to tend the beasts instead.

"We need these folks, or the mission is already over," Harry said, looking away from the whinnies and back to his teammate. "Our kid, as touchy an asshole as he is, isn't used to the gravity yet and doesn't have much in the way of fighting skills, so if he dies on the little giant's knife, we risk the SpinDog' support. If we shoot our way clear, we're done. This duel is the only way I can see to get the mission done. And I'm not going to order you to do something I'm not particularly glad to do myself. So yeah, I'm sure."

Heh, listen to your pulse pounding already.

Okay. Mostly sure.

"If you waste Sonny, Daddy probably won't be inclined to go with our plan."

"Yeah, I'll try to remember."

"Well, then, remember the first rule of a knife fight," Rodriguez cautioned him before handing over the Gerber BMF Harry had carried in Somalia and now on R'Bak.

"What's that, Marco?"

"Losers die. Winners di-di to the field hospital. Only we ain't got a hospital."

The tribal shaman, or medicine woman, or whatever she was, stepped between the two, cutting off the smart-assed retort Harry had been about to deliver.

"Ha-Ree of the Far Star People will stand for the house of all the Sky People in this matter. Grevorg will stand for the

Sarmatchani," she proclaimed, both hands raised over her head. It had taken the better part of an hour to explain who Harry and Rodriguez were. The Terran's advanced weapons awed the tribesmen, and constrained by their chief, the clan had offered no direct threat but neither would they yield their claim. The Sarmatchani had grudgingly accepted Harry belonged, in a distant way, to a high-status offshoot of the Zobulakos by virtue of being "from the sky."

"If Ha-Ree should win, the debt by Stabilo is forfeit," Harry heard her say, and jeers from the crowd answered her.

And I get a chance to persuade Daddy, after cutting his kid up in front of him, to start a revolt with me. What a fucking op.

"If Grevorg shall win, the life of Volo will be in his hands," she said, keeping both hands in the air. Cheers rang out, leaving no mistake as to the preferred outcome.

Gotta love a friendly crowd.

Their response gave Harry a reason to scan the people around the circle. As far as he could tell, the men and women wore nearly identical external clothing, rather like the Inuit on Earth. The shaman's shirt was different, overlaid with a vest, upon which was tied a variety of small sachets, bones and dried plants. She pointed to the hill behind them. "When the sun appears above the grass, the fight will begin. It will end when one fighter yields or dies."

"I'm sorry for fight, star-man," Grevorg said, seemingly sincere. Over his shoulder, the sister, not much shorter, glowered wordlessly at Harry as she passed her brother the knife. "Clan law says I must defeat you. If you yield fast, maybe I don't have to hurt you. Much."

The clan version of K'tor was different than what Harry had learned. The differences in pronunciation and slang were manageable, though, and he got the gist of what the fighter was saying. Grevorg was young, and young men were prone to anger. Harry would use that.

"I appreciate the thought, kid," Harry replied a little dismissively. "I'll return the favor."

Grevorg simply narrowed his eyes, stepped forward a pace and settled into a blade-forward fighting stance. Harry reciprocated, but used his lead hand to guard the knife in his right. For several moments they watched each other, motionless, accompanied by the encouraging shouts of the Sarmatchani.

"The sun has arrived," the shaman-woman pronounced.

Like quicksilver, the tall youth immediately struck, trying to score on Harry's empty hand. Harry merely sidestepped, measuring his opponent's speed. Grevorg tried again, extending his arm further, and Harry dodged again, smiling to goad the younger man. He could feel the adrenaline coursing, and he breathed carefully, willing himself to remain calm.

Several of the clan yipped, urging Grevorg on, and his next attack anticipated Harry's sidestep. Harry merely leaned the other way, making the motion seem negligent and casual, causing a few of the watchers to laugh. Harry watched Grevorg grip his knife tightly, squaring fully up with Harry.

He's getting angry. Good. We know what that's like. Yes, we do.

On the next pass, Harry sidestepped, but this time, he used his own forearm to widen the gap and slashed at his opponent's momentarily unguarded flank, scoring a hit. The leather tunic deflected some of the blow, but Grevorg stepped back a pace and dipped a hand to his side, testing the injury. It came away red. He inclined his head to Harry and smiled toothily, while the tribe screeched in excitement. Harry replied in kind, but a wet feeling on his wrist made him glance down. He saw his left sleeve had been opened from wrist to elbow, as neatly as if cut with shears. Underneath, a cut several inches long traced a red line along the thick part of the forearm. He flexed his arm a bit, and the midpoint of the cut gaped like a jeering red smile. Harry hadn't felt more than a sting. Fortunately for him, the cut ran along the grain of the muscle, and function wasn't impaired. Much.

Harry's rage kindled, sending even more adrenaline surging into his system, making him feel preternaturally alert.

Sharp knife and a fast man with more reach. Gotta watch. Gotta think this through.

The two men tested each other's wounds, shuffling inside the circle, searching for openings. Several more quick passes ensued, and Harry acquired three more shallow but productive cuts in exchange for only one deep slash to his opponent's thigh. He reluctantly accepted that his opponent was both faster than him and learning quickly as well. Only minutes in, Harry was breathing like a slow bellows, but Grevorg was panting, growling in anger. Harry continued to fight his own anger down. Anger bred impatience, and he needed the other man to make the first big mistake. For obvious reasons, both men had carefully protected their face and neck during the fight, but if Harry wanted to win this, he had to do so before blood loss became the deciding factor. He needed to render Grevorg helpless and compel a non-lethal end to the fight. They shuffled in a circle, and Harry's shirt grew sodden with blood.

Firearms, not knives, had been the focus of weapons training in the special ops community, but Harry had trained with the Negritos in the Mindanaoan jungle of the Philippine highlands. Their rough and tumble fighting style accepted punishment as the price to close with an opponent. Harry needed to give the kid a target he couldn't pass up. All he needed was a spark.

"I see you've brought your sister along on a war party," Harry said, trying a sneer on for size. "Is that for your convenience or mine, after I win?"

Grevorg fairly roared and sprang towards Harry, who dodged, but feigned a stumble, exposing the upper end and shoulder of his knife arm. The angry youth leapt into the opening and Harry felt excruciating pain along his knife arm and shoulder, nearly making him drop his weapon, but now he had the distance. In a single, fluid motion, Harry drove into pain, feeling the edge of Grevorg's knife drag deeper as he trapped his opponent's wrist and weapon between his shoulder and the man's stomach. He blocked the man's ankle with his own and used his momentum to flip the bigger man off his feet. In a flash, Harry dropped to his knees, one driving deep into Grevorg's abdomen, forcing all breath from his lungs. Harry used his empty hand to deliver a calculated blow to Grevorg's temple, stunning him. Then he placed his own knife against his target's carotid and pressed hard enough to dimple the skin and open a small incision. His hand trembled slightly as the blood sheeting down his numb right arm blended with the fresh cut on Grevorg neck.

Kill him. Do it.

The urge to finish the stroke was strong, but he ignored the raging voice in his head, blinking sweat out of his eyes.

"Yield. Or. Die," Harry panted into the sudden silence, his head swimming.

Grevorg bit his lip but remained mute, shaking his head once. Harry looked up at the shaman and then the chief, struggling to keep his knife steady. He could barely feel his hand now.

"You claimed blood or treasure," he said, glaring at Yannis. "Here is the blood! How much more will you have? We may find it difficult to discuss the future of the Herdbanes if my hands are red with the last of your son's lifeblood."

"Father, n—!" Grevorg's second spat, but their father raised a hand, looking angry enough to chew rocks. He stared at Harry, then at Volo, who was standing mute, watching from the sidelines.

"Raah!" he suddenly yelled, grabbing his braids tightly enough that the muscles of his forearms bunched, his face contorted for a moment in frustration. "Parlay! So be it. First, you need to bind up your wounds before you expire while my clan is in your debt! And someone look to my young idiot!"

He nodded curtly at the shaman, and the circle broke up. A few clansmen as well as Rodriguez and Volo hastened to the combatants. Harry flopped to his side, rolling off Grevorg, and just like that, his rage rolled up, receded out of sight, like a window shade winding back into a hard roll. Grevorg sat up, holding one hand to his neck. They looked at each other, still breathing hard.

"Thank you for my life, Ha-Ree," Grevorg said, waving off his sister who was trying to see to his neck wound, prying at his blood-stained fingers.

Harry meant to nod, but the ground was in the way and his shoulder throbbed with every beat of his heart. He yelled instead as a great weight clamped against his shoulder. He looked over to see Rodriguez leaning on him, hard, both hands on the wound. Blood had already saturated the battle dressing Rodriguez had evidently held at the ready.

"Shit, this is really deep, El-Tee," he said, "Volo—open that second dressing! I can't tell if the artery is cut, and the wound is too high for a tourniquet. We have to pack it, now!"

He looks a little pale. Wonder how much blood I lost. I wonder how bad my arm is.

Harry let Rodriguez work. The pain was bad but seemed very far away. He vaguely felt his body being manipulated this way and that, but presently he felt very tired. Harry didn't notice when the shaman began aiding his teammate, because he was unconscious by then.

I can make this work! I love you!

I love you, too, but it's too late.

No—it's not too late. I can fix it. I'll come back.

You're gone, my love.

Come back!

It's too late for us, Harry.

No! Noo!

Harry woke up, clutching at the air. Not another hundred years! He fell back right away, breathing hard.

He was on a bedroll combining the synthetic foam pad he'd brought with him and some unfamiliar soft fabric or hide dyed a deep brown. A few candles, tallow by the smell, guttered alongside. Their smoke mingled with a new, astringent scent that filled the concave leather walls surrounding him. His eyes traced the lines of the walls as they tapered to a pointed ceiling a few meters overhead.

Opposite him, Rodriguez had been dozing, but Harry's movement caused him to open his eyes.

"Hello, sunshine," he said, before smacking the heavy skin wall of the tent and shouting, "Hey! Rosha! He's awake."

"How long was I out this time, Marco?" Harry asked, blinking. A small pewter-colored brazier was the source of the bitter smell. It didn't seem to be bothering his faithful NCO.

Another hospital. And more hospital dreams. I hate hospitals.

"All day and most of the next," Rodriguez answered. "You're tore up pretty good. The kid got his knife into your bicep and your delts. Nicked the artery. Bled like a pig and went into shock. I got the antibiotics on it, but you're not going to be good for much for a few weeks and it's gonna be stiff for months."

The flap to the tent was pushed aside and the shaman-woman summoned by the NCO ducked in, her outfit blurring in motion as the assorted decorations and fetishes danced with her movement. She was followed in close order by Grevorg and his sister, Stella. Grevorg had a skin-colored leather patch on his neck, apparently sticking of its own volition. Stella still wore her now-familiar glare.

"You wake at last, Ha-Ree," Rosha said, making her way to his side and sinking onto her haunches. "Welcome back from the dream world. First, I will examine my work. Then you must eat. You lost much blood and need to replace it for your body to heal."

She reached towards Harry's shoulder. Involuntarily, he flinched away and raised one hand. His right hand, on the side gored by Grevorg. Everyone stopped and watched the movement.

"Is there pain?" the shaman asked.

"No," Harry answered, shocked that it was true. He hadn't gotten a great look at the time, but he remembered clearly Rodriguez and Volo working on the wound right next to his face. It had been a massive and deep laceration. He'd seen his own muscle and fascia, clear to the pinkish bone of the humerus.

He shakily moved his arm up and down a little and it began to ache.

"Maybe a little."

"So," the healer said. "Now, we look." She glanced at Rodriguez. "A light, you smelly beast."

"She likes my flashlight better than she likes me," Rodriguez explained, producing a small battery powered Maglite and aiming it down as Rosha moved away the blood-stained padding. "Holy shit! Look at that!"

The wound centered on Harry's upper arm and shoulder was fully closed, demarcated by a bright red, puckered welt, framed by the circle of bright white illumination. He flexed his elbow, and pain, almost like a cramp, bloomed deep in the muscle.

"Good," Rosha said, laying her hand on Harry's arm and gently pushing it down. "Put it down. Now the other arm."

Harry obediently raised his left arm. The deep slashes on the forearms were also closed and were hardly more than red and purple lines. He made a fist and felt a light sting along the skin, similar to what a line of stitches had felt like in the past. Except, there were no stitches. He shoved the blanket down, and the wound on his ribs was similarly closed.

Harry stared in shock, and he could hear Rodriguez's disbelieving mutterings.

"How long has it been?" Harry repeated.

"Nearly two days have you slept," Rosha answered, peering at the wound. She withdrew a little clay pot from a pocket on the belly of her garment and dabbed a finger inside before smearing the line of the incision with a snot-green paste which smelled like a urinal. As she traced the cut, she muttered inaudibly and the touch of her finger grew hot, like a hair dryer left aimed at one's scalp for too long. Rosha continued down every red-seamed wound and then repeated the ritual twice more before settling back on her haunches half an hour later, visibly tired.

"My magic is strong, and as you can see, the wounds are closed and healing."

Harry looked, and sure enough, the redness of the incision lines had faded perceptibly.

"El-Tee, that ain't natural," Rodriguez said in English, staring at impossibly healthy, intact skin. "I've treated every kind of bush injury there is, and I'd have bet my abuela's virtue you'd be screaming in agony without some kind of painkiller. I used the anti-infection stuff we got from the Dornaani, but there's no way the wound is just *gone*."

"Tell you friend not to fear, Ha-Ree," Grevorg said, smiling at the obviously distraught Terrans. "Our shaman is powerful and knows the old ways. See?"

He peeled back the edge of his neck plaster to reveal the shallow cut Harry had inflicted there, and sure enough, it too was barely more than a closed red seam.

"Fool boy, ruining my work!" Rosha said, smacking his hands and carefully resealing the thin leather covering.

"How?" Harry asked in Ktor, not even bothering to conceal his awe. "No disrespect, honored clan-woman, but even our advanced medicines can't accomplish this much, so fast."

"Oh?" Rosha asked, cocking her head. "Truly? The more one uses the old magic, the better it works, and your body responded quite well, as well as our hunters who've used these magics since birth."

She looked at Harry's biggest wound again and sucked her teeth meditatively.

"Perhaps better. I think that apart from scars, there will be no permanent damage."

Rosha peered into the little brazier. She reached down and pulled a little leather sack off her vest. Opening it, she poured a little handful of fine white powder into her palm and weighed it before adding a bit more. Then she tugged a small bunch of dried twigs from the other side of her chest and crumbled one into her palm before upending the mixture into whatever was already brewing. Harry realized her decorated vest wasn't the affectation of an indigenous witch doctor: it was a functional combat medic's harness, complete with pharmacy. A fresh puff of smoke and a renewed astringent odor accompanied her actions. "Your body had been drawing on its reserves and now you must eat."

She snapped her fingers.

"Stella!"

The young woman moved up to Harry's bedroll, body-checking her brother out of the way. She held a small, three-legged pot by a handle, its underside charred black.

"Help him sit, you slow oaf," Stella ordered her brother. "He can't eat on his back."

"What's this, Grevorg?" Harry asked, confused as strong hands helped him to sit upright before more blankets and pillows were stuffed behind his back.

"You won the trial," his former opponent said, his tone making it clear that the answer obvious. "When you spared my life, Yannis accepted your offer of parlay. That can't happen till you are well, so we will help you heal. Clan law."

Stella opened the pot and stirred it.

"Open your mouth, Sky Man," she said.

"Use courtesy, sister," Grevorg said. "The law binds Keepers more tightly than others. As you know."

For a moment the siblings scowled at each other, but Stella relented.

"If you please, Ha-Ree," she said, grudgingly. "I help you eat so you heal more speedily."

"Looks like you get to find out if those immunity shots on the station took or not, El-Tee," Rodriguez said with a malicious smile. "Someone had to be first. I'll be over here, just enjoying some of these delicious SpinDog rations."

Harry looked helplessly at the shaman-woman, who stood, hands on hips. She made little urging motions.

"Eat, eat!"

He opened his mouth to protest he could feed himself, and the girl promptly shoved a loaded spoon into it. Harry chewed cautiously. The texture was meaty, and the taste was mildly sweet and salty. As he chewed, he became aware of a growing level of spiciness, like the Thai food served at Sara's favorite restaurant.

"By the way, I saw what they were cooking an' it had at least six legs, if it had a one," Rodriguez offered, gesturing with a plastic spoon.

Despite a pang of homesickness Harry somehow forgot to be mad.

Volo watched the activity in the camp as it quietly bustled around him. He paid particular attention to the younger women. Even clad in the robes and leathers which protected them from the desert wind, their obvious athleticism was…intriguing. It probably wasn't a good idea, but he couldn't help but imagine some of them wearing the much lighter, form-following station suits worn by the SpinDogs in their off-planet habitat. However, his regard had not been returned, a first for Volo. He'd never lacked for companionship, despite the strictures on sexual relations aboard *Second Spin*. This was particularly true since even the youngest of the Zobulakos family was still an attractive political match.

However, he'd learned on R'Bak, the same wasn't the case. Despite painful preparation, his musculature and endurance did not compare to that of the natives, or even the Terrans. Oh, he was treated politely enough. The outcome of Tapper's duel had ensured it. But the duel had only been necessary as a result of what was clearly a preplanned maneuver by Volo's idiot brother, Stabilo. The next message Volo had squirted up to the orbiting microsat for relay to *Second Spin* had outlined the situation and the reply from his father contained confirmation.

At least his father would see to Stabilo's embarrassment. Knifing your brother in the back, at least metaphorically, was an accepted ritual during the incessant, internecine struggles for dominance among more traditionally-minded SpinDogs. Of course, one was expected to succeed. Failure was gauche, enough so that it reduced one's social desirability. Among the Sarmatchani, allowing a second to stand for you in a duel seemed to have imparted the same taint. And while the duel had extinguished the immediate hostility, the Sarmatchani chief had remained unswayed by Volo's proposals for action against the J'Stull, let alone facing the Kulsians directly, preferring to wait until Tapper had healed.

A movement caught his attention, and Volo followed the headman's daughter with his eyes as she strode into view, lightly stepping between the guy lines along the row of tents, before ducking into the yurtlike structure where Tapper was recovering from the injuries he'd sustained during the duel. The young woman didn't bother to first slap the leather to request entrance, as formal custom required. Volo frowned.

Only two days after the fight, the Terran officer had regained partial use of his arm despite the massive tissue damage and blood loss. Now, he was effectively fully healed, and, unfortunately, the off-worlders couldn't stop talking about it. The power of R'Bak's pharmaceuticals was something Volo's father wanted deemphasized in any negotiations with the Lost Soldiers. More important, the Sarmatchani should build a relationship principally with the SpinDogs, not the Terrans, and that wasn't progressing either.

Volo needed something, but he wasn't certain what. In the meantime, he would continue to persuade the clan chieftain, as slowly and subtly as time allowed, that it was in his people's interest to continue to be of assistance.

After the meal, Rosha and her sidekicks left, promising to return later. Rodriguez had stepped out too, leaving his boss to relax and rest in private. But before Harry could fall asleep, he had a different visitor. A single firm slap on the wall of the tent alerted him even as the flap was swept aside and the gray-maned chieftain swiftly ducked inside. As he straightened, he looked at Harry and raised an eyebrow in restrained greeting before glancing around the space.

"I hate that smell," Yannis said, wrinkling his nose at the vinegary odor wafting from the brazier. "My wife swears it works, but I think she does it just to annoy the young men and encourage them to get out of bed sooner."

"Welcome, honored Yannis," Harry said. The Dornaani language program had emphasized the importance of formal speech, but the taller man made little palm-down motions in response as Harry struggled to sit somewhat more upright. "I wasn't expecting a visit. Please excuse my inability to greet you properly."

"Just woke up after losing half your blood, and still courteous," Harry's visitor observed. "Different from the others we've received from beyond the clouds."

Harry took a few moments to adjust his pillow so he wasn't reclining quite so much. He used the time to give the chief a once over. Yannis has skipped the full cloak he'd worn the morning of the duel. He was also empty-handed when it came to his lance or an obvious gun, though a sheathed knife, similar to the one Grevorg had used, hung on his belt. The man sank easily into a cross-legged position, leaning against the central tent pole.

"Do you receive such visitors often?" Harry said.

"Often enough to see the difference, Ha-Ree," Yannis said. "Rosha has examined you closely, and she confirms what anyone with eyes can see: you are not of the Sky People. Your bones are too heavy. You are too scarred, like a warrior. Your hands are not soft. Your eyes are hot, but you have the *skepsos*, the thinking way of fighting, even when angered. That's how you goaded my son into a loss."

Harry recognized the near-ritual quality of the chief's recitation. This was no casual chitchat and he hadn't the luxury of preparation. The SEAL flogged his mind to full alertness.

"I regret the necessity of wounding Grevorg," he said earnestly. "But, as I explained before the fight, my clan is allied to the SpinDogs, the Sky People, because we must create a refuge on this planet while we wait for our comrades to return. And so, we must find allies among your people."

"Grevorg is fine," Yannis waved away the apology. "He learned something valuable. Know that I have spoken to your man, the other star soldier, Rod-ree-gets. He tells me you know of the legends of the Reavers who land on R-Bak as the second star grows close, scorching the land. He says you would fight against those who murder the tribes. He also says you need us. But he doesn't explain *why* you fight."

"They aren't legends, sir," Harry replied. "They're true, and your enemy is already here. Better to fight while you're strong."

"Yes, yes," Yannis said, acknowledging the statement with a wave of one hand. "But what do you get from the fighting? You didn't have to come here."

"We fight so we might have a base, a safe place for our soldiers to rest and ready for another battle," Harry replied. "We fight so the SpinDogs, such as Volo, might have somewhere to land after hundreds of years spent without a planet under their feet."

The smell coming off the brazier was just too strong, and Harry reached over to replace the lid, at least choking off any more of the fumes from deepening the eye-watering atmosphere.

"I know you're brave, Ha-Ree," Yannis said, a small smile playing on his lips. "Only a great hero would dare to change a treatment ordered by the fearsome Rosha. But bravery doesn't explain why you want to fight. Is it just the sting of battle you seek?"

"I've found the 'sting' of battle to be highly overrated," Harry replied. "I fight when I must."

"Tell me why you must fight for the Sky People, then," Yannis said, looking into Harry's eyes and holding them. "I know what they want. They need land under the suns and our healing plants. They require healthy women who can help them grow their tribe. Most of all, they need allies in order to defeat the Suzerain, his satraps such as the J'Stull, and the beasts who will ravage land. These SpinDogs aren't as strong as the armsmen of my great-grandfather, who wore the colors of the Eastern Hegemon before he fled to become a free man. They aren't as strong as the Suzerain of the North and his army. They have no magic and hope to learn ours. But why do *you, Ha-Ree,* fight? What do you want?"

Harry didn't know whether sharing everything was the smart play or not. What with the blood loss, he wasn't entirely sure he had all of his wits, and besides, keeping track of lies was a pain in the ass. He looked at the little bank of oil lamps which provided inadequate illumination. Tired of the gloom, he lunged halfway out of his pallet and opened the tent flap, letting fresh light—and air—in.

Screw it. The truth it is.

"We want to go home, honored Yannis," Harry replied. "My man and I were stolen not only from our land but from our time by the masters of the Kulsians, whom we call the Ktor. Our families believe us dead. Our country—our tribe—has forgotten our memory and my sons' sons do not know my name. If getting back to our home means helping the SpinDogs, means helping you, means killing every Kulsian on this planet, then we fight."

There was a pause as Yannis digested Harry's reply.

"And how do you propose to help us fight the forces of the Suzerain?" he asked finally. "You are but two, even if you have weapons from the stars. You have no boats, no airships."

The initial orbital surveys had confirmed SpinDog intelligence regarding surface logistics. Harry already knew that as a matter of control, the satraps, including the local J'Stull, largely forbade convoys of ground vehicles, whether mechanized or animal powered. They did operate lighter-than-air, semi-rigid dirigibles and boats, giving them a tremendous advantage and allowing them to dictate terms to both of their less-well-equipped vassals, as well as any barbarian who decided to contest the balance of power.

"We know the Reavers, as you call them, are already here in small numbers," Harry said. "They, and the Kulsians, are preparing the way for many more. They ready their ground *vehicles*."

He noted Yannis' puzzled squint at the new term. "Wagons and carts which move themselves, equipped with weapons like these, and larger. They can carry more than any ten whinnies and need to be tended by only a few warriors. If we can take them, we deny their use to the Suzerain. The Sarmatchani can use them instead, becoming swift, able to strike in many places quickly, as though you were far greater in numbers."

"Hmm." Yannis was skeptical. "Volo has told us he can ask for help only once from his friends over our heads, and that only if he can report a success. The J'Stull are many and there are many vassals like them. Even a small stone town like Chorat has half a hundred warriors, and again as many militia. And then there are the Reavers, who will have weapons which shoot fire and lightning. You ask much of my people."

"We can teach your fighters new ways of war," Harry answered. "If you can persuade more of your tribes to join us, our numbers will be enough to take the war wagons when we, and not the enemy, choose the time and place of battle. And I ask no more of them than myself."

"I admire your courage, Ha-Ree, and I can see something of your character. Yet you've already lost your clan, as you've said. If you lose here, you forfeit only a hope of seeing your own world. If the Sarmatchani fail in battle, we lose everything."

"One can lose a battle and keep fighting, honored Yannis," Harry countered, leaning forward. "If your clan loses hope, then all is lost. Consider this: Your people understand that the approach of the second sun and the enemies it brings will kill many and drive the survivors from your lands. If the stories are true, and they are, then the Scorching will leave the Sarmatchani to fall so far that your children will struggle for years to regain even as much as you already have. Does my offer of an alliance offer any more danger than that?"

Yannis looked at him and didn't reply for a long time.

Finally, he placed his hands on his knees and said, "How shall we persuade my fellow chiefs to fight when hiding is what has allowed us to survive, so far?"

"What if, instead of having to begin afresh as the second star recedes, your people could begin from where you stand now?" Harry asked in turn, holding up a clenched fist before opening it slowly, as though presenting a gift. "And what if you could shelter as the satraps do? How many more Sarmatchani children would grow to adulthood to serve the clan?"

Harry smiled. "Besides, everyone loves a winner, Yannis. There is a saying among my people, from a warrior-poet who died long before I was born: *'It's loot, loot, loot, that makes the boys stand up and shoot.'* Let us show the Sarmatchani and the other tribes just what winning looks like."

Chapter Sixteen

R'BAK

"Remember, we want them low enough so we can reach them with this," Harry said, patting the shrouded contraption in the whinnie-drawn cart. "But not so low they actually hit you. You're just the decoy."

"I can wiggle better than a Saigon cola girl trying sell you a short time," Rodriguez answered cheerfully, using English.

"Marco, English or Ktoran. Pick one, not whatever grunting noises you doggies use among yourselves."

"Bait, El-Tee," the noncom replied in Ktoran as he strode to the small group of Sarmatchani waiting for him. He waved a hand over his head in a tight circle, signaling to Grevorg to get a move on. "We'll be the bait the gasbag can't pass up. You just make sure not to miss."

"Hell, I'm an officer, and you *know* what good shots we are!" Harry jibed back, covering his own tension in the time-honored manner.

"Not helping, El-Tee!" Rodriguez threw the last comment over his shoulder as he reached the front of the small decoy group.

There wasn't any more to be said. Harry and the Special Forces sergeant had rehashed the plan each day of their march. The daily message bursts relayed through the satellites had generated replies from Murphy and the planning cell with the SpinDogs. Their critically important updates made the plan possible. There wasn't a lot of room for error. Of course, that wasn't a new factor, not on this op.

Rodriguez had the easier, but clearly more dangerous of the two objectives. Once Harry had persuaded Yannis, the tribe had moved higher into the low mountains ringing the desert, drawing closer to the commerce routes used by the satrap's gatherers to trade with Chorat. During breaks in the march and after the evening meal, Rodriguez had trained up a few of the fleetest tribesmen. His decoy group was now armed with all three of the tribe's precious breech-loading rifles.

Their projectiles were hand-loaded conical bullets, which were crammed forward into the barrel by the action of closing the breech, and propelled by a limited supply of paper-wrapped black powder cartridges. The nearly prehistoric weapons had been looted during successful skirmishes against the satrap's own bands of hunters. The rifles had limited range and also created a very large cloud of smoke with each shot. Against like opponents, the Sarmatchani employed them no differently than the long bows with which most of the tribe were equipped, which was to say, as part of a general skirmish line. Harry could tell this offended Rodriguez's professional instincts, and the noncom had enthusiastically introduced the basics of coordinated fire and maneuver.

"What does the name he used mean?" Stella asked curiously. She was standing with the rest of the clan, watching the decoy group head toward a convenient gorge. Around them, the land was rock, mostly bare of vegetation. "What is 'el-tee'?"

"It's my rank in our clan," Harry answered. He'd become more accustomed to the local dialect, and now understood some of the vernacular more completely. "I'm a warband leader among my people."

"And you made a death-joke, yes?" she asked. "You laugh, but the smile doesn't reach your eyes."

"I did make a small joke, as a way to acknowledge his bravery," Harry explained. "He knows the danger to his group, and he accepts it, so I offered a joke suggesting the danger was even higher. It's a way to acknowledge his bravery without embarrassment."

"Yes, we do much the same thing," Stella said without particular emphasis. "But the danger *is* great. The Kulsian's skyboat is untouchable. My brother's life means much to me and our tribe. My father's honor means even more. If your plan squanders either, you'll answer to me."

Harry knew he should be more used to Stella's casual threats, which were offered pretty much at the end of every other conversation he had with her. With the ease of practice, he dismissed his irritation and focused on the implications of her words. He'd asked the Sarmatchani to extend a huge measure of trust, after all.

The local vassal of the Suzerain patrolled his territory and maintained order using what the tribes considered to be terrifying displays of power. In truth, the technology was no better than what could be found on 19th century Earth. Spectral analysis from the Dornaani suggested the riverboats used wood-, coal-, and kerosene-fired steam engines at an efficiency level barely sufficient enough to buck the strongest river currents. The few semi-dirigibles which patrolled the most important trade routes and borders were limited in payload and speed. However, to a tribe whose movement was entirely limited by how fast they could hike, the Kulsian's technology was awesome, and like the aeroshells which had delivered Harry's team, it represented a magic they couldn't hope to match. All the Sarmatchani clans recognized and resented the impossible advantages conferred by the somewhat common boats and much rarer airships.

Harry knew it, and was counting on it, in fact. En route, the initial band of Sarmatchani had been joined by representatives from neighboring groups. In order to get them to observe Harry's operation at close quarters, Yannis had spent political capital like water, using a mixture of promises of spoils blended with accusations of cowardice. Nearly all had agreed, though they were more cautious than his band, and so would stand off and watch from farther away.

"The skyboat is nothing more than fabric, wood, and a little metal," Harry explained. He'd repeated his explanation every day, but the tribe only followed his instruction because of Yannis' command. "Like you, they think their machines are untouchable. They won't expect our surprise. When they lose their precious gasbag, they'll grow more fearful of the Sarmatchani and your tribe will gain much status."

"I hear your words," Stella said, glancing at him before letting her eyes follow the dwindling figures of the decoy group as they marched toward the lower of the two morning suns. "My lance waits to believe. So, now lead me to the place my father has selected for this folly."

Harry swept the horizon for the target. Below the rim of the shallow canyon, the decoy group was gathered around a fire, enjoying their afternoon. Harry's first job was simple. The main group would see the airship first, by virtue of their higher vantage point. Then Harry would instruct another to signal those below.

"The breeze is light, as you hoped," Yannis observed, lying next to Harry, covered by a dirt-colored hide which lay across them both, smooth-side up. Harry recognized the blue-black fur from his encounter with the batangs, as the Sarmatchani called the creatures he'd encountered early on. This must have been an even larger specimen whose skin comfortably spanned both men as well as Volo, who lay on Harry's other side.

"*Second Spin* updated the forecast, and winds should remain low," the SpinDog offered. "The message stated the target remains on schedule as of the last satellite pass, a few hours past."

"Thanks, Volo," Harry answered. The satellites had been tracking the surface activity for weeks, even prior to the drop, and the schedule of the boats and airships was consistent. The younger man had seemed content to allow Harry to lead so far. He'd relayed all of their requests for information without complaint and had offered useful ideas which had speeded the construction of the new weapon. "The less wind, the more confident the crew of the dirigible will be," Harry continued.

For a time, they lay quietly, the light breeze rippling along the edge of their covering. Harry left the men to his left and right to their own thoughts. Abruptly, he realized he hadn't thought about Sara for two days. Maybe more.

Even when she'd been angry with him, Sara would listen to his rants, pick apart his rationalizations, and generally help him be a better person. He'd been so wrapped up in this op he'd not realized how much he missed it.

Get busy, forget your wife. What an asshole I am.

Of course, she always said as long as I was in the field, that's where my head needed to be. Just leave the field behind when you come home.

Home.

Harry tried not to think about home for a while and didn't check his Casio until Yannis bumped his hip.

"There."

Sure enough, the oblong shape of a dirigible was edging around the point, a few klicks away. Harry kicked Volo's ankle, and the SpinDog used a mirror to flash the campfire below, soliciting a flash in response. Invisible to them, Harry knew the decoy team would then use their mirror to "give away" their position to the oncoming airship.

He studied it through his monocular as it grew closer.

The main component was a blunt-nosed fabric cylinder more than a hundred meters long. It was dyed a rust color and tapered from front to back. The semi-rigid vehicle was encased and shaped by a grid of heavy ropes, like a coarse fishing net. Around the midsection or waist of the bag, and integrated into the net, ran what looked like a light gray metal frame, possibly aluminum. The rear of the frame supported control surfaces, built kite-style in a cruciform shape. Dwarfed by the bag, and hanging beneath it, was a long, mostly enclosed gondola with actual portholes lining the sides. It seemed to be at least head-high and from the canoe-shaped stern was hinged a huge wooden-framed, fabric rudder. An exhaust stack projected to starboard, trailing a blue-black haze, presumably from the power plant which was kept well separated from the lift bag above. The motive force was provided by two propellers, whose nacelles were hung from the midships rail. It took Harry a moment to figure out they were running on belt or chain drives leading toward the motor section.

Abruptly, the nose of the ship shifted as the craft changed course, steering directly toward the decoy team.

Excellent. It was time for Rodriguez to wriggle. Right on time, one of the Terran's few ground flares ignited below, the red actinic glare visible even in broad daylight. Nothing in the hands of the tribesmen should burn so brightly, and Harry had calculated the anomaly would draw the craft even closer. Sure enough, it began to descend, approaching the level of the canyon rim where the assault team was hidden.

Harry felt his own excitement build as the parts of his plan came together.

"Yannis, ensure the wagon teams keep the covers on till the last moment," Harry whispered, not taking his eyes off the approaching target. Nothing must give away the ambush until the craft was deep inside his range, even as they thought themselves above the range of bows or captured rifles. It descended a bit more, sinking below the lip of the canyon.

Harry saw the first puff of muzzle smoke from the decoy group as they opened fire. A second and a half later, the sound reached Harry. A second puff, then a third. The airship slowed and began to yaw, and movement was visible inside the control compartment. A few more moments, and a corresponding puff of smoke, though smaller in size, bloomed from the gondola. A much sharper report sounded. Then another and another, until there was an intermittent crackling as the gunners on the ship ruthlessly took advantage of their height.

The gunfight was just like a rock fight in a well, only it was Harry's team on the downside. Only two puffs of smoke replied from the ground.

"Now?" Yannis asked, gripping Harry's elbow. "Now!"

"Not yet," Harry said. He wanted the ship to lose even more momentum so if he missed, he would have time for a second attempt before the craft ascended out of range.

Anxious moments passed, and Yannis' grip grew excruciating.

Good enough. Let's see what Mama Tapper's boy brought to the party.

"Now!" Harry shouted, and Yannis stood, throwing off the concealing tarp. Harry remained prone and lowered his head to the comb of his M-14, already laid in front of him. He looked for a porthole which might correspond to the pilot, coxswain, whatever, of the airship. Only two hundred yards away, it was nearly at a dead stop, and even as he acquired his sight picture, he noted the rate of fire from the ship had slowed as lookouts spotted the activity taking place behind Harry. That was a good thing, because the decoy team's fire had dwindled to nothing.

Harry began shooting, punching rifle rounds through the wooden bulkhead of the gondola. Slow, deliberate fire, not faster than one round every two to three seconds. Even without a certain target, his fire would serve to distract the gunners and crew, taking the heat off Rodriguez. After five or six rounds, no more plumes of smoke came from the ship as the rate of enemy fire also dropped to zero, likely in shock. Harry knew his own position would be hard to spot for an enemy accustomed to looking for large blooms of gun smoke. He smiled, imagining the confusion on the airship.

Surprise, motherfuckers. Mr. Murphy would like a word.

Harry couldn't see behind himself, but he knew Yannis and Volo would be exhorting the gunners to get the camouflage covers off the remaining two wagons as fast as they could. He wondered if the torches were lighting from the smoldering tapers they'd had to keep burning all afternoon as they waited. He could hear the clacking as the loaders spun the cranks, drawing back the massive drawstrings of his "surprises." Focused on his shooting, he didn't watch as the improvised Roman-style ballistae, designed and built by the Terrans with considerable and increasingly enthusiastic Sarmatchani wheelwright's assistance, were trained on the target. It had taken nearly as much effort to persuade Yannis to cannibalize half of his clan's wagons for the scheme as it had to attempt the effort in the first place.

Volo had already hustled back to the mechanisms. He was in charge of laying the weapons and alternating fire.

Two ballistae. Why? Because two is one and one is none.

A loud *TUNG!* finally got his attention, and a faint red line arced toward the airship. Amazingly, it tracked true, piercing the bag amidships. Harry waited for a moment, but nothing happened. Both Rodriguez and he had thought hard about the problems of making an incendiary ballista bolt. The SF sergeant, a veteran of myriad booby traps improvised by his Viet Cong enemy, had devised a way to use the burning metal of their red marking flares as a payload that wouldn't be snuffed out by the speed of the ballista bolt. Harry knew—well, believed—the R'Bak satraps were using hydrogen to generate lift. The Dornaani analysis all pointed one way. However, the airship remained intact. In fact, the ship's stack belched a pulse of darker exhaust. Someone was belatedly increasing speed.

I didn't say you could go yet, motherfuckers!

Harry went to rapid fire, using the rest of his magazine to probe the gondola, hoping he was distracting, or better, disabling the crew.

The second bolt fired, also striking the target, but yielding no effect.

They've got to be using hydrogen. There's no way they have enough helium to fill their ships.

He snarled and let a little bit of his bottled frustration and anger out for a glimpse of the world. The bolt locked back on his rifle, so he rocked a new magazine into place and kept firing, this time aiming for the engine nacelles. The airship's acceleration was still building, and the range to target was nearing the limits of their improvised weaponry.

Harry heard a third bolt go downrange, but the unmusical *tung!* was accompanied by a crash and a scream. He looked back to see one gunner facedown and another holding his bleeding arm. The capstan, used to tension the bow, had failed catastrophically, and the parts had been flung in all directions. A materials failure, bad design, the gunners got nervous and over-cranked the machine—it didn't matter. Harry spied Volo at the head of the little crowd staring at the wreckage, and the remaining weapon wasn't in service.

"Volo, make ready to load and fire, goddamit!" Harry yelled. He left the rifle and ran the few meters to the shallow pit that had been used to conceal the wagon-born ballistae. Volo gave him a started look and sprang back into action. Harry snatched the bolt from the Sarmatchani crewman looking askance at the bleeding tribesman on the ground and thrust it at the SpinDog before roughly pushing the chieftain toward the tensioning mechanism. "Yannis, be pissed tomorrow, but spin the crank, now!"

Harry and Yannis worked the alternating handles on the crank, drawing the bowstaves back. Made from the wooden suspension leaves of the cannibalized wagons and inserted into pre-tensioned loops of thick sisal-like plant fiber, they creaked with a strain they'd not been designed to handle. Too much load and they would crack. Too little and the bolt wouldn't reach the airship, which was now gathering enough speed to respond to the rudder and was already turned all the way to one side. The pawl clacked forward one more time, and Harry stopped.

Volo laid the bolt into groove, ensuring the notch was seated.

"Light!" the SpinDog ordered, and Harry watched as Stella, of all people, laid the torch against the little metal cage immediately behind the spiked business end of the bolt. The mixture of twisted plant fiber, animal fat, and signal flare lit with a sullen red glow. "Training. Stand clear."

Harry itched to aim the weapon himself, but Volo had already achieved two hits. This was their last chance and Volo was the right person.

TUNG!

The group held their breath as the bolt described a graceful arc before curving down and disappearing into the stern of the ship. A moment later there was a sudden glow, and then an audible *whoosh* as a brilliant, glaring light bloomed from the stricken ship. The fire was bright enough to make the daylight seem pale in comparison. Immediately the stern crumpled and sank, arresting the ship's forward motion. The fire ate at the fabric, creeping forward toward the bow. The gondola sagged suddenly, and figures were visible at an open door. A coil of rope spilled out, and a man, then two, grabbed at it and slid down.

Unfortunately, the ship was still much too high, despite the accelerating loss in altitude. The lower man arrested his descent as he reached the end, still fifty meters above the ground. He barely had time to consider the calamity. His fellow didn't stop, and both men pinwheeled, doll-like, from the end of the dangling rope. Their screams lasted only a moment before they disappeared against the dark earth.

A second *whooshing* sound heralded the ignition of the forward gasbag, and Harry put up a hand to shield his face. Even at a distance nearing three hundred meters, the heat was intense, yet thankfully brief. The clan around him was screaming in jubilation, drowning out the distant, thin screams of their unseen victims trapped onboard. He looked around, an unaccustomed smile slowly growing on his face, as his body rocked from the joyful pounding Yannis was delivering. Stella was screaming a paean of pure triumph and blood. Harry looked at Volo and offered a casual salute, touching two fingers to his brow.

"Good shooting, Volo!" Harry yelled, but he doubted the SpinDog could hear him, although he saw Volo grin in response.

Well, maybe we can make Murphy's Law the other guys' problem, after all.

Chapter Seventeen

R'BAK

This is even louder than the feast scene from the last Star Wars movie. At least there aren't any of those annoying teddy bears, even if the music is about the same.

Harry gripped his drinking horn tightly as another drunken Sarmatchani slapped him hard enough to bruise, braying his approval and giving Harry a great view of his food-stained mustache, the bristles sticking out at odd angles as the man yelled something congratulatory. Harry just nodded and smiled, since he could barely hear himself think over the sound of the hide drums and buzzing, kazoo-like harmonicas which served the Sarmatchani as musical instruments. He turned carefully, balancing on the three-legged stool propping up his drunken butt, here at the head table. He opened his mouth to address Yannis.

"Well done, boy!" Yannis overrode Harry with a roar, his boozy words accompanied by a bit of spray. "Have I told you how well done that was!"

Yannis caught sight of something over Harry's shoulder and didn't wait for Harry's answer.

"Excellent, the main course is here for the hero's feast!"

The entire assembled clan had been doing heroic trencher duty for an hour already. Immature whinnie was on the menu, and though it didn't taste just like chicken, Harry enjoyed the spices. Some sort of grain dish, whose individual flat grains were shaped somewhat like pumpkin seeds. More unidentifiable meat, tasting like the first thing Stella had fed him during his recovery. Each place setting had a shallow clay bowl with hot coals and Yannis had shown him how to cook the meat just long enough for it to brown before dunking it in gravy and wolfing it down.

Or doing whatever took the place of a wolf on this damned planet.

He looked for Stella in the crowd below, but he was jostled by two men bearing a wooden tray nearly a meter long. Harry almost recoiled in disgust looking at the contents.

The new dish was a bug. A giant, red and black bug shaped like a lobster, if a lobster had extra legs and the giant hooked mandibles of a mosquito larvae. It was still alive, its segmented body pinned to the wooden tray with sharpened dowels. He swore that the damned thing's eyes were watching him, and the jaws clacked together angrily. Harry could hear Rodriguez groaning next to him.

"Oh shit, I was afraid of something like this."

"Like what, Marco?" Harry said, his voice rising an octave or six.

"That, El-Tee, that's lunch," Rodriguez said soberly. "And you can't flunk lunch."

"What the fuck do you mean?" Harry eased back as the bug tried to escape again. He tried a different tack and addressed the chief. "What the hell, Yannis! What's that?"

"We're lucky, Ha-Ree!" Yannis said happily. "I wasn't sure our hunters could find a nest of *astakos* with so little notice. They are quite rare, but tasty. Their flesh gives a warrior new strength and potency! Haha!"

Yannis dug an elbow in Harry's side hard enough to dislocate a rib, laughing so uproariously that Harry had no doubt what kind of potency Yannis meant. Before he could suggest an alternative to this no-doubt great honor, the drunk chief whipped his belt knife out overhand, severing one of the legs. The creature tried to hunch its back in a pain response, and the armor rubbed against itself at the joints, making a grunching noise while the remaining seven, count 'em, *seven fucking legs*, clattered on the table as it tried fruitlessly to escape.

The chief dropped the spasming leg in his cooking coals, holding it in place with his knife until it stilled. The smell wasn't bad, and the carapace was turning a bright white in the heat.

"Go on, you've earned the second piece!" Yannis prodded Harry. "Only the bravest may sample it! Do watch out for the mandibles, they're quite sharp."

Oh, man. I have to eat a fucking giant cockroach.

He looked over at Rodriguez again, but he was no help. The noncom only nodded sagely, trying and failing to suppress a gleeful smile.

"It's not too bad, El-Tee," he said, motioning to Harry to get a move on before swallowing more of whatever the fermented drink was. "Better than cobra-venom gland sushi, like I had to eat in Cambodia. You gotta eat it, or you're refusing the hospitality of the clan. It would mess up that shiny new hero image you made by shooting down the blimp-thing. This meal is a test. You can't flunk it."

"I didn't shoot it down!" Harry said, looking over at Volo, a couple stools over. "Volo shot it down. He should have the honor!"

Harry glanced down at the struggling bug.

Grunch, grunch.

"On no, Harry—I mean, El-Tee," Volo said, folding his arms and standing. "You're the leader. The honor is yours! No one will be surprised if I, a mere gunner, refuse the honor so a great warrior such as yourself can enjoy this…feast."

I can't believe this shit.

Harry grabbed his horn to swig some of the alcoholic-whatever-it-was and fortify his strength.

"Hey, El-Tee, do you want to know where they get this fermented milk?"

"No. No, I do not."

Harry took a breath, drew his knife, and deliberated which leg he'd choose.

Clatter-clatter-clatter. Gruuuunch.

Just fuck me.

"Oww," Harry said out loud. He awoke flat on his back, looking up at the ceiling of the same style yurtlike tent as the one in which he'd recovered. He let his memories reassemble themselves in no particular order.

Finding Rodriguez and Grevorg, injured but alive. Searching the crash site for anything valuable. The elated march to a nearby Sarmatchani tribe's village. What else?

Oh right. The traditional Sarmatchani drinking celebration. Fermented...I still don't want to know what it was. And now the traditional penance...

The scent of last night's fire failed to complement the pounding in his head, as he creakily struggled to his elbows. Gray morning light filtered in from the gaps between chimney and the tent roof, and that hurt a bit, too. "Oww."

"Good morning, Ha-Ree."

He started, nearly falling off his short billet, and looked to his right to see Stella. She was under the covers, curled up on her side. Her long, dark hair lay tangled across her bare shoulder. He was suddenly aware of three things. She was gorgeous, he was utterly naked under the blankets, and *holy crap that's the chief's daughter*!

"You've finally awoken," she said, smiling. "I'm glad. You were snoring like a lovestruck whinnie, and I feared lest one hear you and come searching for a mate. Fortunately, I was here to defend your virtue."

"Uhh," was the best Harry could offer. "Thanks?"

"Now you're awake, and I can finally get warm," Stella said happily, scooting under the blankets and draping herself across his chest and other parts. If she was surprised to find him without the approved Sarmatchani pajamas, she gave no sign.

Perhaps the Sarmatchani didn't wear pajamas, Harry thought. *She certainly isn't.*

An undefinable time later, Harry was still awake, and in much the same position as when he awoke, except this time his head was clear, and his shoulder was decorated with the head of a beautiful woman.

"You demonstrated considerable foresight bringing that jug of water with you," Harry said. After addressing the first round of rather urgent business, Stella had plied him with cup after cup of cool water, and his headache had slowly receded. "Or was it experience? Oww!" he added, involuntarily.

"You think I sneak into tents with drunken strangers as a matter of course, you *skrellig*!" Stella said, her fist cocked back, ready to repeat her punch. "I'm the daughter of—"

"Easy, easy!" Harry wheezed, one hand over his solar plexus. He didn't know what a *skrellig* was, but it probably wasn't a compliment. "I was just asking if you tried that witch's brew we were drinking last night. Maybe you knew that I really needed some water. That's all!"

"Oh," Stella said, suddenly deflating. "I thought that you meant…never mind. Everyone knows that strong drink first brings laughter and then fireside boasting but leaves you with an empty stomach and an emptier head."

She lifted the blanket from his stomach and groin, studying where she'd hit him. "Does it hurt? I don't see a mark."

"No, I'm fine," Harry replied, hastily tugging the blanket back down. "I feel good. Perfect, actually."

"Well, of course you are," she said, matter-of-factly, and rolled away to refill Harry's kidney-shaped canteen cup again from the water jug. "I took some of your anger, so naturally you feel a bit happier. What could be more natural than that?"

"My anger?"

"You hold your anger inside you, like a fist," she said, sipping. "Many could see it. Rosha saw it first. I thought your anger was aimed at us, that you were glad to hurt Grevorg. It's why I didn't trust you. But now we have a great victory, just as you said we would! So, I decided to take some of your anger, to see what's underneath. I should have known."

Harry digested that. About the time he got on active duty, the military was experimenting with psychologists to help operators who had problems. The cost of training a replacement was high enough that it made sense to try to fix the ones they already had. None of his fellow SEALs trusted the concept. Despite having dodged that particular bullet, now Harry was getting his head shrunk by a barbarian girl on an alien planet. It hadn't been what he expected. Maybe if the Teams had beautiful women shrinks, he would have given it a try. Of course, he'd already had a—

"You have a woman," Stella said. It wasn't a question.

"Had," Harry ground out, fighting an intense wash of emotions. Without any warning, his feelings spiraled downwards, like a high-speed canopy malfunction. He attempted to maintain his composure as anger, sorrow, and more anger eroded his failing control. Residual exhaustion, too much drink, and a copious helping of guilt finished him and the anger both, leaving only a surprising emptiness. To his horror, he felt the sting of tears filling his eyes. "She's dead. She's been dead for a long time."

Stella sat up, ignoring any modesty and gently took one of his hands in both of hers.

"Tell me."

So, he did.

He spilled his guts.

What it meant to be in the Teams and how proud he was. How much it cost. His family. Being gone all the time, endlessly deployed. The arguments. The last-moment orders to Somalia, just as he was considering getting out. The absolute wreckage of a country, the lawlessness. The sneering militia who used kids no older than Harry's own sons as cannon fodder, knowing that the soft Americans would hesitate to shoot. The useless UN commanders, padding their careers and lining their own pockets. His decision to make a little justice in a capricious, uncaring universe. How good it had felt, torturing the militia captain who resold the refugees' food, who'd mousetrapped Harry's unit into killing innocents. The consequences. The resulting helo ride. Waking up dead to find himself a century and a half too late to fix anything, after all. All of it.

When he finished he was crying. Big bad, Navy SEAL, leaking all over his own stupid face. Wiping his eyes, he looked at his audience. Stella still held his hand, but she too was crying, tears leaving shining tracks down her cheeks.

"The gods chose you, Ha-Ree," she said with perfect conviction. "I don't know why, or how, but the hand of a greater power is clearly upon you, reaching out to steer your fate."

"Fuck the higher power," he answered vehemently, and then went on somewhat more calmly, gently squeezing her hand. "I didn't ask for this. This moment has been the first decent thing that's happened to me in the last...century."

He laughed as he began his last sentence and then stumbled over the last word as his chuckle nearly turned into a sob. God, he hated being a big wuss. He felt the bedding shift as Stella adjusted something, and he looked up to see her smiling and wiping her eyes.

"So, *this* is the first good thing in your life in so long?" Stella asked, raising one eyebrow, and then the blanket. "And I'm the one responsible? As a warrior-maiden, I find that acceptable. Let's prolong the experience, then."

And she did.

Volo watched as Tapper emerged from the tent, swinging both arms and stretching. The Terran was followed by Stella. Both appeared to be pretty happy with themselves, and to his surprise, Volo found himself sanguine with the prospect of them pairing off. One of the advantages, in his opinion, of planetside life among the Sarmatchani was the absence of social constraints on relations between men and women, like those imposed by *Second Spin*'s genpop council.

Of course, his mellow feeling was probably influenced by the recent break in his own drought of...activity. Following the successful downing of the J'Stull airship—and his role in the operation—Volo had been propositioned rather directly, and he'd accepted.

His wristcom vibrated as it received the download from the satellite, and Volo retreated to a bit of shade, making it easier to read the shiny display.

He shook his head. It must have been too much to expect that having succeeded against all expectations, their run of good luck was going to hold out. Headquarters was reporting—make that *complaining*. Whatever Volo had done to the J'Stull, it had been overkill. The activity at the Kulsian's clandestine vehicle cache had more than trebled. The equipment, secreted away on the R'Baku surface, was updated and re-used each time the planets were at their closest point of approach. With the Searing two years off (the actual periastron was actually a few years later), the Kulsian raiders should have been working at a languid pace, but now both the cargo vehicles and lightly armored escorts were being fueled and positioned for departure. Volo's little group didn't have weeks longer to plan and execute the convoy seizure mission. They only had days, maybe less.

The SpinDogs might have a real opportunity to interrupt the Cycles which had trapped them off-planet, but it was slipping away, and fast.

A portion of *Second Spin*'s message was doubly encrypted, marked only for his eyes. The victory on the surface, and the consequences, had roiled the SpinDog council. The shifting balance of power now tilted toward the faction that favored using the coming war to "use up" the Terrans, decreasing their numbers and influence. Prior to the destruction of the airship, Volo knew he would have been, at worst, ambivalent about this. However, he was feeling something new, a bond of kinship he'd never before experienced.

Tapper, though arrogant and barbaric, had stood next to him. Moreover, he'd actually trusted Volo to shoot the newly invented weapon, when the entire mission was depending on the gunner's accuracy. Rodriguez, for all his uncouthness and indirect threats, had volunteered to be the highly expendable bait, necessary to lure the ship within range. How many on *Second Spin* would have risked themselves like this?

Who were the old men on the council to dictate to whom Volo should give his loyalty? They weren't here, eating this food and sleeping on the ground! Of course, if Volo did anything but dutifully carry out orders, he would be on his own. He wished he could yank the elders out of their council room and bring them on this march, make them open their eyes.

What was that pungent phrase Rodriguez employed when the Sarmatchani trainees complained, wishing for a chance to rest from his demanding military drills? Ah, yes. *"Shit in one hand and wish in the other, then see which hand fills up first."*

"What do you mean, the timetable has moved up?" Rodriguez almost yelled and hobbled a step towards Volo before Harry interposed himself. "We're completely out of position!"

Harry noted the attention they were drawing and gestured to his noncom to stand down. Volo had come to them with the latest download from the comm network.

"Ease up, Marco," he asked, rather than ordered. "Let's have a sit-down. Volo, could you repeat that?"

"*Second Spin* relayed that the complete inventory of vehicles has been withdrawn from storage ahead of the worst-case projections," Volo replied, turning to accompany Harry as he led the way along the dirt path to the trestle tables framing the clan's eating and gathering area. Rodriguez and Stella followed, and somehow Rosha attached herself to the little procession. "The number of artificers and technicians is far higher than we thought. Some of the cargo trucks are even being test driven already. We no longer have several weeks. We must move sooner."

"There's no way we can move fast enough to get to the cache before they roll!" Rodriguez almost yelled from the end of the little procession.

"Hail, Yannis," Harry said, spotting the clan chief sitting with some of his men. Harry suspected the burly chief had simply continued drinking into the late morning, but he appeared fresh and rested. The chief roared a greeting, waving a drinking horn made from a hollow tusk nearly half a meter in height.

"Ha-Ree, do all Sky People need so much rest before they can resume toasting our victory?"

"We have received grave word from our friends overhead," Harry replied, sliding onto the stool across from Yannis. "Despite our victory, the J'Stull have crafted a surprise from their defeat. They have accelerated their efforts to prepare the war wagons, the trucks. If we want to capture them for the use of the Sarmatchani, we can't allow the enemy to move the machines to their city."

"Can we simply not melt back into the hills?" Grevorg asked before taking a pull on his own drink using his unbandaged hand. "This we have done before. Let them strike the empty hills and fields with their fist. We will laugh at them from the wastes!"

"We sure can't, battle-brother," Harry answered, shaking his head. He clapped the taller man on his shoulder. "I know it's worked before, but now we have shown them the strength of our hand, and the J'Stull will not forget. If they collect all their war machines, they can follow you much faster than you can run."

"Are these machines like the *ballista* that you made for us to kill the skyship?" Yannis asked pensively.

"No, sir," Rodriguez answered for all of them. "Imagine a wagon made of metal, which doesn't need beasts to draw it, but can move across the ground twice as fast as the fastest sprinter. They'll have guns that can shoot very quickly, like the one the El-Tee used during the fight, but much larger. Each wagon can carry up to ten warriors and all their kit."

Murmurs greeted this description, several affirming that they had heard of such vehicles.

"Still, if we run, we may live," a voice called from the circle that had accumulated around the informal council. "Who would want to fight such a machine?"

"None of us have the luxury of running anymore, my R'Bakuun brothers." Volo, who'd remained standing, stepped forward and faced Yannis. "We've learned something more. The J'Stull and all the satraps are required to keep a high-ranking member of their dynasty on every boat, whether on the river or in the sky. This is their way to ensure all recognize the authority of the vavasors and the vassals, all the way to the Suzerain himself. One such was on the sky boat which we struck down. His death touches the honor of the J'Stull."

"Well, good!" Yannis said happily, and fresh roars answered his declaration. "Tell them to send more by-blows of their so-called royal J'Stull family. We'll simplify the choice their clan head must make among his heirs!"

More roars of approval.

"It won't happen like that, Chief," Harry said, slipping into briefing mode. "Yannis, it *can't* happen like that. The J'Stull can't afford to ignore such a challenge, not if they want to keep their place among the satraps. They are far more concerned with the power of their peers than the threat posed by rabble that is too stupid to live in the cities—I'm sorry, but that's how they think of you. Once they complete their immediate mission—moving the trucks to safety—the J'Stull must settle the account. They must find us and totally destroy the Herdbanes, root and branch, or suffer the same fate themselves at the hand of the Reavers. Even with the new warriors from the other tribes, we don't have enough trained fighters ready to attack a well-protected convoy head-on."

"You're sure, boy?"

"Perfectly sure, Yannis," Harry answered forthrightly. "But we have options."

"Go on, then."

"Chief, the first thing to know about them is that these wagons need three things to work. They work best on roads, and really bad ground will stop them. They have to have fuel, and that fuel is both heavy and easy to burn. And lastly, they have to have trained men to drive and fix them."

Harry stood and tipped over his stool.

"Without all three, their strength is like that of a stool with only two legs."

"And?" Yannis asked. "How do we fight these trucks, these machines of destruction?"

"I don't want to confront them or their escort if I can help it, Yannis, not while they have all three things they need to work," Harry said, reaching to Volo, who placed the plastic-coated map of the region into Harry's hand. Harry opened it and laid it out on the trestle table, moving a few empty plates and mugs to make room. He traced one finger down the road that led to Chorat. "But there is a way to fight the men."

Chapter Eighteen

R'BAK

"You're getting too close to the head, Ha-Ree," Stella cautioned him, as Harry strode alongside the first whinnie in their column. The Sarmatchani had explained that though the beasts would tolerate a heavy pack saddle and were docile enough to be led, they were dangerously unrideable. "That makes them irritable, and this one will take your arm if you don't move."

Harry looked up at the whinnie. It was mostly tan, though vertical greenish counter shading ran along the rough and creased hide. The great dun beast seemed placid, striding along with the barest serpentine motion. Its colorful neck fringe hung loosely about the long neck, and it didn't look any more agitated than it had at camp, where the Sarmatchani strapped the crates containing a few hundred kilos of improvised charges to its back. None the less, this would be a bad time for one of the explosive-laden whinnies to decide it had had enough. Harry angled his steps to open the distance a bit but maintained the rapid pace that he'd set for the entire task force from the outset.

For a while, only the treading feet of the long column made any noise, apart from the occasional low whistle from a worried or bored whinnie, which was then reassured by a light touch from its handler's goad. Experience had taught Harry that groups would string out during a march, so he looked back over his shoulder to check on the progress of the people behind him. Several Sarmatchani camps had contributed to the force, won over by Yannis' exhortations, and their participation stretched the group out even more. On either side of the road, really not much more than a broad track of rammed earth, rose the grasslands through which Harry had passed much earlier. A curve in the road obscured the back half of the group, though the swaying heads of the whinnies rose above the vegetation, giving the appearance there was a herd of unaccompanied animals passing through.

"I've seen the great bridge," Stella offered after they covered another klick. "It's very big, and very old, older than the Cycles. It's been a part of the land for so long that even the animals make use of it. Do you really think this *demo* you've brought will be enough to damage it?"

"Rodriguez thinks so," Volo announced from his position behind Harry, who was mildly surprised to hear what sounded like genuine admiration in the SpinDog's voice. "And he was right in the matter of the blimp."

"I'm reasonably sure we have enough," Harry answered Stella, working to sound confident. The last thing he needed was second-guessing. "Both Rodriguez and I have a lot of experience. Our modern explosives should enhance the effect of the black powder we've collected from the clans who chose to support us. Plus, I know a thing or two about engineering. If we dig down a bit and bury the explosive, we can tamp the explosion and direct the force. We've got enough people to dig. Easy-peasy, we drop the bridge, and the J'Stull will be trapped on their side of the river until they can repair the bridge. All we have to do is wait for our friends, who will bring many warriors and guns. Then we can force the convoy to surrender."

"I like this plan," Stella replied. "It's simpler than the plan to destroy the airship."

"Simplicity is good," Harry agreed, feeling a bit chuffed by her approval.

"Indeed," Stella replied pertly. "The less time spent on it, the better. No hunting plan goes perfectly. Always, there's a surprise. Why spend so much time on the plan when the warband leader will have to change it?"

"Well, you have to have a plan," Harry answered, automatically stilling the old anger when it made a half-hearted attempt to rise before it was easily quashed by the chuckle that rose in his chest, unbidden, hearing the surety in Stella's voice. "Things don't *have* to go wrong every time."

As they talked, they had approached the crest of the latest ridge they had to traverse. Waiting for them was Yannis.

"Take a look, Ha-Ree," he said, holding out the monocular Harry had offered him as a battle-gift. "There's a change."

Harry used bare eyes to stare in the direction indicated by Yannis' finger.

Squinting against the glare, he could make out the bridge, describing a dirty white arc across the darker color of the chasm it spanned. It was closer than the horizon, but still several klicks off. He used the monocular to enhance the view.

"Ah, shit," he said, as his vision cleared. "That is new."

"What's new?" Volo asked, catching up to the trio.

"There's a guardhouse on the end of the bridge. We're going to have to deal with it first. We can't just walk up and plant the charges."

"See?" Stella asked, perhaps a little smugly. "Always the plan changes."

"All you have to do is get their attention." Harry repeated the instruction to Volo, who was nodding earnestly. "Wait for full dark, then sting them. Get them angry, then run back up the road just fast enough to stay ahead of the reaction force. Do *not* engage with these guys. They outnumber our entire force, and all of them have guns. At some point they'll get tired and break off pursuit, or they'll hear the explosion and turn back. Then you head to the rendezvous."

The young man had insisted on leading one of the three groups Harry had created, and the SEAL officer wasn't spoiled for choice. Harry wished Rodriguez was on hand, but even Rosha's miraculous treatment couldn't restore his leg quickly enough to accompany the forced march, which had lasted a day and a half so far.

The first team had already been dispatched. It included the minimum number of Sarmatchani required to keep the whinnies calm and be ready to lead them to the bridge with the explosives. Hidden behind a hill, they would stay well back until Harry called them in by runner. Harry had asked Yannis to stay with the mixed crew of Sarmatchani. The towering chieftain's presence would be more than enough to enforce discipline among the clansmen, ensuring that they didn't move prematurely and compromise the operation. Now that they were nearly at their destination, the big lizard-like animals actually *were* becoming restless, as though they could sense the impending action.

The second group was led by Volo. He would be responsible for the largest number of Sarmatchani, who had to stage a noisy demonstration against the force guarding the bridge. Then, they had to *appear* to flee, encouraging pursuit. Harry just hoped that the kid would keep his head. Volo needed to retreat in time to allow the Sarmatchani with him to not only serve as tantalizing bait, but actually remain outside the reach of the reinforced company of J'Stull who'd materialized at the vital bridge.

The third group was the smallest, led by Harry. It would sweep the bridge of any residual guards and call in the whinnies. Harry would lead the diggers and expose as much of the two key trestles as possible before burying the explosives and lighting the fuse.

"No problem, El-Tee," Volo said, slapping Harry's shoulder. "We'll make beaucoup demonstration, and Mr. Charles will chase our pretty asses all the way home!"

"Kid, you've been spending *way* too much time with Rodriguez." Harry wryly shook his head, before gripping the SpinDog's hand for a quick shake. "You don't want to end up like him. Good luck, and watch your ass."

Volo flashed him a quick smile and trotted back to his command, rapping out orders in a low voice. Harry watched the thirty Sarmatchani melt into the dusk, already shaking out into skirmish order as they disappeared into the grass. He looked at the eight men he'd kept to sweep the hopefully empty guardhouse. All right, six men, two boys who could run like hell, and one very determined woman. Harry had picked the kids because he needed someone to get word to the explosives team. Stella had picked herself, appropriating her injured brother's rifle, but wearing her own knife. All of them wore their hunting leathers and had shovels or spades slung rifle-fashion. They'd kept their lances to hand and had dulled the shine of their faces with ashes.

"We wait for the shooting to die down and swing in behind the J'Stull," Harry reminded them. "Then we clear the shack on our side of the bridge and four of us dig like hell while the rest pull security. As soon as the holes are halfway, the two runners carry the word to Yannis. He brings in the explosives, then we backfill and boom! Got it?"

Harry looked around the little circle, receiving nods from each man and, for once, a serious look from Stella.

"All right, let's settle in and wait. Stay close enough to touch the man to your right. When you feel the tapping, pass it on and be ready to go."

His team briefly milled about before finding a spot for the wait. Sitting down, Harry couldn't see any further than the person next to him. Stella was sticking close. The group quieted down as the night sounds resumed around them. Harry knew that they had at least an hour before Volo would start anything, and then another ten minutes or more before the commander of the bridge security company decided to do something about it. If Harry had learned anything in the Teams, it was to take advantage of small moments like this, so he tilted his head back and looked at the stars.

Here he was on another battlefield, hell, another planet. So much for getting out of the Teams. In a little while, he was going to lead a mostly untrained assault team on a night demolition assault. Good thing night operations were simple and *never* went wrong. By way of an unexpected twist, he was taking a woman with him. At least that was a first. He looked over at the dark shape of the woman next to him. Of course, Stella wasn't your average girlfriend. Like the rest of the warriors, she'd simply settled in, waiting quietly.

No chitchat, no last-minute fidgeting.

I wonder what she thinks about us?

Us? Is this a relationship?

Man, this is the weirdest pre-mission pep talk I've ever given myself. Time to get the game-face on.

Harry mentally shook himself, and then rehearsed all the steps needed to close the distance to the gatehouse and clear it. He was checking off the list for the umpteenth time when the crack of rifle fire seized his attention.

"Volo's getting started," Stella whispered.

"No need to whisper," Harry said in a more normal tone of voice. "No one is going to hear us over the sound of that."

"That" was an impressive fusillade. Harry knew Volo's group didn't have many firearms, so the J'Stull security company was as heavily armed as Harry had feared. There was a brief *whooshing* sound and Harry grinned. The kid was doing all right. Harry had shown the Sarmatchani how to make black powder bottle rockets and Volo was using several of the things to create even more noise and confusion. The J'Stull would be surprised since they'd never encountered their like before.

"What's going on?" Stella asked.

"Volo's doing his job," Harry answered. "Don't worry. It all sounds good, so far."

The rockets were simple noisemakers, but their mere presence increased the pressure on the commander to do *something*. At least, that was the plan. A loud horn was sounding from the bridge now and the gunfire from the road sounded like only a few rifles remained, using slow fire. Good. Volo had probably pulled part of his force a short distance back so the front line could simply turn and run under the cover of the first group's fire. Rodriguez had done a good job training the kid.

The horns sounded again, and this time Harry could hear harsh yells, unmistakably the sounds of leaders marshaling their men in the dark, getting ready to chase the irritating Sarmatchani.

A few more rifles cracked, and there was a brief silence. Harry could actually make out some of the shouted commands.

"Close up! Close up!"

"Let's get those shit-eaters!"

Then the Sarmatchani's deeper, booming fire picked up again, just enough to goad the J'Stull into accelerating their pursuit, trying to close the distance to these savages that dared to attack them on the J'Stull's own ground. Harry could make out the jingle of equipment as small units trotted past on the road to his side. The rifle fire sounded further away and still he sat, waiting.

After his Casio showed the ten-minute mark, he tapped Stella on the arm.

"All right, brothers," he said, standing, "let's go bag a bridge."

The good news was that the J'Stull left behind were neither especially numerous nor skilled. Harry's group had approached quietly and fallen upon them with the fury known only by those who've killed with cold steel. Harry led the assault, padding down the track toward the yellow glow of the guardhouse windows. The external guard had been standing at the edge of the area cleared of the tall grass, twenty meters from the adobe building. Unfortunately for the sentry, he was looking back at the building he was supposed to guard. At the last second, he jerked his head up, perhaps finally hearing the tread of the assault group or the sound of their passage through the dense foliage.

He was the first to die, dropped with a single round. Harry used the follow up shots from his M-14 to hollow out the cluster of organized defenders rushing out of the building, while the howling Sarmatchani swarmed, spears forward. The six J'Stull survivors had the presence of mind to return fire but the nomads screaming out of the darkness made for poor targets. Only one tribesman died and three more, including one runner, were seriously injured. In moments, all twelve defenders were cut down and Harry quickly organized the bloody aftermath. He ignored the bodies of the enemy, but adrenaline-fueled rage tingled in every extremity as he contemplated the death of men who had been his teammates. Instead of yielding to his anger, he organized the remaining Sarmatchani who were gaping at the electric light, rudimentary radio, and the firearms laying there, *just for the taking*.

Harry led them and the surviving runner topside before he and the diggers scrambled down the steep bridge abutment, seeking the first upright pier. It loomed in the darkness, cool to the touch. The pier was rectangular in cross section and a meter thick. Harry quickly organized two of the Sarmatchani to dig on the uphill side while he, the last clansman, and Stella searched for the next pier. Ears ringing, Harry could barely hear the sound of his spade biting the dirt, but his battle adrenaline fueled his efforts. For once his anger served a good purpose. As soon as the hole was knee-deep, he turned to order the last Sarmatchani to dispatch the runner while he and Stella finished digging.

Before he could get the words out, fresh gunfire shook the narrow canyon.

"The fuck is that?" Harry yelled at no one in particular.

He exchanged a shocked look with the man he'd been about to address. All three fought their way back up the steep abutment, swearing at the loose, treacherous footing. Above their heads, more fire was being exchanged, and Harry readied his weapon to the sound of screaming.

The Sarmatchani cleared ground level first, just ahead of Harry panting in second place. A heavy caliber bullet tore through the man's head, painting Harry with a hot spray of blood. Ahead of the fresh corpse lay the cooling bodies of the other diggers. Harry dove to one side, rifle up, searching for targets.

There were plenty. Fully another half-dozen J'Stull soldiers were in view, spanning the clearing which faced the end of the bridge. They were still firing into the guardhouse where Harry'd left the survivors of his first attack. There was no return fire. Harry rolled sideways and down, seeking the concealment of the tall grass at the lip of the canyon. Leopard crawling along, he heard a couple rounds rip through the grass waving over his head in response to his passage. He needed to move even faster, so he rose to get a look and bounded forward, using the age-old mantra of the combat infantryman.

I'm up, he sees me, I'm down.

Just in time, because about half the J'Stull fired at his momentarily visible shape. Harry moved a few meters laterally, and then popped up to return the favor, hitting one J'Stull high on the shoulder and spinning him down to the grass. Harry looked for Stella, but she wasn't visible. He'd last seen her on the final climb up the slope. Had she assaulted forward without him? He peeked but didn't see her body.

Where is she?

He fingered his only fragmentation grenade, brought all the way from Earth. Between his superior rate of fire, and the little olive drab sphere, he had a chance. First, he needed the enemy to bunch up. He'd have to make sure he didn't hi—

"Skyman!" an unfamiliar male voice cried out. "Skyman, I know you are there!"

Harry jerked so hard he popped his neck.

"Skyman! I have your woman!"

What the hell? Are you fucking kidding me?

Harry moved very slowly to the edge of the guardhouse. The view stopped his heart. A very tall man, as tall and as broad as Yannis and a J'Stull officer by the richness of his uniform, stood just outside the circle of yellow light cast by the surviving electric lights in the guardhouse. He was clearly daring anyone to chance a shot. He could afford to because he had a firm grip on Stella's bloody right arm. Harry quickly scanned around, spotting two hidden guards who'd stayed further back in the grass, but the bulk of the enemy were arranged around their commander. They must have attacked across the bridge and chased some of the Sarmatchani back into the brush before turning around to spot the dig team.

Harry's anger bloomed anew. His woman, his team. His mission. He began to breathe deeply, fully, adding oxygen to the fire of his rage.

Harry looked back at Stella. She was bleeding heavily from her arm and shoulder and though her face was tilted forward, partially obscured by her hair, he could see blood there, too. Where had this asshole come from?

Harry's stomach fell when he realized there must be two guardhouses. He'd missed the second one from a distance, and by the time they were close enough, the light had already begun to fail. This force would've been a couple hundred yards away, across the causeway. It had taken them this long to decide to move over, likely because they hadn't been able to raise friendly forces on Harry's side.

"Skyman! I know who you are! I know about your plan to shame the J'Stull, to attack the property of Kulsis, rightful overlords of R'Bak. Surrender, and I'll spare this bitch."

This guy was way too well informed. Harry and his anger wanted time, more time, ask me for anything but time, but this fucker was going to shoot Stella. Harry desperately flogged his brain for any combination of tactics and weapons that could turn this around. He might be able to drop the commander, but it wasn't a sure thing, since he was shooting over open sights at night at a moving target. But then Stella would die at the hands of the others. If he used the grenade, he'd probably frag himself. It would kill Stella, for certain.

Dying wouldn't be so bad, his anger whispered.

"Let her go, and you can have your bridge!" Harry yelled from behind the adobe wall, staying deep in the shadows. He saw gun muzzles snap in his direction and then weave, looking for a definite target. He mastered his rage one more time. "I'll leave this place."

"You'd give me what I already have?" the officer said, sneering. "How generous. Perhaps your woman can convince you."

With that, he dug a finger into the wound on Stella's arm, and she screamed, high and breathless, hanging from her captor's iron grip.

"No!"

Harry didn't even think, he stood and drew a perfect bead on the man's face. Before he let this bastard hurt her again, he'd drop the man, consequences be damned. He began slowly pacing forward, heel-and-toe, carefully maintaining a sight picture. The front sight was razor sharp, his target a bit blurry and the night-blanketed grasslands behind were just a dark blur.

"Let her go or die, asshole."

"Careful, hero," the J'Stull soldier said, giving his limp captive a shake.

Harry stopped a few paces away. He could see Stella better now. She raised one hand to sweep her hair aside, revealing her unexpectedly composed features and as he watched, her eyes slitted as she evaluated their predicament.

Harry checked the position of the two snipers, but one was missing. While he watched, the second was yanked sideways, snagged by an invisible, irresistible force whisking him out of sight and deeper into the grass. A dull *thud* and grunt punctuated movement.

"Sir, sir! Behind us!" cried one of the J'Stull.

"Call them off or she dies!" the officer yelled, shaking Stella like a terrier shakes a rat.

Harry could see the source of the motion now. Hulking blue-black forms were ghosting forward, staying outside the circle of illumination. Harry lowered his rifle to the ground, slowly, slowly, and kneeled. His rage howled, but Harry shoved it down, down deep, and reached for their only chance.

"Harry, no!" Stella cried.

"Baby, just be quiet and relax," Harry said, his voice low and urgent.

The J'Stull officer was clearly puzzled, looking left and right for his missing men, but he kept the gloating smile on his face as he surveyed his kneeling enemy.

"Fool. Your life is mine n—"

And the first batang bounded into the clearing, smashing into the nearest soldier. It hooted like a base trumpet as it knocked him down, and then grabbed his arm and neck as the soldier thrashed, trying to escape. The burly animal straightened its arms, like a washer woman spreading laundry on a line, and detached the man's limb before discarding his victim on the ground.

Hoots and whistles came from every side as dozens of the creatures, including a particularly huge specimen, shuffled quickly into view. Shots rang out and some batangs screamed, sounding like steam whistles. Harry lay flat, arms at his side, watching as the officer released Stella and raised his own weapon. Another hairy form plowed into him, driving the man into the grass as Stella slumped motionless to the ground. The officer disappeared from view. Then his head bounced back into the clearing.

In moments, no men were left standing, and the clearing was full of grunting, hooting, and agitated batangs, slapping the ground. A few would dash up to a warm corpse and strike it before dashing away again. The largest batang, a huge monster that towered nearly three meters tall, shuffled forward, snuffling from its nasal slits.

Harry held very still as the batang drew within touching distance. It stamped the ground, and snorted. The rest of the troupe grew quiet. Harry remembered Volo's words, and kept his eyes down, staring at the horny, spiked digits that tipped forearms many times thicker than his own legs. A procession of animals moved past, seemingly endless but in reality only taking a minute or two. Slowly, almost ponderously, the largest batang moved off. After another moment, Harry turned his head to see the tall animal shuffle-walk onto the bridge and disappear into the darkness, going about the important business of migrating, and leaving human business to the humans.

Around him lay bodies and parts of bodies, but heedless of the gore he scrambled over to Stella, who was curled into a tight fetal ball. As he approached, she looked up and then lurched to her knees to embrace him.

From out of the darkness, a final hooting call echoed across the canyon.

"Are you sure you're supposed to be standing?" Harry asked, carefully holding his arm around Stella without actually resting his full weight on her. This was the first that he'd seen Stella up since she got shot. "Rosha seemed quite specific you were to rest. Most of what comes next is just waiting, anyway."

"It isn't every day of my life that I get to see, what did you call it, a *shuttle*, land next to my camp," Stella retorted, reaching up and tugging his arm more fully onto her shoulders.

"The bones have knit and the holes from the bullets are closed. I can even move the arm as long as I'm careful."

"That arm is staying in the sling," Harry insisted.

A double *crack* sounded across the sky, causing two rabbit-sized creatures with long legs and tails to take flight, their membranous wings pumping furiously.

"Ah, Ha-Ree, your friends come now, yes?" Yannis said, ambling over and scratching the hairy stomach peeking from behind his vest. "Soon we attack the J'Stull city?"

"Yeah, that's them, honored Yannis," Harry replied, looking upwards for the tell-tale contrail. Once the bridge had been blown, Harry had uploaded the sitrep on the next satellite pass, and Volo had received it even before they'd met at the rendezvous. Overhead imagery had confirmed that two full spans had failed on the ancient, inexplicable structure, trapping the J'Stull convoy. "Soon you'll meet my comrades and we will take the war to Chorat, and then across the face of R'Bak, itself. But first, we will have to take the vehicles we have stranded on this side of the bridge."

"They cannot run! Their fate is sealed!"

"Yes, but they can still shoot." Harry smiled. "However, when the sun sets and they cannot see..."

Stella slipped free her arm around Harry's waist, a motion detected by Yannis.

The chief concealed a smile behind a cough, and clapped Harry on the shoulder, though much more gently than he'd ever done before. "We will have a tremendous victory feast tomorrow, Ha-Ree!" Yannis exulted. "We will drink to the death of all J'Stull and their works! Your friends will attend! And then we shall seize the war wagons together!"

None of it was a suggestion. Harry winced internally, wondering how he was going to introduce the mixed bag of rugged individualists from old Earth to this nomadic chieftain. Then again, he'd like to see Major Murphy deal with it. It wasn't his problem, anymore.

And that's worth a smile.

"How did you know about the batangs, Ha-Ree?" she asked, reclaiming Harry's attention.

"I didn't." He glanced at Yannis just as the older man hid a crafty smile, looking away. "But I'm pretty sure your father did. Probably why he was so confident. How thc heck did he—?"

"It was Rosha who summoned them and marked Father as an alpha. But I was not asking how you knew the batang were paralleling us; clearly, you did not. I mean, how did you know how to react when they appeared? Batang are particularly dangerous when they are traveling with young. Yet you knew to neither flee nor fight. How?"

"Volo warned us early in our trip," Harry replied. "He insisted that we remain calm and let the batangs pass. It worked the first time, so…"

"I could see that you were ready to loose your anger," Stella said firmly. "I was angry you might sacrifice the quest just because that *skrellig* gave me a small hurt."

"There she is!" whooped Rodriguez from atop one of the clan's wagons. "Hell yeah, bring me that dust-off, boys! I got me a ride on the freedom bird!"

Harry looked, and high up in the brilliant blue sky, he saw the contrail left by the shuttle, describing arcs across the sky as it turned, bleeding off excess speed.

"I will never again trade your blood for anything," Harry said, looking back at Stella. He watched her eyes widen fractionally. "No hurt to you is a small hurt, my love."

"So, I'm your love now?" she answered, smiling broadly, even joyfully. "You will give me all of your anger? You will be my mate?"

Holy crap, she's proposing to me!

Harry heard the crowd murmur, so he looked up again. The tiny cruciform shape of the dropship was barely distinguishable, drawing the long white line behind it as if by magic.

"Yes," he said, still looking at the ship. He looked back down at his woman and slipped his arm from around her shoulders to face her fully and take both of her hands in his. "Yes. And you'll be mine."

He noted in passing he was trembling like a racehorse before the gate. Big bad Navy SEAL was as nervous as a virgin.

Damn. I've heard of getting the shakes during a drop, but this is ridiculous.

Chapter Nineteen

SPIN ONE

The news Murphy had been waiting for arrived as the deck in the outer docking bay opened up. The third tilt-thruster interface shuttle—even boxier than the ones Bowden was turning into attack craft—swiveled its engines and dropped through the opening into free space. As it did, the report scrolled across the top of his dataslate: "Captain Moorefield reports safe landing in AO. Currently surveying site recommended by Sarmatchani for FOB Stark. Second shuttle now entering high-angle polar descent, five-by-five. All systems nominal."

Murphy exhaled the breath he'd been holding for…well, it felt like two hours: the approximate time it had taken for Moorefield's lead shuttle to go from atmospheric approach to landing. "Blazing a trail before I ask my guys to follow it," the armor officer had explained when he'd insisted on taking point during the descent. It wasn't really risky, and Murphy was glad he had cadre who were willing to lead from the front, but damn: if something happened to Moorefield or Tapper, the whole operation would be over before it started.

Murphy tapped an acknowledgement just as the inner loading bay doors groaned open behind him.

Yet another shuttle was wheeled in on a platform; it was off-white and looked like it either had a fresh paint job or was brand new. He stepped forward to get a better look—

"Don't do that, sir," rumbled a voice behind him. Murphy started and turned.

A bear of a man was two feet behind him, carrying an old-school M16. It looked like a toy in the meaty paws of his ostensible bodyguard, Maximilliano Messina. The sleepy-eyed fellow shook his head. "Another step back, sir."

Murphy smiled. "Max, I don't think they're going to run me over with a shuttle." Although given his treatment by the SpinDogs to date, he wasn't as sure of that as he'd have liked to be.

But Max was still shaking his head. "Not what I'm worried about, sir."

"Then what—?"

Before Murphy could finish his question, Max pointed with his eyes toward a doorway along the catwalk that provided access to the high, square gantry of the frame crane which moved small craft around the loading/staging bay. "Sir, anyone who opens that door has a clear line to you. And you're standing in the way of my preemptive shot. So, it's better if you stand a little forward or back." And with that, Max became completely immobile once again, his eyes moving slowly but constantly around the bay and all the chambers and entries that communicated with it.

Murphy nodded—not that Max noticed—and stepped back so that he stood alongside the hulking soldier.

Maximilliano Messina's story was a strange one, even among the Lost Soldiers. His dossier started normally enough, noting that he'd arrived in Vietnam right after the Tet Offensive. After being shuffled from one training facility to another, he did a short stint with a LRP team. He proved himself to be an expert—one officer used the term *artiste*—with an M16 and was uncannily quiet in the brush, despite his size. But for reasons unspecified, he was withdrawn from the team and assigned to security.

That's where the story got really strange. Usually, a security assignment meant either duty with or in support of MPs, but not in Max's case. He never spent a minute guarding any of the innumerable bases and depots and wharves that led both locals and GIs alike to assert that "US" stood for "Uncle Sugar." No, Max was given a special role, one for which the Army didn't even seem to have a designation: VIP over-watch.

In short, when Big Brass or a senator or a diplomat arrived in Saigon, Max Messina was never far off. How many of these usually clueless and incautious big shots he had saved was unknown. Because the would-be assassins were only rarely preempted or apprehended; instead, Max racked up an impressive number of one-shot "suppressions."

But it was his after-hours efforts that truly defied quantification—because they were never reported. Max not only had the eye and alertness of a sniper, but the mind and instincts of an undercover cop. The number of times that suspected VC death-squad operatives showed up as corpses in an alley or a brothel or a shuttered bar just before one of Max's VIPs arrived was, as one Embassy security officer put it, "nothing short of eerie."

To be fair, Max himself was a little eerie. Those who didn't know his record—which included almost all the other Lost Soldiers—actually thought that because he was big and soft-spoken and droopy-eyed that maybe he wasn't the sharpest knife in the drawer. Murphy had discerned that Max did nothing to counter those low opinions of his abilities; he enjoyed the quiet…and the surety that he would be underestimated by any who might oppose him. So, after being held at gunpoint in the SpinDog Ops center, and to stifle Makarov's consequent, if sensible, nagging to accept a bodyguard, Murphy acceded to the inevitable and made Max his shadow and guardian angel.

SpinDogs were now swarming the shiny new shuttle as the wheels of its carrier-trolley were locked off and chocked. As its rear bay opened, a pair of vehicles rolled toward the ramp extending from its interior. They were a weird cross between an ATV, reconnaissance car, and pickup truck. According to Nuncle, they weren't of terrestrial manufacture, which explained why they were too big for easy operation and had manual controls that sure as hell weren't designed for human hands or feet. But at some point, the Lost Soldiers who'd commandeered them on a planet called Turkh'saar had fitted them with grips and pads and extensions that made them usable. But comfortable? That was *never* going to happen.

The next load wheeled toward the shuttle was what he had actually come to see; the first crates of locally manufactured 7.62x51mm NATO ammunition were winched up into its aft cargo section. He'd inspected the shipment just yesterday. Except for the absence of any manufacturing stamps, it was indistinguishable from the original ammo. And the SpinDogs only had the design specs for five weeks.

And by next week, the first Huey was supposed to show up. Advance reports indicated that the first production models would, in fact, fly pretty much as expected with little or no adjustments or retooling. Compared to the months or years of teething problems that were typically associated with factory production of new aircraft, this wasn't just amazing, it was downright suspicious. Anyone capable of creating all the internal systems of even a Vietnam-era Huey, that quickly and that accurately, didn't just have some truly impressive replication technology, but damn deep pockets. Making parts was one thing, whistling up all the necessary materials for a Huey—plastic, rubber, dozens of different alloys—could mean only one of two things. One: the SpinDogs had diverse material stockpiles in reserve, although God knows how, living in deep space. Or two: they had sold their souls to the devil. And given that these were the descendants of the Ktor, well…

There were limits to what they could achieve, of course. In fact, it had been none other than Bramath—now his liaison from the primary producer, Family Kormak—who had offered an explanation of those limits in a voice so measured that Murphy had immediately tagged the tone as "plausibly deniable condescension." Nothing overtly insulting, but there was a subcurrent of spite and contempt running underneath, and the oh-so-patient tempo was exaggerated to the point of patronization. As if Murphy had been a clueless kid of seven.

"Yes," Bramath had said, "we can replicate many machines, and very quickly. But it is much more efficient to create a great number of just a few models than it is to produce a small number of many different models. Each model requires special adjustments to the automatic fabrication—we call them autofab—machines. Much time and effort are spent identifying and solving any problems in the process."

Assembly was another bottleneck. If it was just a matter of making the parts, that could be accomplished quite quickly. But when the emphasis was on creating *completed* units, setting up and troubleshooting the automated assembly robots was a real time-sink.

The only unusual, or at least unexplained, limitation was that the SpinDogs seemed incapable of replicating anything that would qualify as "information technology." No computers, no logic-driven automation, no expert systems, no "smart" encryption or sensors, and not a single digital control or device. It was the same with their own machinery: 21st century mechanical engineering slaved to 1960s analog controls and systems.

But despite that, what the SpinDogs were achieving was nothing less than amazing, and when one of the pilots approached the new shuttle, Murphy asked, "How old is this craft?"

The SpinDog was evidently too enthusiastic to remember to be surly or dismissive to one of the "trogs." "It is new! First mission, other than its proving flight."

Murphy nodded, may have said something congratulatory, but all he could think was, *Either this was in storage, or they just built a spacecraft in a little over five weeks. And the SpinDogs don't seem to have much in the way of reserves, so…*

"Major!"

Murphy turned; Makarov was running towards him. "Personal relay of messages is not required, Captain."

"With all due respect, Major, I believe this one is."

Murphy felt his pulse quicken. "Tapper? Has he done it?"

Makarov nodded slowly: not exactly enthusiastic. "Yes, sir. And he is ready to make his report. On the 'special' line."

Murphy's pulse sped up even more, but for a very different reason. The Dornaani or 'special' comm channel was to be used at need only…where need was defined as urgent opsec control. Makarov put the Dornaani comm relay in Murphy's hand.

Tapper's voice emerged from it. "Seeker Six is standing by, as requested."

"Seeker Six, this is Glass Palace Actual. Good to hear from you, Harry. Sitrep. Append opsec risk."

"Roger all, Glass Palace. Objective vehicles seized. Casualties light. None among Lost Soldiers. Two vehicles compromised. DX'ed on site. Full list of commandeered enemy equipment is attached. It's long, sir. And pretty interesting."

So far, so good, and absolutely by the numbers. "Are you able to make planned rendezvous with Saber Six at transfer point?"

"Affirmative." A pause. "Are you alone, sir?"

Murphy looked at Messina and Makarov, who looked at each other, exchanged shrugs, moved back a step. Messina's head remained on a slow but steady swivel. "I am alone."

"Opsec issue, sir. You are familiar with Stabilo, First Scion of Primus Zobulakos?"

"I am."

"He was here before us, sir. Almost poisoned the well with the Sarmatchani. And while I have no actionable evidence, I think he dropped the dime on our plans. We got caught with our pants down at the bridge. The J'Stull knew we were coming."

Murphy felt the hairs standing up on the back of his neck. "Anything else, Harry?"

"Just an observation: Stabilo's involvement could change the game board. Big time."

"I agree, Harry. We don't get a lot of information on the situations in the Spins, but I'm getting the distinct impression that there are a lot more elbows out than usual."

"Because they're realizing that their days of hiding are numbered?"

"That, but also because the Otlethes Family is now trying to find a new leader. And the Hardliners are nervous about cooperating with us."

"Nervous enough to try to sabotage the alliance?"

"That's what I hope to find out."

"Sir, I'm not sure which of us is in more immediate danger."

"I'm not so sure myself, Harry. And if we talk too long, our 'friends' are going to wonder why they're not able to find the signal. So good luck with the hand-off to Saber Six, and although I'm not Navy…Bravo Zulu, Lieutenant."

"Appreciated, sir. Watch your six."

"You, too, Harry. Glass Palace out." Murphy pulled up the list of commandeered equipment, thought for a moment, and then turned to Makarov. "Captain, I need you to send a general communique to our officers regarding our intel-gathering priorities."

Makarov had his dataslate at the ready. "New directives, sir?"

"No. I'm bumping up several items to top priority."

"We already have many 'top priorities' on the list, sir."

"Understood. Bump down those having to do with local customs, trade, and identifying and relaying coordinates for additional water sources and useful flora discovered in the Ashbands."

"The what, Major?"

"Ashbands. The local term for those areas that are vegetated most of the time but are almost fully defoliated by the Searing."

Makarov nodded, scribbled. "Done, sir. Which items are now top priority?"

"All information on the technology level of equipment in caches." The list and descriptions that Harry sent indicated a wide range of age and sophistication in the vehicles and their systems. "I particularly want to know the upper limit of those we're likely to find. Append this conjecture: if I was an Overlord, I'd save the best equipment for the more organized and competent operators to follow. So, I suspect that these initial raiders have not been given coordinates for all the caches.

"All information sources are to be considered, including indig hearsay and legends."

"Sir, there could be a great deal of misinformation in there."

"Absolutely, but there are ways to detect and exclude a great deal of it. But at this point, all information is good information. We need to get a fix on the most formidable tech we could encounter—or acquire. And the most desirable information would be any information about cache locations that are traditionally not exploited until the actual Harvesters arrive.

"Next intel priority: what is the upper limit of technology that the satrapies themselves can produce? Or maintain, in the case of any items they've salvaged over the centuries? Is there any limit that the Kulsians impose? If so, how severely and actively do they enforce that limit?

"Lastly, I want to know why the satraps of the Ashbands are usually more powerful than those in the green regions. The SpinDogs told us that was the case, and Tapper's report seems to confirm it. But why? There's a power dynamic here we don't understand yet, and we need to. ASAP. You have all that?"

"I do, sir. Anything else?"

"New directive. Makarov, I want you to talk to Max and compare notes on the respective indig vetting procedures you guys used in your respective wars and AOs. Once you've got that together, pass it on to me and I'll add anything that seems appropriate from my time in the Mog. Then we put those into effect at Camp Stark and our other sites as they come online in the Hamain and Ashbands."

"Sir," Makarov said hesitantly, "that will change our current relations with the indigenous peoples. It has been very open, and they have reportedly appreciated that."

"I understand, and I hope our cadre are up to explaining why we've got to put them in place. Only to be applied to the indigs who enter the bases. Nothing else changes. In fact, I am encouraging increased off-base contact to compensate. Of course, buddy-system and anything else you guys want to add."

"Or you could just send me down to have a look around," Max rumbled.

Murphy smiled. "I wish I could, but Makarov would have kittens if I didn't have a bodyguard."

Makarov nodded, added, "Sir, regarding the new indig directive: do you expect saboteurs? Informers?"

"The latter. And not just because of the Sarmatchani or other peoples. Officer and enlisted alike, our unit is anything but a bunch of choir boys—" a phrase he'd picked up from Moorefield's top kick, Whittaker "—and they're in the ass-end of nowhere with only rudimentary language skills and no local support staff or providers. As I hear it, everyone dirtside is already hankering after a few beers and a few hours of pleasant company. In three months?" He shrugged. "Soldiers are soldiers. Add that to the growing need to hire locals for support functions on the FOB, and that some of them are poor or corrupt enough to work as spies for the satraps." Murphy shook his head. "Better we get out ahead of it now, put policies in place while everyone is still passing the jug and singing kumbaya. And frame it as just an annoying necessity because our foes are so sneaky and dishonorable."

Makarov almost grinned. "You would have had an excellent career writing occupation pamphlets, sir."

"Watch it, Makarov. I've got a thick skin, but some insults cut too deep."

Max shrugged. "Yeah, but…he's right, sir."

Murphy glared at the two of them, glanced at this slate, saw Moorefield's update: the second shuttle had completed insertion and was now in level flight, making for what would soon be Camp Stark. "Makarov, send Captain Moorefield advance warning that we'll be forwarding indig security and vetting protocols within the day. His camp is going to attract all sorts of Sarmatchani almost as soon as it's set up."

Makarov poked the screen of his own device. "Message already drafted, sir. Flagged for priority delivery. Will send pending your approval."

The message popped up on Murphy's screen. He didn't get as far as the communique's content; his eye was snagged by, and stopped on, the routing information. "I…I never noticed this before."

"What's that, sir?"

"Moorefield—Bo—his real name is Hubert? *Hubert?*"

"Yes, sir."

"Well," commented Murphy as he pressed the "send" tab, "I see why he goes by 'Bo.'"

PART THREE:

MOOREFIELD

Chapter Twenty

R'BAK

I can't keep doing this, Bo. I love you, but you're never here. I knew you'd be away a lot with the Army and everything, but when you're home, you're not here either. I can't do it anymore. Please try to understand. Don't come looking for me.

Bo Moorefield folded the brittle, yellowed paper carefully and slipped it inside a plastic bag. After sealing it against both time and the elements, he tucked it into the angled pocket of the uniform blouse hanging beside his creaky bunk. That Sharron had written the letter over one hundred thirty years before didn't dull the pain of that wound. Neither did the thought of her being long dead. Nothing helped. His careful romantic plans—to pick up Sharron's favorite tulips, two bottles of her favorite champagne, and surprise her at her mother's cabin on Lake Watauga in the Appalachian Mountains—never had a chance. She hadn't wanted him to come for her, and fate had stepped in to ensure she got her wish.

One moment, Bo had been in 1992, leaving Somalia on a UH-60 Blackhawk after having accused a Turkish general officer of cowardice. The next, he was waking in a sterile room next to a bored medical technician who told him that it was 2125, that he was light years from home, that there was intelligent life in the galaxy, and that some of it wanted him and the rest of humanity dead.

After awakening six weeks ago with other "lost soldiers" hijacked from various wars in the twentieth century, Bo did spend some time wondering about Sharron's reaction when she'd received the news that the Blackhawk had crashed with no sign of survivors. For a few seconds, he thought about the money she would have received from the Servicemembers' Group Life Insurance policy he'd arranged: a cool $400,000. Because divorce proceedings hadn't even started, there was little doubt she'd taken that check and smiled all the way to the bank.

What was it Sergeant First Class Gleason had always said? Nothing moves as fast as a cavalryman's paycheck in the hands of his spouse?

Or was it to never, ever, let a woman fuck up your life?

Bo snorted and rolled off the heavy, green sleeping bag and stretched before straightening his bunk. There was no one to inspect his quarters; no one would have seen him leave the bunk unmade. Still, it was a habit to make his bed and be sure that at least one thing would go right that day: finding his bed made at the end of it.

He reached down and worked the leather straps of his roughed-out tanker boots through their buckles and tightened them. They weren't his original boots, but they were reasonable facsimiles and just as comfortable to wear. In fact, almost everything seemed a bit more comfortable. For having slept over a hundred years, his body felt better than ever. But still: a hundred and thirty-three years and a whole life, lost in an eyeblink.

Solace came in odd places, in simple things. Familiar boots. A squared away bunk. Divorce papers he'd never have to sign. A body mysteriously devoid of the nagging injuries he'd acquired living the life of a soldier. With a sigh, he reached for his uniform blouse out of habit. As he did, his left thumb rubbed the smoothed skin where his wedding band had been just a few short weeks—and more than a hundred years—before. He winced at the realization for the hundredth time, with a similar result.

Fuck me.

He pushed through the flaps of the Vietnam-era tent (General Purpose, Medium) and into the calm, cool morning of the desert tableland. The storms overnight had cleared, and the sky blazed with starlight. Given the mission underway, the small forward operating base was quiet, even at 0300. He moved down the slight incline toward the headquarters tent at the center of the small, oblong compound. Concealed by alien scrub brush, the base was tucked into the shadows of a shallow, rocky bowl, surrounded by low slopes that were eerily similar to those of eastern Africa. On the other hand, the air was totally without the humidity and stench of the cities that seemed to permeate miles in every direction. At its core, the small base reminded him of the UN compound outside Mogadishu. But instead of being filled with ineffective bureaucrats playing soldier in comical uniforms, there were actual soldiers around him for the first time in years. Uprooted from their own times, each had been believed killed or missing in action. But now they found themselves being moved about as pawns in a conflict much larger than themselves. What mattered were their shared experiences—past wars and present homelessness—and the mission at hand. All they had was each other, and to survive, they would have to stand together.

Given that Murphy had already had their first mission roughed out by the time Bo awakened, there had been little for him to do except to observe, learn, and deploy from a hidden spaceside facility to the surface of R'Bak.

The operation was almost unthinkable. Their own transportation assets were few. The supplies of POL products—petroleum, oil, and lubricants—were critical to maintain and ration. They used their few trucks and other vehicles sparingly to maintain stocks in case of some emergency or combat action. However, as if nature had decided to compensate for all the man-made shortages, they had plenty of local pack animals—*whinaalani*—which were able to serve in multiple roles. Bo tried not to think of them as lizards, but they looked like something out of the reptile display at the Iuka Mall back home, except about twenty times the size of their counterparts on Earth.

More precisely, the whinaalani resembled a mixture of an iguana and a Komodo dragon. From the tip of their tail to the rounded nose at the front of their triangular head, a typical whinaalani body was about three and half meters long and stood just over a meter tall at the saddle point between their four muscular legs. Wide, clawed feet gave them great traction for both climbing and digging. A long, strong tail gave them grace and balance. They'd evolved to suit peculiar weather cycles and climatic shifts and appeared to survive the periodic Sears by going far underground. They were the largest of the natural fauna observed in their area and they'd responded very well to the Lost Soldiers.

Saddling them and riding them came even easier, much to Bo's surprise. Raised on a farm in northeastern Mississippi, he'd ridden horses his entire life and discovered that the whinaalani not only took to being ridden more quickly and with less agitation than horses or mules, they seemed to enjoy carrying a rider on their strong backs. Still, without Bo's accidental discovery of their other abilities, the whinnies would have been nothing more than a work-around for their transportation shortages, rather than an increasingly vital part of his unit's table of organization and equipment.

A herd of wild whinaalani always seemed to be near them. While they seemed every bit as disinterested in Bo's indigenous allies as the whinnies already broken to the yoke, the untamed ones were genuinely curious about the Lost Soldiers. They often followed dismounted patrols at a distance and occasionally ran alongside any of the vehicles out for their short, routine maintenance rides.

So when one of them followed Bo on a scouting hike a month before, he'd not given it much thought. He'd started hiking to clear his mind and try to make peace with Sharron for her decision, but before long, his interest had shifted to assessing the available supply of water. With the Sear approaching and ambient temperatures rising, the nearby lakes and streams were already starting to shrink and recede. He'd tried to locate signs of an aquifer or some persistent, potable water, but Murphy's orders were not to leave an area five kilometers from the base without security. Carrying a weapon wasn't enough. There was far too much about their surrounding environment they didn't know.

Bo had climbed a rocky embankment to peer across the waves of rolling terrain to the south and west of the base. Near the top of the exposed stone, a flash of movement caught his eye and he'd recoiled. His mind told him it was an angry snake, and Bo raced down the rocks, not expecting the slithering, black and green thing to chase him at a frightening speed. He looked over his shoulder, saw the creature racing toward him with a single bright white fang glinting in the sunlight—and ran into the leathery hide of a whinnie. It looked at him curiously and Bo's mind raced to figure out why it seemed different, until he realized the whinnie had knelt.

Knelt.

He'd scrambled onto the back of the whinaalani as the slithering thing closed to strike. Bo kicked a leg over the whinnie's back as naturally as he'd done on a horse. The whinnie pivoted, let out a throaty cry, and stomped down with one rear leg repeatedly until the snakelike thing lay trampled in the sandy ground.

"Holy shit," Bo had sighed as he patted the whinnie's neck. It seemed natural, and the whinaalani seemed to like it. When the whinnie didn't buck him off, Bo rode bareback for nearly two hours before heading home. He'd ridden into the compound that day to the shocked stares of his compadres.

He got a similar, if more understated reaction, from Murphy during his brief uplink later that day. The major replied to Bo's report with an unexpected, albeit thin, smile. "Seems like we've found something for you to do, Captain Moorefield," Murphy had said. They identified a half-dozen of the Lost Soldiers with experience on horseback and found them mounts. One moment, Bo had nothing but daily hikes to clear his mind, and the next he had a squad of mounted soldiers. His very own cavalry.

The whinaalani enabled longer searches for water sources and the local medicinal flora Murphy identified as a commander's critical intelligence requirement. They hadn't located any of the pharma plants, but they did come across several potable springs in the desiccating landscape as their search area widened. As the Sear approached, having a constant, reliable source of water morphed from a want to a critical need. Water, though, was only one of the unit's problems.

Bo glanced up at the clear night sky as he walked and tried to remember where Murphy told them to look for Earth. Nothing about the sky seemed correct. He knew it was a product of distance and perspective, but it made his mind swim in confusion.

You always said you would be there for me, Bo. But you were there for the Army instead.

Jaw clenched, Bo looked down at his feet as he made his way to the headquarters area. There was movement in the darkness off to his right and he turned that way to see a whinnie watching him intently. He smiled.

"Hey, Scout. Hey, boy."

The whinnie padded toward him, strangely silent for something so large. Scout was the largest of the males in the herd which had now attached itself to the Lost Soldiers. As with terrestrial fauna, the female whinnies were slightly smaller, but no less exceptional. Most of his riders rode female mounts because each herd resembled a pride of lions with many females and only a few males. Bo reached up and patted its warm neck affectionately and smelled the big animal's unique scent, like a slightly sweeter version of a burning tire. The odor never ceased to take his mind back to Somalia for a brief moment before he shook away the past. Except when he could not.

"Always taking care of me, huh?" He ran a hand over the warm, rough skin.

They stood there for a moment, and Bo felt an immense sense of pride and love for the big animal. From their appearance, he'd assumed them to be a reptile, but they were warm-blooded and exceptionally intelligent.

Bo patted the whinnie's neck again. "Get some rest, big guy. We'll ride this morning."

Scout made a sound that was something between a purr and a growl and silently walked away. While he always enjoyed the company of friends, Bo felt better about being marooned in this perilous future because of his mount. He couldn't explain it to anyone who'd never owned a horse, but those who had understood. The bond was something unspoken and true.

He looked up into the strange, clear sky and drew a long, deep breath of the cool air to clear his mind. He looked forward to the daily mounted patrols, and the whinnies seemed to enjoy the exercise, too. This morning would be different. With a mission against hostile R'Bakuu forces to the north underway, his commander's plan to lure them out relied not only on his mounted cavalry, but on Bo himself. He wanted to think he was ready.

Bo walked down the gentle slope toward the headquarters enclosure. There were soft red lights on the exterior and Bo knew the staff manning the command post would set watches outside each of the entrances. Murphy wasn't the type to let security get lax just because there appeared to be no close, imminent threat. Since he'd roused out of cold sleep, they'd been working with and sometimes against the local populations in their area. The pursuit of resources as the Searing approached presently defined life on R'Bak. The indigs' enemies on Kulsis were preparing for wholesale rapine and their local allies were grabbing whatever they could scavenge. Stopping them was the only prayer the Lost Soldiers had of going home.

Home. Bo shook his head. *What's that quote? You can't go home again?*

At the west entrance to the headquarters, the two Lost Soldiers standing guard held their rifles at the low ready. In the darkness, they appeared almost the same, and yet Bo was certain that, back in their own world and time, neither one of them had ever learned to hold a rifle at the low ready, muzzle pointed at the ground and firing hand hugging the weapon's grip tight to their stomach. Much had changed between the time when they'd been hijacked to when Bo himself was disappeared.

But some things *were* timeless. He couldn't help but smile as he heard the whispered conversation: "No. You're talking about Chicago-style pizza, man. That's called deep dish. No way. Too much bread. Give me a big New York thin crust with cheese and extra pepperoni any day. Nothing else. No salad on it. No fruit either. Cheese and pepperoni only, as the pizza gods ordained."

The other soldier grunted in a Russian accent. "Cheese and tomato sauce on cardboard is what you are describing, Devolo."

Bo chuckled as he walked around the corner. "Make mine thin crust, too, when you find it."

"Captain Moorefield." The soldier on the left drawled with a sleepy New York accent. "Good morning. See? The captain has good taste."

Bo grinned. "Devolo? You staying awake out here?"

"Too pretty a sky to fall asleep, sir. I've been telling Orlovski here all about Vietnam."

The Russian grunted. "I have listened to the same stories twice and now we argue about food. I am eager to end this watch and get some sleep."

Bo couldn't hold back the laugh in his throat. "We all agree with you, Orlovski. Just wait until he tells you about that one special prostitute in Saigon."

Orlovski turned his head to Devolo. The smaller American's face screwed up in discomfort. "You haven't told me this story, Devolo."

Devolo shook his head. "Rude, sir. Just rude."

"You're the one who shared it, Devolo." Bo glanced at his G-Shock. "Besides, I'm guessing you still have about an hour on your watch. That story should help pass the time and keep pizza off your mind."

"I am very interested now, Devolo." Orlovski nodded at Bo. "Thank you, sir. I trust Devolo does not like this story?"

"Not at all." Bo grinned. "Just try not to laugh too loud, okay?"

Bo stepped through the tent flap and into the headquarters, hearing Devolo sigh and utter the words familiar to every soldier when a great story is starting: "No shit, there I was…"

As his eyes adjusted to the red lights, Bo saw Staff Sergeant Yarbrough standing at a crude mapboard. Topographical maps were the backbone of ground operations, and while they had nothing precise regarding the ground they occupied and operated on, the renderings were good enough to show relative distance, key terrain features, and other points of interest. Next to him was a satellite communications terminal unlike anything

Bo had known in his time. He was equally sure Sergeant Yarbrough had no clue what it was. The Vietnam veteran, like so many of the others in Bo's little command, had a special term for the advanced technology they used alongside their more familiar weapons and gear: PFM.

Pure fucking magic.

"Home Plate, Oscar Papa One. Negative contact. Out."

Bo heard Yarbrough sigh before the older non-commissioned officer nodded at one of the few indig radio operators on the base. He spoke a mixture of English and other words from a local dialect that Bo did not understand. The indig RTO, radio telephone operator, did not reply but busily scribbled the time and message in a green, bound logbook.

"Keeping records?" Bo asked as he approached from behind the sergeant's right shoulder. "For posterity's sake or to pass the time?"

Yarbrough snorted. "A bit of both, sir. What are you doing up at this hour?"

Bo shrugged. "The usual. There's a mission underway. Even if they aren't mine, I can't sleep. You know how it is."

Yarbrough looked him over for a long moment and then turned to the map. "OP One should be tucking back in soon. The other forward observation posts haven't seen anything yet. Soon as we have comms with them, we'll update the board."

Bo studied the map. "The OPs won't see anything for a while. Even from the top of the pass, there's too much rolling terrain in the way. We could move OP One down to the bottom of the pass on the far side, but that puts them at risk if anything is out there."

The older sergeant frowned. "The real risk is if they are still out there come daylight. No matter how well planned or supported they are, something always goes wrong with night raids."

Bo didn't say a thing. He'd learned as a second lieutenant when not to say anything. There was more behind Yarbrough's comments than the sergeant let on, and while Bo suspected he knew the source of the veteran's worries, he didn't want to assume anything. Even though the sinking feeling in his own stomach said everything.

Yarbrough turned to the PFM radio set and looked at his watch. "Glass Palace should be overhead in about two minutes, now. The window will be about a hundred seconds."

Bo nodded and kept his face as straight as possible. Either Major Murphy had already signaled a desire to talk to him directly, or Staff Sergeant Yarbrough, his operations NCO, thought it would be best for Bo and Murphy to speak at the earliest opportunity. Time to find out which. "Anything happen on their last orbit and comm check?"

Yarbrough shook his head. "The mission team talked to Lieutenant Tapper after comm check with us. Just before Tapper initiated his final raid."

Bo took a deep breath. Too much could happen in ninety minutes.

A minute and a half later, the PFM radio squawked to life.

"Starkpatch, this is Glass Palace, over."

Bo had to smile. Mississippi State University, his alma mater, was located in Starkville, Mississippi. The students had a myriad of names for the quaint, quiet town that dwindled in population when the semesters ended. He'd named their forward operating base Camp Stark, for other reasons, and the radio callsign worked well and brought some daily levity to his world.

Bo picked up the microphone and pressed the transmit switch. "Glass Palace, this is Saber Six actual."

Ten seconds passed before Major Murphy's voice replied. "Bo? You're awake early. You ready for this?"

Bo brightened. "Yes, sir."

"I want you to take the mounts out ahead of your main body. Just in case Tapper's convoy runs into trouble," Murphy replied. "Once those vehicles he's grabbed have made it back up the pass and are on the way to Camp Stark, I'll feel better about covering them with ground forces and what artillery we have. It's their distance from your position I'm worried about. So I want you in the field, leaning in their direction. You can use your movement to search for water sources, but nothing that puts you out of position to provide immediate support to the convoy as it moves to the rendezvous."

"We expecting resistance? Pursuit?"

"Yes, to resistance. As for pursuit? I'm hopeful," Murphy replied with what sounded like a smile. "Once they're here, you're going to have to be ready for phase two."

Bo nodded. "You're poking the bear."

"Exactly. How many can you mount?"

Bo took a deep breath. "I can mount twelve, easy. There are another five or six leg infantry who are learning to ride the whinnies now. I can take them along, too."

"You can't recon and teach riding at the same time." It wasn't a statement as much as an unasked question with something behind it.

"It would slow us down a little, sure."

Murphy paused. "I want you to take Aliza Turan with you. Do you know who she is?"

Bo's stomach flopped and rolled on itself. "I do. She's one of the Israelis."

"That's her," Murphy said. As he continued, his voice was firm and direct. "She's also a trained equestrian. I know that's not the same thing as a teacher, but she's taken lessons and can keep an eye on your new riders while you keep an eye out for water."

"With respect, she ain't the kind of rider we need." Bo frowned, thinking of all the trained equestrians he'd known who were pure crap on even simple trails. "Plus, she's a terrorist by her own admission, sir."

"She's going with you. She has asked to be involved in operations, and we need everybody in the organization supporting the mission. This is a good place to start. As for what she was doing when she was captured? Read up on your history, Bo."

"I don't think this is a good idea," Bo blurted and added a perfunctory "sir" at the end.

Murphy's voice was low and firm. "Take Miss Turan and your troops out at first light. Patrol sector four and be prepared to support the convoy as it approaches. Keep your eyes out for enemy pursuit of any kind and stay in contact with me through the relay at OP Two." Murphy paused. "Plan to recover all forces back to the FOB by dark."

Bo nodded. The mission was as clear as any he'd run in his career. "If the enemy comes after the convoy? What do you want us to do?"

"Let's cross that bridge when we get to it," Murphy said. "Find us a good watering hole if you can. Just stay ready."

"Always ready, sir."

The connection faded out, and Bo replaced the microphone on the top of the radio set. He turned to Yarbrough. "Who's your relief?"

"Lieutenant Meehan, sir. Takes over in an hour. Said he wanted to be on the comms when the recovery went down." Yarbrough didn't look happy, and it matched the return of a snarling feeling in Bo's stomach.

Great. Just great.

Aliza Turan woke at the first sounds of activity beyond the thin sides of the small tent. She clutched the scratchy green wool blanket to her brow, fearing the voices were finally coming for her. But…the voices she was hearing now were not those voices. Because *this* place was certainly not that place.

She took a deep breath, lowered the blanket, and opened her eyes. The other women were not yet awake. They were still snug in their cots and makeshift beds. Their sense of security in this strange land, and under the circumstances, amazed her. Soldiers, she understood all too well, could make anyplace their home in a matter of hours, sometimes even less. All they needed was a cot and a blanket to feel as if they were meant to be there. For Aliza, a cot, and even a blanket, were luxuries. Trust and security were not.

Fully awake, she forced herself to lay there for several minutes listening to the sounds of the morning. A mission was underway, that much they all knew, but it didn't seem to faze her counterparts. They all had their jobs to do—even the ones who spent more time getting out of their work than what it would have taken them to actually do it. The hard labor projects, particularly filling sand bags, shuffled from one soldier to the next. In her frustration at seeing men and women gleefully shrug off their tasks, she'd ultimately taken up their shovels and gotten to work. Before long, the unrelenting heat forced her to shed her familiar outer blouse and work in a short-sleeved shirt. Surprise at what that revealed gave way to guilt, and the modern soldiers eventually began to work alongside her.

Modern soldiers. She tossed that adjective around in her mind. They were certainly more modern than she, having been removed from battlefields in the later years of the twentieth century. But here on R'Bak, they were all antiques, long confirmed as missing and presumed dead. She snorted softly. When they told her that not only was it 2125, but that she was far from Earth, she'd laughed in their faces.

You sound like the Nazis, she'd said only to watch them recoil in shock. *You want us to believe whatever you tell us. To believe your lies. So you can cut into us. Experiment. Never again.* The recovery technicians blanched and covered their mouths with nervous hands as she showed them her left forearm and the blue numbers that would forever adorn her skin.

Gray-uniformed soldiers had taken her from her home, a small village named Tegernsee south of Munich, five days after her seventeenth birthday. At gunpoint, the Nazis loaded her and her family into squalid railcars and moved them toward a place she'd remembered as a vibrant city that was now only mentioned in whispers: Dachau.

Aliza fought tears remembering her parents' faces as the Nazis separated them. In the first few weeks, they saw each other often enough that the camp seemed a hardship and not a prison. But as the tide of war changed, there were fewer people in the camp from those early days. Time blurred into months and then a year. The Nazis marched her father off to the gas chamber when she was eighteen. Her mother disappeared three months after that. Her siblings…all of them in the last days, mostly to typhus.

Somehow, she was spared. Food became so scarce that, when the Americans approached the gates, Aliza and the others didn't have the strength to cheer. She saw the revulsion and horror in the soldiers' faces as they tried to help her and the others. Even as she started to heal and her strength returned, she knew she could not trust them. Free and supposedly able to return home, she couldn't bear to go back to her village and see the same people who'd given her family up on the street. She couldn't forgive them, but more importantly, she couldn't trust them. Trust would never come easily again, if at all.

Aliza opened her eyes anew and saw a few other women moving in the tent. She sat up and shrugged the blanket away. There was enough light that she could see the numbers on her arm as if to remind her she might be in the distant future, and on a planet very far from home, but she was who she was and the others, especially the soldiers, weren't to be trusted any more than necessary.

Her head snapped up at the sound of a loud, almost purring noise, and she smiled. Like her, the whinaalani were early risers. While the animals weren't horses, they were enough of an analog to settle their roles in her mind and inspire her to get out of her bunk every day. The whinnies were intelligent and docile when mounted, except for when the locals attempted to do so. Then they seemed agitated and almost angry. As she watched the creatures in the makeshift paddock, they were playful and wild. She'd grown up with horses and learned dressage from a very young age, so being around the whinaalani was comforting. And the memories they evoked, both at home before Dachau, and her life after it, were not unpleasant. Not at all.

There was a crunch of footsteps outside, and the door flap was pushed slightly, and modestly, to one side. A man, silhouetted against the compound outside, spoke softly. "Miss Turan?"

Aliza replied, "Yes?"

"Ma'am? Captain Moorefield needs to see you. As soon as you can, please?"

"I'll be right there," she said. The man ducked away from the door, pulling both flaps discreetly closed.

Since her awakening four weeks before, she had had exactly two conversations with the overall officer in charge: Major Rodger Murphy. He had taken a keen and genuine interest in her, and once she had been convinced that the improbable future was real, she met with the chief medical officer, Doctor Arthur, to go over her medical history. When that had concluded, Major Murphy had stopped in to speak with her a second time and affirm that she had a place among the Lost Soldiers. It wasn't much, he said, but it was better than the alternative. Murphy had been kind but also very frank, evidence that he understood her from the outset. Captain Moorefield? Not so much.

Aliza dressed quickly, tugging on the boots that somehow weren't her size but didn't hurt her feet, and left the tent. Her mind drifted back to Murphy's last conversation with her. He'd asked several details about her life, especially after leaving Dachau. Where had she been? What had she done? What was her last memory? He had listened intently to the last story, even smiling at one point when there was nothing particularly happy about it. She'd asked him why he was smiling, and he'd said it would be something the Lost Soldiers could use in the very near future.

Apparently, that near future is now.

Chapter Twenty-One

R'BAK

Dawn broke in a spectacular display of purples and orange like nothing Bo had ever seen on Earth. He caught himself staring to the east, into the almost blinding beauty, and forced himself to look away. Mounted on Scout, he'd intended to move around the paddock and check on everyone—what an old brigade commander had called MBWA, or management by wandering around. In his service, especially during his time attached to the United Nations effort in Somalia, the technique had proven invaluable for seeing how work was being done. Around him, the soldiers familiar with their mounts were helping the rookies with the tack for riding whinnies. The long cold sleep hadn't affected the ability of those who had ridden on Earth, and it turned out they were solid examples and adequate teachers. They handled the job with the aplomb of old soldiers teaching the new recruits, probably what each of them had experienced in their first days wearing a uniform. In the paddock, the din of the new recruits' nervous activity contrasted with the focus and quiet resolve of the experienced riders. Combined, the feeling was electric and excitement coursed through Bo's veins in a way it never had before other mounted patrols. Until, that is, he saw Aliza Turan walk into the paddock with a bright smile on her face.

Her dark hair tied into a ponytail, Aliza wore the green olive drab fatigue pants the Vietnam veterans knew all too well. Her black, polished boots had straps instead of laces, exactly like his own. Where she'd gotten the tanker boots he didn't know; they were only supposed to be worn by those who had earned them.

As fast as the thought came up, he squashed it. Nothing from that old Earth mattered anymore.

You always said I mattered, Bo. What happened to us?

He blinked and kept staring at Aliza Turan. Her matching green fatigue shirt was open but tied at the bottom in front, revealing a black shirt underneath. Bo clenched his jaw and nudged Scout toward her. The whinnie trotted her direction, almost happily. Turan waved to a couple of the others and stopped to talk with Sergeant First Class Whittaker. She smiled and touched his arm and the grizzled old sergeant grinned.

"Captain Moorefield," she smiled up as Bo rode up. "Good morning."

He nodded and touched the wide brim of his boonie hat. He would have preferred a more traditional cavalry Stetson, but it would have to do. "Miss Turan."

"Major Murphy asked me to join you today."

Bo pressed his tongue against the inside of his teeth for a long moment. "I'm well aware of what Major Murphy asked, ma'am."

Her smiled faded at his tone, and her dark eyes became serious. "I will assist you as needed."

"Sergeant First Class Whittaker is my NCOIC. All I need you to do is assist the newbies." He jerked his head toward a group of unsure soldiers watching others saddle and prepare to mount up.

"NCOIC," she squinted. "You mean your second in command?"

Bo frowned at her. "Yes. That's right."

"I'm sorry," she replied with a quizzical raise of her eyebrows. "This new terminology is confusing."

"Don't apologize. It's a sign of weakness," Bo said with a grunt.

"I'll try to remember that." She smiled at him and turned toward the whinnies. "You have any recommendations for my mount today?"

Bo studied the collection of whinnies in the paddock. "What can you handle?"

"They're much like horses, yes?" Turan said. "I rode dressage growing up and can handle almost anything."

"They're wilder than horses when you first get started. Not like broncos, but close," Bo said. He pointed toward a whitish-gray whinnie with a thin blaze of red along its triangular forehead. "That one. She's a solid mount. We call her Athena."

Turn nodded and followed his gaze. "She looks good. I trust your judgment."

"We're leaving in ten minutes. Let's get the newbies mounted up, Miss Turan." Bo jerked Scout toward the compound's front gate. "Sergeant Whittaker? Ten mikes. I'll meet you at the front gate. I need a SITREP from the CP."

Whittaker nodded. "I'll see that Miss Turan gets everybody in the saddle, sir. She seems to have a good handle on things."

Bo frowned. "I want to get moving. Put the newbies in the center of the formation and keep her there."

"Respectfully, sir? That woman will go wherever the hell she wants. You'll be hard pressed to stop her."

Bo sighed. "Just get them saddled up, Top."

"You want her armed?"

He thought about it for a long moment. The effort involved with taking an untrained civilian on a patrol was one problem. Providing that civilian with a loaded weapon bumped it up to another level entirely. But Murphy mandated that soldiers remaining planetside on R'Bak had some weapons training and that they had all "qualified" at a modified weapons range built into the west side of the compound. "Did she qual?"

Whittaker grinned. "Expert on the M1911, sir. Shot thirty-nine out of forty, if memory serves me right."

"Good for her," Bo grunted. "Make sure she has a sidearm, then. Standard load. Pull extra water for everyone, too."

"You thinking it'll be a long day, sir?"

"Yeah." Bo glanced toward the high ground. "Pull a ration, too. Just to be safe."

"Done, sir," Whittaker said. He jerked his head in Turan's direction. "She'll be fine, sir."

"I'm not worried about her," Bo lied. "Have the patrol ready to move out, Top."

"You got it, sir."

As Bo turned toward the command tent and readied himself to nudge Scout into a trot, he noticed Whittaker smiling. He clenched his teeth. This clusterfuck was Murphy's idea and as much as Bo wanted to get back on the PFM and give the major a piece of his mind, he knew it wouldn't do any good. They needed more riders, and while a training program was something he and his squad could do, they couldn't do it fast enough. Not without help. He glanced back at Turan, surrounded by smiling soldiers as she taught them how to mount the whinnies from the side, like a horse. Not a man in the group was paying attention to the training as she climbed up and swung a leg over the whinnie's back in one smooth motion. Her fatigue pants were baggy, but not enough to hide her athletic figure.

Sharron loved horses.

She rode dressage, too.

Bo mentally slapped himself even before her words came into his mind.

You always argued with me about my horses. You were never willing to hear that the Army cost us more in time and money than my horses ever did. You knew how important they were to me and that didn't matter. All that mattered was the Army.

He nudged Scout and said to himself, "I will be glad when I don't hear your voice anymore, Sharron."

A whoop sounded from behind him. He whirled in the saddle, just in time see Turan cheering and leading the others in applause as the first of the recruits, Private First Class Boyd, vaulted into the saddle.

"Whoa, Scout." He spun the big whinnie in place and trotted over. "Miss Turan. This is not a cheerleading competition. Getting the recruits into the saddle and prepared to ride doesn't merit a celebration."

"They need confidence." She met his gaze. "And a good leader's encouragement."

Bo clenched his jaw as he felt blood rushing to his face. "Then encourage them to get their asses onto their mounts so we can move out."

Turan smiled up at him. "And what would you have me do then, Captain Moorefield?"

"Once they're mounted, I expect you to stay in line and keep your interval, Miss Turan," he replied and forced a tiny smile onto his face. "Keep the FNGs in the middle of the formation and do what I ask. Is that clear?"

"And what is an FNG? I do not understand your American love of acronyms."

Bo frowned and let out a quick sigh of frustration. "Fucking New Guys. The inexperienced riders. The ones you've been assigned to *babysit* in the hopes they can someday ride patrols without adult supervision. Can you understand that, Miss Turan?"

The mirth drained away from her face. "Perfectly."

"Sergeant Whittaker!" Bo called and looked up at the old sergeant now astride his whinnie. "Get the patrol mounted and ready to LD."

"LD?" Turan asked. There was a hint of a smile on her lips, and it nearly enraged him.

"Line of departure. As in crossing it and starting the mission sometime today," Bo growled. He turned his mount away and made for the command post.

"Yes, sir," Whittaker grunted and called for the veterans to help the newbies. Bo didn't watch. He trusted his NCOIC implicitly, but he also wanted to get an update from Major Murphy. He checked his watch again for the next communications window and frowned. The force conducting the operation should have returned to Camp Stark by dawn, and they were nowhere in sight. Bo felt a familiar knot develop in his stomach. Fourteen months with the UN, the last six of which he'd commanded convoy operations in Mogadishu, had taught him one simple lesson. Retrieving a stranded convoy was difficult enough in friendly zones. Where the enemy had a foothold? Damned near impossible.

When Bo stepped into the command post, Lieutenant David Meehan was standing before the mapboard, arms crossed and frowning. The young, dark-haired lieutenant adjusted his "birth control glasses" with their thick, myopia-correcting lenses and shook his head.

"What's the problem, Dave?" Bo asked.

Meehan turned to face him. Despite being taken by the Ktor from the jungles of Vietnam in the heat of mid-summer, every inch of him was a pasty, dough-like color. Severe acne dotted his face. Meehan had been twenty-two days into a disastrous tour when he'd fallen behind after an ambush deep in enemy territory. "Sir? Glass Palace reports the convoy is having major issues moving some of those vehicles. They are way behind schedule."

Bo nodded. "That hasn't changed from my conversation with him on their last orbit."

"Oh," Meehan's mouth worked silently for a few seconds. "It's just that Major Murphy ordered us to hold our other forces back behind the pass in case the enemy attacks."

"Again, that hasn't changed." Bo tried not to frown. Meehan was like every other second lieutenant he'd ever met, including the one he'd faced in the mirror years before. "What are you over-thinking?"

Meehan blushed. "Well, sir, logistically, we *can't* support them out there. But you've been ordered to go out there on a patrol *to* support them. Even though you're the OIC of this camp. You should be here monitoring the radio and making decisions."

Bo almost smiled. "Just because I'm out there doesn't mean that I will not be making decisions."

"But I can focus on, and handle, activities here in the rear." Meehan brightened. "Give you one less thing to think about."

Oh, hell no. "Negative, Dave. You are manning the CP until I return. No other duties or distractions. Not even making sure that the men are memorizing the enemy equipment manuals that the indigs passed on to us. Your job is to corral information that we'll need out there. You and Sergeant Yarbrough will oversee base activities, yes, but you will let *him* handle the priorities of work. You remember that term?"

"Vaguely." Meehan frowned. "Officers work on plans and command while the sergeants handle the business of the post?"

"Close enough." Bo grinned. They were far from any government they'd ever known, and while invigorating, it was scary, too. They were alone—to a point. "Whatever Major Murphy wants to happen will come, and it's not just us who will respond to it. We have one mission right now: to go support that patrol. I'm taking it for two reasons. One, I'm the most experienced rider in camp and using the whinnie cavalry is my idea. Nobody else can handle that. Two, the commander in the rear is almost always wrong. I'll be out front where I can see the terrain and shape the operation. That's new to you, I get it. Just because you're in the rear doesn't mean that you can take it easy. I need you monitoring the situation and keeping me informed of what the other OPs and forces may do as this thing unravels."

"Unravels?" Meehan squinted behind his glasses. "You think this mission will fall apart, sir?"

"I do, Dave. That's what we have to be ready for. You're here to lead that effort. Not everyone gets to wield the sword of destiny, son," Bo drawled theatrically.

Meehan shook his head. "I have no idea what you're talking about, sir."

"Old movies, Lieutenant." Bo grinned and pushed through the tent flaps and into the morning light. "It's a fine cavalry day."

Camp Stark sat slightly back from the edge of a tableland that overlooked a five-hundred-kilometer-long valley which flowed up and into what the locals called the Hamain: the highest and most arid region on this part of R'Bak. Although well-hidden in a small basin nestled between the slopes that wrinkled the top of the shelf-like plateau, the outpost's position and altitude was optimal for providing early warning for the bulk of the aviation and heavier assets that would soon be gathering in a sheltered canyon well behind it to the east.

Five kilometers to the southwest of the camp, pushing up from the rim of the two hundred and fifty-meter-high walls of the tableland, was a small hill covered in the alien scrub. The exoflora looked eerily like sage on the western American plains but smelled entirely different. Bo had positioned one observation post atop that hill, from which observers could look down into the pass that led up to the tableland. They could also watch the termination point of a steep, dry gulch that carried occasional highland run-off south and then west to the ocean. The intermittent lakes and streams in the wide valley, like most of the water sources on the continent, were slowly receding. Where there was water near the surface, the alien vegetation seemed to be in almost constant bloom, as if trying desperately to stay alive before it died under the intense heat of the Sear.

Surveying the stark landscape from the front of the patrol as it edged downward, Bo steered Scout through a series of craters that indicated the use of heavy artillery sometime in the past. In the dust lay rusted shards of shrapnel from a massive shell, far larger than anything he'd seen used on Earth. As time and distance passed with no update from the convoy, Bo moved the patrol south of the main pass and chose to leave the rim by a narrow cut he'd seen the whinnies use.

At the top of the trail, Bo reined up Scout and moved to the side. Specialist Sublete took point and confidently coaxed his whinnie downward. Several of the newer riders went by. None of them spoke to Bo and only one dared to look up as their whinnies loped down the brush-covered trail. In the middle of the formation, Aliza Turan was coaching one of the new riders. Her eyes never left him and though she forced a smile as she spoke, Bo could sense her anger from twenty meters away.

"That's it. Now, just lean back a little and try to relax. He'll be just fine on the descent," she reassured the soldier as she nodded him onward and brought her mount, Athena, to a stop next to Scout. The whinnies glanced at each other and purred.

"Miss Turan," Bo said. He touched the brim of his boonie hat and nodded politely. "Nice day for a ride."

"Why aren't we on the north side of the pass? That area is almost entirely unexplored." She stared holes through him. "We should look there for the medicinals the indigs taught us to identify and collect."

Bo forced a smile onto his lips. "The terrain over there is much steeper than here. It would take us twice the time to descend it and four times as much to climb back up. We don't have that kind of time today."

"But those medicinals are valuable. Some of them are priceless in this culture."

"So is water, Miss Turan. That's what we're scouting for until the patrol gets back."

She scoffed. "You're not trying to find anything. You're just hoping the whinnies do it for you."

"This is a migration route for them. I'm not sure if you understand how game trails work, but they often connect to water sources." Bo looked over the passing formation again. Sergeant Whittaker and the rear element were in sight now. "You should get moving."

"Fine." She shook her head. "But I'm guessing there's no water source down there close enough for our use."

"Maybe so." Bo removed his hat and wiped his brow with his left sleeve. "But I know for a fact there're no medicinals along this side of the valley for the next ten kilometers. You can stop looking for them and keep coaching the newbies, Miss Turan."

"And you'll be doing what, exactly?"

Bo leaned forward in the saddle and nudged Scout forward. The whinnie moved as if he wanted nothing more than to get away from the woman. Bo knew how he felt. "We're meeting an indig guide at the bottom of the trail. He's taking us south, along the base of the rim. It's a path we've never ridden before that skirts the outside edge of sector four."

"You're taking us out of our sector? And you won't search for medicinals in a brand-new area?"

"Yes, I am. And no, I won't." Bo turned his back on her. "We've patrolled out here for three weeks now. The river valley is our best shot for a water source, even if it's an aquifer."

"Searching the same area repeatedly and expecting a different result sounds very much like insanity, Captain

Moorefield." Her voice rose as she added, "Just because it's steep doesn't mean there's nothing of value out there."

Bo pointed with his right hand, "Get back in line and keep your interval."

Damn that woman.

Aliza clenched her jaw and pressed her tongue against the back of her front teeth to bite back a reply even as what she'd said dawned on her. For a moment, she heard Ben Mazza's voice across the dark desert north of Jerusalem.

Just because it's steep doesn't mean there's nothing out there.

He'd said the same words in the moments before her memory stopped, and she'd woken in this distant future and impossibly far from home.

Except she really hadn't had a home in years, not since the Nazis forced her onto the train to Dachau. After liberation, she knew that her town was not her home anymore. Germany wasn't either. The few Germans she saw soon after the Americans freed them wouldn't even look at her in their shame.

Amongst the other emaciated survivors, she'd found very few women and no one younger than herself. While the Americans nursed them back to life, she'd found Ben gnawing on an American chocolate ration bar as he sat against a low stone wall. They'd looked at each other for a few seconds before he held up the candy and waved her over. She'd sat down next to him, nibbled on the chocolate, and spoke her first words in over three months.

From there, they'd been fast friends and looked out for each other. As her color returned and her ribs disappeared back inside her skin, there'd been more than one occasion where she'd caught the attention of American soldiers only to have Ben step in front of them. One day, an American officer saw several of his men approach and circle her. He'd stepped to her side with a level of anger which surprised and shocked her. He raged at them for even thinking about her, or any of the other women in the compound, sexually. If they didn't remember that they were here as rescuers, they were no better than the Nazis.

The men had averted their eyes in shame and apologized, but the officer had not let it go, swearing that he would be watching them. Every day.

That officer had worn the gold oak leaf of a major, as she learned later, but she'd never learned his name. The only other thing she remembered about him was the screaming eagle patch he wore on his shoulder. The same one that Major Murphy wore, along with the same gold oak leaf. She doubted that she could have made herself trust the men who awakened her into this strange future had she not seen those two symbols and felt the faintest pulse of trust, of safety, that they quickened in her heart.

A day after waking, she'd eaten a full breakfast and reported to a small room for an interview. There were only two chairs in the tiny space. One was empty and Major Murphy sat in the other. He'd smiled at her.

"What's your name?"

She'd told him and immediately asked, "Where am I? Where is Ben Mazza?"

Murphy shook his head. "There's no Ben Mazza here, Miss Turan."

"I was with him before..." Her words trailed off. "Am I dead?"

"What is the last memory you have?" Murphy asked quietly. "Before waking up here?"

"Ben went down the hill toward the railroad tracks." She blinked and shook her head. "He went to check the explosives."

Murphy sat a little straighter in the chair. "Explosives?"

She nodded. "We'd emplaced them on the end of a bridge."

"Why?" Murphy frowned. "Was this during the war?"

She snapped her eyes back toward his. "After."

"When? What was the date?"

"The 16th of June 1946," Aliza replied. "Our target was a railway bridge over the Nahal Kziv in Lebanon."

Murphy said nothing for a moment, instead consulting a small, glass device in his hands. "The Night of the Bridges."

Aliza shrugged. "Those were the targets, yes."

"That's what the operation was called, Miss Turan."

"We called it Operation Markolet."

Murphy shrugged. "History seems to change when the victors write it. The attack on the railway bridge was by the Palmach. Were you working with them?"

Aliza nodded. "My friend Ben Mazza and I were scouts for them. The bridge was heavily guarded, and the Palmach came under fire as they laid the explosives. We were atop a hill with rifles, providing covering fire. Ben saw something on the steep terrain below and went to check. I tried to follow him and found only a man with dark glasses. Then I woke here."

Murphy nodded again, his face straight and open. "You were fighting against the British, yes?"

"Their policies stopped Jewish immigration to Palestine. For those…like me, there was no home to return to, so we chose Palestine. When we tried to go there, the British detained us and put us into camps. It was almost as if we'd never left the Nazis, that they had simply passed us along to another captor," Aliza replied, her voice thick with emotion pent up for far too long. "All we wanted was a home."

"Well," Murphy said and placed his palms on his knees. "This is your home now, Miss Turan. You are part of what we call the Lost Soldiers."

"I'm no soldier. I will be of no use here with you."

He laughed. "And yet there you were, atop a hill providing covering fire during an insurgent combat operation. I think we'll find something you're both good at and willing to do."

And despite her silent certainty that he was wrong, within two weeks, she was putting her first saddle on a whinaalani. Working with them, first as pack animals and then as mounts brought her horsemanship skills back. She relished the opportunity to ride almost any animal, and the whinnies were agile and graceful despite their size. Teaching the soldiers to ride hadn't been easy, at first. There was a familiar gleam in some of their eyes, but like the nameless officer at Dachau, Major Murphy quickly ended any predatory ideas by ordering her trained with the M1911 pistol and allowing her to carry one at all times, if she wished. After a week on the ground, she'd eschewed doing so, especially after meeting Sergeant First

Class Whittaker. The no-nonsense sergeant made sure everyone knew she was not only good at what she did, but he considered her to be one of them.

Whittaker's gruff voice shook the memories away and brought her back to the present. "Everything okay, Aliza?" Like Murphy, Whittaker wore the screaming eagle patch on his right shoulder.

She let her eyes linger on the patch for a long second before she smiled and met his eyes. "I asked the captain about our route. I'd hoped to search the high ground to the north for medicinals. Not areas where you've patrolled before."

Whittaker nodded, and there was a hint of a frown at the corner of his mouth. "There'll be time for that."

"Not today, though. Right?" She smiled, hoped that the older sergeant would reciprocate.

He did not; the radio headset attached to the shoulder of his load-bearing straps crackled to life. "Saber Nine, this is Oscar Papa Two, relay follows. Over."

Whittaker grabbed the headset and spun the round microphone of the radio they called a prick seven. She'd had to learn so many things quickly. Whittaker depressed the transmit button. "Oscar Papa Two, send it. Over."

"Saber Nine, relay from Glass Palace. Seeker Six established brief uplink. They report significant mechanical issues on the patrol. Recovery requested. They do not have Class Nine and Class Three is critical. Position two decimal five clicks from bottom of Charlie Papa Five. Enemy recon assets may be converging on the area. Quantity and type unknown. Over."

The military discussed everything in an abbreviated fashion, including supply and materiel. Class three referred to fuel and petroleum products. Class nine were repair parts.

"OP Two, how do we know OpFor elements are coming if they can't identify them?"

"Saber Nine, they're reporting biologics scattering behind them. Probably due to fast approach of OpFor, over."

Whittaker's face went from a frown to a scowl. "Good copy, Oscar Papa Two. Relaying to Saber Six. Standby. Saber Nine, out."

Aliza looked him in the eye. “Is everything okay?”

Whittaker shook his head. “I knew being under the command of a guy named Murphy was a bad omen.”

“What do you mean?” Aliza asked and then mentally slapped herself. “Oh, I’ve heard you all talk about Murphy’s Law. ‘Everything that can go wrong will go wrong.’ Yes?”

Whittaker grunted and nudged his mount toward the trail at the top of the rim. “That’s about it.”

“And things just went wrong?”

He looked over his shoulder. “Things just went to shit, Aliza. There are only two options and neither of them are good.”

Chapter Twenty-Two

R'BAK

"Halt!" Bo called as soon as he handed the radio handset back to his RTO, Specialist Sublete. He frowned at the wide-eyed young man before turning to the patrol and making eye contact with his leading two section leaders. "Set a coil. Leaders on me."

The riders and their whinnies formed a circular position with their noses pointing out in all directions for security. No one raised a weapon and there was no threat identified, but the simple action kept everyone involved in the patrol's security. All eyes were alert and everyone quiet enough to listen to the surrounding environment. All Bo heard was the blood rushing through his ears in anticipation.

There were two options. The first was the most dangerous—rush the patrol down the trail to the bottom of the pass to rendezvous with Seeker Six's raiding party ASAP to determine how bad things were. But if the enemy came swooping down on them, his small cavalry force wouldn't be able to hold off the attack long enough for reinforcements to arrive.

The second option was the least palatable. Remaining on the high ground gave Bo the freedom of communications with the observation posts and the ability to see and command the field. Staying in place, however, didn't provide security or covering fire to the friendlies limping through the valley toward them. He'd seen far too many soldiers die outside the protection of their nearby units, but the risk to his small force was great. Probably too great.

For a split second, he remembered watching Somalis scampering through alleys with their assault rifles and RPGs to swarm the next convoy from behind. Frantic radio calls to speed up went unheeded or unheard. The leaders of that second convoy had never known why, thirty seconds later and on the block Bo's convoy had just passed through without issue, the vehicles from their nonprofit medical organization were destroyed. With no survivors.

Bo's leaders—the four section leaders, Whittaker, and Turan—gathered. He met Whittaker's questioning eyes. "We move further down, to the next overlook. Set a hasty defensive perimeter. We need to see what the enemy forces are doing. If they're really coming or not."

Whittaker nodded and his facial expression didn't change. "Yes, sir. How are you intending to figure out what the enemy might do?"

"Observation," Bo replied. "And we'll be in radio contact with our guys soon."

"But they're at least a terrain feature away." Sergeant Cook from the first section blurted. "They may be out of sight when an attack comes, sir."

"Noted," Bo frowned. "Look, I'm not happy about this situation either and—"

"We need to go down there," Turan said. "You're leaving them out in the open. Abandoning them."

Jaw clenched, Bo tried to hold back the comment that burst through his lips. "And what would you know about protecting friends in combat, Miss Turan?"

Her eyebrows rose. "What do you mean?"

"How about you leave military operations to those familiar with them? I don't need any advice drawn from your experience as a terrorist," Bo snapped.

Turan stepped forward, her eyes blazing. "You have no idea what I went through, Captain Moorefield!"

"Keep your voice down," Bo replied.

"I will do no such thing. You know nothing about why I did what I did. You cannot imagine what I lost." Her arm shot out and pointed down the hill. "We must go get them!"

Bo wasn't listening. The bluish numbers tattooed on the inside of her arm stunned him silent. He'd not known she was a

Holocaust survivor, only that she'd tried to emigrate to Palestine after the war and violently resisted the British authority. His mouth dropped open, and he closed it before looking up at her eyes.

"I had no idea."

"You don't care," she snarled. "Like you don't care for those men out there. You sit here and wait, doing nothing when we should search for water. Medicinals, too. You preach about gathering your—your 'intelligence requirements,' but now, when your men are in great danger, you will not make them the first priority? You will not help them?"

Impatience flashed into anger. Bo stood. The woman took a step back as his hand came up and pointed at her chin. "Make no mistake, Miss Turan, I know there are soldiers down there who need our help, and that supersedes any other mission on this godforsaken planet in this future we didn't want. I'm prepared to do whatever it takes for my friends, and while it might seem contradictory that I am not presently doing so, you are still on this patrol and under my orders. The simple fact is that I *can't* order this patrol to the bottom of the pass until I know more about what we're facing."

She blinked. "But you said that helping them is your priority, that it supersedes—"

"I know!" Bo blurted. "You're missing my point."

Aliza flinched back. "Does this 'point' mean we must sit up here and wait, instead of—?"

"Yes, damn it: that is *exactly* what my point is. I can't risk something catastrophic happening to this untrained and lightly armed unit." It was the truth, but it sounded—and felt—weak; he pushed harder. "Hell, we're little more than a bunch of trainees on mounts with pistols and rifles. If we're going to remain a functional unit, there is no other tactical choice. We set a defense, care for the whinnies, and let the situation develop. Let's make it happen."

The group broke up. Bo turned back toward Scout and prepared to climb into the saddle. The feeling of a stare burning two holes in his back was so strong that he turned around. Aliza

Turan's flashing eyes followed his every move. But the voice in his head was not hers.

You said you cared, and you wanted to make things work, but your actions never showed it. You were too busy waiting for the right time.

Bo Moorefield sighed and shook off the memory as best he could. He turned and mounted Scout, then moved down the trail with Specialist Sublete to reconnoiter the immediate surroundings. He didn't see Aliza Turan do the same.

The descent proved more difficult than Aliza first thought. The white and brown scrabble reminded her of the rocky hills of Palestine, although much steeper. The loose rock made Athena rumble with discomfort as they made their way carefully down the slope and kept a good fifty meters distance from Moorefield and Sublete. Athena shuffled gracefully as the rocks slid out from under her feet before springing to solid rock in a fluid movement that almost took Aliza's breath away.

"Easy, girl," Aliza cooed and patted the lizard-like creature's neck. "Easy."

Reins in hand, she gently guided the whinnie back into the center of the trail while keeping her eyes on Moorefield's back as he made his way down the hill. The whinnie responded like the best dressage horses she'd ridden as a child. The big animal wasted no energy. Every step was fluid and sure. It made every movement with purpose and intent—strong and agile. While a whinnie would never win a dressage competition, there was something about the animal that filled her with joy, and not merely because she had never known so wonderful and exhilarating a riding experience. Mounted on a whinnie's flowing, almost serpentine, back drove away the memories and salved the loss and pain she fought to overcome during every waking moment.

Ahead of her, Moorefield stopped on an outcrop of rock and she instinctively pulled back on Athena's reins.

Stay here, Aliza.

The voice was Ben Mazza's, and it threatened to bring tears to her eyes.

His last words to her, before he'd disappeared over the small hillock toward the railway bridge, rung in her heart. The firefight there, between the British and the Palmach, erupted in seconds and caught them by surprise. From their position in over-watch, they had calculated the likelihood of a prepared British response was low. She and Ben carried rifles intending to eliminate any approaching threat as the Palmach moved to plant explosives. The appearance of the British platoon changed the dynamic. Pressed against the dirt with stray bullets whizzing through the air above their heads, she looked into the eyes of the only friend she had in the world.

"Stay here, Aliza." Ben grimaced as machine gun fire tore into the small, narrow valley below. He'd tried to smile at her, but everything in his expression was pained. His dark eyes glittered in the dim moonlight. There was dust in his scruff of beard and dirt on his face. He placed a warm hand on her forearm and nodded once. Before she could respond in kind, or say what she'd wanted to say for weeks, he was gone.

She'd started to follow him when the firefight reached a crescendo. Her memory ended there. She wiped a sleeve at the fresh tear sliding down her left cheek. Eyes squeezed shut, there was nothing she could do for the sudden pain in her chest except to breathe.

A distant, crunching sound from the valley below snapped her attention back to the present. She opened her eyes and nudged Athena forward. Moorefield did not turn around as she approached. His eyes scanned the valley below. As she came alongside, she looked up at him and saw the concerned grimace on his face.

"Miss Turan," he said without looking in her direction.

"What was that noise?" she asked.

Moorefield shook his head. "No idea, but it sounded bad. If the patrol can't get up the pass…" He let the words trail off, and Aliza understood. Anything unable to get up the pass would be left behind, and the raid would have been for naught.

"There has to be something we can do," she challenged, intending to add more. Instead, her eyes caught sight of several small flocks of nameless bird-like animals flapping toward them. As her gaze shifted in that direction, she caught sight of a smudge rising up over the horizon: the unmistakable sign of a dust cloud. "The J'Stull are coming."

"What we do depends on the shape Tapper's guys are in right now," Moorefield said. "Without them, I'm not sure we can do much out here. This patrol would be really outgunned in a direct fight."

"We have to go down there and help them."

Moorefield turned to look at her. He acknowledged her comment with a solemn nod. "I'm sorry for what I said up there."

She looked up into his blue eyes and saw something different. His intense eyes always seemed to stare at something far away, and yet they were softer somehow. More present. "I know you care for those men and women. I shouldn't have said what I said, either."

He looked back at the distant cloud. "I think this day is about to get longer than we ever imagined. So much for finding water and medicinals."

She laughed. "The army conspires against us."

"Captain Moorefield!" Behind them, the RTO approached waving the radio handset. "Sir, update from OP Two. They've got line-of-sight with the vehicle column now."

She squinted at Moorefield and he saw her expression. "Means our radios can see each other, if that makes any sense."

"It does. I think?" She smiled involuntarily. "What do you want me to do? Take the recruits back to base?"

"Hang on," he replied and reached for the radio handset the moment Specialist Sublete got close enough to hand it over. "Seeker Six, this is Saber Six. SITREP, over."

"Saber Six, we're stopped two klicks from the bottom of the pass. I've got four vehicles non-mission capable at this point."

"Good copy, Seeker Six. Report status of other vehicles."

"Twenty vehicles mission capable. Full loads ammo and fuel. Minimal crews. I have four KIAs and six wounded to get up the pass immediately. Requesting assistance."

Moorefield clenched his jaw for a long moment. As he turned to look at her, the softer look in his eyes was gone and replaced with something she hadn't seen in the young captain before. "Miss Turan, return to Sergeant Whittaker's position. Tell him to have the leaders ready for a mission brief when I get there. I'm going to figure out how to skin this cat."

There was nothing she could say to him. He meant business in every sense of the word. The sudden determination reminded her of Ben and the Palmach soldiers they'd supported. Committed to the task at hand, they would give their all to ensure the others survived. She shelved the uncertainties that persisted in her attitude toward the young officer. He'd trusted her with a task, and she would complete it.

"What are you planning to do?"

Moorefield stared at her, and she realized she liked the confident look on the man. "Whatever it takes."

Aliza snapped the reins. Athena spun in place and trotted forward. They leapt from rock to rock as they climbed up the hill. Once again, Aliza felt the thrill, the joy, of riding the whinnie run through her. It didn't matter that danger was close and everything she knew in this improbable future was at risk. She felt alive again, truly alive.

And she wasn't going to let anything disrupt this second chance at life.

The rising dust cloud bothered Bo, but not nearly as much as the mechanical breakdown of so many vehicles. Murphy's intent had been to grab everything that they could to assemble combat power. If they could not get the convoy to the top of the pass, amassing the key components of that combat power—specifically, fast vehicles equipped with heavier weapons—would not be an option. While they could attempt to defend their final approach with a mostly infantry force, everything in Bo's experience told him that, whether or not his men had the high ground, it was a bad idea. What they actually needed was that most perishable asset in the universe: time.

Dammit.

Bo studied the valley below, noting the higher terrain stretching north and south to his right and left. The flat-topped bluffs resembled the familiar mesas of Colorado and New

Mexico. While the vegetation was not the scrub oak and piñon of the higher altitudes, the terrain was not unfamiliar. That's why it had been so easy to choose the ground where they'd established Camp Stark; as on Earth, they sought—and found—a site on the upper reverse slope of a wide tableland with rocky bluffs, cuts, and draws, protecting the summit. There was only one pass wide enough for vehicle travel, and that qualified it as an avenue of approach and key terrain.

Key terrain.

Bo wanted to slap himself. He'd been so accustomed to convoy operations in Somalia, following main supply routes back and forth and pulling security against the near targets close by in the rubble and war-torn buildings, that he'd forgotten a simple mnemonic device. OCOKA. Observation. Cover and Concealment. Obstacles. Key Terrain. Avenues of Approach.

You're an idiot, Bo. He laughed at himself and studied the terrain around him once more, and a plan formed quickly. He couldn't help but smile.

"You okay, sir?" Sublete asked him.

Bo met the concerned young man's eyes. Sublete, like so many of the others, came from Vietnam and his short career hadn't given him much trust or confidence in officers. "I am, Sublete. Let's get back up the hill. You take the lead."

Once the young soldier had moved a good thirty meters ahead, Bo nudged Scout, and they shot up the trail quickly. Bo looked back over his right shoulder as they passed into the concealment of some vegetation. The dust cloud in the distance had doubled in size.

No doubt about it. They're coming.

As they climbed, he adjusted his hands on the reins they'd bought from the indigs with C-rations. He brought his right hand to his mouth and whistled like they had taught him on the farm as a boy. The shrill sound caught the soldier's attention and Bo waved at him to stop in place. As Scout came alongside Sublete's mount, Bo reached out for the radio handset.

"Seeker Six, this is Saber Six. We're coming for you. ETA is fifteen mikes. How copy? Over."

"Saber Six, good copy. We're continuing repair operations and will be ready to move what we can. Seeker Six, out."

Chapter Twenty-Three

R'BAK

Bo swung out of the saddle into the center of the formation and stepped a few paces away from Scout. With a boot, he cleared a small piece of ground. Kneeling down, he drew the ridgeline they'd descended in the center and then added the path of the mountain pass just to the north of them.

There was a sudden crunch of footsteps rapidly approaching. "Why are you scratching in the dirt?"

Bo looked up and noticed something different. Aliza was talking to him with a little smile on her face. He smiled back. "Miss Turan, we call this a sand table. It's a hasty, visual way to make a plan."

She laughed. "And what are we planning? To save the day?"

I remember all those times you said you had a plan, but you really didn't. I think you just wanted more time for things to sort themselves out in the hopes the Army would be done with you. You knew they wouldn't, but you kept lying to me about your plans. You and your goddamned plans.

His own inner voice blotted out the ghost of his ex-wife. *Aliza said "we."*

We.

The section leaders gathered. Bo caught the looks on their faces—something between amusement and worry—as they made their way to him. His temper threatened to flare, and he tamped it down. He'd not given them any reason to trust him beyond taking them on mock patrols, so he looked down at the sand table again and took a deep breath.

Whittaker stepped forward. "All accounted for, sir. What's the plan?"

Bo met the older sergeant's eyes and nodded. Without a thought, he fell into the familiar litany of a mission briefing. "We're going after the raiding party. They're stranded at the bottom of the pass with broken-down vehicles and some casualties. I'm taking first and second sections with me. Experienced riders only. For the first phase, we're going down to rendezvous with Seeker Six's lead elements and get a SITREP from them."

Aliza moved to raise her hand, but Whittaker interrupted. "SITREP is a situation report. What's their status and what can we do about it."

Bo kept talking. "Behind us, Sergeant Whittaker and Miss Turan will bring down third and fourth sections. Before you ask, Miss Turan, I can't spare the manpower to take you and the newbies to camp. You're with us and you're in charge of that section. Once we know what the situation is with the Seeker Six's patrol, and their pursuers, we'll plan our next move. We need to see what the bad guys send after our folks, adjust our plan to counter it, and give Camp Stark a chance to evacuate."

"Evacuate?" Turan blurted.

"That's right," Bo replied. "We may have to pull out of Camp Stark and move back toward the area we were reserving for final force consolidation. I'm guessing Major Murphy is already working that piece of the puzzle right now. We'll make sure they prepare the camp to evacuate and beat feet to the rear. That's step six or seven on the list. We've got more important things to handle between now and then."

"You think the…the J'Stull will attack?" Aliza asked.

Bo nodded. "I think they're gonna come after our raiding party with everything they have. But a good cavalry arm always protects the main body. We'll simply do this the old-fashioned way."

Whittaker nodded. "I don't suppose you mean artillery and air support, sir."

"Not at all, Top," Bo replied. "Fire and maneuver. That's really all we have if we can't get those vehicles moving. And we're gonna have to bust our asses to get them to safety."

Whittaker nodded. "Our indig guide never showed, sir."

"A sure sign of an attack," Sergeant Cook remarked under his breath. "I knew we shouldn't have trusted those guys."

Most of the section leaders murmured their assent, though none of them would make eye contact with Bo. They didn't trust anyone but themselves. Bo didn't believe that to be a bad thing, necessarily, but the sergeants didn't seem to trust him or any of the officers, either. He met Whittaker's eyes and the older sergeant nodded confidently at him. He hadn't felt as proud since he'd been a second lieutenant and managed not to screw up being a platoon leader on the first try.

Another crunch sounded in the distance, this time much louder. The whinnies, normally docile and quiet, shuffled and stamped their feet. Two trumpeted nervously. Some newbies appeared on the verge of panic in their saddles, but the more experienced riders all went to their aid and calmed their mounts quickly and, most importantly, quietly.

Aliza spoke up. "The indig: do you think the J'Stull planted him to spy on us? Determine strength and position for the enemy to gauge the attack?"

Impressed, Bo shrugged. "Great question. We don't know. But right now, it doesn't really matter. We have to get down there in order to help the raiding party get those vehicles up onto high ground and back to our compound. If I'm right about the attack, we don't have much time at all." They all nodded, even Turan, which he took as a good sign. Bo pointed at the sand table. "If they hit us while we're moving the vehicles, here's what we're gonna do."

Bo led the patrol down the mountain as fast as he dared let Scout run. A look over his shoulder proved that both the newbies and the experienced riders were having trouble keeping his pace. Brush tore at his sleeves as Scout bounded down the narrow trail toward the valley floor. Bo relaxed and allowed his hips and lower body to remain attached to the whinnie's side and his body to follow every move the big animal made without expending too much energy. He gave Scout a kick with his right heel, urging him to go faster. The whinnie responded with a lurch forward; Bo snapped backward in the saddle. The nearby flora blurred as Scout accelerated down the steep hill, and Bo smiled and tried not to let out a whoop of excitement.

Barreling through the scrub, they burst onto the valley floor about two hundred meters from the trail leading up the tight pass. Behind a small hill, they were hidden from both the approaching patrol and the enemy. He'd ridden Scout a few times at as full a gallop as the whinnies could go, but bouncing through the brush and from rock outcrop to outcrop left him slightly out of breath, if exhilarated.

Sergeant Cook's section was the first down the trail; his soldiers were all experienced riders. Bo motioned them to move ahead of him and pointed along the base of the hill in the direction of the raiding party. As Cook met his eyes, Bo held up two fingers and pointed them at his eyes. Holding his arm still, he then rotated his fingers to point out, he pointed with his other hand in the direction of the potential enemy patrol. The hand and arm signal to set far side security communicated exactly what Bo wanted them to do without having to either use a radio or use their voices in a tactical environment. Cook and his section of four mounts moved off in the direction he'd indicated.

Second section, under the leadership of Staff Sergeant Stewart, came next. Bo repeated the hand and arm signal, but only pointed at his eyes to indicate near side security. The four mounted soldiers were a mix of experienced riders and newer trainees, but as they galloped toward the convoy, Bo noted that all of their faces were confident and ready.

Third and fourth sections finished their progress down the slope last and almost at the same time, though, technically, he hadn't outfitted a fourth section. Sergeant First Class Whittaker led third section, but with the addition of the newbies under Miss Turan's tutelage, they'd made her a section leader by default, and Whittaker moved those new riders into a fourth section. As they reached level ground, Bo walked Scout out and had them follow behind him. With the security deployed forward, he was again in the lead of the formation as the patrol moved toward the convoy.

Bo heard the convoy before he saw them. The sounds of the vehicles differed vastly from anything he'd heard. Some of them sounded like internal combustion engines. Others sounded like turbines. None of them sounded particularly well-maintained or reliable. As they rounded the ragged bottom of a bluff, Bo stood in his saddle for a first glimpse of them…

And thought, *Well, shit.*

At least three of the vehicles were smoking and one sat askew on the trail, its front end deeply jammed into the loose dirt. Sergeant Stewart appeared to be talking to Lieutenant Tapper. He looked up, saw Bo approaching, and came riding as fast as his whinnie could go.

"Sir!" Stewart reined up the whinnie and skidded to a stop a few meters away. "The El-Tee says they got priority wounded. At least two are critical. They're taking three of the lightest vehicles up the pass to get medical attention. There are seventeen more remaining behind with drivers. Most of them aren't fully crewed."

Bo chewed on the inside of his cheek for a moment. Moving the wounded was the most prudent action they could have taken. "They leaving anyone else behind?"

"Besides the drivers and gunners? A few indig crewmen," Stewart said. "They're trying to get the four dead-lined vehicles moving again."

"Why? What are they?"

"Tacticals." Stewart frowned. The heavy assault vehicles were one of the critical requirements for Tapper's team to capture in their raid. Two bore missile systems and two had multiple rotating machine guns: all weapons that would improve their chances against anyone who might thumb a nose in the Lost Soldiers' direction. Recovering them was a mission requirement.

Dammit. "Get back to Tapper and have him get the seventeen ready vehicles into a defensive line, facing those dust clouds. Maximum concealment. Use the terrain and the brush as much as you can. We're gonna figure out a way to get those four busted tacticals up the pass. We'll need everyone else pulling security in case the enemy recon assets fix our position and strike while we're moving those platforms."

Stewart nodded. "How many of the ready vehicles do you want for towing the tacticals, Captain?"

"None."

Stewart flinched as if he'd been struck. "Sir?"

Bo hooked a thumb at the winding, rock-strewn pass behind him. "Look at the width of that pass and the width of those vehicles. Some of them will barely fit. And give their engines a listen, Sergeant. I'm not sure they'll make it up as it is. But towing those tacticals?" Bo shook his head. "It would be like a go-cart trying to pull a car. One failure and we've got two vehicles blocking the pass. We have to get the tacticals up another way."

Stewart's face clouded. "Begging your pardon, sir, but how?"

"We'll tow them with the whinnies," Bo replied. He had no idea if the whinnies could actually drag the vehicles behind them or not, but the leap seemed logical. Or at least unavoidable. "We may have to tear apart some saddles to get enough rope and cords, but we can do it. Tell Cook to bring in his security as tight as possible and, as soon as the ready vehicles are deployed, find out which of them need crews. On the double."

"You got it, sir," Stewart replied and galloped back toward Cook's position near the bottom of the pass.

Bo looked over his shoulder and caught the eye of his RTO. Sublete moved forward on his mount. "Radio." Sublete passed him the handset. Bo nodded his thanks before holding the ancient piece up to his face like a telephone. "OP One, this is Saber Six. SITREP to relay. Over."

"Copy, Saber Six. Send it."

"Relay to Starkpatch: convoy minus four vehicles secured. Friendlies moving up the pass. Time now. Multiple wounded requiring further evac. Break."

Bo released the transmit button. Whether the J'Stull or anyone else could direction-find their UHF transmissions was an unknown, but prudence said to maintain communications discipline as they always had. And there just wasn't the time to wait for orbital assets to be in a position for secure ground-to-bird and then bird-to-ground relays.

He pressed the switch again, "We are executing recovery operations to move four dead-lined vehicles. Push security elements forward to receive wounded and prepare to support my patrol by indirect fire. I want all mortars on the line and ready to send it. Prepare to execute contingency Charlie. I say again, prepare to execute contingency Charlie. How copy?"

The observation post RTO read back Bo's message verbatim and added, "Saber Six, relay commencing. Please confirm contingency Charlie."

"Contingency Charlie is confirmed. Danger close is authorized, if necessary."

"Copy that, Saber Six. OP Two reports there is biologic activity in your AO and other indications that there is an unknown size force moving this direction from north-northwest. Over."

"Copy," Bo replied. "We've seen it. Report change in size or identification when you can. Saber Six, out."

He passed the handset back to Sublete. "Keep a good ear on that, Sublete. Unless they call for me directly, just relay the information. Stay close. Got it?"

"Will do, sir," Sublete replied. "I'll be your shadow."

Bo grinned. "You do that."

He made a fist, raised it over his head, and brought it down like he was miming it hammering the top of his helmet. The signal for "form on me" brought Whittaker and Aliza Turan forward, their whinnies moving at a trot.

Bo gave them a bare-bones SITREP. When he mentioned the four disabled tacticals, Whittaker raised an eyebrow. Bo nodded grim agreement. "Yep. Gonna be rough. But I think the whinnies could be the answer. Using tow chains, we hitch them two or three per vehicle."

Whittaker's face remained still. "How?"

"We lash together harnesses, using pieces of the newbies' saddles and tack."

"We need those saddles to keep training," Aliza objected.

Bo shook his head. "If these vehicles don't get up the pass and integrated into our overall defenses, we won't have any opportunities to train anyone on anything."

She frowned but did not reply. Her eyes were serious and calm, and she'd taken his comment without a shred of contempt or challenge. Her demeanor suggested that she was prepared to listen to him and act responsibly.

No, that's not it. He chided himself as the answer bubbled up: *She's acting like a soldier.* "Can either of you lash? Or weave? Good with knots? Anything to make those harnesses?"

Whittaker grunted. "Willing to bet we have at least one Eagle Scout in the bunch."

"What is that?" Aliza asked and then shook her head. "Not important. We'll make it work."

Bo smiled. "Aliza, some of your newbies may have to dismount and help crew the ready vehicles, anyway. Use their saddles first. See what you can do."

"I will."

Bo looked at Whittaker. "We need two whinnies per tactical, minimum. I want good riders up there, too. If that means we can only send two vehicles at a time, so be it. I want the first ones moving as soon as they're ready."

"What about them?" Whittaker cocked his head toward the rising dust cloud to the north.

Bo looked over his shoulder for a long moment. There really wasn't any option. "First and second sections are providing security now. The minute we get the tacticals moving up the pass, we'll focus on how to skin that cat."

Or maybe, kill it.

Whittaker had been correct. Two of the newbies, a private from the American contingent of Vietnam vets and one of the Brits had been Scouts and knew their way around ropes and straps. Aliza watched them strip saddle materials and reins, tie them into ropes, and rig up makeshift harnesses for two of the largest whinnies. She watched as Moorefield and Whittaker set about hooking them up to the lead tactical. The first whinnie, with a black-tipped tail, stepped into the trail and backed into the harness with ease. A darker male with a crimson blaze on its angular forehead took some coaxing, but finally, anxiously, backed into position. With quick work and quiet, purposeful direction from Moorefield, they tied the harnesses into place. The young captain clearly had experience working with animals, and the whinnies were surprisingly compliant.

The riders nudged the whinnies and the tow straps snapped tight as they strained against the weight of the broken-down vehicle. Its wheels inched forward. A cheer erupted from the group as the whinnies pulled harder, gaining momentum.

"Hey! Step in there and push it," Moorefield ordered a group of soldiers standing nearby. "Get them moving faster."

The soldiers stepped behind the vehicle and put their hands and shoulders into it. The vehicle rolled forward faster and faster. The black-tailed whinnie snorted a call and leaned into the weight hard, its head low to the ground. Almost immediately, the darker male did the same and the rate of the vehicle's forward progress doubled and then doubled again. They were moving up the steepening hill at a good pace.

"Stay behind it!" Bo pointed at the soldiers pushing the vehicle. "All the way to the top."

Whittaker's voice boomed nearby. "Get the second vehicle hooked up!"

Aliza watched the first vehicle move up the pass and then almost disappear when it went around the first curving switchback. While the towing appeared to work well, it was slow. Too slow. She nudged Athena and walked over to Moorefield. His eyes followed the effort to hook up the second vehicle and get it moving.

"This is too slow," she said in a low voice. "We won't get all of them up the pass."

He turned to her with a frown on his face. "I know. We just have to do the best we can, Aliza."

She didn't respond. His casual use of her first name sent a ripple of excitement down her spine. Her own reaction shocked her—until she started at a whinnie bellowing directly behind her.

Aliza spun to see one of the more experienced riders holding on to his saddle for dear life as his whinnie bucked and thrashed in the makeshift harness. Several soldiers shouted commands and advice, but there was panic all over the rider's face and he half-fell and half-jumped clear. He hit the dirt, rolled, and scrambled away from the whinnie. Without its rider, the animal calmed down, but twisted and shook like a wet dog, trying to throw off the ropes connecting it to the second disabled vehicle.

Moorefield dismounted his whinnie and ran toward the distressed one. A few meters away, he stopped, and she could hear his low voice talking calmly. She lost his words in the slight breeze and the ambient noise around her. His whinnie, still at her side, trumpeted softly and a few others repeated the noise with their own distinct voices. The anxious whinnie calmed, stamped two of its feet in rapid succession, and then turned to stare unpleasantly at Moorefield as he stepped closer.

Chapter Twenty-Four

R'BAK

When he was eighteen, Bo and his father took in three horses from a neighboring farm that had fallen into disrepair. The lush green fields of northern Mississippi gave the animals enough in their pasture to eat, but they hadn't had real interaction with human beings in the several months of their previous owner's illness. When Bo and his dad arrived, the old mare of the group trotted over happily and let them get a lead onto her without much trouble. The other two horses stayed a good hundred meters away, eyeing them warily.

It took more than an hour to get the older male calmed down and led to the gate. The younger stud stomped in circles as Bo talked to it like his father always did. His father leaned against the front fender of the old Ford truck and watched for an hour as Bo tried and failed repeatedly. Disgusted, he'd walked over, leaned a hip against the nearest headlight, and spat. His father smiled.

As Bo stared down the whinnie, he heard his father's voice as clear as ever. *No two animals are the same, Bo. What works for one doesn't always work for the other.*

With Scout, he'd never raised his voice or violently spurred the animal. The whinnie had always responded. The anxious one appeared to take little notice of Bo's attempt at soothing words. He stayed quiet and walked forward confidently and slowly. The whinnie watched him approach and stilled.

Easy. He didn't say the word aloud; it was more a matter of *willing* it at the big lizard. *Easy, boy.*

The whinnie looked up and over Bo's head. He resisted the urge to follow the animal's gaze; he stepped forward and grabbed the reins. When the whinnie didn't respond, Bo grabbed the saddle and swung himself up into the seat in one smooth motion. That was when he saw that the whinnie's eyes were on Scout, twenty meters away. Who stood alert and staring at the whinnie he'd climbed aboard. The intensity of Scout's eyes struck him.

They're not just smart. They're almost—or actually?—intelligent.

In the next breath, he mentally shook himself. Intelligent wasn't necessarily the word he was looking for: they were sentient. They communicated verbally with their hoots and other noises. Like horses, they moved as a herd. Maybe they even had alphas and omegas. Societal instincts, intelligence, and communication spoke to something much more than they'd assumed the whinaalani to be. His mind reeling at the discovery, Bo forced himself back to the present and backed the whinnie into position for the harness.

He pointed at Stewart. "Hook him up."

The sergeant and two others did so quickly. "Good to go, sir."

Bo leaned back in the saddle and looked over at the other rider, Specialist Davis. "You ready?"

Davis, a tall and lanky Alabaman, nodded and drawled. "On you, sir."

Before he could respond, Specialist Sublete waved at him. "Sir, the first vehicle has reached the top of the pass."

Bo replied, "Tell them I'm on my way with the second. I'll get back here as fast as I can. Sergeant Whittaker, you're in charge until I get back. Let's see just how much time we have."

Before he nudged the whinnie into action, he caught sight of the dust cloud along the northern horizon. It had doubled in size against R'Bak's sky.

Let's hope it's enough.

As Moorefield and Davis disappeared around the first bend of the trail with six soldiers pacing them on foot, Aliza caught Sergeant Whittaker's eye. The old soldier sat astride his mount, Casper, staring at the dust cloud.

"Are you okay?" she asked.

He nodded once and looked back beyond her to the horizon. "The better of the four vehicles are headed up the pass. That means we're fifty percent complete with this part of the mission."

"That's a good thing, isn't it?"

He laughed. "In ordinary circumstances, yes. This isn't ordinary. Looks like we've got the whole damned J'Stull army headed this direction. And we're forward, located away from the rest of our own ground forces. Gonna be a long day."

She followed his eyes to the dust cloud. There was no doubt the J'Stull were coming now. Word was that Tapper and his team had hit the enemy hard. The enemy would not merely want to eliminate their attackers, but make examples of them and, so, would accelerate across the valley floor. She looked over the defensive line of vehicles—all random shapes and weapons—and wondered how they could hold off an assaulting force of any size.

"Is he thinking about using those vehicles down here instead of moving them up the pass? I don't think they have a prayer of delaying the J'Stull, no matter how well we fight them."

"When the time comes, we'll do what we have to do, Aliza." Whittaker sighed. He spun his mount and called to Sergeant Stewart. "Set one hundred percent security. Push out a section to recon the north side of the pass, but no farther than Phase Line Sheridan."

Aliza squinted at him. "What is a phase line?"

He laughed. "A control measure. We call it a phase line, which, in this case, is an intermittent creek bed about two klicks north. Giving it a code helps us relay information faster."

"And Sheridan?"

"American Civil War general, Union side." Whittaker grinned. "He was the quintessential cavalryman. Very colorful guy."

"Why use his name?"

Whittaker's grin faded. "He's one of Captain Moorefield's favorite generals. Gave the Confederates fits in West Virginia.

Unpredictable and elusive. Exactly the guy we could use right now."

"And is Moorefield 'that guy?'" she asked.

Whittaker shrugged. "Could be. But he's gotta have the heart for it."

Aliza wondered what the sergeant meant but did not have time to ask as Whittaker rode out to set the patrol into their duties.

The ride to the top of the pass went more smoothly than Bo would have dared to imagine. Once the whinnies snapped the towlines taut, they kept a constant, measured pace all the way up the two-kilometer trail. As they crested the top, Bo sent the walkers down the pass. Bo intended to join them as quickly as the recovery team from the camp could unhook the vehicle.

Fortunately, Lieutenant Meehan had come through. The recovery team—a half-dozen mechanics and maintenance specialists with two vehicles from the motor pool—came forward with heavier tow chains. A squad of infantry was detailed to both sides of the trail, standing security. As soon as Bo and Davis had the crippled tactical over the lip and on mostly flat ground, the recovery team unhooked the hasty harnesses, draped them over the front of the two riders' saddles, and started connecting the chains. The two strange vehicles—crude diesel command car-truck hybrids—rumbled to life, belching black exhaust into the air as they backed toward the tactical to put a little extra slack in the chains. Once attached, the recovery team mounted up, and the first vehicle gunned its engine, building the torque required to tow it swiftly to the rear. The smell of diesel exhaust never failed to bring back memories of the first time Bo had climbed aboard an Abrams main battle tank at Fort Knox. What he would have given for a few of those beautiful beasts on R'Bak. The ability to see, positively identify, and then engage targets thousands of meters away would have been a beautiful thing.

As the first recovery vehicle started towing the tactical away, Bo turned to Davis. "Get down the hill with these harnesses. Get the next one ready." The young specialist pivoted his mount and galloped back toward the men readying the last two vehicles. Bo glanced around, found the RTO for the security patrol Meehan had sent, and waved him over, making a "give me" motion as he reached for the handset. "Starkpatch, this is Saber Six. Fifty percent of the disabled tacticals are on the plateau. We're heading back for the rest now. Over."

"Saber Six, be advised. OP Two says enemy forces are heading that way. Not sure you'll have time to recover them all. Over," Meehan replied.

"They are mission imperative. We're not leaving them." Bo frowned. "We'll just have to move faster, Starkpatch."

"Sir, all due respect, you can't buy time you don't have."

"The hell I can't," Bo snarled into the handset. "Saber Six, out."

With a nod at the RTO, Bo whirled the whinnie back toward the trail. This male didn't respond like Scout did, but it moved well enough, and fast enough, to settle Bo's mind to the task at hand.

You can't buy time you don't have.

A force of unknown strength was bearing down on them. His cavalry patrol couldn't fight them off, and the retreat from Camp Stark back to the main assembly area was poised to start. If the enemy kept coming at the rate Bo thought they were, even the retreat could fail. The paltry forces forward at Camp Stark, or any of the other smaller posts Murphy had set out for different missions, wouldn't be able to develop a concerted defense. Everything dirtside was in danger.

I have to buy time.

As quickly as the thought crossed his mind, he smiled. It could be done. All he had to do was sell it to Sergeant Whittaker and Aliza Turan. She'd wanted to check out the higher ground for trails and viable passes. Well, now she would have her chance.

When he turned the corner at the bottom of the pass, Bo saw the dust cloud from the enemy advance rising higher than before. He caught sight of his patrol hooking up the third vehicle under the watchful eyes of Aliza and Whittaker. As he closed the gap, he saw her looking at him and his stomach churned. She would not like what he had in mind. Using her and the bulk of the patrol—the rest of the newbies—as bait didn't set well with him. Something in his gut said she would like it even less, and he realized that was exactly why it bothered him.

"You want me to *what*?" Aliza asked Moorefield, dumbfounded. She raised her palms to him. "Just so I understand you, please."

The young captain licked his lips and started again. "You and Sergeant Whittaker will take your sections north along the skirts of the tableland at a gallop. I want you to raise as much dust as you can and make the enemy think there's more of us with you than over here at the pass. A *lot* more. It will buy us additional time to get these last two vehicles up to the recovery team."

She shook her head and a nervous laugh came out. "You're making a big assumption."

"More than one; I am aware," he replied. "But the whinnies *will* find a way up into the middle slopes at the edge of the plateau. All you have to do is to attract the enemy's attention for fifteen minutes. The whinnies will do the rest. When the J'Stull turn and chase you, we'll counterattack into their exposed flank."

"And what about when the enemy storms our position on the slopes of the tableland, Captain Moorefield? What then?" The anger in her voice surprised her, but she'd seen firsthand the consequences of poor planning and uneven execution.

"You let me handle that, Aliza." He lowered his chin and frowned, but there was still a twinkle in his eye. "Whittaker has command. All you and the newbies have to do is make your patrol look like a herd of elephants."

"And if we don't find a way up?"

"You will. We'll be there before they can attack you with any strength, I promise."

The calm, confident look on his face and the slow smile threatening to crease it made Aliza smile involuntarily. A sudden grit-laden gust made her blink and sweep her hair away from her face in one movement. When she opened her eyes, not more than a second had passed, and he was still looking at her in the same manner. In the next heartbeat, she realized that she liked it, and it only made her smile wider.

"Well…" She paused. "We'll have to raise some dust and find a way up between the cliffs."

His smile widened and his teeth shone. "You do that, Aliza. We're counting on you."

She nodded. "We won't let you down."

"Trust the whinnies," he blurted. She frowned, not certain what he meant. "I think they're smarter than we think."

She squinted at him. "In what way?"

"When I took that other mount…well, whatever Scout and Athena vocalized got through to it. I'm pretty sure I wasn't the one who calmed him."

"They *are* very vocal animals," she replied, but the rest of the thought stopped on her lips. They'd casually assumed control over the whinaalani, as if they were little more than clever farm animals trained to submit to human dominance. She took in a breath in a sudden flash of realization. "What if we've gotten them all wrong?"

Moorefield nodded and took a long breath. His voice was low when he said, "I think we have from the very start. I'm not sure if they understand what we're saying to them, but I think they understand our emotions somehow."

"That's fascinating." She shook her head even as recollections of Athena's behaviors when being ridden and called played through her memory, like quick clips from a newsreel; the speed and surety of her responses were unlike any horse she'd even known. "You think they are sentient?"

He shrugged. "I don't know. Honestly, we don't have time to think about it. Just trust them. Get ready to move out as soon as Sergeant Whittaker is ready."

"Yes, Captain."

"Thank you." He tipped the brim of his boonie hat and nodded to her. "Just one more thing? Call me Bo."

He turned away to direct his soldiers. Heart trip-hammering in her chest, Aliza turned back to Athena and heard the distinct purring sound the female whinaalani made when content. Athena's angular head turned toward her; the wide, dark eyes studied her for a moment before their focus turned back to the others. Soldiers from the third and fourth sections who'd dismounted to assist with the tow operation climbed aboard their whinnies. Across the road, Whittaker spoke with Moorefield and pointed first in the direction of the game trail they'd used to descend from the tableland and then out across the ragged bluffs to the north and east.

"Third and fourth sections, mount up," she heard Whittaker call. She climbed aboard Athena smoothly and nudged the whinnie toward the soldiers. Astride Scout once again, Moorefield trotted toward her.

"One more thing," he called.

"Yes?"

His lips were a tight, thin line. "If Sergeant Whittaker asks you to do something, please do it. There will be a good reason he's asking. I know you've had some experience in the field, but this is one time I can't have you not following Top's orders—or even his advice or requests. So if, for example, he tells you to stay somewhere, we need you to stay the hell there. Do you understand, Aliza?"

A bolt of electricity shot down her spine. Aliza's mouth fell open, and she snapped it closed. With a nod, she acknowledged Moorefield's request without trusting herself to speak. Her words wouldn't have been something she could explain in the time they had. Try as she might, she could not stop hearing Ben Mazza's voice insisting she do the same thing, just before he'd disappeared over the hill above the Nahal Kziv.

And never came back.

Bo watched the screening party under Whittaker and Aliza gallop east along the edge of the bluffs. He hoped they would quickly find a viable route up the steep sides of the tableland. He chuckled. "Hope" was not a term he associated with combat. His last Army squadron commander, before he'd done his tour in Mogadishu, had been a career light infantryman placed in charge of a cavalry unit almost against his will. His view of mounted operations skewed far into the negative range. Lieutenant Colonel Peabody wasn't a negative person, but his view of things was both realistic and memorable. Among his favorite sayings was that hope was not a method. No real comeback for that axiom, Bo admitted.

He gave the departing patrol one last long glance and then turned back to the towing operation, intent on getting the last two vehicles up the hill as quickly as the first two so he could support—and protect—his screen as soon as possible.

Sublete was waiting, radio handset outstretched as Bo turned in his direction. "Sir? OP Two."

Bo took the handset from Sublete. "Saber Six, go."

"Saber Six, OP Two. Relay from orbital assets via Glass Palace. Regimental-sized enemy force moving your direction. Estimated distance to your location is twenty-three kilometers. Estimated speed of lead elements is forty-one kilometers per hour. ETA to you is less than three zero minutes. Acknowledge. Over."

The gnawing sensation in his gut threatened to burgeon into nausea.

"OP Two, roger. Relay to Glass Palace: acknowledged. We are Charlie Mike. Over." Charlie Mike meant continuing the mission. He'd picked up the slang from the Vietnam veterans and while not established procedure, it seemed to fit best.

"Saber Six. Acknowledged and wilco. Out."

Thirty minutes.

Shit.

There wasn't time to lament the timing or the situation. The third stalled vehicle, towed by two whinnies and their riders from the second section, strained against the straps for a moment before the broken platform rolled forward slowly.

Bo watched the creeping progress. Every rotation of the platform's wheels produced a squealing sound.

"Sounds like a bad bearing. Maybe a few," Sublete said.

"You have a maintenance background?"

The young sandy haired soldier shook his head. "Not in the army, sir. But around the farm, everything had a bad bearing at one time or another."

Bo nodded and analyzed the entire operation for a moment and tried not to wince. The pace of the third vehicle was nothing like the previous two. Bo calculated the two whinnies had towed both previous vehicles up the pass in less than fifteen minutes. That would not be the case with the remaining two tacticals.

"Sergeant Cook?" Bo called over to the section leader. "Get the last one tied up and moving. We're short on time. Might be tight up there, but it's necessary to reduce the interval."

"Aw, hell," Bo heard Sublete mutter under his breath.

He glanced toward the moving vehicle and saw that's its forward momentum was half of what it had been in the loose soil. Even with four soldiers pushing it at ground level, the vehicle barely moved forward.

"Cook! Get a third whinnie on that vehicle. Push it if you have to."

"Copy, sir." The young sergeant whirled his mount and called for another whinnie and rider to get behind the vehicle and push. As awkward as that position was, the whinnie used its chest and left front leg to grab the rear of the platform near the ammunition supply deck and pushed. Moving on three legs didn't seem to bother the animal, and several of the other whinnies made low, rumbling sounds. Bo heard and felt Scout make the same sound, and he instinctively patted the animal's neck.

"You like what you're seeing, don't you?" Bo said in a low voice. "You get us, don't you? I don't think you know what we're saying, but you get it, huh?"

Scout turned his long neck hard to the left and faced Bo for a short moment. He snorted once and returned his gaze to the towing of the third platform, as did Bo. It was moving at a better pace, made the first switchback turn, and headed up the winding, two-kilometer trail. Bo looked around. There were a few indigs and soldiers left from the raiding party along with two whinnies from the second section and himself. It would have to be enough.

"C'mon, Scout." Bo nudged his mount toward the rear of the fourth vehicle. "We're gonna do the same thing, buddy. Give it a push."

Scout moved forward without being nudged, and Bo shook his head. Murphy and the others needed to know what they'd discovered. There was no doubt the whinnies understood the situation. Several of them stamped their feet anxiously.

If we had more harnesses, we could lash up a whole damned team of them. That would get these things moving.

"Hey, sir?" Sublete called behind him. "That one's in pretty bad shape."

Bo glanced back over his shoulder. "The vehicle? What's wrong with it?"

"Sir, I ain't sure it's gonna move much at all," Sublete said. "Both of the back wheels look shot and the axle is bent. Looks like it took a hit or two on the retreat. Got shot up good."

Bo turned back to the vehicle and saw exactly what Sublete meant. He hadn't had the time to give the vehicles more than a cursory look at first. But as luck—*or Murphy's Law?*—would have it, the first two vehicles had been the good ones. It was the last two that were much worse for wear. In fact, where the rear axle should have run straight through the rear of the fourth vehicle's frame, there was a definite curve.

The damned thing's gonna wobble like one of those wooden duck toys. Bo shook his head. *We're lucky it made it this far.*

"Sergeant Cook!" Bo yelled. "Give me one rider back here. We're gonna double the push on this one with the whinnies."

"Yes, sir," Cook replied and spun his own whinnie toward the soldiers who remained at the base of the trail.

Bo looked over the dismounted troops left from the raiding party: they looked tired and dehydrated, but still ready. "You men, get moving. Stay between these two vehicles in case we need your help to recover them. Lock and load. Grab anything else that needs to get up the trail and move out."

Scout took his position next to another whinnie, a lighter-colored female, behind the fourth vehicle. With two whinnies in front and two behind, the vehicle lurched forward and moved up the trail. It wobbled worse than Bo had predicted, but it kept moving. After a minute, they lurched into the first of the winding turns, clearing the close rock outcroppings on either side by scant inches. Bo risked a glance at his ancient ticking watch.

We're gonna make it.

Chapter Twenty-Five

R'BAK

Away from the tight draw where the main trail ascended to the lip of the tableland, the scrub brush thinned. At the head of the column, Aliza saw Whittaker gesture with his arms out like wings and the rest of the experienced riders swung outward in a triangular formation the soldiers called a wedge. As she rode, she saw at least a couple of her section looking at her for instruction or direction. She repeated the same gesture as Whittaker at the front of the formation. Her section of six riders swept out behind her in a similar wedge of their own, doubling the amount of dust kicked up by the formation.

She couldn't help but grin. Athena galloped forward at a steady, manageable pace, and the sensation she was truly and absolutely free washed over her. R'Bak was a far cry from southern Germany, but that didn't matter. In fact, maybe that helped. For the first time since Palestine, she felt like she belonged. The joy of their ride was palpable. Every time she'd been astride a whinnie, she'd almost forgotten about Dachau.

Back on Earth, all she'd wanted to do was go home, but there hadn't been a home. She'd listened to Ben Mazza and others that their future was in Palestine, but ultimately that hadn't even been an option. Alive in a future so removed from that earlier time and place, it was easier to simply focus on moving as one with Athena and, for the first time in as long as she could remember, being in and enjoying the moment. Just that and nothing else.

The dust cloud to the west continued to grow. Riding hard, they kept a steady pace that would have fatigued a modern horse within twenty minutes. They pushed north, following the near-vertical face of the tableland's margin. Red-orange cliffs glowed in the light of R'Bak's star. Along the edges, at almost symmetrical distances, bluffs extended from the escarpment into the lower plains. Whether wind, water, or something else had carved them, the rocky spurs shielded at least a part of the terrain between each. One of those tight, dark draws had to have a trail up to the tableland and from there, a way home.

A way home.

That she considered R'Bak and the Lost Soldiers as her home didn't strike Aliza as ironic. It was a progression, of sorts. Acceptance of the fate dealt to her was no small task. Yet, with no one around her dedicated to the project of exterminating her and the people from which she was descended, there was hope, once again. And as long as there was hope, she remembered her father saying often, there was light. And light would always prevail.

Given time and heart, Aliza, anything is possible.

Racing east along the bluffs, Aliza saw Whittaker turn his whinnie to the right, toward one of the rocky bluffs. There was enough of a curvature to the hump of rock that a pass, whether washed out by erosion or something else, was likely. That would give them a way up to the higher ground. Above the draw, the pitch of the terrain increased to near vertical in places. If they could get up there, the enemy might not give chase. In the shadows of the morning light, there seemed to be some open areas near the bluff. Perhaps they were even enough to maneuver around and through.

Aliza felt her mount pivot toward the draw without any pressure on the reins and grinned. Bo was right. They knew. Somehow, the big friendly animals knew more about humans and their intentions than should have been possible.

Let's hope that's enough to save the day.

A kilometer up the pass, the tight scrub brush along either side of the trail dwindled enough that Bo could see the entire northern horizon. What he saw chilled him. The dust cloud marking the enemy's approach hadn't only doubled in size, but it appeared to be broad enough that it might still span the distance between the ready vehicles and his patrol, and the screen line being raised by Whittaker and Turan's rapid transit across the front of the tableland. Time was always the most perishable resource in a combat operation, and now, with the enemy already maneuvering to intercept, it was against them.

"Sublete!" he called over his shoulder. The RTO had taken up a position a few meters behind the center of the vehicle that Bo and Scout were pushing from the left rear. "Call OP One. They are to fall back up the game trail and plot TRPs along the way. Authorize them to call for fire as necessary. I want our mortars covering that pathway. Got it?"

"Word for word, sir," Sublete replied. Almost immediately, Bo heard the young radio operator giving OP One the instructions to shutter their operations forward and race back to the tableland proper. Target reference points would provide the limited mortar support from the rear with a means of rapidly zeroing in on that likely avenue of approach. Every single way up the tableland's escarpment had been targeted, just like the pass they had been operating in. Every good defensive plan provided a contingency to deal with every possible avenue of attack. In this case, they had to rely upon mortars. The only other way to deter enemy advances would have been minefields and obstacle emplacements, but they hadn't had the time, supplies, or equipment for those. The lack of emplaced obstacles was particularly unfortunate because that meant there was no way to slow down attackers. The only option was to distract and lure them into a pre-selected engagement area. Assuming Whittaker and Turan found a way back up to the top of the tableland. And assuming it was a place where contingency Charlie could be applied to maximum effect.

Scout shuffled in the loose soil and rock of the path, and the vehicle's forward progress hitched. The other whinnies at their side and the two in front strained and kept the vehicle moving. Bo felt rather than saw Scout get his feet under him. The big whinnie leaned against the broken vehicle with an audible grunt that sounded distinctly angry. Bo couldn't help but smile.

"C'mon, Scout." He leaned down over the whinnie's neck. "You got this, buddy."

The second switchback up the trail—at roughly the halfway point of the two-kilometer journey—was the narrowest part. The two towing whinnies rode shoulder-to-shoulder as they made the turn. Bo and Sergeant Cook struggled to fit their mounts in the space. Large rock formations shielded both sides of the trail, pinching its width down to three meters. To make matters worse, the pitch of the trail increased to a good seven percent incline. Back on Earth, powerful tractor-trailers with full loads struggled to make it up that kind of hill. The wobbling axle ground against both wheels and the vehicle lurched in multiple directions at once.

"Yah!" To his right, Bo saw Cook kick his whinnie hard in the side. Nothing changed. His mount was working as hard as it could to shove the vehicle with its left foreleg while digging its rear legs into the dirt for any kind of purchase. "Yah!"

The mount trumpeted again, and Bo heard Scout snort loudly and flinch his neck to look over his shoulder. The flash of anger caught Bo off guard, but he understood. They were doing all they could and didn't need outside encouragement.

"Cook!" Bo leaned over. "Don't kick her again."

Cook's entire face was a question. "Sir?"

"They're giving it all they can already. They're not like horses or mules." Bo pointed at his reins. "When's the last time you really had to guide her?"

"What do you mean, sir?"

"Have you done a damned thing to get her to put a shoulder into that vehicle? To push with three legs like that? Did you even think that was possible?"

Cook's face regained composure and realization at the same instant. "Oh, shit! Er…Sir. You're right."

Scout trumpeted softly. Bo wondered if he meant to say something like "Finally." Or maybe Scout had recognized that the entire unit at Camp Stark seemed to use "Oh, Shit" as their motto.

"Let them do their thing. All we gotta do is—"

Metal squealed as the axle bent sharply near the left rear wheel. The gun platform crashed into the dirt just as Bo and Scout, driving forward and right behind the wheel, saw it shear away. The sound was similar to an explosion, so loud that the whinnies flinched. Scout, leaning heavily into the vehicle, only had enough time to flinch backward.

Bo couldn't seize the reins fast enough. There was the brief sensation of flying backward, untethered through the air until he hit the ground. And then—

Nothing.

Do you remember that night at the enology lab? Out in the vineyard? I do. I remember the clouds were indigo in the reflected city lights. The rains were long gone, and we sat out there on a blanket and watched soundless lightning race along the underside of the thunderheads up toward Tupelo. You tried so hard to be romantic. Roses and wine. It was sweet, but for a second date it wasn't much. You asked me about it later. Why hadn't I been ready to kiss you? Do you remember where we went after that? That I needed to drop off an assignment at Justin's apartment? And he wasn't there, so we went back to my apartment and watched a movie?

I think about that night a lot. If Justin had been there, I wouldn't have come back to your car. I wouldn't have gone out with you anymore. I shouldn't have kept going because I knew. I thought—I told myself—you were good enough.

But I knew better.

Bo came awake with a start, wiping at his warm, wet face frantically and checking his palm for blood. Instead, he saw thick globs of clear liquids filled with the tiny bubbles of spittle. Above him, Scout was staring down at him with an expectant, if not concerned, look on his angular face. The whinnie made a deep-throated sound oddly like a cat's purr and stepped back as Bo sat up, rubbing the back of his head.

"Easy, sir." Sergeant Cook was at his side with a compress. "You've got a nasty knot back there, but no blood. You okay?"

As he sat up, the world swam from left to right and back again violently. He blinked several times in succession to clear his vision. The pain began as a small buzz and grew until it filled his head and threatened to block out everything.

"How long was I out?"

Cook shrugged. "Less than a minute. Gave us a good scare, though. Never seen a whinnie get so scared, either. He was all over you, licking your face and scratching the ground. I think you're right about them, sir. I think they really care for us."

Bo nodded and instantly regretted the slight movement of his head. He blinked again, and his dizziness abated. "Help me up," he asked Cook. The sergeant stood and extended a hand, which Bo took. As he stood, Bo felt better but still wobbly. He'd hit his head plenty on armored vehicles and knew the feeling and how to operate with it. He rubbed the back of his head and gingerly probed the swollen spot. It wasn't an open wound, but he'd still need it checked.

"Bird went with the first vehicle, didn't he?" Bo asked. The diminutive medic was nowhere in sight.

"Yes, sir."

Bo laughed. "Dammit. You don't have any aspirin, do you?"

Cook shook his head. "You want me to send for Bird? He can get back down here and throw it over to us from the other side of the wreck."

"No time," Bo grunted.

He studied the collapsed tactical that was wedged solidly in the middle of the tight trail. There was no way it would move in any direction without divine intervention or serious explosives.

"Mission failure," he said and spat in the R'Baku dirt.

"That ain't your fault, sir." Cook replied.

"The hell it's not." Bo fought the urge to kick at the dirt he'd spat in.

"We did the best we could," Cook offered.

Bo slapped at the dirt on his legs with both hands. "We should have gotten down the pass faster."

Cook said nothing in response. He didn't have to. The commander was always the one to blame. No matter if his intentions were honorable and good. The mission had been to recover the entire raiding party and the vehicles they'd secured. Of paramount interest were the gun platforms, and while twenty-three out of twenty-four wasn't bad, they were not going to get the final vehicle up the pass. For Bo, that was tantamount to failure.

"Saber Six, this is OP Two, over."

Bo gestured for Sublete and the radio handset, reached up for it with a grunt, and got a fresh bolt of dull, throbbing pain down his spine. "Saber Six, go."

"Saber Six, we've got visual contact with lead enemy elements. Estimate they're fifteen klicks out and have slowed their advance. The lead formation has sighted the screen and diverted almost fully in that direction. How copy?"

Bo took a breath and held it for a moment before releasing it. The plan was working so far. "Good copy, OP Two. What else?"

"Sir, confirming the lead element is a regimental-sized force. Two battalions are line abreast in the front of the formation."

Bo blinked. "Say again your last?"

The RTO repeated the report and Bo almost wobbled back to the ground. A *regiment*? Heading straight toward sections three and four? He exhaled slowly. He'd been right; this was not a cat he'd be able to skin. This was a cat he had to kill. He nodded, depressed the key on the handset. "Copy, OP Two. Relay that SITREP to Starkpatch, coded for immediate relay to Glass Palace. Relay to Saber Nine, I am en route with reinforcements. Time now. Saber Six, out."

He ran his fingers through his sweaty hair and realized his hat was missing. In the intense radiation of R'Bak's two stars, skin cancers and melanoma were all too real a possibility. He turned a slow circle and found his boonie hat. With the care and patience of a much older man, he bent forward and grabbed it from the ground. As he stood up to his full height, the pain and the wobbling sensation weren't anywhere near what they had been before. His adrenaline had kicked in at the most opportune time. If they didn't get a move on, his idea to counterattack the J'Stull as they chased the screen wouldn't materialize.

Bo took a quick breath and exhaled it just as quickly to clear his mind and felt one of his ears pop involuntarily. He shook his head, albeit gently, and looked up at Cook who was the only senior leader on the downhill side of the vehicle.

"Get everyone on the other side of the wreck up the pass, right now. Send a mount to the vehicles. Tell them to stand by and not start any engines until I tell them to. We're gonna ride for the screen and hope like hell they've found a pass."

Cook nodded and bounced his whinnie up to the vehicle and called over the platform for the others to fall back to the vehicles. As he looked around, Bo counted: Cook, Sublete and their whinnies were with him on the downslope from the wreck. Four soldiers from the raiding party and two indig guides were with them as well. He gestured at them and then back down the trail. "Double up on the whinnies and get to the bottom ASAP. Mount up on a vehicle and get ready to attack. We're not playing defense anymore."

Seeing the dismounted troops scramble aboard the available mounts took some of the weight of command off his shoulders. He raised the handset again. "OP Two, the pass is blocked. Personnel upslope of the block are recovering in your direction. Report when they rendezvous with recovery forces. Break."

He released the transmit button and then pressed it again two seconds later. Old habits died hard. "Relay to Saber Nine, we're en route. Need their location and route. Over."

"Saber Six, OP Two. Good copy. Will relay to Saber Nine when we can see them again. Over."

"You don't have eyes on them now?" Bo asked, incredulous.

"Negative, sir. We haven't seen them for over ten minutes. They're too close to the bluffs down there. Lost radio contact at the same time. Over."

Bo ran a hand over his face and placed his tongue between his teeth as though intending to bite his words back. He had failed.

"Sonuvabitch!"

Chapter Twenty-Six

R'BAK

As Athena bolted up the narrow gap and bounced from outcrop to outcrop, Aliza clenched the reins with every ounce of strength in her hands. She clamped her legs in the saddle to hold her in position atop the whinnie. Hands and legs burned from the effort, and she realized she'd been holding her breath. Forcing herself to breathe, Aliza bounced in the makeshift saddle again as Athena scrambled toward, and then up, a vertical face only a few meters high. Aliza gasped at the speed and audacity of the move. The speed of the climb shocked her. On the mostly flat, rocky ground of the tableland and surrounding desert, the animals were graceful and fast. But she'd seen no evidence of the almost gravity-defying climbing ability that Athena had demonstrated. Slipping over the top of the wall in less than three seconds, the whinnie moved uphill and deeper into the brush, the other whinnies trailing behind her.

Aliza pulled back gently on the reins. "Slow down, girl. Let's wait for the others."

Athena grunted and continued moving forward at a slow walk. The whinnie didn't want to slow down but understood Aliza's intent. As they climbed up the hill through the scrub brush, the narrow passage around the craggy bluff opened onto a wider area. While the brush seemed thicker and more pervasive, Aliza realized that Athena's meandering path was purposeful. The whinnie chose her path to avoid thickets and anything that would distract her rider.

To their left, the draw climbed up the mountain into a thicker forest that appeared to level out into a tight, but extended, valley that curved toward the northern rim of the tableland. There was no sign of how far it stretched. On their right, toward the summit location of OP Two, large, recent rock falls covered most of the area. Boulders the size of automobiles littered the landscape that would have given them the fastest way up to the high shelf of land. Aliza saw Athena stare up that slope for a moment before angling back to the left.

"What have you got, girl?"

Athena pressed ahead, faster now. Aliza looked over her shoulder and saw the rest of the patrol scrambling up the hill toward the vertical face they'd climbed. None of the whinnies appeared to have any trouble duplicating her feat. Aliza relaxed and let Athena pick up her pace.

As they climbed into the forested area, the intense heat relented and Aliza could feel a cool—well, less hot—breeze on her skin. She wiped a sleeve across her forehead and reached for a canteen on her load-bearing equipment harness—olive drab canvas "H" straps attached to a pistol belt with a metal clasp. It wasn't the most comfortable apparatus she'd ever worn, but it carried canteens, ammunition, her M1911 pistol, and a couple of other pouches with ease.

The water was cool and good, and Aliza drank greedily. As she slipped the canteen back into its container, the rustling of the taller tree-like plants filled the little valley with a peaceful sound. But there was something else on the wind.

"Whoa, girl." Aliza tugged the reins and Athena stopped. Closing her eyes, Aliza put her entire focus on the sensory input from her ears. In the breeze, there was a barely audible trickling sound.

Water.

She smiled. *I knew it! All we had to do was search up along this side of the tableland.*

Turning her head slowly, Aliza tried to locate the sound. She tugged Athena in that direction and the big whinnie trotted up the slope and between several copses of trees. In the center of a group of five trees was a small pool only a few feet across. On the uphill side of the pool there was a rock overhang. The water in the pool emerged from underground.

A spring.

She followed the flow from the overhang, through the pool, to a narrow stream that flowed for about five meters before it darted back underground. There was no sign that the spring returned to the surface anywhere in their vicinity. A lucky find.

Aliza laughed to herself and shook her head in disbelief. She studied the pool and her eyes grew wide in recognition. Several very familiar and very rare plants blossomed at the edge of the water. She wanted to dismount and see them up close, but she remained in the saddle. There was no way of telling if the water was safe enough for them to—

Athena stepped forward and lapped at the pool for several seconds. Satisfied, the whinnie raised her head and turned back to look at Aliza. Her dark eyes almost glittered. If it could have laughed, she imagined the whinnie would have.

Aliza's mouth fell open. "You knew."

Athena made a purring sound and stepped to the left of the pool and the tiny stream and continued up the valley. Dumbstruck in the saddle, Aliza didn't react until they'd gone twenty meters beyond the spring. She looked back toward the pool and couldn't see it.

"What the hell?" She listened for a moment and could still hear it. The perfectly camouflaged pool wasn't something casually seen or located. A very lucky find.

No. A deliberate one. They led us here.

The sound of an approaching whinnie at a fast trot caught her attention, and she turned to see Whittaker riding toward her.

He pointed over at the hidden pool. "Aliza? Did you see that?"

She smiled. "I did. Athena drank from it. They knew it was here."

He shook his head. "I'll be damned."

Aliza brushed her dusty clothes. "Seems that way. What do you want to do?"

Whittaker pointed up the valley. "Follow this around the bend as far as it goes. There has to be another way up to the tableland. If Athena wants us to go that way, we probably should."

Aliza pointed at the radio handset on Whittaker's harness. Unlike Captain Moorefield, he'd chosen to carry the heavy radio himself. "We should report this."

Whittaker grunted and reached for the handset. "I'll try. Line-of-sight to OP Two has been terrible."

Aliza swept back a lock of her hair the freshening breeze was fluttering across her face. She turned toward the west and saw a low cloud on the—

Not a low cloud. An enormous dust cloud. *They're coming after us.*

"Sergeant Whittaker?"

He paused and looked where she stared. "OP Two, Saber Nine. Over."

A static-filled voice replied. "Saber Nine, OP Two. Be advised enemy attacking in your direction. Saber Six is en route to your position now. Advise you find a way up to the tableland fast. Over."

Whittaker turned back to the curving, narrowing valley. "Negative, OP Two. Relay to Saber Six, we're preparing a hasty defense. Tell him to bust his ass and join us. I'll hang a lantern for him. Out."

"A lantern? It's full daylight?" Aliza asked.

"An expression. I'll post a guide down below to get them up here in a hurry. We've got other things to do right now."

"As in preparing a defense instead of climbing up and over?" Aliza asked. "Isn't that Captain Moorefield's decision?"

"He knows the stakes, Aliza." Whittaker frowned. "They're moving too fast, and we have the advantage of the high ground here. If they get up on the tableland, they won't stop until they roll up everything we have. Our job was to deceive *and delay* the enemy, and that's exactly what we have to do. We hold them here at least until he can slam those stolen vehicles into their flank."

"You're certain?"

Whittaker grinned. "It's what I'd do."

Whittaker's report was exactly what Bo wanted to hear and his own plan of action crystallized. The immobile gun platform sitting utterly broken in the middle of the trail's tightest section had become a solution, rather than a problem. The craggy rock formations pinning it from either side restricted movement in the immediate area. Leaving the trail to cut a new path up the pass would take a significant investment in time and blood. While their enemy might have the resolve to do so, the trail's blockage could be used to channelize them to wherever Bo wanted them to go.

Until they get the vehicle out of there, that is. Which they might very well be able to accomplish, given the larger vehicles they'd seen in reconnaissance. Yanking the broken vehicle out with something more powerful than a handful of whinnies wouldn't be that hard. Bo studied the rocks on either side and smiled.

Unless it is so jammed that even vehicles can't get it out of the way.

He grabbed the handset from Sublete and thumb-stabbed the transmit button. "OP Two, relay to Seeker Six. Need their sappers or demo team at the block point to detonate this vehicle and the surrounding rock formations. I want them to collapse the pass completely at this location. Over."

"Saber Six, OP Two. Roger all. TRP set on location and we'll get the sappers moving that direction immediately. Over."

"OP Two, roger that. I'm moving to Saber Nine now," Bo said. He took a quick breath. "Contact Saber Nine for grid coordinates in front of their positions and standby for contingency Charlie at my command. Saber Six, out."

He handed the handset back to Sublete and nodded at the young man. The young soldier projected confidence. "Ready to move, sir."

Bo pointed at Sublete's mount. "You've ridden him at a full gallop before?"

"A couple of times. A few minutes, tops."

"Then hang on for dear life, son." Bo wheeled Scout to the east and waved at Cook. "When we get to the bottom, dismount and find a vehicle. Leave your whinnie; it'll be fine. We'll mount up and attack to the north, into their flank. Once we blow up the pass, they'll take the bait and commit fully toward our screen. That's when we'll hit them. You'll be the lead vehicle in the attack."

"Yes, sir!" Cook nudged his mount, and the whinnie launched into a trot that quickly became a full gallop across the desert.

"Go, Sublete. I'm right behind you." The RTO and his mount sped after Cook with a good interval between them. Anything they could do to confuse, confound, and slow down the enemy would be the priority. From the upslope side of the collapsed vehicle, Bo heard a group of whinnies approaching.

He didn't wait for them to dismount and prepare the explosives. "C'mon, Scout!" He tapped the whinnie's side gently. "Time to put steel on target."

Once out of the pass, Bo rode straight for the ragged line of vehicles concealed in the rocks and scrub. Cook was near the center and gestured toward a six-wheeled vehicle with a fat, wide turret on top of its hull. Its two large cannons pointed out over the front windows. They moved slightly from left to right and Bo knew they were already seeing, and tracking, the enemy.

He was already working his feet out of the stirrups and Scout's harness as they slid to a stop. He dismounted the whinnie and saw Scout's triangular head turn his way. The animal's eyes were calm and focused, and despite their frantic pace down the mesa, he appeared to be breathing normally.

"Go home, Scout." Bo turned around and made for the vehicles. The whinnie didn't move. He pointed up the steep skirts of the tableland toward their compound and paddock. "Scout! Go home."

Scout trumpeted softly. The tone was deep and mournful, but the whinnie turned and trotted toward the bottom of the slope and made its way to the north. The other dismounted whinnies followed.

Bo watched them for a second until Specialist Sublete appeared at his shoulder. "Sir, Saber Nine."

"Saber Nine, Six, go," Bo said into the handset.

"Confirm that OpFor regiment is advancing in three echelons. Forward elements are two, I say again, two mechanized infantry battalions. More or less. They're moving toward our position now in a line abreast formation. Third echelon is behind them a couple of klicks or so. They appear to be heavy indirect fire weapons. Not artillery pieces, but with elevated tubes and smaller bores. Probably mortar carriers. How copy?"

Bo clenched and relaxed his jaw. "Good copy. Anything else?"

"We're in a solid defensive position, sir. What are your intentions? Over."

"Counterattack. We'll hit the southernmost echelon first. Either kill them or turn them toward the others. Based on the cloud, I don't think we'll intercept the further echelon until they're on top of your position."

"Looks like that to me, too, sir. We'll hold the second echelon provided their artillery isn't accurate." Whittaker paused. "If it is, we've got some secondary positions identified."

It will have to do.

Cook pointed at the big vehicle. "Sir, you're in this one. Sublete is on the next vehicle over."

Bo nodded and turned to Sublete. "Flag me down if the shit hits the fan."

"Yes, sir," Sublete replied and went to his vehicle.

"You've got Private Jackson and Private Cleric onboard this one, sir. It's rough around the edges but can hammer armor from what the indigs tell us." Cook moved toward the vehicle and kept talking. "There's a hatch up top. You'll probably want to use it: old-school everything in this bucket."

"Thanks, Cook. Good hunting," Bo said and scrambled up onto the quiet vehicle using rungs on the right rear of the vehicle's hull. He crossed over the engine deck and stepped easily onto the turret. An oval hatch in the center of the turret beckoned. He stooped and swung his legs down, putting his body halfway into the turret. He felt around with his soles and found a small shelf where he could stand. *Some things are the same wherever you go*. The amount of bodily exposure while standing in the hatch reminded him of the M1 Abrams.

There was a rudimentary headset hanging on the lip of the hatch. He slipped it over his head and heard the two soldiers talking over the crew intercom.

"Crew report," Bo said.

"Driver ready, sir," Jackson replied.

"Gunner ready, sir," Cleric said. "I'm below you and to your left. Jackson is in the hull. We have eighty rounds aboard and we're ready to go."

Bo smiled. *Not bad for making it up as we go.*

"Standby for ignition short count," Bo called. "We have no radios with the others, correct?"

"Not really, sir. Some data sharing at my console, but direct comms are inoperable," Cleric said. "Gotta do it the old-fashioned way."

"Roger that," Bo replied. *Let's hope everyone remembers hand and arm signals.*

He stood in the hatch and looked in both directions. Every vehicle had at least one crew member looking his way. He waved the signal for "attention" and followed it with the sign for "prepare to move." As he made the circular motion, he called to Jackson. "Start in three, two, one."

The vehicle growled to life under him. The other vehicles seemed to answer with their own roars and turbine-screams. Bo held both arms out to his sides indicating a line formation and ensured that all the crews saw him. He gave them the signal to move forward, and the line rumbled into the scrub and picked up speed.

"What can you see, Cleric?"

"It's got a decent thermal type sight, sir. I can see the first battalion now. We're coming in on their flank."

Bo kept his eyes on the formation. He pumped his fist into the sky several times. "Floor it, Jackson! As soon as we're in range, Cleric, pick your targets and start firing."

"Yes, sir!" both men answered in unison.

The vehicle picked up speed and bounced across the rocky terrain. Bo grabbed at the edge of the hatch for safety and wished there was any type of machine gun mount there to hold on to. His time aboard the Abrams, with its .50 caliber machine gun mount on the commander's hatch, had spoiled him.

Cleric fired, the twin cannons discharging a half-second apart. What rounds they fired Bo could not track as there was no tracer element. However, when they impacted the side of a similar vehicle in the attacking column, the results were spectacular. Along the line, Bo watched his vehicles fire and adjust into the marching battalion. The attackers never had a chance.

"Hell, yeah!" Cleric yelled over the intercom. The turret swiveled to the right and fired again. Another vehicle, this one a dune-buggy-thing full of infantry, detonated in a bright orange fireball. "They've gotta be seven hundred meters away!"

Bo agreed based on what he could see. As the surprise effect waned, the enemy formation did not veer off to flee, but instead turned into the approaching Lost Soldier formation for a counterattack. From his position at the center of the line, Bo saw the edges starting to slow and push his formation into a vee shape. He flagged down the vehicles on the extreme left as Cleric kept up a steady rate of fire, locating, ranging, and engaging one target after another. The line sped up and closed with the surprised enemy.

As the distance between the formations closed, the firefight began in earnest. One of Bo's vehicles on the right side of the line exploded as they charged into the enemy flank. They hit another on his left, which heeled to a stop, smoking sullenly. But his attack kept moving forward and putting rounds downrange. Accurate rounds, whereas a great deal of the J'Stull shots went wild. *Because it must be just like the locals told us,* Bo thought with a nod at the absent indigs: *almost none of the OpFor have any significant training.* In fact, if the intel was as correct as it seemed to be, most were just strong-arm enforcers.

Cleric fired again and again. Dust and smoke obscured more and more of the enemy formation. Bo frantically signaled his line to slow down, but they kept charging forward into the cloud. One second, Bo could see the battlefield and the next, the white and brown cloud encircled them. A flash of movement caught his eye, and he spun to see an enemy vehicle with a wide-bored gun tube pointed in his direction.

"Contact left!" he called.

Cleric swung the turret hard left as Jackson yanked the vehicle in the opposite direction. Bo lost his grip on the hatch ring. One moment he was standing in the hatch; the next, the vehicle's lurch sent him skittering across the top of the vehicle. He slid off its side toward the rocky ground two meters below.

Shit!

He hit the ground and instinctively rolled away from his vehicle's wheels. Pain swam in from every limb and almost every part of his torso. Eyes closed and face pressed into the desert floor, Bo quickly evaluated his body by feel. Nothing was broken, but he'd have a damned hard time moving as he recovered from the impact.

He rolled over and sat up. The dust and smoke continued to swirl around him, and the sound of the battle seemed more distant to his left and right than in his immediate position.

We cut right through them.

Bo stood and patted his holster; his pistol was missing. He searched the ground nearby but didn't see the weapon. A round of some type whistled through the air above his head. Scared into action, he dashed forward to a rock outcropping only a meter high and flung himself behind it. He pushed up close to the rock and peered over its jagged edges.

There was nothing worth seeing in the nearby dust and smoke. Vehicles were burning. The sound of weapons firing and vehicles moving had almost faded to nothing. As elated as he was that the first stage of the attack had gone so well, Bo realized he was alone and unarmed amid an enemy formation's route of march. He slumped against the rock, pressing his face against the warm, rough stone. His thoughts were a sudden whirl of recollected survival skills, escape and evasion techniques, and how to find his way back to the tableland. The intense heat of R'Bak's stars hammered through the dust, but he didn't move. Instead, he took a deep breath, and with his head throbbing, sighed dejectedly.

Well, shit.

Chapter Twenty-Seven

R'BAK

No sooner had the captured vehicles attacked when the first rounds of indirect fire fell across Saber Nine's position on the high ground at the back of the draw. Aliza, with Sergeant Whittaker behind a rock outcropping, had a good view of their entire defensive front. The first rounds fell in the vicinity of the upper positions from which riflemen were laying down fire over and across the rest of the patrol. Shrapnel from the enemy shells ricocheted off the rock walls and caused little damage. Others missed their position entirely. A few made it to the more exposed positions at the top of the wall and tore them to bits.

As soon as the first barrage ended, Whittaker leapt off the front of their position to gather the wounded. His eyes looked back and caught hers as he dragged one soldier away from the forward positions; his glance was both a question and a summons. She jumped into action and helped the sergeant.

Working at different points along their line, they dragged three of the injured to more protected positions, finishing just as the second barrage fell. The enemy had improved their targeting, and the shells dropped with greater accuracy but still had little effect.

As the interval between explosions slowed, Aliza saw Sergeant Whittaker jump up from cover. As he began sprinting in her direction, a mortar round exploded ten meters behind him along the top of the escarpment.

Time seemed to slow. She saw, in terrible detail, shrapnel tear through his right leg as he ran. His next step with the left leg was fine, but as his right leg went forward to meet the ground again, it buckled and he crumpled to the ground, his shocked and anguished face just ten meters from hers. He panted, blinked—and another round detonated almost on top of him, flinging him in her direction.

Before he'd even stopped tumbling, Aliza dropped her pistol atop the rock and bounded toward him. Adrenaline flowing, she grabbed him by the shoulders and dragged him backward, to her position. More rounds rushed down, sent shrapnel sleeting. It was as if she could feel every fragment passing through the surrounding sky. One passed close enough that she felt it tug on her hair. Another missed penetrating her left boot by a fraction.

Halfway to the outcrop, she looked down at Whittaker as she strained backward, her rush of adrenaline almost expended. His eyes were closed, and his mouth was a tight, white line. Then his eyes opened, locked onto hers for a moment, and then squeezed shut again. Blood seeped from innumerable wounds and turned his olive drab fatigues a slick, wet black.

She screamed before she had even registered the frustration and rage which sent the violent sound out of her. Tears blurred her vision as she pulled Whittaker into cover and collapsed by his side. Lungs burning with the effort, she blinked away her tears and reached for Whittaker's first aid compress. His right hand touched hers, and she stopped.

"It's okay, Aliza," he wheezed. His eyes were bright and clear. Where there had been pain across his wrinkled face there was now acceptance, almost peace. "It's okay. I lived…twice. Don't mind dying twice. Not for—"

She took his hand, squeezed it. "Don't…don't leave me. Please!"

Whittaker smiled and there was a beauty to it she'd never imagined. She took his hand in both of hers. His grip weakened, failed, and his gaze became a sightless stare over her shoulder into the cloudless sky.

She lowered her face to her hands and cried. As she did, Aliza realized her tears were not just for Sergeant Whittaker, but for her family, her friends, and Ben Mazza. They were tears she'd never shed. They came with a force that surprised her, and in her grief, there was something new. In the months since Dachau—months a century and a half in the past—she'd experienced rage and frustration tinged with tiny glimpses of hope and love. Instead of clinging to those glimpses, she'd embraced the anger, tried to let it fuel her.

But tears? They were new. She could feel what they meant, what they were telling her: it was time to let them go. As she cradled Whittaker's lifeless hand in hers, a warm trickle of blood ran down across her wrist and into the crease of where her slender hand clutched the hard, broad palm of the dead sergeant. Almost calmly, she realized her right arm was bleeding from the muscles in her forearm. The pain was considerable and getting worse by the second. She also realized the barrage was over.

Aliza stood, started unevenly toward the most heavily shelled positions, determined to do exactly what she and Whittaker had done before. There was risk of course, and they might all be trapped in a future none of them wanted, but they were here and the only way they'd ever see Earth again was to take care of each other.

And that, she decided as she scrambled forward, was better than rage and frustration.

Bo took off his uniform blouse and draped it over his head and shoulders. The sounds of the attack intensified in the north. Every report sent a bolt of pain through his head. As much as he wanted to follow it, he was alone and there were still enemy vehicles and personnel surrounding his position. Either they would retreat or move to re-consolidate with their surviving forces. It was a matter of time. Without a weapon, transportation, or water, Bo knew his best choice was to stay put even as the clouds of failure swirled through his mind. It hadn't been a perfect plan, but he'd been confident in its success.

It could be succeeding. You're just stuck out here because you fell off your fucking mount, Bo.

On cue, Sharron's words came to mind. *You always think things rely on you. You're so self-centered sometimes I can't even believe it. All I wanted was for you to care about me. About us. You cared more about things you thought had gone wrong or that slighted you somehow. My life isn't about you, Bo. Not anymore.*

He shook his head and strained to peer over the top of his rock-strewn position. Movement caught his eye in both directions. There was no way he could move. Not for a while at least. He settled back against the rock and hung his head to his chest in resignation. The breeze freshened slightly in his face and he raised his eyes enough that he saw his missing boonie hat caught in a cactus-like plant a few meters away. He crawled forward and reached for the hat—

The sound of several rifles firing nearby rang out. Bo flinched away from the hat even as his brain told him they weren't firing at him. He leaned forward and snatched the hat away from the plant and heard a deep, throaty roar. A whinnie charged directly toward him at full gallop.

Not just any whinnie. Bo grinned and got up to a low crouch. He slapped the hat on his head and worked his arms through the sleeves of his blouse. There wasn't time to finish buttoning it up before Scout reared up and bounced to a stop in front of him.

As Scout settled in front of Bo, streaks of dark purplish blood streamed from several wounds on the whinnie's side. Bo stood and went to him. The bullet holes were small, and he counted ten of them on the right side of Scout's neck. His first impulse was to grab his field dressing and tear the package open to press it against the worst of the wounds.

Scout hooted and slammed Bo's shoulder with his triangular jaw. The whinnie jerked its chin toward the saddle and hooted again, this time much deeper.

He wants me to get aboard.

"You sure, buddy?"

Scout made the deep purring sound and then shook his head and body, not unlike a dog trying to dry itself after a dip in a lake.

He's telling you he's okay, Bo. He's shaking it off.

My God, we're communicating.

Rounds impacted nearby, but Scout held his ground. A gun-shy mount would have bolted, but Scout stood resolute. Bo climbed aboard and patted Scout's left forward shoulder, the one opposite of the wounds. "We can do this, buddy. Get me to Athena and the others."

Scout took off again, this time back to the east and the distant tableland. From the very first time he'd galloped a horse at fourteen, Bo learned a valuable lesson. Moving that fast astride an animal, especially one built for speed, distorted time and distance. On the farm, he'd intended to only ride his first horse, Maverick, for two minutes at a gallop before slowing down. He'd judged that he could ride to the far posts of the main pasture and back in that timeframe. When it had taken almost double that time, and Maverick was surly at him for a few days afterward, Bo had realized what had happened. A full-out gallop took a lot of energy for a horse, especially when they weren't used to running like that. Aboard Scout, he kept wanting to hold the big animal back, but Scout never relented. Though it seemed impossible, as Bo hunched over the saddle to be more aerodynamic, he thought the whinnie kept a pace far faster than they'd done on the tableland.

"Atta boy, Scout!" Bo called as they raced across the scrub. Branches tore at his boots and pants, but Bo didn't care. His eyes remained locked on the high plateau. He turned once when the dust and smoke started to thin, saw the second enemy echelon approaching a draw that appeared to be where Whittaker and the others had prepared their defense. In that same direction but in the middle distance, Bo saw a pale whinnie standing and looking toward them. He didn't immediately recognize the mount or its rider but headed toward them.

Less than a minute later, Scout skidded to a stop next to Private Morton, a gangly kid from New York with shockingly red hair. Bo smiled; Whittaker had indeed hung out a fire-topped lantern for him.

"Captain Moorefield? They reported you dead," Morton blurted.

"Not yet." Bo smiled. "Get us to Sergeant Whittaker and the others."

The redhead grinned and tugged his mount up the trail. "Follow me, sir."

They bounced up the trail for a minute, and the draw came into view. An escarpment spanned the back of it like a dried-up waterfall. About five meters tall, the wall it created was imposing and perfect for defense. At the top of the wall, and atop the nearly sheer valley slopes flanking it, Bo saw the soldiers of sections three and four manning hasty defensive positions. He smiled to himself. Whittaker had chosen those parts of the high ground with good observation and fields of fire. The experienced sergeant had also placed firing teams above them on the rocks for air defense and better geometry for the attacking force at the valley's mouth. The position was utterly defensible despite the dust and smoke swirling about them from the enemy's indirect fire attempts.

This might just work.

Whittaker had positioned the sections of four in multiple locations. Two were on the rocks above the tight valley in prone positions behind cover. They appeared to be in good shape as they opened fire. Bo couldn't see the enemy infantry, but he could hear them screaming as they ran up the draw.

Several explosions drowned out the sound of battle for a few seconds. The OpFor's indirect fire weapons weren't dropping accurate fire on the position. They couldn't see it from their position out in the valley and with no forward observer to actually plot and correct their firing solutions, they were firing blind and hoping to have some, if any, effect.

It's meant to deplete us. Harass us. Rattle us enough that their infantry rolls all over us.

Not this time.

They kept moving toward the position as a new barrage of indirect fire came down. This time the fire was more accurate. Soldiers scattered in all directions as the small, powerful explosions rocked the draw. Morton had frozen in the saddle of his mount. Bo bounded Scout around the shocked pair and raced into the position as the enemy infantry came into view at the wall below.

The artillery fire ended abruptly, and she heard the forward positions engage the infantry again as she stood. A whinnie clambered down from the rocks above. She recognized the rider and felt fresh tears fall on her cheeks as he approached at a gallop. Moorefield dismounted his whinnie and ran toward her. Words failed her and all she could do was shake her head. The young captain knelt by the body of Whittaker and touched his neck. Finding no pulse, he simply put his hand on the sergeant's shoulder and squeezed. She couldn't see his face under the brim of his floppy hat, but she felt his grief. The *crack!* of a single rifle fired from the points above them snapped both of their heads back to the wall at the mouth of the tiny valley.

He stood and looked at her. "You're in charge here, Aliza. Sergeant Cook is your platoon sergeant. I'm taking Stewart with me. Move everyone who can fire into position behind cover up here in case any of them get up here. Tell them to shoot whatever they can see and keep shooting until we come across the valley. Don't hit us."

"What are you doing?"

He smiled grimly. "Sounding the charge."

She blinked. "You're what?"

He pointed. "The whinnies can make it down the slope with us on their backs. We just have to hold on and trust them not to dump us. We'll surprise the infantry and drive them toward our vehicles. You pin them down, and we'll smoke them out."

"But that's crazy!"

"Not really." He turned back to her. "We have the advantage of moving downhill. With speed and as much firepower as we can pour on them, we can pin their infantry between us and our vehicles down there. If the mortars are ready, we can rain steel on their heads and push their regiment back long enough so we can escape up the tableland and evacuate Camp Stark."

There was a clinical logic to his thinking. Before she noticed it, she was nodding.

"You want us to stay here and harass the infantry below. Hold them in place for your charge to sweep them across to us, yes?"

"Precisely. Can you do that?"

She felt a genuine smile cross her face. "If you'd said to sit still and wait for rescue, I would have said no. We'll hold them down, Bo. Go sound your charge."

He grinned at her and reached down to Whittaker's radio. He hesitated for a moment, grabbed and holstered the fallen sergeant's pistol, and then picked up the handset. "Saber Six Romeo, Saber Six. You read me?"

"Holy shit, sir! We thought you were dead," Sublete replied.

"Alive and kicking," Bo replied. "I want you moving toward the valley entrance. Slowly. We'll scare up the infantry in your direction with a little cavalry charge. When you see that, you call for contingency Charlie. My authority. Tell the vehicle commanders to lift and shift their fire until we find cover and then let anything escaping to the west have it. Over."

"Roger, Saber Six. Good copy. Give 'em hell."

Bo dropped the radio handset and turned, shouting orders to all the riders. From up the valley, the whinnies ran back to the soldiers and knelt to be mounted. Something seemed off and after a second of staring wide-eyed, she could see there were more whinnies than riders. At least twenty had no saddles on their strong backs. They'd come with the herd.

To charge our common enemy.

The electricity of the thought spurred her to action. "Sergeant Cook!"

He looked over at her. "Yes, ma'am?"

"Gather the wounded. Everyone that can shoot gets in position behind these outcroppings. If we've got a few more who can get up on the high ground, get them up there. We don't have much time to lay down fire for the charge." She didn't wait for a response. Instead, she spun and reached down for Whittaker's radio, remembering their radio procedures by heart. "OP Two, Saber Nine, update on the mortars. Over."

There was no response. She snorted. "Then we'll just hope they get in position soon."

She grabbed Whittaker's M14 and spare magazines from his load-bearing equipment. The peace on his pale face had settled as slight creases and deeper wrinkles, like an old man who had fallen deep asleep in a hammock. She smiled and placed her hand on his. "Let's hope you're right about dying twice, my friend. Thank you. I will see you soon, but not today. Not if I can help it."

No tears came, which surprised her. There would be time for more of them, but it would not be now. She stood, cradled the rifle at what the soldiers called the low ready and ran forward toward the wall. She took up a firing position and saw the enemy infantry dismounting their vehicles and rushing toward the opening.

A sharp whistle from above caught her attention, and she spun to the right. Atop the rocks and back from the upper firing positions, she saw Bo and the others. He waved at her, and she checked the soldiers to her right and left and those at the other outcroppings. She gave him a thumbs-up and turned to the soldiers under her unlikely command. It was time to do what she hadn't been able to do for Ben Mazza and the others.

"Open fire!"

As Aliza's defensive positions rained direct fire on the infantry below, Bo turned to Sergeant Stewart halfway down the poised line of whinnies. The ones without riders surprised him, but he said nothing. Scout and the others evidently understood the stakes and, given their intelligence and disposition, they had brought the rest of the herd into the fray. The wounds on Scout's neck seeped blood, but there was no sign that the whinnie was in pain or even distracted by them. Several others had more serious wounds yet stood alongside the others on the upper surface of the eastern wall.

"We'll sweep downhill like a swinging door," Bo said. "Stewart, your side stays pinned close to the bottom of the wall as we go across. This end will sweep out, all the way toward the enemy vehicles. Move as quickly as you can. The whinnies will bound down these rocks faster than anything you've ever seen. Just hold on for dear life until you reach the floor of the draw. Once you're there, commence firing and stay in your lane. Once we hit the enemy flank, all hell will break loose. Push them south toward our vehicles. They will eventually regroup. When they do and start to return fire, find cover. Until then, watch out for each other and good hunting."

The soldiers all nodded, and their faces were more serious than he'd ever seen. Gone were any expressions of bored indifference or guarded resentment. Some of their friends lay wounded below them. A few were dead. They all knew the cost and there was nothing in their present demeanor to suggest they would shy away from it. Still, he sensed trepidation.

Bo smiled, made sure his nod was one of casual, and therefore absolute, confidence. "It'll work, guys. The 20th Maine did the same thing at Gettysburg. Won the field and likely the whole damned war that day. Just stay in line and keep firing."

Stewart waved a hand. "Sir?"

"What is it, Stewart?"

The sergeant slowly smiled. "Was just wishing we had a bugler. You know? To sound the fucking charge?"

The soldiers laughed together and their tension broke.

Bo waved one last time to Aliza. "Hell," he said loudly, "who needs a damned bugle?" He nudged Scout forward and shouted, "Charge!"

Around him, the soldiers and the whinnies raised their faces in a matching cry and raced down the hill together, straight toward the flank of the J'Stull infantry.

"Go, Scout! I'm with you." Bo wrapped the reins around his hands and squeezed the whinnie tightly with his legs. Scout bounced between two rocks and then shot downhill in a series of bounds that took Bo's breath away. The last leap took them to mostly level ground. Through the brush on both sides, he saw the line was intact and starting to swing. From his position near the far end, he saw the unmounted whinnies charging forward of the line.

Beneath him, Scout roared. It was a sound he'd never heard from any of the whinnies. The ones charging forward slowed to stay in formation, to keep with the line as it pivoted. They charged over a slight rise and descended to the flatland of the draw and toward the loosely arrayed enemy infantry.

The surprise was complete. Intent on finding a way up to silence the stiff fire from Aliza's defenders and to reach the tableland higher up, the enemy hadn't seen or heard the whinnies coming. Turning to discover a charging line of cavalrymen and ferocious animals bearing down upon them, the enemy infantry panicked and ran. They scattered, some falling back toward their vehicles but most simply fleeing away from the charging whinnies. If any of them realized that the direction of the charge was actually herding them south of the attacking vehicle column, there was no sign of it.

In seconds, Bo and the others were among them. Pistol in hand, Bo kept hold of the reins with his left and fired with his right. Some of the enemy stood their ground only to be cut down by weapons, or in more terrifying ways by the whinnies. A man Bo hadn't seen appeared on his left side. Before he could pivot with his weapon, Scout darted that direction without breaking stride. He snapped his jaws, and the man fell to the ground, both hands amputated in a spray of blood.

Holy shit!

"Go, Scout! Get 'em, big guy!" Bo yelled. It felt good enough that he screamed from his diaphragm. The others joined him, and the whinnies roared. The enemy infantry's panic became absolute. Those who had fled without any initial direction now raced for the imagined protection of their vehicles.

The gun platforms on the enemy carriers opened fire. Bo and the riders leaned forward to lower their profiles as they charged. A whinnie on his right went down with a howl. He heard a *smack* as a bullet missed his left leg and tore a gash in Scout's hide. The big whinnie roared again, and Bo expected him to bolt further forward when he dashed hard left instead. The entire line moved that way without a command and ran east toward the sheer, soaring sides of the tableland.

"Scout! What are you doing?" Bo tugged the reins hard to the right, but Scout wouldn't change course. "Scout! You're going the wrong—"

WHUMP! WHUMP!

Bo whipped his head to the right and saw a series of explosions around the enemy vehicles as mortar rounds fell among them.

Contingency Charlie was on time and on target. And was very close—or would have been, had Scout and the other whinnies not heard and understood the significance of the incoming mortar rounds.

Between the withering barrage, the captured vehicles roaring out of the south, and the line of whinnies that had slowed and stopped just beyond the mortars' beaten zone, the enemy infantry threw down their weapons and fled west. Still in a line abreast formation, they faced as one into the rising dust cloud of explosions and watched the steel rain fall.

The barrage hammered down for several minutes, completely obscuring any view to the west. A trooper from third section appeared out of the thin smoke from the direction of the wall, the unit's radio on his shoulder. "Sir! Sir! We've got comms again!"

Bo reached for the handset. "OP Two, Saber Six. Relay to the mortars cease fire. I say again, cease fire. Over."

"OP Two, roger, out."

A few more rounds moaned through the sky above them, chasing after the dim shapes of the J'Stull vehicles, and exploded on impact among them. Silence fell across the valley. Bo pressed the handset again.

"Saber Nine, Saber Six. SITREP, over."

Aliza's voice came back a little shaken, but steady. "Saber Six, we took more casualties, Bo, but we're okay."

"Roger, we'll be back there soon." He glanced at Stewart. "Post an OP and observe them. See if there are survivors and such. Let them collect their dead and wounded. If they mass forces or start any movement east of their line, I want to know about it."

"Yes, sir," Stewart replied. "On it."

"Make it happen," Bo said. He watched with pride as the young sergeant raced back toward the mouth of the valley with a section of four riders.

"Saber Six, OP Two with a relay from Starkpatch, over."

"Send it, OP Two."

"Starkpatch relays Glass Palace. All enemy elements withdrawing at speed. Evacuation of Camp Stark delayed pending further observation of OpFor movement. Major Murphy sends outstanding work. Orders are for you to maintain reconnaissance and prepare for next phase. How copy? Over."

Bo grinned and wiped his chin with a sleeve. "Good copy. We'll start extraction immediately. I'm positioning OP One forward again to observe the enemy here. I want you to move to the mortar platoon to augment their security. Over."

"Roger, Saber Six. Displacing now. Will report from mortar position. OP Two, out."

He passed the handset back to the trooper and put his hands on his hips for a moment and then thought better of it. There wasn't time to relax.

"Back to the wall. Good job, troopers. Move out!"

Chapter Twenty-Eight

R'BAK

The scene at the top of the wall was not what Bo expected. Aliza and the others had the wounded ready for evacuation. Those who could walk moved up the slope toward the top of the tableland where a truck-become-ambulance was standing by. Those who could not walk were carried atop the whinnies. The remaining soldiers silently collected the dead and secured their weapons and equipment.

Aliza saw Bo approach and walked in his direction. "Six dead. Fourteen wounded. Only two seriously. We're moving them up to the rim as quickly as we can. Lieutenant Meehan has vehicles standing by to recover us."

Bo nodded. "Anything else?"

"There's a potable spring just up the draw. The way it flows back underground suggests there might be a cave system here. Maybe an aquifer, too. That could be useful during the Sear." Aliza said. She tucked an errant lock of hair behind one ear and kept talking. "There are some medicinals at the spring. We've identified several species including *londau'd* and *ogh-ul*. They are perennials, but extremely rare. Rare enough that when the actual Harvesters arrive, they are almost certain to know to come here in search of them. And I think there are more nearby."

"Get what you can, Aliza," Bo replied. "But you have to hurry. If the J'Stull don't keep running, they'll soon realize that we've blocked the fastest ways up to the tableland. If they can, they'll come after us again. We'll be ready for that, but if they do, they've seen our positions and know the kind of force and tactics they'll need. So, we've got to be gone if and when they get here."

Aliza sighed and a faint smile crossed her lips. "I've been wishing to not be here since I woke."

He squinted at her. "But you feel differently now?"

She nodded. "It's not something I can explain."

For a moment, Bo wanted to push the subject, but something held him back. "Would you take me to the spring and show me the medicinals? You're better versed on them than I am. I wouldn't know what to look for if it was sprouting right in front of me."

She grinned. "It's right over there."

Bo slid off Scout and absently brushed the dust and dirt from his pants before falling into step alongside the young brunette. They walked in silence. With a fresh breeze rustling the vegetation and the wind pushing the smells of battle away from them, the early afternoon was almost pleasant.

The tiny pool of water looked cool and inviting. They stopped and Bo knelt by the water's edge and studied the clear liquid and the various multicolored and very alien-looking plants there. "And we're sure it's safe to drink?"

"Athena drank from it with no ill effects," Aliza replied. "The whinnies have always shied away from the water sources we determined to be bad. It bodes well for this one."

"That's still taking an awful risk, Aliza."

She knelt beside him, stuck both hands into the water and made a reservoir with her palms. Before he could stop her, she brought her hands to her face and said, *"L'Chaim!"*

"What did you just do?"

Aliza made a satisfied sound and laughed. "I took your risks for you, Bo. Sometimes the greatest risk is to take none."

He reached out and took her hand. When she didn't flinch away, he smiled at her. "That's not something I want you to do for me, Aliza. What does that mean? *L'Chaim*?"

"'To life.'" Her smile slipped away. "Every moment you have it is a moment worth celebrating."

"I suppose so," Bo said. He wanted to stare into her eyes, but he glanced away.

When she spoke again, her voice was faint, tentative. "Sergeant Whittaker said you needed to find your heart, Bo. What did he mean?"

Bo chuckled and shook his head as he brought his eyes back to hers. "None of us started this new future with a blank slate. Some of us have carried more pain than any human should carry."

"Maybe there's a way past that pain?" She squeezed his hand, and he returned the gesture.

He looked at her for a long moment. "I can't even imagine what you went through, Aliza."

"You won't have to." She smiled. "This life will differ from our old ones."

Bo chuckled. "I haven't looked at it that way."

"Whittaker said—" a tremor of grief passed across her features "—he said that dying twice was worth it because he lived twice. I think I know what he meant. Living again makes all of this new pain worth it. Particularly because we can use our past to show us how to live better now, rather than allow it to define us all over again." She frowned slightly but was also smiling. "Does that make sense to you?"

"It does."

"I know we're here for a reason and on this mission for a reason." Aliza took a breath. "But I think we're supposed to do much more than hold this ground. We might not be obligated to complete the work, but we cannot abandon it. At least that's what the Talmud says."

"That ain't exactly my department." Bo smiled at her. "I agree that we're part of something much bigger than just us. But I think you're right. To achieve anything, we have to be here for each other."

She smiled, and it captivated him. Aliza Turan was as beautiful as she was genuine and resilient. He'd been very wrong about her.

His heart hammered in his chest when she asked, "So assuming we do not have to flee and keep fleeing—something with which my ancestors were quite familiar—what do we do next?"

Bo tried to force himself to focus on the larger mission. "Two things. One, we really need to understand the whinnies and just how smart they are. Allies out here are scarce, and we haven't even scratched the surface of what they are capable of. Two? One of my lieutenants used to say the simple things were always hard and the hard things were always simple. I think in this case he's right." *About more things than one.*

"What do you mean, Bo?" Aliza squinted at him.

He looked at her but heard Sharron saying the words that, had she been here, he might now have said to her: *I've found someone else who is everything you are not. I can't help but wonder if I'd met them first would I ever have married you? I settled for you, and I was wrong. I've found someone who'll be here for me. You never were. They'll love me in a way you never could.*

Bo looked down and opened the slanted pocket on his uniform blouse. He removed the yellowed paper from its plastic bag and, without unfolding it, slowly tore it into thin strips and then into tiny squares. He scattered them into the freshening wind.

I can't carry the past anymore. The future is too important. Goodbye, Sharron. Bo took a long breath and exhaled slowly.

Aliza put a hand on his arm. "What was that?"

"The letter my ex-wife sent to tell me it was over. I opened it the morning the Ktor snagged me. They kept it and made sure I had it."

Her face twisted in a question. "Why would they do such a thing? Surely they read and understood it."

"Maybe." Bo shrugged. "Maybe they thought it would anchor me to who I was or to whatever they had planned for all of us. Or to focus my resentment and anger at her, even more than at them. Either way, I'm done with that."

She smiled again and rolled her left elbow outward, revealing the blue numbers on her smooth inner forearm. "I can't get rid of this so easily."

"It doesn't matter." He looked down at her. One hand traced the line of her jaw and she did not flinch away. Her eyes were dark brown, almost black, yet very bright. So bright that, like mirrors, he saw himself in them, and something far greater, besides. "Like you said, our past doesn't define us, Aliza. We don't have the time to even give it another moment's thought."

She nodded. "Because this isn't over." Aliza stared into his eyes. "It hasn't really started, has it?"

"Not at all. They're coming for us, Aliza. Maybe not today or tomorrow, but they're coming. So, if we want this second chance at life, we have to be ready for them. For anything, really. Even the things we never thought would happen again. There's too much at stake now. Like you said, we might not be obligated to this unexpected future, but we damned sure can't abandon it."

Chapter Twenty-Nine

SPIN ONE

"Report, sir." Makarov's voice a little more clipped than usual.

Murphy kept reading the reports on the final trials of the first replicated Huey: damned impressive. "Just send it to my slate, Makarov."

The Russian captain cleared his throat. "It is the after-action report from Captain Moorefield, sir."

Already? Damn, Bo didn't waste any time. He looked up and reached out a hand. "Thanks..." He almost said "Mak," but he'd had to retire that nickname. Not only was the Russian persistent in his dislike of it, but it sounded too much like "Max," which confused Murphy's bodyguard no end. But Messina had helped out by coming up with a replacement nickname for the Muscovite, which Murphy remembered to use: "Okay, Pistol, hand it here." Makarov actually smiled as he handed over the file.

Murphy was slightly annoyed that he hadn't thought of the moniker "Pistol" himself, but Max had enjoyed the advantage of having been born in the time when the underlying phrase had come into use. "Pistol Pete" had apparently been a TV character or sports figure. Maybe both. Whatever the origin, it was definitely more suitable. With a family name of "Makarov" and a first name of "Pyotr" it was difficult to think of a more apt name for the Russian.

Murphy pulled Bo's AAR out of the sheaf of hardcopy documents and skipped all the introductory copy to get to the nitty-gritty:

"Commandeered vehicles and supplies transferred to Cpt. Moorefield, CO Camp Stark, at rendezvous point Lima. J'Stull pursuit/attack repulsed, suffering heavy losses. Abandoned and reclaimable enemy equipment includes APCs, light ACVs, company-level personal gear, including Kulsian small arms. Note: otherwise unbreakable draught creatures (designated as *whinaalani* in prior comms) allowed themselves to be ridden into combat by our personnel. Unit casualties: 11 WIA, 1 WIA/ND ("non-deployable"), 4 KIA."

Makarov gave Murphy a full minute to peruse it and the intel addenda before almost chirping, "Only 4 KIA and one WIA permanently disabled. That may be the most efficient, one-sided battle I have ever heard of. It is quite the triumph, sir."

Murphy nodded and sighed. "Yeah, it is, Pistol…and if we have another ten triumphs like that one, half of us will be dead or cripples."

"Sir?" Makarov sounded surprised and a bit miffed.

"Captain, it's a great victory and the one we needed, no doubt. But it's also a wakeup call. There's going to be a lot of fighting to be done on R'Bak, and if we do the bear's share every time, we'll be putting ourselves out of action. No, we've got to transform our table of organization. Make sure it's filled out by indigs, with our own personnel reserved for command positions or as 'embedded technical advisors.'"

Makarov had no reply; frowning, and apparently confronting the unpleasant and deflating context that Murphy had brought to what had seemed a cheer-worthy outcome, he wandered out of the CP.

Sorry to be a downer, Makarov, Murphy thought after him. *Bo did a hell of a job, but we're still in deep shit and can't afford to have victory celebrations just because our second battle wasn't anywhere near as costly as it had every right to be.* He kept reading the observations that Moorefield had deemed worthy of mention.

It turned out that the casualty count was even less representative than it appeared. It had been significantly impacted by two variables which might have cancelled each other out. On the one hand, even some of the most severely injured WIA were expected to be fit for duty in no more than two weeks. Judging from their wounds, several should have been out-and-out KIAs. But the Sarmatchani healers—almost exclusively women—were surprisingly near at hand when the battle came to an end and were ready with roots and other exotic plantforms that healed most wounds so quickly that Murphy found it hard to believe the reports.

But Tapper and Moorefield were two of the steadiest Lost Soldiers Murphy had, officer or otherwise, and their accounts of the efficacy of these 'native remedies' included specific details of both the compounds used and hourly observations on the progress of the wound reversal. Bottom line: if the Sarmatchani healers hadn't been there and ready to offer their help, the list of fatalities and permanently disabled WIAs would have been at least twice as long as it was.

On the other hand, the actual Kulsian raiders, whom, it was said, the satraps and their Kulsian overlords dubbed "coursers," not only had impressive personal weapons, but some extremely effective ammunition. So effective that two of the KIAs could not have been saved by any herb in the universe; they'd been hit in the torso by dum dums. According to the wounded abandoned by the fleeing J'Stull, the ammunition had been reclaimed from the same cache as the vehicles that they'd used to chase Tapper's column.

Other dum dums were found scattered among those J'Stull troopers furnished with refurbished Kulsian weapons, but those had been reloads or, as Bo had labeled them, "local remanufactures." So much of the satrap materiel fell into that category that Bo had created a new term to shorthand it: "reman." In the long list of battlefield spoils, that word figured very prominently and provided further insight into why the satrap troops inspired such fear.

Over the centuries, they'd had the opportunity to clean up various battlefields as well as come across the remains of Harvesters who had either been ambushed or fatally stranded due to weather, vehicle failures, or other misfortunes common to the wastes. The salvage the satraps had acquired was not restricted to weapons, but included advanced optics, simple electronics, and other useful equipment, all of which was hoarded, lovingly restored, and given to their best troops. It conferred a significant edge on the battlefield.

A timer toned. Murphy had to start moving or he'd be late for his meeting with the new replication liaison down at the staging bay. He put his slate to sleep, reached over to turn off the formidable computing and communications array that reminded him of a desktop PC and mission control all rolled into one…

And blinked when the screen went dark before he even touched it. The saving and buffering wait screen came on, then went dark, and was replaced by an inquiry he had never seen before, in an unfamiliar typeface:

"If alone in a secure environment, enter assigned access code. N & N."

Murphy fell more than leaned back in his chair. The N & N access code? The identifier he'd been given by Nuncle and Nephew, and then never used? Exhaling slowly, he remote-activated the door lock, turned on the home-built white noise generator Makarov had cobbled together—apparently, you learned all sorts of strange lessons in Soviet Russia—and entered the code.

The screen illuminated. Nephew's face was suddenly smiling out at him. Murphy leaned back as the Terran started to speak.

"Hope this is a surprise, Major Murphy. If it's not, then Alnduul over-sold the security of his software monitoring AI. And no, I'm not going to say anything more about that because, frankly, I don't have the information myself.

"At any rate, the system is sure it's you, and not just because of the code you entered. More about that later.

"First order of business: there is new data at your disposal. Only two things are required for you to access it: that you enter this code and that you are at this computer. And when I say 'at this computer,' I mean exactly where you are sitting right now, plus or minus half a meter.

"The new data are schematics, about ten times the number we left with you. Part of the reason these are being freed up for your use is because you have already been sparing with the ones you have. Had they all been shared out, all at once, this system's AI would have been highly suspicious of the activity. Either it would mean you were being careless or being pressured into providing access to schematics you hadn't shared yet, or someone had in fact hacked this supposedly unhackable system.

"Since that did not occur, and since you are personally sitting in front of this computer, I am told that by monitoring all traffic that comes into or is sent from your linked systems, the AI has deemed it is both a safe and useful time to release this information to you.

"If you're getting angry right about now, all I can say is that I'd feel the same way. But this was the only secure method we had of continuing to support at a distance: by giving you access to information that would not only prove useful for your operations, but good leverage in dealing with your hosts.

"These schematics are far more varied than the ones we left, which were mostly from American defense industries during your Vietnam era. These range across not only more time periods and nations, but other species. I think you will be interested in both human and Ktor designs for transatmospheric vertibirds. Nothing revolutionary, just smarter and more efficient designs. The one constant that cuts across all these schematics is that they do not require or contain any scientific or engineering insights that the SpinDogs do not already possess."

Murphy swallowed. *Problem is, how do I get the SpinDogs to build them? They're already bitching about exceeding their capacity. But, damn it, with the increased rate at which the raiders and satraps are completing that transmitter....*

Nephew hadn't stopped. "We anticipate that sharing these schematics could entail increased risk; your hosts are pretty greedy and ruthless. Again, we've taken that into account and placed your final recourse protections right inside the most valuable asset under your control: the Dornaani satellite network.

"You already know that neither the system nor the individual birds can be hacked. What you don't know is that there are a few other features which can be used to protect you from exploitation if hostile push comes to deadly shove.

"Before waking you and your cadre fully, you all had nanite-scale biosamplers implanted. They not only routinely signal that you're alive, but function as a distributed network. Think of it as the biological equivalent of a dead-man switch. If any of your biosamplers stop sending the 'everything's okay' signal, the satellites turn off unless they get a countermand from you. Same if you, or any of the others, are registering extreme emotional or physical duress when you attempt to access the satellites; again, no go.

"One last thing we didn't advertise: the satellites are also transmitters. Each of them is capable of a battery-depleting comm burst to Kulsis. If anyone tries to take control of the satellites, either with you or without you, and no matter the method, the Overlords will find out—and find the SpinDogs. So, if anyone on the Red Team decides to pull the trigger on hacking the system, there is no calling back the bullet."

"You might be wondering: why is the transmission calibrated to deplete a satellite's battery? Because there's no way for an enemy to reactivate a dead bird. And even if they manage to get their hands on one and, by some miracle, do an end-run around the anti-tamper system, they'll need to provide a correct biosample and the scan of a functional retina to reinitiate the network."

Nephew looked thoughtful before finishing. "This is all grim stuff. A real joy to hear, I'm sure. And I wouldn't want anyone screwing around with my freedom of choice and action the way this system's AI is set to do. But in the end, these decisions were taken to ensure that you always had another rabbit to pull out of your hat—and one that only you could grab by the ears. If we've done our jobs correctly, this should keep any would-be backstabbers at bay. Take care, Major. We will be back as soon as we can. My word on that. Even if I have to return alone."

The screen blanked and resumed the program Murphy had been about to exit.

He reached the loading bay only a minute ahead of schedule. Max was following further behind than he liked to and doing so under protest. But this was the first meeting with the liaison from Primus Kormak whose replication plants had now begun cranking out Hueys at a prodigious rate, the first post-trial example of which was soon to be loaded for transfer to R'Bak.

Murphy had originally tried to line up a meeting with the primus himself: Dolkar Kormak, first among the Hardliner Family heads. But his requests had been ignored and a liaison had been assigned instead: none other than the suspicious bastard from the ops center stand-off, Bramath.

Murphy wasn't sure which he liked less: having to make nice with a guy who'd held a gun on him for no sensible reason, or the brush-off from the Primus. Because by sending a second-tier Scion in his place, Kormak had actually sent a definitive response to Murphy's request for a face-to-face meeting. And it was: *You are in no way my equal, so I will not meet you. I will not even send my son to meet you. I will send you my second nephew. And you should be glad for that.*

So much social dancing when a simple "fuck you" would have sufficed. Murphy would have liked to beat the tar out of something or someone, but instead took a deep breath, released a long sigh, and entered the bay.

Bramath was waiting at the side of the Huey while cargo-hands checked the straps that kept its rotors tied-off for loading: it was going to be a tight fit in the shuttle's hold. The Second Scion saw Murphy, nodded.

Who nodded back and began walking very, very slowly toward the liaison.

Who eventually became so impatient that he, too, began walking to close the distance, and ultimately met Murphy halfway.

Which had been the whole point of the exercise.

"Are you injured?" Bramath asked with a smile that was all shark.

"No. Are you?"

Bramath frowned. "Of course not. I feared you might have suffered some mishap."

"I thought the same of you when you did not move at all." *You prick.* But it was time to play nice, so..."You and the Primus must be very proud of the helicopter. I've seen the trial results. Extraordinary by any standard, particularly for a first production model built from schematics you'd never seen before a month ago."

"It was a modest challenge," Bramath allowed with patently false humility.

"Even more astounding, then," admitted Murphy. "And singularly encouraging given the recent events on R'Bak."

"To which events are you referring?" Bramath asked carefully.

"Our seizure of the J'Stull convoy, and a great deal of equipment left on the battlefield by the following force they routed. The powerplants of the vehicles and the capabilities of the weapons are very impressive. I suspect the greatest difficulty will be to select which ones should be slated for replication. I was hoping we might schedule a meeting to discuss that." Murphy stopped as Bramath's incipient consternation became an extremely deep frown.

"Do you mean to embarrass us?" the Second Nephew asked in a low voice.

Murphy did not have to feign perplexity. "What do you mean?"

"Do you not realize this touches on our limits? That in broaching such a subject, you may ask more than we could manage?"

"You consider that an affront?"

"I do. More importantly, *we* do. If you were of the Spins, you would know this. You would also know that such an offense might warrant a challenge." Bramath allowed his frown to fade slightly. "However, I am a patient man."

Yeah, right. "Bramath, I meant no offense, and apologize for any I might have given. But how can we productively discuss future replication projects, if you do not share your production capacity?"

At that moment, Bramath Kormak's frown became more thoughtful as he grappled with that conundrum. Then, as if realizing that his frown wasn't quite dour enough, he pulled his brows down again.

Murphy managed to keep the surprise off his face. Bramath wasn't trying to come to terms with his "allies'" alien value system; he was…acting. In that brief moment, the veil of his "injured honor" had slipped and revealed that it was mostly, if not entirely, a charade. But performed to what end? To see how Murphy would react…?

No: to surprise *me—and so, make it easier to throw me off the topic you wanted to avoid: the Kormak Family's replication capacity.* So, the strategy had been to distract the alien newcomer by feigning a possible diplomatic insult, thereby derailing any strategically sensitive discussions. *And since Bramath is supposedly pissed because my inquiry would have "embarrassed" his Family by revealing its limits...*

It meant he was trying to conceal the opposite. Which was consistent with the speed and quality of the production they had been achieving. *Hell, these guys aren't at the edge of their capacity; they're not even close...*

"Major Murphy?"

"Er, yes? My apologies, Bramath. I repeat: I meant no offense. I retract my query. In the interest of friendship between our peoples, I hope you will agree to overlook my misstep."

Bramath made a gesture of dismissal, offered an easy, agreeable smile…but Murphy spotted the careful, assessing glint in his eye. *Watching to make sure he hasn't overplayed his part...So, my best move is—* "Let us proceed in a different fashion, then. I shall relay copies of the most tactically useful new equipment to you, for study. So, when you find it convenient to do so, perhaps *you* will approach *me* regarding which would be the best candidates for eventual replication, and when."

"That is agreeable," Bramath consented.

Murphy nodded eagerly "And I intuit that will also be the most appropriate and polite moment to share our own more complex schematics with you," Murphy added.

Bramath squinted. "You have…more schematics? Ones you have not shared?"

"Of course. I thought that was intimated by our commanders before they left. Perhaps not, or perhaps that detail was not widely shared." It wasn't a lie, exactly; more like a wild exaggeration "I suspect that is why our respective leaders settled on the UH-1 helicopter as a trial platform: it was, as you say, only a modestly complex replication challenge. I don't mean to diminish its tactical and even strategic importance, of course, but compared to the other schematics we may share—vehicles, aerospace craft, weapons, power plants—it is but a humble beginning."

In fact, the Huey's status as a dirtside gamechanger was largely due to its comparative simplicity. It was also comparatively easy to store, which meant the SpinDogs now had the option to create their own planetary caches with smaller, less expensive vehicles that were optimized for atmospheric operations.

Murphy concluded with a wide, innocent smile. "I suspect you will find many items in our inventory that will be of intense interest to you, when that time comes."

"Doubtless," Bramath muttered as Murphy nodded, gave a short bow that was in keeping with SpinDog customs, withdrew…and had the distinct impression that the other man was now no longer entirely sure of just who had played whom.

As Murphy headed back toward his point of entry, Max peeled off his post just beyond the blind corner of the bulkhead. As he swung in behind Murphy, Messina muttered, "So that guy's a well-greased dick, isn't he?"

"Sure is."

"Where now, boss? The fabrication bay for an update on how Lieutenant Bowden's, uh, 'project' is coming along?"

"The captain doesn't need me looking over his shoulder." *Or seeing the face that might have to give him orders he'd rather die than receive, if push comes to shove.* "I'll just send him today's update from the CP."

Chapter Thirty

SPIN ONE

The command update flashed across Bowden's slate just as he was about to enter the fabrication bay where the modifications to the three interface craft were under way:

> First ground operation completed. Sufficient enemy weapons and vehicles commandeered for phase two. Ground attack remains primary/preferred tactical option for mission completion.
>
> However, regional and orbital recon suggests enemy is outpacing initial completion estimates. Continuation of that trend could promote air attack contingency to primary option for mission success.
>
> Murphy.

Bowden stared at the data slate. *Well, shit. Of* course *this whole mess is going to land in my lap.* After all, everything *was* going to follow Murphy's Law, right?

But there was "no time to cry over spilt milk or flying shit," as one of his flight instructors used to say. And he had to present a calm, collected, confident face to the locals who were actually going to fly the mission.

Once inside the bay, Bowden found Ferenc studying the lead aircraft. They'd spoken frequently over the weeks, mostly about the additional electronics it needed to be able to drop ordnance with any chance of hitting the target. As it turned out, the SpinDogs had a variety of lasers they used in space, so the development of the needed emitters and receivers hadn't been an issue, nor had the necessary rocket technology.

Or so he'd thought. As Bowden approached the craft, though, he could see a number of new pieces of gear scattered about—in addition to what was obviously the SpinDogs' versions of the AGM-123 Skipper and the AIM-9 Sidewinder—and they *weren't* what he'd discussed with Ferenc.

"What do you think?" Ferenc asked with a big smile.

"Well…uh, I think they are good demo versions," Bowden said, trying to keep his comments positive. Ferenc had complained—at length and often—about how much trouble he had getting the components into the production line, and how much grief he had received from the leading families for disrupting their normal operations.

"I like what you did with the rockets." Bowden pointed to the bomb, which now had small rockets mounted between each pair of rear fins. "The problem is going to be if one of them fails to fire or doesn't function correctly. You have the guidance fins mounted mid-body on the bomb; that isn't going to work as well as if they were mounted on the nose."

Ferenc made some hand motions as he went over the aerodynamics of the bombs in his mind. A pilot himself, it didn't take him long before he blushed. "I should have thought about that," he said. "They asked me where we wanted them mounted, and I didn't give it any thought."

"But you see why they would work better on the front?"

The SpinDog nodded. "It will take less movement of the fins, and it will be more precise."

"Exactly," Bowden said, happy to be able to compliment the man on something. "We want the bomb to fly as smoothly as possible. The more corrections it has to make—especially the big ones required in this configuration—will cause it to use up all its energy, and it might not make it to the target."

Bowden wiggled the receiver to test its movement. "Can we power it up and see how it works?"

"Uh, I don't know how to do that. I will have a technician here tomorrow, and he can show you."

"Okay, that's fine," Bowden said. He turned toward the air-to-air missile. Unlike the bomb, it was hanging from a hardpoint on the wing of the craft. The missile was easily twice as thick as the Sidewinder he was used to seeing, and—at almost five meters tip to tail—was easily half again as long. "So, tell me about this."

The man sighed as he looked at it. "The guidance fins will need to move to the nose of the missile."

"Yes, they will. What is the warhead made of?"

"Warhead?"

"Yes. What happens when the missile hits a blimp?"

"Well, it goes through the blimp, making a big hole, and the blimp deflates."

"There's just one problem with that."

"Which is?"

"Assuming the seeker is an IR seeker like we discussed, this is going to hit the hottest part of the blimp, which is the exhaust for its motor. If it hits it hard enough and accurately enough, it may knock the engine out, but there will still be people in the gondola firing at you. They'll be at the same level as you, so shooting you will be easier for them. *And*, if they have any handheld missiles…"

"We'd be easy targets." The SpinDog slumped, obviously seeing more modifications and production time needed. He studied the weapon with tired eyes. "We have missile warheads, of course, but they are for ship-to-ship use in space. No streamlining, and their only purpose is to breach the hull and inflict structural damage. No fragmentation or incendiary effects." He sighed. "So, what do we need to do to fix it?"

"Well, I've been thinking about that," Bowden said. "The standard blast-frag of your Sidewinder copies will do less against a blimp, and the odds are we'd probably have to hit one with several missiles to knock it out of the fight. We could either make the missiles even bigger than this one—which I don't want to do because of overloading the aircraft—or we can change the warhead."

Bowden thought for a moment. "Pretty much everything on a blimp—especially the gas bag, but even the gondola—is going to react pretty poorly to fire. Do you have anything we could use as an incendiary charge?"

Ferenc smiled and nodded. "I will talk to my people, but I have some things in mind. We have plenty of flares."

"Great. Flares would be wonderful." Bowden pointed to a new, smooth-edged box hanging under the port wing, closer to the wing root. "Is that…is that the laser designator?"

"It is. At least this should not need many changes. It's a laser we use for ranging on our mining craft. That is something we didn't have to make new."

"Well, uh…I like that you can use existing gear, but is it possible to redesign it a little?"

"In what way?"

"I don't know what it originally came from, but the wires stick out from the side of the box. They're just begging to have a bird, or something, hit them and tear them off. Hell, even maneuvering through the atmosphere is going to be hard on them."

Ferenc peered critically at the wires. "It was originally in a small spacecraft. Maybe the wires can be moved…"

"They need to be, because—"

"I know," the SpinDog said with an exaggerated sigh. "If it can go wrong, it will."

"Do you have the handheld laser designator?"

"I should have it tomorrow."

"Great! So we can test it tomorrow with the Skipper. It would be best if we could mount the weapon to the plane and run the test from inside the cockpit."

"I…uh…I don't know if that will be possible. The wires haven't been run yet…"

"Okay. Well, do the best you can. Will you have a PRF analyzer in the cockpit?"

"A what?"

"You'll need some method of setting and receiving the pulse repetition frequencies—the PRFs—of the lasers in use."

"What is that and why do we need it?"

Bowden forced himself not to sigh. "When the weapons are fired, we'll be going for two separate targets, with two sources of illumination guiding the bombs onto the target. If one designator is high power and the other is low power, what is to keep all the bombs from going for the same target that's being illuminated by the high-power designator?"

"I don't know," Ferenc said. "Dropping them at different times?"

Bowden shook his head. "By using different PRFs, you don't have to worry about separating the aircraft or which laser is firing at which time. If you can change the PRF that the bomb is looking for to match what each laser designator is sending out, the bombs will go where you want them to. We'll need at least two settings, but six is probably better."

"How does your Murphy know all this?"

"He's a smart man."

"I will see what I can do, but I do not think the engineers will like it."

"The Terran says the guidance fins for both the bomb and the missile need to move to the nose," Lotho Ferenc said.

"So?" Primus Dolkar Kormak asked.

"We have the data packets for replication of the Earth weapons he is trying to build."

"I ask again, so?" Kormak did not try to conceal his annoyance. "Why are you wasting my time with this?"

"Because it would be much easier to simply replicate what he needs, Primus, rather than to cobble them together from scrap. Not only easier, but they are more likely to function correctly. The same thing goes for the targeting lasers Bowden is looking for."

"No. I do not want the disruption to the production schedule, nor do I want them to know the depth of our true capabilities."

"I understand, Primus, and I respect that. However, in this case, the things they are asking for will help them destroy the transmitter the locals are building to communicate with the Kulsians. You have indicated that it is far better for us to prevent, rather than permit, that outcome. It also will make it less likely we will lose the interface craft you have allotted for this endeavor."

Kormak frowned, considering. Although the production schedule was normally sacrosanct, it would be better if the remaining raiders weren't able to make contact with Kulsis. Adding in the costs of potentially losing an interface craft swung the decision for him. "I will permit it," he said. "You can make the guidance fins for the missiles and bombs, but that is all. Everything else must be assembled from existing parts."

"Thank you, Primus. The Terran also has issues with the wiring protruding from—"

"Let him have issues! They are living off my largesse!" Their daily needs were actually provided by all the Families, but Kormak felt he had taken a greater part of the burden than the others. "If this Bowden person does not like it, let him rewire it himself. You are not to ask for anything else. Am I clear on this?"

"Yes, Primus," Ferenc said, then he bowed and left.

Chapter Thirty-One

SPIN ONE

Bowden didn't get the word that the equipment was ready for testing for another five days. In the interim, he had asked the major for a couple of troopers to attend the next briefing, so he could familiarize them with the handheld lasers. No decision had been made yet on whether a squad would be sent to attempt a ground designate for the targets, but Bowden wanted people prepared for the mission. They probably wouldn't know until it was nearly "go time," and if he waited, there wouldn't be any time to train them. It was now or never.

He wasn't surprised, therefore, when he showed up at the craft for the operational testing and found three troopers in addition to Ferenc and the SpinDog technician who'd been assigned to the project.

"Lieutenant Bowden?" asked one of the soldiers. "I'm Sergeant Young. I'm the squad leader who's been assigned to this, if we get the go-ahead to do it." He nodded to the other two men. "Here are your two victims, Dork and Renaldi. Try not to poke too many laser holes through them." He walked off, chuckling to himself.

"Uh, suh, you're not really gonna poke holes in us, are you?" asked a large, hulking man. The accent placed him from rural Alabama. The other soldier snorted in derision.

"You're Dork?"

"Yes, suh, Private Dorkhouse, but they all just call me Dork, 'cause I, uh, get lost sometimes."

"I see." *Probably not the only reason.* "No, Private, I'm not going to poke any holes in you. Although you'll need goggles while dealing with the laser to protect your vision, the laser isn't strong enough to hurt you. Right, Alak?"

The SpinDog tech, Alak Lekral, looked up from the wire he was running to the bomb. "No, we tuned it to your specifications. You could stand in front of it all day and not be injured. Although I would not recommend it."

"Told you Sarge was just fucking with us," said the other trooper, Private Adam Renaldi. His accent marked him as a New Yorker. An interesting pair.

"Okay, thanks. Just didn't want to get home and have to explain to my mama why I had holes in me."

"Your mama's long dead," Renaldi said.

The big man shrugged. "Maybe, maybe not. That's what they say, but we won't know fo' sure 'til we get home."

Renaldi started to say something else, but Bowden held up a hand. "You guys can argue that later; I'd like to see what Alak's put together for us."

The SpinDog tech nodded. "First, we were able to design some new fins for both the bomb and the missile," he said, pointing to the guidance assembly on the bomb, "moving them to the nose on both."

Bowden stepped up to the bomb. He'd never seen a real-life Skipper before, but the guidance section looked just the way he'd imagined it—a laser receiver followed by movable fins. This was attached to the bomb's main body—about 1,000 pounds of high explosive—then larger, fixed fins, and the rockets. The rockets still looked stupid in that configuration, and with four, there were multiple opportunities for failure. He shrugged. If this was the best they could do, it was pretty close to what he'd wanted. Assuming the guidance section worked, it'd be fine.

They could always press in closer to the target if the motors didn't work. It would suck for the pilots—flying through triple-A was *not* fun—but it could be done if they had to.

He walked over to where the air-to-air missile sat in a cradle of its own. While he'd never seen the Skipper guidance package before, he *had* seen the Sidewinder's, and the one that was now attached to the missile looked *exactly* like an early Sidewinder guidance section from back home, including being the same size as the original missile's. Although the SpinDogs had designed a step-up section to mate the smaller guidance section to the bigger missile, it was obviously not intended for this missile. It was a lash-up.

"Where did this come from?" Bowden asked.

The tech shrugged. "There was actually an original missile seeker head in with the Lost Soldiers' equipment. That allowed us to replicate it much more closely."

Bowden inspected it. "This looks like a real Sidewinder guidance section all right. It's not as sophisticated as the ones I had—it looks like an earlier model—but it looks like a genuine AIM-9 seeker head. Right down to where you filed off the serial number."

The tech shrugged again. "I do not know."

"You must come over here," Ferenc interrupted, gesturing toward the handheld laser designator, "so we can provide a quick demonstration." Once Bowden and the two soldiers had drifted over, he continued, "As you can see, it is the same device as the one hanging from the aircraft, so there will not be any interoperability issues between them."

Bowden nodded appreciatively. *If true, that would be the first thing* without *any interoperability issues.*

"We developed a tripod for it to sit on so the operator can keep a steady spot on the target," Ferenc continued. "The battery on it is the weakest part. Since it is normally wired into a spacecraft, we had to add a battery to it, and the one which worked best will only fire for about ten minutes before you have to recharge it or put on a new one."

"That's not too bad," Bowden said with a shrug. "I think that's comparable to ours back home."

"Good. I was worried that it would not be long enough."

"That's what we're here for?" Renaldi asked, looking critically at the gear. Bowden couldn't blame him; it looked big, bulky, and—what was worse for the troopers—heavy. "What is it? And please, tell me I don't have to carry that damn thing."

"That is a laser designator," Bowden said, "and that's what we're going to use to destroy the antenna the indigs are building to call back to their bosses on Kulsis."

"But you said it was safe," Dork said. "How are we going to blow up the antenna with it if it is safe to stand in front of?"

Bowden smiled. "That's a good question. Here's how this is going to work. When it's turned on, this box emits a beam of laser light. You're going to carry this box—and another one just like it—to the target, and then you're going to point the laser at it. The beam will hit the target and bounce off. Meanwhile, Mr. Ferenc here, along with several others, will fly some of those aircraft behind us into the target area and drop a bunch of bombs. Those bombs will see the laser light that's being bounced off the targets, and they will follow it all the way down and blow up, wiping out the antenna and the control station."

"What's it weigh?" Renaldi asked.

"It is only about twenty kilos," Ferenc replied.

"*Only* twenty kilos, says the man who doesn't have to hump it around on his back all day," the soldier muttered. The man's eyes widened as a thought came to him. "You said the bomb follows the laser beam down?"

Bowden nodded.

"How does it know to hit the target and not this giant piece of shit I've been carrying around all day?"

Bowden smiled. "It's all due to the geometry of the attack."

"I'm sorry, suh," Dork said. "I wasn't very good at math."

Bowden chuckled. "You don't have to *know* math to use it. What I meant was how things will be arranged." He pointed to the objects. "Here's you, standing at the designator, and the target is over on the bulkhead over there. The bomb is coming from behind us. If you're pointing the laser at the target, the only light the bomb can see is what is reflecting off the target. As long as the bomb can't see the front of the designator, it can't see the beam, and it won't guide on you."

"Okay," the big man said, nodding. "How does it work?"

The tech moved forward and handed everyone goggles. "Put these on, please. The laser will not burn you, but it is not good for your eyes." Everyone put on the goggles.

The tech flipped a switch on the left side of the box, and it gave off a low hum. "First you turn it on. Then you dial in the code." He typed in "1666" on the pad between the two switches. "Then you activate the laser beam." He flipped the switch on the right. "Now you just point it at the target, and the bomb will follow it in. We could not make it any simpler."

"The box is on?" Renaldi asked. The tech nodded. "I don't see a laser beam."

"It is invisible. Trust me; it is on."

"Great," Renaldi muttered. "A heavy fucking box that you can't even tell is on. Probably won't be working after a day on the march, and we'll never know."

"I can show you it is working," the tech said. He walked over and plugged a wire into the bomb, and its laser receiver popped up. "See? The bomb can see the reflected laser light, even if you cannot. Move the designator around."

Bowden turned the designator to the right and the laser receiver on the bomb followed it. He moved it back to the left, and it tracked left. Then he jerked it to the right, and the laser receiver went back to center.

The tech nodded. "You have to be smooth with any corrections, or you will break the lock on the bomb."

Bowden looked to the soldiers to see if they understood. Renaldi was still frowning, obviously still annoyed about having to carry the box, but Dork's mouth was open, and his eyes were wide. "It's just like magic…"

"Well, not really magic, just science and technology," Bowden said. "Let me take you through how all this is going to work…"

"Okay, so what do we know?" Bowden asked two hours later.

"After carrying the heavy piece of shit all day, the mule shoots a laser beam that we aim at the target," Renaldi said. Bowden nodded, ignoring the soldier's constant grousing. He'd learned hours earlier that acknowledging it only made the soldier bitch more. He remembered what one of his earliest chiefs had said: "A bitching sailor is a happy sailor," and let it go.

"The laser bounces off the target," Dork said. "The bomb sees it, and it flies into the target and blows it up." Bowden had almost been to the point of asking for someone else when Dork had finally figured it all out. Although the man could easily lug the box around, Bowden was less sanguine he could operate it correctly. Finally—on the last battery they had before having to recharge them all—the light had gone on for Dork.

"And what do we need for the bomb to see the laser?" Bowden asked.

"The correct angle," Renaldi said. "It's best if we're on close to the same line as the attack run."

"And you have to punch in the right magic code into the box," Dork said happily. Bowden had given up on saying "Pulse Repetition Frequency" or even "PRF." Dork thought of it as a magic code, and that was okay with Bowden, as long as he entered the right code at the right time. As it turned out, Dork could remember a number pattern, he just couldn't manipulate the numbers. Remember "1555?" No problem. Multiply eight times eight? Dork was more likely to give the answer "apple sauce" than "64." If he wanted to think of it as a magic code, that was fine with Bowden.

"And what's the most important thing?" Bowden asked.

"Timing is everything," they both answered. "The box has to be on and pointing at the target at the correct time," Dork finished.

"And we care about that because?"

"Because the battery only lasts ten minutes," Renaldi replied, "and we'll only have two because they're damn heavy, and I ain't carrying any more than that."

Bowden smiled. They'd go over it again every couple of days to ensure retention, but it seemed like at least the ground component of the attack understood its part of the mission.

"So," Primus Hesheth asked, pushing his plate away, "the Terran captain-of-pilots got his newest batch of toys today?"

"Just a few hours ago," Primus Dolkar Kormak muttered, his own meal untouched.

"So, you have complied. As we all have had to." Hesheth's tone and smile were facetious. "Do you wish me to pour out drinks of commiseration?"

Erkuk Hesheth's sardonic grin fell away when he saw the look on the more powerful Primus' face. "Because we are 'peers,' I shall let your asinine japery go unaddressed." Kormak paused, waited to see if Hesheth would challenge him. The lesser primus had the dignity of a self-soiling halfwit but was evidently not stupid; the man just stared. In shock, apparently. Good. Shock was needed if they were to change course before it was too late.

"My Second Nephew Bramath was in here again, also," Kormak explained, "pushing me to initiate our second production phase now. The third such entreaty this week, if you can believe it."

"Why does he feel it should be accelerated?"

"Because he spoke to Murphy and heard starry glory in the hints of the other toys our new 'friends' may offer us. But any discussion of that can only proceed if we reveal our *full* production capacity."

"I believe you mean *when* we reveal our full production capacity, Primus."

"I said what I meant." Dolkar put his fists on the table. "Hesheth, this will not end well."

"Of what do you speak?"

"This alliance with the Terrans."

"You fear they shall fail?"

"No. I fear they may succeed."

Hesheth squinted, as if that might help him better see Kormak's point. "Yes, and, as we have conjectured, that is likely to give the shit-eaters on Kulsis a reason to pause, possibly to forego their coming Harvest. And in the meantime, with the Terrans leading the effort, we might secure and utilize the surface of R'Bak and its peoples. We would have almost a century to grow powerful and possibly fend off Kulsis come the next Searing. It would be the realization of a long-held dream."

"Would it?" Kormak muttered. "Listen to yourself; you are starting to utter the same starry opiates that have blinded the Expansionists, thanks to the whispers of these Terrans. And if their coalition should succeed at these first, simple steps? They will come to believe they *can* prevail against the Overlords of Kulsis. They will be incautious, will overreach—and that will be our doom."

Hesheth nodded slowly. "I have had similar reservations. It is certainly a far more uncertain enterprise than the Expansionists are now envisioning it to be. I agree that they are overly optimistic—"

"Which is why they must not be allowed to go further with this deluded madness."

Hesheth stared at the tabletop; Kormak saw that the lesser primus had clearly heard the implicit call to internecine action. "So, what of *Second Spin*? Does Arko Primus Zobulakos agree that the current Expansionist plans must be…curtailed?"

Kormak resisted the urge to spit. "He is 'deliberating.'"

"What has undermined his prior resolve to diminish the Expansionists' power?"

"The life of his fool son, Stabilo. The Expansionists detained the young idiot, pending 'inquiries' over the nonsense he perpetrated on the planet."

"So, our fate is in the hands of a weak-willed father who should be glad to be rid of a Scion so intemperate that he can neither conceal his actions nor contain his ambitions?"

"If you do not see the greater complexities, Hesheth, then your sight is as dim as your thought. Zobulakos is not only thinking of his son. His dominion on *Spin Two* has been kept dependent upon our support since its inception. Largely at our insistence, you may recall."

"It was sound policy at the time," Hesheth objected gruffly.

"Indeed. It was sound policy up until a month ago, at which point unforeseen interlopers and events made a ruin of all our fine calculations." Kormak sighed. "We were necessarily tepid in our support of Zobulakos's maneuvers to accrue greater power on his own spin. He is now, not surprisingly, tepid in his commitment to moving against the Expansionists."

"In short, he is not for our cause."

"In short, he is for himself. Which means he will wait to see which way the shadow falls before he makes a move to support either side. However, I am certain he would be happier to join with us."

"So, if we make a strong start, a bold set of first moves—"

"Yes, that might decide him. But regardless of *Spin Two*'s ambivalence, we must be decisive and swift in our actions. The Expansionists have ever been soft-headed and never more than now, as their various Family Primae strive for overall leadership. But the situation becomes more urgent the longer this disastrous alliance with the Terrans goes on. The more short-term success their coalition realizes, the more supporters they will gather from among the undecided. Their delusion that we could survive a direct confrontation with Kulsis will become universal, and so, complete. We must act now. Agreed?"

The Primus of Family Hesheth sounded resolved, rather than resolute. "The trend bodes ill indeed."

Dolkar Kormak kept staring at his nominal peer. "I did not ask you for your observations. I asked if you agree to act. Now."

The other sighed. "Agreed."

Kormak finally addressed the food on his plate. "I will eat as we make our plans."

"Have all the cadre acknowledged receiving the revised estimate on the transmitter's completion?" Murphy was sending them almost daily, now.

"All but one: Captain Lee." Pistol's tone was concerned, almost brotherly.

Frankly, Murphy was concerned himself. After that one clusterfuck dirtside, she'd spent an unusual amount of time with the Matriarch's Family. He had the sneaking suspicion that she was almost using them as a refuge.

"Shall I resend, sir? Perhaps call her to the CP?"

"No," Murphy replied flatly. "She'll be going back to R'Bak for the next training cycle. If she wants to keep to herself right now, I intend to give her the time and space to do just that."

Even if I have to staple my lips together to keep from asking what put that tough-as-nails chopper jock into an apparent tailspin. "Has everyone else replied?"

"Everyone except Chalmers, sir."

It rankled just to be reminded that Chalmers was technically part of the cadre. *Had* to be, since he was the only Lost Soldier with the necessary skillset and experience for counterintelligence and investigations. Murphy sighed. "Give him a few more hours, Pistol."

"Yes, sir. It would not be the first time he has been…slow to acknowledge a general communique."

Or to get with the program. For a guy who was supposedly a wizard at sussing out other people, he did a pretty crappy job when it came to handling his own shit. That had been obvious the first time Chalmers was being briefed by SpinDogs. Right away, he'd butted heads with them. Particularly the lead trainer, Stabilo, who was a piece of work himself. *And if I hadn't been there to short-circuit whatever antagonism had been building between them, well…*"Has Chalmers at least confirmed he's on schedule to deploy dirtside?"

"Not yet, sir." Makarov paused. "He hasn't made things easy for us, has he, sir?"

Murphy usually rebuked anyone who passed that kind of comment on a soldier under his command, but in this case, he could only sigh. "No, he hasn't."

"But you believe he can determine which locals may be undermining our operations on R'Bak?"

"Better than anyone else we have. Or at least, anybody else we can spare."

Makarov paused. "And do you trust him?"

Murphy stared at the question. "Trust," he replied slowly, "is overrated."

PART FOUR:

CHALMERS

Chapter Thirty-Two

R'BAK

"Trust but confirm. Trust but confirm. Trust but confirm," Chalmers grunted the litany into his helmet.

"What?" Jackson gasped.

Chalmers didn't answer right away, fighting for breath after saying so much.

Their shuttle had been burning for what the SpinDogs termed, "a narrow drop window to orbital insertion." This "Spaceman Spiff" speech translated roughly as, "An absurdly fidgety three-hundred-pound trucker will be sitting on your chest, gut, and bladder for at least thirty minutes; have a nice day." By all accounts, the Dornaani ship on which they'd arrived in-system compared to their current ride much like a Ferrari compared to a Mustang. Both were powerful and looked pretty, depending on taste, but one certainly seemed a lot more refined than the other. Even so, the shuttle *looked* more advanced than anything Earth had been sending into orbit in his day, and it was certainly powerful enough to push his eyeballs through the back of his skull.

He'd just decided that concentrating on speaking would at least take his mind off the struggle to breathe when the thrust suddenly cut back to something like one gee.

Chalmers breathed in and out, repeating the process twice, just to be sure his ribs were in their proper place, before he finally replied, "I was just wishing we could have confirmed this thing was safe before being packed in like sardines."

Jackson pulled a face, his expression clearly visible through the visor of his space suit's helmet.

"What was that, Space Man?" Chalmers asked, more than a little freaked out by the fact that he was in a fucking space suit, too.

"I fucking *hate* sardines."

Chalmers laughed. "I'm sure they love you."

"Naw, man. My pops, he used to make us get them on our pizza."

"On pizza?"

"Yes."

"You sure you're talking about sardines? I heard of anchovies on pizza, but not sardines."

Jackson's eyes were a little wild. "I'm talkin' sardines. You know: those fish in oil. Stink to high heaven."

"Both are packed in oil. Anchovies are smaller, I think."

"Sardine, anchovies, whatever, man," Jackson said, calmer for having something other than their predicament to talk about. "They used to stink like nothing else. Would make the whole house smell, even when he only got half the pizza covered with that crap."

"That's…unnatural," Chalmers said, meaning it. "In fact, it should be against the Geneva Conventions."

"I *know*!" Jackson sniffed, shook his head. "Miss that guy. Not the pizzas, though. Not those fish-smelling, nasty-ass pizzas!"

"Pizza," Chalmers said, reminded of the best he'd ever had. "Knew this place in SF made a killer slice: pineapple and ham."

"Fruit? You put *fruit* on your pizza? Talk about violating the Conventions, man. That's just wrong, man. Just *wrong*. At least fish is meat."

"Fish ain't meat, man."

"The fuck it ain't. Who the hell asks the asshole who thinks putting fruit on a piece of pie is a good idea, anyway? No one, that's who!"

"For God sakesss—" Chalmers' retort was pressed out of him in a distorted *hiss* as the pilot piled on the gees again, and the tremble of touching the top of R'Bak's atmosphere started rising up through his gut.

And then, suddenly, he was on the back of a whacked-out bucking bronco, trapped in an elevator plummeting straight to hell.

"Hands-on experience is essential, Jackson," Chalmers said, jutting his chin at their ride and glad the brush fire burning almost three miles to the south wasn't likely to be along their path. Of course, any of the more naturally occurring ones might become a problem.

Wishing to limit their exposure to hostile eyes, the big, snub-nosed shuttle had landed in as sparsely settled an area as possible. The main mission, of course, meant they were still fairly close to one of the satrapies, as those states were the ones that protected Kulsian interests in their overlord's absence. An anxious-looking SpinDog crew had thrown the two Lost Soldiers and their equipment out as soon as the vehicles from Camp Stark—including one serious dune-buggy—appeared on the dove-gray horizon. Then, quite literally in this case, they burned for orbit. The massive dual-phase engines of the shuttle had ignited the stretch of scrub that still smoldered in the distance.

"'Hands-on experience is necessary?' You tryin' to sell me that? Really?" Jackson asked, his expression making it all too clear he knew Chalmers was full of shit. Chalmers sensed his partner was arguing as much to distract them both from the oddly astringent brush smoke being carried on the morning wind as any strong desire to drive the buggy himself.

"Look, dude, I drove these things all over Baja." It was an exaggeration, of course. He couldn't be sure, but Chalmers was reasonably confident he'd driven one for an hour or two one drunken week in Mexico. He'd done a *lot* of drinking on that vacation, as he'd been celebrating—or trying to forget—the demise of his second marriage. Come to think of it, he just might have spent more than a couple hours behind the wheel.

He shook his head, unable to recall. There had been *lots* of mescal.

"Fine," Jackson grunted.

Chalmers nodded, more to himself than Jackson. It *was* fine. Even this shitty mission on a shitty desert planet was *totally* fine. He, more than any of the rest of the men and women stolen from their own times and places, was happy as hell to be anywhere but home. Sure, they might be at the ass-end of nowhere, but the fate he'd been facing at the end of the helicopter ride that had ultimately landed him here had well and truly sucked. Sucked bad enough to have made one Horace Earl Chalmers consider suck-starting a shotgun, truth be told. And now, here he was, about to drive a dune-buggy that looked so badass he thought he might get a hard-on just from looking at it.

The all-wheel weirdness was every kind of post-apocalyptic *Mad Max* cool: seating for four with a steel tube chassis riding high on beefy shocks. The buggy made his hands itch with desire to drive it.

He bent to examine the tires, which proved to be perfectly tailored to the sand, dust, and loose, stony soil composition of the terrain. They were even partially deflated to provide the best possible purchase, and a spare was mounted on each side behind a rank of jerry cans.

And the cool didn't end there. The large, exposed engine had made a satisfying growl when it was driven up to them by a gearhead from Camp Stark's new motor pool. The grease monkey might have been ex-army, but just whose army it had been was hard to say; he'd had Cyrillic tattoos across his fingers. He also looked resentful at having to part with the stolen machine as he climbed into the truck that had accompanied him out into the godforsaken wastes and was now carrying him back to the forward operating base. Might have just been jealousy over the fact the two new arrivals were being given *any* kind of vehicle to complete their mission, but Chalmers doubted it. Neither fuel nor spares were easily come by, and their operation was being carefully controlled to avoid waste. Once the Lost Soldiers ran out of those logistical necessities, the vehicles liberated from the Kulsian cache would go from being indispensable to oversized paperweights.

"You acting like this thing is a saddle-whinnie, Chalmers," Jackson said as he removed his pack and settled it behind the rear passenger seat. The cargo area was small, and he had to move the strap of a come-along to get it in place.

"Am not," Chalmers said. "Though I would pay money to see you try to ride, city boy."

"Look at you, talking shit like you some kinda John Wayne or something."

"Naw, just a part-time redneck. We like gears and engines more than steers and horses."

"That why you rednecks have all them broke-down cars and refrigerators and shit on your front lawns?" Jackson asked as he loosened another come-along strap to make room so Chalmers could drop his pack next to Jackson's own.

Chalmers chuckled. "Must be."

The combined communications and GPS—or whatever—unit attached to Jackson's pack pinged.

Jackson glanced at Chalmers, who nodded. The sergeant unclipped the carabiner securing the device to his bag and held it up. A touch of his thumb activated it.

"Gentlemen." Murphy's voice was clear and cool, like the pre-sunrise air. "Are you ready?"

"As much as we can be, not knowing where we're headed," Chalmers said, keeping his tone as light and non-confrontational as he could, even as he wished for video so he could read Murphy's expression.

"Sorry about that. OpSec has to be very tight on this one." The major made a point of pausing.

Jackson and Chalmers both perked up at this, making a check of their surroundings. No one was close enough to listen in without being obvious about it or using vanishingly rare electronics.

"You're to meet with a couple of the kinsmen from the Sarmatchani tribes. They're from the next tribe over and have more contact with the settled peoples we are eventually going to have to get on our side. The tribesmen will help you make contact with the people of Clarthu."

The device in Jackson's hand lit up with a map and coordinates.

"Orbital SIGINT intercepted a radio transmission during our last movement near Clarthu. The same guys decoded the message, and it was a fairly accurate report of our movements and numbers during and since we started seizing cached Kulsian vehicles and equipment."

"Shit," Jackson muttered.

"The indig tribesmen we've been dealing with say the villagers are predisposed to support us, too, which tracks generally with the HUMINT the SpinDogs have been sharing with us. Therefore, both intelligence streams believe it's only one, or possibly two, collaborators."

"But how much can we trust the SpinDogs?" Chalmers asked.

Murphy paused again, clearly aware their hosts would know exactly what he was saying over their own comm system. "While the SpinDogs have been…less than entirely forthcoming on certain matters, they have fully supported the mission. I think this particular situation might have something to do with the RockHounds faction or the friction between the Expansionists and the Hardliners. Frankly, I don't know." A thoughtful pause. "There's a lot of political complexity up here, and we've only begun to scratch the surface."

"Poles," Chalmers said, equally thoughtfully.

"What's that, Chief?" Murphy asked.

"Just thinking we have to be wary of being used up like the Polish Paras in WWII," Chalmers explained.

Murphy was silent for a long moment, then said, "There could be some parallels to Operation Market Garden, but I hope to keep everyone from dying because we over-extended and reached for a bridge too far. Or further."

Chalmers smiled weakly. Murphy still intimidated the shit out of him, but it was good to hear the major recognize the quality of his assessment.

"At any rate, gentlemen, I need you to collect your tribal guides, obtain their best assessment of who might be radioing in our dispositions and why. With that information in hand—or not—you will then proceed to the village where you will locate and confiscate any radio equipment before our next movement.

You will accomplish this while minimizing any damage to our future relations with the villagers as potential future allies. I am told that Bruce—er, Captain Lee—is done with her shakedown flights of the new, replicated Hueys and will be standing off for emergency extraction during the meet with the Kedlak."

"You suspect the Kedlak's people will give us trouble?" Chalmers asked, relieved there was some kind of plan to get them out if things dropped in the shitter.

"No, but I know I wouldn't want to meet with a tribe of unknowns without some kind of extraction team, and I won't send people to do things I wouldn't do myself." The major paused. "And before you ask, I considered having Bruce loiter near the meet, but we don't know precisely where the camp is, and I don't want to spook them."

"Spook them?" Chalmers asked.

Jackson shot a look at Chalmers the latter interpreted as, "Why don't you pay attention to the briefings?"

Murphy, unaware of the silent byplay and apparently willing to overlook Chalmers' ignorance, said, "The only people with air power on R'Bak are the bad guys, and we don't want our first impression to be tainted by that association." Murphy then added, "Look, I know this mission's a dog's breakfast, but I need you to execute, copy?"

"Copy that," Jackson said.

"Any questions?"

"What kind of toast you want with that order?" Jackson asked.

"Blackened rye," Murphy drawled.

"And how long do we have to accomplish the mission?" Chalmers asked, glad the major was cozy with one of them, at least.

"Oh, I'm sure two crack investigators like you can sew this up in forty-eight hours. In forty-nine and one-half hours, the lead elements of our force will be transiting the valley in full view of the village. Gentlemen, I would really hate to level a village because of one asshole. Find the radio. Find the operator. I'm not too concerned about the condition of either. Stopping the transmissions is priority one. Hooah?"

"Hooah, Major," the partners chorused, even though neither of them were, or had been, Rangers. The query-and-response had been ubiquitous among the Airborne guys in Mogadishu, and some things spread—and stuck in the head—like herpes.

The link went dead.

"I'm still driving," Chalmers said, rushing around to the driver's side of the buggy.

Jackson let Chalmers go, ratcheting the come-along until their packs were held firmly in place.

Chalmers hopped in and started the little rear-engined vehicle, which came snorting to life.

Startled by the sudden, angry growl from so close at hand, Jackson banged his head against a roll bar and spat a string of invective at Chalmers in multiple languages.

"Sorry, man."

"You nuthin' but a redneck fuckup, you know that?"

Chalmers kept staring ahead. Jackson's tone had been at least three-quarters gruff banter but that's not how he'd heard it.

Not from the moment the word "fuckup" had left the little sergeant's lips…

Chapter Thirty-Three

SPIN ONE
FIVE WEEKS EARLIER

"Chalmers, do you know how many times the words 'fuck up' appear in your dossier? And that's coming from officers who are not given to profanity."

Chalmers shook his head. "No idea, sir."

"I don't suppose you would. And I don't suppose you'd care. That's also a common theme in the assessments of your COs." Murphy sighed. "But you're the only asset we have who can smoke out one or more informers among our indig allies. And build rapport with the locals while you do so."

"Rather not have to, Major," Chalmers said, carefully suppressing a flinch as Murphy snapped an angry stare his direction. He wasn't sure why he felt the urge to shy away. Murphy wasn't particularly imposing, and Chalmers knew that proper command authority to back Murphy's orders was, at the very least, way the fuck out of reach. Like, *light years* out of reach.

But upon learning just how lucky he'd been waking up here and now, Chalmers had taken a sober look at his life and the shit show it had become. In light of the messes he'd made, Chalmers decided to do better. To *be* better. So, despite a strong natural inclination to tell the major some bullshit about being eager to take on the mission, Chalmers was not going to lie to get off the hot-seat.

Murphy's stare was still fixed on him. "What's that about you 'rather not' doing your *job*, Chief?" The major's tone was not angry, but coolly detached. Which was worse.

"With respect, Major, I'd rather not be dropped in the shit again. I mean, 'hearts and minds?' You've got operators for that. Hell, from what I hear, some of the men were around when the term was coined."

Murphy's tone chilled from unpleasantly cool to icy. "Warrant Officer Chalmers, I'm fairly certain I didn't ask what you'd 'rather.' In fact, I'm certain I give not one fuck what you'd rather." The major paused, whether for effect or to prevent giving vent to his temper, Chalmers couldn't say.

Despite knowing the man lacked the legal authority to do much to him, Chalmers swallowed the disrespectful response that threatened to spill from his lips. His goal of being better was not going to just *happen.* No one was going to just hand Chalmers the respect he'd always craved. More important in this moment, Chalmers realized he actually gave a shit what this guy—what all the men—thought of him. He didn't like the mission, but Chalmers liked this man's contempt even less. And he wasn't sure what, exactly, he'd done to earn it.

Unless.

"Major, I apologize. I misspoke. W—"

"Did you?" Murphy snapped.

"My experience is almost exclusively CID," Chalmers explained. "Criminal investigation is my area of expertise. I've got no experience getting people to come around to our si—"

Murphy's waved Chalmers' protest down, his icy demeanor taking on the weight and majesty of a glacier as he slowly leaned forward. "I don't need you to win their hearts and minds, Warrant Chalmers. I need you to investigate, to identify, and to root out the equivalent of a local crime ring and, if possible, help us locate hidden caches of Kulsian tech before their lackeys can empty them. You do have a proven track record of rooting out such networks, of properly identifying and seizing their contraband. Your selection for this mission was precisely due to certain moral ambiguities with which you seem perfectly comfortable, given the…activities that led to your presence on the helo that was taking you out of Mogadishu."

Chalmers swallowed a protest, knowing it would be a lie. Desperately seeking to ingratiate himself—and not entirely sure why—he ventured, "I'd be careful, Major, about how much you reveal of people's backgrounds."

Murphy's wintry smile accompanied the confident regard of a man entirely indifferent to any leverage or bluster. "Is that a threat, mister?"

"Fuck, no, Major! I just meant—Look, I wasn't on my way home, but being transferred pending the results of their investigation. An already-completed investigation. Sending me out on orders was just a face-saving measure my CO and—" Murphy opened his mouth but Chalmers raised a hand, eyes pleading as he rushed on. "I know what I did. Here and now, I ain't denying it. But the information of what I did would only be available *after* we were shot down. You being in possession of that information tells a suspicious person you might be a participant in the program that kidnapped us. If you have similar information on others of us, you'll want to be careful about what and how you reveal it. I'm telling you, I've interviewed enough shitheads to know they're always looking to lay the blame for getting caught at someone else's feet. In this case—" he shook his head "—I know the rest of the soldiers aren't likely to be shits like me. But even for a straight GI-fuckin'-Joe, getting stuck in this whole fucked-up situation is gonna feel like they 'got caught'…by something or someone. So, whatever you can do to keep people from automatically thinking you're part of that 'something or someone,' the better."

Murphy's right eye twitched, the only sign the major wasn't carved of ice. Then again, it actually looked more like an involuntary tic.

"I know you weren't party to it," Chalmers blurted, hands up in surrender. "I'm just saying, well, those 'Nam-era snakes did coin another term, something about, 'fragging' COs."

Murphy blinked. Both eyes this time. Definitely not a tic. A moment passed. Another. The major's sharp nod was more the calving of an iceberg than anything resembling an acknowledgement that Chalmers might have a point or had managed to thaw Murphy's disdain in the slightest.

"Frankly, I don't have any choice but to plug you in. If ever I discover you've jeopardized the mission—a mission intended to secure the survival of every single one of us—I will find a way to make certain you are put out of my misery. Besides, your ability to think around certain corners like that is just the turn of mind this particular mission requires, Chief. *If* you can stay on mission?"

Chalmers, noticing the major had resumed calling him 'chief'—the honorific by which warrants were usually addressed—started breathing again. Not trusting his voice, he nodded mute understanding.

"Mission-specific briefing materials and your training schedule will be available after lunch. Language training begins tonight. Sergeant Jackson—I presume you'll want him—will join you once medically cleared. He'll have to play catch up."

"Shouldn't be a problem for him. He's a lot better at languages than me," Chalmers said, fighting a wave of relief that Jackson would be on his side again.

"Very good. Dismissed."

Chalmers stood, saluted, and left.

It was only when he started reading the briefing that Chalmers realized the mission was already on the operational timetable. This kind of local shit-sifting usually took months to prepare for, but Major Murphy had acted as if they could reach a useful level of language competency in weeks.

Instead of whining to command right then and there, Chalmers read the rest of the briefing materials and in due time discovered just why Murphy thought they'd be up to speed.

Virtual language instruction at ten-to-one time compression? He rubbed his forehead. Fucking unreal, the things the Doorknobs could do.

SPIN ONE
TEN DAYS LATER

A gesture turned off the alarm while Chalmers tried to summon the will to rise from his rack. He'd drunk too much last night. Way too much.

Jackson had needed it. It had started out in good fun: a few drinks, some shit-talking, a few more drinks. Chalmers had been happy to be out from under the fate he'd known awaited him at the end of the helo ride. Jackson had been happy to have survived the crash but was wounded behind the eyes. The liquor had pried the pain out into the open, allowed the small sergeant to begin to express it like the rot at the center of a boil: the two kids and pregnant wife left behind, hundreds of years and more miles away than anyone without a physics degree could even begin to comprehend.

Chalmers glanced across at Jackson, who was snoring, hard, in the next bunk. There at the end, Jackson's anger had boiled over, directionless but still volcanic in its heat.

An unfamiliar guilt washed through Chalmers, made his guts churn even more than the remnants of last night's liquor. Guilty because he, and he alone, should have been the focus of his partner's anger. He could only suppose that Murphy hadn't told the sergeant why, exactly, they'd both been on the helo when they were shot down. Murphy had probably thought telling Jackson would be counter to mission needs or some shit; he might even have been right to withhold the information.

But that didn't make Chalmers feel any better. Indeed, it tested his resolve to *be* better. Should he tell Jackson and blow up the only relationship he'd ever been able to maintain? Just to keep the promise he'd made? Did wanting to be better—*do* better—with this second chance at life give him the right to fuck with Jackson's peace?

Unable to find an answer, Chalmers coughed and, head pounding, sat up. He wouldn't have moved, but two needs drove him: to relieve his bladder and drink something to float his brain, the pan of which was dry-humping every neuron into oblivion. Carefully, oh so carefully, he got up and took care of those needs, then fumbled for the medication the SpinDogs had supplied them with. They said the stuff was harvested on R'Bak, but frankly, Chalmers didn't give a damn. Just so long as it dealt a killing blow to the hangover that threatened to make him hurl.

SPIN ONE
TWELVE DAYS LATER

The hatch to the bay Chalmers shared with Jackson slammed open.

"Nothing," Chalmers said automatically, feeling as if he'd been caught with one hand in the cookie jar. "Nothing useful," he amended, slowly returning his hands to the oddly-designed SpinDog keyboard.

Jackson snorted. "Man, you have a shit startle response." The sergeant looked, and sounded, much better than he had before his outpouring of drunken vitriol. Since then, the virtual reality language training had pretty much consumed all their time. And time, even virtual time spent slogging through the odd complexities of devolved Ktoran grammar and syntax, had apparently healed many of the festering wounds that Jackson's binge started draining. "In fact," Chalmer's roommate continued after a dramatic pause, "you may have the worst startle response of anyone I've ever worked with. Totally useless."

"Might be, Jacks, might be." Chalmers rubbed his chin and the five o'clock shadow there. "But it's only a result of my need to protect my pretty face."

"Keep telling yourself that, man," Jackson said, casting a meaningful look at Chalmers' display.

"I was looking at the history files," Chalmers said carefully. They'd been cooling their heels since the SEAL's mission had launched, attending a seemingly endless string of mandatory briefings and planning sessions. Despite all the meetings, Murphy was being cagey about when, exactly, their deployment would happen. Tonight had been their first time off in a while, and Chalmers had decided to turn over a new leaf and started researching their space-dwelling allies. What he'd found hadn't satisfied him, not at all. He'd looked for more juicy material, something equivalent to a gossip rag or tell-all book, but the SpinDogs either didn't have such things or were keeping the Lost Soldiers locked out of the public information stream.

"Not much there," Jackson said. "Makes you think they got shit to hide."

Chalmers nodded at the computer screen. "Maybe we can hack it, you know, like *War Games*? You get much time on computers as a kid?" he asked, hoping against hope the younger version of his partner would have acquired some hidden skill at computers he didn't know about.

"'Course, man!" Jackson chuckled. "Growing up on the South Side in the early eighties got us kids all sorts of time on them mainframes. In fact, I was gonna go straight to work for IBM right up until I signed my first contract with the Bulls."

Chalmers was laughing well before Jackson finished his sarcastic rant. He held his hands up in surrender. "All right, all right! I'm an asshole."

"No, you just showing your vanilla," Jackson said, smiling.

"All right, I deserved that…" He gestured at the terminal as well. "But you've been reading up, right?"

"Damn straight."

"The files they gave us; they're pretty scant on who hates who."

Jackson shrugged narrow shoulders. "Well, kinda understandable."

Chalmers looked a question at him.

"They're making a mistake like the one mistake *you* just made. Only on a lot bigger scale."

"Not sure I follow," Chalmers said.

"The SpinDogs all seem to think their way is *the* way, so why bother learning what others think or do?"

Chalmers shook his head slightly. "Yeah, but these guys are supposed to be all, 'survival of the fittest' and warrior culture. Seems like holding back basic information would create issues of survival for anyone who was that blind, and those acting on that blindness."

"Crackers gonna be crackers." Jackson delivered the words with a southern drawl that he seemed to think should underline his meaning.

Underlining or no, Chalmers missed what he meant. "What?" he asked.

"Look at their history—at least what we've been told of it. They were bound to think of themselves as the best and brightest thing going, and their arrogant asses won't let them admit that losing their own civil war—or whatever—was their own damn fault. So, they get kicked out of the house and come here, finding all these backward people, a lot of who've descended into some kind of worse-than-Thunderdome shit. They all set to claim themselves the new masters, but then the Kulsians appear, who haven't descended quite so far, and they got big guns, too, and better numbers. But our friends were lucky enough to be in space, so they hide out, bide their time, all the while thinking their truth is the only truth that matters. When really, what's goin' on is one cracker sees the other cracker got a bigger whip and knows, deep in his bones, that he wants to hold that whip, but can't."

"You lost me again, Jackson," Chalmers said.

Jackson sighed, thought about it a moment, then said, "These SpinDogs have had nothing smack them in the face to tell them how wrong their outlook is."

"But they were kicked off their home world or whatever."

Jackson nodded emphatically. "Sure were. But to their minds, they got beat by people who were *better* than they were at being the ideal of their culture. They come here, see the people that lost some of the motherland's stink, all descended into barbarism, and the folks that didn't sink *as* low still in charge, still adhering to the Old Ways. Nothing has ever told these crackers their system is whacked. They don't even think to question that. The only lesson they've learned is the wrong one: that *they* weren't good *enough* at working that system, which only served to *confirm*, in their eyes, the values of the very same system, man."

Chalmers blinked. He'd always known Jackson was smarter than he, but he'd rarely been shown just how *much* smarter. If the man had been given a better education, Chalmers had no doubt Jackson would have been some kind of staff officer or civilian bigwig.

Guilt followed the thought. Guilt that, had Jackson not fallen in with the wrong crowd, so many things might have been different. Especially since, in this case, the wrong crowd was one Horace Chalmers, Warrant Officer, US Army.

"Yeah," Jackson mused, staring at the bulkhead, "Murphy seems to think things are going to be fine once we put our hosts in charge of the planet. Maybe it's just my blood talking, but I'm thinking we just putting *our* crackers in charge, nothing more."

"Is that a problem?"

Another pensive shrug. "Not really. I figure the government in D.C. used to do the same shit all the time, right? So long as we know what our crackers want, we can be looking out, I guess…No, thing I worry about is this: do we really know our crackers, or are they gonna be stabbing each other—and us—in the back to get the best bits of the pig?"

Chalmers leaned back, suddenly wishing they hadn't had this conversation in what was probably their bugged bay. Not that there were any sureties of privacy elsewhere, but if Jackson was right, Chalmers was certain all of the competing interests would act to make sure their agenda was served. And that could interfere with the mission. Almost certainly would, in fact.

He didn't think he was being paranoid, but just because you couldn't see threats didn't mean they weren't there. That's why he'd been diligently searching through the records they'd been given. Wanting to name his fear made Chalmers a far better student than he'd been before.

Come to think of it, the emphasis all the non-Terran humans—SpinDogs, Hardliners, R'Baku, and Kulsians alike—placed on clan loyalty was a lot like Mogadishu, what with its powerful warlords and would-be kings.

No, this could end up *being* the Mog all over again, no matter who they wound up backing in the end.

SPIN ONE
SEVEN DAYS LATER

"Man, this mission just keeps getting better and better," Jackson said, replacing the headset on the terminal.

"What's that?" Chalmers asked, mopping a sweaty brow with one end of his towel. The .75-gee maintained in the quarters of most SpinDog habs wasn't enough to maintain real muscle tone, not on its own, so the afternoon workout he had just returned from had quickly become a habit. His body had likely been in the best shape it had been since AIT on his awakening, and it was easier to start from that high level of fitness than it had been at any time since his youth. He needed *something* to be easier, too. This changing his life for the better the second time around wasn't exactly easy, so he figured making a habit of healthy practices was better than trying to play catch up later.

"You see the latest mission brief?" Jackson asked, leaning back in his chair to avoid getting sweat dripped on him. The Coriolis effect made it hard to predict just where shit was gonna hit.

"No. What happened?" Chalmers asked, his gut suddenly churning.

"Murphy said we're no longer going to be tasked with locating black-market dealers and their suppliers, but uncovering spies in the local populace."

Nodding, Chalmers finished wiping down and, wadding the towel in one fist, chucked it into the reclaimer built into the wall of their quarters.

"You don't seem surprised."

Chalmers shrugged and skinned off his sweat-soaked shirt. "Nope. Murphy doesn't know any better than us what we're gonna see on the ground until…well, until we're boots on the ground. I figure we could end up doing anything from carrying beans and bullets for the shooters to driving one of those goofy armored vehicles the local warlords tool around in. There's just no way of knowing until we are down and doing it. Murphy's Law screws with even the simplest plans, and this one has way too many ifs for comfortable planning."

"How are you so chill, man? No offense, but your ass wasn't exactly known for coolness…"

Chalmers smiled. "I figure I got a second chance at doing this right. Being…better, I guess? Life being life, that don't mean the chance doesn't have a heavy price tag attached, but I'd rather get it right, you know? For me."

Jackson smiled. "You got all wise and shit, Chalmers."

"I'm trying, Jacks. I'm trying."

Chapter Thirty-Four

R'BAK

And I'm still trying, Chalmers thought, trying to bring his focus out of the past and back on to the mission. But the heat when the sun—no, check that—when the *suns* came up was pretty awful. Only two hours on R'Bak and the problem was not that it was too alien, but too damned familiar. It was hot like the Mog, dry like the Mog, and even had terrain like the Mog. Shit, maybe this was just some long, booze-born hallucination, and he was still *in* the Mog.

But no, the locals who rose out of the gray and red rocks in front of them were not properly cast if this scene was set in Somalia. Wild diversity of genotype, better fed, crap weapons, and sparing of both motion and sound.

Chalmers grunted and slowed the buggy to a crawl as sentries waved to him from a guard post located just below the crest of the pass. They'd been under observation for at least the last ten kilometers, from well-concealed watch posts they only knew of because of the images the SpinDogs had given Murphy and by roving patrols they had caught glimpses of once or twice in the hours it had taken them to come this far.

A large man, with dreadlocks, a broad, scarred face, and wearing the loose, flowing tunic and pants that seemed something of a uniform for the indigs, came out of a rampart-like arrangement of felled timber, earth, and stone. He barked something that Chalmers lost the meaning of somewhere between the thick accent and missing teeth. Again, just like the Mog.

Chalmers put the buggy in neutral and braked to a stop but kept the motor running.

Jackson smiled and called back in the same language, "We're here to see the chief."

The man smiled, showing dark spaces where his front teeth should be. "The Kedlakis-Ur waits for you with son and daughter at tent *something* the *something*."

"Can get this in?" Jackson asked, gesturing at the buggy.

The guard nodded and said, "I send warrior with you to make sure you not *something* on *something*."

"Understood," Jackson said. Chalmers really didn't want to think how hard his life would be without a good partner. Jackson truly had the gift of tongues.

"Mayal, you go with *something*. Guide past the *something*."

A skinny warrior—Chalmers did a quick double-take as he made out the fine features and beardless chin—woman came out of the defenses and eyed the buggy suspiciously.

Jackson smiled and waved the woman to the back seat, which she promptly climbed into. Chalmers eyed her in the rear-view. The woman named Mayal held herself tightly and didn't strap in until Jackson leaned back and showed her how to work the three-point restraint. She seemed a lot younger perched nervously in the unfamiliar seat, one of the long-barreled single-shot rifles favored by better-equipped nomads held muzzle-down between her knees. She smelled of nomad, too. A not entirely unpleasant tickling of the nose that fell somewhere between sweat and sage.

Once she was situated, Chalmers put the buggy into gear and eased past the guard post. About a hundred yards on, the saddle at the top of the pass narrowed to the width of a football field.

Mayal tapped his right shoulder and pointed to the right.

Chalmers obeyed, and, after they covered about twenty yards on the new heading, she tapped his other shoulder, pointing to the left. He changed direction, but she tapped him again, directing a harder left.

"Shit!" Jackson said, looking down.

"What?" Chalmers asked, taking his foot off the gas.

"Didn't you listen to the guard boss?" Jackson spat.

"I fucking listened, man," Chalmers answered, mildly angry at lying. "I just couldn't understand him past the lisp."

"Right," Jackson said, shaking his head and gesturing at the ground to the right, "Pits, man. Covered pits. Big enough to swallow a rider…or us."

"Jesus." Chalmers made sure to drive slowly for the next ten minutes as Mayal guided them through another series of changes of direction. When she relaxed in her seat, he relaxed. By then, though, they'd climbed to the top of the pass and turned up a defile that was only a few feet wider than the buggy.

They drove out of the shadow of the defile into a larger box canyon, a narrow, side-hugging shelf that descended to the canyon floor, which held the tents of the encampment.

Chalmers nervously kept the driver's side wheel next to the wall of the canyon. The last thing he wanted was to go over the edge and down the two hundred yards or so to the floor. He whistled after a moment. What he'd first taken for a scattering of only twenty-odd tents resolved, after a more careful study, into nearly a hundred.

"This is a freaking town, not a camp," Jackson said, his eyes on a forge being worked under an awning of one of the larger pavilions, located hard by the spring that had presumably helped carve the network of draws and canyons that made up the territory Chalmers and Jackson had just come through.

Their engine noise attracted the interest of a great number of the locals, who paused to watch them as Chalmers navigated the narrow track. Some started moving onto the trail head.

"Major Murphy did say something about the tribal leadership summoning the clans after the beating Moorefield gave the J'Stull."

Jackson nodded, but the sergeant didn't otherwise answer. Chalmers could see the sergeant's fingers twitching as he kept counting tents.

"Figure a family a tent, a hundred tents…" Chalmers mused. "What do you figure, one or two military age males per family?"

"Stop throwing numbers at me. I'm trying to count."

Chalmers shut up.

"Jesus," Jackson said after another minute. "There's ninety-six tents in view. Call it at least two hundred, two hundred and fifty, military age *people*," Jackson said, hiking a thumb at the woman in the back seat.

"I wonder how things ended up that way," Chalmers said. "No religion's saying it's a no-no, maybe?"

"Gotta think it's more than that," Jackson said, sounding thoughtful. "They inherited their way of living from the Ktor. And I think the decline in tech was faster and mentally easier to accept than the disintegration of social norms."

Chalmers chuckled.

Jackson shot him a look. "What?"

"You talk a good game, but I think you had more schooling than you let on," Chalmers said, navigating the last turn of the trail before reaching the bottom of the canyon.

"I had occasion to read a lot," Jackson said, looking sidelong at his partner, "and a library card is free, yo!"

Chalmers was prevented from talking shit when Mayal pointed at a nearby tent and said, "There."

A large number of indigs were already gathered around their destination, with more arriving every moment. The crush of bodies forced Chalmers to slow to a crawl. All ages were represented, though the people were generally thinner and just a little shorter than most 20th century Americans. Everyone was armed in one way or another, the richest having some form of rifle and smoothbore muskets for the slightly less affluent.

"Lots of bandoliers filled with shells, almost enough to equip the extras on *Blazing Saddles*," Chalmers said nervously. The crowd was parting for them, but slowly, and everyone was eyeballing them like they wanted to cut a flank steak from their bodies.

"Not that many bandoliers in that flick. You're thinking *Three Amigos*, man," Jackson said, nerves making his voice high.

"That the one with Chevy Chase?"

"Yup."

"Dammit," Chalmers said, shaking his head. "I always get them mixed up."

"Good way to keep 'em separate is to count n bombs. Not an n-bomb in *Three Amigos,* while *Blazing Saddles* has them all over the place. Then again, that's 'cause there's not a single black person in *Three Amigos*, and Mel's always interested in punching people in the face with their own racism and bigotry. Love that old bastard."

"Probably dead, now, though," Chalmers said as he parked in front of their destination.

"Why you gotta be a dick, Chalmers?" Jackson shook his head. "Mel will live forever, man! *The 2000 Year Old Man* is immortal!"

"Sorry, Jacks. Guess I'm just not that nice a guy." He shut the motor down.

"At least you own it," Jackson said as a tall woman stepped from the tent. The crowd quieted. Not that they'd been that loud to begin with. The newcomer looked about forty, which meant she was likely in her mid- to early thirties. A nomad's life wasn't easy, not even for the wealthy, not unless they were filthy rich, by which point they'd carefully *chosen* to remain nomads.

"Who is the chief, again?" Chalmers asked.

"Not sure Murphy had a name for us, but the guard said Kedlakis-Ur, right?"

"Awesome."

"Just like the regular Army," Jackson said, grinning.

Shaking his head, Chalmers concealed his own smile until Jackson wasn't looking. No use letting Jackson know in just how high a regard Chalmers held the small sergeant.

Chapter Thirty-Five

R'BAK

"Focus on the mission," Chalmers told himself as the indigs of Kedlakis continued to gather. He tried not to shove too hard at the onlookers as he came around the buggy to stand next to the passenger side.

Being surrounded by so many armed strangers would make anyone nervous, and Chalmers already had a suspicious nature. Even if they'd had an extraction team and pair of Blackhawks ready to rain death on anyone who stepped out of line, he'd have been anxious. As it was, Captain Mara Lee—call sign "Bruce"—was supposed to be paralleling them in the next valley over, ready to come in hot should they call for her, but that was cold comfort. Chalmers respected the pilot, but even if she could get to them in two minutes, anything more than a minute was an eternity in close quarters battle. Things were so tight with the indigs that if anything popped off, they were done for.

"Is that Kedlakis-Ur?" Jackson asked Mayal, nodding in the newly-appeared woman's direction.

The young warrior nodded but quietly added, "*The* Kedlakis-Ur, yes."

Jackson glanced at Chalmers, who gave a slight nod and started pushing against the crowd to make room for his companion. The sergeant climbed out of the buggy and stood in the space provided as the Kedlakis-Ur approached. By the time he was standing next to Chalmers, the Kedlakis-Ur was before them; the crowd had parted for her without a command.

She was thick-wristed and sleekly muscled. Tall and powerfully built in the way of ranchers back home, her long, dark hair was bound in what looked like a complicated network of braids that were allowed to fall down her back after passing through a yellow stone ring. A real man-eater.

Chalmers liked the type.

"Greetings, Kedlakis-Ur," Jackson said. "I am Sergeant Jackson, and this is Warrant Officer Chalmers. We were told you are expecting us. We bring the promised gifts."

The woman studied them both for a long moment. Chalmers didn't usually feel uncomfortable when women looked at him, but there was something about this woman's regard that left him with the sense he'd been weighed and found wanting.

"I am the Kedlakis-Ur. Welcome to the camp of the Kedlak. You have my protection and welcome." The woman's voice was gravel on rose petals. The kind you wanted to hear raised in song.

Chalmers and Jackson waited for more, but the woman stood silently regarding them.

"We…ahh, have the promised gifts," Chalmers said, after the silence had stretched too long for comfort.

The woman nodded, and Chalmers gestured.

Jackson climbed into the back seat and grunted as he pulled the bag of SpinDog-approved goodies from the foot well. Never ones to trust REMFs—especially someone else's REMFs—to provide everything they might need, Chalmers and Jackson had both added a few hopefully high-value items from their personal rucks.

The Kedlakis-Ur gestured for a young man at her right to pick up the pack when Jackson dropped it at her feet. The youth easily hefted the pack and slung it over his shoulder, retreating toward one of the nearby tents.

The indigs crowding the Lost Soldiers began to disperse. Their steady withdrawal made Chalmers more nervous rather than less. He wasn't sure if the behavior was due to the indigs observing some unknown social formality, but it seemed odd the indigs didn't hang around to see what these outsiders were offering their chief and, ultimately, them. It made him feel as if it were Jackson and Chalmers themselves the locals had come to see…like they were a low rent freakshow that hadn't lived up to the barker's claims.

Chalmers was anxious enough that when he looked back at the Kedlakis-Ur and found her staring at him, an electric jolt ran from the base of his spine to his skull. She really was quite attractive, with eyes of a deep, burnt amber he'd never seen the likes of before. His earlier discomfort was gone, leaving a different sort of ache in its place.

"We thank you for your protection and welcome," Chalmers mumbled, hoping he didn't misspeak. "And hope you will accept the gifts offered."

"They will no doubt prove sufficient, War Technician," the Kedlakis-Ur said, turning away. Chalmers, released from her magnetic gaze, stumbled forward after her, noting the same delicate, sage-like scent in her wake and a very feminine sway to her hips under the wide belt she wore.

She walked them toward the tent to which the younger man had taken their offering.

Jackson nudged the warrant, giving Chalmers one of his patented "What the fuck?" looks. Chalmers just shrugged and followed the woman into her large tent.

The interior was more like one of the surgeon's barracks-tents from *M.A.S.H.* than the Arab chieftain's harem tent he'd half-expected. Sure, it was decked out with all the amenities the upper class could get, but there was still something unmistakably military—and spartan—about the interior.

They were offered seats on low benches that Chalmers recalled were multi-purposed as racks for stowing tents when on the move as well as frameworks for hasty defenses that, when filled with earth, made excellent barricades. The benches bore cushions that doubled as containers when traveling, and currently stored other fabrics and filler that could be sat upon without damaging them. Indeed, from lamps to seating, everything the nomads made for themselves had multiple purposes. It said something about their mentality that Chalmers sensed must be important.

"Be welcome in my tent," the Kedlakis-Ur said, once they were seated. "Please take food and drink."

"Thank you, but we are neither thirsty nor hungry," Chalmers said, grateful he'd retained the SpinDog briefing on this, at least. They were to refuse the first offer, and second, but refusing the third offer of food and water would give grave insult.

"Please, you must be weary from your travels, we have plenty."

"We are healthy and strong, and our travels short."

"I do not doubt it, but comfort is offered, and for it to be received would be our pleasure." She clapped her hands, and the young man who had taken charge of their bag at the buggy entered with a large, shallow, and elaborately-chased silver bowl in his hands. If the fine silverware was incongruous against the bandoliers and still-slung rifle across his back, the Kedlakis-Ur gave no sign.

"We would not deny you your pleasure," Chalmers said.

He could feel Jackson relaxing at his successful completion of the ritual and cast his own patented look the sergeant's way, the one meant to tell his partner, "See, I'm not completely clueless."

Unaware of the silent byplay, the young man came forward and offered the bowl, which was filled with alien fruits and what looked like jerky. Chalmers took a selection of both and ate enough to, he hoped, avoid rudeness, not because of any distaste for what was offered—it was quite tasty, the fruit in particular—rather, getting a case of the R'Bak Runs was high on his list of shit to avoid, if he could. The SEAL, whatshisname, had reported it as a thing, despite the conditioning medications the SpinDogs had given them. It made sense to Chalmers there'd be something about the food that was hard on Terran digestion, given that R'Bak was a lot farther from Kansas than the Mog, and acclimating to what the warlords had fed their guests there had put some folks in line for the latrine for days. Even the smallest amount of the wrong food could make a man wish he were dead.

He filed such concerns under, "the things a soldier had to do to survive," and moved on.

"Your messenger did not offer many details of what would be expected of us in the coming days," their host said, gracefully plucking what looked like a green grape the size of a tangerine from the bowl and biting into it.

Chalmers smiled and wished, not for the last time, that he knew more about this place and these people. "The mission changed not two days ago. Even we did not know what was to be done until Major Murphy told us."

"You do not answer the question I did not ask," she said, a broad smile lighting up those exceptional eyes.

Chalmers returned his own, more cautious grin. All his raging successes with women had been short term. Once they got to know what he was really like, they always grew to hate him. It was one of the things about this second life he hoped to change. "To be honest, we need guides who can—" he paused to be certain of the word: verb tenses were such a bitch, "—introduce us to the people of Clarthu."

"And then?" she asked, taking another bite of the fruit. The juices made her lips glisten. They were nice lips.

"Then we will find the one who reports our movements to our common enemy."

"*We* will find?" the Kedlakis-Ur asked, arching an eyebrow that had a thin scar running its length.

"It is hoped your guides will help us track down the spy, yes." Chalmers finished less confidently than he'd hoped, unable to gauge just what this woman wanted from him.

"The people of Clarthu will not look kindly on us *something* in their *something*," she said, too quickly for him to understand.

Chalmers glanced in puzzlement at Jackson, who said, "Can you clarify, Kedlakis-Ur? Do you mean they will not like us, collectively, interfering, or that they will not like *your* people interfering?"

The Kedlakis-Ur finished her fruit and licked the last of the juices from her fingers before responding. "Both. But they will not want interference from my people. We are seen as *something* to them." When she saw that Chalmers had lost her meaning, she explained the term, "A thing or person that is needed, but not wanted."

"I see," Chalmers said.

"I will give you the help you ask for. The guides will be told to try and avoid *something* the villagers," Chalmers figured out the word he'd missed as "antagonize" a beat or two after she said it.

"Our thanks, Kedlakis-Ur."

"For now, take your ease. You will sleep here."

"Do you not want to see our gifts?"

She waved dismissively. "It can wait until after you've rested. I will select your guides while you rest." She stood with the same fluid grace she'd exhibited from the first.

Chalmers got an elbow in the ribs as he watched her leave.

"What?" he complained, rubbing his side and glaring at Jackson.

"Please don't let a need to dip your wick get us in trouble, man."

"I won't," Chalmers said, swallowing against a suddenly-dry throat. "She's something, though."

"No doubt." Jackson's smile cracked his concerned expression. "No doubt. Still, we need to watch our shit. These waters are deeper than Lake Michigan, and we don't know half what we should."

Chalmers nodded and cocked his head. "Speaking of which, you notice she didn't seem too concerned with the bribe we offered?"

"Nope. Definitely has her own reasons for helping us."

"We should report in; let Murphy know we've made contact, and that she's agreed to assist us."

"Copy that. You want to, or should I?"

"Go ahead," Chalmers said, looking out the tent flap in hopes of catching another glimpse of the Kedlakis-Ur.

"Quit thinking with that dipshit between your legs, Chalmers. You'll get us both killed."

"I won't jeopardize the mission, man," Chalmers said, earnestly.

Jackson looked askance at him.

"What?"

"Man, what the fuck is up with you?"

"What?" Chalmers said, more defensively than he meant to. The genuine concern in Jackson's voice made the man's question a real one, not a jab of their usual banter, to be deflected and laughed off.

"Time was you'd have told me to go fuck myself and gone on to get us in a world of shit. It was how you rolled."

"Well," Chalmers said uncomfortably, "I'm trying to change."

The reply silenced Jackson, but only for a moment. He muttered something Chalmers couldn't quite make out.

Chalmers thought about letting it ride but remembered the promise he'd made to himself. "What was that?"

Jackson's expression was a cracked mask of barely-suppressed emotion. He did an even worse job of controlling his voice, which throbbed with rage. "Now, Chalmers? *Now*? You choose now to change? I'd have thought you might have made better choices before. Before we were in this—this…situation. You see, Chalmers, I know. I fucking *know*."

Chalmers couldn't answer, knowing his partner's anger was fully justified, that he—the man he'd been before—fully deserved it, and he could only begin to pay the bill his old ways had run up among his friends, family, and colleagues. He sat silent, hoping Jackson would unload, yet desperate his partner would not explode.

"I *know*, Chalmers," Jackson repeated, jabbing a finger hard into Chalmers' chest. "Murphy told me when I woke up. I *know* I wouldn't have even been on that godforsaken helo if it weren't for your shitty play with that warlord. I *know* you fucked me. The only thing that stopped me from putting a bullet in your head when we woke up was the fact you were in it with me, and I kinda hoped you might catch a bullet meant for me. More than that, though, I wanted the option of fucking ending you myself if you fucked up again. That, and my momma taught me it's always better the devil you know than the devil you don't." Jackson's tirade was getting loud, but Chalmers dared not tell the sergeant to lower his voice.

"And!" Jackson nearly shouted the word, eyes wild. "And if there was ever half a chance of surviving this fucked-up situation it would be helped by knowing the man beside me, even a shithead like you. And even knowing just *how* his shit floats, you asshole!"

Scarred hands drew into tight, angry fists as Jackson lowered his voice and rasped on, "But, God help me…but I've also come to realize you know how to paddle up Shit's Creek like no one else. And…and…" The sergeant heaved in a great, shaking breath before releasing it more slowly and continuing, "And…the way I see things, that's what we need to survive right now: someone who knows how to paddle."

Chalmers, overwhelmed with an unfamiliar emotion he eventually identified as gratitude, nodded and looked away from his partner's still-smoldering gaze.

"Dick," Jackson said.

Chalmers nodded, meeting his partner's gaze again. "Trying to be better, man."

"Whatever, man, just make sure you don't fucking forget to paddle while you're 'trying.' Paddling against the shit is the one thing that's kept you alive so far," Jackson grunted roughly.

Chapter Thirty-Six

R'BAK

Maybe it was the way Jackson had cleared the air, but Chalmers woke feeling pretty damn good about things. Could have been that, could also have been that he'd only had to hit the latrine once during the night, and there'd been no discernible difference in that visit to the usual, despite overindulging in some of the local fare before bed. It was good. Halfway between Tex-Mex and some of the Palestinian food his neighbor used to make.

The stuff he'd been helpless to resist had looked like a whitish celery stalk, tasted like honeyed lemons, and smelled like really good chocolate. He'd mentioned the stuff was the perfect Valentine's Day gift, but Jackson's dark stare had forced him to put away any thoughts of trying his theory out on the Kedlakis-Ur. Their host had been generous with her time and company, and Chalmers woke to the very real desire to spend more time in the camp, if only to discover whether the Kedlakis-Ur was truly a man-eater or just looked like one.

Seeking diversion from the nascent erection brought on by thoughts of the tribal leader, Chalmers sat up and looked around.

Jackson was standing just outside the tent, drinking something hot from an earthen mug.

Chalmers rubbed the sleep from his eyes and joined the shorter man under the awning.

"Morning," Jackson said.

"Morning," Chalmers returned, yawning. The nights were short, but blessedly cool in the highlands, and the lingering cold did as much to wake Chalmers as the mug of hot liquid Jackson handed him.

"Any new instructions from command?" Chalmers asked. He sniffed, glad the fragrant tea covered the scent of stale sweat and dust that had permeated his clothes.

"Only to repeat that the timetable is tight, and we will need to move fast once in Clarthu. The unit left Camp Stark yesterday at 0500 and is on schedule."

Chalmers nodded. "We really don't know enough about the villagers to guarantee even a qualified success, do we?"

"Not yet, no. I plan on picking the guide's brain while we drive."

"Speaking of which, any idea who the Kedlakis-Ur is sending with us?"

"I think we're about to find out," Jackson answered, nodding toward the three figures just emerging from the chief's tent. The Lost Soldiers had been hosted there for another, later meal after their initial interview, and then treated to entertainment from a pair of young singers accompanied by the Kedlakis-Ur on a stringed instrument that looked positively medieval. Jackson and Chalmers had nodded along like two Catholics at a Baptist church on Sunday, unfamiliar with the words, but grooving to the music and feeling the sentiment. When the party had ended, the pair of them had been escorted here, to what they presumed was a guest tent of sorts, as it had none of the embroidery and decoration the Kedlakis-Ur's had, but was comfortable enough.

One of the figures accompanying the Kedlakis-Ur was the young man who had served them the night before, the other was a woman about the same age as the man. Both were armed with breech-loading rifles and wore matching expressions of, if not anger, then intensity. As they drew closer, Chalmers realized the pair looked a lot alike, though they could just have a strong clan resemblance rather than be siblings. Their erect carriage and self-assurance gave the impression of competence.

Then again, Chalmers had always made a point of *looking* competent, too. Especially when fucking around.

He supposed that in this case, though, appearances would not be deceiving. Those that had to hunt, gather, and fight to survive were less likely to successfully hide any failings. He dimly recalled some nomad group on Earth leaving those too old or infirm to make river crossings and such-like behind to die.

"Your guides," the Kedlakis-Ur said, drawing him from his observations.

Chalmers put his tea down and smiled at her. "I thank the tribe, you, and our guides for the gifts of your aid."

She cocked her head, lovely eyes narrowed on him. "The tribe is not involved. Solely the Kedlak."

"I beg pardon. I misspoke." Chalmers said the words without knowing what, exactly, he'd said that was incorrect. He'd thought the Kedlak were the tribe. He suppressed the urge to glance at Jackson and decided to shut the hell up. Clan politics, he decided.

The Kedlakis-Ur waved a hand. "There is nothing to pardon. My *something* will see you to Clarthu and help you uncover the traitor."

"Thank you," he said, restraining the urge to hit on her. Much as he wanted to chat her up, now was not the time. Not for the new, better Chalmers, anyway. Old Chalmers would have followed where this attraction led at the expense of just about anything.

"Travel easily and lightly," she said. The Kedlakis-Ur then turned to the guides and nodded once to each, repeating the benediction. The bows they gave her were the most formal thing Chalmers had seen from an indig thus far.

The Kedlakis-Ur walked away, Chalmers trying not to stare after her in case it offended the young pair.

"Head's up," Jackson said, shoving Chalmers' bag into the warrant's hands with a quelling look that made the older man wonder what he'd done now.

He loaded the buggy while Jackson topped off the tanks from the jerry cans. Their guides looked on, impassive, as the partners prepared for travel. The rest of the camp paid them no more attention than they had the night before.

"A little less than one and a half cans left, Chalmers," Jackson said, the impact of one knuckle drawing a muted bong from the partially-empty jerry can.

"Copy that. Should be plenty, so long as we don't have to fight sand or something." He looked a question at the guide.

"No sand," the guide said, shaking his head. "No big rocks. Some small gravels when we get down the *something,* and then green lands to Clarthu."

"Green lands, eh? Sounds nice," Jackson said, looking at the sere beiges, browns, and grays of the mountains surrounding the camp. "Though I suppose, growing up here, anything would look green."

Chalmers checked the tautness of the tie-downs keeping their packs in place, slung his M-14, and hustled to claim the driver's seat. He really enjoyed driving the buggy. Driving it made him feel both useful and in active command of his own destiny. In control of something that was, in fact, hard to manage. Like exerting control over his lifelong inclination to lie and fuck things up, only safer.

His rush caused the slung M-14 to bang into the steering wheel and shoved him off balance.

Or maybe *not* so much safer, after all. Murphy's Law always found a way of leveling those who started thinking too highly of themselves or their skills. Flushing, Chalmers removed the weapon, carefully slipped it into the rifle scabbard between the seats, and secured it.

"What?" asked Jackson with a grin. "I thought you were getting ready to lay on some dumbass redneck shit, driving with a gun in one hand like a wild man."

Chalmers did not respond, but put the buggy in gear and accelerated smoothly—and slowly—back toward the open wastes.

Chapter Thirty-Seven

R'BAK

Chalmers was going too fast to do more than brace himself against the wheel as the herd of alien whinnies appeared in front of the speeding buggy as if by magic.

A cop he'd once known said that was what all the responsible parties said in car accidents: "The other car just appeared in front of me!" when they might have seen that shit coming if they hadn't been going too fast for the conditions.

He supposed the big lizard-like creatures did not deserve the moniker "alien," at least not here, not on their home turf.

They certainly resented the buggy's sudden intrusion into their midst; a couple of the herd sounded a loud resonating threat-whistle while the others ran for it, scrambling up the side of the draw.

Chalmers tried for a clear spot in the herd, the big tires of the buggy spitting grit and gravel in their wake. He couldn't help but grin madly under the goggles. This was the most fun he'd had in almost a hundred and fifty years, for God's sake!

Then one of the whinnies feinted toward the nearest wheel, mouth open. The red-orange interior of the throat and finger-length opalescent teeth were all the encouragement he needed.

"Fast fuckers," Chalmers muttered, shifting gears and hammering the accelerator. He spent the next moment counter-steering against the shuddering skid he felt through the seat and wheel, then aimed for an opening in the rocks ahead.

They made it, but the gap ended up being a yard or so above the lower slope, and the buggy left the ground doing a feather under fifty.

They were airborne before Chalmers realized the animal—the freaking animal—had *feinted* an attack at the buggy, just like he used to mess with his stepmother's pissy old cats.

The landing pushed the buggy's occupants, both Terran and local, hard into their seats. The broad tires slipped before biting into the patchy turf of the uneven slope they bounced along. Chalmers adjusted his steering three times in as many seconds, fighting the inertia and momentum that threatened a roll-over. His efforts and the heavy-duty off-road suspension finally steadied the buggy, the uphill side compressing as the lower smoothly traveled to give them a more-or-less steady platform.

"Bastards know how to make a damn good buggy," Chalmers mused, taking a hand from the wheel to wipe something green-brown from his goggles.

"What?" Jackson shouted, his brown knuckles lighter where he clutched at the roll bars.

Chalmers would have to talk to Jackson about that. Chicken bars were there so you didn't lose digits holding onto the roll bars during a roll. It was yet another example of how little training they'd had before going on this mission.

But for now, Chalmers just shook his head, grinning madly behind his scarf as his downshift made the engine throb loudly. He'd been doing that a lot recently—smiling, not downshifting.

He glanced in the mirror at the well-equipped, by local standards at least, indig warrior riding in the rear passenger-side seat. Kenla was another example of the varied advantages this place and time had over Fort Leavenworth's prison: women.

"What?" Jackson repeated.

Chalmers raised his voice over the wind and engine noise. "How we doing for time?"

Jackson checked the pad in the hand he was not using to clutch the sissy bar. "Not bad, Chief!" he shouted. "So long as you don't wrap us around a tree, we're golden…" he continued, quietly enough that Chalmers could pretend he hadn't heard.

He glanced at the shiny display. The miniaturized computer was the only piece of modern Terran tech Chalmers had access to—well, it *and* a feed from the tiny spy sats crisscrossing overhead in whacky orbits. Seeded in advance of their arrival, the Dornaani satellites were almost entirely plastic—or something like it—and not much larger than a hubcap. Non-reflective and sheathed in some kind of temperature-equalizing material that made them thermally invisible, they sounded like something straight out of Area 51. If the locals did manage to detect them, though, they were reportedly programmed to take a swan dive into the atmosphere: burnt to ash in minutes. Still, Chalmers figured that if the opposing team found one, they'd look for more until the last one committed re-entry suicide. And then the Lost Soldiers would be well and truly on their own.

But, hey, as long as they lasted, there was no way Chalmers was going to rely on barely remembered land navigation courses when his continued survival was on the line. Not when such wonders were available. Not on an alien planet with a different diameter and magnetic pole. GPS systems had first made an impression on him back in Desert Storm, and while Chalmers wasn't sure it operated on the same principles, this device was even more accurate and less bulky than what he had used back then.

He slewed the buggy around a stand of tree-sized plants that looked like a clump of insanely large blades of lawn grass pulled from the ground by a giant's shitty golf swing. Passing close enough to reach out and touch it, he realized the earthy clump at the base of the lawn grass was some kind of weird root-ball of dense-looking fibers.

The passenger directly behind him asked something like, "Fight wanted?"

Chalmers wasn't sure of the indig's name, just that he was the leader of the local resistance cell, and as such, was one of two "types." Either a guy with too much hero and too little common sense for his liking, or just another hopeful warlord in the making. Neither were high on Chalmers's list of people to hang out with, so Chalmers pretended not to hear the question.

Thoughts of warlords sent Chalmers on a trip down memory lane, remembering the big souk in Mogadishu, where you could buy anything, including some of yesterday's shipment of food, fresh off the UN relief trucks. These people had yet to prove themselves, so he wasn't about to go out on a limb for them.

Because if he did, Murphy's Law made it a sure thing the locals would saw it off at the trunk. From the sticks, himself, Chalmers understood one immutable law of insular cultures: outsiders were afforded neither the respect nor care that insiders could rely on. He wasn't one of them, and there was no telling when they would decide to saw Chalmers' own shit off at the trunk if he did go out on limb for them.

"Fight wanted?" the indig repeated, loud enough that Chalmers couldn't ignore him without offending him.

"What's that?" Chalmers asked, working his way up through the gears as the way ahead became clear. They were still heading downhill toward where the valley debouched onto a wide floodplain crisscrossed with canals fed from a huge, shallow lake. The dry land between the waterways was the source of most of the local food production for the region. At least, that food which the nomads didn't herd through the mountains they were leaving behind. The village itself was visible now: twenty to thirty low edifices, water mill crouching on one edge of the largest, all surrounded by fields of ochre-green crop lands.

"You want fight, Warrant Officer?" the local repeated more loudly, emphasizing Chalmers' official title.

The locals were intensely rank conscious. It was almost as bad as the regular Army had been. Worse, even. Chalmers had no idea how to identify an indig's status at a glance. Not yet, anyway. He supposed he'd have to learn soon enough.

"I hope not." He slowed his speech, careful with his diction. "Not a straight fight, anyway. Want to get there and catch them with their pants down."

The male indig spoke equally slowly and carefully, clearly wanting to be understood. "Respectfully, then, may I ask you to slow, Warrant Officer Chalmers?"

"Why?"

"Because if you go fast, like raiders, they open fire. If they see me and Kenla, they less likely to shoot first, question later."

"Less?" Jackson said, jumping on the word before Chalmers could.

"Clarthu not friendly. Not all the time. We raid them from time to time. Nothing so bad to make them hate, but they not like a surprise."

Chalmers downshifted and let engine braking slow them. "I don't want to give the people we're looking for time to bail or hide their comms."

"Bail?" the indig war leader asked.

"Run away," Chalmers clarified. There were still some errors in translation, but the weird tech they'd been subjected to sure beat shit out of attending Defense Language Institute courses for months on end. Then again, DLI had been close enough to San Francisco to hit the clubs on weekends, so it had that going for it. Had. Very past tense. He hadn't even thought to ask if either place still existed.

He dropped the buggy into first gear and slowed even further as they came into range of the big-bore weapons the indigs used. And there were armed men and women manning the earthen berm surrounding the village. Some had no doubt fled to the fields when they heard the buggy's snarling approach.

Jackson grunted and turned to look at their guides. The male indig unbuckled and stood up in the seat.

"The Kedlakis-Ur sends greetings and *something*," he shouted through cupped hands. "*Something* of the Kedlakis-Ur wish to meet with the hetman."

One of the guards, a tall, wasp-waisted woman, waved them on.

Chalmers kept the buggy at a walking pace as they crossed the last few yards to an opening in the berm. There was talk between some of the other villagers and the woman, but she mostly ignored it and waved them through the gap without any further discussion.

Chalmers, mildly astonished that a brief statement was all the villagers required to give them access to the village, almost caused the buggy to stall.

"You insisted on driving," Jackson said. "Least you could do is keep us from looking stupid in front of these people."

Chalmers just drove on, his head on a swivel.

A space Chalmers assumed was the equivalent of a village green lay just beyond the berm. A brief drive between low, adobe-brick buildings followed. They entered a small square with a well in the center and a larger building on the left.

"Stop there," the talkative guide said, pointing to the building opposite the large one.

An older, richly dressed man stood at the entrance, a fruit of some kind surrendering its skin to a wicked-looking knife wielded by capable hands.

Chalmers stopped the buggy and shut her down. The hot metal of the motor pinged as it cooled. Chalmers immediately felt the sweat, held in check by the wind of their passage, begin to run down his flanks.

"This is the village *something*, Larn Clarthu, Warrant Officer," their guide said, waving at the fruit-peeler.

Jackson, always the superior linguist, handled the niceties of the introduction, providing the SpinDog countersign.

Chalmers tried to act casual as he took stock of their surroundings. There were a couple of oldsters staring at them from around the well, but on the whole, the villagers seemed a lot less interested in their arrival than the nomads had been. There were some kids watching, sure, but they were chivvied back toward the fields and work abandoned in the excitement.

"The *somethings* will come," the hetman said, turning to enter what appeared to be his home.

Chalmers swallowed fears they were being set up and nodded at their guides. "Stay here, please?"

Both guides nodded, though there was something in the woman's body language Chalmers didn't like. His tolerance for things he didn't like had been mightily adjusted by circumstances, so Chalmers ignored the feeling and followed Jackson.

The half-underground lodge was cool after the growing midday heat, and carpets of some beautifully-dyed material softened sound and lent an air of civilization to what would otherwise be a spartan, cave-like dwelling.

The village hetman was a hard-looking fifty-ish. Thinking about it, Chalmers couldn't recall seeing an older indig, which fit the briefing. Namely, that those locals who didn't collaborate with R'Bak's elites lived neither well nor long. The SpinDogs had provided fairly good intel, but it wasn't updated often enough to give more than deep background and a few points of contact for their area of operations. As Chalmers had reliably found reason after reason to doubt the accuracy of every intelligence briefing he'd ever been party to, he was always on the look-out for those moments when reality matched the brief. Of course, just because the SpinDogs had given the straight dope on the lay of the land didn't mean they hadn't spun the shit out of the details.

The hetman likely wasn't the collaborator they were looking for, since the village seemed too far from any real center of power for it to be worth the cost of buying him.

Distance didn't mean they were safe, though.

"A lot like Mogadishu," Chalmers muttered.

Jackson shot him a look, but Chalmers waved him off.

The hetman asked something too quickly for Chalmers to understand.

"No, not yet," Jackson's answer was slow, and far easier to understand than the local's.

"Not yet what?" Chalmers asked.

"Not here to overthrow the satrap," Jackson clarified.

Chalmers smiled at the hetman, nodding slowly. "Not yet, anyway. We want to catch—" he sought the word a moment "—spies."

"No spies here," the hetman said. His tone was level, but his gaze hardened.

"I'm sure everyone in this village is super happy with leadership," Chalmers said, in English.

"What does he say, Leader-Of-Ten?" the hetman asked.

Jackson shrugged and lied easily. "He quotes a general."

The hetman's suspicious gaze eased.

Chalmers noted the reaction and stored it under useful confirmation of information the SpinDogs provided. Specifically, that the indigs were militant in a way that most of Earth circa 1990 AD had gladly forgotten.

"Did anyone leave town as we came in?" Chalmers asked.

"No one, War Technician," the hetman said.

Chalmers liked the man's translation of Warrant Officer into the local lingo and decided not to correct him.

"Did anyone ask to leave, Larn Clarthu?" Jackson asked, glancing at Chalmers.

Smiling and nodding encouragement, Chalmers watched the villager and decided that, even more than before, he was glad Jackson was so much better with languages.

Larn Clarthu didn't answer directly, but picked up an ancient-looking rifle that had been hiding among the cushions at his knee and stood with a fast, fluid grace. Chalmers dimly recalled that, in R'Bak's outback, place-names were often taken from the clan that held dominion over them, and a hetman's title wasn't hereditary but earned in battle.

"Come," he said, when he noticed the visitors had not followed suit.

Jackson got up with similar ease and gave a hand to help Chalmers to his feet. As much as the body armor they'd been issued in the Mog made getting up and down a pain in the ass, Chalmers wasn't about to give up the additional protection it offered.

The hetman gestured with a scarred hand for the off-worlders to follow.

"He look like Ked to you, too?" Jackson asked quietly, pointing with a stubbled chin at the retreating back of the hetman.

"Who?" Chalmers blurted before realizing his partner meant the male half of their indig guides. He shrugged. "I guess so, yeah. But then they're all bound to be cousins or some shit."

"No wonder you're so cool with them. I forget how you rednecks are all related," Jackson shot at him. The sergeant pushed his way through the heavy leather curtain covering the first dogleg of the entrance to the hetman's home.

Remembering his promise, Chalmers swallowed a shitty remark and followed past the tight corners. Initially he'd thought the construction was intended to restrict airflow and keep the interior cool, and it probably helped with that, but now

Chalmers suspected the primary intent was as a choke point in the event of an attack.

He was rounding the final corner when someone outside started shooting. A pretty big gun, from the sound of it, and a distinctive report.

A report he'd heard once before, almost a month ago on *Spin One*…

"How many shots?" Chalmers had asked, glancing from the display to the SpinDog briefing officer who had the most personal experience with the tribes in their probable area of operations. He'd been brought over from *Spin Two* to share his knowledge.

The officer nodded at Chalmers' question. "Most of the native long arms are single-shot breech-action, but there are more advanced arms in production, and the satraps and their lackeys have not been able to keep control over *all* of them."

Chalmers listened, but his attention was back on the display. A rifle-armed woman was belly-crawling toward what looked like a cross between a turkey and a toothy lizard: it was one freaky-looking predator. Despite the awkward appearance, however, it was *definitely* a predator. The opening of the video had shown the alien things chasing down and dispatching one of the woman's equally-alien looking livestock with a single bite to the back of the critter's short, muscle-bound neck.

Preoccupied, the bird-thing slashed the belly of its prey with one claw, then thrust its smooth head fully into the gaping wound.

Chalmers, aware of the mixed company, carefully did not verbalize the crack every soldier ever would make on seeing the images.

The woman in the display carefully rose to one knee, leveled her long rifle, and took aim while the thing had its head *inside* the other thing.

The predator withdrew its bloody maw, a massive piece of organ meat distending the scaled throat as strands of bloody tissue quivered and stretched all the way back into the wound cavity. It was easy to imagine the sound of that mouth snapping closed around a human victim, given how wide and powerful the man-eating jaws were.

The woman fired.

The thing seemed to flinch. The dun rocks behind it were suddenly painted with oddly-tinted blood.

The shooter wasn't watching. She was already reloading, breech open, trigger hand reversing and dropping a palm-length cartridge into the breech.

"Jesus, what is that gun, a fifty?"

There followed a brief explanation and comparison of Kulsian versus Earth's "Imperial" caliber nomenclatures. The briefers were two dudes and a tall, spindly woman he had a hard time not staring at.

"So not quite fifty caliber," finished Stabilo, the lead briefing officer and higher muckety-muck. Or the son of one. Chalmers didn't know and didn't like him. First, he was handsome, and second, he said everything with an air of certainty that rubbed Chalmers the wrong way.

On the screen, the bird-thing stumbled, possibly already dead on its feet.

The woman shot again, just to be sure.

A second, throaty almost-fifty-caliber roar sounded well after the first, as if the shooter wanted to be sure their target was dead. Or maybe, wanted to give them enough time to realize what was happening to them.

Jackson just about bowled Chalmers over trying to get back inside the hetman's home. They'd both thought it was safe to come out, but were jacked up on adrenaline and fear, eyes wide and nuts tight when the shot cracked the quiet. Jackson had only succeeded in shoving the Warrant Officer back toward the entrance before bouncing off Chalmers and onto his ass.

"We good?" Jackson asked, getting back on his feet almost instantly.

Chalmers swallowed and nodded.

When in the shit, Jackson somehow always found cover first. Growing up rough on the South Side of Chicago did that to a kid. Chalmers didn't begrudge it; following his partner's nigh-preternatural instincts had saved them both more than once.

The pair blinked a few times in the harsh afternoon light. Unlike most terrestrial towns that had a square, Clarthu was fronted on all but one side by the low buildings the briefings told him were villagers' favored abodes in the Ashbands of R'Bak. The fourth side, where a place of worship would normally sit, was taken up by the village storehouse.

By the time Chalmers' vision adjusted, Larn was already entering the trench before the door to his neighbor's place, two armed villagers on his heels.

There was some muffled shouting, but no more shots from inside.

A heavy local rifle—the kind Chalmers expected—was tossed out the open door. It landed in the dust, breech open and empty. A woman emerged a second later, her hands up. She offered no resistance as several villagers pulled her from the doorway.

"Damn," Chalmers said, hastily holstering his sidearm as he recognized the woman.

It was Kenla.

Chapter Thirty-Eight

R'BAK

Jackson picked up on the identity of the shooter a split second later. "Shit."

Chalmers nodded, wished he could understand any of the angry words being exchanged. None of which were spoken by the shooter, who remained serenely aloof in the thicket of murder-eyed villagers.

"Where is Ked?" Chalmers asked quietly.

Jackson shrugged, eyes on the woman and her captors.

"Order!" the hetman shouted.

The villagers quieted instantly.

Such discipline impressed Chalmers. In the Mog, a shooting like this would have the whole city rattling off rounds, but the R'Baku didn't seem to have a *khat*-analog, thank God. Then again, rampant stimulant use wasn't the only reason people felt the need to get trigger-happy, not when simple greed with a side of racism and religious fanaticism would do in a pinch.

Chalmers blinked back memories of Somali kids leaving their shot-to-shit homes and only begging for chocolate or digging through UN trash barrels for goodies. When you were a third-generation bullet-dodger used to scavenging for basic necessities, it was easy to miss the big picture, let alone see the root causes of a fucked-up life. Chalmers reminded himself—as he'd had to a few times before—that he was here for a specific mission, not to fix everything.

Beyond the tableau and visions of old memories, he caught sight of a sweating Ked jogging into view from between a couple of buildings.

"What was *he* doing?" Chalmers asked.

"Not his job, that's for sure," Jackson replied.

"You *sure*?"

Jackson's eyes didn't leave Ked. Lips thinning, he shrugged and said, "Fuck. No way to know."

"Right," Chalmers said, eyes sliding back to the hetman.

Larn was in the process of almost reverently disarming the woman.

She said something Chalmers didn't hear.

Larn nodded, said something equally quiet. The crowd started to hurl what sounded like threats at the woman, showing the hetman's control was not as complete as it seemed at first. Kenla was smart enough to remain still, her expression frozen in what Chalmers took to be resignation.

"What should we do, Chalmers?" Jackson asked, head swiveling between Ked and the mob around his sister.

"I don't know," the warrant officer said, certain only that he didn't want to be between the villagers and the target of their anger. He looked again for Ked and saw the warrior shoving his way through the crowd to get to the woman.

Two of the larger villagers pointedly blocked his path. One pushed him. Ked's expression darkened, anger overcoming his initial shock and surprise. The villager ended up flat on his back.

"Shit, we gotta do something, right?"

"Damn it," Chalmers said, watching Ked use a slick move to dump another of the locals on his ass.

"Stop!" Larn barked as several of the villagers turned to deal with the threat charging into their midst.

But Ked was already putting down the next man who laid hands on him; only a few bodies separated him from Larn and Kenla.

Larn wasn't having it, though, and pushed the still-unresisting woman behind him.

Chalmers was moving, but knew he was too late to do anything but witness whatever came next.

Thankfully, Ked hadn't completely lost his senses and tried to get around Larn rather than through him, as he had the other villagers. The older man barely moved, but Ked stumbled away, blood spurting from his nose.

"Cease!" Larn shouted, raising a hand to stop two of his villagers trying to grab Ked. "If you wish to challenge my authority, you must do it properly, Kedlak."

Challenge my authority...

Like a homing pigeon arriving unexpected but with surety, those words summoned a memory—one of the few useful ones from the long briefing sessions with the most arrogant SpinDog he'd yet encountered...

"Stabilo, I'm not challenging your authority." *You self-important prick.* "I'm trying to get a proper answer."

"And I am giving you your answer, Chalmers," the SpinDog said, glancing past the "class" toward the hatch at the back of the chamber.

He wanted to call bullshit, but Chalmers wasn't willing to turn his head and see who was there. Murphy, probably, and the warrant officer *really* didn't want another run-in with the major if it could be helped. But a straight answer could mean the difference between life and death, or, more to the major's interest, success or failure.

The initial team—a SEAL, a Vietnam-era Army Special Forces soldier, and Stabilo's own brother, Volo—were already boots on the ground. Chalmers assumed the SEAL had accepted—or been forced to accept—two datapoints Chalmers couldn't take for granted. First, that Volo's life was important enough to the SpinDogs to act as surety of their intent to see the mission through. Second, that Stabilo's family had the full cooperation and endorsement of all SpinDogs. Chalmers knew better. Just because some political boss said everyone was pulling for you, it did not necessarily follow that anyone but the boss was actually pulling for you. Even the boss was suspect until proven otherwise. Especially given the nature of most SpinDogs'—hell, most *humans'*— rise to power. And Chalmers had worked under his fair share of shit-climbers.

These data points in mind, he needed to know a lot more about who they would be working with once he and Jackson became thc next boots on the ground. "So how do we know we can rely on the locals?"

"Because my family, your hosts, and it being the sole chance of success, assure you of it," the SpinDog said, leveling another quelling look at Chalmers.

Chalmers suppressed a snort. This guy was more arrogant than just about anyone he'd ever met, and he'd been around a lot of arrogant bastards. Almost every single officer he'd ever interrogated as a suspect, for example.

"All right, and why is it *you* are so sure?" Chalmers asked, in his best, "don't bullshit a bullshitter" voice.

If looks could kill, Chalmers would have died right there, been painfully resurrected, and killed a few more times. Stabilo's glare only ended when Murphy cleared his throat. The young SpinDog's gaze flicked up to the older Terran and back to his tormentor.

Chalmers couldn't help but smile beatifically.

"Rest assured, the people of Clarthu will be amenable to contact," Stabilo tried again.

Chalmers shook his head and looked to Murphy.

"Warrant Officer Chalmers has a need to know, Stabilo."

"Very good, Major Murphy." Chalmers didn't miss the way Stabilo's lip started to curl before the younger man got control. "We've been in contact with the villagers for generations. They provide us information and certain biologicals we cannot easily obtain elsewhere; we provide them with certain technological items they cannot make themselves."

"Like what? How much? How often?"

"I am afraid I cannot answer those questions with specificity."

Chalmers shook his head again, hoping the major would jump in and stomp the local into a more cooperative mood.

But Murphy, rather than piling the pressure on, asked, "Maybe if you explain exactly what you want, Chalmers?"

Chalmers answered Murphy directly, ignoring a fuming Stabilo, "I need to know what these people value so I can either predict which way they'll jump if someone offers them a deal to sell us out or where to apply pressure if I have to question one of them regarding a crime they commit."

"Question?" Stabilo's smile was a razor. "I think you overestimate how civilized these people are. There is no 'rule of law'…as I think you call it?"

Chalmers nodded.

A wider, predatory smile from Stabilo. "No, none of that. Like as not, if accused of some crime, the average R'Bak nomad will insist on trial by combat."

"And the villagers, the city-dwellers?" Chalmers asked.

"Most will have ground staked out for such, and formal judges to rule in those cases where both parties die as a result of the trial by combat."

"Trial by combat! I demand trial by combat!" the woman shouted in answer to something Larn said to Ked, who was still prone on the ground.

"Who will stand in the circle?"

"I, Kenla Aksinos, will stand for myself in this. Your son raped me. I avenged myself upon him. I am innocent of wrongdoing under the laws of both the Kedlak and the Clarth."

The hetman raised his voice as well, arms lifted to silence the gathered people. "I dispute your right to vengeance, as you provided no proof to the people of his wrongdoing. As my son's widows are both with child, they cannot stand in the circle. Therefore, I will face you myself."

"Shit," Jackson muttered. "Does that mean—"

"She killed his son?" Chalmers said, finishing the thought.

The villagers shouted bloodthirsty encouragement to their leader, and the mass of them started toward the staked grounds at the far end of the village.

Ked, forgotten in the drama, climbed to his feet and edged through the crowd to join Chalmers and Jackson. His expression was guarded but calmer than that of either of the off-worlders.

"What the hell, Ked?"

The indig nodded toward the last of the locals as they departed, bringing one finger to his lips to ask for silence.

Chalmers and Jackson waited impatiently for the last of the villagers to leave the small square before the hetman's dwelling.

"You wanted to check the homes, no? Look for radio of collaborator who communicates with the City?"

"What?" Jackson asked.

"You mean you arranged all that?" Chalmers asked.

The indig's shrug was eloquent. "My sister wish revenge." He gestured at the hetman's residence. "She will make the fight last as long as she can, but we waste time."

Jackson's eyes were a bit wild. "She's not likely to survive, is she?"

Ked shrugged again, and the bone charms decorating his bandoliers clicked as he moved to the hetman's door. "Honor demanded this action."

Chalmers hurried after. "But not of *you*?" he asked, hearing Jackson follow.

Ked's surprised glance told Chalmers he'd put a foot in it. "Of course not. Kenla was attacked by Lornsos. As she is not with child as a result, she avenged herself, removing the stain to her honor."

Chalmers shook his head. "But the trial?"

He shrugged. "She is better at blades than I." He bent and led the way into the hetman's home.

Chapter Thirty-Nine

R'BAK

The central room where Larn had received them was as they'd left it: quiet, comfortable, and spartan. Ked quickly crossed to the curtained alcove at the back where the hetman slept, presumably.

"What size thing do we search for?"

"A very small chest. Might have a crank on it." This much, at least, he'd accepted from the SpinDog briefer: while the Kulsians had some machinery that was far more advanced than what he was used to, they were not likely to give any high-end technology to the indig collaborators this far from centers of power. The rig was supposed to look something like a transistor radio, with a hand crank similar to those on AM/FM survival sets from Chalmers' own era.

Ked rummaged around in the alcove while Chalmers searched the main chamber and Jackson watched the entrance.

It didn't take more than two minutes to search. The villagers were maybe one step up from nomads themselves, and even the hetman's possessions offered very little in the way of hiding places.

"Nothing?"

Ked shook his head. "Nothing."

In the end, splitting up to search several additional houses still didn't produce the radio. Chalmers stalked out of his third, still empty-handed. Even if they'd had a Gestapo-like disregard for the personal property of their allies, hastily tossing a place was no substitute for a careful, thorough search.

They needed time they simply were not going to have, not if the noises rising from the dueling ground were the bad sign they seemed to bc. The ritualized, chant-like shouts had become more frenzied since the three had split up. Any long fight was a hard fight, Chalmers knew.

"Chalmers!" Ked said, emerging from the large building across from the hetman's home.

The crowd noise changed again, became a series of rousing cheers as Chalmers jogged over.

"Is this it?" Ked asked. He held what looked like a metal-framed bread-box with a dynamo crank protruding from one end.

Chalmers smiled at the younger man. "Sure is! Where was it?"

"Inside. Village grain store. Buried about arm-length."

Chalmers cursed. Right where it would make it impossible to single someone out as the owner, so long as you didn't leave fingerprints. For perhaps the third time since wakening in these strange circumstances, Chalmers lamented the fact he had no evidence kit with him.

Another cheer rose from the dueling ground. Chalmers glanced at Ked, wondering how the man could be so cool while his sister was fighting for her life a few hundred yards away.

"Jackson, come on, man," Chalmers called as loudly as he darted into the doorway of the home belonging to the hetman's son.

"I'm coming, Chalmers," Jackson grunted. "Hold your shit."

"Ked found the radio, man."

"Right," Jackson said, walking backward out of the building. Chalmers could hear him dragging something.

"What the shit, Jacks?" Chalmers asked as he saw the trunk his partner was dragging. Except, on second glance, it wasn't a trunk at all. Covered in whinnie-hide, the thing looked like a treasure chest out of one of his old D&D books, five feet long by three feet high.

"Check this shit out," Jackson said, flipping the lid up.

Chalmers whistled. "That ain't right." And it wasn't.

Nestled within the chest was a shipping crate full of what looked like anti-tank missiles. Five of them and the single-tube device that, judging from a button-studded box which extruded from one part, had to be the launcher.

"Shit, man, those had to come from—"

Another cheer, this one louder than those previous, erupted from the grounds. It was cut short by a collective gasp that left a silence as troubling as anything that had come before.

"Thinking we should put it back, no?" Chalmers said, wondering what the villagers would make of them looting a dead man's possessions.

"I don't think so. I figure we give the hetman a look at what his son was up to," Jackson said, patting the lid.

"And if they bought them?" Chalmers asked, looking hopefully at Ked.

The warrior scratched at his sparse beard thoughtfully but ultimately shook his head. "Nothing the villagers have in trade is worth so much as these."

"And then there is the why. These are not so useful against men, but against machines," Jackson mused.

"But the J'Stull don't come out to these parts—"

"Not according to our friend Stabilo, anyway," Chalmers said.

The crowd noise had receded to a lower, steady volume.

Ked sighed, the set of his shoulders easing.

"What is it, Ked?"

"My sister is victorious," he said, pushing the radio into Chalmers' hands.

Chalmers blinked. "How do you know?"

"They do not cheer for her as they would for their hetman. I go to see if she needs healing. I will return."

"Wait! Should we put this back?" Chalmers asked, gesturing toward the chest.

A shrug. "I do not know. The hetman may be dead. We will find out in a few moments. His son is already dead, and so beyond caring if caught with these weapons."

Chalmers stared after Kedlak. "Jacks," he mumbled, "we are standing in broad daylight holding two pieces of evidence that prove some local is a traitor."

"Yeah," the sergeant agreed sourly, "which means we are the only ones holding the bag that someone's ready to kill over."

Chalmers spat. The mission just kept getting better and better.

"I'm trying to *something* from your point of view, but I just can't seem to give a *something* begroag shit, Ked," Kenla said, a toss of her head making several of the tiny bones in her dreadlocks click against one another. Kenla's right arm was in a sling and there was a bandage around her midriff, but the bandage showed surprisingly little blood, especially since the trousers she wore still glistened with the stuff down to her knees. A third wrapping covered the place where her neck joined her shoulder.

"You overcame and survived, did you not?" Ked asked, sounding defensive and, from the flushed reddening of his ears, knowing it.

"No thanks to your medicine! I had to be treated by the village healer, here," she gestured with her unbound arm at one of the women walking behind her. The hetman was being carried into his home, and the healer's progress was slowed by the bearers and their charge as they negotiated the entrance. "They showed honor, though, treating me before their own."

"Is he alive?" Chalmers asked.

More clicking of bones followed as she shrugged. "He was when he fell at my feet, though just barely. I cut him many times, but he is tough as old leather," Kenla opined.

Deadlier than the male. The quote crossed his mind before Chalmers could remember where he'd heard it.

"He will live," the village healer said. "I have given him the *patheos-pak*, and his natural endurance will replenish his blood within a day or two."

"The what?" Chalmers asked, but the healer ducked into the entrance, and Ked and his sister had their heads together, speaking quietly.

Amazingly, the rest of the villagers seemed uninterested in the chest Jackson had dragged from the dead man's home. Chalmers had been watching. No one seemed to take any undue notice or care.

He'd hid the radio in his pack, so there remained three possibilities: one, the collaborator responsible for the transmissions was smooth enough to avoid gawking; two, the collaborator who had the radio had not been responsible for the weapons as well; or three, the collaborator and man killed by Kenla were one and the same.

"You see anything?" the warrant officer asked Jackson, in English.

"No. You?"

Chalmers shook his head. He considered a moment, then added, "We'll have to watch tonight, then. I can't see this going unreported to whoever provided those missiles."

Jackson nodded. When the siblings had finished their quiet conference, he repeated the plan in the local dialect. The more of it they heard and spoke, the more they realized it had a lot less Ktoran in it than what the SpinDogs spoke.

Kenla considered the instructions. "It will not be easy to watch unobserved, War Technician Chalmers."

"I will do it," her brother said.

Chalmers did not miss the glance she leveled at her brother. Wondering what it meant, he decided to keep an eye on both of them as well as the grain store tonight. He would, as Ronnie RayGun had said, "Trust but confirm."

Chapter Forty

R'BAK

Chalmers rolled his eyes; the hissing and grunting had resumed.

"For God's sakes!" he muttered, kicking the grunting little alien lizard-goat off his foot for the tenth time.

The goat—well, *begroag*—was a tiny, more stupid, and, if this one was a good example, more inbred cousin to the whinnies that the locals used as pack animals. Normally this would not have impacted Chalmers one bit. Normally.

But Murphy's Law was in effect, and this begroag had decided Chalmers' boot was a fine source of food or sex; Chalmers wasn't sure which. Both, maybe? Every few minutes Chalmers was forced to kick it away, and it would get the hint for a little while before coming back at odd intervals to bite, then hump and shimmy against his foot. He was leaning toward the idea it wanted to make babies, simply because it was so utterly persistent. Nothing was that hungry. Horny, yes. Hungry…nah.

It was obvious the creatures had been domesticated for the same reasons humans—well, *Terrans*—kept goats, for food and keeping the weeds down, so it was definitely someone's property. Which made it out of bounds for a more permanent solution than a boot to the head. He could think of no better way to piss off a farmer or herder than killing their livestock, so shooting the damn thing off his boot was not an option, even if he could do it silently.

The stakeout was one of the least onerous he'd ever been on. Unadjusted to R'Bak's shorter days, he'd found it easy to stay awake well into the nine-hour night, even without the constant attempted boot-buggery of the begroag and despite the warm earthen berm he was stretched out and hiding on.

Jackson was on the far side of the village, watching the eastern approaches to the grain store. Ked was supposed to be watching the western side of the village, and Chalmers was watching him from what he hoped was a concealed position. Something had been off in the man's responses after the duel, and Chalmers didn't trust him. Kenla was still in the healer's hut, recovering from blood loss, though she seemed awfully chipper for someone who'd been cut so many times. Chalmers had no doubt these people were hard. It remained to be seen if they were trustworthy.

Shaking clear of other concerns, Chalmers focused all his attention on what he could do. A moment later he was grateful he'd decided to pay closer attention. He wasn't sure what it was, but something was different. Movement? He peered into the twilight, but couldn't pick out exactly what had triggered the feeling.

He slowed his breathing, straining to hear.

A maddening itch started just above the top of his left boot, distracting him. He reached down to address the issue and found something wet, warm, and sticky left behind by the begroag. He brought his hand up and stared at glistening fingers in the dimness. Fighting the urge to shriek in horror, leap to his feet, fetch the nearest flamethrower, and *burn* his fingers, leg, and boots clean off, he caught movement out of the corner of his eye.

Overcoming the urge to incinerate, Chalmers again tried to concentrate on the sound heard just moments before.

Among the shadows and blank darkness where Ked had hidden, there was a flicker of movement, then another, then Ked's slim figure emerged into the dim light of R'Bak's distant secondary star. He crouched, peering intently toward the storehouse.

Scrubbing his begroag-scummed hand on the rough soil of the berm, Chalmers slowly, and as quietly as he could, raised himself from the ground. As the begroag started to amble closer for another go, he set out toward the building more quickly than quietly, not wanting another sliming.

Ked, meanwhile, had moved from one shadow to the next, and was nearly at the door to the storehouse. The indig disappeared into shadow again before briefly reappearing alongside the black rectangle that marked the storehouse's recessed entryway.

Chalmers could see another figure—Jackson—closing on the same spot.

A muffled cry and then a thump sounded from inside as the partners arrived within a few steps of each other.

Jackson drew his sidearm and glanced at Chalmers, who had decided to remain empty-handed in case he had to go hands-on. Timing smaller nods to reach a shared, final 'go on three' nod, they entered as quickly yet quietly as they could.

But only one step in, Chalmers' foot came down on something higher and softer than the floor: a body, he realized as he stumbled, righted himself—and got slammed in the back. He stagger-stepped aside, turning toward the possible threat.

But no, it was just Jackson, who'd been following so closely that he had inadvertently jammed the muzzle of his .45 into his partner's back.

"Sorry, man," Jackson said.

"Fuck you," Chalmers grunted, rubbing his back just above the kidney, knowing he'd have a muzzle-shaped bruise there in the morning. He knelt next to the body just inside the door; it was Ked.

Reaching blindly with his left hand to feel for a pulse at the young warrior's throat, Chalmers drew his own pistol with his right. Trying to do too many things at once, he failed at all of them. Forcing himself to slow down, he found Ked's neck and the carotid. A strong pulse pushed against his fingers.

"Lights," Chalmers hissed, fumbling with his left hand for the newly manufactured Vietnam-era, L-angle, red-lens flashlight they'd been issued for the mission. He slid the switch to on. If the other Lost Soldiers were as troubled as Chalmers was over using a device manufactured on a fucking asteroid some hundred and more years after the original design was considered completely outdated, they hadn't shown it. Then again, Li-ion batteries and LEDs were not always better than alkaline and incandescents and second chances didn't always result in improvement. It was another sign that, regardless of whether it was a second chance, it was fucking weird, this life. Then again, the same could be said for Army life, though there had been more people to look at and shrug in silent commiseration back in the Green Machine.

Immune to his thoughts, red light illuminated the short hall to the storeroom. Unlike Clarthu's homes, the storehouse didn't have a doglegged entrance. Rather, the hallway was broad, probably to facilitate transportation of the harvest in and out of the place. One of the two rough-hewn wood doors at the end of the passage was ajar, a few inches of blackness showing in the opening.

"Cover," Chalmers said.

"Covering." Jackson modified his stance, the pistol steadied with the hand holding the flashlight. He'd been to the range with some of the Vietnam-era boys, it seemed.

Chalmers looked down. Ked's head was damp, slick with blood that looked black under the red light. There wasn't a pool under his cheek, so he wasn't bleeding that much.

"No one got past you, did they?" Chalmers whispered.

Jackson shook his head.

"All right. Let's clear it."

"Copy."

The pair advanced on the doors, each to one side of the hallway, Chalmers on the side with the door ajar.

Ked started snoring, the sudden noise shattering the quiet and nearly startling Chalmers into pulling the trigger. He shook his head and, grinding his teeth in frustration, watched the doors as they advanced.

The doors opened toward them and Chalmers nodded at them as they drew close enough to pull the big wooden handles. Sweat began to prickle his hairline.

Jackson reached across and pushed the one in front of Chalmers all the way open with his flashlight.

Gun up, Chalmers rolled in as swiftly and smoothly as he could. A long, empty aisle stretched about twenty yards, ending on a wall. Every third yard an opening yawned on either side of the aisle, each providing access to a bin-like holding area, fronted by a knee-high pony wall.

Jackson entered and went to the other side, pistol and flashlight up and at the ready.

Sweat began to roll off Chalmers' brow and threaten his vision as he sliced the pie to take a look inside the first chamber opposite.

There were great big—he did a double-take; no, Indiana Jones-sized—baskets stacked two high across the width of the chamber, tight fitting lids in place to defy any monkey that might give away their quarry. He was tempted to shake his head to get rid of the movie image. "Hope this guy brought a sword to a gunfight, too," Chalmers muttered.

Jackson's stifled "What the fuc—?" was interrupted as a figure trailing a fog of grain dust burst from the opening he was covering and ran straight at him.

The sergeant's .45 didn't *bang*, it *BOOMED*, straining Chalmers' already-frayed nerves to the breaking point and just beyond. The warrant officer, never a steely-eyed gunfighter, yelped and flinched, yanking the trigger on his own Beretta. It *BOOMED*, too. Missing both Jackson and the person rushing him, the fat lead round *spanged* off the bricks beside Jackson and ricocheted down the corridor with an evil *wheet-wheet* sound that made Chalmers' sack draw up.

Meanwhile, the silhouette rushing Jackson folded and fell into him, wheezing wetly.

"God damn!" Jackson yelled, shoving the wounded figure back, hard, with the muzzle of his still-smoking gun. The person toppled over onto their back.

Ignoring the persistent *EEeeeeee* in his ears, Chalmers steadied his flashlight on the target, saw it was a woman and blinked, wondering where he knew her from.

"It's the medic or whatever," Jackson said, the .45 in his hand rattling loudly as he lowered it. The after-effects of adrenaline were making the weapon—an exact copy of the

Vietnam-era .45s carried by some of the older Lost Soldiers—shake.

Chalmers nodded. It was the healer. The one who'd treated both Kenla and the hetman. She coughed, blood touching her lips, a knife gleaming wetly in her left fist.

Jackson fell to his knees, then across the woman's legs.

"What the hell?" Chalmers grunted, strode toward them, then started running when he realized that the small sergeant wasn't moving at all.

When the indigs barged in a few minutes later, Chalmers was still holding Jackson in his arms, tears streaming down his face as he tried to come to grips with the fact that he'd gotten his only friend in the world killed.

Their response to the situation was strange: they did not seem angry. Not in the least. They picked up their healer, causing her to cough up a great gout of blood. He thought sure it was her death rattle, but she was mumbling as they carried her from the storehouse. They left him almost alone and feeling entirely desolate. Almost alone because one of the villagers stayed behind. He was a thin-faced guy with a sparse beard and pockmarked cheeks. Chalmers was pretty sure he could take this local easily, even without the Beretta they hadn't bothered to confiscate. To his surprise, the man knelt and gently disengaged Chalmers' arms from around his friend.

The villager surprised the warrant officer once again by grinning at him, eyes laughing.

"What the fuck you smiling at?" Chalmers hissed. He said it in English, forgetting his debased Ktoran in the moment but trusting that, regardless of language, his tone conveyed his meaning.

Maddeningly, the man smiled more broadly and said something Chalmers didn't understand.

"Fuck you!" Chalmers snarled.

The bastard snorted and, lifting Jackson's arm at the elbow, slapped Chalmers in the face with one limp, warm hand.

Chalmers surged to his knees, spilling his friend to the ground. "You mother—"

Which is when it dawned on him that Jackson's limp hand was warm, not cold. And not cooling, either.

"He's alive?" Chalmers asked, in English.

The man grinned wider still and mimed wiping away tears, then laughed at Chalmers.

"Get your shit together, Warrant," Chalmers told himself, pressing a shaking hand to the sergeant's neck. Sure enough, a slow, steady pulse was there.

"What happened?" Chalmers asked.

"She gave him the slap of sleep. Like Kedlak," the other man said, once he'd stopped laughing. The bastard was wiping actual tears away. When Chalmers clearly had no idea what he was talking about, the man pointed a red-ochre stain on the other side of Jackson's neck from where he'd taken the pulse.

"Why did Ked have a-a head—bad—" he struggled to find the right word "—a head-*hurt* then?" Chalmers asked, glad he hadn't touched the stuff, and angry the man had given no warning.

A careless shrug. "Hit head when he fell."

Chalmers wanted to choke the smirk off the man's face, not least because he'd been such an unsympathetic witness to his moment—okay, moments—of weakness.

"When will he wake?"

Another shrug. "Morning."

"Can we wake him up before?"

"Safer not to. You want help carrying to tent?"

"Yes, please."

They gathered Jackson up. Chalmers stared at Ked as they carried Jackson past, confirming he was still snoring.

"You put in good word with his sister?" asked the helpful villager.

"What?"

"I like her like you like him," the man said, nodding at the unconscious Jackson slung between them.

"What?" Chalmers, addled by his evening, simply could not comprehend what he was being told.

"Man like you," the man waggled one scarred brow, and said very slowly, "with begroag *something* juices marking his leg, has hard time looking for love, no? That's why you let begroag *something* your leg, to show you are ready for love."

Unsure what the man was talking about, Chalmers looked at his pant leg, noting for the first time the oily, glittery sheen on the fabric from just below the knee to the top of his booted foot. In short, it looked like a glittered-up and oily stripper had humped his lower leg and the top of his foot for an hour.

"What the?" Chalmers cried, dropping Jackson's arms. The unconscious man's head thumped hard on the packed earth floor, but Chalmers was too busy trying to figure out how to get the stuff off his leg without touching it to give his friend's comfort much thought.

"The scales of begroag are pretty when still moist, no?" The man was laughing again.

Furious, fed up, and just a little frightened by how little he knew of this place, these people, and these times, Chalmers stomped around swearing at the top of his lungs for the next little while. The tirade included choice words from four different languages and a couple he made up on the spot to better describe his disgust in the best possible fashion. It didn't achieve anything other than making him feel better, but that was enough. Eventually he ran out of words, if not steam, and stomped back to the still-unconscious Jackson and the indig.

"All right, Laughing Boy, get his legs."

"Laughing Boy?" the man asked, all trace of humor gone from his face. "I am a man. Full warrior of the clan. You, who are not a full warrior, do not call me boy."

Chalmers stared at him, grinding his teeth. Eventually, he threw his hands in the air and said, an edge of hysterical laughter he hated in his voice, "If you would tell me your name, I would not have to give you insult!"

The man cocked his head, considering whether or not to continue taking umbrage. Chalmers let his hand settle on the holstered pistol at his belt, fully ready to shoot anyone who gave him the least bit more shit.

But the man's good humor returned as he smiled and said, "Artzhimaklid is my name, War Technician."

"All right, Archie, get his damn legs. Don't want another begroag to come along and decide to ride him like a pony."

"Pony? What is pony?"

"Small riding beast."

Archie chuckled at that. "Watch his head."

Navigating the narrow passage, the pair carried the unconscious man into the hetman's home and placed him on the bedding Jackson and Chalmers had set up there before the stakeout. Kenla and the hetman were still asleep. Something about her victory over the man had made them all a guest of his for however long her wounds required to heal.

*Speaking of which...*Chalmers checked and saw that Kenla had not stirred from the makeshift bed in which the healer had treated her. Wishing there was someone he could talk to other than Archie, Chalmers led the way back outside and returned to the storehouse.

It wasn't until they had Ked laid out in his own bedroll that Chalmers realized just how weird the whole situation was. Within barely twelve hours, Clarthu's four visitors had killed the hetman's son, stabbed the hetman near to death, and shot their healer. Oh, and said healer was clearly reporting their movements to the enemy while the son of the hetman had either sold something or, more alarmingly, been bought to the tune of an anti-armor weapon and ammunition.

Something was wrong. No, so many things were wrong that Chalmers couldn't sort out just what he should focus on.

Chapter Forty-One

R'BAK

Jackson grunted roughly as he sat bolt upright, then shouted, "Whotoleyoutoputhathere!"

Chalmers snorted. "You having crazy butt sex in your sleep again, Jackson?"

"Only with yo momma," Jackson muttered, scrubbing his face with his hands. "Wait, what the hell? Did I kill someone last night?"

"No, Kemosabe, you did not. Not for lack of trying, though."

"I missed? He was so close."

Despite the absence of the young man who knew the full story, Chalmers decided not to lie and instead took the high road and said, "Nope. You tagged them. Right in the chest."

Just because Chalmers wasn't lying didn't mean he had to admit to Jackson that he had missed so badly as to endanger them both with the ricochet, or that he didn't want to distract him from the impact of shooting someone, something Jackson had only had to do once before, if Chalmers recalled correctly. And that hadn't been a woman. Not that it should matter when you are threatened with deadly force, but some folks needed reassurance they wore the white hats, even when they were entirely within their rights to defend themselves. And some guys, Chalmers included, had a hard time reconciling harming a woman with being the good guy.

"In the chest? And he ain't dead?"

"Not yet," Chalmers said with a shrug. "And if the way these freakish villagers are acting is any indication, she's likely to live."

"No shit?"

"No shit," Chalmers answered, glad Jackson had missed his gender slip.

"How?"

"A couple of followers—I think they're apprentices or something—took charge and have been working on her ever since."

"Surgery?"

Chalmers shrugged. "I guess. I had to drag you in here while you were sleeping on the job."

"Wait…*her*? I shot some chick?"

Cursing inwardly, Chalmers qualified his partner's statement. "No, you shot an *attacker*, thinking they were about to kill you."

"The healer?"

"The healer," Chalmers confirmed.

Jackson shook his head in confusion. "So, the villagers weren't pissed?"

"I know, right?" Chalmers asked with feeling. He'd sat up all night spinning his wheels between concern for Jackson and wondering when someone would come to kill them both.

"But one of our party offs the hetman's kid and then I shoot their healer?"

"Yeah, it's starting to make me think there is something seriously wrong with these people."

"Starting?"

"Jacks, I am freaked out. Haven't slept all night."

"Wait…what did she knock me out with? I don't feel like I was cracked in the head," Jackson said, hands investigating his shaved skull.

"She used some kind of drug on you."

Jackson looked more confused, not less. "Bullshit. That kinda shit only happens in movies."

"What's that, you getting knocked out by a woman? 'Cause I'm pretty sure there was tha—"

Jackson interrupted him. "Naw, man, a drug knocking someone out that quick." The smaller man stood up and cracked his neck by the simple expedient of grabbing his head in both hands and twisting one way and then the other.

"I don't know; doesn't chloroform work that way?"

"Sure, but it's risky as hell. Killed a lot of people even when used by doctors." Jackson pulled his pistol, press-checked it, and popped the magazine. "I don't feel any the worse for wear."

"No shit?" Chalmers asked.

"No shit." He looked a question at Chalmers, who gestured at the pack behind the bedroll Jackson had been lying on.

"Okay, but why is it important?"

Jackson shrugged as he rummaged in the pack for the box of ammunition. He palmed a cartridge and closed his pack up. "Aside from my mouth tasting a bit of ass, I don't feel any real side effects, and any medic who can do that for our wounded would be worth their weight in gold."

Chalmers nodded. "I see. Well, guess we oughta hope you didn't kill her then?"

The question elicited another shrug from Jackson as he slid the fat .45 cartridge into the magazine. "Street rules: come at me, I go at you. Happened before, will happen again. Street rules." He slid the magazine into the well and tapped it with the heel of his left hand to make sure it was properly seated, then holstered up.

"Copy that," Chalmers said, wondering again what kind of life Jackson had come to the Army from.

Jackson crossed his arms over his chest then said, "Besides, her doctor's bag probably has enough of whatever she used on me and maybe even more useful stuff. We can take samples back to the major."

"And then what?" Chalmers asked. "The SpinDogs aren't as advanced as the freakshows that brought us here, and I didn't see anything that would let us synthesize tea like on the *Enterprise*."

Jackson shook his head. "Your momma never accused you a thinkin' too far ahead, did she? I want to make it past this shit show and somehow make a life. To do that, I think we gonna need everything we can get: ideas, dope, weapons, allies, whatever. Every damn thing we can get. When you up against it, street rules apply."

"Makes sense," Chalmers said, unsure he still wanted to know what Jackson's childhood had been like. He'd always known the sergeant was smarter, a little more ruthless, a better planner, and simply a better man than he himself was, but the hard edge to Jackson's voice made Chalmers shiver. And neither the tone nor content of Jackson's statement had been directed at him, but rather at an uncaring universe. It seemed to Chalmers at that moment that it was just possible Jackson could bend that universe to his will.

Maybe.

Grinning like a wild man, a villager trotted toward the partners, a bottle in one hand.

The partners had walked the village from one end to the other. Ostensibly searching for Ked—who they'd left near Clarthu's main gate—but they were both hoping for some clue to leap up and tell them just what the hell was going on.

As the running local approached, Chalmers smiled, asked "For us?" and reached toward the bottle.

The villager swerved to avoid the warrant officer, shooting him a dirty look as he trotted the rest of the way to the gate, where he immediately handed the flask to Ked. Their guide had a leather strap holding a bandage to the wound on his head from the previous night's misadventures.

"Was that the good stuff?" Chalmers asked absently, watching their guide talk easily, casually to the newcomer and a couple of the villagers guarding the main drag into town. The young nomad took a deep swig from the bottle.

"Is it the good stuff? Good stuff?" Jackson's laugh was a derisive bark. "There's no good stuff. Not here."

"You know what I mean," Chalmers said. He gestured at Ked. "What the hell is going on here, you think?"

Jackson shook his head. "I ain't sure. Somcthing stinks, though."

Ked's smiling face was suddenly painted a bright, wet red.

"Holy—" Chalmers shouted, gaping at the man that had been standing next to Ked. A good part of the man's face was gone, or at least mangled beyond all recognition.

Chalmers blinked, his brain catching up even as the sound of the shot reached his ears: a large caliber bullet had entered the back of the man's head blasting out a spray of skull, teeth, and skin. It was his blood, not paint, that had splashed all over Ked.

Chapter Forty-Two

R'BAK

"Down!" Jackson bellowed, already yanking Chalmers into a crouch beside him.

That part of his brain not reeling from the sudden violence and death in front of them was amazed at how fast Jackson's reflexes were. His partner was already kneeling beside the front wall of the hetman's place, scanning for the shooter.

Ked was also in a crouch and moving to cover even as something raised a puff of brick dust against the wall beside him.

This time the sound of the sniper's shot was drowned out as Jackson opened up right next to him. The four fast rounds from his M-14 made Chalmers jump. The warrant officer knew his hearing wouldn't be the same after a few more close shots, but couldn't care less, so long as Jackson kept the sniper from shooting again.

Chalmers risked a quick look over the wall at the area Jackson was firing upon. A largish stand of the tree-like grasses he'd almost hit on the way in lined a juncture of two of the irrigation canals about a hundred and fifty yards from the village. It wasn't much as cover, but it had obviously provided great concealment up until the moment the sniper had fired. Now, though, a thin, whitish cloud of smoke marked the sniper's hide.

Another puff of smoke. Chalmers ducked. Someone yelped off to the left and the sound of the gunshot rolled in a heartbeat later.

Chalmers risked another look as Jackson returned fire again. A sapling-sized blade of the tree-grass fell a yard or so above the smoke. Jackson was shooting straight.

He ducked back down as another puff of smoke erupted, this one from a few yards to the right of the earlier, slowly-dissipating ones. Either there were multiple shooters, or the sniper had displaced a few yards.

Chalmers had no idea where the round went because he was busy flogging his brain for an approach to the stand that wouldn't get him shot. One of the canals ran parallel to the low stone wall surrounding the village, flowing from the millrace that powered the village's mill.

Ked and a couple of the villagers with him thumped backs-first into the wall to the left of the partners. One raised his rifle—no, musket—and fired. A flash in the pan, then nothing. The man cursed and lowered his weapon, which decided to discharge at that very moment. Thankfully the round didn't hit anyone, just buried itself in the mud brick in front of him, but the misfire did throw the gun out of the frightened villager's grip.

"Jesus," Chalmers grunted.

Ked's breechloader proved more reliable as the grinning nomad *banged* a round downrange at the enemy and dropped back to reload.

"Who's shooting at us?" Chalmers shouted.

"Enemy," Ked shouted back.

Rather unhelpful, Chalmers thought. "Try and leapfrog up to them?" Chalmers asked Jackson, hoping the answer wasn't yes.

"Don't like the odds without a better base of fire and some grenades," Jackson said, far more calmly than Chalmers felt. The sergeant displaced a couple yards along the wall, popped up, and fired another fast semi-auto flurry before ducking back behind cover.

"What you want me to do?"

"Fuck if I—" A ragged clatter of gunfire from the far end of the village cut him off.

"What the hell!" Chalmers blurted, swinging his head that way.

A flat *CRUMP* came next, scaring the shit out of him.

"Mortar!" he shouted, unnecessarily.

"Get the buggy under cover!" Jacks shouted, his cheek still along the receiver of the M-14 as he laid down fire.

"*Cover? Cover?* There is no fucking cover!" Chalmers screamed even as he started toward the vehicle. It seemed to require far too much time in the open to cover the ground between buggy and wall, though that was probably because of the insufficient air wheezing through his fear-constricted windpipe and the fact that he couldn't seem to stand up straight.

CRUMP! Another explosion threatened to deafen him. Dust and smoke. Still on the far side of the village, thankfully.

"Jesus!" Chalmers screamed, jumping the last few yards to the buggy. He dropped the key trying to get it out, get in, and get the vehicle started all in one go. He bent, retrieved the key, and jammed it in, starting the motor.

Jackson dropped into the passenger seat. "Jesus!" Chalmers screamed; the sound startled from his lips.

"Not Jesus! Just drive!" Jacks shouted.

CRUMP!

The engine revved high before Chalmers remembered to slam it into gear. They shuddered into motion.

An absurd feeling of relief struck Chalmers. Moving targets were harder to hit, and they could always simply get the hell out of Dodge if push came to shove.

"They must have only the one tube," Jackson shouted. "Get us out of town."

Only too happy to comply, Chalmers worked the buggy into second gear as they blew past the last building of the village proper and out onto the beaten earth path that led toward the closest satrap city.

"The shooter!" Jackson's shout was nearly lost in the *CRUMP!* of another shell exploding, but his pointing arm was clear enough.

The track they were on curved away from the enemy positions. Chalmers hadn't driven this way and wasn't sure how to get across the—he counted quickly—two canals to the stand of giant grasses Jackson was pointing at. Then he saw there was another canal that connected the two, like the cross of a giant H. The near juncture of the H was close, maybe two hundred yards. Conscious of the adrenaline pushing him to go faster, Chalmers tried to keep the buggy at a safe speed, but the noise of repeated gunshots and explosions made him want to crush the accelerator with the heaviest lead foot across seven star systems.

It looked like the far end of the village was the focus of the assault while this end was pinned down by a squad or war party or whatever.

"Where the hell you going, Chalmers?"

CRUMP!

"Gonna go out and around, come back at them from behind," Chalmers shouted, the words carrying them almost to the place where the connecting canal ran under a wooden bridge. He went off road for a better look at the canal.

"Can we use it?" Chalmers shouted at Jackson.

"Shallow enough," Jacks shouted back.

"The slope?" Chalmers asked, figuring Jackson was answering how deep the water was, not the slope.

"Oh. Steep, but where the wall meets the bottom looks gentle." He cupped a hand to show Chalmers.

"Fuck it," Chalmers said. Not wanting to roll the buggy, he slowed and angled the vehicle so as to drop into the canal as smoothly as possible. Even with his careful approach, the buggy nearly tipped. The violent change of direction made their shoulders slam together, the impact nearly launching the lighter Jackson out of his seat. Chalmers grabbed him one-handed by the web harness and yanked him back to safety.

The buggy chugged, nearly stalling as his foot came off the accelerator with no downshift. By some miracle he managed a gear change before they hit the sluggish flow at the bottom of the canal and watery mud rocketed up all about them. He let the water slow them to a walking pace as the buggy's fat wheels pushed matching bow waves of stinking mud before them. With any luck, the bad guys would think they wrecked. Failing that, Chalmers guessed the canal would mask their engine noise, make it harder to tell where they were in relation to the attackers. Unless there was someone in the canal with them.

A wide-eyed and cursing Jackson rested his M-14 muzzle in the foot well and started putting the four-point restraint on. Steering with his knees. Chalmers followed suit, or tried to.

"All right, we follow this to the junction, then turn right and we're behind the bastards," Chalmers grunted. He lifted his ass to get at one half of the buckle he'd been sitting on. "We go straight at them and we nosedive into the next canal."

Jackson nodded.

Chalmers clipped in and was suddenly breathing easier. Then the absolute absurdity of the feeling of safety he had from putting on a seatbelt on in the middle of a gunfight struck him, making him giggle madly.

Jackson spared him an old-fashioned look.

"Buckle up, bitches!" a smiling Chalmers brayed, hammering the accelerator. Rooster tails of sludge shot up, behind, and all around them.

Jackson, either buying into his madness or too busy holding onto the chicken bar to say anything, just nodded. Nodded and, once the acceleration steadied, raised his M-14 to rest the forestock on the roll cage's crossbar.

CRUMP!

The crackle of gunfire was muted by the steep banks around them but still accompanied their progress. They soon reached the far juncture. Chalmers turned into it, decided this canal was too deep to push along the bottom, and forded it.

They'd covered maybe a hundred yards before Chalmers started looking for a way up. If his estimate was correct, they would now be about a hundred yards west of the position from where the sniper was firing on the villagers. Close enough to take the attackers under fire, but far enough to take full advantage of the M-14's greater accuracy and higher rate of fire. He really liked the idea of coming in behind the enemy's shooters.

Chalmers eyed a spot where more earth had settled into the canal, gentling the slope considerably. He needed that easy gradient because, as it was, he had to hit the gas hard to climb the sloppy surface. The engine gave a throaty grumble as he horsed the buggy up it, mud, gravel, and loose soil ricocheting from the far side of the canal in their wake.

"Fuck," Jackson said without heat, wiping the M-14's receiver clear of muck.

Unsure whether to blast out of the canal or ease his way, Chalmers dithered so long he did neither in the end. The front of the buggy dropped flat as they crested the top and bounced down onto the field, revealing three men crouched behind a tripod-looking thing Chalmers required a moment to identify.

"Mortar!" Chalmers bellowed, flooring it.

Two of the men, mouths round Os of surprise, reached for their weapons as the partners bore down on them at twenty-five and accelerating. Chalmers couldn't tell what the third guy was doing.

Jackson pointed and fired a few rounds, but only succeeded in giving his partner an earful, as far as Chalmers could tell.

Chalmers redlined it. He didn't bother to shift into second. Best not to if you were about to hit something. He tried not to think about what he was about to do.

Two of the mortar men figured it out, though, and tried to jump aside. One made it, though it didn't make any difference as the buggy crashed first into the rest of the crew, then into the mortar, which, in turn, was flung off its plate, crushing the third man's chest. He went down in a welter of blood, an oblong, finned object spinning in a lazy arc from his hands.

Chalmers slewed the buggy into a hard left, a last-ditch effort to keep himself between Jackson and the expected explosion. He was only partially successful as the dead loader's burden struck the ground and exploded with what Chalmers hoped was the final *CRUMP!* of the afternoon. Hot, hard needles traced lines along his arm, cheek, and shoulder closest to the blast, while his chest rattled with the shockwave.

The buggy, which he decided deserved a name after today's action, barely slowed. Something sounded wrong, but Chalmers couldn't be sure if it was just his abused ears shrieking their death song to his brain or actual damage to the motor. It wasn't until he tried to draw breath to laugh in relief that he realized what was making that alarming rattle: his own breathing. Well, maybe the motor was fucked up, too, but he was really having trouble getting his wind.

"Threat right!" Jackson shouted.

Chalmers turned the buggy—had to decide on a name for her, and sooner rather than later—hard in that direction. His estimate had been off: they were about four hundred yards from the mill and closer to two hundred from the tree-grass stand from which the attackers had started their ambush. Five or six warriors were still sheltered behind the rootballs of the stuff as they fired at the village, but were turning to face the growling mechanical beast that had done for their mortar team.

He watched one warrior raise his rifle and saw the puff of smoke. Chalmers supposed the shot was a miss, given the lack of a whistle, thump, or thud. Then again, his ears were truly fucked, so there was no telling.

The field was a reasonably flat couple of acres on a mild diagonal approach to the enemy position, allowing Chalmers to build some speed. He slammed the buggy—or maybe "The Beast?" Naw, sounded too masculine—into second gear, gathering speed despite the atonal complaint of steel on steel somewhere in either the gearbox or engine.

Taking advantage of the comparatively level ground, Jackson took aim as best he could and started shooting.

The guy who'd made a try for them fell. Whether shot or stumbling as he scrambled for cover, Chalmers couldn't say.

"Rumblekins," Chalmers muttered.

"What?" Jackson said, reloading with a speed and skill Chalmers knew he couldn't have matched. Hell, Jackson himself would probably be amazed at how smoothly he was able to manage the process once they got through this.

"Name—" Chalmers coughed. The pain was excruciating. He decided this coughing thing was excessive and unpleasant. He would not allow it to happen again.

"What?" Jackson asked again.

"Names for the buggy," Chalmers answered, sure his partner wasn't listening, because the sergeant was busy servicing targets again. "Beefeater," he muttered to himself past wet lips.

He licked without thinking, tasting copper and salt instead of the muddy water he'd expected. "Nah," he decided, patting the wheel. "You ain't ginned up, are you, girl?"

Oh!

"Man-eater!" The mad cackle that followed the thought ended on a painful cough that left him slumped in the seat, wondering where the last little while had gone.

He heard Jackson shouting, but his partner wasn't in the passenger seat anymore. There was a flurry of shots from his left, not the sharp cracks of the M14's 7.62 NATO ammunition, but the more throaty booms of Jackson's .45.

Chalmers wanted to help, tried to get out, but found he couldn't. Reality kept blinking in and out, like a light switch played with by a sadistic five year old. He struggled mindlessly for far too long before realizing what the problem was. He fumbled with the buckle on the four-point restraint, his shaking fingers strangely cold.

He looked for Jackson, waiting—no, *wanting*—to hear a crack or two about how shitty his coordination was, and instead saw his death standing a few yards away. It was the warrior that had first shot at them a million years ago but less than five minutes of clock time. The raider dropped the great yawning blackness of his gun's muzzle to point at Chalmers' chest.

Reality stuttered again.

The warrant smiled redly. "Fucking shoot straight."

"Fuck you!" Jackson shrieked, leaping out from between two monstrous blades of grass. Chalmers watched, fascinated, as the pistol in his partner's hand barked and bounced, its big slide racking back and forth.

A great blossom of pain bloomed and grew to a full flower of agony rooted in the left side of Chalmers' chest. As he closed his eyes against it, he really wished his last words had been something pithy. Something worthy for his partner to remember, if not with pride, then at least with a smile. Not something that would piss the little guy off. Chalmers had done enough of that. He was trying to do better.

Chapter Forty-Three

R'BAK

"Do better!" Jackson's angry shout was muffled.

"I'm doing muh best, Sergeant," the man's accent was pure Missouri redneck, "But do you see an X-ray machine here? We barely know what we're dealing with when it comes to the alien fungus 'n shit. An' that shit they'uns did to close up'n his wounds don't quite track with what'n I learnt in school, unnerstan'?"

Alien fungus? A cold thrill of fear ran down Chalmers' spine. He tried to clear away whatever was covering his ears, only to discover he couldn't move his arms. He tried to speak, at least mumble, but found his mouth full of something.

"Fuck you, man," Jackson shouted. "Worst Army doctor ever!"

"Imma corpsman, not a doctor, *boy*."

"Boy? *Boy?*" Jackson's voice went very high, very fast.

Chalmers' grin made something wet and hot trickle down the side of his head. He kept grinning anyway. From the ascending tone of Jackson's question, someone was about to get *very* messed up. Just because he was short, people tended to think they could get away with shit around Jackson. They were wrong.

He heard a clatter and a surprised yelp. Then, far more quietly: "You apologize, you cracker motherfucker or I'll break every bone in your goddamn hand."

"Look, I ain't even a doctor, just a corpsman!" the other man whined, the last parts of the sentence run together by both pain and a fervent desire to end it.

"Apologize, Cracker."

"I'msorrysosorryplease."

"Sorry, *Sergeant*."

"SosorrySergeant," the man moaned.

"That's better. See how easy that was?" A faint noise, another moan, then, "See to my partner, you cracker, or I'll see to you."

"Yes, Sergeant."

There followed a few minutes of fussing and tending from the medic, corpsman, whatever, whom Chalmers dimly remembered as some Vietnam-era redneck with a full set of tattoos and teeth that hadn't been a full set since shortly after his twelve year molars had come in. The medic or corpsman or whatever left quite quickly after that.

Chalmers tried to say something again, but not only had his mouth been stuffed, they'd wound something around his jaw. He didn't remember anything hitting him in the head enough to break any bones, but then the boxer never saw the punch that knocked him out, did he? Fear made his heart race. Was he gonna look like the Elephant Man? Uglier? He'd never considered himself model-pretty, but he'd known himself to possess a certain dark, rakish charm.

He heard what sounded like a stool being dragged over, and then Jackson's voice, clearer now that he was closer. "Hey, partner. You awake?"

Chalmers' attempt to answer came out more like a whining moan than the manly grunt he'd been trying for.

"Hey, that's good," Jackson said.

Chalmers could hear the lie in his voice.

"You lost a lot of blood, and if it weren't for another one of those Clarthu healers, we'd have lost you in those first hours. As it was, they had a hell of a time putting you back together. And now, Chalmers, there's this whole other thing…" Jackson trailed off, clearly at a loss for how to tell his partner his face was being eaten by an alien fungus.

"Hwww lnnng?"

"How long? Well, let me think. Shit, better part of two weeks, more or less? Hard to keep track."

More lost time. Chalmers thought about asking what his prognosis was, but hesitated, not really wanting to hear about how his flesh was being devoured by a mushroom.

Jackson helped distract him. "I bet you're wondering what the hell happened?"

Chalmers managed an, "Mmmmmhmmmm," that sounded a lot less emphatic than he liked. He was desperate for any kind of distraction, and his mind, never predisposed to dwell on bad news, leapt at the chance to learn what had happened in his absence.

"The hetman hadn't been paying tribute to the top dog, so the platoon-level attack we interrupted was meant to tell them who was boss."

Chalmers managed a tiny shake of his head.

"I know, right? None of the briefs said they kicked up to the satraps or their lieutenants. No, they all said Clarthu was more or less independent, that the people there could be relied on to a certain extent. And the briefs, they were correct, too—more or less—because the bosses they were supposed to be appeasing weren't R'Baku at all, but top dogs for real. Which is to say, the SpinDogs—or rather, an isolationist faction among them."

"Ergh?" Chalmers managed, unsure whether it was painkillers, blood loss, or simply native stupidity that was preventing him understanding Jackson's explanation.

"Remember Murphy telling us there was a potential problem in that the SpinDogs were *mostly* backing us?"

"Mmmm-hmmm," Chalmers managed. His cheek was starting to itch abominably, making him bite back a sob.

"Well, it stood to reason there was another faction, one that didn't want us to interfere in their profitable and long-established dealings with the R'Baku."

"Ergh?"

"Some people can't be trusted with power," Jackson said, then swallowed loudly and let go a sigh that was tired but satisfied. "Just can't trust them at all. Want to stay there no matter what the cost is to their own organization. Apparently a group called the Hardliners are spearheading the faction that wants everything to remain status quo." He chuckled. "That means 'the same,' Chalmers."

"Fthk Uuuu," Chalmers managed.

Jackson's chuckle deepened, then became a laugh. Chalmers liked to hear it, though he didn't feel much like doing anything other than scratch away the itch that was crawling along the side of his face like shark skin rubbed the wrong way. Tears welled as Chalmers considered they might actually have to use something like sharkskin on his face to scrape the fungus out of his wounds. No more man-eaters for Chalmers. Likely no companionship ever again. Not unless he purchased it. Self-pity made silent tears flow, or try to. The bandages soaked most of them up.

Another loud swallow was followed by the sound of liquid swishing in bottle. "Damn rude of me to be drinking without you, but you can't have a drink in your condition. Something about it lowering your immune system."

Chalmers didn't even try and tell his partner to fuck off. He didn't want to aggravate the itch any further than necessary.

"Where was I?" Jackson asked after a brief wait to see if Chalmers would rise to the bait. "Oh, yeah, the Hardliners. So these fuckers realized that their source for the drugs the healers used to fix your broken ass was about to either dry up or, worse yet from their point of view, end up in the hands of the Expansionist faction: their main rivals.

"So, the Hardliners decide to make sure we failed. Spectacularly. They contacted their people on the planet—apparently they've got a network like the main SpinDog liaisons have—and activated a couple of dead drops. Murphy is pretty sure—"

"Ergk?"

"What's that? Oh, yeah, Murphy and me had a long chat after the battle and a couple of rather interesting discussions with some people here. Something went on up there, on all of the SpinDog rohabs; something heavy. Murphy was vague on specifics, but I got his drift: the shit they tried to pull here became known up there and bad blood boiled over. Anyway, the guys who attacked Clarthu may not have been following direct orders from the Hardliners—they may have had some motives of their own—but they definitely got the mortar and shells from them."

"Huuu?" Chalmers asked, the desire to know more momentarily overcoming the need to avoid more itching.

"How? Not sure of the delive—Oh, you mean how do we know?"

"Essss."

"You know how exacting their copies of our weapons are, right? That's why my .45 rattled like the ones I trained on at Basic despite the fact it was a SpinDog-made copy. Well, the mortar was straight US Army, circa Korean War, but no serial number. Not even the stamp that the SpinDogs put on their knock-offs. Meaning the Hardliners found a way to get the plans we shared with the SpinDogs to their own fabricators—probably black-market operators among the RockHounds." Jackson shook his head. "Leastwise, that's what we think. Not a lot of real evidence left. You fucked the tube up good driving through the crew like you did."

Chalmers heard another swig and swish as Jackson drank. Silence remained in its wake; Chalmers was unable to speak and struggled to avoid recalling the feel of Man-Eater as she bucked over the bodies. He wasn't sure what Jackson was thinking, but hoped the silence was recognition of Chalmers' sacrificial act, interposing himself between Jackson and the exploding shell.

"Anyway," Jackson said after another pull on the bottle, "I think Murphy is layin' too little at the feet of the Hardliners, but he may just be taking a page from General Powell: tryin' to avoid breaking up the alliance despite the shit our allies be pulling."

"Buuuht?"

A theatrical sigh. "You talkin' too much, Chalmers. Let me get a word in edgewise, man."

"Funk uuuuu. Wheeer frm?" Chalmers managed. His bonds were loosening, which might be of concern. He probably wasn't supposed to scratch at any of his infected wounds.

"Where were the weapons from? I already tole you," Jackson was slurring a bit now, the drink obviously taking effect.

"Mnnn."

"Oh, the men were militia from the villages in the regions north of Clarthu. Fuckin' weekend warriors. Apparently, they were called up by the satraps' local underlings—called vavasors—but hadn't shown much enthusiasm for taking on the Clarthuuns or the Kedlakis until they got the gear from the Hardliners."

"Tang?"

Jackson snorted. "Space OJ?"

"Nnnmmm. Traneng," Chalmers said carefully.

"Training?" Jackson asked.

Chalmers didn't answer, fully occupied with suppressing a resurgence of the itch.

"I'm just gonna take your trembling for a yes. We're still trying to run that down, but it looks like some of the satrapies allow locals to guest-train on the equipment they keep stored in their city armories. We couldn't ask questions of the mortar men, for reasons you know already. The rest either got away or got themselves executed by the Clarthuuns, who were straight *pissed*. Oh, and in case you're wondering where we are that I'm able to knock back Wild Turkey like the good ole days, then wonder no more: we're in the new camp. All of us. The Kedlakis-Ur and her people came, too, once they heard from Ked that vengeance had been taken for the affront to her niece—that'd be the little badass, Kenla—and we'd settled the rest of the matter for them."

Chalmers stirred.

"And about the scores getting settled? Apparently that was part of the plan from the get-go. At least, according to the Kedlakis-Ur. The village hetman's kid, the one Kenla killed? He wanted to take over from his pops but had been refused by the village council. So, he gets all angry and shit, and starts shopping the village to the, uh…the vavasors. Real dirtbag, this fucker.

"Somewhere along the line, a vavasor puts him in touch with the local satrap's fixer, who hooks him up with those RPGs. It was part of a deal to not only get control of the village, but as many of the nomads as he could convince to come over to their side. And, get this! He apparently approached the Kedlakis-Ur's niece to negotiate a deal that would betray us all to the satrap. When the niece told him to pound salt, he attacked her."

Another pull on the bottle, then a bourbon-rasped, "I remember thinking, given how easy she was about dueling the hetman and *controlling* that fight to buy us time, that his rat-fuck son must have had a trick up his sleeve to even think about attacking Kenla himself. Didn't make sense at the time, but then enter the drug the healer used to put me down."

Jackson coughed. Another slosh. Chalmers heard the bottle thump on the ground.

"So…so then. What am I missing?" Jackson's slur was fairly strong now. "So…so the healer, right? She's pissed about her son—oh, yeah, the healer and the hetman were a couple back when. But she'd made her peace with the break-up. She wasn't happy about her boy making deals with the enemy and then stealing her drugs to mickey the Kedlakis-Ur's niece. Oh, no, not the kind of shit a wise woman or whatever can take lying down. Goes against her oaths and whatnot. So she's pissed, right? But it's her kid, right? So, she decides to get rid of the evidence that shows he's working for the wrong side…and that's when we show up and I put a round in her chest." Chalmers heard Jackson's hands scrubbing the stubble of his cheeks. "Fuck, me, but I'm glad I didn't kill her…"

Silence settled around them.

Chalmers wasn't sure he understood all of it, or that it all made sense, but what he did comprehend jibed with the behaviors he'd seen from the principal players in this little intertribal drama.

"Cmmn?" he asked.

"Common?"

Chalmers nodded.

"I'm afraid I don't understand you, Chalmers. Maybe if I take that off." Chalmers heard a *thump*, like the front pair of a chair's legs hitting a wood floor after someone leaning back came fully forward. A clinking, as of scissors being taken off an aluminum tray, then, "Hold still."

Chalmers, helpless to do anything but, did as he was told. A few seconds later he was blinking into a lantern hung from one of the tent's supports while Jackson got rid of the remaining bandages that had swaddled his head so tightly he couldn't speak.

Jackson sat, returned his chair to the preferred angle of lean with his boots on Chalmers' bed, and allowed a big shit-eating grin to slowly spread across his face.

"What?" Chalmers asked. Surprised at the lack of pain, he tried to raise an arm to touch his face and survey the damage, but Jackson hadn't cut his hands free.

"Nothin'," Jackson slurred.

"Wait, why am I feeling no pain?"

"'Cause you're in heaven?" Jackson ventured, fixing Chalmers with a leer.

"Fuck you. We both know I'm going to hell when I die." He blinked, struggling to get his hands free, still feeling no pain—at least from his face, despite talking. "Wait, why was my jaw tied up?"

"Already told you. I wanted to get a word in edgewise."

"Jackson!" Chalmers shouted, the deep breath that followed and the struggle to get his arms free causing a harsh throb from deep beneath his ribs.

Jackson laughed, hiccupped.

"What the fuck, Jackson?" Chalmers wheezed.

"You like that shit? I'm particularly proud of the alien fungus bit I came up with, though I think I might have oversold the cracker shit Sonningen wanted to act out." He looked a question at Chalmers.

"B-b-but, you said I was out for weeks?"

"Jesus, man!" Jackson snorted, waving a dismissive hand. "You just lost a shit-ton of blood, had some deep lacerations, and broke two ribs. The crazy drugs they have here did for the lacerations, and you're wrapped pretty tight around the chest. The face wounds are already pinked scars. You've only been out uh, a little less than two days, I think." He paused, thinking. "Yeah, two days. Shit did really get fuzzy at the end, there."

"Wait, so no alien fungus?" Chalmers asked, bewildered.

Jackson laughed. "Fuck no!"

"Untie me, then, you asshole!" The shout drove a spike of pain through his ribs. Chalmers decided not to shout, ever again.

Jackson only laughed harder as he watched Chalmers' face contort. "Nah," he eventually gasped, wiping at tears, "I think I'm gonna enjoy this a while longer." He reached down and plucked the bottle from the ground. Saluting Chalmers with it, he took a long swig, swallowed, and said, "Not every day I get to shut you up at will."

Jackson made a face as the liquor went down. Now calm enough to note the bottle wasn't Wild Turkey, but some of the local rotgut, Chalmers let go of his earlier jealousy.

He also didn't repeat himself. Didn't beg. Now that his temper had cooled, Chalmers knew better. Old Chalmers might have begged. More likely he'd have raged and cursed. But new Chalmers wasn't about to beg. Not that Jackson wouldn't accede to a properly worded beg-fest, but because that was exactly what Jackson wanted.

No, Chalmers' choice was about himself. New Chalmers had, ultimately, been better. Done better. He'd sacrificed his body to save Jackson from injury, and they both knew it.

The whole purpose of Jackson's charade was to distract them both from the changes wrought on their relationship by surviving the shit show together. They both knew their lives had rested in the other's hands in ways they never had before, that whatever sins Chalmers had committed in the past, they were just that, in the past, and he had done better with his present.

Against all previous experience and expectation, Chalmers had made good on some of the oaths he'd sworn, both to himself and to Jackson.

Neither of them could acknowledge what they had done for each other, not openly. To do so would break the unspoken contract. Jackson had come close to breaking it back in Kedlakis, but he'd been justified. Anger and honor wore a completely different set of responsibilities than gratitude, and it demanded a different set of rules. Gratitude was not to be spoken of, not to be displayed. Not between them.

So instead they would continue this complicated dance, neither admitting to the other exactly what the other meant to them until one or the other was dead.

And that was fine by both new and old Chalmers.

Really.

"Can I get a sip, Jacks?"

"Sure, sure," Jackson said, holding the bottle out to his partner.

Chalmers reached, but his hands were still tied.

Jackson fell out of his chair laughing.

Chapter Forty-Four

SPIN ONE

"Major?" Mara Lee's voice called from just beyond the open hatchway.

Murphy leaned away from the plotting table until he could see her. "Bruce, what are you doing here?"

"Hoping to speak with you a moment, sir."

Murphy checked his G-Shock. "A moment is all I've got. Meeting with the new head of Family Otlethes in fifteen minutes."

"I know, sir. That's why I'm here."

Murphy motioned her in. She shut the door behind her.

"You've got that look on your face, Bruce."

"What look is that, sir?" Her tone was forced jauntiness layered on top of trepidation.

Murphy met and held her eyes, kept his own tone serious. "The look you were wearing when you came back from the first training cycle dirtside."

Lee dropped the jauntiness, paused, then nodded. "Yes, sir. That tracks. Probably because it's connected to what I wanted to ask of you."

"Ask of me?" *That's new.* Captain Mara "Bruce" Lee made it part of her job to be all about finding solutions and answers instead of making requests and asking favors. Murphy sat on the edge of the table. "So, I can give you two minutes, but that's really all I've got. Particularly after getting Chalmers' report."

"Actually," she said, "that's part of what I'm here to talk to you about. I know you're getting ready to take news of that to Anseker, the new Primus Otlethes, but…" She took a deep breath. "Let me do it. I can make it right."

"What do you mean?"

"I mean, I think I can guide how the dominoes fall."

"Still don't know know you mean, Bruce."

"I mean that what Chalmers dug up at Clarthu will be…will be easier for Family Otlethes to hear if it comes from me."

"Because you're closer to them?" Murphy shook his head. "Bruce, that might be one of the main reasons *not* to let you be the bearer of the news. Stabilo's creation of an insurgency against us, of attacking our columns in the region, could tear our alliance with the SpinDogs to pieces. Particularly since there are indications that his father, the Primus Zobulakos, pointedly looked the other way. Which makes him complicit in his son's treachery, at least to the extent of aiding and abetting it. And given that the mortar used in the attack was produced by RockHounds that subcontract for Family Kormak—"

"Sir," Lee interrupted, eyes closed tightly; she didn't open them until she continued. "Major, please. I understand the political dynamics at work, how this news is going to be heard, the repercussions it's going to have. So please, trust me on this." Her carefully controlled expression didn't disguise the pleading in her eyes. "Have I steered you wrong yet?"

Murphy considered. "No. No, you haven't. Very well, Captain. You will proceed as our formal conveyer of—"

She shook her head. "No. Nothing formal. I'm just going to visit the family. As I normally do. That won't raise any suspicion. And trust me, we want to keep this as low-profile as possible, for as long as possible."

Murphy sighed, nodded. "The whole pound, then."

"What?"

"Brit expression that an English diplomat in the Mog used: 'in for a penny, in for a pound.' I guess if I can let you be our messenger for this news, I can let you do it on your 'private time.'" He smiled faintly.

Her answering smile was larger, but also, very serious: not an expression he often saw on "Bruce" Lee's face. "Thank you, Major Murphy."

"No reason you should thank me, Captain."

She stopped at the hatchway, shook her head. "I didn't say 'thank you' for me, sir. I'm thanking you for all of us."

Puzzled, he frowned after her receding back before gathering up the classified hardcopies. It was going to feel damned odd, asking to step up the rate of replication while knowing that the Family responsible for eighty percent of it—Kormak—was probably trying to sabotage the very campaign it was enabling.

But there was no way to put off the conversation, no matter who wound up handling the production. One of the linchpins of the ground campaign wasn't carrying the strategic weight that they had all hoped it would support. The SpinDogs had been certain that the satraps would be slower to react, would not realize what was happening until Moorefield and Tapper had cleaned out all the caches the Sarmatchani knew about or suspected existed. The Harvesters took considerable precautions to keep their locations secret, but the odds were low that any construction or changes—either in the Ashbands and Hamain—would escape the notice of those who called the wastes their home.

And at first, everything went according to that plan. Sarmatchani scouts had led Bo and Harry to three caches, each of which was promptly emptied. But when they arrived at the fourth, it had already been opened, stripped—and booby-trapped. Apparently, it had only taken the remaining Kulsian raiders two weeks to realize that their caches were being breached and emptied. Possibly they'd been alerted by embedded alarms, or maybe they'd sent satrap patrols out to keep their untapped caches under observation.

But that hardly mattered now. What was to have been a fast find-and-grab campaign to equip the Lost Soldiers and their Sarmatchani allies at the expense of their enemies was now a race of who could get to which caches first. And whereas the Sarmatchani were the masters of the region and knew much of what went on in it, the Kulsians had exact coordinates.

So, the mission clock had been impacted again, and now, more replicated gear was needed since there was going to be less coming from pilfered enemy reserves. Which made the ground campaign that much more uncertain and turned the dial more in the direction of having to rely on Bowden's air attack—in concert with a mechanized assault or not—to take out the transmitter.

Step one in the attempt to salvage the situation was to brief the most sympathetic leader amongst the Expansionists: Anseker, the new Primus of the preeminent Otlethes Family. It would be their first face-to-face meeting—not the best time to announce problems and make requests—but the situation required prompt action. If there was any way to make more of what was needed, either through the present arrangement with Family Kormak, doubtful, or by shifting to a different provider, likely—that option had to be identified and activated immediately.

Tucking the sheets into the folder, Murphy checked his watch again, discovered he was going to be late, and was secretly glad that he'd sent Max ahead of him; waiting on every security precaution the big bodyguard wanted to take kept eating into his schedule.

Hustling out of the CP and code locking it behind him, Murphy swung onto the corridor that followed the long axis of *Spin One*, pushing through the momentary balance and orientation glitch that was part of learning to live with the Coriolis effect. In this case, it was the result of the rapid repositioning of his inner ear in relation to the direction of the habitat's rotation. The little things one got used to…

From further up the corridor, there was a sound of a hatch swinging back. Not opening, just swinging on its hinges.

Murphy frowned, took his first step toward the meeting with Anseker, resolved not to fret and flinch at every sound that might be out of the ordinary; *Spin One* was a big habitat with new sights and sounds that still surprised him and the other Lost Soldiers. Even so, he let his right hand drift toward his sidearm—and realized that he hadn't shifted the folders to his off hand.

Shadows appeared in the passageway, one emerging from either wall. No, not the walls, from maintenance access panels that connected with crawlspaces that snaked like rat warrens throughout the habitat.

Murphy dropped the papers, grabbed at his holster—but knew he was too late: the shadows—black-clad and -masked—had already raised the square, big-gripped weapons that were standard issue for SpinDog troops and security personnel.

Two quick reports…and Murphy was surprised to find he was still alive, still upright. He was more surprised to see the two shadows fall forward. What the—?

"Down!" yelled a voice he recognized only as he was hitting the deck—because he'd never heard Max Messina shout before now.

Staccato machine-pistol fire was behind him, answered by a flurry of three round bursts from an M16 in front of him, rounds wheeting and whining through the space he'd just occupied. A second later, Murphy heard a leaden *thump* back where the submachine gun had been stuttering.

To Murphy's front, Max emerged from an already open hatch, just a few steps beyond the maintenance access panels. He checked a small data slate, nodded. "Video feed and motion sensors say we're clear, Major. For now. Let's get moving."

Murphy wanted to run the last few hundred meters to the comparatively safe precincts of the Otlethes Family. Max, still jogging slowly, shook his head. "No, sir. Not a good idea. Sounds of running carry pretty far in these steel tunnels. Better go a little more slowly and a lot more quietly."

It made Murphy nervous, but he'd learned from the platoon sergeant in his first command that a smart officer allowed experts to do their job and to realize that he probably wasn't an expert at anything. So, he followed Max's lead, literally and figuratively.

Gunfire rang down the metal passageway. Murphy crouched. Max didn't. "Not theirs," he muttered.

"What do you mean? It sure as hell isn't one of our M-14s!"

Max shook his head again. "Those are Otlethes' seven-millimeter assault rifles. Not as good as the lighter Kormak carbines in zero gee, but they're better dirtside, and about equal up here in the Spins."

Murphy listened again, wondering how and when Max had become acquainted with the sounds and characteristics of the local firearms. "That's a lot of gunfire. It's picking up."

It stopped suddenly…and then resumed at twice the intensity.

Max straightened, made a rough upward gesture. "You wanted to run, sir? Well, now's the time!"

They sprinted—but Max was leading them toward the sound of the guns.

Three minutes later, they came up short at a corner and Max called out, "It's Major Murphy, coming in!"

"Advance and be recognized!"

Max put up a hand blocking Murphy's progress. Murphy looked at it, then him. "I thought you were sure that these are the good guys."

"I am."

"Well?"

Max almost smiled. "I could be wrong." He took a big step into the open, left hand holding the M16 by the carrying handle, right hand well away from his body.

"Well, don't just stand there!" said a thickly accented SpinDog voice. "Come forward. Anseker will be relieved the major was not killed."

Max waved for Murphy to follow. They passed through a gauntlet of armed men and women, most in Otlethes colors, but a few wearing symbols and signs of allegiance that Murphy did not recognize. He glanced up at Max, muttered, "Let me guess: you know who the new players are, too."

Max shrugged as they followed a tween-aged girl through barricades and over bodies—mostly wearing Kormak colors. "I get around, sir."

"I don't see how. Seems like you're my shadow every waking hour. Only time you're not there is when you're asleep."

Max cocked his head philosophically. "Sir, you're making the assumption that, when I clock out and head for my rack, I actually go there." He leaned down toward Murphy. "Truth is, I don't sleep much."

Murphy swallowed, wondered what martyr's sacrifice he'd made in an earlier life to deserve a guardian angel like Maximilliano Messina. "And that's how you know about Anseker's new allies."

"Not new, sir," Max corrected. "Just quiet. They knew this was coming, y'see. I kinda had hints, too, once some of the other side's guys started following you around."

"Some guys were doing *what*?"

"They were good, I'll give 'em that. And because they were pros, I knew they wouldn't be the ones actually making the hit. Good assassins never appear near their target; someone else does that. And the two guys watching you always worked alone. They were never in the same place, never at the same time. Always at distance. Didn't move with us; that was too obvious. But they had hand-offs, one calling ahead to the other to pick us up as we changed location. SOP when you're tailing suspects…or targets. They also passed near the CP way more than any local would have reason to."

"Which you knew how?"

"Video feed. Scored some of the local cameras from the Expansionists. Anseker heard, reached out to me in his role as their defense chief. We talked and he clued me in on what was about to go down. And he asked me not to tell you."

"And you agreed to that?" Murphy stopped, barked, "Sergeant, fact check: who the *hell* is your CO?"

Max slowed to a halt, regarded Murphy solemnly. "You are, sir. And you made it my job to keep you alive. If doing that to the best of my ability meant keeping you out of the loop for three days, then that's what I was willing to do." He gestured forward, resumed walking. So did Murphy. "Sir, I'm sure you noticed I didn't last long in the field, back in 'Nam."

"I did. But there were no reports or charges of insubordination."

Now Max did smile. "Kinda difficult for officers to report you when you save their asses by doing what needed to be done. Particularly while they were still trying to get their thumb out. And when everybody in the field and up the chain knows it." He sighed. "Look, sir, I don't mean to sound cocky. I had good officers, but sometimes I clue in to a growing threat like I'm coming up on a highway intersection socked in by fog that no one else can see through. And there's never a good way, or enough time, to explain what I see or how I saw it. By that time, we'd all be dead."

"Well, okay…but keeping me in the dark for three days?"

Max shrugged. "Sir, if I'd told you, you would have reacted to protect all of us, because you'd have been right to fear that every Lost Soldier was either going to be tortured for information or sent out an airlock as soon as the Hardliners got control. But those changes would have made the Hardliners suspicious and they'd have learned that the Expansionists were ready and waiting for them." He grimaced. "Then the plans to read you in at today's meeting with Anseker got fubared by what just happened dirtside."

"Which you know about how?"

"Don't know the details, sir. But even though you have your own secure line, the SpinDogs have their own operators and sympathetics on R'Bak. Word came up about a mortar attack. Word was the mortar was not of local manufacture; no surprise there. It also meant that there was only one source from which the locals could have scored it: Kormak or some middleman of his."

"And that set off a war?"

"Sir, first off, the war was already coming. According to Anseker, the more you started talking about increasing replication, the more antsy the leading Hardliners became. Even without the informers who came forward, the Expansionists saw the writing on the wall—the wall against which they were going to be lined up by Kormak and his pals."

Murphy nodded. "So, they came up with their own plans. Which they had to keep totally off the radar."

"Yes, sir. I'm guessing the civil war is just about over by now. Because while the Hardliners had a plan, the Expansionists knew it, made their own, and managed to keep it quiet. That 'watching you watching me watching you' bullshit could have gone on for weeks, probably."

"But then the mortar report came up from R'Bak."

Max nodded as they rounded a bend that put them inside the stronghold of Family Otlethes. "Kormak and Company didn't have to be geniuses to know their fingerprints were on that smoking gun…well, tube. So Kormak made the logical move: attack early, before the Expansionists could react to the evidence that the Hardliners were trying to sabotage the very mission they were apparently working to support. Only problem was, they had no idea the Expansionists were already waiting for them."

Murphy nodded, slowed as they approached what looked like blast doors, flanked by automated defense turrets. As the two slabs of bulkhead began opening to admit them, he caught sight of Makarov inside…along with Mara Lee. He glanced up at Max as they resumed their approach. "Lee knew about this, too, didn't she?"

For the first time, Max looked uncomfortable. "I don't know, sir. But I suspect she smelled something was up. She's—well, they treat her almost like she's one of them."

Yeah, and that's just what I'm afraid of. The question was, why? Ever since Lee had returned from the first training rotation on R'Bak, it wasn't just that she'd been acting differently. The Expansionists—and the Otlethes Family in particular—had been behaving differently toward her: regular and less formal contact, including meals. A measure of contact, of intimacy, that hadn't yet been shown to any other Terran. Which was exactly what Murphy had hoped she would achieve, but he hadn't anticipated she'd also become more distant from the Lost Soldiers as a consequence.

Murphy suppressed a sigh as they approached Anseker and his Terran guests, who now stood before a wall map festooned by unit markers. Almost all the markers carried the colors of the Otlethes Family. Lee, receiving information from the Primus himself, glanced at Murphy and smiled faintly.

Murphy returned it, even as he realized, *It's high time for a heart-to-heart, Bruce.* He didn't want to pry into the details of what had happened during her first tour dirtside, but now, the circumstances had changed. Now, he was watching one of his cadre acting and speaking as if she was the family friend of some very enigmatic and high-handed "allies." Opsec alone made it necessary for him to get the facts of what had happened on R'Bak. *All* the facts.

And there was only one way to get them.

PART FIVE:

LEE

Chapter Forty-Five

R'BAK

Reminders of home are a double-edged sword.

For some reason, that thought popped into Mara's head, fully formed and apropos of nothing as the song on her Walkman flipped from her usual hard-driving classic rock to a poppy, groovy number by Deee-Lite. Her son had loved the song, though he'd innocently missed all the innuendos involved in the lyrics. That's how it worked when you were only four.

"Captain Mara Lee?"

Grateful for the distraction, Mara hit the pause button on the Walkman and pulled the headphones off. She levered herself up on her bunk and looked toward the figure silhouetted in the doorway.

"Yeah?"

"Major Murphy's compliments, and he wishes to speak with you."

A chorus of *oohs* arose from the other women in the bunk bay, and Mara snorted and grinned, despite the melancholy direction her thoughts had started to take. She got to her feet and lifted both middle fingers in response, laughing along with the others as they rolled over and went back to whatever they'd been doing. Mara shoved her feet into her boots and tied them quickly before walking toward the hatch, twisting her hair up into a bun as she went.

"Any idea what he wants?" she asked.

"No, ma'am," the young man said, his accent crisp and British. He wore a khaki uniform and the insignia of a WWII-era commando. He was stiff, and seemed not entirely comfortable looking directly at her. Mara glanced down at her own attire and realized her sand-colored flight suit was unzipped nearly to her waist. She let out a tiny sigh and zipped it to the level of her nametag.

She'd been relaxing! Why did it suddenly feel like she'd done something wrong? A discontented mulishness trickled into her mind, and she fought to keep her facial expression pleasant. Realistically, though, the best she could probably hope for was "neutral." She'd always had a wicked case of "Resting Bitch Face." Murphy never seemed to care, at least. She supposed that was a silver lining of sorts.

Mara followed the young Tommy to the section of the station Murphy had claimed for his headquarters.

Tommy rapped his knuckles on the door frame as the hatch slid open. He slipped inside. Mara heard the murmur of voices, but since she was standing back from the opening, she couldn't make out distinct words, other than Tommy's clipped, "Yes, sir."

The young soldier stepped back out and turned to her. "You're to go right in, ma'am." He said it in that strange Brit way that made it sound like "mum."

"Thank you," she replied, resisting the urge to be sarcastic or otherwise snarky. Tommy couldn't help what decade he'd been born in any more than she could. She flashed him a smile he probably didn't see—given that he was still avoiding eye contact—and slid past him into the boss' office.

"You wanted to see me, sir?" she asked.

"Bruce. Yes. Please come in. Have a seat." Murphy gestured to the cluster of chairs and a small table that dominated one corner of the room. "Can I get you anything?"

"No, sir," she said. "Thank you." His use of her callsign indicated this wasn't the most formal of meetings, but Mara still had no clue why he'd called her in. So, she sat, but lightly, balancing on the edge of her chair.

"How is your part of the mission prep coming, Captain?"

Mara let out a breath and dutifully took him through the primary and contingency plans she and her fellow crews had worked up over the past few weeks. She was careful, thorough, and detailed, and damn sure she didn't miss anything as she filled him in.

Murphy nodded thoughtfully, his eyes on the tabletop. Then he raised them so they were boring straight into her own.

"That sounds very promising. But it all hinges on one detail you've assumed in your report. Namely, that all the SpinDogs will show up to play their part." He leaned back in his chair, his eyes unblinking as he waited for her response.

"They'll be there, sir." Mara fought not to fidget under his intense regard, looking directly into her commander's eyes. "I can promise you that." She could, too. She knew it as sure as she knew her own name.

"Promise. The biggest two-syllable word in the English language." He still did not blink. "Strange word, too. Such a straightforward definition in the dictionary, and yet it always seems to have unspoken caveats connected to it. Like the promises made when people get married. Sometimes all the vows and oaths are kept, and no one gets surprised or hurt. But sometimes the words mean different things to different people, and they don't realize it. Some people make promises knowing they'll break them, or they already have—and there's always the escape clause. Because it's kind of hard to know just what 'until death do us part' means when, just a few months later, a couple can sign some papers and get a divorce."

Finally, he smiled. "So, tell me, Bruce, how's our marriage to the SpinDogs? Specifically, how's that final oath? 'Til death do us part?"

Mara saw the smile, saw the way it didn't quite reach all the way to his eyes. She took a deep breath and straightened her spine.

"Sir," she said slowly, careful to shade her tone with respect, "you made me their liaison. You're asking me if we have a good relationship with them? Is that right? If they'll fight beside us? I'm telling you they will, but from the way you're asking the question, it sounds like you don't quite believe me. Or maybe you want proof? Is that it?"

His smile became slightly brittle. "I don't have a degree in theology, but I'm pretty sure that since a promise is a matter of free will, not even God could prove whether or not a person is going to keep it." He leaned forward. "And, as impressed as I am with your abilities, Bruce, I don't think walking on water is likely to be one of them.

"However, you clearly believe that you *know* what the SpinDogs mean when they promise to be by our side in the coming shitstorm. So much so that you are clearly willing to risk your life on that understanding and their oath-keeping. Even though you have only known them for about two months."

The remaining fragments of his smile disappeared. "I've watched you, Bruce. You don't trust easily. Which I consider to be a good thing, particularly in this situation. And yet, you trust the SpinDogs more than you trust the majority of us. So no, I'm not asking for proof that they're going to do what they say; I'm asking why you are so certain they will."

He leaned back again. His expression was disturbingly neutral. "Maybe it's time to tell me what really happened at the end of that first training assignment. The whole truth, and nothing but the truth…so help you God."

Mara froze and willed her face to stay blank, her eyes to be unwavering while her thoughts whirled and spilled over each other in a chaotic jumble. After an interminable moment, she inhaled slowly through her nose and forced herself to speak.

"All right," she said. "You're right, sir. There is more to the story than what's in my report. But it's not military details. It's…personal."

He didn't move. He just waited with that penetrating gaze for her to begin.

Chapter Forty-Six

R'BAK
TWO MONTHS EARLIER

"You sure about this, ma'am?"

Mara didn't turn her head to look in Elroy's direction as he spoke. Instead, she continued standing with her arms crossed over her chest, watching as the SpinDog shuttle made its final approach to the center of their brand spanking-new training camp. She did, however, unbend enough to tilt her head a tiny bit toward him, so he could hear her over the sound of the shuttle's engines. "El, have you been sure of *anything* since we woke up?"

Elroy snorted behind her, acknowledging her point.

"Exactly," she said. "But Murphy's sure about one thing—and he's right. We can't go at this alone. And so far, the SpinDogs seem to be our best option for allies. If that means teaching them to fly helicopters, then I'm gonna teach them to fly helicopters. They can't be any worse than some of the FID students I've dealt with."

"FID?" Elroy asked.

"Foreign Internal Defense. Um…I think you guys called them MAAG in Vietnam."

"Oh, yeah. Those guys. You did that crazy shit?"

"Little bit," Mara said, noncommittal out of habit. "A few years ago. It's why I know how to fly the N-model Huey."

"Nice. I always knew you were a bad mamma jamma, ma'am," Elroy said, and it was Mara's turn to let out a short laugh.

"Always, El?" she asked. They'd known each other less than a week.

"Always since I saw you fly."

"That's just one day ago."

"That's all it took, ma'am."

"And that might be the nicest thing you've ever said to me, El," Mara said. "Now let's smile pretty for our guests."

"Yes, ma'am."

Mara schooled her face into the half-pleasant, half-intimidating expression she'd perfected for meeting new students. She knew that Elroy stood a half-step behind her, in a near-identical pose, with his own menacing scowl firmly in place. Six-foot-five inches and 290 pounds of ebony-skinned muscle, Sergeant Elroy Frazier towered over her, but his placement and posture said clearly that he was on *her* side and subordinate to her in rank.

Little subtleties like that mattered in Mara's experience. Especially during a first impression.

After angling under the camo-netting that mimicked the vegetative cover common at R'Bak's poles, the SpinDog craft set down with enviable lightness and cut its engines. As the noise abated, a hatch opened in the side and a single figure emerged and walked toward them. As soon as she could discern details, Mara found herself blinking in surprise.

"Is that one of our guys?" she asked, voice pitched low. "He looks too big to be a SpinDog!"

"He ain't that big," Elroy said, and Mara had to fight a smile.

Maybe he didn't match up to Elroy's gargantuan frame, but the man walking up to them was quite a bit larger than any of the other space-dwelling men Mara had yet encountered. He had to top six feet, easy, and he was far too powerfully built to have grown up in the .75-gee of their long, rolling asteroid habitats. But he wasn't one of theirs—wasn't a Lost Soldier—and he wore the utilitarian coveralls sported by SpinDog shuttle pilots.

He strode confidently up to Mara and Elroy and came to a rigid position of attention about a meter in front of them. Then he brought his right hand up in the salute that both of the ex-US service members recognized and waited.

"Sir, Pilot Ozendi reports as ordered."

He spoke the English words with a harsh, clipped accent. Softened from the sound of the old Ktoran Mara had learned in the Dornaani's virtual language sims, but its origins were clear. More importantly, she understood the salute for what it was. She snapped to her own position of attention and returned it.

"Please, stand at ease," she said in bastardized Ktoran.

Ozendi dropped his hand, and his face split in a wide grin that flashed white against his bronze complexion. "Your, er, 'classic' Ktoran is very good," he said, speaking in his own language.

"Thank you," Mara said. "We've been waiting for you. Are you alone?"

"Yes," he said. "I will learn your machine and then I will teach others. It was decided."

"That's not what we were briefed," Mara said. "We were expecting a full class."

"The other pilots who passed your remote orientation last week will come after I have completed the instruction here. I had the highest scores in the, eh…'academics,' I think you called them?"

"I did," Mara answered. She drew in a deep breath and took a moment to study the man in front of her. With his size, the color of his skin, and his wide, easy grin, something about him tugged at her memory. Her ex's bronzed, beautiful male face coalesced in her mind's eye, laughing at something she said as he shook seawater out of his eyes. Unexpected pain flared bright and hot in her gut.

"I don't suppose you surf, do you?" she asked, without really meaning to do so.

"I do not know what that is."

"Never mind." She shook her head slightly to clear it. "It's nice to meet you in person, Ozendi. I'm Captain Mara Lee. This is my crew chief, Sergeant Frazier. And this," she said, turning slightly, "is the mighty Bell UH-1 Iroquois. You can call her 'Huey.'"

Ozendi tilted his head to the side and looked from Mara to the helicopter and back again. "Why do you use the word 'her?' It is a machine, is it not?"

Mara smiled thinly. "Yes," she said. "*She* is a machine. But ask any Huey pilot, and they'll tell you that *she* has a soul. You'll learn, and until you do, I'd appreciate it if you'd use the proper terms out of respect. This old warrior, and others like her, have saved a lot of lives over the years."

"Including mine," Elroy rumbled behind her.

Ozendi's eyebrows pinched together in a frown. "But this is not proper. A machine does not have intelligence or a personality. You cannot speak of it as if it does."

Mara's smile grew. "Tell you what, hotshot," she said, "when you're teaching me how to fly your aircraft, you can call it whatever you like. But if you want to fly my bird, you'll do as I say. Sergeant Frazier will get you settled into your quarters and issue you the gear you need. Be back here in an hour to resume the academics."

She didn't wait for a reply, simply turned on her heel and walked back toward the low-slung building that functioned as the headquarters of the tiny operation. She had to call Murphy and inform him that the SpinDogs had changed the plan. And she needed a moment to collect herself and get her shit together.

Why did the damn student have to look so much like her ex-husband?

After half a week of academics, Mara realized that Ozendi didn't look all that much like Cam after all, other than the fact that they were both built like Polynesian warrior gods. Cam had always been light-hearted and easygoing, which had balanced nicely with Mara's driven intensity in the early years of their marriage. Ozendi, on the other hand, was every bit as focused as she and had a healthy dose of the competitive nature she'd glimpsed among their SpinDog allies. Especially when dealing with Elroy, which Mara found to be equal parts amusing and annoying. But it was a personality quirk, and like all personality quirks, it presented an opportunity for exploitation if she paid attention.

And Mara had learned to always pay attention. Which was why she and Ozendi were walking out to the bird alone today, despite Elroy's vociferous protestations.

"Ma'am," he'd said, using his hardest-edged tone. "Major Murphy charged me with your safety. You can't be serious."

"I'm absolutely serious, El," she'd replied, slamming her locker closed for emphasis. She leaned down to stuff her helmet in its bag and straightened back up, her eyes hard. "You're not going. End of story."

"But how can I—"

"Keep me safe? That's a damn good question. Do you have a set of controls in the back, Sergeant Frazier?" she'd asked, raising her eyebrows, and letting her tone dip down into the glacial range.

"No, but—"

"But what? What the fuck do you think you're going to do back there, then, hm? Learning to hover is arguably the most dangerous thing the student pilot will do. Putting you on the bird exposes you to unnecessary risk without any corresponding reward. Whereas I, as a competent and trained instructor pilot seated at a set of controls, have the ability to prevent the student from crashing the aircraft and injuring or killing us both. However, that job will be infinitely easier if he's not also trying to show off for you because of whatever stupid man-competition thing you guys have going on between you. So you, Sergeant, will *sit your ass down and wait for me to land*. Is that clear?"

Mara had watched as a muscle in El's cheek jumped in his otherwise impassive face. But he'd nodded and left without giving her any more grief. She'd have to smooth his ruffled feathers later, she knew. Right now, though, she had other things on her mind.

"So," she said as she and her student approached the nose of the helicopter, "are you ready for this?"

"Absolutely," Ozendi replied, flashing her that confident grin of his. "I look forward to it."

"Remember what I told you," she said. "Soft hands, soft feet."

"Of course, of course," he nodded, but she was pretty sure he wasn't really paying attention. So, she just shrugged and walked around to the left side of the aircraft, opened the door, and plunked her helmet on the seat.

She got her seat set up the way she liked, activated her EFB, scrolled down to the proper checklist page, and then walked back around the bird to join Ozendi. Though she'd been skeptical at first, she had to admit that the concept of having all of her publications on a computer no larger than a pad of paper was a *damn* nice improvement over the paper checklists and pubs she'd always lugged around before, even if it *did* make her feel a little bit like a character on *Star Trek*.

"Right," she said. "Let's preflight her."

Ozendi glanced at Mara's hands where she held her EFB. His face went blank, losing all of the cheerful excitement of the moment before.

"Why do you bring that?" he asked, pointing. "The tablet computer?"

"It's my EFB," she said, startled. He just looked at her, waiting. "Electronic Flight Bag. It's got my checklists and stuff on it. You've seen me use this before. I had it during academics."

"It is merely archival?"

"Y-yes," she said, eyes narrowing. Where was he going with this line of questioning? "But you should know that. Sergeant Frazier gave you one on the first day, when he issued you your helmet!"

"I did not activate it," Ozendi said.

Mara blinked. "Wait—what? You didn't even turn it on?"

"No. I do not trust it."

"But…you went through a whole week of academics! You had to have opened it to study. How else could you possibly have learned your systems knowledge well enough to pass the test?"

"You and Sergeant Frazier taught me. I remembered."

Mara blinked again, her mind reeling. "You mean to tell me that you memorized *everything* we said to you in academics?"

"Yes. So I do not need a computer to tell me what to do."

"The EFB doesn't—" Mara shook her head in frustration. Murphy's initial briefing about this mission, some of which had grown out of her own observations, amplified what she'd seen signs of during the spaceside battle: the SpinDogs *were* incredibly leery of automation or AI-assistance. He'd promoted that to the level of a culture-wide obsession. No surprise, then, that all radio navigation mods had been removed from the aircraft. Hell, even their comms had been stripped down to very basic, line-of-sight radios.

"Okay, look," she said, taking a deep breath. She angled the tablet to let Ozendi see the Before Exterior Inspection Checklist on its screen. "This is just archival, like you said. It's not an augmentation or assist of any kind. It's literally just a book displayed on the screen. But this book is important, Ozendi. You can't fly without it, even if you memorize every word I ever say. There's stuff in here that I've never encountered, thank everything that's good. But if I ever *did* encounter it, my best shot at dealing with it is contained here."

Ozendi nodded slowly, but instead of relief or acquiescence, his face assumed a pained look.

"Cannot we just take the book?"

"You mean a physical copy? I don't—we don't have one printed out, and to print it will take…hell, I don't know…several days? But…" she pressed her lips together and made a decision. Murphy may not like it, but he'd been the one to talk about strategic victories when dealing with their new allies, after all.

"Look," she said. "It's important to me that we don't do anything you're uncomfortable with. If you don't want to fly with my EFB, that's fine. We can postpone the flight until we can get you some physical copies of the publications you need. And I *will* get you those. But if you want to go today, maybe you can just trust me that the EFB is just an archival device, like you said?"

Ozendi stared at her, his eyes dark with conflicting emotions. She could tell he wanted to go. He was a pilot, after all. At a certain point, the yearning to fly saturates the self and makes every delay painful.

She smiled and reached out with her free hand to pat his shoulder. "It is up to you, my friend," she said, using that language for the first time in their acquaintance. He started a little at her touch. "I will not push. I want nothing but trust between us if we're going to fly together."

"I trust you," he said, looking as if he spoke without realizing it. "I want to go."

"All right," she said. "Then let's go! And I promise, on my honor, I'll get your paper pubs started as soon as we land."

His smile grew slowly this time, rather than the flashing, cocky grin she'd seen before. This one seemed like something else, something much more genuine.

"Thank you."

"Of course. Now, let's start up top…"

"Okay, so the first thing we're going to do," Mara said over the Huey's intercom as she smoothly hover-taxied the bird out into a clear field behind the shuttle landing area, "is try out the controls one by one."

"I can take them both," Ozendi said, keying his intercom microphone with his foot after a minute's searching for the switch.

"Well, first of all, there are *three* sets of controls, not two," Mara said as she decreased collective and set them down lightly in the center of the field. "So that's something you need to understand right away. Hovering a helicopter isn't like flying a fixed-wing aircraft. You're keeping the bird in a state of dynamic stability. Here, I'll show you."

She looked over at Ozendi, occupying the seat to her right. He sat up tall, his spine straight, his legs rigid with tension, his feet flat on the heel plates in front of him.

"Look at me," she said. "Turn your head and look. First of all, notice my posture. See how I'm kinda slumped down like this?" She exaggerated the curve of her spine for effect. "Slide your butt forward just a bit on the seat and let yourself bend. She's not the most ergonomically designed aircraft ever, but she gets the job done."

"Like this?" he asked, echoing her posture. Mara grinned and nodded.

"Perfect," she said. "Now, stretch your legs out a little and put the balls of your feet on the crossbars of the pedals—go ahead, you can look. Down there where it says 'Bell' and 'Huey.' And put your heels down on the heel plates. Yes. Good. Now when I tell you to make a pedal movement, I just want you to move your foot—not your whole leg! Just the foot, pivot at your ankle. And if I tell you to 'curl your toes,' I mean just that. Scrunch your toes up in your boot. Understand?"

"Yes, but why—"

"Because, Ozendi, the Huey is a lovely old warbird, but she must be treated like a lady. You have to make very small, very fine muscle movements in order to not overcontrol the aircraft and begin working at cross purposes to yourself. You'll see what I mean here in a minute. Just trust me for now."

She glanced at his face, or what she could see of it beneath his helmet's smoked visor. His lips were twisted in a wry half-smile, but he nodded. Good enough.

"Okay, hands. Put your right hand on the cyclic. Again, look over at me. See how my right forearm is anchored on my thigh like this? That's part of the reason for sitting the way we do. You keep your arm locked down like this, and that helps you to make very small, fine movements with your hands. And don't grip the cyclic that tight! I can see your knuckles turning white from here. Hold it like it's an egg, don't strangle it—better. Now look at my hand again. See how I'm waving my bottom three fingers at you? I'm only holding the cyclic with my thumb and forefinger, so that I can key the trigger mic and talk. See? When I tell you to 'wiggle your fingers,' that's what I want you to do, got it?"

Ozendi obediently waggled the middle, ring, and pinky fingers of his right hand at her.

"Perfect, again. Okay, lastly, the collective. This is your vertical movement, got it? You pull up, we go up. You push down, we go down. It's very simple, but it often feels counterintuitive to people used to flying fixed-wing craft. So just remember, up and down are in your left hand. Lateral movement is in your right, and you control where your nose points with your feet."

"I learned these things in academics," Ozendi said, a thread of impatience working through his tone.

"Correction. You *heard* these things in academics. You're about to learn them now. So just follow along on the controls as I pick us up…"

Mara began to smoothly pull up on the collective as she spoke, feeding in a tiny amount of left pedal as she did so. In truth, she didn't even think about the pedals or the collective anymore. The Huey was the first helicopter she'd ever flown, and, at this point, hovering was merely an extension of her thoughts: Mara thought "up" and her body and the machine worked together to pull them up into a stable hover, with her skids hanging exactly four feet above the ground.

"Now what I want you to do," she said, hearing the dreamlike quality in her voice that meant she was speaking while hovering, "is to slowly take control of the cyclic. Your hand is already in place. I just want you to keep us in a stable hover. When you're ready: 'Pilot has the cyclic.'"

"Pilot has the cyclic," Ozendi said, squeezing the trigger mic to speak. That squeezing was enough to cause the hover to wobble backwards, which Ozendi instinctively tried to correct by pushing forward.

"Less forward cyclic." Mara's command was still dreamy; she concentrated on keeping her hand close enough to prevent Ozendi from getting truly out of control. As she'd known he would, he overcorrected and pulled back rapidly on the cyclic. The Huey responded by tilting her nose sharply up and accelerating backward.

"Instructor has the controls," Mara said, grabbing the cyclic and centering it back up in order to gentle the helicopter's movement. The Huey settled, once again, into a stable hover.

"I barely touched it!" Ozendi said, indignant.

"Yep," Mara replied, smiling slightly. "You barely touched her, and yet it was still too much. Remember what I said about not strangling the cyclic? Hold her gently, like a lady."

"Not all ladies like to be touched so softly," he grumbled.

Mara grinned. "Perhaps not," she said. "But this one does. Gentle, Ozendi. You're doing great."

"Am I?" he asked, but he gamely rested just his fingertips on the cyclic again. This time, when Mara gave him the control, he did much better at keeping the Huey centered and stable.

"Good," she said, feeling a smile as she spoke. Teaching a student, *feeling* them getting it…that was the essence of flight instruction. It never got old. "Okay, now, when I tell you, I want you to move us to the right. I'll tell you 'right ten' and I want you to gently feed in right cyclic. We'll start to accelerate in that direction. I'll count down from ten, and when I get to one, you'll have to stop us. Do you understand?"

"I think so."

"Good." Mara twisted in her seat, craning her neck to look over her shoulder through the pinned-open cabin doors of the Huey. "Clear right ten."

With her fingertips on the cyclic, Mara felt him pull the tiniest bit to the right. As was natural, he pulled slightly aft, too, but she used her hand as a barrier to keep him from going too far. She would address that on the next try. For now, she just wanted him to feel how much input he needed to get them going in the right direction. Her feet on the pedals kept the nose pointed steadily ahead as they began to slide across the ground in a sideways hover to the right.

"Five," she called. "Four. Three—start taking your input out—Two. One. Stop right."

It wasn't particularly smooth, and he immediately started to oscillate fore and aft, but Ozendi managed to bring them to a credible stop at the end of her countdown.

"Instructor's controls," Mara said, taking a firmer hold of the cyclic.

"Instructor's controls," Ozendi agreed, letting go.

"IP has the controls," Mara confirmed, and decreased the collective to gently set them down on the grass. "Ozendi!" she said then, letting a bit of the joy she felt into her voice. "That was awesome!"

"It was?" he asked, sounding faintly exhausted. She couldn't help but laugh.

"It damn sure was! Almost no one is able to do that so well their first time. That was fantastic. I'm really proud of you. Now. Ready to add in the collective?"

By the end of the first day, Ozendi could hover.

Oh, it wasn't one hundred percent stable, but he could pick up and set down where he wanted, and he could move laterally and vertically according to the commands Mara gave him. He was a little shaky on controlling the nose with the pedals, but that wasn't unusual for a brand-new student, and Mara was confident he'd improve rapidly. Especially as he was their only student, and they were planning at least one flight every day.

"As soon as the rotor is still, you can go on inside," Mara told Ozendi as the main rotor coasted to a stop during the shutdown sequence. "Sergeant Frazier will help me put the bird to bed, and then we'll join you for a debrief."

"Debrief?" Ozendi asked.

"Yes. It's essential for your learning. We're going to talk about your flight and all of the things you learned in order to reinforce those lessons," Mara said. She couldn't help but give him a sympathetic smile. "Don't worry," she said. "What's said in debrief isn't personal. It's all about making you a better pilot. And we all had to learn at some point."

"And Sergeant Frazier will come?" Ozendi asked, his voice pitched low, as the man himself approached with the long rope used to tie the main rotor down.

"He will," Mara said, her tone hardening. "His expertise is also necessary for your learning."

Ozendi drew in a deep breath but gave her a short nod and said nothing else. Instead, he released his four-point harness and reached for his door handle.

"Ozendi," Mara said, surprising herself. "It was a good flight."

He hadn't yet removed his helmet, so she still couldn't see his entire face, but his lips curved in that genuine smile again, and something warm uncurled deep in her belly at the sight of it.

"Thank you, Mara," he said. "You are a good teacher."

He opened the door and stepped out of the aircraft. He nodded to Sergeant Frazier as the crew chief caught the rotor blade and pulled it down to hook the tiedown rope to the right place. Mara could see Sergeant Frazier's blank, professional face as he returned the nod. Then, as he walked the blade around to where he'd secure it to the tail, his eyes met Mara's, with a question shining clear: *What the hell was that about?*

Mara shrugged and looked down at the aircraft forms in her lap. Honestly, she didn't know, and she wasn't sure she wanted to find out. Fortunately, she had the perfect distraction available as she turned her mind to the mental math required to calculate the time they'd spent flying and hovering. She put her head down and focused on filling out the forms.

It was no use. By the time she finished up the forms, Elroy had tied down the blades, done the appropriate checks, and was standing next to her cockpit door with arms crossed over his chest.

"Well?" he asked when she looked up.

"It was a good flight," she said.

"It musta been. He was beaming like you'd just asked him to the prom."

"He's a pilot, El. He likes to fly. And he did well for his first helicopter lesson. That was him hovering back in here."

"Hmmph, no wonder the nose was hunting all over like a dog trying to catch a scent."

Quick, hot anger rose up inside her, tangling with the normal post-flight fatigue.

"Damnit, El! This is why I didn't bring you along," she said as she swung her legs over the collective and hopped down to the ground outside the bird. Elroy towered over her, but she put her fists on her hips and glared up at him. "I don't know what Ozendi did to piss in your Wheaties, but you need to get over it. Now. He's our student, and this is an important step toward building the strategic partnership that Murphy—and others—think we need to survive. I don't care what you have to do, but get your shit together, all right? I don't have time for this crap!"

Elroy met her glower for glower, but Mara held her ground. She'd never been one to be intimidated into backing down, especially not when she knew she was right.

Finally, eventually, Elroy wilted just a bit.

"You're right, ma'am," he said softly. "And I'm sorry. It's just…something about that guy rubs me the wrong way."

"Can you put your finger on what?" Mara asked, allowing her tone to soften slightly. "Instincts are important, and I'm inclined to trust yours, but you've got to meet me halfway, here, El."

"It's just…he don't look at you right." Elroy shuffled his feet slightly. "I mean, I don't think he'd ever try anything…but I watch him watch you, and he ain't looking at you like one pilot looks at another. He looks at you like a man looks at a pretty woman."

Mara's eyebrows went up. "Are you telling me Ozendi's checking out my rack?" she asked dryly.

"No, ma'am. He's checking out your ass."

Mara stifled a laugh and a surge of pure alpha female pride. "Well," she said slowly, "can you blame him? I mean, my ass is pretty spectacular."

Now it was Elroy's turn to look shocked. His mouth dropped open slightly, and for the first time in their acquaintance, he appeared speechless. Mara snorted and let the laugh bubble up from inside her and spill out.

"Hell, Elroy, you should see your face! I'm sorry, man, I didn't mean to short-circuit your brain, but damn, I got you good!"

"Ma'am?" Elroy said slowly. "I don't understand…do you want him to be looking—"

"At my ass? Not particularly, no," Mara said, shaking her head and continuing to chuckle. "But it's not the first time, and I'm sure it won't be the last. Unless you think he's gonna do something inappropriate, I think I can forgive him for sizing me up. As long as he performs to standard, right? Because that's the mission, and that's what matters."

Elroy shook his head slightly, his expression faintly disapproving. "It just don't seem right."

Mara took pity on him and reached out to lay a comforting hand on his big shoulder. "Look, El. The Air Force I served in and the Army you served in were very different entities. But men and women don't change. Like I said, he can look all he wants, as long as he's respectful and performs to the standard. The minute he fails to do either of those things, we're on him, right? But people are people, and people are gonna look. Hell, how many times do you think the girls and I checked out your arms and back just after we were all defrosted?"

"You—you did?"

"Mmm hmm. You were Irina's favorite of the MACV-SOG guys. She called you 'Hot Chocolate.'"

He snorted softly, rolling his eyes, but his lips quirked up in a smile.

"So," Mara said, "we good?"

"Yes, ma'am," he said. "We're good. I'll lay off the Spin jock. I'm gonna keep watching him close, though."

"I wouldn't expect any less."

Mara flashed a grin at him, then she turned and grabbed her helmet from the hook above her seat. Elroy fell into step beside her as they headed to the temporary building that had been set up as their operations center. It was just a prefab building, camouflaged with the local shrubs and trees that made up the forest around them. Mara couldn't have said if they were deciduous or coniferous plant forms since they seemed to look like both and neither at the same time. What they were, though, was prolific, which was interesting, given the overall character of the dry, desert planet. Here at the poles, however, the climate was more temperate—a fact for which Mara thanked her lucky stars. She'd done more than enough time in Africa and the Middle East to relish operating in cracked, dusty heat. It was a nice change, having their little training facility tucked in a valley between forested hills and set next to a clear mountain stream; it was pretty, and Mara liked to be in pretty surroundings. Even if they were, according to Murphy, over a hundred-fifty light years from home.

The interior of the building, however, looked much like every deployed tactical operations center she'd ever set foot in:

utilitarian beige walls, ugly linoleum flooring, communications wiring stapled along the corner between wall and ceiling or wall and floor. Mara strode all the way down the hallway to the small locker room on the left, where she dumped her gear before hitting the restroom and meeting the two men in the larger room they used for briefings and lessons.

"All right," she said as she walked in. Both Ozendi and Elroy came quickly to their feet in response. She waved a hand to indicate they should sit and took her own chair at the head of the table. "Let's go through this from the beginning."

As they talked, Mara remained mindful of Elroy's warnings about Ozendi's attitude toward her. She took care to keep her own tone brisk and businesslike, but that didn't seem to faze her student at all. He still smiled that wide, warm smile that shone through his dark eyes. When she spoke, he listened intently, even taking notes here and there. He accepted her criticisms and corrections with good grace, even when Elroy chimed in with his perspective as a back-end flyer.

At the end of the debrief, she sat back in her chair and folded her hands in her lap.

"Now," she said, per her usual custom. "It's your turn. How was my instruction? Was there anything that I could have done to make it easier for you to learn today?"

Ozendi looked up from his notebook, where he'd been scribbling down her last few points.

"Better?" he asked, sounding surprised. "No! Not at all. You are a good instructor, Mara. I said this before."

"Thank you," Mara said, studiously avoiding Elroy's eyes. "But even good instructors can improve. Every flight offers the opportunity to learn, right? That's true for me, too. So, tell me, what should I learn from you?"

Ozendi looked at her for a long moment, his smile softening, then fading away as the look in his eyes grew more intense.

"I cannot think of anything right now," he eventually said. "But I will let you know."

"Good enough," Mara said, ignoring the flutter in her stomach. She was just hungry after the flight was all. She pushed her chair back from the table and stood up. Both Elroy and Ozendi followed her lead. "I'll see you back here tomorrow morning then," she said. "El, walk with me."

"Yes, ma'am," Elroy said. He stepped quickly to follow her out the door, leaving Ozendi staring after her.

Chapter Forty-Seven

R'BAK

Training progressed. Mara taught Ozendi the basics of hovering and forward flight, as well as what to do in a number of emergency situations. The one thing she couldn't really teach was instrument flying. For one thing, R'Bak didn't have a network of radio navigation stations…or really any at all. The SpinDogs were so skittish about stray radio signatures that there was no way for her to build even the most basic of instrument approaches or routes. For the time being, at least, it appeared that they were limited to VFR operations and navigation only.

She largely concentrated on what had been called "mission skills" when she'd learned to fly the Huey. This mostly consisted of VFR navigation at both high and low altitudes, as well as operations in unprepared landing areas under various terrain and threat scenarios. They started with the basics and eventually worked up to flying long, circuitous routes in and around the hilly, forested regions near the pole.

They were still limited, however, by their fuel capacity.

"Mara," Ozendi said to her one day, when they were planning a training route for the next day. "I want to go here." He stabbed his finger down on the terrain map, indicating a valley higher up in the mountains to their west.

"We don't have the legs for that, Ozendi," Mara said. "You know that. We go out that far, we won't get back to the camp here before we flame out from fuel starvation."

"What if we refuel at this location, then? We can fly in these mountains and identify some very good high elevation LZs. Excellent training!" He flashed his grin at her, the one he used when he was trying to be charming and persuasive. Mara smiled back, even though the grin didn't have the same effect on her insides as his softer, more genuine smile.

Not that *that* thought was helpful. Mara forced her focus back to what Ozendi was saying.

"It would be, but I doubt there is a cache of JP-8 in that random mountain valley, Ozendi."

"No, but there could be, if we put some there."

"What are you talking about?"

"This location is known to my people," he said. "It is one of our contacts. I can have fuel positioned there for our use. It is part of the overall plan to establish flying bases throughout this region, yes? My people already cache vehicles there. It makes sense to have helicopters as well."

Mara looked down at the map, considering. He was right about the location. It *would* make an excellent air ops base for mountain training, and its distance from their current location meant that if they *did* have refueling capability there, it would effectively double their range.

"It's a good idea," she said slowly. "But I have to speak to my leadership about it before we do anything."

"Of course," Ozendi said, his smile triumphant. "You must call Major Murphy at once."

She laughed. "Not so fast, hot shot. We're following *your* people's comm security schedule. My next contact is tomorrow afternoon. That's soon enough. In the meantime, go ahead and plan the training sortie. Make sure you pick at least three possible LZs with various characteristics. Make one a pinnacle if you can. We'll see if we can actually get into any of them. We'll talk about terrain masking and threat mitigation along the route, too."

"And what will you do?" he asked.

Mara stopped short, drew herself up and let her face and voice go icy. "Why?"

"Because…" he hesitated, spread his hands and gave a little laugh. "Because I like working beside you more than working without you."

She let her eyebrows go up.

"Well," she said. "That's very flattering, but I have things to do, and you're perfectly capable of coming up with a decent plan."

"Are you sure you wouldn't rather just oversee my efforts? Just in case?"

"In case of what?" she asked. "You know how to do this, Ozendi. You don't need me to hold your hand."

"Perhaps not," he said with a ghost of his cocky grin. "But perhaps I would *enjoy* you holding my hand."

She snorted softly. "Are you flirting with me?"

"Yes," he said, and he blinked his eyes slowly as his smile grew. Not for the first time, she noticed the sweep of his very long, quite beautiful lashes.

It took her a moment to tear her eyes away, but when she did, she rolled them skyward in an exaggerated expression of exasperation.

"Just make a plan, Ozendi. I'll be back later to check on you." She turned toward the door.

"I shall await your return with great eagerness," he called after her.

She ignored him and headed out into the hallway, shaking her head at his audacity.

But she couldn't stop her lips from curving upward in a smile.

Murphy approved the plan and had further information for her, besides. It seemed the SpinDog leadership was happy with their progress and was looking to accelerate the program. Mara had gained a lot of respect for Murphy since he'd been awakened, but he increased in her esteem when he explained how he'd leveraged this desire into building a more robust support team for their surface-based operations.

"So yes, Bruce, by tomorrow afternoon, you will have your fuel at the settlement your student indicated," Murphy had said. Though his face remained composed and blank, Mara thought she could detect a gleam of triumph in his eyes, even through the transmission's induced distortion. "In addition, we're sending you a larger maintenance response team and a few other SpinDog support personnel. Medical, for one. She's also fluent in English, so she can help with any translation problems that may arise with your incoming student body."

"Incoming when?" she'd asked.

"Twenty days, maybe a bit less. You'll have to finish Ozendi's training, have the training syllabus validated, and the logistics worked out by then."

"It will be tight, but I should be able to manage, sir. Especially with the additional assets you're sending my way."

Because, of course, the training support wasn't all that Murphy was sending to meet her in the mountains. Her sleepy, tiny little training base was about to get a lot busier as the majority of the Lost Soldiers' rotary-wing assets unveiled their capabilities. What had been simply her, Elroy, and a part-time maintenance team would eventually expand into a full-blown task force.

All under the guise of training the SpinDogs.

Strategically, it was a brilliant move on Murphy's part, for it allowed them to demonstrate their commitment to these new allies, as well as increase their own lethality and planetside capabilities. And, as Mara and Ozendi continued to develop SpinDog helicopter operations, that increase would apply to *their* capabilities as well. Win, win, win.

If Mara could get Ozendi trained up to the appropriate level quickly enough.

So, the cross-country training that they'd planned had gone from "highly desirable" to "mission critical" in a very short period of time. To that end, Mara dispatched Elroy in one of the local ground vehicles to make his way to the settlement Ozendi swore was there. The SpinDog pilot had given Elroy a flat metal disk he'd taken from around his neck to use as a bona fide when he arrived. Apparently presenting the disk, which was stamped with a design Mara didn't recognize, was the only way to not be executed upon arrival.

The settlement was quite protective of its privacy, it seemed.

Mara pushed down her worry and waved goodbye as Elroy drove away, jouncing and bouncing over the unimproved terrain. The man had been MACV-SOG. He could take care of himself. And anyway, Murphy's maintenance response team and support staff should be there by the time he arrived. It shouldn't be an issue.

As Elroy's vehicle disappeared through the trees, Mara turned to look at Ozendi, who had raised his hand in farewell to Elroy.

"Well," she said. "Looks like it's just you and me."

"How fortunate," he replied with a flash of his grin. Mara snorted softly and rolled her eyes, eliciting a laugh from the man.

"Let's go look at your plan," she said. "Show me what you think we can get accomplished."

Ozendi nodded and gestured for her to precede him back to the operations building. Mara started walking in that direction, but slowed so that she paced beside him, rather than ahead of him.

"So, it seems like you and Sergeant Frazier have mended your fences," she said, her voice softening. This wasn't really her business, and she'd talked to Elroy about it, but she was desperately curious about Ozendi's perspective on the relationship. "Or, at least, the two of you aren't growling and bristling at one another anymore."

"Oh!" Ozendi looked over at her and smiled. "I was wondering what 'fences' you were talking about. Yes, Sergeant Frazier and I have come to an understanding. He is very protective of you."

"Sorry about the fences; it's an expression from home," she said, shrugging. "But yes. We're a crew and good friends as well. Part of his mission here is to be my backup. I'm actually surprised he was willing to leave me, even if only for two days."

"That is part of what we talked about before he left. Part of what you call the 'fence mending.' He explained his obligation to keep you safe and asked me to assume that obligation temporarily during his absence."

Mara's eyebrows shot up.

"Oh?" she asked. "How interesting."

"I was willing," Ozendi said. "Such requests are not unknown among my people. When our missions take us from our home stations, it is common to find a trusted friend to assume responsibility for those in one's care. It is a matter of great honor to be so chosen. I was happy to agree to his request."

"Don't be offended," she said, squaring her shoulders as she prepared to speak bluntly. "But I'm honestly surprised he would ask you, since he's been suspicious of your demeanor toward me from the beginning."

To her surprise, Ozendi threw back his head and laughed.

"Yes," he said. "He mentioned that. I reassured him that in my culture to try to sexually take an unwilling woman was to court death, if not from her retaliation, then from the retribution of her Family. Very possibly from the station as a whole." He glanced over at her and gave a little shrug. "We are a tightly bound community, and most of us are related to each other, however distantly. Such behaviors are incompatible with our existence, and the punishment for them is to be ejected from the station."

"You mean exiled planetside?" Mara asked, fascinated by this glimpse into SpinDog culture.

"I mean ejected naked from an airlock," Ozendi said baldly, no trace of a smile on his lips now. "As I said, transgressive behaviors are incompatible with our existence."

"Fair enough," Mara said. "But I'll be honest, I don't think Elroy was worried you'd force yourself on me. I think he's more concerned you'll try to seduce me…and even more concerned I'd let you."

"Ah," Ozendi said. Mara waited, but he didn't elaborate. When she glanced up at his face, that warm, beautiful smile was stretched across his mouth once again.

"'Ah?'" she asked.

"Yes," he said, coming to a stop before their building.

"Do you have any other thoughts on the matter?" Mara asked, exasperation leaking into her tone. "Besides 'ah'?"

"One," he said, that smile growing, shining from his eyes.

"And?" she prompted.

"Simply this: Sergeant Frazier is not the type to be unduly concerned…about anything." With that, he reached out and twined his fingers through Mara's, and lifted her hand to eye level. He pressed her knuckles to his forehead and then to his mouth. He brushed his lips across the back of her fingers, and the warmth of his touch rocketed through her, igniting fires under her skin that burned like the light in his dark eyes.

She opened her lips to speak, but for once in her life, she couldn't think of anything to say. Ozendi lowered his right eyelid in a wink, let go of her hand, and disappeared into the building before she could do anything else.

Mara dragged in a deep breath, trying to force her nerves to settle. *Get yourself together, girl,* she ordered. *You've flown with beautiful men before! Never mind that none of them made you feel like you were about to combust just from a single kiss. It's not a big deal. Handle your business!*

With that demand ringing in her metaphorical ears, Mara squared her shoulders and followed Ozendi into the operations building.

The next morning, at dawn, Mara felt a fluttering in her belly that had nothing whatsoever to do with Ozendi.

The suns rose bright and clear in a cloudless, golden sky. The air was sweet with a tantalizing hint of the heat to come, but a consistent light breeze promised to keep temperatures within the bearable range. It was, as one of Mara's old flight instructors would have said, a cherry day to fly.

Mara pushed aside memories of other perfect days back home and headed out to the aircraft with an eagerness that vibrated through her entire being. Yesterday, she and Ozendi had gone over every detail of his plan—which had been rather good. In hindsight, that really wasn't much of a surprise: life in space meant you either planned well or died fast. And, she had to admit, he was coming along nicely with his flying skills. Before too long, she'd be willing to certify him as a fully qualified aircraft commander. Then they would see if he had what it took to be a flight instructor—but those were questions and problems for another day. Today, they were going to fly and have some fun.

Their first order of business was to make their way to the settlement Ozendi had indicated on the map. From the beginning of this venture, navigation had been a tricky proposition. Back home, Mara would have used radio navigation aids like VHF omni-directional receivers and TACAN military navigation aids to augment her visual "clock/map/ground" dead-reckoning navigation. Not to mention the Global Positioning System, which had been an aviation gamechanger in the last decade she'd spent on Earth.

But R'Bak didn't have any of those options available. The Dornaani microsats could certainly have served in the same role as the GPS constellations back home, but the SpinDogs' ingrained caution about casual radio contact made that a no-go.

So, she had to rely on other methods. Like most planets, R'Bak had a magnetosphere complete with north and south poles. The Huey had a magnetic—or whiskey, for "wet"—compass mounted high above the pilot's windscreen. She could use that for basic dead-reckoning, although that was a tricky proposition since they were based in the polar region itself. As one would expect, the closer they got to the pole, the less reliable the whiskey compass headings became. Plus, some of the aircraft systems that used electricity induced further errors in the reading, thanks to the electrical current running through the wires also mounted above the windscreen. Basically, Mara could use the whiskey compass as a rough guideline, but she wouldn't want to rely upon it for precise navigation over long distances.

Fortunately, she had two things that *did* seem to be utterly reliable. The first was the incredibly detailed imagery compiled by the SpinDogs over many decades—centuries?—and recently updated by the Dornaani microsats to create excellent navigation maps. Mara had never seen such high-resolution, high-fidelity images, not even from the most highly classified satellite intel back home. With these maps, she could almost navigate tree-by-tree, and, since the indigenous population of R'Bak seemed to be both pre-industrial and—perhaps more importantly—located elsewhere, Mara had little fear of "pop-up" obstacles like towers or powerlines.

The second reliable factor was Ozendi.

"I was born in the settlement we are going to see," he admitted. They were about thirty minutes into their navigation route, winding through the mountains and forests about one hundred meters above the trees. "It is why I was sent to be your first student. I grew up adapted to standard gravity, and it was thought that this would be helpful in learning to fly the atmospheric craft."

"Shit," Mara said as her mind spun from this revelation. "Yeah, it would be. I didn't even think about that, but in order for the Huey to fly, we have to keep a one-gee load on the rotor. If that didn't feel 'normal' to you, that might present difficulties. We'll have to figure that out for the other students."

"It will not be hard," he assured her, flashing a quick grin in her direction before turning his visored face back to look out the windscreen. "We are used to encountering varying gee levels with our other craft. But perhaps it might be useful to install an accelerometer, just so the spinborn may have something concrete to tell them what is acceptable and what is dangerous."

"That's not a bad idea," Mara said. "I'll talk to El and the maintenance team about it."

"I am honored," he said. "But yes, that is part of the reason I wanted to come this way. I know these hills. I spent the first nine years of my life exploring them from top to bottom. Long enough for my bones and musculature to be well established." He thought a moment. "A little too long, actually."

Mara frowned. "Why is that 'too' long?"

Ozendi shrugged. "I should have gone to one of the rohabs—rotational habitats—when I was four or five, but the shuttle sent to pick me up had to be diverted, and it was several additional years before the next one came to this region. So, I came late to living and moving in low- and zero-gee." He smiled. "But as you have seen, I am a swift learner."

"And your body didn't regress once you got there?"

"A little," he said. "But I was already earmarked as a planetary liaison by that time, so I trained very hard to keep my body in condition to return."

"I didn't think you guys had any permanent planetary settlements."

"We do not have settlements, exactly, and those few places that we visit regularly are kept very quiet. I was only authorized to tell you because—because it was necessary for the flight program."

He was going to say something else. Mara didn't know how she knew that, but she did. He had corrected himself and given a different, albeit true, answer. Curiosity burned within her, but she pushed it aside. As much as she wanted to know, there wasn't a reason for her to insist, and to do so could be damaging to the excellent working relationship they'd built.

Because building relationships was their key to survival. Just as the contemporary "Terran" officers—Nuncle and Nephew—had pointed out shortly after awakening her and as Murphy continued to emphasize in all of his communications. Forging those relationships were just as crucial a mission as getting the helicopter training spun up. She couldn't afford to forget that.

Even if it meant that her attraction to Ozendi continued to grow.

She shoved *that* thought aside as well and forced her focus down to her watch and then to the map she held in her gloved hands.

"There should be a distinctive rock outcropping coming up," she said. "A stone spire that's been weathered away from the rest of the cliff. It'll be at your one-o'clock for approximately half a kilometer—"

"Contact," Ozendi said. Mara flicked her eyes up to the windscreen and, sure enough, there it was, a little more than 500 meters away.

"Perfect," she said. "That's our turn point, so keep it out your right door and turn around it. We'll have to climb a little to get through the pass below it."

"Pulling in power to seventy percent torque," Ozendi replied as he approached the landmark. "Right turn…clear right."

Without Elroy in the back to look out the large cabin windows, the pilots had to clear their own turns. Mara had been relentless in her instruction, ensuring that Ozendi developed the discipline to turn his head and look *every time* before he banked the aircraft.

Mara punched her stopwatch button, resetting the leg timer, and glanced at the map again. "Keep your climb at ninety knots if you can, please," she said. "It should only take us a minute and change to clear the pass, and then we'll see the next river valley beyond the ridge. The river is our boundary, so don't cross it. We're looking for what looks like a wide, flat turn in the stream, like the beginning of an oxbow."

"I know the place," Ozendi said. "Leveling off. This should keep us one hundred meters from the highest point in the pass."

"Good," Mara said, looking up again. The terrain really was breathtaking. On either side of their pass, craggy granite peaks rose. Vegetation grew on every slope that wasn't sheer rock, and its dark, cool green-blue colors looked black in the morning shadows. They cruised through the pass and descended down the other side, being careful to keep clear of the uneven terrain as they approached their river valley. This was the last leg of their first flight, the leg that would bring them into the settlement where Ozendi had been born, and where Elroy awaited them now.

They made it to the settlement, which Mara had already christened "FOB Ozendi" in her head. It consisted of a village with a wooden stockade, perched on the wide bank of the mountain stream they'd followed. Like their training site, there was a large, open field which bore scorch marks from the engines of orbital shuttles, not far from one of the gated entrances.

"I'm guessing our people set up near the same landing field," Mara said, glancing down at the satellite imagery and then back out at the landscape. "Yep. That looks like Sergeant Frazier's vehicle at the northwest corner there. Make your approach to the north end of the field."

"Roger," Ozendi said, easing the collective down and beginning a turn designed to bleed off his airspeed to the point where he could make a safe, controlled approach and landing.

Mara called out his altitude and airspeed as they both decreased, until they wound up in a respectable four-foot hover, about fifty meters from where Elroy waited, leaning on his vehicle, arms and legs crossed. Despite her sudden urge to jump out and hug her battle buddy, Mara made herself sit still and help Ozendi step through the After Landing and Engine Shutdown Checklists in a methodical, disciplined manner. Once the rotor slowed to a stop, Elroy came forward and opened the rear cabin door.

"Good to see you, ma'am, sir," he said as he reached under the left alcove seat for the pelican case that held the rotor tiedown cord, among other things. "I've got fuel on standby, and the village put together a lunch for you guys to take with you. I told them you'd quick turn this afternoon but be back to spend the night this evening."

"You're a godsend," Mara said with relief. "I brought snacks, but I wasn't really excited about them."

"You will like the food, Mara," Ozendi said as he pulled his helmet off and grinned at her. His tousled helmet-hair made him look younger than usual, heaping a boyish appeal on top of his other attractive qualities. "It is full of flavor."

"It's good," Elroy confirmed in his usual laconic fashion. "Naliryiz—she's the Doc—has it all ready for you over by my truck."

"Truck?" Mara asked, raising her eyebrows. Elroy pulled the tiedown free of the box and gave her a shrug and a tiny smile.

"Good a name as any," he said. "Y'all go eat. I'll get your bird fueled and turned."

"Naliryiz is here!" Ozendi stowed his helmet behind his seat, his face splitting in the widest grin Mara had seen from him yet. "I was hoping she would be the one to come!"

"You know her?"

"She is my sister!" He reached down and fumbled at his harness release in his haste to untangle himself and get out of his seat. He pulled the door release, kicked it open, hopped down, and broke into a run toward Elroy's vehicle. Mara watched as a smaller, female-shaped figure emerged and headed toward Ozendi. She didn't run, but she did open her arms wide and allow herself to be caught up in a hug that lifted her feet off the ground. Mara snorted softly through her nose as she undid her harness and stepped out of the vehicle. The man was like a puppy sometimes—all endearing exuberance!

Mara spent a long minute or two putting her helmet on her seat and her flying gloves into her pockets before walking around the nose of the Huey to join her copilot and his sister. She didn't want to intrude on their family reunion, but they were on a bit of a tight timeline if they wanted to get all of their training in today, and she was hungry.

"Mara, please, come meet my sister," Ozendi called out. He turned, leaving one arm around his sister's shoulders, and beckoned to Mara with his free hand. His face lit up with joy, and Mara felt a strange, ugly feeling twisting in her gut. She tamped it down hard, anger at her stupid irrationality erupting in her brain. Of course, the man was happy to see his sister! She'd have given anything to see her own family, wouldn't she?

…and that was another thought best locked away. Mara forced her face into a smile and stuck out her hand as she mentally shoved all of her inconvenient thoughts back behind the steel doors of her mind. "Hello, Doctor," she said, keeping her voice determinedly light and cheerful. "It's nice to meet you."

"You as well, Captain," Naliryiz said, taking Mara's hand in her own. She inclined her head slightly, in the way Mara had seen some of the SpinDogs greet each other, and swept her long-lashed eyes closed for a second before returning Mara's frank gaze.

Naliryiz was, to put it mildly, stunningly beautiful. Where her brother looked every bit like a Pacific Island warrior, Naliryiz had an almost ethereal look to her. Part of that was the slender, delicate build of the orbital-born, but there was also something otherworldly about her eyes, with their long, dark lashes and their honey-colored irises. She looked like she could see right into your soul, a thought which made Mara have to fight the urge to squirm.

"Please," Mara said. "Call me Mara. Or 'Bruce,' if you like. It's my callsign. Your brother and I haven't been particularly formal in that way."

"No," Naliryiz said, glancing up at Ozendi, her tone dry. "I can see that. But then you must call me Naliryiz. Or 'Doc,' as your sergeant does."

Some of the tension in Mara's shoulders eased, and she glanced back toward Elroy and the bird with a smile. "He does, does he? You know, that's a compliment, him giving you that title. You must have impressed him."

"I have been made aware of the significance of the nickname," Naliryiz said, her beautiful full lips curving in a smile that sparked through those striking eyes. "I am deeply honored."

"Well, if he trusts you enough to call you 'Doc,' then I do, too. Welcome to the team."

Ozendi looked between the two women, confusion twisting his face. "I do not understand," he said.

Naliryiz looked at Mara, but Mara just raised her eyebrows and tilted her head slightly, indicating that the other woman should go ahead and explain.

"On their world," Naliryiz said, "the warrior caste is but a small part of their society. Those who perform healing arts are not generally part of that caste…except for those who are. When one of their warriors calls a healer 'Doc,' it means they honor the warrior within the healer, and they trust the healer to stand beside them in the face of the enemy, if necessary."

Ozendi frowned at his sister. "Sergeant Frazier does not trust easily."

"No," Naliryiz said, "he does not. But one of their team members suffered acutely during planetary entry, due in part to some past trauma, I believe. I treated the man as soon as we landed yesterday, and Sergeant Frazier was grateful. He began calling me Doc after that."

"What are y'all doing standing here jaw-jacking?" Elroy asked, his deep voice threaded with exasperation. Mara turned to see the big man approaching from where she'd left him at the aircraft. "The bird's got full bags, ma'am. You need to eat and move out if you're gonna meet your timeline."

"Thanks for the reminder, El," she said. "He's right. Shall we?"

"This way," Naliryiz said, gesturing. She turned and led them to the vehicle, now much dirtier than it had been when Mara had last seen Elroy driving it away through the trees.

The big man walked up to it and slapped the front fender affectionately. "This truck ain't a bad rig at all," he said. "She made steady progress through the nastiest terrain. Not the most comfortable ride I've had in my life, but I've had worse, too. And she's got plenty of cargo room."

Mara followed Ozendi and Naliryiz to the rear of the vehicle and saw that Elroy was right. There was ample space for two large, nondescript containers in the back. Naliryiz opened one to reveal a stack of local fruits, a container of something that looked like pine-nuts, and two covered bowls. She reached inside and handed one of these to Mara, and the other one to Ozendi.

Mara watched Ozendi and followed his movements as he pulled the cover—a type of close-woven fabric Mara had never seen before—off. He bent over the bowl and inhaled deeply, pleasure writ large on his face.

"Delicious," he said. "Did you make this, my sister?"

"Iope did," Naliryiz replied softly. Because Mara was watching Ozendi for clues on how she was to eat this dish, she didn't miss the slight tensing of his eyebrows, the deepening of the corners of his mouth at his sister's answer.

"Ah. She's a wonderful cook," he said then, his voice clear of any tension. He turned to Mara and grinned. "This is *debem*. Roasted grain, meat, and local vegetables with spices. You must try it!"

"Use your hands," Elroy supplied quietly behind her. "Like rice and fish."

Mara smiled her thanks at him and reached into her bowl. She had to admit that the contents smelled wonderful: savory with heat and a hint of sweetness. She grasped a portion with her fingers and put it into her mouth, trying not to drop any down the front of her flight suit.

Flavor exploded into her mouth. Heat kissed the surface of her tongue, mingled with salt and a deep meatiness that made her eyes go wide with pleasure. She chewed slowly, experiencing the texture as well as the taste.

"Wow," she said after she swallowed. "This is amazing."

Naliryiz's smile grew and, for the first time, she directed it fully at Mara. "I am pleased you like it! *Debem* has many ingredients that will be beneficial for you. I think you will not need to eat again until you return to us tonight. But you will take these *leob* fruits and roasted seeds just in case."

Mara might have doubted at first, but as she continued to eat, she realized the dish was, in fact, extremely filling. As she used her fingers to sweep the last bits out of the bowl, she found herself full, but not uncomfortably so, and she had to admit that Naliryiz could very well be right. The food was in every way superior to her own stash of dry crackers and spreadable cheese.

"We need to go," she reminded Ozendi as she followed his example and wiped her hands clean on the cloth that had covered her bowl.

"Yes," he said, excitement in his voice. "I am ready. Thank you, my sister," he said, and hugged Naliryiz hard with one arm. The slight healer returned the embrace, and, once again, Mara felt a stab of envy. Though whether it was for the closeness of a sibling or for Ozendi's obvious affection, she couldn't have said. Rather than think too hard about it, she turned to Elroy.

"You're all ready to go," he said. "I'll be here waiting for you when you land. We've got billets set up, and you can meet the rest of the team tomorrow morning. There's a call scheduled with Murphy tomorrow night."

"Sounds good," she said, smiling. "Take care of everyone here."

"Yes, ma'am," he said. "Don't let the SpinDog kill you."

"Fiiine. I promise." She sighed, rolling her eyes in mock exasperation. Elroy snorted softly and gave her a tiny grin. She winked at him and turned to walk back to the bird, her mood restored from its momentary dip. It was time to get back in the air.

Chapter Forty-Eight

R'BAK

Their route initially continued to follow the river as it wound through the mountains and out toward the southern plains. The sun—which was hard to think of as the binary system's "secondary"—angled toward the west as they flew, beams slanting through the terrain and gilding everything below. Mara had taken the controls, giving Ozendi a break and a chance to practice his navigation. She reveled in the feeling of flying as she banked the Huey at a forty-five-degree angle toward a ridge, using the aircraft's energy state to make the climb up and over.

"Continue down and to the left," Ozendi instructed, glancing down at the map. She looked out her left window in response and then turned the aircraft further in that direction.

"Clear left," she announced as the Huey responded to her touch. After so many flight hours, the helicopter was like an extension of her body. She didn't have to think about the mechanics of balancing her cyclic, collective, and pedal inputs anymore. She merely thought *down and left*, and the Huey responded.

"We're going to follow this valley for several kilometers—"

Plink. Plink plink plink...

"Mara! What is that?" Ozendi's voice on the intercom cut through the sudden, high-pitched scream of the number one engine.

Mara ignored him. She knew what it was.

"Breaking right! Ground fire, ten o'clock!" she said crisply as old training kicked in. She whipped the cyclic to the right, and saw the fire light on the number one engine flash orange against the darkness of the dash. She slammed the collective halfway to the floor and dove for the dubious protection of the trees. As she turned, she glanced down to see what looked like a camp hidden in the trees below. A camp with several vehicles mounted with weapons. Weapons that were shooting at them.

"Engine fire in number one!" Ozendi shouted. "I smell smoke!" He started to reach his hand toward the warning light and the handle that, if pulled, would shut down that engine.

"Wait!" Mara ordered into the intercom as she banked back to the left, initiating a momentary climb that would hopefully make them harder to track. A bend in the ridge further to the left held a promise of safety, if she could get the Huey there in time. "She's still giving me power! Let her burn, we gotta get out of the WEZ!"

"Mara! More muzzle-flashes! They're still shooting!"

Mara buried the nose and pulled up on the collective. The scream from the number one engine intensified, and the acrid scent of smoke began teasing into her nostrils. She saw the bend in the ridge draw closer, and she whipped the bird further to the left to put the rock outcropping between the Huey and those determined to take her down. They carved through the air around the terrain and into another narrow mountain valley. Less than a hundred meters below, a tributary stream bubbled over rocks and fallen trees as it flowed to join the river.

She waited for a three count and then eased back on the collective to slow their airspeed into the range that would allow them to fly on only one engine.

"Okay," she said, forcing her voice to be calm, collected. There was no time for emotions. "Boldface. Now."

Together, she and Ozendi did the boldface steps of the emergency checklist by memory, shutting down the number one engine and activating the engine fire extinguisher. The warning light winked out, which made her draw in a deep, shaky breath of relief.

"All right," she said then. "Get the checklist. Let's clean this up and see what we've got."

To his credit, Ozendi had regained his composure and situational awareness, and he had the checklist ready to go. In truth, Mara couldn't fault him for losing it momentarily. Everyone reacted differently to being shot at, and almost no one held it together the first time.

"Power, checked," Ozendi read.

"Roger," Mara said. "You watch the engine gauges; I'll keep an eye on the rotor and the torque. We should have right at fifty percent available."

"Roger," Ozendi echoed. "Copilot is posted on the engine gauges."

"Power's coming in," Mara said, and she began a slow, steady pull of the collective. The number two torque needle rose in response, climbing through thirty percent, forty…

"Stop pull! Number two engine temperature is at maximum!"

"Shit," Mara said, glancing down at the stack of engine gauges to confirm it was true. Sure enough, the number two engine temperature gauge showed the needle right at the red line. Even worse, as she watched, the oil pressure in the number two engine began to decrease at a slow, but steady, rate. "They must have hit number two as well. We're going to have to land."

"Can we fly it back to the settlement?" Ozendi asked, though the sick tone of his voice indicated he already knew the answer.

"I don't think we've got that much time," Mara said. "The oil pressure is already at the minimum. I know it'll run for a little while if it pisses all the oil out, but if it comes apart, it's gonna be ugly. I think we'll have a better chance if we shut it down on our terms and make a safe autorotation."

"Okay," Ozendi said. "Okay. Let me see—" he looked down at the map, and then back up again. "Yes! I know where we are. There is a plateau ahead, into which this stream spills as a small cascade. The plateau is a flood plain. Mostly flat and very wide, without a lot of trees. It is a good space for autos."

Privately, Mara thought that nowhere other than a prepared runway constituted "a good space for autos," but she didn't think saying so would be particularly helpful. Instead she concentrated on flying at sixty knots; that airspeed would give her the maximum rate of climb. Or it should.

It also occurred to her that whoever had shot at them was still somewhere out beyond their six, but that thought was even less helpful at the moment, so she pushed it away and kept flying.

Below them, the mountain stream twisted and turned, cutting through the rocks on either side. It was probably only a minute or two, but it felt like hours before Mara spotted the waterfall ahead.

"There it is!" Ozendi said, the joy in his tone making it clear that he, too, had been anxious.

"Okay," Mara said. "The winds are pretty calm, so I'm just going to shoot this along the longest axis, which is probably going to be parallel with the stream, right?"

"Mostly," Ozendi said.

"Good enough. I've managed to eke out a little more altitude for us, so I'm gonna trade that for some extra airspeed and try to enter this thing as close to ninety knots as possible. I want to make it look as much like what we practiced as I can, all right? As soon as I enter and roll the throttle to flight idle, I want you to shut the engine down, okay? Get that throttle off so I'm not trying to reengage it at the bottom. Don't worry about the pilot not flying calls, I'll make them for myself. Got it?"

"Got it," Ozendi confirmed, and a tiny corner of Mara's mind laughed to hear him solemnly repeat the Earth-born slang phrase.

Mara eased the cyclic forward, pulling in power right to forty percent, and willed the aircraft to accelerate. The airspeed needle crept around the dial, slowly reaching first seventy knots, then eighty…

"Over the falls now," Ozendi said, his voice calm.

"Roger," Mara said, keeping her own voice empty of emotion. "This is real world, crew. Entering in three…two…one. Autorotate. Throttles Flight Idle."

As she spoke the words, Mara slammed the collective to the floor and rolled the number two throttle all the way back to the idle stop. The speed with which she'd lowered the collective helped to spike her rotor speed, which was what she wanted. She felt the throttle move beneath her hand as Ozendi toggled the idle stop release and rolled the twist grip throttle all the way off, shutting the engine down. It got eerily quiet after that, with only the whine of the rotor in the background.

"Two hundred feet," Ozendi said, reading off the radar altimeter. Mara's eyes flicked through her crosscheck, looking first at her rotor speed, then her airspeed, then her trim ball, then glancing outside to her intended landing area. It loomed before them, and only Mara's discipline and years of habit patterns kept her from getting sucked into staring at the ground rushing toward them.

"One fifty," Ozendi said.

Rotor. Airspeed. Trim. Outside…

"One hundred feet. Flare, flare, flare."

As Ozendi made the flare call, Mara pulled back on the cyclic, a little bit at first, and then gradually more and more as she progressively bled her airspeed off and converted that energy into rotor speed. She could hear the whine of the rotor increase in pitch, and she gritted her teeth and forced herself not to pull up on the collective to correct it. This was for real. She wanted all the rotor energy she could get.

"Hold it off," she whispered to herself. "Hold it off…" She kept holding the cyclic aft until it felt like they were about to slide backward onto the Huey's tail, and then she exhaled and let off the cyclic pressure. The nose started to fall back toward the horizon, and Mara glanced at her attitude indicator to make sure she brought the helicopter all the way to a level position.

And with her left hand, she pulled.

She held her breath and pulled upward in as smooth and steady a movement as she could manage. She pulled and kept pulling, forcing the Huey's rotor to use all of the energy she'd shoved at it to cushion their landing as the skids touched down on crack-webbed mud of what looked like a dry lakebed. The rotor noise changed in pitch; the scream became a moan as she converted all of the rotor speed into lift.

The Huey skidded forward for a few feet, bouncing slightly, before shuddering to a stop and rocking first forward, then aft on the skids. Above them, the rotor swooped once, twice, slow enough for Mara to look up through the greenhouse and see the individual blades in turn. On the master caution panel in front of them, several lights blazed, showing that the engines were, in fact, no longer working.

But they'd done it.

Mara drew in a deep shuddering breath and closed her eyes. For just a moment, the memory of her son's face flashed behind her eyelids, and she pressed her lips together to keep from crying. Her hands shook. Everything shook.

"You did it!"

Ozendi's triumphant tone jolted Mara out of her daze. Her eyes snapped open, and she took another breath.

"We did it," she said on the intercom, pleased to hear her voice as steady and calm as before. "I'm gonna do an emergency shutdown. We're not on fire anymore, so you stay put. We probably spread the skids a little bit, and I don't want the rotor taking your head off."

Her hands flew over the switches required to shut down the remaining systems on the aircraft. Once the rotor was stopped and the battery off, she reached up and removed her helmet, hoping that Ozendi couldn't see the tremor that remained in her hands.

"Well," she said brightly, hoping it sounded like she was joking. "I got us here. Your turn; what's next?"

It turned out Mara already knew what was next. Once the blades had slowed to a stop and she'd shut everything down, she and Ozendi got out of the aircraft and took stock.

"Well, she's fucked six ways from Wednesday," Mara said, disgust and anger mingling in her tone as she looked up at the charred ruin of her number one engine. "How does number two look?"

"The cowling is glowing red," Ozendi called to her from the other side of the aircraft. "I can't open it to take a look."

"Awesome," Mara said. "Well, okay. We knew we weren't flying out of here anyway, so I guess this doesn't change anything. Lucky for us, Murphy just sent down a full maintenance response team. If we can get them out here, they might be able to figure out how to salvage her…if we knew where 'here' was, that is."

Ozendi appeared at the nose of the aircraft. "I know where we are," he said, a slightly distracted frown creasing his features.

Mara blinked, then stared at him. "You do?"

"Of course. Remember, I told you I grew up in these mountains. That's how I knew about this flat space where the creek floods in the winter."

"That's right!" Mara said. All of a sudden, she remembered the satellite imagery they'd been using for navigation. She lunged for the cockpit door, leaned in, and pulled the crinkled pages from the map holder on the copilot's side.

"Here," she said, shoving the maps at him. "Can you mark our location on this map?"

"I can," he said. But his voice held doubt, and his frown deepened as he met her eyes. "But Mara, I don't think I should. I know our location, and how to get back to the settlement…but those people who shot at us…"

"Yeah, who were those assholes?" she asked, anger further jacking up the jittery adrenaline dump skittering along her nerves. "I thought the indigenous R'Baku didn't have modern firearms technology."

"Most do not. And those who have it do not reveal or use it lightly."

"So, who—?"

"I do not think those who attacked us are R'Baku. I am not certain, but I fear that they may be raiders from Jrar. If they find us or these maps…"

Mara froze at this unexpected answer. Unable to help herself, she glanced over her right shoulder at R'Bak's slowly setting sun, profoundly orange as it sank toward the horizon.

"Raiders?" she asked softly. "Do you mean a scout team? Like the ones who were stopped by my people when we arrived? Or have the Searing culls come early?"

"One of those. I know not which. What I do know is that they *cannot* be allowed to find our settlement!" Intensity throbbed through his tone, and his dark eyes went hard with controlled horror.

"Yeah," she said. "With my people there, I can see how that would be bad. Okay then, this is out of my realm of experience. What do you think we should do?"

Ozendi shook his head and shoved a hand through his sweat-matted hair. "It's not just that. The settlement itself—" He broke off, shook his head again, then appeared to force himself to focus on her question. "We must get back as quickly as possible. There is a woodcutter's road from the settlement that passes near here, but I am hesitant to use it."

"Yeah, if they're looking for us, we should stay away from roads."

"We should be able to hike out cross-country, but the way is difficult. Sometimes, rock- or mud-slides leave it impassable."

"Then hiking back is what we'll do," Mara said, reaching out her hand to rest it on his forearm. "We'll get what we need from the bird and head that way. We've got a little time before both the sun and the primary set, yes? Let's get as far away as we can and then we'll stop for the night when we find a good spot."

Ozendi nodded. "Yes," he said. "Yes, that is good. That is what we should do."

"All right," Mara said. "Grab your bag, fill it with the fruit and stuff that Naliryiz sent with us. Grab the maps, too, and anything else that's easy to carry in your backpack. Let's keep our hands free if we can. Is that water safe to drink, do you think?"

"It is," Ozendi said. "It comes straight from the ground a day's hike from here."

"Okay, I'll take your word for it," Mara said. "Fill up your water bottle, and we'll get going."

He nodded again, a single, sharp movement of his head, walked past her to slide the cabin door open, and began grabbing his bag. Mara watched him closely for another moment, just to make sure he wasn't *too* tightly controlled, before she walked around to the right side of the aircraft and followed suit. Within a few moments, they had packed up what food they could carry and a few other things, and they were kneeling beside the creek, filling water bottles.

"Oh! One more thing," Mara said. She shrugged her backpack off her shoulders and jogged back to the aircraft. She pulled open the cockpit door and leaned in to remove the tiny key in the side of the center console. She zipped it inside the small pocket on the upper arm of her flight suit and then turned to run back down the bank to Ozendi.

"Ready," she said.

"What did you need?" he asked. He looked so different from her smiling, flirtatious student. This morning, he'd been all flashing grin and easy charm. Now she found a hard determination to succeed.

"The key," she said. "It's a small thing, but at least this way if the assholes find the bird, they won't immediately be able to figure out how to start her. I should have disconnected the battery, too, but it's getting late and we should get going."

"I've always wondered why there was a key, anyway. It serves no other function than to complete the electrical circuit to the starter, right? Why could you not just have a complete circuit without it?"

Mara grinned and slung her backpack up onto her shoulders.

"That's an interesting story," she said. "Lead the way, and I'll tell you while we walk."

Ozendi looked at her, and, for the first time since they'd been fired upon, a ghost of a smile played about his lips. "All right," he said. "This way."

He turned and began following the creek upriver to a spot where it narrowed. Mara shrugged her pack once more, settling it into place, and followed him.

"Once upon a time," she said, "Hueys didn't have ignition keylock keys. But one night, in a place called Tipton Field, Maryland, a man named Robert Preston decided he was sick of being shit upon, and he was gonna do what made him happy…"

They didn't get far before both stars set and it got too dark to keep going, but Mara figured progress was progress and tried not to stress about it.

Ozendi hadn't wanted to stop for the night. She couldn't blame him; it had to be hell knowing that the raiders were out there, close to the vulnerable settlement of his people. She could feel the tension singing through him as it got steadily darker under the canopy of the R'Baku polar forest. She'd managed not to say too much, but their progress slowed to a crawl as he peered through the trees, straining to make out the landmarks that would point the way home.

"Ozendi," she said softly. "I think we need to stop. It'll take us longer to get back if we get lost in the darkness."

"I am not lost," he said sharply, almost snapping at her. "I am just making sure. We must just get up and over this ridge…" He trailed off, but kept walking, pushing through the undergrowth. Branches whipped back at her, requiring her to keep one hand raised up to protect her face.

"Ozendi," she said again, a bit more steel in her tone. She stretched her legs in order to push up beside him. "This is stupid. Let's just find a place to cam—"

The ground crumbled beneath her right foot as she stepped down. Mara tried to throw her weight to the left, but it was too late. She felt the slope collapse under her weight as her ankle, and then her knee, buckled. A strangled scream ripped itself from her lips as she tumbled. She tucked her shoulder into a roll and barely managed to keep the back of her head from hitting a fallen tree trunk. Her face hit the forest floor as she spun. Something sharp stabbed her cheek just below her right eye.

"Mara!"

Ozendi's voice followed her down the slope. Mara skidded to a stop against a piled-up mass of tangled branches and needles that had built up next to a largish rock—almost a boulder, really. She groaned and pushed herself over onto her shoulder, then blinked twice to clear the dirt from her eyes.

"Wh-what?" She coughed, spat out some of the dark, R'Baku forest loam, and squinted up the slope in time to see Ozendi stumbling down the hill in patent disregard for his own safety.

"Are you all right?"

"Mostly," she said, spitting again. She grunted and shrugged out of the straps of her backpack, before pushing herself up to a sitting position. Electric pain shot up from her knee and ankle, and she pressed her lips together to keep from screaming. "That fucking hurt."

"I am sorry," he gasped out as he reached her, sending more of the loose dirt and forest detritus up into the air as his feet slid to a stop. He grabbed onto one of the branches in the deadfall and steadied himself before crouching beside her. "I am so sorry. This was my fault."

"Yep," Mara said evenly. "Sure was." She grunted again and hauled her backpack into her lap. She opened the front pocket and began digging for her flashlight. "Help me see how bad the damage is. Nothing feels broken, but my ankle and knee hurt like hell."

Ozendi knelt down and gingerly put his hands on either side of her knee. Despite the lightness of his touch through her flight suit, she winced as pain shot up through her hip. She gritted her teeth and managed to keep from making any sound other than a hiss as he gently felt her leg from thigh to heel. Eventually, she remembered her plan, and her fingers closed around the thick, textured cylinder of the flashlight in her bag. She pulled it out and clicked it on, shining the red light over her leg. No bones or blood. Those were both good signs. Though she could see her knee was starting to swell.

"Well, buddy," she said, her voice rough with pain. "Looks like we're gonna camp after all. I can't go any further on this tonight. Tomorrow, you might have to continue without me, depending on this swelling."

"Do not worry about that," Ozendi said. He laid her leg back on the ground as gently as possible and then stood and grabbed her backpack. "Let's just find a place to shelter for the night. There are predators in these hills."

"Oh? You might have mentioned that before," she said, rather mildly, all things considered.

"They generally do not bother us. But now you are injured and vulnerable."

"Thanks for the reminder."

He turned to look at her, and in the fading light from the suns and the red glow from her flashlight, Mara could see the self-recrimination writ large on his face.

"Mara," he said. "I—"

"Don't worry about it," she said sharply, cutting him off. "That gets us nowhere. Just find us a place to camp and help me get there. Then we'll figure out a plan."

"I—all right," Ozendi said. She watched him square his shoulders slightly and shift his weight as he started to look around. He glanced to the top of the ridge, from where she'd fallen, and then further down the slope. "Wait here. I will return shortly."

"Leave me my backpack," she said. "In case you don't."

He stared at her, and she let herself give him a tiny, dry smile. She wasn't sure if he could see her expression or not, but she smiled anyway. Eventually, he snorted softly and turned to pick his way carefully down the hill.

Darkness continued to rise up from the forest floor while she waited. Mara's knee and ankle began to throb in concert with one another. She concentrated on breathing in and out, drank some water, and continued digging in her bag. She could have sworn she had a small packet of aspirin…

It felt like she waited forever. The forest began to make what she assumed were its usual night sounds. One of the most disconcerting things about R'Bak were the ways in which things felt familiar. She remembered many happy evenings spent listening to the sound of nocturnal birds and insects chirping as she and her family camped out in forests much like this one. For just a moment, she closed her eyes and inhaled deeply, remembering.

Woodsmoke mingling with the scent of roasting meat and burnt pine pitch. The warm weight of her son, laughing in her arms. Sticky marshmallows and chocolate melting over her fingers…

"Mara!"

Ozendi's voice echoed through the alien trees up at her, jolting her back to awareness. She shifted the red light toward the sound and surreptitiously swiped at her eyes with the back of her free hand. Hopefully, it was dark enough that Ozendi wouldn't see muddy tear tracks through the dirt on her face.

"Here," she called, her voice a rough croak. She cleared her throat and tried again. "I'm here. Did you find a spot?"

"Yes," he said as he drew near. In the weak circle of red light, she saw him bend down and reach out his hands to her. "It is not as near as I'd hoped, but it will work well. Can you stand?"

"I think so, if you help me." She reached up and felt his strong fingers wrap around her wrist. With a heave, he levered her up onto her good foot and managed to duck under her arm to support her.

"It's going to be interesting going down the hill like this," she said as they hobbled the few meters necessary to clear the area of deadfall where she'd been sitting.

"Yes," he said. "I thought about that. It's mostly clear right here. If you sit down again, I think we might be able to slide down the slope in a mostly controlled manner."

Mara laughed a little at "mostly controlled," but since she didn't have any better ideas, she reached out to steady herself on a nearby tree trunk and helped him lower her back down to a sitting position. She'd missed the "we" in his sentence, she realized, or she hadn't recognized his intent, so he surprised her by lowering himself to the ground behind her and spreading his legs on either side of hers.

"Keep your feet together," he said in her ear, his breath warm against the side of her neck. "My legs are longer, so I will act as a buffer for any obstacles we encounter."

"This seems like a terrible idea," she said.

"Do you have a better one?"

"I've been trying…but no. Fuck it. Let's do it."

He let out a short, surprised laugh, his chest rumbling against her back. She settled her backpack in her lap and pressed her legs as close to each other as possible, wincing at the fire in her knee and ankle every time she moved.

"Ready?" Ozendi asked. Before she could say yes or no, he pushed off, and they began sliding down the hill, loose forest debris spilling like a wake behind them. Mara fought down nausea from the pain and felt her body tense, readying for the impact that would surely come when they barreled into a tree, or a boulder, or another deadfall, or…

…or nothing, because the slope evened out at the bottom, and they coasted to a gentle stop in the dirt.

"I can't believe how well that worked," Mara said. Ozendi laughed again.

"You might try trusting me more often," he said. "I generally know what I'm doing."

"I fly with you, don't I?" Mara said. "That's trust."

"Yes, but you keep your hands close to the controls at all times."

"Well." Mara shrugged, looking up at him as he got to his feet behind her. "That's practicality." She couldn't see his face in the darkness, but she imagined he was smiling.

"Come," he said, reaching down to take her hands again. "It is not far."

It wasn't actually that far, for which Mara was intensely grateful.

Ozendi half-carried her a few more meters toward the bottom of the valley and then along the length of it for a minute or two. It felt like an eternity, but eventually he paused next to a place where the valley wall rose up in a sheer cliff.

"There is a small cave back here," he said, his breath coming quickly. "Shine your light on the cliff there."

Mara obliged, and sure enough, she could see a narrow, vertical slit of darkness half obscured by brush.

"That's good," she said. "Nice and hidden. Is it big enough for both of us?"

"Yes," Ozendi said. "Hold on, I will have to carry you." He bent and tightened the arm around her waist, while slipping his other arm beneath her knees. She could tell he was trying his best to be gentle, but pain shot through her at his touch. She pressed her lips together so hard that they hurt, but a muffled sound of distress escaped anyway.

"I am sorry," he said, breathless.

"It's all right," she said. "Just get me there."

Mara tucked her head close to his chest, feeling his warmth radiating through his flight suit beneath her cheek. She felt him duck as he stepped through the narrow cave opening, angling her body so she didn't hit the rock walls. It had been dark outside, but that gloom was nothing compared to the blackness inside the cave. Ozendi took only two steps and then stopped.

"Shine your light," he said. "I want to make sure this is a safe place to put you down."

Mara played her light around them. The dim redness seemed impossibly bright in the full dark as it showed an uneven, undulating wall and a sloping, dirt-covered floor that held nothing but a pile of old bones and branches.

"We are not the first to shelter here, it seems," Ozendi said, his words rumbling through his chest. "But I do not smell anything, so I think the pile is at least a season old. I'm going to put you down now, all right? Then I'll see about making a fire. The cave opens out behind us, so we should have adequate ventilation."

"Is that smart?" Mara asked. "What if it draws the assholes to us?"

"We should be shielded well enough in this cave," he said. "And we could both use a little light and warmth, at least until we sleep."

Since her hands and feet had stopped shivering and gone numb with cold a while ago, Mara didn't argue. She just braced herself for the lancing, stabbing pain as Ozendi bent to set her gently down on the cave floor. She scooted herself backwards so she was leaning against the wall, and then took a moment to congratulate herself for not passing out from the agony as she did so.

She pulled her backpack into her lap and began digging in it for tools and supplies while Ozendi used the piled-up branches to create a small, merry blaze.

"You were right," Mara said softly as the fire crackled in the makeshift pit he'd scratched out of the dirt on the floor. "We did need a fire. I don't know why, but I feel better having one."

"Fire is light and warmth and comfort," Ozendi said, giving her a smile that seemed to flicker in the uncertain light. "We who have spent time planetside crave it on an instinctive level. On the Spins, it is a different story. I have many friends who are not comfortable with fire at all."

"Fire is dangerous in space." Mara nodded. "I get that."

"Do you have those fruits? I will roast some. They're delicious that way."

She held out the bag, and he dug around in it. He grabbed two of the fist-sized fruits and cut them open, then removed the sweet flesh and speared it on the tip of the knife she'd seen him carrying in his pocket.

"The sugar caramelizes with the heat," he said as he held the speared fruit down into the yellow flames. "And the fruit puffs slightly. It's very good. Try it!"

"Like a marshmallow," Mara said as she accepted the offering when he held it out to her. She tossed the hot, sticky mess from hand to hand and then popped it in her mouth, sucking in air to help it cool. It even tasted a little bit like a roasted marshmallow: all crispy, burned sugar. "It's delicious."

"What is a 'marshmallow?'" Ozendi asked as he speared another bit on his knife. "Is it a fruit from your planet?"

"Not a fruit, a candy," she said. "It's basically spun sugar. They're terrible for you, and even worse when roasted. But they're delicious. Donnie used to love them."

"And who is Donnie?" Ozendi asked, a joking edge to his tone. "A lover? A partner you left behind?"

"No," Mara said, her voice going quiet and empty. "My son."

Ozendi inhaled, and Mara could tell he had turned toward her, but she kept her eyes steadfastly on the flames.

"Mara, I am so sorry," Ozendi said. "I did not know you left a child behind."

Mara nodded. "He was four," she said, keeping her voice even. She never talked about Donnie, or much about her old life at all, but all of a sudden, the words seemed to well up inside her, wanting nothing more than to spill out into the flickering firelight of the cave. "His dad and I divorced, but we stayed on good terms. We used to take Donnie camping every summer.

He loved to roast marshmallows and make s'mores. He's dead now, I suppose."

"You don't know that," Ozendi said.

Mara let out a harsh laugh. "Yes, I do," she said. "It's been over a hundred years since that…since I entered cryosleep. He's long dead. He was staying with my ex when I was deployed. My ex wasn't a great husband, but he was always a good dad. Sometimes…"

She felt her lips curve up in a smile. "Sometimes I think about Donnie growing up, going to high school, playing sports, having a girlfriend. Stuff like that. I imagine him getting married and having kids. The Army would have given me a funeral and stuff, given him a flag. I like to imagine him telling my grandchildren about me. Showing them the letters I wrote home to him, telling him how much I loved him—"

She broke off when Ozendi's fingers brushed her cheek. Her eyes had flooded again. She sniffled hard and looked down in embarrassment.

"Sorry," she mumbled.

"Do not be," Ozendi said, his voice rough. "Do not apologize. You are so hard, so strong, all the time. You can…you are allowed to hurt for this."

His words broke the dam. Mara squeezed her eyes tight against the flood and opened her mouth in a scream. Grief swelled within her, pressing out from the center of her skull, from the core of her chest. She pulled her arms inward, crossing them over her heart, her fingers curled in claws of agony as she finally opened the door on the thoughts she'd been pushing aside since she first woke in the Dornaani infirmary, since before she even met Murphy.

Wave after wave of grief and memory washed over her, paralyzing her as she gasped, choking in the dark on pain and loss.

She wound up lying on her side, the stone floor of the cave cool under her cheek. Her knee and ankle throbbed abominably, but her physical discomfort had faded to background noise under the onslaught of the emotional maelstrom. Firelight flickered, painting mobile shadows across the tiny space. Mara sniffed and tried once more to wipe her eyes.

"What I wouldn't give for a shower," she muttered, her voice rough but even as she pushed herself up to a seated position. She felt empty, wrung out, as if the explosion of emotion had burned her clean from the inside out.

"Here," Ozendi said. He reached into his own pack and pulled out what looked like a spare T-shirt. He shook it open and then wet it with some of the water in his bottle. "There are many streams and springs around here," he said, holding the damp cloth out to her. "At least you can wipe your face and hands."

"Thank you," she said. She hoped he understood she wasn't just talking about the cloth. She took it and immediately began scrubbing her face.

"May I look at your leg now?" Ozendi said. "I'm not as good as Naliryiz, but I might be able to help a little."

"Sure," Mara said. She sniffled mightily and straightened the leg as best she could. He came forward and gently prodded at her knee and ankle. "I don't want to take the boot off," Mara said as his long fingers felt around her foot. "I can already feel it swelling, and I'm afraid I won't get it back on."

"It is fine," Ozendi said, his voice pitched to be reassuring. "You will not need to remove it, I don't think. I think you are right; nothing feels broken. This is good news; I have something in my pack to help with swelling and inflammation."

He turned to rummage in his bag again while Mara continued to wipe her face and hands free of the clinging grit. It wasn't the shower she longed for, but she had to admit that she felt better once she was done. Ozendi turned back to her just as she was folding up the cloth.

"Here," he said, holding up a small fabric twist. "This is what I was looking for."

"What is it?" Mara asked, unable to keep her tone entirely free of suspicion.

Ozendi laughed. "Just herbs. A local blend. You dissolve them in your drink. Naliryiz makes this for the liaisons because we're naturally clumsy when we first come back to planetary gravity. It will reduce the swelling and the pain."

Mara eyed the packet with distrust, but since she didn't have a flight doc handy and she really needed to be able to walk tomorrow, she gave a short nod and held out her water bottle. Ozendi opened up the packet and carefully poured in the powdered mixture. Mara capped it and shook. The whole thing turned a muddy, unappetizing brown color in the firelight.

"Down the hatch," she muttered as she uncapped it and chugged. To her surprise, it didn't taste bad. It had a sort of citrusy zing, but mostly it tasted like the scent of newly mown grass. She'd definitely tasted worse.

"That should work quickly," he said. "I think you will feel much better tomorrow."

"Let's hope so," she said quietly, suddenly feeling very exposed. She looked away from him, staring steadfastly at the fire.

"Mara." Ozendi's voice was soft, and he bent close until she had no choice but to make eye contact. "You are all right. Grief is to be expected in your situation. Have you not allowed yourself to mourn yet?"

Mara shrugged one shoulder and looked away again. "It's just easier, you know? Especially with the guys. I'm secure in my position and stuff, but it's never good for them to see a woman crying. They tend to think we're weak. I can't believe I let you see."

"You know I do not fault you. Many among my people think as you do. But living on R'Bak for so long when I was young, I saw that for people like you, the problem is not weakness. Your problem is that you have been too strong for too long. One thing I have learned from my travels in both worlds is that emotions must be felt, Mara. Otherwise, they fester like a wound untreated."

She looked back at him, and his nearness shivered along her skin. "Not every emotion is a smart emotion," she whispered. He quirked the corner of his beautiful lips in a tiny smile and reached out to brush a stray piece of her hair behind her ear.

"We are talking of emotions, not logic. Smart or stupid doesn't apply."

"Maybe not, but they do apply to behaviors. Choices. It isn't smart for me to choose to let the guys see me crying."

"It isn't smart for you to lock your emotions away indefinitely, either." His fingers traced her cheekbone. "You have to deal with them eventually."

"When it's safe," Mara murmured.

"It's safe," he assured her and leaned in. His lips hovered a breath above hers. She could feel the almost electric warmth of his skin. "Yes?" he asked.

She shouldn't. There were a thousand reasons why she shouldn't. But none of that mattered in the flickering light and her sudden, agonizing need for touch, for life.

"Yes," she said, and claimed his lips for her own.

Lightning tingled below her skin as he carefully pulled her close. She reached, her hands frantic, and began unfastening his jacket, opening up his flight suit. She nearly ripped his undershirt in her haste to get to him, to feel that warm bronze silk so delicious against her own skin.

"Stars and ancestors, Mara," he groaned next to her ear. "I cannot stop. I cannot get enough of you."

"Then don't," she said, her breath a gasp of need. "Don't ever stop."

Firelight and shadows danced over their bodies as they tangled one with the other, reaching for the knowledge—the proof—that they still lived. Together, they spiraled toward an aching, almost painful climax that left them breathless, holding onto each other like shipwreck survivors clinging to driftwood.

"You—are you hurt?" Ozendi asked, his words broken as he gasped for air.

"No," Mara said, her voice just as breathy. She could feel the languor that followed sex start to seep in, gilding the edges of her thoughts. "No, not at all." She started to roll away from him, but he tightened his hold and pulled her gently, inexorably back, until she lay stretched upon him once more, her head pillowed in the hollow of his shoulder.

"I don't usually cuddle, after," she said, putting some humor in her tone.

"What is your English expression? Oh, right. Shut the fuck up, Mara."

She stiffened, unsure whether to laugh or be insulted. He went on, his hand playing idly with her hair.

"I know what you are doing. You are trying to put me—this—in a box with all of the other things you don't want to feel. But now that we have come together, I have a say, too. I won't let you lock me away, Mara. You feel this, the same as me."

"I just thought—"

"That is the problem. By the mercy unknown to the Deathfathers, Mara. Stop *thinking*." He stroked his fingers over her shoulder, down her back to her hip, and back up, trailing fire under her skin with his touch. "Just let me love you."

"Love?"

"Shhh," he said and stopped her mouth with a soft, hungry kiss. "You're thinking again. Is not this love? You desired me, and I you. And now we've come together in beauty and pleasure and need. What else would you call it?" he whispered when he was done.

"This is just sex. Love is—I don't—"

"Is not sex a form of love? Just as friendship is love? Loyalty is love? I think perhaps you have been so angry at yourself for waking up that you have severed yourself from all of these things. You deserve to feel, Mara. You deserve to be loved."

She should have gotten angry. She knew that. She should have shoved him away and told him that her feelings were none of his business. She should have threatened him with bodily harm if he touched her ever again…

But he was touching her now, and igniting that need that still slumbered within her, and she wanted…oh, she *wanted* him. All of him. Not just his beautiful warrior's body, but she wanted everything else he was saying. She wanted his laughing eyes and his sweet smiles and his inside jokes. She wanted his presence beside her, bolstering her nerve. She wanted his strength to augment her own. She wanted his words whispered in her ear.

She wanted him. She wanted to feel. She wanted his love.

And she was so, so tired of fighting what she wanted.

"And you," she whispered, hating the vulnerability in her voice, but knowing it needed to be there. "You…want to love me?"

"I have since the first time we flew together," he said. "Since the first time I glimpsed the real you behind the façade of toughness you wear so well."

"Okay," she said.

"Okay?"

"Okay. I want you. To love me."

"Then I shall, I promise."

She felt his hand glide once more down over the curve of her hip. He lifted her, pulled her more fully atop him, and stared up into her eyes. Then he smiled.

And did.

Chapter Forty-Nine

R'BAK

Pre-dawn light filtered through the cave, waking them. Mara felt good, despite not sleeping for most of the night. The herbal remedy seemed to have significantly improved her knee and ankle, and she took a couple of experimental steps, carefully allowing it to take her weight.

"How do you feel?" Ozendi asked. He had extinguished the banked fire and was busy repacking the items they'd pulled out during the night.

"Really good," Mara said, surprise threading through her tone. She turned to him with a grin. "Not nearly as tired as I would have expected."

"There are many forms of rest," he said and gave her an exaggerated wink. She threw her head back and laughed.

"Where did you learn to do that?" she asked. "Is that something your people do?"

"No," he said. "But I have seen your people do it from time to time. Did I get the context wrong?"

"You nailed it," she said, and walked over to him with just the barest trace of a limp. As she'd hoped, he opened his arms to welcome her into an embrace, and she took a moment to breathe in his scent and revel in the replete soreness she felt from the previous night's exertions. Ozendi wrapped his arms around her and held her close.

"Since we are speaking of your people," he said, "do you think there will be trouble for you, because of our connection?"

"Murphy will be pissed," Mara predicted, a grim edge forming around her words. "But he'll get over it. In the end, what can they do to me? I'm one of our few pilots and *the only* one with quals on more modern birds. They need my skills too badly to put me back on ice." At least, she seriously hoped so.

"I will help protect you if I can," Ozendi promised. "There will be no repercussions to me for taking you as a mate. Especially if…well, my people will protect you if necessary."

"I think it'll be fine," Mara said and dropped her arms. "But that's a problem for another day. For now, we need to get back to the settlement and let them know about the raiders…and figure out how to get my maintenance team back to our bird."

Ozendi let her go and smiled down at her as she stepped back.

"I did not feel like you would welcome this before, but I feel that I should tell you: you are quite arousing when you take command."

Mara snorted. "Well, I hope you've got some extra room in your shorts, buddy, because this is who I am."

"Oh, I am very aware," Ozendi said with a satisfied smirk. Which made Mara laugh again.

They started out in high spirits. The day itself seemed to echo Mara's sunny mood back to her. The sunlight streamed golden and green through the trees, and though Ozendi set a brisk pace, it wasn't nearly as punishing as it had been last night. Mara's knee and ankle continued to improve as they walked, too.

"Damn," she said as they stopped near another one of the innumerable mountain streams to refill their water. "Whatever that herb cocktail is, I need to get some. My ankle doesn't hurt at all, and my knee only twinges when we're going up the steepest grades."

"Naliryiz may make some for you," he said. "It works very well and is very safe. Only—well, you will have to ask her about it. I do not know if she will want to share it with all of your people."

"Why not? A secret recipe or something like that?"

"Something like that," he said. She let the matter drop.

The journey took them the rest of the day. They took a short break around midday, stopping to eat and rest for a little bit. They made love again under the spreading limbs of the blue-green forest, while the dual suns heated the air around them in a soundless promise of the Searing to come. By the time the suns dipped below the western horizon, they were nearing the top of another great ridge.

"The settlement is just on the other side," Ozendi said. "Though it will take another hour or so to reach it. Will you walk in with me?"

Mara looked up sharply at the sudden vulnerability in his voice.

"What do you mean?" she asked.

"I mean, I know that you said there could be some trouble for you…"

She shook her head. "Let's worry about that later. We don't have to say anything when we first get there, we've got other priorities. But yes, I will walk in beside you, and if people draw conclusions, they can draw conclusions. Hell, they probably would have anyway."

He smiled, though his eyes seemed troubled, but he said no more. He simply resumed hiking up the slope toward the top of the ridge.

Once they got to the top, Mara smelled smoke.

"Cookfires," Ozendi said when she asked. "Nothing to worry about." But he picked up the pace just a little bit anyway. Once again, Mara mentally thanked the absent Naliryiz for her concoction as she hitched up her pack and followed Ozendi down the slope, into the night-dark valley.

Darkness blanketed the settlement. Mara tasted the acrid tang of smoke in the back of her throat as they threaded through the trees along the river toward the stockade. No firelight—or any kind of light, for that matter—penetrated the smoky gloom.

"Ozendi," Mara said, pitching her voice low. "Something's wrong. There are no fires."

Ozendi nodded but didn't say anything. Mara pushed aside a wistful thought that they should have armed up before setting out yesterday and followed close on his heels. She was right at his shoulder as they broke through the screen of forest and looked at what remained of the settlement where he'd been born.

The stockade was mostly left standing, though it smoldered in quite a few spots. Thick smoke billowed up from the center of the town, blotting out the sky as it rose.

"Dio," Ozendi whispered, and broke into a run. A tiny corner of Mara's mind wondered who had taught him Spanish, but she ignored that and took off after him as he pelted through the stockade's gates. They looked as if they'd been hit by something heavy, for they swung, splintered, on battered, warped hinges.

The town inside was dark, too, and seemed deserted. Fear opened up in a pit in Mara's stomach. Where were her people? Where were *any* of the people?

Ozendi ran all the way past the center of town toward a place near the rear wall of the stockade. He stopped dead in front of a smoking pile of wood and rubble and stared, his face pale in the darkness, his eyes open holes of pain and denial.

"Ozendi."

Mara whirled at the sound of the woman's voice, her hand going for the small knife she carried. Fire flared in the darkness, and relief flooded through Mara as the newly lit torch revealed Naliryiz's symmetrical features, marred by grief.

"Doc!" Mara called out. "Ozendi, look! It's your sister! She's all right!"

Ozendi turned and lunged toward Naliryiz. He wrapped her up in a tight embrace, heedless of the torch she held. As quickly as he'd grabbed her, though, he let go, and stepped back, holding her by the shoulders and peering into her face, his own ravaged by grief and worry and...rage?

"Iope and Dio were alive, the last I saw," Naliryiz said quickly, her voice quiet and even. "They were taken, along with several others."

"Who?" Ozendi asked, though Mara was pretty sure they already knew the answer.

"Raiders," Naliryiz said. "Early and too far north, but they looked and acted like the advance parties we've seen before."

"Were my people taken?" Mara asked.

Naliryiz shook her head. "No," she said. "They joined with our resistance and fought the raiders off. They were most helpful. But Kelrevis was taken, as well."

"I know where they took them." Ozendi said, his voice icy cold but still throbbing with urgency. "We can get them back."

"Wait," Mara said. "Hold on. We'll get them back, Ozendi, but you can't just go barreling in there. Let's take a breath; make a plan!"

"You don't understand!" he snapped at her. Then he shook his head abruptly and let go of his sister's shoulders and stalked away, his chest heaving as he fought to breathe.

Naliryiz looked after him, and then offered Mara a small, half-smile.

"Forgive him," she said. "You are right, of course, and he knows it. But his worry is to be expected: Iope is his mate, Dio is Diozera, his daughter. And of course you have Kelrevis, our Matriarch. Who is also our aunt. This is a terrible blow. His agony is understandable just now."

Mara blinked at Naliryiz as the healer's words registered.

Iope is his mate. Diozera his daughter.

His mate.

His daughter.

An image rose up in her mind's eye, unbidden. Ozendi laughing, his eyes dark with passion as he spoke to her of love. Mara closed her eyes and shoved the image away, pushed it into the box where she'd sworn it would never go and locked it down behind every mental barrier she held.

"Where are my people?" Mara asked, forcing her eyes open, her voice to be calm.

"We have set up a field hospital in your landing area. Many were hurt. Everyone has gathered there."

She should have gone to him. Mara knew that. But in that moment, she just couldn't.

"Bring him when he's ready. Tell him we'll get them back." As she spoke those clipped words, Mara saw Naliryiz's eyebrows furrow. Doubtless, she wondered why Mara was being so cold. But Mara couldn't do anything about that, any more than she could stop the anguished, tearing feeling inside of her.

One problem at a time.

She nodded sharply to Naliryiz and turned away. Let the healer see to her brother. Mara would find Elroy, find her people, and find a way to get her lover's family back.

Even as it broke her heart.

"I understand your position, Captain, but the rest of the task force isn't ready to deploy planetside yet. And if it was, it is far too early for us to show our hand."

Mara glared at the static-blurred shape of Murphy's face and fought the urge to spew profanity. She inhaled slowly through her nose, and then exhaled before nodding her head once.

"Fine," she said. "Then given the *strategic imperative* of our mission here, I request permission to take command and do it my damn self!"

Murphy glared right back at her, and Mara could see icy fury radiating down the lines of the comm link. Or at least, that's what it looked like… "A moment, Captain Lee." The gray screen and soft hiss of a neutral comm channel replaced his face.

He was going to refuse. Or at least, freeze her out. She didn't care. The rage boiling inside her was hot enough to melt any ice he threw her way.

Murphy's face reappeared. "Agreed," he said more readily than she expected, but his words were still clipped. "We must provide assistance, but you should send your student instead, Bruce. Your abilities are far more strategically important than—"

"Ending the call. Enemy could triangulate and locate." She cut the connection before he could complete the order for her to sit this one out. Like hell she was sending Ozendi in to rescue his family and the rest of the villagers without her. He was too distraught. He'd never make it out alive. Truth be told, she would have preferred to leave him out of it altogether, but she needed his local knowledge to get back to the Huey and find the raiders' camp.

She sighed and stepped back, then turned to find Elroy watching her from just inside the flap of the tent where they'd set up the comm set.

"You okay?" he asked, his voice a soft rumble.

"I'm fine," she said, and made to step around him and out of the tent. He moved to the side, and she came up hard against the iron muscle of his chest.

"Don't lie to me, Bruce," he said, using her callsign as he only did in private. "Something happened between you two out in the woods. You won't even look at the guy. Did he hurt you?"

Mara surprised herself with a hacking, joyless laugh.

"No, El," she said. "He didn't try to rape me. I swear, you fucking men think that's the end-all, be-all of 'bad things that can happen to a woman!' Besides, do you think he'd still be breathing if he had?"

"No," Elroy admitted. "Okay, fine. So, what *did* happen?"

She wasn't going to tell him. She had absolutely no intention of telling her 6'5", Vietnam-era badass of a crew chief about her broken heart. But when she drew in a breath, the words tumbled out all over themselves anyway.

"He said he loved me," she whispered. "He told me I deserved to be loved and that he wanted me always, and then I come back here to find he has a family. God! I'm so fucking stupid! Listen to me, I sound like a teenage girl!"

"You sound like a woman who's been hurt," Elroy said, and he reached out and gently pulled her into an embrace. Mara drew in a deep, shuddering breath, and tears of rage and agony started to fall. Elroy held her close, the rock to her storm, and supported her while she let all of her whirling, tangling, distracting emotions out.

"Fucker is right about one thing, though," Elroy said once her maelstrom quieted. She sniffled mightily and swiped at her eyes, then leaned back to look up into his ebony face.

"What's that?" she asked.

"You do deserve to be loved, Bruce. You hold people too much at a distance. This group we're with…well, we're all we've got, now. It's like being in the bush in 'Nam. You can't push people away because you're gonna need them. Eventually."

An uncomfortable thought wormed its way through Mara's mind.

"El?" she asked softly. "Do you—I mean, have I—"

Elroy laughed and dropped his arms from around her. "Nah," he said. "Don't worry, I'm not much into white women. Too dangerous for a young black man where I grew up. We're a crew, though. And I love you like my sister."

Relief washed over her, and she hugged him briefly before letting go again. "I love you, too, El," she said. "And I'm proud to call you my brother."

"See?" he said, white teeth flashing in a grin. "That wasn't so hard, was it? Do you want me to kill him?"

"Who? Ozendi?"

She felt him nod and knew his offer was 100% serious.

"No."

"All right. If you change your mind, just say the word."

She sniffled hard again and wiped her eyes, then her nose with her sleeve. "When this is over," she said softly, stopping him as he turned toward the tent flap. He looked back at her and she forced her shoulders to relax. "When this is over, if you're willing, I'd love to tell you about my son. Donnie."

Elroy smiled a slow smile, sympathy dark in his eyes. "I'd be honored, sis," he said. "When this is over."

"Right," she said. "When it's over. Right now, let's go kick the shit out of some raiders."

"Amen and hallelujah."

By the time Mara had her maintenance team assembled and briefed, Ozendi had rounded up a sizeable crew of fighters and vehicles willing to take part in the crazy mission to get their loved ones back. Mara told herself she shouldn't be surprised. The man was obviously capable of compartmentalizing things in his head.

Just as she was.

At one point, while they were planning and gathering resources, he ran to join her as she walked briskly from the field hospital to the vehicle staging point.

"Mara," he said as he caught up to her. He reached out to catch her fingers. His voice was rough. "Mara, please. I must talk to you."

Mara stopped and pulled her hand back as if his touch had burned her. On some level, it had.

"No," she said, her voice cool iron. "I don't think you must. In fact, it's best if you don't."

"But—"

"One problem at a time." She cut him off, turning the corners of her mouth up in a humorless mockery of a smile. "You want your mate and kid back safely, right? Then stay out of my way and let me concentrate on the mission, Copilot."

He just looked at her, pain in his eyes. She felt her internal self yearning toward him, so she did the only thing she could. She turned on her heel and walked back the way she'd come. She would check on the vehicles later.

In the end, they pulled together eight of them. They were the same rugged tracked vehicles Elroy had lovingly dubbed "trucks." Mara's maintenance team had two pairs of M60D machine guns that were intended to be mounted in the Huey's doors. Some genius had figured out how to rig a pintle mount for two of the trucks, and so one of the pairs of weapons was re-purposed for ground use.

Mara had debriefed Elroy extensively on the damage to the Huey, and he and the maintenance team had packed accordingly. Thanks to the extra engine parts they were bringing along, it would be a tight fit in the vehicles, so most of the fighters elected to ride on top, like Mara had seen old soldiers do in WWII films.

By the end of the second day, they were ready to go, furnished with the bare bones of a plan. Basically, they would convoy through the forest to the plateau where they'd left the Huey. This time, rather than going up and down all the ridges, they would take the woodcutter's road and trust to their firepower and speed to get them there safely.

So that was the plan. Mount up and haul ass under cover of darkness. Fix the Huey during the light of day, then assault the raider camp with the bird providing overhead cover. As plans went, it wasn't the most detailed. Or the most survivable. But it was what they had. The twin suns set behind the western ridge, one large disk and one very small, as she and the maintenance team loaded up with Ozendi and his fighters and moved out down the tiny woodcutter's road into the forest.

She rode with Elroy in the center vehicle, the one carrying the majority of the Huey parts they'd need. Ozendi was somewhere else in the convoy. She didn't know where and wouldn't allow herself to think about it.

"Did you talk to the Doc?" she asked Elroy as they crested the first ridge and headed down the other side. They were about an hour into their journey, and Mara was fighting to keep from letting the steady vibration of the vehicle's motor lull her to sleep.

"Yeah," Elroy said with a little smile. "She's gonna take the survivors back to where we set up our school. It's the best option around here for a population that size, and we can fortify it when we get back."

"If we get back," she groused.

"*When*, sis. Knock it off with them negative waves."

Mara snorted and let the corner of her mouth lift in a smile. Her father had been a big *Kelly's Heroes* fan when she was growing up, so she recognized what would have been a contemporary pop culture reference for Elroy. Instead of replying, she sat back against the crate carrying her new compressor section and pulled out the wrapped bowl of *debem* Naliryiz had pushed into her hands before they left.

"You dig that stuff, huh?" Elroy asked.

"Mmmhmm," Mara said. "It's delicious. Better than anything else I've tasted here."

"Yeah, it ain't bad," he agreed. "I'd kill for a pepperoni pizza, though."

Mara nodded in agreement. "We should try to make one, after this. Pizza's basically just flatbread with cheese and stuff on it."

"Where're you gonna get tomato sauce?"

"Dunno. Ask the Doc most likely. Some of the native stuff might be close. They've got good shit here, El. Ozendi gave me this…tea, I guess you'd call it. I twisted my ankle and knee when we were hiking out; it healed it right up. No swelling at all. And no side effects."

"That you can tell."

Mara shrugged to concede the point. "That I can tell. Still though, it's good stuff. Our medics should take a look at it. They could learn a lot from the Doc."

Elroy shook his head. "She won't teach them. I already asked. She'll treat us, but she won't teach our guys and won't say why."

"Huh. Weird. Maybe some superstition? Like how they don't like AI?"

"Maybe. Who knows, maybe your flight school will soften things up and make them more inclined to share."

"That's what Murphy wants," Mara said. "That's our whole mission here. It's less about teaching them to fly as it is about *forming relationships.*" She couldn't entirely keep the bitterness out of her tone.

"Well, we're doing our best," Elroy said, and reached over to squeeze her shoulder gently. She nodded and focused on eating. She'd need the strength for the night and day to come.

The bad news was the whole number one engine needed to be replaced.

The good news was they'd brought the parts to do it.

The repair was going to take all day, and that was if they really jobbed it, so Mara did her best to help by staying the hell out of the way. She and Ozendi gathered with his fighters to plan their assault on the raider camp while Elroy supervised the work on the Huey.

Their biggest problem was a lack of basic intel. They didn't know where the prisoners were being held, but from what Mara could remember, the camp wasn't very big, and there didn't seem to be a lot of places for them to stash the almost twenty people they'd snatched from the village.

"I'm betting they're keeping them outside," Mara said as she and the fighters went over her maps of the camp's location. "Probably in a stockade of some kind. We'll be overhead as a gun platform, and I'll relay down to you guys on your handhelds."

One of the fighters shifted uncomfortably at the idea of using the handheld FM radios, but Mara had informed them they had no choice. She understood why they were so careful with stray radio signatures, but with this op being such a last-minute, cobbled-together, jerry-rigged clusterfuck of an affair, they *had* to have reliable, flexible comms. Otherwise, it was a suicide mission, and none of their families would get out.

Truth was, Mara still had her doubts on that score, but she buried them deep and kept going. Because how could she not?

She also mostly-successfully avoided talking to Ozendi about anything personal. She saw him watching her, pain in his eyes. She could feel how he wanted to pull her aside and address the gulf that yawned between them, but he didn't. It was a wise choice, all things considered. Several times during that day, she looked up to see Elroy watching her, as well. Once he jerked his head toward Ozendi and raised his eyebrows in a question. Mara gave him a little headshake, and El shrugged and turned back to his work. She let out a long breath, closed her eyes, and massaged her temples.

Sound drifted over from the work area surrounding the Huey. A flow of guitar notes intertwined with an eerie, winding voice spiraling, singing a wordlessly haunting melodic line. The scratch of a maraca…then the drums stepped in, and Mara recognized a song she'd listened to as a kid and loved all her life.

"What is that music?" Ozendi asked, looking up from the group huddled around the map. Mara couldn't help herself, a grin split her face for the first time since they'd found the burning wreckage of the settlement.

"It's 'Gimme Shelter.'" She tossed the answer back to him without looking as she strode toward the helicopter. "It's a classic Huey song."

The maintenance team was crawling all over the Huey, most of them singing Jagger's lyrics or tapping their tools to the beat on the cowling. Even Elroy was grooving along, swaying his hips as he peered into the now-empty engine compartment.

"Where did you guys get this?" Mara asked.

"Bobby fixed it up," Elroy said, pointing to their avionics tech who was working on the center console, wiring in one of the FM radios they'd brought.

"Bobby?" Mara asked.

"Hey, ma'am," he said, looking up. He had a shock of white-blonde hair and a wide, toothy smile. "I had an 8-track player in my bag when I got snatched. I figured since the bird had a psyops rig for the loudspeaker, and I was in here anyway, I'd hook it up and give the guys a treat. I've only got the one tape, though. Hope these guys like the Stones."

"I think your odds are good," she said. "Thanks for doing that, man. Can you leave it wired in?"

He grinned at her. "Sure thing, ma'am. Gonna do a little psyops?"

"Can't hurt, right?"

"Damn straight."

"This is perfect, Bobby, thanks. Good work."

Mara stepped back from the skid and looked up at Elroy again. "Got an ETIC?"

"What? English, ma'am. I don't speak your future shit."

She sighed, but her smile remained, thanks to the music thrumming through her. "When are you gonna be done?"

"Couple more hours. We should be ready for a test flight before sunset."

"Sounds good," Mara said. "Keep going."

Chapter Fifty

R'BAK

Thanks to the heroic efforts of her maintenance team, the Huey was once again flying by sunset. They did a quick check-out flight then landed back on the plateau. They'd brought a little extra fuel in their convoy out, but they didn't want to waste gas, so Mara shut her down and waited for full dark.

Six of the trucks had left at sunset, carrying the local fighters. They'd follow the woodcutters' roads and game trails to a spot upslope from the camp where they could wait unobserved. It would take them an hour or two to get there. By the time they were ready, it would be dark enough for Mara to come in low and fast over the treeline.

Their plan was incredibly simple. Mara would kick off the op by flying in and opening fire from the air. Then the trucks would roll in, hopefully vectored by intel from Mara and Ozendi, snatch up the prisoners, and roll out again while Mara continued to keep the raiders' heads down. Elroy and another MACV-SOG guy named "Bones" would be her gunners. She and Ozendi would fly. The guys on the maintenance team that hadn't gone ahead to join the party would head back to the settlement in the two remaining trucks and hopefully meet up with the convoy on their way out.

It could work.

Probably.

"You ready, sis?"

Elroy's deep, rumbling voice cut through the fog of her woolgathering, and Mara blinked as the cockpit of the Huey came back into focus.

"Yeah," she said, reaching up to pull her helmet off its hook and pull it on. "Just thinking it through."

"Well, it's time to stop thinking and start doing," Elroy said over the intercom. "Bobby just transmitted they're in place."

"Roger," she said. "Scramble Checklist."

Ozendi responded with the appropriate checklist steps, and soon they had the bird in the air, armed to the teeth, and flying south. Moonlit trees and terrain blended into a blur as Mara focused on the task at hand: get in, lay down covering fire for the trucks, get out again.

Five minutes from the camp, Mara made a short transmission to the ground team. She got a single break in squelch as a reply, but that told her all she needed to know. The trucks knew she was overhead, and they were rolling.

"Game time, gentlemen," Mara said, her voice icy calm over the beat of the rotor. "The camp is just on the other side of this ridge. Left gun, right gun, call out anything that looks like it might be our people, all right? And if anyone shoots at us, light them the fuck up."

"Roger, ma'am," Bones said, and she could hear the sound of him charging his weapon through the intercom. Elroy did the same on his side but said nothing.

"Up and to the right," Ozendi said, turning his head to clear in that direction before applying power and banking the Huey. They crested the ridge at an angle, in a bank, so they had multiple options if they took fire on the other side.

"Camp is at the ten o'clock, low," Mara called out, reaching for the cyclic and collective. "IP has the controls." She rolled out of the bank, but continued their descent to the level of the trees and kept her nose buried so they would pick up as much speed as possible.

"I got eyes on the convoy," Bones called out behind her. "Back at the eight. Coming in hot."

"Copilot's contact with the prisoners," Ozendi said, his voice professionally blank. "A pen next to the river at the far edge of camp."

"Left's contact, too," Elroy said.

"Excellent," Mara said. "Vector them in, Copilot. Bones, keep me apprised of the trucks' progress," she added as Ozendi toggled the floor mike and made the transmission to their ground team.

"Let's wake them up, boys," Mara said. She reached overhead and toggled the loudspeaker switch on and hit "Play" on the 8-track player Bobby had strapped to the dash. Immediately, the cascade of notes began falling from the Huey's external speakers, starting up the haunting, twisting melody once again.

"I've got enemy gun trucks in parking on the left," Elroy called out.

"Cleared hot," Mara said, and her crew chief opened up with the thick, snapping bursts characteristic of the M60. Mara felt the floor of the Huey shudder as he methodically walked his fire down the line of parked enemy vehicles. Charlie Watts' drum line kicked in right as lights flared inside the makeshift tents and temporary buildings of the camp.

"I've got the friendlies," Bones said. "They're approaching the pen with the prisoners."

"Roger," Mara said. "Keep any enemies clear of that area."

"You got it." She heard answering snaps from his direction, though they broke off as the aircraft approached the line of friendly trucks barreling down on the objective: a rough animal pen half-filled with scared-faced people. From the quick look Mara got as they roared overhead, most of them looked to be female or very young.

"Targets down," Elroy said as an explosion boomed out, lighting up the sky and blinding Mara for a breathless instant. She blinked furiously and waited for her vision to come back.

"Hard left turn," she announced as soon as she could see again. Bones quit firing and cleared her turn. She pulled back on the cyclic, then banked hard over, using her anti-torque pedals to assist her through the turn. This brought the nose first up, then quickly back down and around as the bird whipped through 180-degrees to come back around toward the bulk of the now very awake enemy camp.

"Left gun, right gun, cleared to fire," she announced again as they passed over the convoy of friendly trucks now pulling up to the pen and starting to load prisoners inside. She could see enemy figures emerging from tents and other parked vehicles, weapons out and pointing at them, but Bones and Elroy continued their steady rates of fire, and as soon as the enemy muzzles came up, the fighters went down under the torrents of 7.62 x 51 mm FMJ streaming down from the Huey's two M60s.

"Climbing right turn, Spooky pattern," she called out, pulling in power to both climb and accelerate as she started a steady spiral up and to the right. Bones ceased firing and began calling out the convoy's progress. Elroy continued raining hate down onto the camp as they flew a circle all the way around it.

"Status?" Ozendi demanded over the FM radio. The radio squawked a burst of static. Then the hurried words "Halfway there" came through.

"Shit! I'm out!" Elroy said over the intercom. Mara immediately turned right, away from the enemy, and whipped the bird around into a left-hand orbit. On the loudspeaker, "Gimme Shelter" faded out and the first rhythmic beats of "Paint it Black" echoed through the night.

"Right gun, cleared to fire!" Mara said, her voice still empty and cold as she re-established the Spooky pattern overhead.

"Last truck's loaded!" Bobby's voice over the radio sounded loud and breathless, and unaccountably clear. "Moving out!"

"We'll give them one more orbit—" Mara was saying, when Ozendi suddenly swore and grabbed at the controls.

"Mara!" he said, panic slicing through his tone. "I see Diozera! In the village! Cease Fire! Cease Fire! That's my daughter, nine o'clock low!"

"Fuck! Left gun's visual! She's in the center of the village, in that cleared area with the torches."

"My controls!" Mara said, her tone losing all its ice and cutting through the intercom like a scorching blade. "Bones, call me on the approach!"

She didn't think. She just moved. Afterward, Mara couldn't have recounted what she did with the controls, but somehow, she brought the Huey screaming down on an approach punctuated by Bones' defensive fire that set them squarely in the middle of the enemy camp…

…where a tiny girl crouched, huddled next to the shot-up hulk of one of the enemy vehicles.

"Dio!" Ozendi screamed. He clawed at his harness restraints and had the door open almost before Mara had the skids fully on the ground.

"El!" Mara demanded.

"I'm on him," Elroy replied, and she heard his intercom disconnect as he hopped out behind her copilot, his personal .45 in his hand. The two men ran to the little girl, who knelt with her face in the dust, her hair whipping around her as she pressed tiny hands over her ears. Mara watched, refusing to feel anything at all as Ozendi lifted his daughter, held her close, then handed her to Elroy before turning and running for a nearby makeshift building.

"Shit! Where the hell's he going?" Bones asked.

"I don't know," Mara said. "Here comes El, help him with the baby."

In front of the nose, Elroy curled over the girl and ran, hunched low, toward the bird. When he reached the open cabin door, Mara turned to look back and see him place the kid—she looked like she was about four years old—on the floor of the Huey.

"Mama and one more are being held inside! He's going after them!" Elroy shouted without hooking his comms back up. Mara barely heard him over the beat of the rotor.

"Go get him!" she yelled back, waving her hand to urge him on. *"Hurry!"*

Elroy gave her a short, single nod, and took off running toward the same building.

"Get the kid secured," Mara ordered Bones.

"Already done," he replied, his voice as calm as ever. "We got company incoming."

"Keep them off us for as long as you can," she said. "El just got to the building."

"You got it, ma'am," the old Vietnam vet said. Under his words, Mara could hear the *pop pop* of enemy fire. Little puffs rose up from the dust, working toward them. Bones answered with another burst from his M60. "If I don't get a chance to tell you, you're a helluva pilot, ma'am."

"Thanks, Bones," she said. "Here they come!"

Sure enough, Elroy and Ozendi appeared, each of them carrying a woman. The one in Ozendi's arms had long, blonde hair that almost brushed the ground. The other one looked older, thin and frail as her head lolled against Elroy's chest. Both women looked bloody and battered to within an inch of their lives.

Someone else's problem, Mara reminded herself. *You gotta get us out of here.*

The track changed again, and Jagger's voice started asking permission to introduce himself as more gunshots rang out, this time from the right side of the aircraft. Elroy flinched and crouched lower, then turned and fired his .45, hunching to protect his burden with his body. Ozendi stutter-stepped, and then slowly toppled forward.

"FUCK!" Mara shouted. *"EL!"*

There was no way under the twin alien suns that Elroy could have ever heard her. Not with the gunfire and the rotor wash and the chaos. But he looked up at her anyway, and when she stabbed her finger toward Ozendi's fallen form, Mara could see a jolt go through him.

Elroy didn't bother with niceties. He took the two steps necessary to get to the bird and half-threw the old woman into the cabin. Then he turned back, crouching and running to Ozendi's crumpled form. While Bones let loose with all the covering fire he could muster, Elroy grabbed the copilot's collar with one hand and got the other under the woman's arms and hauled them the last ten feet toward the Huey, even as Mara heard the *plink plink plink* of shots hitting her fuselage.

"They're in!" Bones said. "El's got the door closed on their side!"

"Don't let them fall out!" Mara warned. "We're off!"

The Huey screamed as she pulled right to her maximum power and shoved the nose over to take off straight ahead. Bones' weapon continued to snap in double-time as she turned to keep the left side of the aircraft pointed at the enemy while she ran, hard, for cover.

Mara dove for the little stream that cut alongside the camp, twisted and turned along its path to present as difficult a firing solution as possible.

"Here they come!" Elroy said, his voice ragged and breathless, but back on the intercom. "Shit, I thought we got most of their vehicles. There's at least five coming after us, two with vehicle mounts."

"Hang on," Mara said grimly, as she put the nose down even further, descending closer to the water, and pouring on the speed. Up ahead, the terrain flattened out, offering her even less in the way of options and cover.

We're not going to make it.

"Bruce! Do you need help?"

The voice came in over the FM radio, staticky and thick with a Russian accent. Mara looked up just in time to see a Hind scream by overhead, releasing its 83mm rockets.

"Hind got 'em!" Elroy cried out, jubilant. "The gun trucks are down!"

Tears of joy threatened to swamp Mara, and she couldn't keep the grin off her face or out of her voice as she keyed the mic and spoke to her two fellow helicopter pilots.

"'Bout time you got here, Sergei!" she said. "Your timing is perfect!"

"You know me," Sergei, the senior Russian helicopter pilot said. "I promise I never miss party!" In the background of his transmission, she could hear the Hind's powerful 23mm gun hammering away at the pursuing enemy forces.

"Yeah," Mara said, laughing as tears ran unheeded down her face. She eased the collective out and started a gradual climb, no longer afraid to silhouette herself against the night sky. "I know, you promised."

"Elroy, how we looking back there?" Mara asked as they crested the ridge and started back down. She forced herself to keep her eyes looking outside the aircraft, no matter how badly she wanted to turn around and see what was going on in the cabin.

"I've got the baby, ma'am," Bones said. "El's doing CPR on the mama. The old lady's breathing and conscious, but barely."

"And the copilot?" she forced herself to ask. Forced herself to keep her voice empty. Forced herself not to think of his name, lest she start screaming.

Bones didn't answer.

"Bones?"

"I'm sorry, ma'am," the gunner's gravelly voice went soft, broken. "He didn't make it."

Mara pressed her lips together and swallowed hard.

"Roger," she made herself say. And then she didn't say anything more until after they landed.

Chapter Fifty-One

R'BAK

Mara radioed ahead. Doc Naliryiz and a team of folks wearing medical masks were waiting for them at the headlight-illuminated landing field. She maneuvered the Huey to land as softly as possible, shut it down, and then waited for all of her passengers, dead and wounded alike, to be unloaded. Then, and only then, did she unfasten her harness and ease herself out of the seat.

The adrenaline rush from the firefight had long since worn off. Fatigue pulled at the edges of her mind, crushed her body under its weight. She carefully gathered up her gear and walked slowly back through the beams of the headlights toward the operations building.

Elroy found her in the locker room, crumpled against the far wall, sobbing so hard she couldn't breathe.

To his credit, he didn't say anything. Instead, the MACV-SOG warrior just walked over and picked her up, cradling her close. For the second time in three nights, Mara screamed silently as a storm of rage and grief ripped through her, scouring her insides with the acid torrent of regret.

Gone.

He's gone.

And there was nothing she could do about it.

Eventually, though, the storm quieted. Mara found herself half-lying across Elroy's lap, his iron-hard arms holding her securely against him. She could feel his chest rumbling as he hummed a wordless tune.

"What is that?" she whispered, her words ragged and raw.

"Hmm? Oh, nothin'. Just a song my mama used to sing to us boys when we was little. 'Specially if we had a bad dream."

"I wish this were a bad dream," she said.

"I know, sis. Believe me, I know."

"He wanted to talk to me. I wouldn't let him."

"I know."

"I was so angry at him. And now he's dead. And I'll never know what he wanted to say."

Mara felt Elroy straighten just slightly, as if something important had just occurred to him.

"Actually," he said slowly, "you might."

"What?" she asked. She felt like Elroy's words should have made her angry, but after her crying jag, she just felt empty. And exhausted.

"I forgot when I saw you on the floor, but I came in here to find you for the Doc. She said she had a message to give to you."

"Naliryiz?"

"Yeah. I told her she should wait, but she insisted you had to come as soon as you were able."

As soon as she was able? Mara was pretty sure that didn't mean "after crying your eyes out for twenty minutes"—or however long it had been. But was she able now?

"I guess," she found herself saying.

"You guess what?"

"I guess I'm able. Let's go find the Doc."

"You got it, sis."

Elroy helped her to stand and finish putting her gear away, then watched her closely as she walked toward the door. Her legs shook like Jell-O at first, but eventually she steadied and moved with a reasonable fraction of her usual purpose.

It's a good thing it's dark, Mara thought as they stepped out of the operations building and headed toward the field hospital which had spread out from the back of the local "alchemist's" house. *I must look like reheated shit.*

They found Naliryiz in the front area of the hospital, addressing several people. Mara recognized two of them as Lost Soldier medics, but the others seemed to be SpinDogs. It hadn't been her intent to interrupt, but Naliryiz broke off as soon as she and Elroy walked into the tent.

"Mara," the doc said, her eyes dark with sympathy. It hit Mara like a hammer blow. *She knows.*

She must have tensed, because Naliryiz immediately turned and dismissed the gathered medical personnel before beckoning to Mara to follow her. Elroy fell in behind them, his expression promising violence to anyone who dared to tell him otherwise.

Naliryiz preceded them down a dimly lit canvased walkway that led to the back of the alchemist's shop. Immediately inside and to the right was a door, half ajar. Immediately across from it, almost fully hidden in shadow, a SpinDog with a weird-looking bullpup carbine eyed them dispassionately.

"We can talk in here," said Naliryiz, gesturing toward the door. "The Matriarch may still be awake."

Mara pushed the door open further and stepped inside, to see that the old woman was, indeed, awake and sitting up in a surprisingly advanced hospital bed. She looked up at Mara's entrance and a strange expression—relief? satisfaction?—flickered through her eyes before fading into something that looked very much like a serene poker face.

"Have you told her?" the matriarch asked, looking behind Mara at Naliryiz.

"No, my Guild-mother," Naliryiz said. "Not yet."

"Told me what?" Mara asked, a shadow of impatience creeping into her exhausted tone.

"There are many things you need to know, child," the matriarch said. "I will ask your patience so that we may explain them in such a way as to make the most sense to you." Her words and expression were kind, but as before, Mara could feel the edge of command in the woman's words. She wasn't used to being gainsaid.

"First, I must ask you a question. I know that you and Ozendi coupled. Are you yet fertile? Is there a chance for a child?"

"I—*what?*" Mara gasped, real anger finally stirring deep within her brain.

"Mara," Naliryiz murmured, her tone half placation, half pleading. She reached out and put a hand on Mara's forearm. "Please. We're not trying to hurt you."

Mara stared at the old, battered woman lying in the hospital bed. The woman stared back, her dark eyes calm and bold and…hopeful?

It was that tiny bit of hope that did it. Mara let out a breath and felt her nascent anger slip away. "There is a chance," she admitted. "I'm not twenty anymore, but…there is a chance."

The matriarch closed her eyes briefly and let out a breath, murmuring soft words of thanksgiving. Then she opened her eyes and smiled a brilliant smile that made Mara's heart ache.

It was Ozendi's smile.

"You must understand," the matriarch said, "forming a romantic partnership with you was never explicitly part of Ozendi's mission. Like you and your *Sko'Belm* Murphy, we *hoped* that a strong working relationship would result, that is all. But when Ozendi contacted us and told us that he wanted to approach you about coming here he confided in me that he felt very drawn to you. He named you 'Skydreamer,' although that isn't exactly right since you are not a planetary native."

"What is a 'Skydreamer?'" Mara asked.

"That is what we call the native people who interact with our liaisons. It gives them a measure of protection, of legal standing within both our society and theirs. *You* already had legal standing as our ally, so the fact that Ozendi felt it necessary to name you thus meant he wanted very much to be with you."

"Is Iope a Skydreamer, then?" Mara said, and try as she might, she wasn't quite able to keep the bitterness out of her voice.

The matriarch smiled, and Naliryiz came forward to take Mara's hand.

"My brother handled this badly," Naliryiz said, her voice soft with regret. "When you returned from the forest, he told me that he never got the chance to tell you about Iope or Diozera. Yes, Iope is a Skydreamer, and she was Ozendi's mate almost three years ago. But you have to understand, Mara, he was no longer romantically involved with her. They loved each other only as Diozera's parents, not as partners for one another."

Grief wrapped around Mara's throat. "You mean—"

"My brother told me he offered to love you, and you accepted. That meant he was yours until his last breath."

Mara bit her lip, hard enough that the copper taste of blood seeped onto her tongue.

"There is more," the matriarch said, drawing Mara's attention back to her. "Naliryiz says that the woman Iope is gravely injured and will likely not survive the morning. She has asked that the two of you—the two women Ozendi loved most—be allowed to take responsibility for the child Diozera. This is a lifetime commitment among our people, Mara. You must think carefully before agreeing."

A memory flashed behind her eyes: Ozendi, explaining his people's customs of caring for one another's loved ones. Her eyes began to burn with regret and loss. She blinked back the tears and straightened her spine.

"I accept," she said, forcing her voice to be as steady and strong as her raw throat would allow. "I know what it means, and I accept. Diozera will be as my own daughter."

"And…if you are with child—"

Mara held up a hand. "Listen," she said, "whether I'm with child or not, you need to understand one thing: I will *never* be parted from a child of mine again. Not ever. So, whether we're talking about Diozera or my own hypothetical baby, that is how it is."

The matriarch's smile grew slightly colder, but it did grow. "That is how we feel as well. These children will form the bridge between our people, Captain. And such a bridge must be unbreakable."

Mara stared down the old woman, willing the matriarch to see the depth of her commitment. "Matriarch and Guild-mother," she said formally, "I give you my word as a mother. I promise to live up to my part of our agreement." Naliryiz squeezed her hand.

The old woman spoke once more, her eyes closing. "Just as we will live up to our promises to you."

Chapter Fifty-Two

SPIN ONE

"I read the report. I'm sorry about your…your student, Captain," Murphy said several beats after Mara finally fell silent.

"Thank you, sir," she said, her voice empty. She felt wrung out, as if she'd just experienced it all over again. She looked down and realized that she'd placed her hand on her abdomen without meaning to do so. She forced it back down by her side.

"I seem to recall reading that the child did make it, though. I take it that's the girl you recently brought to the Spin habitat for the first time?"

"Diozera, yes. Her mother, Iope, lived long enough to personally and formally request that we—me and Doc Naliryiz—look after her Dio."

Murphy leaned forward, his elbows on the tabletop. Mara risked a glance up and found not his usual coldness, but something like sympathy in his striking eyes.

"That's what you said. But why would she do that?" he asked. "You never met Dioreza's mother before she was taken, correct?"

"That's correct, sir," Mara said. "But…" She trailed off, then squared her shoulders and took a deep breath before plunging on. "You're familiar with the SpinDog concept of Skydreamers, right? The native R'Baku who interface with their liaisons? Ozendi's mother was one. The settlement that was attacked was one of a few places planetside where the offspring of the relationships between a SpinDog liaison and the indigenous R'Baku are raised. Ozendi grew up there."

"One of several?" Murphy asked, his eyebrows climbing his forehead. "There are so many of these children?"

"It's not exactly encouraged," Mara said. "But it's not exactly *discouraged* either. You gotta remember, sir, these people are so very invested in their genetics, right? They know they need fresh genetic material every few generations or so to keep their bloodlines strong. And you've said it yourself, humans are human. Relationships are *going* to happen. Claiming the offspring just allows the SpinDog Guild-mothers and Breedmistresses to keep it a little more under their control."

Murphy grew quiet, his eyes boring into hers. "That still doesn't answer my question. Naliryiz is the child's aunt; I understand why she was made responsible for Diozera. Why you?"

"Because," Mara said, "her father loved me. And I'm carrying Ozendi's child." She lifted her chin and met his steely stare with her own. For a long moment, nothing moved. The only sound was the whoosh of air through the life-support system overhead.

"Ah," Murphy said softly. "So, you *are* pregnant. I'd wondered if that was why you elected to assume a command and control role rather than fly in the assault on the transmitter."

"That's part of it," Mara admitted. "The SpinDogs' routine pathogen scan confirmed the presence of embryonic development when I returned from planetside. It's so early I didn't want to risk flying in combat. Although I do believe that I would be useful controlling our air assets."

"I'm sure you will be," Murphy said. "I would have thought that the father might be Sergeant Frazier, or even Vat, though I suppose that's not terribly likely."

"Vat's a friend, and El's my crew chief and brother, but I don't mind if people think the baby is his. It might be easier that way."

"Who among our people knows the child's parentage besides myself?"

"El does," Mara said. "That's it."

"And you think the Breedmistresses will try to claim your child as they do the children of the Skydreamers?"

"I do," Mara said. "In fact, they already have. It was almost the last thing the matriarch said to me before she died. And *that* is why I know that they will play their part. Because I've made it very clear that this child is *mine.* If they want access to him or her they need to meet their end of any bargains they make with me and my people. You gave me this job in part because I'm good at understanding and analyzing cultures, right, sir? Well, here's my analysis: In the eyes of the SpinDogs, when Ozendi gave me his seed, that was an irrevocable act. We're now as married as two Mormons just leaving the Temple."

"And so they'll play their part."

"They will, sir. I've bet the lives of *both* my children on it." Once again, their gazes met, and this time, Murphy's was the first to soften.

"All right," he said. "I believe you. Will you reveal your unborn child's parentage, eventually?"

"Maybe," she said. "It's probably inevitable. But for now, I'll just remind anyone who asks that it's not their fucking business…unless it is. Like with you, sir."

"If that's how you want to handle it," he said. "I'd appreciate being kept apprised of your medical status, please. I realize that's not a typical request, but you've managed to set yourself up as the first real bridge we have with these people, and so—"

"Understood, sir," she said. "Both Doc Naliryiz and Doc Arthur say that everything's just as it should be."

He raised a single eyebrow. "How much could they know? It's only been, what, about eight weeks?"

"It's actually shorter, sir; those eight weeks are made up of eighteen-hour days. So more like six weeks, in terms of actual clock time. But the SpinDog Breedmistresses are way ahead of us when it comes to prenatal medicine."

"Glad to hear that you are in such good hands," Murphy said, sitting back in his chair. "One more thing, Bruce, before you go."

"Yes, sir?"

"You did well on that mission. I told you that before. Under other circumstances, I would say mounting the assault so quickly was hasty. But given the tactical situation, which I didn't fully understand at the time, you made the right call. Not just to save lives and rescue an important leader, but to demonstrate that our people were ready to risk themselves to save SpinDogs and what they hold dear. I realize you had our strategic goals in mind the entire time. I want you to know that I see that."

Mara swallowed past the sudden thickness in her throat.

"Thank you, sir," she said. "I appreciate that."

"And, Mara…"

"Yes, sir?"

"I am very, very sorry for your loss."

Mara inhaled through her nose and fought to keep her hands by her sides. Grief welled up inside her, threatened to come crashing down like a tsunami. She pressed her lips together and pushed it back—not forever, just temporarily. She gave Murphy a soft smile and got to her feet.

"Thank you, sir," she said. "I appreciate that, too."

"You haven't taken any time. If you need to—"

"No, sir," she said, shaking her head. "I'm fine. Work helps."

"All right," Murphy said. "But please remember, you're not alone. We're here for what you need. It's dangerous to bottle up grief."

Her smile grew, even as she willed her eyes not to fill. "Yes, sir; that's good advice." When she was sure they would not spill over, she added, "Seems like I've heard those words somewhere before."

Chapter Fifty-Three

SPIN ONE

"Welcome, Major Murphy…or would you prefer the title *Sko'Belm*?"

Murphy made the small bow that polite appreciation of the offer required. "I shall remain 'Major,' Primus Otlethes. You honor me, but my title is part of my duty and oath as an officer."

Anseker nodded. "I understand. That is why I perceived that it would be incorrect to offer to address you as 'Primus;' you lack the requisite autonomy. *Sko'Belm* simply signifies that in this place, you are the highest-ranking leader of your people."

Murphy managed not to grit his teeth; he had little taste for titles and less for what felt like tribal chest-thumping. "The Primus honors me by indirectly putting his offer before me yet again, but my title is defined by the government to which I have sworn fealty. I cannot take another."

Anseker shrugged. "There is wisdom in that, too, I suppose. At any rate, we are prepared to begin, if you are prepared to bear witness."

Murphy nodded, went into the small, glass-sided pressure module to the left of the large hatch that led into what was usually an airlock. Once inside the module, he sat in the last empty chair. The other four seats were filled by three Primae of other Expansionist Families and one *Sko'Belm* of a Family which had been non-aligned prior to last week's violence, but which the Hardliners had decapitated in an excess of preemptive caution. They faced the chair in which the prisoner—Dolkar Kormak— waited and behind whom an outer airlock hatch loomed large and ominous.

A middle-aged woman entered the airlock-courtroom and exchanged highly formal bows with Anseker. He turned toward the small habitation module. "Be aware that the closest to she who was Primus when the alleged treachery occurred is now here to confer punishment or forgiveness, as is the ancient rite and duty of Breedmistresses. Guild-mother Shumrir hears the Statement of the accused with one ear alert to the call of justice, the other attentive to the needs of our community."

Murphy tried to remember what Lee had told him before she had returned dirtside. Breedmistresses were those women who used whatever weird powers some of them supposedly possessed for predicting the best genetic pairings between different Families and breedlines. Guild-mothers were an executive council of the most senior and/or accomplished among them. A Matriarch was a rare creature indeed, a title conferred upon a Family Guild-mother when she was also promoted to become its Primus. Which explained why Family Otlethes had taken Matriarch Kelrevis' loss like a body-blow: that much leadership and authority concentrated in one person produced a singular spasm of panic and uncertainty when they were lost without warning.

Shumrir bowed low to the gallery in which Murphy sat and then motioned to a smaller hatch opposite the one through which she had entered. It opened and a figure in a black hood and red robes stepped within. A sizeable curved dagger was scabbarded on—his? her?—belt. The smaller hatch closed.

Shumrir pointed at the newcomer. "Behold the Guarantor, oh you Aggrieved," she proclaimed in the kind of droning tone that Murphy associated with ritual. She faced the gallery directly. "If you find fault with the allegations or the preparations made here for the Statement, it must be spoken now."

She waited. No one made a sound.

Anseker shouted. "So begins the Statement of Dolkar Kormak in answer to the allegations."

Shumrir turned to face the deposed Primus. "Your deeds are not in dispute."

Kormak echoed her proudly. "My deeds are not in dispute."

"Then share your Statement, that we may know why you felt it necessary to act in violation of your troth with the Aggrieved."

Kormak faced the gallery. "Imprimis to the Aggrieved: had we become known to R'Baku beyond those few whom we visit near the poles, the whole planet would have had word of us. Accounts of our comings and goings would become commonplace and specific. We would cease to be dismissed as the stuff of myth or wild legends.

"Such word would ultimately have spread to the Harvesters of Kulsis, and that would have been the end of our existence. For the Overlords will brook no rivals, no challenges to their dominion."

Anseker spoke without looking at him. "Points you made during the discussions among all Primae when we were compelled to decide how to manage the aftermath of the battle whereby the Terrans unwittingly revealed our existence."

"Yes," Kormak agreed, "discussions in which consensus had to be reached *swiftly*. It did not afford us the opportunity to cleave to the Death Fathers' axiom, 'Plumb any pool into which you would dive.'" He looked at the faces in the gallery but avoided Murphy's. "Time revealed the problems with that hasty decision, as time often does. Advocates of the extremist delusion that we might somehow accrue enough power to resist the might of Kulsis and exist unhidden were empowered to become policy makers. I remind you of the objectives upon which our coalition with each other—and alliance with the Terrans—were founded and approved: that we should take action to eliminate any spoor, evidence, or report suggesting that the loss of the Kulsian ships might be the work of an unseen force such as ourselves.

"But each further step to achieve that necessitated other, further steps. Instead, we could have resorted to the simplest solution, which we proposed at the outset: a plague. That would have wiped out any credible persons or records that might have made report of us. It would also have been a reasonable explanation for the loss of the Kulsian's ships through infection carried up from the planet."

Anseker frowned. "A solution which was also likely to wipe out *all* human life upon R'Bak, or at least enough to destroy our only source of essential biological products, and so, our future survival."

"An unproven outcome."

"Unprovable, I think you mean. However, the point is moot. The option was considered and rejected during our initial discussion."

"Not so. It was *tabled.*"

"It was, and it was to be left so until and unless our planetary campaign showed no hope of eliminating the transmitter. Yet two such plans continue forward. And because of that, we have no reason or justification to risk our own probable extinction or the near-certainty of the death of all the R'Baku."

Kormak gestured toward Anseker as he turned to face the gallery. "And here, in the mouth of the Voice of the Aggrieved, we hear the same irresolute words that make us undeserving heirs of the Death Fathers' wisdom: he avers that we should concern ourselves with the survival of the R'Baku." Kormak glowered. "They are lesser beings. Their fate concerns ours only insofar as their presence or absence increases our chance of survival, of attaining dominion. Do you, the other Aggrieved, accept your Voice's words as representing your will in this, as well?"

Murphy managed not to blink at Kormak's casual embrace of genocide. He knew the SpinDogs were pretty ruthless, but to hear so extreme an expression of it, invoked as a presumably shared value, sent a shiver down his spine.

No one in the module spoke or reacted.

Anseker did not bother to look at Kormak. "If you have no argument that disproves the proposition that the death of the R'Baku would eventually bring about our own, then the reasons we chose for our present course remain valid. In consequence, your breaking of troths was unwarranted by a change in the bases of our joint decision."

"As if the Kulsians were the *only* threat to us."

It was Shumrir who turned to face the deposed Primus. "You confirmed that your deeds are not in dispute. The matter is constrained to them."

But Kormak was facing the gallery now, his eyes roving across all the faces. Except, again, Murphy's, whose left hand had started shaking; he tucked it tight against his leg.

"The farther down this path we go, and the more we must bend our industries and society to these 'missions,' the more orders the newcomers give, the more authority they acquire and exert.

"Do you not see it? Do you not see that the greatest threat is not from Kulsis but from them?" He jabbed a finger at Murphy. "They have brought war to the very core of our culture. They tempt the soft-headed and soft-hearted with the promise of new technologies, and in so doing, inveigle the susceptible to emulate their own values, their own decadent notions of fawning compassion, of mercy for the weak that must and should die. It is not only the wisdom of the Death Fathers; it is the self-evident law of nature. Yet they have found willing converts in the form of radicals—radicals who call themselves Expansionists, but in fact are something far more dangerous. They are cultural traitors. So, it was our determination that we had to fight both enemies—exposure to Kulsis' might and exposure to the Terrans' insidious ways—at the same time."

Shumrir stood before Kormak. "Your rhetoric is certainly stirring. But you leave out one important fact: that you have long desired our fall."

"We have long wanted to maintain our *independence*."

"That is a polite way of saying that you are culturally averse to any unnecessary coordination with Expansionist families, just as you frown upon any unions that are not necessitated by genetic considerations."

Kormak bristled. "That is because your ways are idiotic."

Shumrir smiled. "And here we see that your breaking of troths was not compelled by new and pertinent needs. Rather, current conditions provided an excuse to pursue a very old agenda: the elimination of us and our ways."

Kormak howled at her. "Because they will be our death! They dull your senses and sap your will so profoundly that you embrace the even greater idiocies of the Terrans. All of which defies the wisdom of the Death Fathers and invites their wrath."

"The Death Fathers are not magical."

"Indeed they are not, yet you doubt their powers. How absurd, when you—of *all* people—know that the powers of Reification are not magic, either." At the word "reification," Shumrir stiffened. Kormak frowned, confused, then his eyes flicked toward Murphy before sharply returning to the Guild-mother. "You—you haven't told them? Not even *him*?"

Shumrir shook her head. "In that outburst, it is you who demonstrate the lack of self-discipline that the Death Fathers warn against as the greatest weakness."

"And you *tolerate* the weak. You negotiate instead of dominate."

Shumrir nodded. "My sister, Kelrevis, saw the value of a balance between those two different approaches, hoped to preserve both truths by working to preserve both sides. She, like so many previous leaders, strove to coexist with your faction, so that each side's strengths might temper the other's weaknesses." She sighed. "But now you have taken steps that have pushed conditions past that point. Those among us who have long argued against that coexistence will now rightly say that you have acted exactly as their worst fears foretold."

Seeing Shumrir approaching the control panel on the bulkhead closest to her, sweat beaded on Kormak's brow. "The problem was not between us, but because of them! They convinced you to—"

"We know better than that," Shumrir interrupted quietly but firmly. "Arko Primus Zobulakos of *Spin Two* told us of your intention to eliminate most of us and diffuse our Families by dispersing the survivors into your own. He also confirmed that this is not a new strategy, but that it has been your goal for almost a century. So recent events simply hastened the inevitable."

"And now you will send me into the void?"

Shumrir shook her head. "You are right that we lack your single-minded pursuit of dominion. We also lack your flair for the dramatic and for grand gestures. No, you shall not be spaced."

"I…I won't?"

"No," Shumrir said, pressing a different stud on the panel. The smaller hatch at the other end of the room opened again and two large men in black robes entered "Spacing is wasteful, and we are prudent. Your water and proteins shall serve us well."

Dolkar Kormak was removed, spitting and cursing and shaking.

Shumrir glanced at Murphy. "About that word you heard: Reification. You are not to ask us about it." He discovered all the witnesses in the gallery were watching him. "It would put our alliance in great jeopardy," Shumrir concluded.

Murphy shrugged. "I can live with that." *For now.* "But about Kormak. He will be…euthanized before you, uh…?"

"Before we harvest the consumables from him? Of course." Shumrir shrugged. "We are not barbarians, after all."

Chapter Fifty-Four

SPIN ONE

Murphy did not go back to the CP after the Statement. He told Makarov to man the desk in his place and headed back to his quarters. Once there, he told Max he was racking early and sent the frowning bodyguard on his way. Murphy managed to maintain a casual pace as he entered his stateroom.

The moment he was inside, his left hand started quaking again. He clutched it, as if that might stop the tremors.

The door paged. *Oh, for the love of...*"Hello?"

"Major Murphy, it is I."

A female voice. Now, who the hell was—?

"It is Nyalriz. We have met in passing."

Huh? He tapped in the code that unlocked the hatch. "Come in, doctor."

Naliryiz entered, looking around as she did; Murphy couldn't tell if her corner-glancing was the result of curiosity or caution. Maybe both.

Murphy gestured to a chair, went to his own, waited until she sat. Which seemed to confuse her.

She leaned forward. "I have been formally asked by Anseker, Primus Otlethes, to assure you that Captain Bowden's attack plans have not been jeopardized by our recent internecine strife. All the necessary equipment had already been replicated and is now under our control. We hope that further replication needs can be handled by the Family Kormak technicians which had already been tasked with the project or by our own, who are studying the schematics even now. However, there were many casualties within Family Kormak, particularly among the replication teams."

"I wasn't under the impression that the battle for control went on for so long."

"It did not. We did not inflict the casualties among their technicians. That was the result of in-family resistance to the late Primus's move against us. Those most involved with expediting your efforts on the surface of R'Bak felt his policy was ill-advised and rose up against him." Her shrug mixed regret with resignation. "The Family is still in disarray, particularly its replication facilities."

"When will they choose a new Primus?"

"Relatively soon, I suspect. We will not exert any influence on that process, but their decision will be subject to our approval." She studied Murphy carefully. "You are concerned."

Murphy nodded. "We need fast replication of key weapons and vehicles to adequately support our plans for a ground attack against the transmitter. It doesn't sound like that's going to happen."

Naliryiz frowned, shook her head. "I am not able to speak to that with authority, but I suspect your conjecture is correct. Since all your replication needs were single-sourced, it will be difficult to restore production quickly." She folded her hands. "I should add that Anseker regretted he could not address these matters before today's Statement. He was grateful for your perception that it would have been improper to mix such business with the resolution of Primus Kormak's Statement."

"He has no need to thank me," Murphy answered with a dismissive wave of his right hand. *And that's no exaggeration. If Lee hadn't clued me in on the Statement and how to behave, I'm sure I would have put my foot in it.*

Naliryiz nodded but did not make any movement to leave. Her eyes did not leave his.

Uh oh. "There is another matter you wish to discuss?"

"Yes. In fact, it is the real reason I came." She glanced at his left hand, which chose that moment to tremble again.

"Nerve damage," he almost-lied.

"So to speak," she replied with a grim smile.

"It's nothing. A little fatigue. That's all."

She nodded slowly. "Exactly what a *Sko'Belm* would say. *Has* to say. Particularly the leader of a small group that is so vulnerable, and yet valuable, that its hosts seem to be unable to decide how it should be treated. Whether it should be made safe and secure—"

"—Or sent out an airlock. Yeah, I get it. I assure you, the Statement didn't leave much to the imagination."

She smiled. "I suppose it did not. Hopefully, there will not be another such occasion for you to attend. I doubt there shall be."

Murphy nodded. "When you guys clean house, you sure are thorough."

"If you mean that we give little if any quarter to our adversaries, that is true. Regrettably so, sometimes. But I am in a distinct minority, even among Expansionists, holding such an opinion. But they tolerate it in me because I am a healer. They presume those of my profession to be less…resolute."

"Are you?"

She stared at him, not angered but surprised. "So direct." She smiled. "So welcome. No, I am not less resolute, but I see a different path to accomplish what we must. A path that makes tools of patience and compassion, rather than presumes them to be weaknesses." She nodded at his hand. "There are those that would see that as an opportunity to overthrow you, sooner or later. To gain commanding influence over your people. Assuming any would accept their dominion."

"Yeah, good luck with that."

Her smile dimmed. "It would not be so easy as the most opportunistic of my people suspect, but neither would it be so futile as *you* think. Your men, and women, listen to their hearts. In the hands of unscrupulous adversaries, that can be a source of considerable leverage."

"Also considerable strength."

She nodded. "My opinion precisely. Which is why, although my medical skills are prized, my counsel is ignored."

"Even by the late Matriarch?"

Naliryiz sighed. "No. She was different. It was fortunate you arrived here when you did, or things would not have gone so well."

A laugh barked out of Murphy's throat before he was aware it was imminent. "You call our experiences since arriving here an example of a new relationship 'going well'? From the start, there's been secrecy, misinformation, and maneuvering over the replication. Which could have undone us. Still could."

She nodded. "And yet, that was the price of having you among us."

"I beg your pardon?"

"Do you think the Hardliners are the only ones with such high replication capability? Do you think the rest of us would remain free of their yoke if we didn't have an equal measure? No." She shook her head. "Accepting you among us was a trade, proposed and driven home by the late Matriarch."

Murphy nodded slowly, felt incredibly stupid not having seen it before. "If the Hardliners were to agree to having us among you, then they insisted on having oversight of replication and supply. They had to be in a position to exert a chokehold on us at a moment's notice. I can't believe I didn't put that together earlier."

Naliryiz smiled. "You have been rather busy."

They laughed together. Murphy liked that feeling…and quickly tamped it down.

"Now," she resumed, "about your hand—"

"I appreciate your concern, but—"

"You will listen to me, now." Naliryiz's steel suddenly shone through, and Murphy discovered he liked that, too. A lot. "I do not broach this matter out of sympathy; I do so out of practicality, necessity. You must continue to lead effectively. The die is cast; the coming days will decide how it falls, but our future is now linked to yours. And, as you have no doubt foreseen, eliminating the transmitter is but a first step. Because Kulsis will not sit idly by and wonder why they have not received a message from their coursers. So, ironically, Kormak was correct in at least one regard: this is just the first step in a long, dangerous dancc that will only become more desperate as it goes on."

Murphy pushed away the image of dancing with Naliryiz. "I suppose you are right, but really, I'm fine."

"So, you will not admit your condition, let alone discuss it." She rose. "No doubt you are wise to resist any action which would reveal it and compromise your position. You think ahead to what would follow if others learned of it. Or if I am observed, or even suspected of, providing drugs that might control or at least lessen the trembling. Questions would be asked, and your condition revealed." She nodded and headed toward the hatch. "I frankly expected no different. Not today, at least."

"Not ever, so far as I can tell," Murphy said. Even he could hear the tinge of mournfulness in his tone. *Wuss.*

Naliryiz turned as she reached the coaming; seen sideways, her narrow, space-born body almost seemed to disappear. "Every day reveals new problems and possibilities. We shall speak again."

"So those are your weapons," Bowden said, completing the walkaround of the interface craft. "Any questions?"

"Nope," First Lieutenant Thomas Byrd, said. "A super-size Sidewinder and a flying bomb that I need to guide into the target or show it a laser so that someone else can." Byrd, a former US Marine F-4 RIO, had understood the Sidewinder immediately and had quickly picked up lasers and how the laser-guided bomb worked.

His pilot when he'd been downed, Captain Sam Hirst, had understood the bomb almost as quickly and had identified the Sidewinder seeker head as coming from an AIM-9B.

The third American aviator, USAF Captain Dave Fiezel, an F-105F pilot, had picked up the laser-guided bomb mission by likening it to suppression of enemy air defense, or SEAD, missions, where he'd fired anti-radiation missiles at Vietnamese SA-2 surface-to-air missile radar sites. Fiezel had Bowden's respect; anyone who dueled with SAMs was a serious badass, even if he'd ultimately lost to one in the end.

"I'm sorry," Bowden said as he led them aboard the craft and into the cockpit, "but the cockpit controls we've put together for this are pretty bare bones. Nothing's integrated very well, and none of it's digital."

"Hah," Byrd said with a laugh. "You've obviously never been in the cockpit of a Phantom."

"Hell, the Phantom's state-of-the-art," Fiezel said. "*You've* never been in a Thud."

Bowden chuckled. "Actually, I have; I saw it in a museum one time." He smiled at the other aviators. "Okay, maybe you won't be out of your element as much as I thought. Regardless, I'm going to have to teach you how to operate all this so that you can, first, fight your way into the target area and, second, blow up the giant antenna they're building to call Kulsis."

Hirst nodded to the dual-piloted cockpit. "Will I be flying with Byrd?"

Bowden shook his head. "No, you'll each have a SpinDog who will fly the plane, while you work the weapons systems."

"RIO appreciation flights!" Byrd exclaimed happily. "Welcome to my world."

"Yeah, well, you're finally going to get to fly in the front seat," Hirst said, "instead of being a backseat driver like you normally are. Were. Welcome to *my* world."

Bowden smiled. It was obvious the two men had been a crew; they had the easy camaraderie that developed between two men who had flown together often.

"Byrd, you'll be flying with Lotho Ferenc. Hirst, you'll be with Jukhal Samkamka, and Fiezel, you're with Burg Hrensku."

"All right," Byrd said, sliding into the copilot's seat on the left. Unlike the US military, where the fixed-wing "pilot-in-command" was normally on the left, the SpinDog lead pilots sat on the right, like in US helicopters. He looked down at the switches labeled in English. "What have we got here?"

The pager in Murphy's quarters toned. He rolled up into a sitting position, tapped his data slate, saw Makarov's face. "What is it, Pistol?"

"Sir, you asked for me to notify you when I had a breakthrough on the black-market activity among the men."

In retrospect, since the SpinDogs didn't seem to be part of the transaction chain, Murphy had mentally relabeled it as a "unit barter economy grown large." But he had asked Makarov to keep an eye on it and find the ringleader, so…"Tell me what you've got, Pistol."

"A sharp drop off in missing items and stores. Also, no mention of illegal card- or dice-games."

Murphy thought. "Did this start about, oh, four days ago?"

Makarov paused for a full three seconds. "Why…yes, sir. How, how did you know?"

"Remember that guy you tagged as your suspect, the one who was on my chopper when it went down?"

"Yes, sir."

"Well, he went dirtside five days ago."

"And you think he could be responsible for so much of this illegal activity?"

Murphy couldn't smother a rueful bark of laughter. "'Responsible for so much of it?' Makarov, I'd take long odds that he was behind *all* of it."

And good luck to the fresh marks waiting to be fleeced down in Starkpatch…

PART SIX:

VAT

Chapter Fifty-Five

MOGADISHU
NOVEMBER 1993

The Range Rover had seen better days, as had the streets it was navigating. Back home in Romulus, Michigan, the ratio was about one pothole for every yard of road. Here it was about one yard-sized pothole for every foot of road. The heat in the back seat was sweltering, but the Rover had probably never had air conditioning, and you were crazy to drive through Mogadishu with the windows down. The truck caromed over a particularly deep pothole, and his head bounced off the roof.

"You good, boss man?" the driver asked. He was about 6' 9", maybe more, and would have been considered skeletal back in the States. If he had been born there, he might have been a high school basketball star. Here, he looked decades older than he was and was missing his left leg below the knee, probably courtesy of some unknown close encounter with the indifferent nature of high explosives.

The man was definitely speaking a version of Afar; it wasn't pure Somali. African dialects weren't in his collection, so when this opportunity opened up, he started learning them. He'd gotten pretty good with Somali over the last two weeks, but Afar was trickier.

"Yeah, A-OK," Victor said in Afar and flashed the man a thumbs-up. The driver beamed at him, his brilliant white teeth offset by his ebony skin. He couldn't tell if that meant he was speaking the correct language or not. *Knowing my luck, he works for Aidid.*

A shrill squawk from his backpack made him jump. He'd forgotten about the sat-phone. Despite the literature, it didn't work in Somalia often and almost never in Mogadishu—there was too much electromagnetic garbage in the air with the US military in town.

He fished it out and flipped the huge antenna up. The signal bar showed minimal. With a shrug, he stabbed the Connect button with his thumb. "Talk quick; signal sucks."

"Vat? Damn it, man, about time. Where you been?"

"Snap, you idiot, it's three o'clock here. The meeting, remember?"

"Jesus, I forgot. Look, man, you gotta get outta there. *Now.*"

"What the fuck you talking about? General Aidid is interested in the bees. Like *really* interested."

"Yeah, well, the FBI just cleaned your place out."

Victor felt his blood run cold. He licked his lips and sat up straight in the seat, something a white guy in fatigues shouldn't do when riding down a street in Mogadishu, especially in daylight. "What did you say?"

"I said the F-fucking-B-I, just hit your place. I'm on a burner phone at the airport. I'm getting out of Dodge. This is your only warning. Good luck."

"Snap!" Vat yelled into the phone, but a series of clicks and a rapid beep told him that half a world away, his long-time buddy Sammy "Snap" Baker had just broken the disposable phone in half and tossed it into the garbage. "Fuck," he said quietly. Someone had dropped a dime on his operation. It wasn't Snap, or he wouldn't have risked everything calling him. Who then?

Doesn't matter. Not now.

"You good, boss man?"

Vat looked up at the driver. Did the man know more than four words of English? He'd been taking Vat to the hotel—more like armed compound, really—provided for him upon arriving in Mogadishu. Vat didn't know the driver's name. He'd just gotten into the car General Aidid's aide had pointed to.

"Can you take me to the American base?"

The man's big friendly smile disappeared in an instant. *Yeah, definitely Aidid's man.* "You go hotel." Vat made a face, and the driver repeated the statement in Afar, confirming Vat's earlier guess.

Vat shook his head hard. "No. The American base," he said in the driver's language. He reached into his duffel, fumbled around, and pulled out a pouch. He held up two crisp $100 bills. "Base." The look of hunger on the man's face was unmistakable, still he hesitated. Vat added two more bills. The hesitation disappeared as the driver reached for them. Vat handed him two and held two back. "You'll get these when you drop me at base."

"Okay, boss man," the driver said, in English this time, his face hard but determined. $400 US in Mogadishu could buy you a new life, or better yet, a ticket out. Vat wondered what his own ticket would cost.

A bullet came through the side window as they turned onto a side street.

The driver gunned it. Vat fell sideways and let his momentum carry him to the floor, pulling his bag with him. His hand went back in and came out with his pistol. In a couple of years, it would be known as a Glock 26. Right now, it was an un-serialized preproduction present from a friend. Super lightweight, super compact, and loaded with 9x19mm parabellum, NATO standard. The 10-round magazine and small size had been a surprise to more than a few people with ill intentions toward him.

What fucking good will it do against a sniper?

He briefly wondered if Aidid had targeted him. No, he was being paranoid. Aidid would just have the driver pull over and a couple guys would have blown Vat's brains out in the middle of the road; no need for the cloak and dagger shit. Someone had probably seen the camos. *Shit.*

The Range Rover's motor slowed. Vat dropped another hundred over the front seat. "Do. Not. Stop," he said, carefully pronouncing every word. The engine coughed and roared again as the driver punched it.

No more bullets followed.

Vat stayed on the floor.

He dug through his bag and grabbed the folder with his proper documents and secured the gun in its Velcro retention strap inside the bag. He destroyed the ID he'd entered the country with beyond recognition and stuffed it under the driver's seat. Nobody would have any idea who *that guy* was.

He risked looking up from behind the seat and saw they were approaching the base's checkpoint. A pair of armored personnel carriers flanked the concrete barriers, and he realized how fast the taxi was moving.

"Whoa, slow down!" he barked in Afar. "We don't want to give the guards the wrong idea."

"Okay, boss man."

The driver slowed and soon a young soldier on one of the APCs waved them to stop.

"Stop and identify yourself!"

"I'm good from here," Vat said and pushed seven $100 bills at the driver. The man took them, amazed. "Good life, my friend." The driver nodded as Vat slowly got out, holding the bag in one hand, high and to the side.

"My name is Alex Finnigan. I'm a US military contractor!"

"Keep your arms raised, turn around, and slowly back toward the APC."

He did as he was ordered.

Five minutes later, the Range Rover drove off.

An hour later, he was climbing into an idling UH-60 Blackhawk.

"Get me out of here," he said to the pilot.

"As soon as my other passengers arrive," she replied.

Vat grunted, sat down, and strapped in. At least he was on his way out of Mogadishu. Soon he'd be on a chopper back to the world. Once there, his papers would have him on a flight to the Czech Republic in a few hours. He would put the shit back in the horse once he got there.

It wasn't too late.

He kept telling himself that, even as he stepped up into the Blackhawk…

Chapter Fifty-Six

55 TAURI B
AUGUST, 2125

Vat blinked and sat up with a start, the after-images of a horrific scene spinning away from his conscious mind. He was in a Blackhawk spinning toward the water. There was fire, smoke, and the screams of people and tortured metal.

"What the fuck?" he asked and looked around.

He was in a gray room. It was obviously a hospital, though it lacked all the usual technological accoutrements. The air smelled funny, like a military flight but not, and the light had an unusual quality to it. All the furnishings were utilitarian, cheap and drab. A sandy-haired man in a strange flight suit was sitting nearby. He didn't have any insignia, and the Velcro patches were missing except rank and name. Vat instantly recognized him from the helo, though he was dressed differently now, making the dream real with a sudden lurch.

"We crashed," Vat said, his throat dry.

"Sort of," the man said. He had bronze oak leaves on his shoulders. So, a major then. The name tag said, "Murphy."

"Care to explain?" Vat asked.

"In good time. How do you feel?"

"Fine, for a dead guy."

"You're obviously not dead," Murphy said.

"Did I miss my flight?"

"You could say that," Murphy said under his breath, but Vat caught it and narrowed his eyes. Murphy plucked a file from a case sitting on the floor next to him and opened it. Printed on the front was an image of Vat from his DoD contractor dossier, taken two years after his departure from the US military. He'd always hated that damned picture.

"Alex Finnigan," Murphy said, reading. "Contractor with the Department of Defense." He read the appropriate number. "You've done dozens of mid-level operations over the previous six years, and all reviews were favorable. You make a modest income, have a house in Tulsa, lease a 1990 Corolla, and pay your bills on time. It doesn't say here if you help your neighbor take out the trash."

"Sure, all records with the DoD are public. You going to—?"

Murphy held up a hand, silencing him. "Let me finish. A review of your dossier in 1991 revealed several inconsistencies, such as rental receipts not matching locations and a link to a Cayman Island offshore account. In essence—" he held up the file, "—this is all bullshit." He dropped it into the case.

Fucking hell.

Murphy pulled out another file. This one had Vat's old US Army file picture. He hated that one even more. "Victor Allen Thomas, First Lieutenant, US Army." He read off Vat's serial number. "You generally go by an acronym of your three names…Vat?" He looked up at Vat who nodded. "Graduated high school in Romulus, Michigan, summa cum laude, went to UM, where you got a Bachelor's of Science in Global Logistics and Supply Chain Management.

"ROTC. Commissioned August 1984. Branched 92D, Aerial Delivery and Material, but you often worked with the quartermaster's office."

Murphy went on to detail Vat's career until the end. "Promoted to first lieutenant in 1987, and you received a general discharge the same year." Murphy moved the papers around, and Vat realized they were not the typical US government printouts. These had a strange metallic look to them. "Interestingly enough, there is no detail on the reason for the general discharge, be it court proceedings, JAG, or general officers' notes. Just a separation order."

Murphy looked at Vat, who merely shrugged. He didn't feel like giving the major any more information than he had given anyone else over the years. The major could go pound sand.

"Well, fast forward to your alter ego, Mr. Finnigan-slash-Thomas. Under the guise of your contractor license, and with contacts no doubt made during your time as an officer in the US military, you embarked on a career as an international arms dealer. A rather lucrative one, based on the aforementioned Cayman Islands account. At the time of your accident, you had a balance—"

"So, the helo did crash? We were shot down?"

"Yes, Vat, without a shred of doubt. You, me, and everyone else aboard that helicopter should have died. But only the copilot and crew chief were killed."

"How is that possible?"

Murphy put the file into the case, sat back, and sighed. He looked at Vat like a principal would a student who'd landed in his office for the umpteenth time. "I don't know what to do with you, honestly."

"Maybe if you fucking explained what's going on?" Vat asked gruffly.

Murphy met Vat's stare. "You, along with the rest of the survivors of the attack on that helicopter, were abducted by an alien race known as the Ktor and subsequently smuggled off Earth." Vat shook his head and started to laugh. Murphy continued, "Our group represents what we believe are the last taken before the Ktor ceased such operations, likely because our technology was becoming advanced enough to spot their ships.

"There are about a hundred more like you in this station who were abducted from Earth."

"You know," Vat said when Murphy stopped, "I always loved science fiction. You should have made this into a movie!"

"Nothing ever written is as real as this," Murphy said.

"You mentioned aliens?" Murphy nodded. Vat recalled the word. "Ktor?"

"You got that faster than I did." Murphy shrugged. "I believe I was puking, at this point."

"Why?"

Murphy's face darkened. "Long story."

"Right. Anyway, aliens. I suppose they're all photogenic? Look like little teddy bears, or can make bicycles fly?"

"No, in fact, they look just like us."

"So, you went with the *Star Trek* model huh? That saves on special effects."

"Vat, we need to move this along. The evaluation of your file said you would accept this as well or better than many of the others. But you're being quite a bit more stubborn when it comes to grasping the basic principles."

"What, that I've been abducted by aliens, and a handy Army major is here explaining everything?"

"No, that you are in space now, part of a group of soldiers taken from Earth. We're fighting an interstellar war with the aliens who abducted us. You are light years from Earth and it's 133 years since the chopper went down."

Vat opened his mouth to reply, closed it, opened it again. "Oof," was all he could muster.

"Getting the picture?"

"Yeah, I don't know if I believe it, though."

"That's sensible," Murphy said. "Doesn't any of this bother you?"

"Not really," Vat said and shrugged. "I didn't like anyone back then, anyhow." *There was that one general...*"Tell me what's going on."

Murphy nodded and took a device from his bag. It was not made on Earth. Vat quickly realized it was a computer far more advanced than anything available in 1993, even more than the stuff DARPA had hidden away.

Murphy began laying out the facts.

Chapter Fifty-Seven

SPIN ONE

The habitat, a hollowed out asteroid, was straight out of science fiction. Vat was pretty amazed, at first. But soon it was just boring and cold, just like the SpinDogs who lived in it. They were a group of cliquish assholes, too.

The so-called "Lost Soldiers," were housed together while most of them got ready for some hare-brained mission on the local planet, R'Bak. The vast majority of their equipment had been snatched by the Ktor at the same time as the humans they'd kidnapped. Some gear was higher tech, either current-day Earth or provided by the Dornaani. There was precious little of that, though. The brains behind the operations, some guys named Nephew and Nuncle, had taken off before they'd woken Vat, leaving Murphy and his odd balls to hold the rear and establish a base for them to return to, despite plenty of local opposition. And once the planet-scorching Searing began, an even bigger bunch of bad guys from the neighboring system would arrive to raid R'Bak for resources.

"Just gets better and better," Vat had said as he read the reports. The reality was, he didn't want a fucking thing to do with the clusterfuck Murphy had taken charge of. Not in the least. Of course, he'd promised Murphy he'd help, so he did odd jobs, helped newly thawed soldiers to adjust, and tried to find an angle.

They had access to a machine from the Dornaani which allowed you to learn things in your sleep. Or at least it seemed like you were asleep. Dream learning, some of the Lost Soldiers called it. Vat refused to get hooked up to the thing. It was mainly used for languages anyway. He didn't need a machine to learn languages.

"Hey, Vat, your bid, comrade!"

Vat snapped out of his reverie and glanced at his cards. He tossed a stick of chewing gum into the growing pile of assorted items without a second thought. The coin of the realm was different items they'd had on them when they were put into the freezers. Several curses ensued, and cards hit the table.

"*Ublyudok*," Artyom spat.

"I know who my mother was," Vat replied, in Russian. "Do you?"

Artyom's eyes grew hard in a way most Americans had never seen. He'd told Vat his last memory of Earth was Kursk, where'd been visited by a strange man in a suit with sunglasses offering him a chance to live, before he'd spent almost two centuries asleep. He'd survived the siege of Stalingrad too.

"*Da*, I know her. She was a bitch," Artyom said and laughed uproariously. He took a deep drink of *chaat*, which was basically vodka or close enough that Artyom didn't care. "I want to see your cards." He tossed in a cigarette: Call. Men's eyes bugged out at the sight of the smoke. They all looked longingly at it.

Nobody else at the table was interested in raising; they all folded. It was just Artyom and Vat. Vat put down his cards: two, seven, nine, king, and ace. All spades. A flush.

"*Blyad*!" Artyom spat and threw his cards down. He had a straight. "You have the luck of the devil," Artyom said and watched Vat collect the booty. There wasn't much of a currency among the Lost Soldiers: a problem for every plan Vat had conceived.

"I have it on good authority there is no devil," Vat replied. "He'd be in this star system if there was one."

The other five who'd been playing drifted off, but Artyom didn't. He watched Vat secure his winnings and carefully put the cards back into a holder. He'd traded a RockHound for the cards. It cost Vat a cylinder of helium, which wouldn't turn up missing for some time.

"I have question," Artyom said.

I assumed as much when you didn't leave. "What is it?" Vat asked.

"You believe it?"

"Believe what?"

"All of this," Artyom said, waving his big, hairy arms. "This is a *spaceship*, and we are long way from Earth. Everyone we know dead. How can this be?"

Vat knew Artyom was one of the Lost Soldiers who was still struggling with the situation. There were a dozen of them, and they were his nominal responsibility.

"Shepherd them," Murphy had said. "See if you can move them along the pathway to acceptance. We need every man and woman we can get. The older ones, the PreBooms, are the hardest." PreBoom, or pre-Baby Boomers, was shorthand for anyone who'd been snatched before Vietnam. The societies which were pre-spaceflight seemed the least able to just accept it and move on. In his own way, Artyom was a poster child for them. Kind of an Extra-Lost Soldier.

"Yes, Artyom, I do believe that all this is real."

Artyom nodded for several seconds, slowly. It was distinctly Russian and didn't mean he agreed, but that he was thinking about it. "If this true, then I would like to kill these Ka-Whores who took me from my Natasha." It was a bastardization of Ktor, but Vat thought it was amusing.

"Wife?"

"Bah!" Artyom spat on the polished rock floor of the room. "She left me for party boss when war started. No, Natasha is my little girl." The hard eyes softened and became moist. Vat knew what he was thinking. Natasha was dead. Any children Natasha had were dead, and probably their children, too. None of them were so much as a footnote in a history book.

Artyom finally stopped nodding. "Well," he swept his arm at the gray walls, "I think about this more." He took another deep drink of *chaat*. He'd already had enough to launch a rocket. "You sleep well, friend."

"You, too," Vat said and watched Artyom get up and leave. The man didn't even stagger. It was a few seconds before he realized Artyom had called him friend.

"What was that all about?"

He turned around and saw a woman in a flight suit standing in the hallway. The impromptu poker game had happened in a little alcove not far from the refectory. It wasn't hard to find privacy anymore; most of the Lost Soldiers were either in other areas training, preparing to deploy to R'Bak, or already there.

She was short, with dark, close-cut hair and a curvy build. The flight suit fit her well. She had captain's bars on her epaulet, and a pair of embroidered wings rode over the name patch: Bruce.

"Bruce is a strange name for a woman," Vat said as he finished putting the cards away.

Her sharp eyes took notice of what he was doing before flicking back to his face. "My callsign," she said. "Mara 'Bruce' Lee."

"Ah," Vat said, nodding.

"I'm into karate, too; it all came together."

Vat looked at her again and finally recognized the voice. "You were the helo pilot out of Mogadishu."

"Correct," she said. "And you were John Q. Public."

Vat laughed and nodded. He rose, walked over and offered his hand. "Victor Allen Thomas. Call me Vat."

"Pleased to meet you," she said and gave his hand a firm shake. None of the female service members ever offered a soft shake. "I never found out: NSA?"

He laughed and shook his head. "Contractor."

"That explains why you had a different name on the flight roster."

Fuck. Good memory, too. "Okay, I might have been doing some secret-squirrel shit."

"You're prior service, but not very old."

"I left the service for medical reasons." Well, it wasn't a lie, really. Anatomy was involved. Sort of. "Army. Logistics. Made first lieutenant and then made my exit." No need to mention that he'd been led to the door.

She nodded, taking it all in. "So, what was the Russki yelling about?"

"Who, Artyom?" he asked, gesturing in the direction his new friend had taken. She nodded. "He's one of those who haven't adapted well. He was taken from the Battle of Kursk."

"Holy shit," Mara said.

"Yeah. I think I made progress tonight."

"You only had to get him shitfaced and take all his cigarettes."

Vat gave her an overly sheepish look. "Don't turn us in, we're not supposed to have smokes. Not that there are very many anyway. The SpinDogs would shit themselves if they knew we were smoking up the place."

"SpinDogs have this herb they smoke, hookah-style." Vat's eyebrows went up. He'd heard rumors. "It's not quite like marijuana, but similar."

Vat made a mental note to look into this lead.

"You don't smoke, though," she said, not a question.

"No, filthy habit." She looked confused as he finished carefully stashing the smokes, gum, and various pills in a plastic container. "Long story. You don't, eh, report to Murphy…do you?"

"Don't we all?"

"True."

"I'm just a pilot getting ready to head back dirtside."

"Dirtside?"

"Down to R'Bak." Her voice hardened; her eyes became distant for a moment. "They have some new Hueys down there, and I'm training SpinDogs to fly them. What about you? Going down soon?"

"No, I'm fine up here." She cocked her head and narrowed her eyes. "You be careful on the planet, okay?"

"Sure. Maybe we'll cross paths again sometime."

"You know," he said, "I'd like that." He watched her go. She was by far the best-looking female he'd seen since they woke him up. No doubt every soldier in the place was following her around like a puppy dog. "I wonder who does her hair?"

Chapter Fifty-Eight

SPIN ONE

Two weeks passed, and Vat's nightly poker crew became steady. Despite a breakthrough in understanding, or at least acceptance, Artyom kept on feigning psychological instability. Not a very hard act for him, Vat reflected, and it kept him on *Spin One*. He, too, had decided it was preferable to the insanity down on R'Bak. People were coming back now, some shot up pretty badly. Considering the amazing stories about the R'Bak's healing herbs, you had to really work to outstrip the native healers' abilities.

Atryom had been assigned to move cargos around the docking bays; not an exciting job, but better than the alternative. "If I'd wanted to get filled with bullets, I would have told commissars to fuck off at Stalingrad," Artyom said as he saw and raised the bid. They'd found little bottles and filled them with *chaat* when the meager supply of cigarettes disappeared. Most of the Lost Soldiers decided they didn't want to part with the few they'd brought through time. Vat had managed to win quite a few of them before that, though. There was interesting stuff that had made the trip through time with the Lost Soldiers in the stasis devices Murphy called symbiopods. However, like the smokes, there was not a lot of it.

"My office was in Nagasaki, where we researched submarine technology," Taiki said. He looked at Vat. "If I had made it back to Japan, you Americans would have blown me up with your bomb!" Taiki Komatsu was a former private of the Imperial Japanese Military Kenpeitai, the secret police. He'd been on a submarine returning with German technology in a late war exchange. They never made it. Last he remembered, his boat was being bracketed by depth charges soon after leaving Vichy France. Then he woke up here, like Vat.

Taiki wasn't much of a patriot; he'd become a technician at a shipyard, like his father. Then, because he knew German, he was recruited for the Kenpeitai because his father insisted. He hated boats and had admitted to Vat he couldn't even swim. He'd joined Vat's group shortly after Vat met Mara.

"Japs had it comin' after Pearl, you ask me," Sam Potts said. A fellow American, Potts had been a corporal with the 101st Airborne defending Bastogne during the Battle of the Bulge. He'd ended up in a freezer after meeting another mysterious man in sunglasses.

Vat was still trying to make sense of Pott's accent. It sounded like classic Georgia from the 1940s, but it had a strange pacing and inflection. He figured it was some older family member, probably recently immigrated to the US, which had influenced young Sam Potts as a kid. It wasn't uncommon.

"I told you," Vat said, "no hacking on each other's country. They're all gone now anyway."

Potts snorted and examined his cards.

The Lost Soldier beside him snorted in response. "You Americans, always setting the terms."

"I said be nice, Lech, or you can find someone else to play with."

Private Lech Kowak was the last to find his way into Vat's orbit. He'd been aboard the storied Polish submarine *Orzel*, which had escaped to Britain but was later sunk by a British plane by accident. The Ktor had taken the crew before the ship went down.

"Poland didn't bluster," Lech said and waved a hand at Potts.

"No, Poland surrendered," Artyom said.

Everyone laughed, except Lech, who grunted and took a drink of *chaat*.

Vat liked the group, and they'd quickly become loyal to him. The four had been the only Lost Soldiers who'd taken off the sleep learning helmets when they were left alone; none of them liked the possibility that their minds might be manipulated, as well. So they'd only become passingly familiar with what the SpinDogs called 'first' or 'old' Ktor. The problem was that passingly familiar wasn't enough for most things. There were ten or more languages between the Lost Soldiers, and quite a few regional dialects.

When they got together, Vat quickly and fluidly switched between Yiddish, Russian, Japanese, English, and Ktor without missing a beat. He didn't think about it, and his ability in each language steadily improved. Lech, who'd been the equivalent of a junior professor before the war, labeled Vat a "Linguistic Metamorph." Vat figured it was pseudo-intellectual gobbledygook. Still, they'd all become better at Ktor, thanks to him.

But he had a new problem: no assignment, not since all the "acclimatization" cases he'd been helping had disappeared. Vat suspected they'd been frozen again. The only Lost Soldiers left on the habitat were either working in their specialties, recovering from injuries after battles on R'Bak, or part of his motley crew. He kept his head down, but sooner or later, Murphy would catch up with him.

"What do you think Murphy will do with us?" Taiki asked, seemingly reading Vat's mind as Vat shuffled the deck between hands. "He seemed anxious last time I see him." Taiki had spoken in Japanese, like he usually did when he wasn't thinking about it, so Vat repeated the question in slow, clearly pronounced Ktor for the others' benefit.

"You have these atomic bombs, no?" Komatsu asked. Vat nodded. "Use them on this planet and be done with it."

"We need the planet," Vat explained again. "As well as some of the assets stashed there. It's a fall back and resupply location while the attack is going on elsewhere in the galaxy." It was three-quarters bullshit, but it sure *sounded* cool.

"Better someone else dying than us," Lech said in Ktor. This time they all nodded.

The game broke up when most of the *chaat* had been won or drunk. Vat left and wandered the corridors carved from space rock. His mind worked furiously. Every day that went by meant it was increasingly likely that his hand would be forced. Vat had gotten away with his trade for as long as he had without letting his hand get forced. *Always have options,* were his watchwords.

Not paying attention to where he was going, Vat ended up in one of the busy operational areas where they were staging ships deploying to R'Bak's surface. A dozen large storage rooms were being used to store the Lost Soldiers' equipment. He'd spent a fair amount of time there, talking with other Lost Soldiers, and "finding" certain things. He hadn't intended to end up there, but he decided to take a look around. Just on general principles.

On a large pallet lashed together with Vietnam-era cordage, he spotted a case which instantly got his attention. He felt a wide smile growing as he glanced around. He was alone, which wasn't unusual since it was late in the day by habitat time. The small space-bound human contingent was eating and relaxing prior to the sleep cycle.

After another quick glance around the area, he dug a small knife out of his pocket and made a couple of quick cuts. Then he heard the shouts. He made the knife disappear and walked to the storage room doorway. Four people were yelling at each other while a woman held back, fear on her face. Two of the men appeared to be SpinDogs, the other two were Lost Soldiers.

What the hell?

Vat left the storage bay and slowly walked toward to the group. One of the SpinDogs was the first to spot him. The man's eyes narrowed, and Vat put his hands up, not wanting the already hostile encounter to turn violent.

The two Lost Soldiers wore WWII-era uniforms and appeared to be fully or partly Asian. As he got closer, he recognized the Filipino being spoken by natives. The standardized version of Tagalog had a distinctive cadence he found particularly easy to pick up.

"We should kill these ancient relics!" one of the two SpinDogs said, his Ktor fast and clipped, the way they spoke when they didn't want anyone else to understand them, especially humans. Vat understood enough Ktoran that this tactic no longer worked with him, not that he let on during his wanderings.

"There are few of them remaining," the other said. "We could be tangling with a batang without realizing it."

The first one scoffed.

"Are they crazy or something?" one of the Filipino men asked the other.

"Must be. We should go." He switched to Ktor. "We go."

"Where do you think you're going, relic?" the first SpinDog snapped. "To find more women to harass?" He reached out and gave the soldier a shove.

Quick as a flash, both Lost Soldiers produced knives and moved far enough apart to avoid getting in each other's way. Vat knew from his time in the Philippines that the hand-to-hand combat training they got was first rate. Not ones to be intimidated, the SpinDogs likewise produced blades. The woman shouted for both sides to stop, but if anything, that just made everyone more agitated.

Vat moved in fast, taking a desperate chance by interposing himself between the two groups. It was impossible to keep an eye on all four blades, and the intensity on their faces left little doubt that this was seconds from turning lethal. *What the fuck are you doing?* he wondered. His personal credo was simple: *Never get between potential customers when they are about to throw down.*

"Hey, easy," he said in Filipino. "My friends." Quickly he switched to the same form of Ktor the SpinDogs were using. "This is not the time to fight."

"What do you want, human?" one of the SpinDogs snapped. "Are you here to help these two eye-bleeders?" The two Filipinos cocked their heads, trying to understand, but their meager Ktor wasn't up to the task. The woman stood behind the two men, her hand on the shoulder of the older one; the fear had not left her eyes.

"I am on the side of peace," Vat said in Ktor and bowed his head slightly. He held up his hands to show he was unarmed. The Ka-Bar he was using moments ago would not be visible unless he really needed it.

"Peace?" the second SpinDog asked, then pointed to one of the soldiers. "That one made a disgusting offer to the Primus' daughter!"

Daughter of a Primus. Shit, Vat thought. *But...a disgusting offer?* "May I speak to these men for one minute?"

"So you can see if their offer is attractive to you, instead?" the SpinDog demanded.

"No, so I can understand what happened."

"We told you what happened!" the other SpinDog yelled.

"There are multiple languages involved. You must realize many of us do not speak Ktor well."

"You speak well," the first one said. Despite the anger in his voice, Vat could see that though his words had not defused the situation, perhaps the men were a little calmer.

"Then let me talk to these other men," he repeated. The SpinDog gave a single brief nod, allowing Vat to give the two humans his complete attention. "These two men are upset," he said in Tagalog.

"We figured as much," the older of the two said. "But we don't know why. They went insane when we spoke to the young woman."

"You did speak to her, then?" They both nodded. "Did you know she is the daughter of a Primus, a leader here? It is inappropriate to interact with her."

"We did not know this," the younger man said, appalled. "We meant no disrespect."

"What did you say?" Vat asked.

"We said she is a lovely woman and asked her name," the older man said. "We did not see her escorts—they were down the corridor and around the corner."

Vat's eyes narrowed as he considered. "You spoke in Ktor, of course?"

"Of course," the younger man said. "We learned from the sleeping machines."

Vat nodded. "Can you repeat exactly what you said? Exactly."

The older man shook his head, obviously not understanding how it mattered, and yet he did just as Vat asked him. Vat instantly realized the problem.

"What you said, inadvertently of course, is this: 'You have a pretty body. Will you take my name?'"

"My God," the younger man gasped.

"It is not what we said!" the older man said.

Vat explained the particularities of tenses and possessives in Ktoran. "It is the kind of thing you pick up after time," he said. "Many coming back from the surface have learned to do it naturally. You haven't seen many locals, have you?"

"No," the older man admitted. "We only speak Ktoran with other Lost Soldiers for ease of translation."

"As I thought."

"How do we fix this?" the younger man asked, glancing at the girl then looking away, his face reddening.

"Let me," Vat said, and turned to the SpinDogs. "I am sorry; there was a terrible mistake. This is what these men *meant* to say." He said the phrase correctly. "While it might have been improper for them to address the lady, it was not meant as an improper solicitation."

The two SpinDogs listened, and Vat saw them visibly relax. The explanation was simple and offered earnestly. He spoke slowly so the two Filipino soldiers could follow along. Out of the corner of his eye he saw them nod when he explained their meaning and the mistake.

"This is true, then?" the older SpinDog asked. Both human soldiers nodded. "Then no harm has been done." He looked at the two men. "I suggest you practice the language and avoid unaccompanied women."

The Lost Soldiers nodded solemnly, and the SpinDogs left with the young woman.

"Thank you," the older soldier said. "We didn't want to spill their blood."

"Not a problem," Vat said, glancing toward the storage room. The two Lost Soldiers left, and he turned back to the storage room.

"That was interesting."

He spun around to see Major Murphy standing a short distance away. The older man was watching him from the shadows, an appraising look on his face.

"Just a friendly disagreement," Vat said. "No big deal."

"I was looking for you," Murphy said. "We need to talk."

"Sure," Vat said. With a last, longing look at the storage bay, he followed Murphy.

Chapter Fifty-Nine

SPIN ONE

"Have a seat," Murphy said, and gestured to one of the two simple chairs at his desk. Several modern computer tablets sat on the desk. Vat glanced at them, then at Murphy, who'd settled into his chair and appeared to be thinking.

"What do you need?" Vat asked.

"I need you to be useful."

"Wasn't what I did back there useful?"

"Useful? Sure. Intentional? I doubt it." Vat started to speak, but Murphy cut him off. "Vat, you aren't fooling me."

"Sorry, fooling you?"

"I know you've been helping yourself to things. Oh, don't look offended. The SpinDogs' tech might not be impressive compared to the Dornaani, but it's enough to have cameras everywhere."

Shit.

"I let you play your games because I was hoping something would come out of it which I could use to put you to work."

"You already do."

"That's make-work, and you know it. I can't assign you anything that requires you to risk your precious hide because you'll weasel out of it. And maybe leave a good soldier or two twisting in the wind when you do."

"So this is your solution? Entrapping me?"

"Call it what you will, Vat. I have to use every tool at my disposal to do this job." For a moment Vat thought Murphy looked far older than he was. "I kept track of everyone's language training. All the hours logged, by every Lost Soldier. Both in the Dornaani virtuality language simulator and later refreshers. Almost from the very start, one person stood out. One Victor Allen Thomas…with a grand total of *zero* hours."

Vat shrugged, and he thought he could see a vein bulging on Murphy's forehead.

"So that's why I was looking for you: to give you an ultimatum."

"Then why don't you give it to me?"

"I'll give you an indefinite vacation in a windowless cell, if you give me any more lip," Murphy said in a chilly voice Vat hadn't heard before. "So, I went looking for you. I found you in the midst of your little encounter."

"How much of it did you see?"

"I was right behind you when it started."

"Ah."

"You could have just walked away," Murphy said. "Instead you walked into the middle of a potential knife fight. That alone surprised me because it didn't fit your psychological profile." Vat snorted. "Don't hold much stake in those profiles?"

"No. Do you?"

Murphy laughed; another first. "Actually, I don't either. They do, however, offer a useful snapshot of the individual, if you don't get obsessed with the details. At least from my experience. Anyway, I was a second from stepping in when you pulled a rabbit out of your hat." He looked Vat in the eye. "How did you learn Ktor so well?"

Vat shrugged again.

"Mister Thomas, this is your come-to-Jesus moment. I'll lay it out as simply as possible. You can either become part of what we're doing here and help—"

"I've been helping—" Vat started.

"Shut up!"

Vat closed his mouth.

"You've been helping yourself, is what you've been doing. Now: you can either help out with everything you've got, and I mean full commitment, or…"

"Or what? Gonna put me back in the freezer like the other PreBooms who haven't adapted?"

Murphy's smile looked as cold as February in Romulus, Michigan. "What makes you think any of them went back into cryostasis?"

"Then what…?" Vat trailed off, blinking. *No, he couldn't—he* wouldn't*—do that.*

"We're in space, Vat. Options are limited, as are resources. As wonderful and charming as you are, I don't have time for you if I can't utilize your skillset."

"I have a natural skill with language," Vat admitted.

"Nothing in your file mentions that, not in education or military service."

"Because I didn't study languages. I tried, in high school."

Murphy tapped on his pane of glass. "Yes, I see a D in French."

"Yes, that's it. I've always been good at figuring out dialects. Detroit has a lot of immigrants. I figured it would translate into book learning. I was wrong. What classwork taught me is to avoid talking about how I pick up languages."

"Came in handy selling arms, didn't it?" Murphy held up the tablet showing Vat's NSA arms license under yet another name. "You were working it seven ways to Tuesday. Legal contractor under your real name, travel permits to war zones under one alias, ITAR permits under another. You were in Somalia to sell anti-aircraft missiles to the warlords."

"How long have you known?"

"I knew you were one step ahead of arrest before you were thawed out. The Dornaani computers are very efficient."

Vat shook his head. "I don't get it. Why bother letting me fuck around up here for weeks if you knew what I did and who I was?"

"Because our mission on this planet requires all sorts of talents, all sorts of people." He gave Vat a wintry half grin. "Even your sort." He looked at his computer then back up at Vat. "We're making inroads on R'Bak, but not as quickly as we'd hoped. The main problem is that we haven't found all the weapons and equipment caches we know are there. And shortly after the satraps figured out that we're here and we're dangerous, they got busy activating them. So we're falling behind achieving force parity at the same time that they're stepping us the speed with which they're completing their transmitter."

Vat stared. "And I figure into all this…how?"

"You have a way with people. Sure, both good and bad, but you knew how to use your special skills to cut deals, make alliances, and get what you want. Most people in your old profession don't fare well."

"Neither did I, in the end."

"You know, I'm not so sure you wouldn't have come out of that as well." Murphy shut off the clipboard-sized computer. "Go down to the surface of R'Bak, sniff around, see what you can find out from—and about—the R'Bakuu that we've missed."

"That's about as nebulous of a mission as you could give me."

"It's what I have. Will you do it, or not?" Murphy asked.

"Do I have a choice?"

"You always have choices."

Yeah, Vat thought, *bad and worse.* "Sure, I'll go on your scavenger hunt. I have to do it by myself?"

"No, take your four poker pals with you." Murphy reached into his desk, put a box on it, and slid it toward Vat.

Vat picked it up and opened it. Two silver bars were inside.

"You'll need those. I'm reinstating you as a first lieutenant."

"You have the authority to do that?" Murphy shrugged, and Vat laughed. "Why trust me with a commission?"

"Captain Lee talked to me. She seems to think you deserve a chance. So you get one." His face became as emotionless as a manikin's. "Just one."

The interface craft came to a stop. As soon as the engines cut out, the crew came forward to open hatches and prepare it for another flight. The air base was small but bustling, and Vat took a moment to take it all in.

The first thing he noticed was the heat; it was damn hot. Not humid hot like Georgia or Louisiana, but Phoenix hot. He looked up and shielded his eyes from the two stars blazing in the sky. One was similar in size to the star he grew up with, Sol, only orange. The other was much smaller and yellow-white. In the coming months, the small one would get closer and closer until it burned nearly every living thing off the planet's equatorial belt. *I'm on an alien planet,* he thought. A little smile crossed his face. *This is kinda cool.*

The patchy ground cover near the field was a strange shade of green, and the sky was not quite blue. By the sad look of the not-quite grass, it was already feeling the effects of the approaching Searing. A small flying insect went by, and he swatted at it, hoping R'Bak didn't have mosquitoes.

"Do you need a ride, Lieutenant?"

The man had to say it twice before Vat realized he was the lieutenant in question. He glanced at the bar sewn into the epaulets on the worn Vietnam-era camouflage duty uniform he was wearing. The only thing new was the nametape: Vat. He'd insisted on it instead of Thomas. He looked at the speaker, a kid no more than 25, with a decidedly Middle Eastern appearance—though no accent—who was driving some sort of box truck.

"Sure," he said. "Where's the FOB?"

"It's just past that point of land sticking out from the mountain," the kid said, pointing.

Vat got into the truck for the short drive. "You can just drop me off at the edge of camp," he said. "I'd like to get a feel for it."

"Sure," the kid said, and he drove to the base, humming the whole time.

The truck stopped at the first tent. "Anything else?" the kid asked.

"I'm fine, Corporal," he said. "Can you aim me at the recon tent?"

"Yes, sir. Go around the chuckwagon, and it's just past the showers."

"Thanks," he said. The corporal gave him a salute, which he returned, then the kid drove off.

The activity at the camp varied, depending on where you were.

The motor pool was nonstop busy. Vat didn't recognize any of the vehicles and guessed they were all local, taken from the satraps by Lost Soldiers. Mechanics and drivers were working and examining what looked like APC-Mad Max hybrids. Others were inventorying parts and stacking the strangely designed local fuel cans; they reminded him of hexagonal insect cells.

The field hospital was quiet. A few people were being treated for non-life-threatening conditions. One of the native healer women sat with a man, held his hand, and talked quietly. He'd love to have listened in to try and pick up the dialect; instead, he moved on.

At the far side of the camp were the helipads. A single helicopter that was vaguely reminiscent of a Blackhawk squatted on an expanded metal pad. Seeing the bird brought back memories and reminded him he was trillions of miles and over a hundred years from what he'd called home. The pilot was in the cockpit, and he wondered if was Mara before remembering she was flying Hueys. And he was pretty sure the pilot was a man.

He found the chuckwagon, a big truck which opened up into cooking and prep facilities for food. It was mid-afternoon, and it smelled like the crew was working on dinner. A big haunch of meat was hanging, and a local woman was filleting pieces from it. The section of animal had a tail as thick as a Burmese python.

Welcome to R'Bak.

Only a few meters farther were the showers, constructed of plastic-coated tarps and wooden frames. The plumbing looked weirdly resinous, and the stalls were all empty.

Finally, he reached his destination. A line of Vietnam-era tents with "Recon Country" spray painted on one. The sound of someone yelling in Russian gave him his final bearing. When he reached the tent, he found Artyom and Lech in a shoving match; they stood inches apart and yelled so intensely that spittle was flying.

"*What in the cursed afterlife is going on here?*" he yelled in Ktoran. While they probably didn't understood all of it, his command voice was sufficient to be recognized by the noncoms. All four of his crew came to attention, though Artyom and Lech glared at each other one more time before casting their eyes at him. Slowly, they all realized who he was.

"They cut your hair," Taiki said and smiled. "You look like an officer now."

"Murphy insisted," Vat said. He'd let it go way past his shoulders and the high-and-tight cut felt as strange as the bars.

"Officer," Artyom snorted. "Naturally."

"I was this rank in the army," Vat pointed out. "At ease, you idiots." They smirked and relaxed. Based on the pitiful attempt of at-attention from Artyom and Lech, it was probably just as well Murphy didn't hold a lot of stock in proper military decorum, outside of haircuts. "Murphy gave me my commission back. I left the Army five years ago. I guess I'm back in it now." He repeated it in Japanese, then Russian. Lech was passable in Russian, so he nodded, understanding.

"Seems like we never left," Lech said. Artyom nodded; whatever he'd been arguing about with the Polish man seemed forgotten. Judging by the ration packs and dice scattered on the floor, Vat could guess what was going on.

"When they brought us all down, we knew you must be involved," Sam said and grinned. "What kind of an angle are you working?"

"No angle, just working." They all laughed, but he held up a hand. "Murphy pretty much told me we needed to work, or we're gone."

"Gone where? Back to outer space?" Sam asked.

"Think about it," Vat said. They all stared at him, uncomprehending. He mimed opening and closing a door, then holding his breath.

"My God," Taiki said in Japanese.

"Did he threaten to throw us into space?" Lech demanded.

"Not explicitly," Vat replied then shrugged. "He didn't have to. He just said we need to get to work or something might happen to us."

"Are we to fight?" Artyom asked. Despite his bearish appearance and the well-known Russian temperament for being willing to punch you in the face, he wasn't a fan of being shot at. He was more of a shoot first, then shoot second kind of guy. Most of them were.

"We're going to do some recon."

"So, they shoot at us?" Artyom asked.

"Hopefully, nobody shoots at us, and we don't have to shoot them. You know the main mission here?" They all nodded, and Vat explained how their group was tasked with locating unfound caches and making advanced contact with villages that might be sympathetic.

"I understand why you would be good with this mission," Sam said. "You can speak a dozen languages, and you understand Ktor better than anyone I know, but what about us?" He waved at the four of them and the tent they'd been assigned.

"Well," Vat said, delaying a second, "you are here in case someone shoots at me."

"I knew it," Artyom said.

They all nodded, and Vat sighed.

Chapter Sixty

R'BAK

Vat pulled his boots on—Vietnam-era army surplus like everything else he wore—and walked to the door of his tent. As an officer, he was assigned a smallish tent that he only had to share with another guy that was never there. It seemed a luxury until you realized it held his cot, a locker for gear, and a desk, along with the various equipment he needed as a small unit commander. Once everything was factored in, he had less personal space than those in his command.

Pulling aside the flap allowed the early morning light to flood in. The orange-hued sun was already a thumb's width above the low hills in the distance, and the temperature was climbing fast. He'd been sweating in bed half the night. It only cooled off well after midnight, though the planetary clock didn't follow the 24-hour cycle he was used to.

After more than a week on the planet, he'd yet to completely adapt to the 18-hour days. Most of the Lost Soldiers stuck to twelve or thirteen hours awake, and slept for five or six. He'd decided on twelve and six. He always felt a little tired, though maybe it was lessening.

Hot was the norm on most of R'Bak. Unlike Earth, there were no icecaps, so it went from really hot in the equatorial region to warm temperate at the poles. When the second sun approached, the equatorial band would be uninhabitable, although there were rumors that people survived there, even at the height of the Searing, and had for generations.

"Those hidden tribes, or whatever they are, may be the key," Murphy had told him. "Find them, make allies of them. At least find out how they've survived, and you'll have paid your way."

"Easier said than done," he said as he yawned and stretched. A group of indig recruits ran by, following a cadence set by a DI at least twice their age. He grinned. *Things could be worse.*

He followed his nose toward the chuckwagon. The smell of lemony eggs and the local equivalent of bacon was carried on the wind. He'd never asked where it came from, and, frankly, he didn't want to know. As he passed between lines of tents, a chuffing sound warned him whinnies were nearby. He made a face and stopped as a team of the big Komodo dragon-looking things moved past with riders on their backs.

"Afternoon, Lieutenant," the team leader said.

"Captain Moorefield," Vat said with a nod. The rider and his people grinned at Vat, knowingly.

Vat scowled until they were past. Riding horses had been popular in his circle growing up in Michigan. Everyone who was anyone went out to the stables in the surrounding counties every spring and took riding lessons. He'd resisted it until he was twelve when his aunt insisted. In front of all his friends and the riding instructors, Vat was thrown and landed in a giant heap of horseshit.

He hadn't liked the great hairy, stinking beasts from the moment he'd laid eyes on them. The animals likely sensed his disquiet and reciprocated the sentiment. The instructor insisted horses could sense fear. Vat wasn't afraid of them; he just didn't like them. Either way, as humiliated as he was, he never went back.

Naturally, his first recon out to meet a band of passing locals was with Captain Moorefield and his team. It didn't help that Moorefield was incredibly handsome and knew it. The whinnies, for all their resemblance to giant lizards, were a lot like horses. Too much, in Vat's opinion. He'd been distracted and barely managed his beast, falling off not once but twice.

The boys didn't care. Taiki had even less experience riding and still took to it right away. Sam had ridden as a kid and loved the lizards. Artyom and Lech managed well enough. Vat was in the unenviable position of being in command of his unit and simultaneously the worst rider.

"I'd happily take Private Komatsu off your hands," Moorefield said afterward.

"Leave my team alone, Captain," Vat growled as he limped away. His ass had hurt for days. His ego still ached.

Once Moorefield and his patrol had passed, Vat continued to the chuckwagon. Fifty or so Lost Soldiers and local volunteers were in clusters around it, eating, talking, and joking. He found the boys sitting together, as usual. Today they were all making eyes at a pair of local women who were trying to ignore the attention, though only halfheartedly.

"You guys having fun?" he asked. All four heads turned toward him, grinning. Their Ktoran had improved quickly over the last few weeks of work. Having so many locals around helped, of course.

"These Ktor women is pretty," Artyom said, gesturing with his head toward the pair. "They are fun to lie with, too."

"They are," Lech agreed. Taiki shrugged and Sam looked a little embarrassed. Artyom saw Vat was looking at the girls, too, and elbowed Lech. They nodded knowingly.

Vat ignored the boys' interplay; he was listening carefully to the two women talking. They were probably sure he couldn't hear them over all the dozens of conversations ten meters away. Along with his natural ability to quickly learn languages, Vat had also developed the handy trait of filtering out any noises he didn't want to hear. In essence, he heard the women as well as if he was sitting at the same table.

"The outworlders are winning," one woman said.

"They are winning for now," said the other, holding up a finger as if she were holding off a negative fate. They both spoke with the regional R'Bak dialect of Ktoran common in this area. Vat had, thus far, identified eleven separate flavors of R'Bakuun Ktor, all distinctly different from the version used by the RockHounds, which was also different from the SpinDogs. The more time he spent among these people, the more it reminded him of Russia with its many regional dialects, though still close enough to understand each other. Several waves of Ktoran exodates had melded over millennia to create a linguistic hodgepodge similar to colonial English, while also resembling central-use Russian.

"Grandmother will not listen," the second one continued. "She says even these outworlders will not stand against the satraps, and when the Kulsians arrive, they will be slaughtered."

My worry exactly, Vat thought. Kulsis might not have super-advanced tech like the Dornaani or the genuine Ktor, but they had resources, numbers, and local reinforcements to back them up. The Lost Soldiers had no reinforcements. The SpinDogs said they would help, but Vat wasn't confident of their assistance if it came down to a real war. The space-based inhabitants had survived there for centuries by running and hiding, not by fighting.

"What is she going to do?" the first girl asked. "Your hetman listens to her."

Vat had come to understand that the hetmen were tribal leaders in this society. However, they listened to their elder women, the moral compasses for their clans and villages. You didn't go against one of those matriarchs without taking a chance. She could pull in favors from her supporters and there might be a new hetman. Of course, not every tribe worked the same way. Yeah, it was a *lot* like rural Russia in the 17th century.

"She says we will go to the Daaj."

Vat's ears perked up. He didn't know what the Daaj was, and he'd never heard the term before. There were hundreds of words and specific terms in regard to their dialects, but this was of a particular category he'd tentatively categorized as non-conforming. They didn't match the structure of Ktoran.

The first time he'd heard such a word he put it down to an aberration. All languages had them; hell, English was practically made up of them. Words stolen from other languages, words morphed into words that didn't even sound like their original.

The only problem was that 55 Tauri was an isolated system that had never had contact with anyone but the Ktor. Successive waves of exiles—the formal term was "Exodates"—had come from the distant home worlds but they were all just more Ktor.

If he understood their cultural norms, major deviations in language wouldn't have been tolerated. So where had 'Daaj' come from?

"The Daaj is just a dream," the second woman said. "Nobody even knows what it is. Not in my mother's mother's mother's time."

The first woman shrugged. "You know Ooshwelo; she has always known what she knows." The other woman grunted and, much to Vat's frustration, got up and left.

"They are beautiful, yes?" Artyom asked and poked Vat in the ribs.

He looked at the Russian, perplexed until the other waggled his shaggy eyebrows meaningfully. So he thought Vat had been staring at the women because he found them attractive? Really? Vat grunted and closed his eyes a second, committing the women's facial features to memory. He had to talk to someone later. Without commenting to Artyom, he started eating. The others looked at him, confused, then returned to their banter.

After he'd seen to his men and made sure they weren't involved in any shenanigans he'd have trouble undoing, Vat made his way to the base coordinator's tent and looked up the "local liaison specialist." A pretty-sounding euphemism for HUMINT analyst/wrangler. Vat described the two women he'd seen and listened to.

"Yes, I know them. Miizhaam and Salsaliin. They're with one of the tribes that supply whinnies to us."

"Good," Vat said. "Give me everything you've got on their tribe."

Chapter Sixty-One

R'BAK

It was probably inevitable that he ended up saddled on a whinnie again. Vat was just glad the patrol wasn't under command of Captain Moorefield. Instead it was a second lieutenant named Roberts. Like Corporal Potts, he was a WWII-era soldier and had been taken at the Battle of the Bulge. Roberts had been with the 2nd Infantry Division, so the two hadn't known each other before awakening, but Potts showed no interest in Roberts or any of the other Bulge survivors. He kept to himself.

The other ten men in Roberts' command were from various eras; also uninteresting. Rather, Vat spent what time he could talking with the two women accompanying them. Each night they made camp, using Vietnam-era tents and cooking on tin mess kits. He never told Miizhaam and Salsaliin that he had overheard their earlier conversation, but between riding the damned smelly lizards across increasingly patchy plains of wilted ground cover and camping each night, he talked with them, getting details about their family.

Theirs was one of the oldest tribes in the area, claiming to have roots back a thousand years. Of course, the further you got from the poles, the more havoc the Searing caused. The Kulsians' success was owed in part to R'Bak's entire civilization experiencing a hard reset every three generations or so. And since that was also when the "Harvesters" arrived to rape, pillage, and "cull" the locals, technological development had been taking two steps back for every two steps forward for centuries. How many, Vat had yet to figure out.

The only problem he'd encountered was Salsaliin. She'd taken a shine to him and wasn't trying to hide it. She'd catch his eye every chance she got, look over her shoulder at him, and she'd even rubbed a breast against his arm last night at dinner. *What am I going to do about this?*

"The Ka-whores who stole us are bitches," Artyom said from his whinnie. "Locals say they are crazy killers."

Vat glanced back from his position, just behind point. The others in his team nodded in agreement even though several were sleeping with the locals.

"They like to kill," Taiki agreed. "They don't care about people. We know their type; they started war with America."

Vat agreed. Everything he'd heard about the Ktor from Murphy and had since read in the briefings confirmed they were real scumbags. Their ancestors had been taken from Earth some time in the distant past—nobody seemed to know exactly when—by a galactic power-player that was no longer around, for reasons unknown. Maybe they'd been grabbed for labor, maybe as the ultimate fighting force? Whatever the reason, they were eventually left on their own, grew into a power, and found a way to sneak back to Earth to follow in their masters' footsteps and start stealing more humans.

Around and around we go, where we stop, nobody knows.

Thunder rumbled across the plains. Far to the west, one of the rare storms was moving parallel to their path. They never seemed to deliver any rain, just lightning high up in the sky and thunder rolling down.

"Where is this first village, Lieutenant?" Corporal Potts asked from behind.

"About five klicks ahead," Vat answered. As he pointed to a notch between two hills, he noticed smoke curling into the sky. More than you'd expect from a couple campfires. "Lieutenant Roberts!"

"Yes, Lieutenant Thomas?"

"Smoke, in our direction of travel."

"Shit," Roberts said. He urged his whinnie into a low-bellied run. "Double-time!"

Vat gave the reins a little flip and made a clicking sound. The damned lizard turned its head and looked at him reproachfully. "Look, I don't like it any more than you do, but let's hurry it up." It gave a chortling sound and kept pace with the rest of the detachment.

As the column raced up the hill, the cavalry patrol began readying weapons. Having been among the last to be equipped, they didn't get the Viet Nam gear that had been the Ktoran standard issue to the Lost Soldiers. Nor did they get the knock-offs the SpinDogs were making, but which had been bumped down the list of cargo priorities. Vat and his men had to pick from the few remaining odds and ends. Artyom had grabbed not one, but two AK-47s. Taiki didn't find any Japanese rifles, so he'd settled for a Mosin Nagant and a Colt 1911. Lech had gone with an MP-40/Luger combo, and Sam discovered a scoped M1 Garand and picked up a 1911, to stay with what he knew.

Vat wasn't much on long arms. He'd qualified on the M-16, of course. However, there weren't any available, so he ended up with a Thompson. He liked .45 ACP. "Hit something, it goes down." However, the absence of his once-beloved Glock 26 hurt. The 1911 was a piss-poor substitute. The armorer glared when Vat helped himself to a dozen magazines for each weapon. At least he had uniform ammo, which was probably the same thing Artyom and Lech had been thinking.

Wherever they'd acquired the lizards, the same source had worked up tack as well. The saddles were equipped with holsters and places to attach infantry packs or web gear. His Thompson fit well in the holster after a simple retention strap was added. As the whinnie raced along with its weird serpentine gait, Vat looked at the gun indecisively. Everyone else had their long arm cross-body, ready to use as they rode. He simply wasn't confident enough in the saddle. *Damn it.* Now he wished he hadn't quit the riding classes so many years ago.

The detachment, with Lieutenant Roberts at its head, crested the ridge five minutes after Vat first saw the smoke. Everyone spread out to look at the village below. Some of the settlement was at the bottom of a shallow valley obscured by another low hill. A few huts were visible, and one was burning.

"The village!" Salsaliin cried out, pointing into the valley. "It must be the J'Stull."

"Why?" one of Roberts' men wondered. "They don't attack villages, only tribal camps."

Roberts looked at Vat who returned the gaze. The same thought ran between them. *We have a mole in our camp.* The satrap's forces hadn't messed with the Sarmatchani who lived in permanent villages because they likely didn't know or didn't suspect that stationary tribes might risk retribution for helping the unknown off-worlders. Maybe their cover story was blown.

There was no sound except the rumble of the distant thunderstorm. Vat looked toward the clouds and saw the storm was getting closer. Maybe it would be a problem in a few hours after all.

Sam had his Garand up and was surveying the village through its scope. "I can't see any movement. That little hill is blocking the view."

"I'm taking my detachment down to assess the situation," Roberts announced. "Take your team to the north," he said to Vat, pointing. "The road leads toward the J'Stull's area of operations. Scout it and report."

"Lieutenant, is it wise to split up our forces?" Vat asked. A first lieutenant, Roberts was in operational command. On the other hand, while Vat wasn't a combat officer, his training had included small-unit tactics for use against the insurgent-style adversaries of the 90s.

The younger man considered for a second, then looked at Vat's "team." Unfortunately, he was clearly making a decision based on appearance, not ability. Vat would put his hardened crew up against any of Roberts' men in any situation except the parade ground.

"Your people aren't as used to the whinnies," Roberts decided. "Riding and shooting is the trick. Please take your people to scout and cover the enemy's possible line of attack. If the opportunity presents itself, set up an ambush."

Vat considered again for a second before nodding. It didn't seem like the best tactical decision, but he deferred to Roberts' rank and experience. "Okay. Sir."

"Please take the local women with you," Roberts added, looking toward the village. "It's more likely we'll see combat than you."

After taking a moment to check weapons, Roberts and his detachment whisked off down the slope on their whinnies. Their mounts yipped and hissed with the excitement of just running.

"Okay, let's get a move on," Vat said. "We need to get to the road ASAP in case they need help."

"In the rear with the gear," Sam said.

"Dis is saying with Americans, too?" Artyom wondered.

"I think it is with any military," Vat said as they turned their whinnies toward the distant road.

Getting to the road wasn't as easy as Vat thought it would have been. Despite being able to see where it was, the ridgeline separating them from it was far too steep to ride along, so they had to go around it. It would have been easier to approach from the side that faced back toward the valley and the village, but anyone watching the slope would have spotted them.

The far side of the hill was rocky and treacherous, partly made up of several scree fields in which even the surefooted whinnies struggled to maintain their footing. Miizhaam and Salsaliin took the lead, being experienced on the reptilian mounts, and the rest fell in behind them. With everyone busy controlling their whinnies, Vat didn't have to worry about them noticing him hanging on for dear life.

Gunshots echoed over the hills, the rifle reports bouncing around the crags above them.

Vat glanced up unconsciously and ground his teeth. The whole purpose of riding days out into the plains was to talk to village elders, gain intel, and maybe get clues to locations of Kulsian caches watched and now tapped by raider-directed satraps. His side mission was to learn more about the non-conforming language elements which might lead to the mysterious Daaj. He resisted urging the whinnie on faster, knowing it wasn't a good idea. Halfway across a particularly bad section of crumbling scree, Vat's whinnie cast an eye back at him.

"What?" Vat asked. He swore the lizard almost sighed as it found its own way through the debris field. After a couple more echoing shots, the shooting stopped.

"Guess the fight is over," Artyom yelled back at him. "Good. I had enough of people shooting at me at Stalingrad."

They reached the other side of the valley without losing anyone or any of their equipment. The seven whinnies stood breathing hard for a short time on the road, which was just dirt, hard packed from routine use. It ran in from the north and over the hill to the village south of them.

"What now?" Artyom asked. Thunder rolled through the air, surprisingly closer.

"We need to set up a position for an ambush," Vat said and examined the rock outcroppings near the road where it cut through the hill.

"Better get set up before the storm gets here," Lech pointed out as the rumbling got louder.

"Isn't the storm to the west?" Sam asked.

Vat looked south in confusion as the rumble crested the ridge, and a pair of big trucks rolled into view. Then the shooting started.

Chapter Sixty-Two

R'BAK

At his first glimpse of the trucks, Vat's thought was of their utility. Just like the ones in camp, they all had a boxy look, a little like the transports used by Russia in his era. *Maybe to load them into spaceships?* The backs even had fabric or leather tarping to cover them. *Maybe form follows function on any world? It's amazing the stupid shit your brain comes up with when you're about to die.*

Vat felt like he had an hour to notice details. The windshield was clear glass, no tint, and also had no angle to it, unlike terrestrial trucks. There were two occupants in the front. The driver caught his eye. He was blond with blue eyes that were wide with surprise. A second later, a bullet shattered the windshield and punched through the unknown man's forehead.

Vat wasn't a combat vet. He'd been shot at, but not as a soldier. Disgruntled customers had tried to kill him, but his solution had always been escape, evasion, or just avoid the situation entirely. However, with the exception of Taiki, his guys *were* combat vets. They'd learned that most important lesson of battles: the ones who shot first were often the winners.

Though Artyom may have been unfamiliar with the specifics of the lesson, he clearly understood the practicality. The single shot from his AK-47 had been perfectly on-target, as proven by the fate of the first truck's driver. Lech was a half a step behind his friend and put a long, ragged burst of 9mm from his MP-40 through the windshield from left to right. Both the passenger and the already-dead driver were hit several times.

Sam fired a single, booming 30-06 round from his Garand past the truck. Vat assumed the paratrooper was firing at the second one, which he couldn't see.

That brief flurry of gunfire was followed by a chorus of shouts and screams, both from the trucks and his own people. It broke Vat out of his momentary shock, bringing back his small-unit tactical training. "Get off the road!" he yelled. Taiki and the two local women immediately spun their whinnies, which leaped up and over the rocks lining the road. Lech and Sam followed suit. Artyom laughed, switched to full-auto, and dumped a mag into the lead truck.

Vat's whinnie was confused by his rider's mixed signals. Vat had learned from Moorefield that the lizards were incredibly intuitive, even intelligent to a degree, and took implied directions from their riders. Vat was trying to unlimber his Thompson while simultaneously pulling the reins to the left in order to lead the animal off the road, thereby screwing up everything.

As Vat got his weapon clear and raised it to provide cover for Artyom, the whinnie wheeled left, jerking toward the side of the road. Vat was catapulted from the saddle. "Shit!" He grunted as he hit the ground and rolled. He had just enough presence of mind to keep the gun away from his face. The weapon's magazine jammed him *hard* in the ribs and a sharp rock cut his left arm, even through the heavy fatigue jacket.

People began pouring out of the lead truck as Vat sprawled to a stop. A few wild shots zipped through the air around him. Artyom's magazine ran dry and he rocked a new one into place.

"Damn it, Artyom! We're supposed to be capturing assets, not filling them full of holes!"

The second truck tried to pull off the roadway. Its front wheel mounted one of the large rocks lining the packed dirt, but the bottom of the chassis didn't have enough clearance; metal barked as the stone shrugged it off and sent it bouncing back into the roadway toward the rear of the stationary and now smoking first truck.

Bullets flew. Vat crawled painfully toward a rock only half his size as his whinnie pranced away, sending a reproachful look over its shoulder. Artyom finished dumping his second magazine into the first truck, running dry just as the second one rear-ended it.

The truck's dead driver had never set the brake, so the bump pushed the vehicle over the crest of the hill and it started rolling down…toward Vat's team. Bullets whizzed past as the big Russian, eyes still on the truck, casually stepped to the side, reloading as he moved. The smoking truck slowly rolled through the space he had occupied seconds before.

As it passed him, survivors began jumping out the back. Some of them were armed and shooting at anything they saw; others were empty-handed and ran for their lives. Vat was surprised any were still alive after 60 rounds of 7.62x39mm Commbloc. Then he saw that the sides were made of steel, which showed dozens of bright impact points, but few penetrations.

Artyom, who had finished reloading, kneeled and sprayed bullets at both groups of survivors. One of them managed to jump clear, get his bearings, and raised his gun toward the Russian.

Vat didn't stop to think; he brought up his Thompson, flipped off the safety, and fired. The selector was on full-auto. The man targeting Artyom took four rounds in the abdomen and chest; he was dead before he hit the ground. Vat swallowed around a dry mouth. Vat had fired Thompsons before—a friend had owned several—so he knew what to expect, but this wasn't like shooting paper targets. Not at all.

The rolling truck slammed to a stop against a boulder. More men poured out of the back. Vat's people were fully engaged now, firing singly or in pairs at anyone they saw. It was easy to distinguish Artyom's and Lech's weapons from Sam's Garand, with the roar of Taiki's Mosin Nagant adding an occasional, sharp exclamation point to the gunbattle. He was unable to discern the reports of the women's breech-loading rifles from those of the enemy. Vat fired several more times: detect a target, fire, acquire a new target, fire. He lost count and soon his magazine was empty. He reloaded.

There were bodies everywhere. At least ten men were running down the road, their weapons abandoned along the road. Vat was about to call for anyone left in the truck to surrender when Artyom, leaned over and threw a grenade into rear.

Where the hell did he get that? Vat wondered, his mouth hanging open in surprise. The grenade was not as loud as Vat expected, but it blew the fabric cover off the cargo compartment. No more men came out; there were only the screams of the wounded and dying.

"Stop shooting!" someone yelled.

Vat, still kneeling, turned. Up the hill was a pair of men. One had his arm around Miizhaam's neck and a pistol pointed at her head. The other was holding Salsaliin by her long, braided hair, her head pulled back, a knife at her throat. The arm holding the knife was bleeding freely from a long gash. Salsaliin's eye was swelling and turning black. It didn't take a detective to understand what had happened.

"Stop or we kill these bitches."

Only Artyom and Taiki were within view. One of Artyom's AK-47s was missing, but he started to raise the other.

"No, wait," Vat said. He lowered his own gun slightly. "This fight is over," he called to the man who had spoken. "Surrender."

"You are some of the thrice-slaves who've been attacking us! You use women? What kind of fools are you? All of you off-worlders will die."

"I really doubt that," Vat said.

The gunfire had stopped entirely, and he had no idea where Lech and Sam were, if they were even still alive. They must have finished off those in the second truck or the satrap troops would be rushing in. Taiki was on the far side of the ruined truck. Vat could see him feeding a new stripper clip into his ancient gun. They had the two upslope J'Stull in a crossfire…except there were hostages.

"Shoot the fool," Artyom said in Russian, so the satrap man couldn't understand.

"Nyet," Vat replied. "We could hit the women."

A hushed mutter in English announced, "I have a clean shot on the one with the knife."

Vat didn't turn his head. The voice was Sam's, nearby. Vat didn't know where he was hiding or how good he was with his rifle. Sam had been impressed with the new scope and practiced on the firing range with it, but 30-06 ammo was in short supply. How many rounds could he have expended in practice? And bull's-eyes at the range was no guarantee of pinpoint accuracy in a hostage situation.

He looked between the girls and hesitated, but Miizhaam caught his attention. She caught his eyes, then cast hers down. He followed their gaze; she had a knife in her hand, held low and out of the man's view. Once she knew he understood, she closed her eyes and nodded.

"Do it!" Vat barked in English.

The M1 Garand's 30-06 spoke from just behind him, near the other truck. The man holding Salsaliin jerked as his head exploded into a red mist; he fell limply. At the same time, Miizhaam doubled over, slamming her knife into her captor's thigh as her head cleared his pistol's muzzle.

The man screamed as she spun away. He started to track her, then reversed, raising the gun toward Vat and Artyom. They fired simultaneously; the man went backward and did not move.

Salsaliin was on her knees, her face in her hands, crying. Miizhaam took a couple wobbly steps then collapsed to her knees.

"Are you okay?" Vat asked Salsaliin. He was shaking so hard it took three tries to swap out the magazine in his Thompson. She nodded but didn't look up.

Artyom calmly walked over to the man they'd just killed, his body still twitching as blood pumped out. The Russian reloaded his AK-47, looked down at the body, then spat on it. *"Ublyudok."*

"Where did you get the damn grenade?" Vat asked.

Artyom took out a cigarette and lit it, then shrugged. "I won in card game." He shrugged again. "Thought it might…eh, come in handy." Vat was impressed, if also chagrined that one of the assets they had orders to secure was now a burning wreck.

Sam walked past the ruined truck, gun held low against his shoulder, looking for more targets, but there was no more screaming from the back. Vat shuddered as he realized it smelled a little like bacon.

Sam glanced at the wreck and shook his head. "Who had the grenade?"

"Who do you think?" Vat asked. Sam looked at Artyom, who grinned. Sam shook his head, bemused. "Taiki, you okay?" The man didn't reply. Vat walked around the burning truck and saw why; a bullet had found the Japanese man. He lay on his back staring into the strange alien sky, eyes wide. The bullet had torn out his jugular. He had probably died in seconds. "Fuck."

"We heard the shooting," Roberts called out as his patrol rode up the hill behind the surviving truck. Rather than soldiers, its cargo bed was filled with prisoners: ten young women from the village. "I guessed you'd run into them. Everyone okay?"

"No," Vat said. "Private Komatsu is dead. No other serious injuries." Sam was quietly applying a bandage to a cut on Miizhaam's arm while Artyom tended to the gouge in Vat's bicep.

"My whinnie bought it, too," Sam said, pointing to the motionless lizard a hundred meters off the road.

Considering how much gunfire there was, Vat was surprised more hadn't been hit. The pseudo-reptiles hadn't run off when the battle began, like horses might have. In fact, he noticed his own mount was eating something: one of the dead satrap troopers. *Oh fucking hell.*

Roberts dismounted and surveyed the slaughter. "What happened to that other truck?"

"I think it must have had some explosives in it," Vat lied. "It just blew up."

"Good ambush," Roberts complimented. "They had you at least five to one."

"Wasn't an ambush," Vat admitted. "We just rode into them. I guess we managed to act quicker."

One of Roberts' men was examining the burning truck for salvage. He came back with a bottle from the cab. It smelled of alcohol. Vat nodded; now it made more sense. The satrap forces had probably been drunk, or at least some of them.

"We got four prisoners from another truck," Roberts said. "Three of my men will take them back to basecamp in the vehicle."

"Ten more guys ran off that way," Vat said. "We going to get them?"

"No, it's not worth the risk. This terrain is perfect for ambushes. They're a long way from home, on foot. You said they're mostly unarmed?"

Vat nodded.

Roberts considered. "I'll only have seven men once I send those three back. I wouldn't normally want to be out here with so few." He looked over Vat and his three survivors with a new look in his eye. "Now I'm not so worried."

"Don't sell the women short," Vat said, and told Roberts what Miizhaam had done. "They're tough characters."

"I believe it. Even better, then. Let's get the women and salvage back to their settlement, and get my men sent off. It'll be night in a few hours; we might as well spend it at the village."

The village was ecstatic to have the young women back. Three of its men were killed in the raid and two huts burned. Despite the losses, they threw a party for Vat's and Roberts' soldiers. It turned out to be quite the shindig. There was music, dancing, and a fair amount of alcohol. As more of the latter came out, more clothes came off.

Vat wasn't interested in joining in. He buried Taiki on the hill where the raid took place. He would rest forever on a lonely hill, under an alien sun, trillions of miles from Earth. He guessed when the Searing came, his body would be burned to ash. He didn't know the Japanese man's beliefs, so Vat, alone, simply asked God to care for him.

Once he'd returned, Salsaliin tried to get him to dance and succeeded once. She was very energetic. The local dancing involved lots of body contact, grinding actually, and she was eager to teach him. He was eager for the dance to be over. An hour past sundown, once he was sure he'd shown enough respect for their hospitality, he retreated to where they had set up their tents.

Firelight from the celebration made exotic patterns against the shelter as he undressed and slid into the slightly musty sleeping bag. The planet was warm, even at night, so the bag was mostly to keep the bugs off and avoid the late-night chill that spiked just before dawn. He lay awake, staring at the peak of the tent for hours before his eyes slowly closed.

Something touched his foot and made his eyes snap open. He saw the outline of someone at his tent entrance, and his hand came away from the 1911 under the pillow of his bundled clothes. "Hello?"

"Greetings." It was Salsaliin. Her voice sounded odd.

"What can I do for you?" he asked.

"You saved my life."

"Corporal Potts did that. He was the one who fired the shot."

"Makes no difference." She turned slightly and closed the flap. The fire outside was still going, though it had dimmed, as had the festivities. When she turned back around, a naked breast was in perfect profile.

He sat up a little. "What are you doing?"

"Closing the tent," she said and pulled back the sleeping roll. He wasn't fast enough to stop her. There was little light, but enough for her to see he was naked. "Ahh, good," she said, and slid down next to him.

"This is a bad idea," he said, making more room for her without making it obvious he was pulling back.

"Why?"

"B-because I am an officer and—" her hand wrapped around him and made him jerk in surprise at the intimate contact. "Please, stop."

"You are nervous?" she purred into his ear. "Am I your first? You do not look that young."

Oh, if you only knew. "Yes," he said too quickly. "I didn't want it to be like this."

"You are not my first. This is good for a man, I think."

His mind froze as he tried to find a way out of the situation. Her mouth went to work, and he groaned, which she took to mean something else. Telling her the truth was too dangerous without knowing the social and cultural implications it had among their people. In short, he was trapped, and there was only one thing he could do.

Chapter Sixty-Three

R'BAK

They left the village early the next morning after Roberts sent a report to Murphy by relaying it to Camp Stark which then sent it to one of the Dornaani satellites. Included in the report were casualty counts as well as Roberts' intention to proceed. The satellite went below the horizon before Starkpatch got a reply.

The patrol climbed back out of the low valley and descended onto the plains again. The grasslands were broken up by rocky outcroppings that extended as far as the eye could see.

Sam and Lech both had the typical morning-after look you see on young people returning from leave; equal parts sexual gratification and hangover. It takes effort to look pleased with yourself and like your brain is about to explode at the same time.

Artyom just looked surly, as usual. This was despite a report of how he'd done his best to sleep with every female in the village and empty every container of alcohol available. The longer Vat spent around him, the more he doubted his first impression of the Russian.

"I thought you didn't like to fight?" Vat asked as the big man sat astride his whinnie in the early dawn.

"I don't," he replied. "That does not mean I am not good at it. I kill many Germans because I need to. So now I kill many Ka-whore allies because I need to." He shrugged and laughed. "I not get laid as much killing Germans; I think I like this place." Sam chuckled nearby from his new whinnie, provided by the villagers. They rode on for a few minutes before Artyom spoke again. "You do some laying yourself last night, *nyet*?."

Vat's felt his expression harden, and he nodded glumly. At the front of the column, Salsaliin was talking with her friend Miizhaam. The two laughed, then looked back at Vat who felt his face growing hot. Salsaliin looked slightly confused, but she smiled at him, and he gave the barest smile in return. He'd never had to work harder to have fun in his life than he had the previous night.

The women of the tribe had been extremely grateful for the Lost Soldiers' arrival. They'd expressed that gratitude to all the men with Roberts and Vat, some of them several times. He tried not to dwell on the mixed message of showing appreciation for being saved from a bunch of sexual predators by then giving the rescuers sex in return. *My species has issues.* Then he remembered how Salsaliin had felt under him, how different it was, yet somewhat the same, and sighed. *You're a fine one to talk.*

He'd spoken with the village hetman. He didn't know what a Daaj was. He thought he'd heard the word once from an old woman in another village, but he wasn't sure. Maybe it was a hiding place. The word also didn't have the same dialect feel as their version of Ktor. Nor of any other, for that matter.

It was like an itch Vat couldn't scratch.

By morning, he was sure there was no more to learn from the village, so they moved on. But as the kilometers slowly crept by, he found himself continually seeing Private Taiki Komatsu's spartan, unmarked grave on the ridgeline where he'd died.

Unable to shake the image, Vat took out the small data recorder Murphy had given him, the only high-tech item he had. Vat had recorded some of the hetman's speech, as well as others in the tribe. He passed the hours listening to them, comparing them. He overlaid recordings of Ktorans from the Dornaani archives. While he had no formal linguistics training, he had his own shorthand for the elements of language. He made notes, slowly isolating elements of Ktoran and how it compared to the version spoken on R'Bak.

Before they stopped for their midday meal, Sam moved his whinnie next to Vat's and got his attention. "Whatcha doing,

Lieutenant? I see you've been wearing your headphones all day."

Vat didn't want to tell the young man he was trying to forget their dead comrade, so he said, "Going over some of the Ktoran language and comparing it to what we're hearing from the R'Bakuun villagers."

"Sounds the same to me," Sam said. "Maybe a funny accent sometimes, like someone from Louisiana."

"That's an interesting analogy," Vat said.

"But they're an isolated society, right?" Vat nodded. *Or so we've assumed.* "So, where would differences come from?"

"Good question. I don't have an answer. I'm just listening and trying to isolate the differences. Maybe something will click."

"You like languages, don't you?"

Vat shrugged. "I'm good with them, but never went to school for them. It's something I can do rather than something I love."

"What do you love?"

Vat grinned. "Figuring things out."

Near the end of the day, they spied a dust cloud coming toward them, indicating others were on the trail. What they were following now were merely trails through the scattered ground cover, not like the road through the hills behind them. Ruts had been ground into the rock, which meant it had seen a lot of people passing that way

"There's nowhere to hide," Vat said, drawing his whinnie up next to Lieutenant Roberts'. He was getting better at riding the lizard, though he wondered if it was the whinnie getting better at carrying him.

"No," Roberts agreed, holding a hand above his eyes to shield them from the afternoon glare. "There are some rocks over there. They're almost a kilometer away, though. Might as well just spread out and prepare."

After a few minutes, it was apparent the oncoming dust cloud was not caused by another group from the satraps, but by a caravan of locals. As they got closer, Vat could see they were in bad shape. Roberts and the soldiers approached them to render what aid they could.

"The J'Stull attacked us," the oldest in the group said; he was maybe fifteen years old. All the adults were gone, including any females over the age of twelve. It was pretty clear the same sort of raid they'd prevented at the previous village had also targeted theirs, only this time, the satrap forces took the men, too.

"These are mostly kids," Vat pointed out to Roberts.

"I know that." He was looking at the map of their route and rubbing his mouth.

"We can't just leave them."

"What are you suggesting?"

"That we abort and escort them to basecamp." Vat didn't like it. They were still a long way from the village where Salsaliin's and Miizhaam's grandmother lived. They had spent days on the damned lizards, and one of his team was dead. He hated the idea of giving up the whole thing, but they couldn't leave this group of kids by themselves. It was, however, a decidedly suboptimal outcome.

"My mission was to take you to these villages," Roberts said.

"Yes, and the satrap must have found out. They're ahead of us and have trucks. The whinnies are good, but they don't have the endurance of a fueled vehicle." *Don't make me pull rank, damnit,* Vat thought.

Roberts looked up from his map at the wounded survivors his troops were tending. Two were trained medics, applying bandages and rendering whatever first aid they could. Normally, there wouldn't have been much for them to do: R'Bak's medicines were amazing—almost magical, really—which was why the Kulsians came to steal them. The problem was that all the healers—along with any stores of the medicines—had been taken by the satrap forces.

"Fuck," Roberts said. "Let's head back. I'll update Murphy as soon as I can raise Camp Stark through the atmospheric garbage from the storms to the west. They'll relay to Murphy, and maybe Moorehouse can send a helo."

There were no helicopters available, so after tending to the wounded, they headed back.

Chapter Sixty-Four

R'BAK

It was three days back to Camp Stark. Midway through the second day, a helicopter was able to meet up with them to take the worst of the casualties. They had lost a nine-year-old girl during the night from sepsis; she'd been stabbed in the stomach by one of the satrap bastards because she'd objected when they took her mother away. Vat was beginning to feel Artyom's opinion of their adversary was apt.

As fate would have it, the bird was a Huey with "Bruce" painted on the pilot door in blue letters.

"Hey, Vat!" she yelled over the idling turbine. "I thought it was your op when I got the orders."

"Yeah, things went to shit."

She nodded, looking over the stretchers of the wounded who couldn't move, and the ones who could still walk. She saw the body covered with a sheet and her face darkened. "I'm sorry we couldn't get here sooner. We were evaccing our resident SEAL after he shot the shit out of another satrap patrol."

"Good; I hope he fucked them over good," Vat said.

Bruce looked at the face of a young boy being helped onto the helicopter by her crew chief and nodded. "How are you doing?"

"Well enough," Vat said. "I lost one of my men in a fight a couple days ago."

"Sorry to hear that," she said, then looked at his face. "This was your first, wasn't it? You've never lost someone under your command."

"Yes," Vat growled. "And it was just a fucking stray shot. Pure bad luck."

"Doesn't matter how it happens," she said, putting a hand on his shoulder. Vat looked down and she cupped his chin, pulling his face up. He felt tears form and hated himself for it. "What you are feeling is *normal*," she said, locking eyes with him. "You wouldn't be worth a mouthful of lukewarm spit if you didn't feel what you're feeling."

"How do I function, feeling like this?" he demanded.

"That's the other half of being a commander: finding the strength to go forward." She looked over her shoulder. The helicopter was almost ready. El, her crew chief, was belting down the casualties while her copilot made sure the walking wounded had their seat belts in place. She moved in quickly and gave him a brief hug. "It's bad decorum, but this isn't exactly a typical deployment."

"You can say that again."

"Hang in there, Vat. You brought the rest of them through."

He watched the Spindog-manufactured Huey take off, spin around, and fly off. He stood by his whinnie for five minutes until the horizon ate the helicopter, and they were alone.

The last two days of the return were uneventful. They saw a small pack of wild whinnies several kilometers away—actually, their whinnies spotted them first—and the mounted lizards' neck furls stood up at attention. A few warning hisses were exchanged, and the other lizards moved off. For the rest of the day, the humans' whinnies seemed quite pleased with themselves, almost prancing down the dirt ruts.

The nights were challenging for Vat because Salsaliin kept trying to invite herself into his tent. So far, he'd avoided it by staying up as late as possible, driving Roberts nuts in the process. He was short as hell on sleep, but at least she was too tired to try and jump him.

About half the refugees had to stay with the patrol. Hueys were great birds but couldn't hold more than the injured, and there were always more calls going out than there were slicks to respond.

Vat spent a lot of time talking with the kids. He didn't pump them for intel; he already knew that would be a wasted effort. Instead, he listened to their speech patterns. Most of the key elements he was looking for were missing, which told him what he needed to know. The outlying speech pattern was something the adults passed to each other; it wasn't used with the kids.

When they got back to the FOB, he wrote a report and began searching out older natives. The older, the better. Unfortunately, the combat operations they were running didn't call for many old timers. Strong young backs were needed to carry gear, strong young legs to run up hills, and strong young fingers to pull triggers.

Two days after returning, he had his first chance to talk with Murphy in weeks.

"So, how's it going?" the major asked via satellite link.

"I've made some progress in understanding their language. I feel confident there is definitely something we aren't seeing."

"I thought I sent you down to help scope out hidden caches?"

"I am. You saw my report on the 'Daaj?' I believe these are linked; that word is one of the non-matching types."

"Fine. As long as you're not going off on a tangent. I need you to find us some pearls."

"What?"

"You know, the old saying: blah and etcetera blah, a pearl of great value? That's what I need you to find: that invaluable, game-changing pearl."

Vat's mouth became a thin line. He didn't like Murphy. Period. The man was, in many ways, the epitome of the sort of officers which made his time in the service a living hell. They always played their little games, testing, checking, and pushing you along. Assholes.

"I wanted to say I'm sorry about Private Komatsu. He seemed to be a good soldier."

"He was," Vat agreed. "I can't even write his family a letter."

"No, they got one from the Emperor two hundred years ago. It comes with combat, and the first is the worst. Except for every other one that comes after. Are you okay?"

"I'm fine," Vat lied. "I wish it hadn't happened, but it wasn't because anyone screwed up. Artyom kind of went off the deep end, but I've talked to him."

"I saw that in your report, too. Based on Lieutenant Roberts' AAR, I'd say Sergeant Volkov's actions, while inadvisable and brash, probably helped you carry the day. It would have been nice to have the second truck, but your team's survival is more important."

Vat nodded. He agreed with the major's assessment. Even though he was an asshole, Murphy was at least giving Vat enough room and material to operate. Vat really did think he was onto something big. It was just going to take some time.

Murphy cleared his throat. "We're going to have to put a hold on another recon in that direction."

"But we never got to the village where Salsaliin's grandmother lives."

"I understand," Murphy replied. "Resources are needed for other operations right now. We're running out of time to talk, here and in general. We are starting to get behind our timetable…way behind. So we need results. I'm inclined to let you continue pursuing your leads. I don't need you for conventional ops. Frankly, I'm not a fan."

"Permission to speak freely, sir?"

"Let me save you the trouble: 'the feeling is mutual.'"

"Correct. Sir," Vat growled.

Murphy paused for a second then said, "So, as General Patton once said, we have an understanding, one son of a bitch to another. Keep looking for those pearls. Murphy out."

"Pearls? Right. Fucker," Vat said to the dead air and left the comms tent.

Chapter Sixty-Five

R'BAK

"Why have you avoided me?"

Vat rolled over and looked at Salsaliin. The sun wasn't quite up outside, but there was just enough light coming into his tent for him to see her face. She was a lovely woman with an athletic yet feminine figure. Most of the Lost Soldiers would have been thrilled to wake up next to her. "I told you, I'm an officer. This doesn't look right."

She snorted and kissed him. He almost made it look like he enjoyed it. "Many of your soldiers are lying with our women. I hear one wants to marry her." She looked at him in the morning gloom. "Do you not find me attractive?"

"You are a lovely woman," he said. She snuggled up against him. Her body was warm and curvy. He sighed. Shortly, she fell back asleep. He didn't. This was a problem he had to deal with, and sooner rather than later. The second time with her had been easier, and the third easier still. *Easier to lie,* he thought. *Just close your eyes and think of...*Even though he'd made a living from deceit, this fake relationship with this clueless but kind woman made him feel dirtier than anything he'd ever done. *She doesn't deserve this.*

While she slept, he slipped out and visited the communal showers. The sign hanging outside said "Men," so he was okay to go in. Later it would change to "Women." Even though more stalls had been added, there weren't enough for separate showers, so they alternated. Since it was early, it was crowded with naked men, some just back from patrol, and others who just wanted a clean start to the day. It might have been an enjoyable tableau if his mind wasn't aflame with a thousand other issues…

As he dried himself from the lukewarm shower, he noticed a pair of men he'd not seen before. He thought the older of two was staring at him as he dressed. Outside, he was talking to another Lost Soldier when he saw the pair again. They were not Lost Soldiers; their dress was R'Bakuun. At the chuckwagon, he asked a group of Lost Soldiers about the newcomers.

"They're from a tribe far to the east," a scout told him in Russian.

Vat wondered if Artyom knew the man. To his knowledge, many of the Russians had been picked up at the same time as his man, at Kursk.

"Why are they here?"

"Word has spread of our success against the satrap, and they want to know more about us."

Vat nodded, understanding. He verified where the newcomers were billeted and looked them up. They had a tent close to the whinnies' corral. The musky, alien smell of the lizards and their droppings permeated the camp, though it was much stronger at their tent.

"The one from the shower," the older of the two said, the one Vat had caught watching him.

"That's me. Lieutenant Thomas, but call me Vat."

"What does Vat mean?" he asked.

Vat explained, and the man shook his head.

"Your people are as strange as we were told you were. My name is Illapt. This is my younger cousin Tevweret. My father is hetman of our village. He might want to help you against the satrap, especially if you can stop the Sky People before they invade."

I don't think we can stop the invasion any more than we can stop the Searing. "Glad to meet you." He talked with them for a time. Both spoke about their concerns for their village.

"You don't seem very worried," Tevweret complained.

"Now, cousin," Illapt said, "our every concern cannot be theirs. We met one of our family here also. Another cousin, Salsaliin."

"Small world," Vat said. "She came in some time back to trade whinnies." The man gave him a strange look.

Vat knew the Lost Soldiers were stretched thin. They couldn't spend a lot of resources defending villages while scooping up all the caches of equipment *and* looking for hideouts to make it through the Searing, and these two might have information he could use.

Then he had an idea.

"Have either of you heard of Daaj?"

Tevweret looked at him blankly, but Illapt showed a small but clear reaction. "Why do you ask?" Illapt asked.

"Just a word I heard," Vat said, carefully concealing a smile. "Let's talk about your village."

"Vat, I can't authorize a mission so far afield."

"Major, this is what you ordered me to do." Vat bristled at the thought of Murphy up in space, so far away from the action, yet pulling his strings. "These villagers are risking their lives for us. The satellite images shows—"

"I know what the imagery shows, Lieutenant; it goes through me first. We don't know if those satrap groups are heading for the village you are interested in."

"There's nothing else in the area," Vat argued. "Several groups have already been hit in the area, including the one we fought for. We've put them in the crosshairs. I have two local men who just came in from the village I was trying to reach."

"I saw the report. They're reaching out for us to help them, but they won't necessarily reciprocate. They're trying to take advantage of our superior fighting abilities. Ironic, since we couldn't convince them when we first landed. Several other groups have done the same, and then refused to pitch in afterwards. So for now, we must remain focused on the ones closest to our AO. Overextending is dangerous."

"You know there's a spy here, right?"

"It seems likely, yes. Too many locals; I'd be surprised if at least a few aren't on some satrap's payroll. I have people working on it. Either way, we don't have the resources to deploy a couple hundred kilometers away on your hunch. Find out what you can from the locals in the AO. If you can give me intel—*solid* intel—then I'll support a mission to this remote village. Murphy out." The signal faded.

"Mother fucker."

Vat walked out of the comms tent with such an expression of rage, the officer in charge moved out of his way without a word. Vat's men were lounging against a wagon on the other side of the road that ran down the center of the camp. He liked to think of it as the Parkway.

"Well?" Artyom asked, always the most vocal of the five. He was still mystified how Miizhaam and her friend Salsaliin had simply joined the group, without request or approval. Maybe it was the brief but deadly battle they'd fought together, or possibly Salsaliin was behind it.

"He said no," Vat told them.

"Ublyudok," Artyom snarled in Russian.

"He's being 'the commander.'" Vat put up fingers like quote marks as he said commander. "He said we can't risk going so far afield with the local tribes in trouble."

"They came here for your help," Miizhaam said, a look of astonishment on her face. "It is our village, too. You will not help?"

"It's not my decision," Vat said.

"Isn't it?" Sam asked, a calculating look on his face.

"I've been playing cards with the man in charge of the whinnies," Lech said, a cigarette dangling from the corner of his mouth.

Where do they keep finding smokes?

"I know where we can get some gear," Artyom said.

"You schmucks have this place wired," Vat accused them. They grinned back at him. "I need to make some inquiries first." Their grins grew even wider. He had to laugh at their expressions. A motley crew indeed. The women weren't sure what was going on, but they seemed game for just about anything, especially Salsaliin.

Vat nodded at the map printout and rubbed his chin. He needed a shave, but the damned medieval razors they had were like using a machete. If Murphy hadn't insisted they maintain a military bearing, he would have worn a beard like some of the local tribes, although only a short one because of the heat.

Illapt pointed at the map. "This is Ikaan hill?" He described the hill near their village and the direction from it.

"Yes, it must be," Vat agreed.

"These maps you use, they are so strange," Tevweret said.

Vat nodded. The topo maps had finally been upgraded to include corrections from the Dornaani microsats. He, like many others, had tried to teach the locals to use the computer maps. Tried and failed. Except for firearms, a lot of these people at the edge of the Ashbands were closer to early Iron Age in their abilities. Going from the simple hand-drawn maps he'd seen to computer-generated interactive touch screens was just too much of a leap for them.

"If this is Whinaalani Peak, as you called it, and this is the little dry riverbed, then this must be Ikaan Hill," Vat explained.

"I love the face you make when you're concentrating," Illapt said. His cousin lifted his head from studying the map and narrowed his eyes. "You screw up your nose like a man who discovers a pile of whinnie shit in his bedroll."

Vat opened his mouth to say something then stopped when he saw the expression on Miizhaam's face. The boy glared at his older cousin. For Illapt's part, he looked chastened and turned back to the map. *Is he blushing?*

"Illapt, I need to know something," Vat said.

"Anything."

"Will your people fight?"

Illapt looked up at him and the bemusement turned to uncertainty. *Yeah, that's what I was afraid of.*

"Illapt, I want to help, both because I think your people deserve our help, but also because I think there's something you can help me with."

"What can we possibly do for you? You have ships which fly in space and in the air, and your weapons. Everything is so much beyond what we have."

"I can't really say until we get to your village. But if we go there, I'm all in."

"I don't understand."

Vat sighed. It was difficult to word it correctly in Ktoran. "'All in' means I will have to do things which will get me in trouble. I am a military officer; I have responsibilities. If I help, I am going against orders." He shrugged. "I could be shot for insubordination." *Or when I get back, Murphy could send me out an airlock.*

"I cannot promise what my father will do," Illapt said, looking forlorn. "He sent us to meet your people and bring back help after hearing of the attacks."

"You expect help, but don't offer it in return?" Vat asked.

Illapt was clearly at a loss for words, and Vat nodded. "Right, you see my problem—we're supposed to risk everything at the whim of your father."

"I understand," Illapt said, looking dejected. "You cannot help."

"I didn't say that," Vat whispered. Illapt looked up, and Vat's heart thundered in his chest. In that moment he knew he had to help. Stupid and foolhardy though it might be, he was going to help. He just hoped there was a way to make it work without getting himself and everyone with him killed.

Later, as he walked down the Parkway, Artyom fell in next to him. "What is it with you?" he asked in Russian.

"What do you mean?" Vat replied in turn.

"You come down to do what Murphy says you must. We look for ways to make some advantage; it is your way."

"You think you know me so well?" Vat snapped.

"We know you well, Lieutenant Victor Allen Thomas. You never say what you do, back where we come from, but I know it scam of some kind."

"I was an arms dealer, okay?" he blurted, rounding on the Russian. "I sold guns to whoever wanted them and didn't give two fucks who got shot by them."

Artyom took out yet another cigarette and lit it with a vintage Zippo adorned with an airborne logo. He had scrounging skills, no doubt about it. Vat hoped he wasn't stealing them. Artyom took a deep drag and blew out the smoke. A native passing nearby looked askance at the smoke and moved to the other side of the Parkway. Artyom took the butt out of his mouth and looked at it. "You know, I enjoy your American smokes, but they are old, they taste funny, and we run out soon."

"What does that have to do with anything?" Vat grumbled and started walking.

"It mean," Artyom said, keeping pace, "even though they are stale and old, and do bad things to you, I still like them. You are good person, gooder than any of us. Maybe you not know this, yes? Maybe something bad happen and make it hard for you to be good? Maybe Salsaliin bring out good." He took a big drag and blew the smoke out his nose. "Or maybe someone else?" He shrugged and walked off, leaving Vat completely mystified.

Chapter Sixty-Six

R'BAK

Twenty-four hours later, they were ready. Because Vat had to hustle to arrange for their sudden disappearance, he wasn't able to help Sam, Artyom, and Lech get their tasks completed. He had to stretch himself to allow them to operate on their own.

When he left his tent and walked to the corral it was still dark. A few people were out and about, mostly Lost Soldiers. The early hours of the morning were popular among the refugees from Earth because it was the coolest part of the day.

He was a few tents away from the corral when he came across Lech. The man was supposed to be getting their whinnies ready. He looked upset, and Vat could tell there was a problem.

"What's wrong?" Vat asked, trying to sound casual.

"That officer, Captain Moorefield, showed up fifteen minutes ago and took his patrol out suddenly."

"So?" Vat asked.

"There aren't enough whinnies left." Lech gestured at the corral across the street and shrugged helplessly. "If we take the ten animals we need for riders and supplies, there won't be enough left if anyone else needs to run a mission." Vat cursed. "You said to make sure! If you don't mind having fewer…"

"No," Vat said. "No, we'll have to delay."

"Won't that put us in risk of not being able to link up afterwards?"

"Yeah," Vat said. "Catch Artyom and Sam, tell them what happened. The women should be there, too. Tell them to hold; I'll see if Roberts' patrol has come back. We might still make it out this morning."

"You didn't hear?"

"Hear what?"

"Roberts and his team got shot up by one of the satrap's balloons. They survived, but they lost almost all their whinnies."

"Right," Vat said and sighed. "Tell the others. I'm going to get some breakfast and see if I can think of a way around this."

"Breakfast?" Lech asked incredulously behind him. "Are you crazy?"

Vat walked down the Parkway to the chuckwagon. He followed the smell of bacon and eggs. Sure, the eggs were lizard eggs and the bacon was lizard bacon, but it tasted pretty good. Better than the stuff up on the SpinDog habitat, anyway. Some of the shit those people called food wouldn't pass for it even if you covered your nose. The food here was always hot and usually good. Better than he'd had in the army most of the time, though that wasn't exactly saying much.

He loaded a plate and sat at the first table he came to and poked at his food. The sun was beginning to touch the horizon when he heard a voice. "You really shouldn't waste food."

Vat looked up and saw a familiar woman in a well-worn flight suit standing next to his table holding an empty tray.

"Hey, Bruce," Vat said offhandedly and went back to his mostly ignored food.

She lingered for a second then spoke again. "What's up with you?"

"Just issues," he said.

"Tell a friend?" she asked.

"Looks like you're heading somewhere," he said.

She sat down. "I have a flight in about twenty minutes. El, my crew chief, can handle preflight."

Vat almost voiced a complaint, then shrugged. He looked at the woman staring at him, then chuckled. "You don't take 'leave me alone' very well, do you?"

"If you had said that, maybe. But you obviously need help from a friend."

"I haven't had many friends since they boot—I mean, since I left the service." A light went on behind her eyes, and he silently cursed.

She leaned a little closer and spoke. "Vat, I don't care that you're gay."

He jerked back like he'd been slapped, looking around quickly to make sure nobody had heard before speaking. "First, there's a lot of Vietnam-era people around here, so you know better. Second, I don't know what the locals think of..." He shrugged.

"Understood. But Vat, I said *I* don't care. You're my friend, period."

He felt unshed tears and looked down, giving her the barest of nods. In a flash, she moved from across the table to sit next to him. She put a hand on his and leaned in so he couldn't avoid looking at her.

"Nobody is near. Tell me what happened, why they ran you out of the service?"

He wiped away the tears that slipped through, and he told her. How he'd been outed by a fellow officer he'd trusted. The man had caught him at a gay bar in Atlanta and turned him in. How a general he'd been *good* friends with saved him from any charges and got him a general discharge.

It ruined him; wrecked his trust in the military. He'd turned to contacts he'd made in logistics to make his first illegal arms sales, and it had ballooned into selling to the worst of the worst. He'd made a small fortune.

"Something in me was dead," he admitted. "I was hurt, and I didn't care who I hurt in turn."

"Were you doing that in Mogadishu?" she asked, her voice level.

"I was trying," he admitted, then shrugged. "My contacts at the CIA were working with me. They wanted to tie certain warlords to arms traffic. I'd do them a good turn; in return I'd make a good piece of change. The deal didn't go through, at least it hadn't before some FBI investigators broke through the shell company I was running for it."

"Hence the fake name," she said.

He nodded. “I was scum. I became pretty bad. Did some despicable things.”

“What’s changed?”

She reminded him of his late mother. “I got to know these people,” he said, gesturing expansively around the planet. “I lost a man under my command. I only came down here because Murphy made noises like he might blow me out into space.” She laughed. “Yeah, but it worked, I guess. Now I’m stuck.” He explained his current situation.

“Some of that shit you sold might have killed people I knew,” she said quietly.

“Maybe,” he admitted. He took his tray and stood. “I understand why you might not want to be my friend.”

“Not all friends are great people,” she said. “Also, I believe there’s always a chance at redemption.” Bruce glanced at her watch, an old Timex digital. “I have fifteen minutes before takeoff. Can you get your gear into a cargo net?”

He gawked at her in surprise.

“Cargo net? *Da*, I have one of those.”

Vat followed Artyom to an apparently empty tent, only to find it full of stuff. Boxes of ammo, grenades, supplies…and cartons of some local plants? “Sergeant, where did all this come from?”

“You know,” the Russian said as he dug around, “sometime things just appear here. I don’t ask why or how.” He moved a sack, which Vat thought said, “sesame seeds” in Taiwanese, to reveal a hemp cargo net folded on a pallet. “Amazing. There is net.”

“Artyom…”

“You going to help? This is heavy.”

As he helped lug the net to the corral, Vat tried again. “Artyom, what would you do if someone found all of that?”

“All of what?”

He would have made a hell of an arms dealer.

They arrived at the corral as the sun began to crawl over the horizon, but a light fog was clinging to the ground. It reminded Vat of a scene from a spy movie. It felt as shady as what he was trying to pull off. Lech and Sam came out from behind a fence, staring at the two men in confusion.

"What's that?" Sam asked.

"It's a cargo net," Lech said. Since he'd served in the Polish Navy, it made sense he'd be the one to recognize it.

"Right," Vat said. "Okay, quickly, get all the gear piled in the middle, but leave enough room so the net can be pulled up on all sides."

"Why are we—?" Sam started to ask.

"Quit asking questions and *do it!*" Vat barked, giving them a true order for the first time. All three men looked surprised, but quickly moved to comply. Less than a minute after finishing, they looked up at the distinctive thumping of an approaching helicopter. Miizhaam and Salsaliin arrived with Illapt and Tevweret following behind them. They had expected a line of whinnies; a helicopter hadn't been part of the bargain.

Vat could see Bruce in the pilot's seat as someone leaned out from the right-side door and waved. Bruce slowly lowered the helicopter to hover over them, a cable hanging down. With the men's help, Vat got it attached to the cargo net. It wasn't easy since his assistants had neither done it before nor even ridden in a helicopter.

Vat stood back and signaled to the man above. The helicopter lifted the cargo net and moved sideways past the paddock of whinnies. He figured the helicopter would scare the hell out of horses, but the lizards just watched the hammering machine disinterestedly.

Bruce set the craft down, first settling the cargo then angling to land next to it. Then it was Vat's job to get his team of wide-eyed people aboard the huge, noisy, whirling death-machine.

Artyom just shrugged and climbed in. Sam practically crawled across the grass, continually looking up at the blur of rotors. Lech started twice before committing. Illapt and Tevweret were amusing; both men half closed their eyes as they walked, trying to appear calm so they weren't out toughed by the off-world humans.

Last was the women. Neither wanted to approach the helicopter. Vat walked back and held out his hand. "You have to trust me," he yelled over the idling machine. Of course, it was Salsaliin who ended up taking his hand and allowed herself to be led to the helo. Miizhaam slowly followed, though she looked terrified. Bruce gave him a thumbs-up once they had all climbed aboard. She had them airborne in seconds.

The four locals, men and women alike, all gawked in stunned amazement as they rose into the sky. Vat was worried they'd freak out, but once they were flying, the four seemed to enjoy the experience.

"This is amazing!" Illapt yelled, an ear-to-ear grin on his face.

Vat had thought Blackhawks were loud helicopters; he'd never been in a Huey. It was noisy and rough. The engine behind his head roared like an enraged dragon. If it hadn't been for the headset, he'd probably have gone deaf.

"You doin' okay, Lieutenant?" It was Bruce's crew chief, Sergeant Elroy Frazier, whom she called El. He was the man who'd been signaling as they hovered. There hadn't been time to meet him the previous outing. He was a massive black man with a permanent grin on his face. Another Vietnam-era soldier.

"Just peachy," Vat replied over the headset. The cargo compartment was nearly full, with boxes of ammo in the center between benches. El showed Vat how to talk to the pilot. He leaned toward the mic. "I really appreciate this, Bruce."

"You owe me, Lieutenant."

Vat grinned and agreed. She was pretty awesome in his book.

Artyom was looking over the boxes with interest. Vat caught his eye and shook his head decisively. The message was clear; don't even think about it. The big Russian roared with laughter, then nodded in understanding.

What would have taken them days of riding, the helicopter covered in less than two hours. When they were about a half-hour out, Vat spotted an unusually pointy hill. It looked like a pile of rocks, just off to one side of their course. His examination was interrupted when Bruce rapped on the divider and pointed out her side door. Vat turned and looked. It took a second to spot the line of dust.

"Trucks?" he asked over the intercom.

"Sure looks like it," El answered. "I'd say at least five of them."

"They have air cover," Bruce said. "Check nine o'clock."

He shifted his gaze and saw it immediately: one of the satrap's damned dirigibles. It was trying to turn toward them, probably not realizing how fast the helicopter was going. Now he knew for certain they were heading for the same place.

"What are we going to do?" Sam asked, using a pair of binoculars to examine the column. "Five trucks, for sure."

"We help those people," Vat said.

The younger man met his gaze and slowly nodded. Vat took the glasses and examined the column. One of the trucks was towing a tank of some kind. Probably fuel. *Shit.*

Soon the village came into sight. It looked pretty typical: a couple dozen huts, a few of them made to be easily broken down for transport.

"Our village!" Tevweret yelled in amazement, pointing. "It took us five days of riding to get to your base!" El grinned from his fold-down seat by the door.

Bruce circled the village, looking for a landing site, as locals poured out of the huts, staring up at them. Many were armed, and Vat was afraid they were about to come under fire. Bruce finally found a spot and lowered them until they were hovering just above the ground. Vat heard a loud snap, and she side-slipped to settle to the ground. The cable holding the cargo net which had ridden underslung the whole way from the base had been released.

Thirty or more tribesman were waiting a dozen meters beyond the blades' rotational diameter, weapons held ready without being threatening. Vat purposely had Illapt and Tevweret dismount the aircraft first. A big man yelled and raised his arms as he ran toward them.

Bruce leapt out of her seat and rushed to the man, screaming. He looked alarmed and stopped. Vat saw her gesturing at the deadly blades whizzing overhead. She leaned close and said something in his ear. The man's eyes bugged out, and he nodded profusely. Vat knew she had just told him what would happen if he ran into them with his arms high enough. Illapt was reunited with his father soon after, albeit a little more subdued than originally intended.

The Huey idled as Bruce came over to Vat. "There you go," she said. "You sure you're okay with that trouble coming?"

"Not in the least," he answered. "But I'm not leaving these people to die, or the women to be raped. Period."

"I knew you were a good guy," she said. "Even if you didn't."

Vat didn't agree, though he kept his peace. "You aren't going to get in trouble for this, are you?" he asked, gesturing at the supplies.

"For what?" she replied and winked. Vat smiled, and she gave him a hug.

It was then he noticed the difference in her posture, and the fit of her flight suit. He leaned in and said into her ear to be sure nobody heard, "How far along are you?"

She pulled back, her eyes narrowing.

It was his turn to wink. "Just a secret, between us."

"Not for too much longer. You be careful, Vat," she said, and trotted toward her bird.

"You, too!" he yelled after her.

El was sitting in the door, feet dangling over the side. Vat gave him a salute, which the man returned crisply. In moments, the helicopter's engine noise grew, and the brand-new model of the ancient Huey pounded its way into the air. Bruce spun it around, tipped its nose forward, and raced away as it climbed into the sky. He hoped he see her again someday, and her baby, too.

For now, he was on his own.

Chapter Sixty-Seven

R'BAK

"Lieutenant," Illapt said, "this is my father, Bafguur, hetman of our village."

"Please to meet you, sir," Vat said, bowing his head. "You may call me Vat. It is the way I prefer to be addressed."

"It is good to meet you too, Vat. My men have spotted the satrap's forces in their smoking wagons. They will be here tomorrow. Are more of your soldiers coming in the thumping birds?"

Thumping birds, not a bad way to refer to a Huey. "We are it," Vat said and gestured to the three men and two women. It was apparent Bafguur was disappointed. "You have heard of our ability to fight?"

"Yes, but four men and two women against the hundred or more the satrap will send?"

"We are more than they are expecting." Bafguur scowled, but Vat pushed on. "Your son could not guarantee you will fight. We came on the hope you will."

"If this is all you will send to help us, I do not know if I should. Maybe we should flee."

"You cannot outrun them." Bafguur's scowl turned to a serious frown. "You've heard stories of our abilities, have you not?" Bafguur nodded. "The offer I make is a simple one: commit to assisting us against the satrap, then the invaders from Kulsis, and we will defeat your enemies with you."

"Such a promise, you can make?"

Vat smiled. "Yes."

"The satrap's forces *and* their sky ship?"

"Without a doubt."

"Then we will *fight*."

"Good to hear." He turned and saw his team was unloading the cargo netting. One case had already been set aside. He patted the case. "Then this is for you. I need your ten best fighters." Vat explained what he needed them for and opened the case. Bafguur's eyes went wide when he saw the contents. The frown he'd worn since hearing how few people Vat had brought slowly changed to a grin.

"For us to keep?"

"If you fight alongside us, yes." The grin turned to a big toothy smile.

Murphy isn't going to like this. He watched the hetman gently pick up the M3 and examined it. *Yeah, he's gonna be really pissed.* "Get your men together; we have to work quickly."

Vat had never handled the old M3, or Grease Gun, as the soldiers nicknamed it in WWII. They'd started phasing it in at the end of 1942 as a simpler, lighter, and less expensive replacement for the Thompson. If it had a downside, it was less accurate at medium range. It used .45 ACP, the same as the Thompson, so it had a good punch, but at a slower rate of fire. It also had 30-round box magazines, unlike his Thompson which had the smaller 20-round sticks. A Thompson could empty a 20-round stick in about a two-second burst. Vat had made sure to take only 30-round boxes for the new weapons.

Due to his lack of familiarity, he let Sam and Artyom give instruction in the gun. Sam had trained with one and, ironically, Artyom had one for a time in Russia—part of the lend-lease exchange.

"I do not like much," the Russian admitted. The M3 looked like a toy in his massive hands. "The aim is strange." Instead of the front sight being positioned at the end of the barrel, the grease gun forward site was at the front of the receiver, four inches back from the tip, and it was tiny, which made for a difficult sight picture. "Harder to hit things further away."

"It's really a close-quarters gun," Sam pointed out.

"This close quarters, too," Artyom said, patting one of his two AK-47s.

"Why don't you just help Sam get these men up to speed?"

Artyom's eyes gleamed, and he went back to work. Vat sighed and listened to their lesson for a minute before going to look over the rest of equipment. Everything had been disbursed based on the plan he'd put together. Villagers were busily getting wagons ready and their possessions packed. It was going to be tight.

"Vat?"

He turned around. It was Salsaliin. He looked around; there was no easy way to escape. "Yes?"

"I spoke to my grandmother. She will talk to you."

He'd nearly forgotten his main reason for coming to the village. "Take me to her, please."

Salsaliin nodded and walked through the frantic activity of the village.

"You want backup?" Sam asked.

"No, I'm good. Keep up the training, conserve ammo, and follow up with Lech after he's done scouting."

"Roger that, sir."

Salsaliin maneuvered through the chaos of the camp under duress. Vat saw dozens of the tribe's members loading women and children onto modified whinnie saddles. Almost all their mounts were going to take the non-combatants away in the opposite direction of the advancing forces at night so no prying eyes would see. However, they couldn't move everyone and everything, and they couldn't do it fast enough to avoid the satrap's forces.

"If we run, we'll have to abandon almost everything we need to survive," Illapt had said. That was what had sold Vat on intervening. With the enemy forces breathing down their necks, he was glad now there hadn't been enough whinnies at the camp. He and his team would still have been days away when the satrap attacked.

Eventually, he spotted Miizhaam standing near a tent. Unlike many others, this one showed no signs of people being packed out.

"This is our Atii, or old-one, Ooshwelo," Miizhaam said.

"I thought you said she was your grandmother," Vat said to Salsaliin.

"We sometimes refer to extended older family in such a way. If they have no surviving family, they are all our grandmothers. You should simply refer to her as an old-one."

Atii, Vat thought and mentally added it to the column of non-conforming wordforms. Miizhaam held the tent flap open, and he entered.

The interior was dark and warmer than outside. A shape he'd thought was a pile of blankets moved, and he saw a head, stooped over and missing much of its hair. As his eyes adjusted to the gloomy interior, he could see she was looking at him.

"Sit, please. You are the one from the stars," she said.

He sat, listening to her speak. Her voice was full of the inflections he'd been recording, the non-conforming elements. He slid a hand into his jacket pocket and activated the recorder, determined to get the most out of this situation in case he didn't get all the answers he needed. He could at least get a good recording of all those strange language elements.

"Yes," he said and bowed his head. "It is a pleasure to meet Ooshwelo, the Atii."

Her face cracked into a slight smile. "Your speech in our words is pleasant to the ears, though it is obvious you have learned from the Fraa."

Vat blinked and thought. The word was similar to Fri, which meant new. "Fraa?" he asked.

"New ones," she said.

"Are there many Atii?" he asked.

"No," she said. "Very few of us."

"Can I ask how old you are?"

She smiled again. "I have seen one hundred and thirty-six years."

Vat's first thought was *she's senile*...but her demeanor and eyes said the opposite. *So how could she be—?* And then he realized: one hundred and thirty-six local years was only—*only!*— one hundred and two Earth years old. "You lived through the last Searing," he said, his voice almost hushed. She nodded sagely. "You have traveled to the pole and back?"

"No, I have never seen those lands."

He leaned closer. "I-I don't understand."

"When you are Atii, you learn a few things." She was quiet for a long time. He began to wonder if she'd fallen asleep, but then she blinked and spoke. "What would you like to know of this old Atii?"

Old and Atii? It came out as a redundant statement, like saying an old old house. He couldn't wait to listen to the conversation again. "I would like to know about the Daaj."

"Oh," she said, slowly shaking her head. "Salsaliin mentioned your curiosity. I'm sorry, I cannot. You are an outsider."

He was disappointed—very—but he couldn't argue with her. How could he? "Can you tell me why your language seems different than the rest of your people?" He gave her several examples. "Even your title, Atii, doesn't match Ktoran in form."

Her smile returned, though more subtle this time. "You believe Atii is a title? How interesting. I would say you have much still to learn about us. I am glad you have come to help. I'm tired now, though; please go away." She lowered her head and appeared to immediately fall asleep. He sat for a long moment then felt a hand on his shoulder. It was Miizhaam, gesturing for him to come. He got up and followed her out of the dark, warm tent.

"Did you learn what you wanted?" she asked once outside.

"No," he admitted. "Do you think she will talk again? After the battle, and they bring her back?"

"Back? She is not leaving."

"But we'll be in a pitched battle!" he complained. "We cannot protect her."

"Atii do not run away. They stay in the area they are born. It is their way."

He didn't know what to say so he headed back to his people.

Chapter Sixty-Eight

R'BAK

As night fell, scouts began to come in. Bafguur had five men out on fast whinnies, trying to track the approaching forces. Vat was provided ten of the tribe's fighting men and women to use on his team. Preparations were largely complete as the suns began to set, which allowed Vat time to check in with Bafguur and his scouts.

He found them next to the small corral for the tribe's whinnies, speaking to three trail-weary men with locally-made guns. The riders looked at Vat suspiciously as he approached. Bafguur offered a warm welcome.

"This is Lieutenant Thomas, known by the name Vat. He leads the people from the stars."

The three scouts examined Vat curiously, their eyes lingering on his uniform, gear, and particularly the Thompson submachine gun he had slung over his shoulder.

"What news?" Vat asked. "Have the other two scouts come in yet?"

"They won't return," one of the scouts said.

"This is Kejern," Bafguur said. "He is my best scout and hunter."

"The satrap's flying bag killed the other two. It is over in that direction, not far."

"Show me?" Vat asked.

"It is too far to see in the last of dusk; we would have to ride out. They can shoot you as far as you can see them, at this hour."

"We have these." He held up a pair of binoculars. The scout looked at them in confusion. "Loan me a whinnie, and let's ride up to that hill," he said, and pointed. Bafguur nodded, and they were off. After a minute, he had to admit the whinnies were nicer than horses. Funny, since they were carnivorous reptiles.

At the top of the hill, Vat spent a minute searching. While mostly dark, the sky and wispy clouds to the west still showed light. Using the powerful Vietnam-era field glasses, he quickly found the satrap dirigible.

He guessed it was about two kilometers away, hovering 500 meters above the ground. He could just see ropes being tossed down. "Do they ever attack at night?" Vat asked.

"No, never. They have their smoking wagons, so they move faster. They don't risk the night."

He showed Kejern how to use the binoculars, and while the man marveled at them as he examined the dirigible, Vat's smile grew predatory. The whinnies were not spooked by gunfire, unlike horses which took extensive training to get them used to weapons. "Kejern, how much can a whinnie carry?"

As the other man considered his answer, Vat looked at the horizon and calculated. *There might be enough time.*

Panazar watched as the bundle of gear was carefully maneuvered out of the gondola. The dirigible was tethered to the ground and had descended to 100 meters, as was necessary when heavy equipment or personnel were being transferred. If you unloaded something heavy and the craft wasn't tied down, it could shoot upward. The blimps gave them a huge advantage over the primitive dung-divers who scratched their food from the ground. That is, until the off-world interlopers had arrived.

He'd been placed in charge of this operation, sweeping out and around where the interlopers seemed to be centered. Nobody was certain of the new enemy's location, only how effective they'd been against his satrap.

"If we don't get control of this before the Searing, our heads will roll," one of Panazar's superiors had warned him. "So, we circle them, pick off the little tribes, have some fun, maybe get some answers. Do what you will with their women but bring me answers about the off-worlders."

It was a simple enough mission, and Panazar anticipated an easy job of it. Yes, he'd lost a two-truck patrol several days ago. The surviving men had come crawling in, weaponless and complaining about being ambushed by a massive force of off-world warriors. Panazar knew better. There were not many of the off-worlders, possibly as few as a hundred, but they were well armed and schooled in strange tactics. Like his leader said, the Suzerain, first satrap among the J'Stull, demanded that the others just beneath his rank—the vassals and vavasors—regain control before the Searing.

"Be careful with that!" Panazar yelled up at the crew on the dirigible. If the motors had been running, they would never have heard him. As it was, someone waved acknowledgement. He wanted to get some sleep before they attacked in the morning, but if he left it to his subordinates, they would make a mess of it. Plus, the larger of the two moons was about to come out; although its light was weak, it would be enough to work by.

Above, the man attached a rope to the overhead pulley, took the rope in hand, and someone else pushed the load out. The rope quivered as it was lowered. A second later there was a thumping sound from above and someone fell out the door.

"Watch out!" the loading crew yelled, and the body plummeted toward the ground. The suspended load, without sufficient manpower to hold it aloft, began to drag whoever else was holding the rope. This person, deciding they didn't want to join the first man, let go. The bundle of gear fell.

"Damned fools!" Panazar yelled. Then a crack echoed across the camp at the same time the body hit the ground with a sickening *crunch. That sounded like a gunshot.* Above him the glass in the dirigible's gondola exploded and rained down. Another *crack* echoed several seconds later. It wasn't the booming sound of their guns; it was how he'd heard the off-worlder's weapons described, like a very loud whip.

"We're under attack!" A line of bullets cut across the camp, tearing through everything in its path.

Sam's shot was dead on. Vat could see inside the dirigible clearly; the man who'd been standing at the controls clutched his chest and pitched over. "Bullseye," he called out.

"Artyom," Vat said. "Open fire."

"*Da*." The big Russian had a hand-rolled cigarette clenched between his lips. He reached forward, racked the bolt on the PK machine gun, and squeezed the trigger. He didn't bother with bursts; he unleashed the 7.62 belt-fed machine gun in a continuous roar. His chin was tucked against the old wooden buttstock as he located concentrations of movement and raked them with fire. The belt had red tracers interspersed every four rounds; it was a wonderful for adjusting aim.

The PK machine gun was fired from a tripod as a crew support weapon. However, he'd had the villagers arrange a mount that attached to a whinnie's saddle for the weapon's integral front folding bipod. Artyom stood at the whinnie's side and held the gun, working from a slight crouch. "I wish I met Kalashnikov," he yelled as the first box ran empty. "I would like this man!"

The whinnie took the rain of empty casings with indifference. They would be hot enough to burn a man's hand, but the lizard's tough, heat-resistant skin wasn't bothered in the least.

"Just reload," Vat said.

"I think I have the commander," Sam said. He was also firing over the back of a whinnie, using his saddle as a shooting stand. The lizard didn't even jump at the first shot.

"Do not, I repeat, do *not* hit the commander. We want cohesion in their ranks. For now." Vat used the binoculars. "And anger, lots of anger."

Artyom was through his second 100-round box of ammo before the first enemy bullet snapped through the air near them.

"That's good," Vat said, "mount up!"

"One more box," Artyom said. "This is so much fun!" He was fumbling the box into place in the gloom, forgetting to lift the belt holder after the receiver cover. He got it in place as a flurry of bullets swarmed around them, and one hit his left arm. *"Blyat!"*

Despite the risk of hitting whoever was in charge, Vat lifted his Thompson and emptied the 30-round box, raking it back and forth across the camp a hundred meters away. "Get him on his whinnie," he yelled at Sam as he changed magazines.

Incoming fire fell off just long enough to allow Sam to get Artyom in the saddle. The big guy was putting pressure on the wound and cursing profusely as they turned the whinnies and urged them into a run. The one with the mounted PK followed without any urging. Vat hoped the PK stayed attached; he didn't want to lose it.

The incoming fire from the J'Stull camp continued as Vat, Sam, and Artyom made their escape. Artyom didn't stop cursing the whole time.

"You know they're gonna be coming now," Sam said.

"I'm counting on it," Vat said. Behind them, the gunfire stopped, and they could hear engines revving to life.

Chapter Sixty-Nine

R'BAK

"Stop shooting, stop shooting!" Panazar yelled over and over. Slowly, the gunfire tapered off. "Someone find the team leaders and get them organized! I want everyone in the trucks and ready to move!"

"But the dirigible!" someone yelled, pointing up.

In the near darkness, Panazar saw the dirigible rocketing upward, completely out of control. He wondered if the crew had been killed in the shooting. It didn't matter; it would be of no use. "Get me a body count and prepare to attack!" All those gunshots, so close together. Then it just…stopped. They had to be out of ammunition. He had to act before they got away. The first truck started with a roar, and he went to find his gun belt.

One of the tribe's healers looked at Artyom's arm and made a *tsk-tsk* sound. Vat felt a little sick looking at the wound. The bullet had taken a chunk of meat out of his triceps the size of a shot glass. The healer brought her bag over, found some chopped up leaves inside it, and started stuffing them into the still-bleeding hole. Artyom revealed he had not yet reached the end of his lexicon of Russian swear words. Vat was impressed.

"You smoke, yes?" the healer asked. Artyom cursed and ignored her. She slapped him across the face.

"What?" he demanded.

"You smoke, yes?"

"Yes, why?"

She handed him a little hand-rolled cigarette, and someone forced a brand under the end. He convulsively puffed, and his eyes went wide. "What is this?"

"A pain killing herb. Shut up and smoke it," the healer said, cramming more leaves into the wound. A second later, Artyom's eyes crossed, and he sighed.

Must be some good stuff, Vat thought. "Is he going to be okay?"

"Yes," the healer said. "The *gii* leaves will stop the bleeding and begin healing."

"Don't let him get too stoned; we need him."

"Stoned?" the healer asked.

"Intoxicated," he said. *Guess some words don't translate from Ktoran.* She nodded and took away the cigarette after one more puff.

"Hey!" Artyom complained.

"How'd it go?" Lech asked, coming up behind Vat. Then he saw the bloody mess. "Oh, damn. He going to be okay?"

"Based on what I've heard about their medicine, probably. They gave him some drugs to smoke for the pain."

"Is goooood stuff," Artyom said in slightly slurred Russian.

"Let me try some." Lech leaned in to reach for the butt.

Vat intercepted him. "I don't need you wasted, too. Is everything ready here?"

"I have them in place. We heard the shooting. How much damage did you inflict?"

"Hard to say," Vat said. "He put two belts into the camp, and I'm pretty sure Sam took the blimp out of the fight."

Sam nodded as he stood to one side and watched Artyom being patched back together. "I capped at least two of them in the blimp, including the pilot."

"You finish setting your surprises?" Vat asked Sam.

"Good to go. I only had enough for the two escape routes."

"It will have to be enough."

"I heard you were back," Bafguur said as he ran up. He saw Artyom being tended to. "How is he?"

"He'll be okay," the healer answered.

"Kejern just came in and said he hears the smoking wagons coming."

"Good," Vat said.

Bafguur shook his head in bemusement. "I hope you are right about this."

So do I, Vat thought. "I am. Have everyone who's still here take cover. This is going to get messy."

Panazar rode in the first truck, his rifle cradled in his lap, his pistol in its holster. The rifle was one of the best they had, a gift from one of the advance scouts from Kulsis. "A taste of what is to come for our loyal forces." It used a lever to load one bullet after another, five shots before reloading. It was an amazing weapon, the envy of everyone in his command. He planned to use it to kill all the off-worlders, one at a time.

The truck rumbled over a hillock, and the campfires of the village came into view. They would only have had a few extra minutes by the time the bastards returned after attacking him. Attacking him, in the dark? How dare they be so dishonorable?

Panazar leaned out the door and signaled the other trucks; it was time to begin the attack. His men whooped from the back of his own truck. The eleven men who were killed were friends and comrades, and the dung-diving villagers were about to pay the price for allying with the off-world scum.

They came abreast of the first huts and the men in the back started flinging glass bottles full of petroleum, each with a burning rag attached. They smashed against the huts, which burst into flames. Within seconds, a dozen huts were aflame. The driver brought the truck to a halt in an open space, and his men began to pile out.

"Wait," Panazar said, confused. "Where are all the villagers?"

"Safe from you," someone said. Panazar spun around and saw a strange man in strange dress holding an even stranger gun. "Goodbye, asshole," the man said with a snarl.

Vat stitched the leader from left to right in a controlled 5-round burst, killing him instantly. He was no longer of any use, having delivered the prey into the trap. The empty huts had been filled with dry grass and arranged in a convenient circle, the few still occupied were a hundred meters away, behind him and, hopefully, out of the field of fire. The second truck was just grinding to a stop when the villagers he'd armed opened up with their M3 Grease Guns.

They were arrayed in an arc to either side of Vat, to make sure none of them would overlap their fire on their neighbor. Sam led a group of five villagers and had armed himself with an M3 for this operation. The Garand's small magazine and long reach were not the right fit for a close-range ambush. Lech had the other five villagers and his own AK-47. In all, thirteen guns poured bullets into the lead trucks, chewing them apart. Dozens of men were mowed down before they could touch the ground.

To the side, firing across the advancing trucks, was Artyom. Vat had almost changed the plan, but the crazy Russian was better with the machine gun. So Artyom had his new girlfriend, PK, and they were dancing to their favorite tune. The drug had taken away the pain, as well as the ability think, at first, but the rush was short lived, even if he was still pretty high. However, he seemed to be handling the weapon well. Unlike the last time, he was actually aiming more carefully, working the muzzle back and forth over the crew compartments while avoiding the cab and engines.

Bafguur and his scouts were concealed among the burning huts, the scouts with their native weapons, Bafguur with Sam's Garand. The hetman had taken a liking to the venerable WWII rifle, so he and his men were targeting the enemy drivers.

The ambush was only a few seconds old when the driver of the third truck realized what was happening and tried to change directions, plowing through one of the burning huts in an attempt to escape. He found a "roadway" between huts and accelerated, only to go up in a ball of flame from one of the improvised landmines Sam had set.

The men who'd managed to get out of the trucks were firing at anything that moved. Vat saw one, then another villager go down. He took a knee and started picking off the enemy survivors. He felt a tug at his side and ignored it, except to acknowledge, *That was close.* His Grease Gun was empty, he reloaded it. Repeated that sequence again, after a brief yet interminable time.

Eventually, the survivors threw down their guns and put their hands in the air. "Cease fire!" Vat yelled in Ktoran. The villagers were unusually well-disciplined and stopped shooting far faster than he expected. "Secure the prisoners," he ordered.

Before the battle, Vat had explained to Bafguur how his people needed prisoners to interrogate. It was part of the agreement for the soldiers' help. He started walking the circuit of their positions, getting a casualty count. Five of the ten villagers had been hit. Two were dead, one didn't look like he'd survive, and two had minor injuries.

Artyom had been shot again, twice. Neither hit was life-threatening, and the Russian had no idea it had happened. The drugs were apparently still doing their job.

"You're bleeding," Sam said and pointed at Vat's chest.

He looked down and saw the side of his camos was dark with blood. He unbuttoned his shirt and saw a shallow crease along his right ribs. The tug he'd felt hadn't missed after all. He wondered why it didn't hurt, and then he felt the pain. "Shiiiiit," he hissed. *Yeah, now it hurts!*

"I'll get the healer," Sam said.

"No, let her take care of the others." Vat dug out a compress from his first aid kit and pressed it against the wound, which felt like someone was holding a hot brand against his side. Sam looked at him and raised an eyebrow. "I'm *fine*, damnit. Let her take care of the seriously injured."

"As you say, sir."

Salsaliin came running up and looked around at all the dead and wounded before spotting him. She raced over, and he held up a hand.

"I'm fine," he said.

"I can see that."

He was a little annoyed she didn't seem worried about him, but realized she was distraught. "What's wrong?"

"It's Ooshwelo."

"Oh no," he said and ran. Salsaliin and Sam both fell in behind him. He raced toward the huts where the few who'd stayed behind were sheltered. Had they not gotten all of the satrap's forces? Had some circled around and attacked from behind? He didn't have enough people to leave a rear guard and was kicking himself for not doing it anyway. If the J'Stull had a second force nearby…

He reached the Atii's tent and found no signs of damage. He slipped inside and found everyone was fine except Ooshwelo. Miizhaam was cradling the ancient woman's head in her lap and humming. She looked up when he entered and spoke.

"I think the excitement was too much for her," Miizhaam said.

"I yet live," Ooshwelo spoke, her voice barely a whisper. Miizhaam caressed the ancient woman's forehead. "Did you succeed?"

"Yes," Vat said. "Some of the fighters died, but the satrap's forces are defeated." *So far as we know.*

"I grieve for the warriors but sing for the victory." The words were full of the non-complying speech elements. Vat wished he had the recorder handy, then hated himself for the thought. "I wish to die at the Daaj," she added, her voice surprisingly strong. "Will you take me there?"

Salsaliin nodded.

"Whatever you want," Vat said.

"Then hurry, I do not have much time left."

"I wish I could go," Vat said.

"Then come; you have earned it."

Chapter Seventy

R'BAK

Miizhaam went out and arranged to have a whinnie brought with a large saddle usually used to move families. It was fitted with a platform in front of the rider where children could sit. Ooshwelo was tiny and frail; there would be more than enough room.

It took longer than Vat thought it should, so he left Salsaliin with Ooshwelo and went to help. The villagers seemed indifferent to Ooshwelo's condition. It was not the attitude he was expecting. He found Bafguur and explained what was happening.

"There aren't many Atii," he said, then shrugged. "Maybe the sooner they die, the better."

"She wants to go to the Daaj," Vat said. Bafguur made a face halfway between a frown and a sneer. "She wants to die there."

"Kejern," Bafguur called. "Get some whinnies for this man." He looked at Vat. "I do this for you."

With the help of the women, he got Ooshwelo bundled up and onto the whinnie. She was shivering though the evening was almost uncomfortably warm.

"I'm coming along," Salsaliin said.

"What about Miizhaam?" Vat asked.

"Just my granddaughter and you," Ooshwelo whispered.

Vat made a face. It would be more difficult with only one person to help. And there was still the risk of more enemies who might not have been swept up in the ambush, or part of a reserve force. As they prepared to depart, the village healer packed Vat's bullet graze with the same stuff Artyom had received. Now Vat understood why the Russian had screamed bloody murder. It *hurt*. By the time she was done torturing him, the whinnies were ready, and the three left. Ooshwelo told him what direction to ride.

"Southeast," she whispered. "Look for a craggy hill."

Salsaliin rode alongside Vat. He kept a hand free to be sure Ooshwelo didn't fall off. She was so still he couldn't tell if she was alive. "Do you know how far?" he asked across the darkness to the shadow of his riding companion.

"Not far," Salsaliin said. "The Atii are never far from the Daaj."

He burned with the desire to question her about it. She shared the speech elements which had brought Vat out on this fateful journey, no doubt learned from her grandmother. But now, riding in near darkness with an old—no, ancient—woman near death's door, he began to think Murphy was right. Chasing his wild hunch had been a waste of time.

No. He shook his head. *It wasn't a waste of time.* The enemy forces would have slaughtered the village and taken the women away as slaves or short-lived distractions.

"Are you okay?" Salsaliin's voice drifted to him from the darkness.

"Fine," he said. "Just…conflicted."

"I don't know of an outsider ever being invited to the Daaj," she said. He could see her looking at him, staring, and wondered what she was thinking.

The whinnies had excellent night vision and with their ground-hugging gait, were smooth to ride. They didn't jostle the saddle like a horse, not even when they ran. There was just a little more side-to-side motion at slow speeds.

They climbed a slight rise, and he spotted a hill, not more than a big pile of rocks against the star-littered sky, backlit by the small rising moon. Vat immediately recognized it as the same hill they'd flown over on their way in.

"Is that the Daaj?" he whispered to Ooshwelo. She didn't reply, but he could feel her breathing, so they continued onward.

Vat was afraid "not far" meant an all-night ride, but it turned out to only be a little over two hours before they encountered the house-sized boulders. Ooshwelo finally spoke, but he missed most of it and had to stop the whinnie so he could lean over and put his ear next to her mouth.

"Look…for…the…black…rock."

"Black rock?" he asked. It was dark so he wasn't sure how would he spot a black rock in the middle of the night. He asked her but she remained silent. He could barely feel her breathing.

"What did she say?" Salsaliin asked.

"Look for the black rock," he said, straining his eyes against the gloom. The tiny moon was directly behind the hill now that they were at its foot. He thought frantically until he remembered he wasn't from this planet. He had technology. Cursing to himself, he dug into his pack and retrieved the big flashlight stashed there. You didn't think about using them in a combat zone. There was no faster way to get a permanent hair parting than by firing up a flashlight.

"Oh!" Salsaliin cried and covered her eyes.

"Sorry, I should have warned you. It's called a flashlight." He played the beam over the mound, taking a few seconds to adjust for the stark shadows it threw into the crags between the rocks. After moving the flashlight around for a minute, one of the rocks reflected like a mirror. It surprised him almost as much as the flashlight had Salsaliin.

He got off the whinnie and walked to the rock. As he got closer, he understood why it was throwing the beam back; facing him was a massive piece of volcanic glass with a sheared, concave side. The rest of the rocks that made up the hill were sedimentary, like the majority of those in the region. Or so he'd been told, anyway. The nearest volcanoes were thousands of kilometers away.

"I found it," he told Ooshwelo. "It's a big piece of black volcanic glass."

This time she only managed one word. "Behind."

Realizing she was near the end, Vat took her down from the saddle. She was as light as a feather, and all skin and bones. Very, very old skin and bones. He doubted she weighed 30 kilos.

Salsaliin followed without comment. After a few steps, Vat almost tripped over a rock. "Take the flashlight and show the way?" he asked her.

"Yes, of course," Salsaliin said.

Vat waited while Salsaliin leaned to peer around the far side of the rock. "There's an entrance here!" she called excitedly. He went to examine it. There was a V-shaped archway where the obsidian rock leaned against a larger boulder; beyond it, a tunnel was clearly visible. More interesting was the unmistakable evidence of tool-worked stone steps.

The entrance was large and there was plenty of room. He had Salsaliin play the light around the cavern. One side sloped down to some steps, the other led to a chamber. They went to the chamber—it was one of the satrap caches, a huge one. At least a dozen trucks were covered with tarps, and there were stacks of gear as well.

"This is the Daaj?" he asked, confused. "This is a satrap cache."

"No," Ooshwelo whispered. "Below."

"What do we do?" Salsaliin asked.

Vat looked around one last time. "We go down," Vat said, gesturing for her to go first as he followed, carrying Ooshwelo.

On the surface, it was around 28 degrees Celsius, as cool as he'd seen it at any time, down from the day's high of 35, which chased everyone to shelter in whatever shade they could find. But only a couple of steps beyond the hidden entrance, the temperature began to drop. Salsaliin used the flashlight to light the way. They reached a bend, and Vat spotted cuts in the rock wall. A cool wind blew through the holes and out matching ones on the other side.

"Why does the air smell wet?" Salsaliin asked.

"It's a moisture trap," he said. "There's an aquifer down here somewhere." She looked back at him, confused. "An underground lake."

"There are no lakes this far south," she said.

"They are underground," he said. "Murphy said they were likely here, but we didn't have the tools to drill for water."

Down they went, passing through four more switchbacks, each with another moisture trap. It was ingeniously built. The multiple traps made sure very little water leaked out from the exit. He recalled seeing a boulder near the entrance. He wouldn't have been surprised if it were the perfect size to seal the entrance for when the Searing came. No doubt the Kulsians would have thought it a great place to hide their equipment, too, but why hadn't they found the Daaj? It was hard to believe nobody had gone down the steps after hiding their gear above.

The tunnel finally leveled out, and they followed it for a short time. Parts of the passage looked natural; others were carved by tools. There was no sign of rock drills or explosives. This had all been excavated by hand with nothing more than picks or other small tools, swung by manpower. Or something else? Had R'Bak once been the home of a non-human species?

He remembered reading a report of the strange healing plants and unusual animals. Someone had noted a lack of seemingly uniform evolutionary trends, though the same person noted nothing on Earth would evolve in a region burnt to a crisp every 88 years. So who was to say what such an environment might yield?

They came to a dead end. A boulder was wedged into the tunnel, fitting its dimensions almost perfectly. *Had there been a cave in?* he wondered.

"The roof must have fallen in," Salsaliin said.

"...push the black rock..." came Ooshwelo's tiny whisper.

Still carrying her in his arms, Vat moved to the boulder and leaned next to it. A tiny cool breeze brushed his cheek from around the edge of the rock. There was no way he could move this; it had to be at least ten tons. More, probably.

"...push..." Ooshwelo repeated.

He had Salsaliin shine the light around again. Like before, they found a piece of black volcanic glass in the wall. He pushed it, and the boulder moved.

"Shit!" he gasped, backstepping just fast enough to avoid falling to the floor and sending his delicate charge flying. A slight *whoosh* of even cooler air passed him. It was no more than 17 or 18 degrees inside.

"It's a door!" Salsaliin said.

Regaining his balance, Vat walked through the opening and examined the "door." The boulder was just as massive on the inside and appeared perfectly balanced. He could move it with a fingertip. "Better close it," he told Salsaliin, who nodded and gently pushed the boulder closed. It settled into its niche with barely a sound. *How old is this?*

After traversing a short passageway, similar to what was on the other side of the door, it opened up. Salsaliin shined the light around…revealing a massive chamber. No, chamber wasn't the right word. It was a *cavern* hundreds of meters across. The roof was covered in stalactites and was fifty or more meters above them. They were inside the hill. As she moved the light along the roof, it left a pattern of glowing phosphoresce behind.

A frail whisper: "…shut off…the light…"

"Do it," Vat said.

They were plunged into complete darkness, but after a few seconds, a glow appeared. It continued to grow until they could see each other again, then details in the distance. Finally, it was as bright as dusk, enough to read by if you strained your eyes. Somewhere, he heard the drip of water.

"What is this light?" Salsaliin asked.

The illumination had a faintly greenish-yellow tint. Not unpleasant, it reminded Vat of an old CRT computer monitor. "It's bioluminescence," he explained. "A fungus growing on the walls. The flashlight made it shut off."

"Welcome to the Daaj," Ooshwelo said. "I am home." She sounded better, as if arriving had given her a temporary burst of energy.

"What do you want me to do?"

"Take me to the Piik," she said. "The hall." Her almost skeletal hand emerged from the wrapping and pointed. He followed the direction indicated by the gnarled forefinger and, to his surprise, saw a village.

Buildings. Underground. Built in orderly rows, made from the same stone as the hill above and around them. Ooshwelo's finger pushed toward the largest building, long and wide but lower than most.

"What is this place?" he asked as he walked, Salsaliin following behind them.

"The Daaj is where we came from. Homes made long, long ago."

"Made by the first exodates?"

"No," she said, looking up at him and smiling. "Older. Before any of them."

He was about to ask another question, but they had reached the building. There were openings with no doors, and holes for windows as well. Inside, it was bare except for a large stone table. "On that," she said, pointing again.

Vat gently set her on the table. He removed his combat vest and bundled it to make her a pillow. "What now?"

"Now I go to my rest," she said. She reached and took his hand. "You were meant to find this place because you came to me at just the right time. Your sacrifice to save my tribe confirmed it for me." She reached with her other hand and took Salsaliin's. "You, my dear, are now Atii. Raise your child as one and use the Daaj to protect the people."

With the last of her strength, she put their hands together. There was a small amulet she'd passed to Salsaliin. It appeared to be carved from stone, rather like an uneven pyramid. Or maybe, a pile of rocks. She patted their hands gently and closed her eyes. Vat leaned close, but there was no breath. She was gone. Salsaliin began to cry.

Vat left her to mourn her grandmother and went outside to explore. The buildings were all open designs, made to allow as much of the bioluminescent light in as possible. It appeared doors and windows had once held fabric to close them off, but it was hard to tell. Everything felt incredibly *old*.

"How long?" he whispered. There were grooves worn into the walkways between the buildings. The only other times he'd seen things like this were the ancient Aztec ruins and places in Egypt. It took untold thousands of years to erode stone from foot traffic.

"Before the exodates," he said. "Before..." Could humans have come to R'Bak before the Ktor came here? He hadn't read anything about that. He didn't know what to think about such a possibility. "I'm just a damned failed arms dealer," he said, looking up at the glowing roof high above. "What does it all mean?"

He eventually returned to Salsaliin, who was wrapping her grandmother in a sheet he hadn't known she carried. *Part of their funeral rituals.* There was a shovel in his kit, up on the surface. He guessed he needed to go get it. There was likely a burial ground down there somewhere. As well as a stash of some sort of foods.

The Daaj was where some of the natives hid from the Searing. Unless he missed his guess, it would only grow slightly warmer down here, even at the height of the solar assault on R'Bak.

"Salsaliin, how many of these are there?"

"I don't know," she admitted. "It wasn't my place to ask. I only knew it was somewhere around here, because the Atii never leave this area."

Vat surmised the area would circle around the Daaj, and there must be others. The language, of which little bits still survived, had come from the Daaj. Maybe it was all that was left of an ancient culture that settled, or was planted here, first.

This was the pearl he'd been looking for. The underground city was large, big enough for hundreds, or maybe thousands. It was indeed a pearl of great price. He needed to get in touch with Murphy and tell him everything. *Hopefully, with all this, he won't have me blown out an airlock for taking off on my wild hunch.*

He blinked as something occurred to him. "Salsaliin, what did she mean by your child?"

She looked up at him and smiled.

"Oh, hell."

Chapter Seventy-One

SPIN ONE

Well, Murphy temporized, Vat may be a huge pain in the ass, perpetually cruising on the edge of insubordination, but damn, he has a nose for the kind of intel we need. Yes, his reports were totally unprofessional from a military standpoint. He dipped toward breezy prose and no small amount of sideways snark, but his final report on the Sarmatchani, the "related" tribes, their customs, and best of all, their hidden refuges for use during the Searing, was a positive gold mine.

Best of all, and something he included as an almost deleted footnote, was that there was a spiderweb tunnel network that connected almost all the subterranean shelters to which the indigs retreated. If Murphy could get a map of those, it would put the legendary Viet Cong complexes to shame. Some of the networks had reportedly linked as many as half a dozen small sites using over a dozen passages. But what Vat was describing linked almost one hundred subterranean towns with several thousand kilometers of improved tunnels across a region almost eight hundred kilometers east to west and about three hundred kilometers north to south. What that might mean from a strategic perspective—moving large masses of troops and materiel in complete secrecy and safety throughout the entire salient—left Murphy's head spinning with possibilities.

Murphy rubbed his eyes and wished the day was over, but he still had to go through Makarov's comparatively dowdy, carefully parsed and tediously detailed Spin-focused intelligence summaries. They were the very model of proper military report writing. They also made Murphy want to gouge his eyes out with one of the ubiquitous SpinDog sporks. But he'd tasked "Pistol Pete" to gather useful insights from his increasing exposure to, and interest in, the culture of the Spins.

In the wake of the snuffed out Hardliner junta and increasing Expansionist suspicions (bordering on certainty) that Mara Lee's pregnancy was the result of a union with a SpinDog, more info had started to flow. Not a lot, and every move toward more casual, routine relations carried the risk of committing some offense against customs, manners, or decorum that necessitated the soothing of local feathers.

Still, every once in a while, Makarov scored some important insights. One emerged from his linguistic background and led to easier instruction of both new SpinDog helo jocks and the pilots Bowden was preparing for the attack on the transmitter. Specifically, while the Dornaani translator had done a damned impressive job of preparing the Lost Soldiers to communicate with the locals, it had left a couple of absolute blind spots, one of which was aeronautical terminology for describing movement, direction, and relative position. This despite the fact that the aviators of both cultures had near-identical concepts of the particulars of flight.

Enter linguist Pyotr Makarov who made no headway until he noticed the nearly universal etymological origins of such terms among the many languages of Terrans: they were adapted from the language of mariners. In English, it was particularly pronounced: roll, pitch, and yaw had their origins in the motion of ships at sea. So too did terms like "sheer off" and "headwind" and many, many others. So, didn't such terms exist in Ktoran?

Well, in fact they did—but they had fallen out of use among the SpinDogs once they left R'Bak and its oceans and rivers. Over time, they had evolved a far more precise, vector-oriented lexicon derived from the different conditions and circumstances encountered in zero gee and vacuum. Thanks to Makarov's work, the translation of the terms became a genuine equivalence among meanings rather than a baffled acceptance that two sets of entirely different phonemes had the same meaning without having any appreciable analog in their roots.

Improvement of flight training was the immediate practical benefit of Makarov's linguistic detective work, but it also engraved a small footnote into the back of Murphy's mind: that in order to truly understand the SpinDogs, one had to remember that they were almost purely creatures of space—and the ramifications of that difference were as deep as they were broad.

That difference played a role in yet another of Pistol's useful observations. It was presumed that one of the reasons the SpinDogs were so focused upon R'Bak was because they knew that one day they could live there and so, leave behind the almost innumerable impediments and dangers of space all around them.

In fact, almost none felt the pull toward a green world as a longing or a need, though, and perhaps only a third of them felt that they would like to try living on one. In fact, the great majority of SpinDogs were of the considered opinion that planets were dirty, crawling with bugs and disease, and impossibly primitive…so much so, that many believed that merely living on a biogenic planet would somehow induce evolutionary regression.

That revelation also led to the discovery of its profound opposite in a small section of the SpinDog population: those who had aspirations to become liaisons. For those who were already curious about the world, the possibility of increased access was an exciting opportunity. The only problem was that it was too soon to expand routine contact with the R'Baku, even those in the comparatively isolated polar regions that neither the Kulsians nor the satraps' traders visited.

But for all of those who were fated to be disappointed in their ambition to become a liaison, a whole new avenue of dirtside access opened up: pilots and crew for both interface craft and the growing inventory of Hueys. Now, anyone who had started investing time and effort in an accelerated full-gee or partial-gee exercise and preparation regimen was eagerly sought after. Even those who could not master the academics could hope to find roles as crew.

News of this increased need for personnel who could work and live in a planetary environment spread like wildfire: a term that, ironically, had to be explained to the SpinDogs. At Makarov's last count, the number of candidates was about five to one for every slot, but the opportunities kept expanding, so those who came too late or needed more gee-acclimatization were not rejected, but put on a re-testing list. It seemed that crewing air- and spacecraft on and to R'Bak was not going to present the staffing problem that many had feared it would…

Visions of satrap troops fleeing before waves of approaching Hueys popped like soap bubbles as Makarov came rushing through the hatchway into the CP.

"Major, this just came, in right after Vat's final report."

"Can it wait?"

"I think not, sir."

Murphy heard the tone, glanced up. Makarov looked even more dour than usual. Murphy stuck out his hand for the folder clenched in his staff officer's white-knuckled grip.

Murphy set it down on the center of his desk, flipped it open. Satellite images from the Dornaani birds. Murphy leaned over to look more closely. "Shit!"

"Very much so, sir. Shall I schedule a meeting with—?"

"Can't wait," snapped Murphy, jumping up from his chair unsteadily. He told himself that was the Coriolis Effect, but knew that was a lie; he'd adapted to that long ago. *Christ, how long can I keep the MS under wraps if it's starting to affect my balance?*

Suppressing the cold stab of fear behind his sternum, he grabbed the most damning photos and strode past Makarov.

PART SEVEN:

BOWDEN

Chapter Seventy-Two

SPIN ONE

Bowden sighed as he sat down to a well-earned dinner that he had silently tagged as, "hydroponically grown pseudo-food menu number four." It was okay, but the lack of variety in the rohabs was only one of the reasons why Lost Soldiers were eager to get planetside. It helped that he was hungry; a long day in the SpinDog flight simulators were pretty tiring. Not because it was exhausting, but professionally terrifying: the interface craft were really designed for ascent and descent. Level flight was far less stable than what he was used to; cruise really didn't have a sweet spot. And anything vaguely like a combat maneuver quickly brought the aircraft—if you could call it that—to the edge of aerodynamic stability. Sighing, happy the day was over at last, he lifted the first spork of bland mystery food to his mouth…

"What do you make of this?" Murphy's voice asked from over his shoulder.

"I'm sorry?" Bowden managed not to start, looked up from his abortive first bite, spork frozen halfway to his mouth. "What do I make of what?"

"This." Murphy slid some imagery onto the table. "This is the latest imagery of your target."

Bowden pursed his lips as he inspected the pictures and pushed his plate to the side. "This is bad. They're almost ready to use it."

Murphy nodded. "Almost all the tiles are in place in the dish."

Bowden shook his head. "I'm not talking about that." He pointed to a pad off to the side of the suspected control station where at least 20 vehicles sat. "You know what this is?"

"That's what I'm asking you."

Bowden frowned and looked at the arrangement of the vehicles. He'd seen a lot of vehicle pools and armor depots—right before blowing them off the map. These didn't look like his former targets. The way the vehicles were parked was not only too tidy, but too tight, as though no one had any intent of having them deploy with any appreciable speed. Not a one of them. Bowden tapped the antenna. "How are they going to supply power to the transmitter? Do they have some sort of generator nearby?"

Murphy shook his head tightly. "Not that I'm aware. They're pretty low tech. Like I told you before, I'm surprised they were able to make the antenna."

Bowden shrugged. "We built Arecibo in the early 1960s. It's hard, but not really that hard if you have some idea what you're doing. They've been visited by space-faring societies, after all. They have to have some concept of the principles involved."

He tapped the image with the vehicles. "That's what they're going to use to power it—those vehicles. They are probably charging some sort of battery or maybe a capacitor they're going to use to power the transmitter. Or, if they're some sort of fuel-cell variants, they could be plugged into it directly. And these shiny panels on the back of all these APCs they've got parked here? It doesn't look like our models, but I'm betting that's some kind of solar panel." He leaned away from the images. "That's why they're at the site, now: they're the transmitter's power plant. Instead of running around doing whatever it is they would normally do. This means the system is very close to being operational." Murphy did not look happy, but neither did he look surprised. "You knew?"

He shook his head. "I wasn't one hundred percent sure, but you just convinced me." Murphy frowned, kept examining the map.

"And?" Bowden prompted.

"And it means the enemy just leap-frogged us and grabbed the initiative. We'd been planning to bring all the vehicles and trained indigs we could to this site. Slowly, in the hope that we wouldn't give ourselves away until we were within a hundred klicks or so." He waved at the pictures. "But this changes everything. We still might be able to get two light mechanized columns there to attack, but not to achieve what we'd hoped."

"Which was what, again?" Bowden had given up keeping tabs on the ground campaign since, with every passing week, it had looked more and more like that option was starting to circle the bowl.

Murphy shrugged. "Screen off the entire site with aggressive patrols, mount a feint to pull the enemy into the field, and get them to reveal any heavy weapons or positions. They'd probably have shifted their triple-A into an anti-armor role—and that would have given us the ability to clear your path. Also, we would have been able to suppress or interdict any air defense launches, whether SAMs or MANPADs." He shook his head. "But now, we'd be lucky to gather sufficient numbers to get there when you do. If we were to send everyone in dribs and drabs, the local defenses would probably tear them to pieces. But waiting for a reasonable mass of force means we could be slipping behind the enemy's mission clock. We've got to get the strike package down to the planet and hit this thing ASAP, because the stakes are even higher now."

"Higher than knocking out the transmitter?"

Murphy shook his head. "No. That supersedes all other considerations. But look at all these vehicles: all electrics. Solar panels, hydrogen powered fuel cells. We really didn't know they had these, and certainly not so many that they could gather them together like a mobile powerplant. But it also means that the satraps are gambling big. They've not only put all their best vehicles on the line and all in one place; they're hooked up as batteries or, like you say, pumping a capacitor. So when we hit, they can't pull these back into combat; they're wired up and committed. And if we actually capture all or most of them, the satraps of Hamain Ashband will go from being the masters of the wide open spaces to a scattering of isolated princelings bunkered into their cities and huddling behind their walls. So, like I say, we need to get this show on the road. Yesterday."

Bowden folded his arms. "I agree. The sooner, the better. But we're not ready yet. We haven't done any of the live weapons testing, and we don't have our people in place to designate the targets."

"We'll try to get you time to test once you're down there, but if this thing is ready to go, you may not be able to get the ground force in place. You may just have to go and throw bombs at it, and at least delay it becoming operational."

"You mean we'd just be pitching bombs into the reflector panels?"

"If that's what it takes, yes. Then we follow up with the ground forces—if they can get through the defenses…on which we have next to no intel." He sighed. "But the bottom line is that we can't let the satrap get a message off to Kulsis."

"If we hit it early, though, it's going to be a bitch going back. Once we've tipped our hand and shown them our capabilities, they're going to ring the antenna with every gun and missile they have."

"Yes, they are. But we'll have to do it anyway, if it comes to that."

"Well, fuck."

"Exactly."

Bowden sighed. "Okay, so what's your plan? You said we're going to go down to the planet for the attack?"

"Yes. We'll get you planetside via a high-angle polar insertion, then equip the craft and get them ready for the mission."

Bowden nodded. "Makes sense. Trying to develop some sort of heat shield for the weapons systems would have been a bitch, and no one likes having ordnance go off alongside you." He smiled. "Back when I did—" he stopped with a wince. "When I flew—before that day—I never thought it sounded like fun, anyway."

"No, I'll bet not. Bottom line is we're going to get you down to the planet ASAP, along with the personnel and equipment you need for the mission. Once you get set up there, you can do whatever testing you need, assuming there's time."

"So," Bowden asked with a wry smile, "when do we leave?"

Murphy's grim expression remained unchanged. "Funny you should ask…"

Chapter Seventy-Three

R'BAK

Bowden walked off the interface craft and got his first look at R'Bak. It reminded him of his weapons detachments at Naval Air Station Fallon, Nevada. Hot and dry, with an emphasis on hot and dry. And, if he understood correctly, it was going to get *a lot* hotter and drier as the Searing approached. A number of people were working to unload the supplies the interface craft carried, and he pulled one aside.

"First time here," he said. "Where do I go?"

The man—his rank was unknown since he was working in a sweat-stained T-shirt—pointed toward a point of land to the west. "It's just around there…uh, sir," he added.

"Is there any sort of transportation?"

"Sorry, sir. The trucks are for carrying the bombs and stuff you guys brought down." He nodded to Bowden's legs. "Your only transport is what God gave you, unless you can ride a whinnie."

"A whinnie?"

"Big-ass lizards. That are really mammals. I think."

"No thanks."

"Then I'm afraid you'll have to walk. It's how we get back and forth, too. You'll also want a hat, and soon."

"Thanks," Bowden said with a resigned sigh and a glance up at the dual suns. He started walking. The air wing had to do a lot of walking around Fallon, too, during their periodic trips there. You got used to it. As long as you didn't work hard, you didn't even sweat much, since the ultra-arid air wicked it off as soon as it appeared on your skin.

As he approached the point of land, he saw a large figure who had stopped and was looking around.

"Hi, Dork," he said when he recognized the soldier.

"Hi, suh," the trooper said, saluting.

"What are you doing?"

"Well, I was told the camp was this way, but I don't see it, and I wasn't sure if it was this way or around that point of land over there." He sighed. "I'm lost, suh."

Bowden smiled. *His sense of direction is really bad if he can't go from one point to another.* "You're on the right path. It should just be around this point of land."

They started walking again, and the tent city began to materialize from behind the rocky outcropping a minute later. "See?" Bowden asked. "You were almost to it."

The big soldier smiled. "Thanks, suh. Directions are hard."

Bowden smiled but privately worried. Hopefully, the soldier could remember the directions he'd been given on operating the mule.

Camp Stark was nestled back in a small, sheltered area between two slopes a short way from the edge of the tableland that overlooked a long valley. In addition to the tents that marked the Terran presence on the planet, Bowden could see a corral as they approached, and he got his first look at the whinnies.

The massive creatures resembled a cross between an iguana and a Komodo dragon, if they'd been fed steroids from birth. From head to tail, they were over three meters long, and stood well over a meter high at the shoulder. They had wide, clawed feet, which were obviously made for digging, and would probably help with climbing some of the arid landscape nearby.

A pretty, olive-skinned woman was teaching a corporal how to ride as they walked by. Although her instruction seemed patient and well thought out, the corporal was having difficulties, and the more the corporal fought, the more the whinnie stamped and snorted.

Bowden stepped up to the railing and chuckled. He'd happily take an F/A-18 over one of the bucking lizards any day of the week. *If we weren't a gazillion miles and a couple of centuries from the closest Hornet, that is.*

The woman turned. "Want to give it a try since you think it's so funny?"

"No, ma'am, I don't," Bowden said. "I was just wondering, though, how hard it was to teach people to ride those things. We have a mission where people will need to go a long way, fast, and those things—whinnies, right?—are probably the best way to get them there."

"They're not hard to ride," she said with a smile, "even if the corporal is having difficulties. As soon as he stops fighting the whinnie, he'll be fine."

Bowden nodded to Dork. "Even someone as big as him?"

"He'd need one of our bigger whinnies, but I don't see any reason why not."

"I love horses," Dork said. "I rode a lot back home."

"Then you'll do fine with a whinnie," the woman said. She patted her whinnie's shoulder. "Athena and her friends are a lot smarter and easier to ride. If you could sit a horse, you can easily ride a whinnie."

"Okay," Dork said, brightening. "I'll come over as soon as I can."

"Good," Bowden said. "Make sure Renaldi gets over here, too."

Bowden sighed as he looked at the interface craft's laser designator the next morning. Despite the number of times he'd asked to have the wires run through the box and directly into the wing's hardpoint, the designator looked like a bowl of spaghetti, with wires hanging out of it and running every which way, not bundled up in nice zip-tied runs like he was used to with US military aircraft. If there was time, that still had to be fixed. If the stupid box hadn't been welded shut, he would have done it himself a long time ago.

"Hey, Kevin, got a moment?" a voice asked from behind him, and he turned to see Tom Byrd.

"Yeah," Bowden said. He nodded to the designator. "That's still not the way I asked for it to be."

Byrd nodded after a quick glance. "It's just begging for something to come by and rip all the wires out of it."

"My thoughts exactly. What's up?"

Byrd looked at him for a second. "This may not be any of my business," he said finally, "but why aren't *you* leading this mission? You seem to know all the tech better than any of us, and you've done all of the target analysis…just seems like you should be leading it, and you're not even going."

Bowden turned back to the laser designator, unable to meet Byrd's eyes, and smoothed one of the wires. "I can't," he said. "I just can't." He played with another of the wires, waiting for Byrd to leave, but he could tell the aviator was still standing behind him. Bowden sighed and turned around.

"My last mission didn't end well. It was in Somalia."

"*Somalia?*" Byrd asked. "I'm not even sure I know where that is. Africa, maybe? What the hell were you doing there?"

"I don't know. I'm not sure anyone really knew." He shrugged. "It *is* in Africa by the way, and if there is a place that is the direct opposite of Vietnam, it's Somalia. Dry, arid, and very few trees." He sighed, remembering.

"The place went to shit in 1991, when the country's dictator was overthrown in a military coup staged by a coalition of opposition warlords. Then the warlords began fighting among themselves, and the country fell apart. Everybody there was starving…it was pretty awful. We went in as part of an international humanitarian and peacekeeping effort, but nobody really wanted us there. The various militias disregarded the cease-fires that were in place, and all of them looted and pillaged what they could. Basically, the place just sucked ass.

"Right at the end, there was a guy we wanted to catch—a guy named Aidid—who we knew was responsible for a lot of the badness. We sent in a bunch of guys to grab some of his folks, but the indigs shot down a couple of helicopters and killed a bunch of our people. Newspapers had lots of pictures of the locals doing awful things to their bodies. We decided to kill him, and I led a mission to bomb the building he was hiding in."

Bowden sighed, a lot heavier this time. "Only it turns out the guy that sold us the location didn't play straight with us; he gave us Aidid's chief rival, who was attending his daughter's wedding at a place outside of town. We couldn't get anyone close to the building to confirm Aidid's presence, but the chain of command went ahead and authorized the strike anyway.

"Just as my bombs hit the building, a little girl, all dressed in white, ran out the front door of the building—a church—and the force of the explosion threw her almost thirty meters." Bowden saw her small limbs spread wide as she cartwheeled through the air, and he choked back a sob. "She…" He swallowed, reliving the end of the memory, then set his shoulders and continued, "She was impaled on the wrought iron fence that went around the yard." He sniffed and wiped his eyes.

"The last…the last thing I saw on my targeting camera was her twitching, broken body on the fence, her hand outstretched to the mother she'd never see again."

His breath shuddered out of him. "The newspapers back home ran the picture of the little girl the next day, in color, calling for blood. My blood. I'd have been happy to let them have it. The chain of command sent me home for the official investigation, but I ended up—" he waved a hand at his surroundings, "—here."

Byrd looked away. "Yeah. Shit happens in wars sometimes. Just be glad you never saw napalm used, or anyone who got it on them. That's a sight." He swallowed. "Let me just say it's unforgettable, even if it wasn't your bombs that did it." He turned back to Bowden. "In your case, even though the bombs were yours, hitting the wrong target wasn't your fault. You couldn't know the targeting was bad or that the guy lied. You're not to blame for the girl."

Bowden shook his head and poked himself in the chest. "*My* plane. *My* bombs. *My thumb* on the button. That's how the little girl got impaled on the fence. So, bottom line: *I* did it. And I won't do it again. *I can't.*"

"Lieutenant Bowden!" a voice yelled as someone shook him. It seemed like he'd just gone to sleep after a second day of trying to get the aircraft the way they were supposed to be, so the new weapons systems could be tested out the next day. And the laser designators *still* hadn't been rewired.

"Mphf?" he asked.

"Lieutenant! You're needed at the command tent for a radio call. Quick—there's only a couple minutes of, uh, connectivity!"

He rolled out of his cot and started pulling on his boots.

"No time for that, sir!" the private standing by his cot exclaimed. "We have to go *now*!"

Bowden didn't bother lacing the boots; he got up and raced after the private, who waved at the people standing guard at the command tent, and they held open the flap. Not even a framed door, yet.

The Army captain he'd been sitting next to in the doomed Blackhawk—Bo Moorefield—nodded when he saw Bowden. Not even a smile as he waved him to come over to the comms console. So: it was *that* bad.

Moorefield barked into radio handset, "Glass Palace this is Starkpatch. Lieutenant Bowden is present, over."

"Bowden, Murphy here. We only have a minute before we run out of line-of-sight comms, but H-Hour is right now. Last pass had the vehicles in the target area wired up and running; they're charging the transmitter. We have to stop that from happening. I need you to get the mission underway ASAP!"

"I'll take care of it," Bowden said. "We'll get the aircraft loaded and out as quickly as we can."

"Understood. Three updates for you. First, the two mech columns—one that Captain Moorefield is readying now, and another under Lieutenant Tapper—will not get to the target as soon as you do. The most optimistic estimates put them an hour behind.

"Second, Captain Moorefield is sending a squad with the two handheld designators on whinnie-back, led by Aliza Turan. They're going to try to get into place by the time you reach the antenna."

"Good, glad to have them. A ground designate ups the chances of mission success exponentially."

"It's good for something else."

Uh oh. "What's that?"

"I need you to fly the mission," Murphy said. "Captain Hirst broke his ankle last night playing soccer and can't do it. You have to fill in for him."

"I can't—"

"*You have to.* Byrd will hit the control station, Fiezel the antenna. You are only flying airborne back up. Even if you're needed, there will be a ground designate. Your bombs will go where they're supposed to."

"I don't—"

"Lieutenant, you *must*, and you know it," Murphy said, his voice noticeably fading. "I don't want to make this an order. But if you don't fly the mission, we'll all be—"

Static.

"That's it," Moorefield said when Murphy's voice didn't come back again. "What do you need from me?"

I can do this, Bowden thought, squaring his shoulders. *I don't have to drop bombs; just go along as the spare. Byrd is a RIO—he knows his shit. He'll flatten the control station. I won't have to drop.*

"Kevin?" Moorefield asked. "What do you need from me?"

And there's a team on the ground to designate the target. It's their fault if a bomb goes astray, not mine. I can do this. It won't be my fault.

"Lieutenant Bowden, you heard Murphy. We're on a countdown clock, now. I repeat: what do you need from me?"

I can do this. I have to do this. Everyone is counting on me. All I need to do is fly, not actually drop bombs. I can do this. I will *do this.* Bowden focused his eyes on Moorefield. "Just thinking about what needs to be done," he lied. "Murphy said you can send someone to lead my two ground designate guys?"

"I'm sending Aliza Turan and Sergeant Cook's squad along with them. They're our most accomplished whinnie riders. If anyone can get your guys to where they need to be, it's them."

"Good. Get them moving right away; they'll take the longest to get there. Then call over to the airfield; we need the aircraft prepped and loaded, ASAP." And the bombs and missiles still had to be assembled, and there were a million other final details that needed to be overseen. This was the clusterfuck to end all clusterfucks. He looked down and realized he was still in his pajamas. "I guess I ought to get dressed, too." He smiled, trying to push back the feelings that rose up, trying to overwhelm him, drag him under, drown him in paralyzing fear. Fear of flying a bombing mission again, even as an observer. "I can wake up the crews on my way."

Okay. This is just like the last-second surprise missions they'd add to the flight schedule in Fallon, just to see if the air wing could rise to the occasion, Bowden thought. *Except here, I'm missing all the people I would normally have to support me. But dammit, we're naval air. Can we do it? You bet your* ass *we can!*

Chapter Seventy-Four

R'BAK

Aliza Turan woke to voices in the dark and froze for a second until her brain was awake enough to focus. She'd thought the memory had been put behind her, but vestiges of it were still obviously lurking in the dark places of her mind.

"Over there," a woman said grumpily, pointing to Aliza.

A shadow moved from the woman who'd spoken to Aliza's bed. "Miss Turan?"

"Yes?"

"Captain Moorefield needs you at the command tent."

"Be right there," she said, now fully awake. She smiled. Being needed always catapulted her out of the past and into the present; it made everything right and reminded her that, yes, she had a purpose in life again.

As soon as the man left, she pushed off the scratchy blanket, dressed quickly, and made her way to the command tent. Even though she'd hurried, she saw as she entered that she wasn't the first to arrive. She frowned slightly as she caught sight of Sergeant James Cook and Corporal Bob Parker already talking with Moorefield; she'd hoped to talk privately with him. There was obviously a mission or crisis to deal with. So, no moonlight walk, then.

Damn it.

Moorefield's smile when he saw her, though, alleviated her disappointment a little. It also made her heart flutter.

"Thanks for coming," Moorefield said. "We just got immediate tasking, and I need your help."

Even better than a moonlight walk. "What is happening?" she asked, nodding to Cook and Parker.

"You know the interface craft and pilots that arrived yesterday?"

She nodded. "I met one of the pilots and one of the ground team. They asked about riding whinnies."

Moorefield nodded. "They're here to blow up the transmitter the J'Stull are building. There are two ground guys who are here to designate the targets so the aviators can drop bombs on them."

"Designate them? Like put a big orange piece of material with a bullseye on the targets? One that reads, 'Drop here?'" She smiled.

"Not really," Moorefield said, and she could see he was determined to keep the conversation absolutely serious. *Too important for even a small joke. That's a bad sign.* She dropped the smile.

Moorefield nodded, acknowledging the change in her bearing. "There are two men who have lasers. Their job is to point the lasers at the targets. The bombs the aviators are going to drop will see the reflected laser energy and guided down to them, eliminating the targets."

Cook's and Parker's presence made sense. They led the squad with the best whinnie riders, and, along with her, were the best riders in the camp. Except for Moorefield, himself, who probably couldn't go because he'd been up all day and was currently on duty.

"We need to get them to the target?"

Moorefield nodded. "The two ground guys have both ridden in the past, but they've never ridden whinnies, and they need to be able to if we're going to get them where they need to be in time. I don't want to send you on this, but you're the most experienced person I have for teaching people how to ride whinnies, and I need Cook and his men to provide protection for them and get them to the target. If you're willing, I need you to keep them in their saddles while Cook's squad gets them to the target."

"Very well. When do we leave?"

"As soon as possible," Cook said. "We've got a lot of ground to cover, and most of it—especially once we get near the target—is pretty forbidding terrain. It's going to be a hard ride getting there and may be an even harder ride on the way out if we attract the attention of the J'Stull."

Aliza nodded. There was no way in hell she'd turn down a chance to make herself useful. *Or to turn down Bo, at all, if the truth were known.* "I shall gather my gear. Tell them to meet me at the paddock."

She already had the whinnies saddled when the two privates arrived with Private Ivan Petrov from Cook's squad. Both of the newcomers had big packs on their backs.

She nodded to the packs as they carefully set them aside. "Are those the designators?"

"Yes, ma'am," the bigger one—Dorkhouse—said.

"They look heavy. Want me to saddle another whinnie to pack them along?"

"No, ma'am," the other—Renaldi, she thought—replied. "Bad enough to have to carry it along. It'd be worse if the damn lizard sat on it and broke it or something."

"The whinnies are quite smart," Aliza said. "They'd do a good job with them. Probably better than you'd do if you fell off your whinnie and landed on the box."

"All the same, ma'am," Dork said, "I'd rather keep mine close to me."

"Me, too," Renaldi added.

"As you wish. Now, I'm going to give you a crash course in riding whinnies—"

"Can we do it without the crash?" Dork asked.

He sounds like he means it. She smiled. The man seemed good natured, if a little slow. His partner, while more mentally agile, sounded like an annoying New Yorker she'd had the displeasure of knowing once. "Of course," she replied when Renaldi rolled his eyes. "This will be the quick, no-crash version. Whinnies are easier to ride than horses, because they're smarter…"

Aliza stood from fastening the saddle's belly-straps as Moorefield approached Cook's squad to see them off. "Good luck," he said to Cook. He turned to Aliza. "Be careful."

She nodded. "I will. I'll get them there and back, safe and sound." She smiled. "With Sergeant Cook's help, of course."

Cook nodded. "Ready to go, ma'am?"

Aliza looked to her two charges. Dork was on Scout, Moorefield's mount, as it was the biggest one they had, while Renaldi was on Trigger, a smaller male that had a more golden color. Dork gave her a thumbs-up, while Renaldi nodded. He was less comfortable on whinnie-back and probably didn't want to let go of the reins. "We are ready," Aliza said.

Moorefield stepped up to Scout. "Take care of them, boy," he said, slapping the whinnie's shoulder. The whinnie purred.

"Keep a light on for us," Cook said, then turned to the formation. "At the canter, forward *harch!*"

Moorefield watched Aliza's back as the squad rode off across the plateau. It was never easy to stay back when you sent men out to do something dangerous, and this time, it was even harder. "*Vaya con Dios*, Honey," he muttered quietly.

"Not sure you really want to do that," a voice said as Bowden gave a tug on the last missile. He turned to find Byrd smiling at him.

"Strangest preflight I've ever done," Bowden said. "I don't know how it was with you, but before I ever got to touch a new model of aircraft, there were a bunch of ground school classes, emergency procedures trainers, and simulators out the ass."

"I got some ground school, but all that whiz-bang computer shit was long after my time."

"Yeah, I guess it would have been." Bowden smiled and slapped the interface craft. "I barely know anything about the craft. If we have an emergency, the pilot will have to handle it, because I don't know shit. The oddest thing, though—from my point of view, anyway—is that we *never* got to touch live ordnance until we knew it inside and out. I barely know what to look for from these weapons, and none of them have the orange 'Remove Before Flight' tags."

"Yeah," Byrd commiserated, "I don't even really *want* to look at the weapons, because then I see how everything is cobbled together, and I start thinking, 'There's no way this shit's going to work.' Weapon safety isn't a big thing with the SpinDogs, which is why I said I'm not sure you really want to tug on the weapons. Fiezel had one of the latches on a Sidewinder fail when he did that, and it came off in his hands."

"Holy shit! What did he do?"

"The other latch on it held, or it would have dropped to the dirt, as there's no way he could have stopped the 400-pound missile. While I don't *think* it would have gone off, I wouldn't say the same about one of the Skippers if they hit nose-first."

Bowden shuddered. He'd shaken all four of his, along with the two Sidewinders, and he realized the drop to the ground was longer than the arming wires. If one had fallen, it would have been armed when it hit, and the 1,000-pound bomb probably *would* have gone off. *Oh hell!*

Byrd took a couple of steps closer. "Hey…you going to be okay with, umm, going along?" he asked quietly.

"Yeah, I'm fine," Bowden said. *Mostly.* "I'm just the airborne spare."

"I'll make sure I take out the control station," Byrd said with a smile. "That way you don't have to worry about it. Even if the Zoomie misses his target, the transmitter will be out of commission until they build a new control station. If they even have the parts to do so, which they might not. It'll take them time to rebuild it, and by then we can have more people trained to fly the mission." He chuckled. "Maybe we can even test out the weapons a few times, too."

"Yeah, that would be nice." Bowden smiled. "I guess, since you're here, you're ready to go?"

Byrd nodded. "Fiezel is almost done, too." He looked at his watch. "And right on time. We're supposed to be wheels-up in twenty minutes in order to be there when we told the people riding the giant Komodo dragon things."

The column was riding down a dry riverbed which had cut a crevice through the foothills when it narrowed suddenly. Aliza

Turan rode forward to get a look at why Sergeant Cook and Corporal Parker had reined in their whinnies. "What's up?" she asked as she pushed her mount alongside theirs in the narrow fissure.

Cook nodded to the landscape in front of them. The crevice divided into three separate, smaller paths. "The map we have only shows the terrain near the target, and we're not close enough yet to be on the map. We're not sure which of those crevices is the right way forward, and we're trying to decide which one to follow."

"Can't we send scouts up each of them?" Aliza asked.

"No time, ma'am," Cook said. "We're already behind timeline. If we get there after the planes go by, Johnson's loss is for naught." They'd surprised a group of J'Stull soldiers, who had made a small camp in a place where the crevice widened significantly. Cook, Parker, and several of his men had charged the camp, riding through and killing the enemy soldiers, but they'd lost Corporal Johnson to a lucky shot by one of the enemy.

"What have you decided?"

Cook ran the back of his sleeve across his forehead to wipe away the sweat. "Nothing yet, ma'am. The one going to the right heads up toward some higher terrain and is probably impassable, which leaves us two. Parker thinks that we'd be better off going to the left as it's less likely to get closed off, and I think the center one is more likely to keep us away from the indigs."

Aliza sighed and looked at her watch. Cook was right; they didn't have time for this…yet they had even less time to make the wrong choice and have to backtrack. Without warning, Athena, her whinnie, stood up on its back two legs, and Aliza had to grab the saddle to keep from being thrown. The whinnie trumpeted loudly, then it dropped back onto all fours.

Within a couple of seconds, another whinnie replied from somewhere ahead, and all three whinnies backed away from the split. The three Terrans looked at each other, then refocused on the center passage and the fast thudding of an approaching whinnie. Everyone drew their weapons as an enormous specimen rounded the last corner, side-winding swiftly toward them. The creature didn't have a saddle or any other equipment to show it had been around humans before.

Athena turned her head and pushed the muzzle of Aliza's pistol away from the approaching lizard. "Cook, Parker, put your weapons away. My whinnie's saying this one is friendly."

The soldiers reluctantly holstered their rifles as the strange whinnie approached and came to rub noses with Athena. It then turned and moved to stand at the entrance to the crevice on the right.

"Huh. It seems to think we should take the pass to the right," Aliza said.

"I don't know, ma'am," Cook replied. "I know we've seen some pretty strong indications that the whinnies are smart, but I don't know if we can trust them to make this choice. I mean, how do we know your whinnie really knows what we're trying to do and where we're trying to go? And how would it send that information to this, eh, wild one?"

"I don't know," Aliza said, "but I say we trust them."

"I'm with the Sarge on this one," Parker said. "I've done a lot of scouting in these hills, and that gulch looks like it's going into some pretty significant terrain."

Athena blew out her breath in a snorting noise and walked forward into the crevice on the right. The large male whinnie stepped ahead of her, jogged forward, and Aliza's whinnie picked up her pace to match. "It seems," she called over her shoulder, "that the decision has been made!"

She risked a glance behind her, and she saw the two men shrug and start after her. She turned back in time to lean into the turn as Athena negotiated a rocky outcropping, and she hunched forward to pat the whinnie's shoulder. "I just hope you know what you're doing."

Chapter Seventy-Five

R'BAK

"Rocket assist in five," Lotho Ferenc said once the tow vehicle had moved off the runway, leaving his aircraft—the mission's lead platform—with its nose aimed down the long, groomed strip.

Although usually reserved for old-fashioned ramjets that had to be accelerated to generate the airflow necessary to ignite the engine, the RATO—rocket-assisted take off—modules had been mounted on each of the three combat craft. Conventional take off—vertical or otherwise—consumed a great deal of their dual-phase engines' fuel, and Bowden's flight was going to need every drop in its tanks since they would have to loiter near the target until they got the go-ahead from the laser designation team. Although built for operations in-atmosphere, the SpinDog craft were not optimized for it, and they consumed fuel rapidly, even during the most normative missions—and this one was going to be anything but.

Five seconds later, the dual rockets on the back of Ferenc's craft fired, and it leaped forward. Halfway down the runway, both of its dual-phase engines rose to a low burn, trailing additional plumes. Ferenc rotated with about a quarter of the runway remaining, and the craft soared up and away as the rockets died out. Ferenc turned downwind and jettisoned the spent rockets, which deployed parachutes and descended to be picked up and used again.

As the second craft bearing Fiezel and Burg Hrensku leaped forward, though, Bowden could immediately see something was wrong. Only one rocket plume emerged from underneath the tail of the craft.

"Bad rocket!" Jukhal Samkamka yelled on the radio next to him. "You've got a bad rocket, Burg." No second rocket meant extremely uneven thrust, and that meant disaster. The only remaining question was: how bad?

There wasn't enough time to correct with thrust from the vehicle's own dual-phase scramjets, and frankly, this wasn't the sort of failure the SpinDog pilots had ever had to worry about and for which there simply hadn't been enough time to train.

Fiezel and Hrensku were on a runaway craft, and it was unstoppable until the rocket burned out. There was no sense hitting the brakes until it did—it would only have blown out the tires and stripped the brakes as the craft skidded along.

The rocket burned out just over halfway down the runway. Instantly, the craft's spoilers popped up and smoke poured from underneath; Hrensku had jumped on the brakes, trying to keep the craft on the runway. But Bowden could tell it wasn't going to stop in time. He'd once seen an F/A-18 go off a runway, and it had looked just like this. The two vehicles that served as fire engines—stationed at the 3/4-point on the runway—churned up a cloud of dust as they chased after the runaway craft.

The bird was still going about 50 miles an hour as it left the prepared surface of the runway. It traveled about 30 meters, and then the left main mount either went into a hole or hit a soft patch of dirt; Bowden couldn't tell which. The left main mount stopped, but the craft kept going. The mount was torn off in a spray of shredded parts, and the left wing dropped to the surface. The sudden increase in off-center drag spun the craft about 90 degrees before it stopped.

Bowden sighed. "And *that* is why we have a spare." The full significance hit him a moment later: his was no longer the spare third craft. It, and he, were now a "go" asset. It was like he was waking from a nightmare, only to realize he hadn't been dreaming at all.

"Wait…uh…maybe they'll want to come and fly this craft instead," Bowden said as his lunch threatened to come back up.

"After they just wrecked, they are going to want to try it again?" Samkamka chuckled. "Even if they are uninjured—

which is unlikely—I find it improbable they will be eager to take our place."

"Uh…yeah," Bowden said lamely.

"There is a problem, though," Samkamka added.

"What's that?" Bowden asked, feeling like a drowning victim who's suddenly been thrown a life ring.

Samkamka motioned down the runway. "They are still in the way. If we experience the same malfunction, it is likely we will run into them. Our normal procedure would be to not attempt a takeoff until their aircraft is towed clear." He shrugged. "As they are missing a wheel, that will take some time."

Bowden looked down the runway. It would be hours before they got the aircraft moved, and—even if they launched then—it would be dark when they got to the target. Who knew if the ground force would still be there, or if they would be able to see the cables anymore. To say nothing of the fact that the first craft would have to come back, refuel, and get new rockets. Which might also fail.

No. If we're going to go, we need to go now. As much as Bowden wanted to cancel the flight, he knew he couldn't. The weapons were untested, and some probably wouldn't work. They had an airborne spare for a reason—if something went wrong with Ferenc and Byrd's craft, then all of this had been for nothing, and the J'Stull would be able to call Kulsis before a second strike could be mounted.

He had to go. All the Lost Soldiers, both on the ground converging on the target and those in space, were counting on them to get the mission done. As scared as he was, and as little as he wanted to go, he knew there was only one thing he could say.

"We have to attempt it, even with the other plane sitting in our abort lane. It's now or never."

Samkamka nodded. "Yes, it is." He started moving switches. "Ten seconds."

Bowden pressed himself back into his seat. "Hey, Samkamka?"

"Yes?"

"If we get a rocket failure, swerve right to miss them, okay?"

"I will try."

That didn't give Bowden the confidence he was looking for, but he had no time to comment or object. Samkamka pressed the red button in front of him, and the rockets lit off underneath them. With only the launching of the other two craft to go by, Bowden was pretty sure both rockets had ignited as he was smashed into his seat, and he saw stars as his head slammed against the back of his helmet.

"Uh…past one quarter," he said. They'd already passed the marker by the time he was conscious enough to notice and call it out. It was like a catapult launch, but one that didn't *end.* A catapult stroke was over in 300 feet—about three seconds—and then the feeling like you were being crushed was over. This one extended past 6,000 feet, and—finally—ended up with them going considerably faster than what a Hornet was traveling at the end of the catapult stroke.

"Engines increasing to nominal…now," Samkamka said through gritted teeth.

"Rockets out…now." Bowden confirmed, watching both the timer and the runway markers.

The pressure on Bowden's chest diminished as Samkamka eased the craft off the ground and put it into a right turn so they didn't overfly the wreckage of the second aircraft.

"Jettisoning." Bowden pushed the two release buttons and felt the *thumps* as the rockets were kicked away.

Bowden shook his head to clear it. He'd always thought being a naval aviator was the pinnacle of "badass." He now knew he'd been wrong. "Let's see if our weapons systems made it through that ride without shaking loose."

Samkamka nodded. "Beginning systems checks."

The ground continued to drop away as the horizon rushed at them.

Athena stopped alongside the wild whinnie as the trail ended in a near-vertical outcropping of rock and sandy soil about 100 feet high. Aliza looked up the hill as Cook moved alongside her.

"Just what I was afraid was going to happen if we came this way," he said. "We're not getting up that hill."

Aliza sighed; Cook was right. No matter how strong and powerful the whinnies were, there was no way they were getting up the incline with riders and loads. It was so close to vertical that even ascent by a human was going to be perilous, at best. And with their current loads…

"I can try climbing up with a rope," Parker said, reining in beside them. "Once I'm up there, I can help pull you up. The gear will still make it dangerous, though," He assessed the steep slope again. "But this will be as far as we take the whinnies."

Cook frowned at the long climb Parker was proposing. "If you can make it up there. The ground looks really soft. Pretty good chance of a landslide."

"We're not getting any closer to the target, Sarge, and going back will take too long."

Cook looked over to Aliza, who shrugged. "You might as well let him try, Sergeant. As he said, we are running out of time."

Parker started tying several coils of rope together. As he was working on lashing the third 20-meter section to the second, the wild whinnie grabbed the first rope in its teeth and sprinted up the slope. Although it had to step on some of the looser soil, causing clods of dirt and small stones to slide down the side of the hill, the whinnie was able to use the rocky outcroppings to turn and leap upward to the crest.

The rope was yanked from Parker's hands as the whinnie achieved the summit, and the end of the rope pulled forward to rest at the base of the hill.

Aliza looked over to Cook, whose jaw was hanging open. "One stairway, no waiting," she said, pleased that her use of American idiom had been, apparently, accurate. She dismounted. "Gentlemen, as you observed, time is short."

The squad made it to the top of the rise and found another crevice that led in their direction of travel. Unfortunately, half the whinnies weren't able to make the leaps necessary to get up the cliff, and the crevice that led forward was too narrow for the ones that could.

"We will go on our own from here," Aliza said with a pat on Athena's shoulder. They had taken off the saddles. Hopefully, the whinnies would wait for them; if not, it was going to be a long walk back to the base. As there was a chance of enemy action, though, they didn't want to leave the whinnies tied up. Athena made a purring noise as she rubbed her nose on Aliza's shoulder, who smiled and murmured, "Thank you, my friend." Athena purred again.

Aliza walked over to the large male and patted him on the shoulder, too. "Thank you for showing us the way."

The male also purred and turned to rub his nose on Aliza but wasn't as gentle and knocked her back several feet. "Ouch," she said, rubbing her shoulder. "We will have to work on your people skills."

"All right," Cook said, calling down from the top of the slope, "I've got the first good news of the day. I just found where we are on the map, and we're closer to the target than I thought. We can still make it in time, but we're going to have to hurry."

Chapter Seventy-Six

R'BAK

Samkamka rendezvoused with the other aircraft and flew in a loose cruise position on it. Bowden pursed his lips as the airspeed indicator continued to climb through 800 kilometers an hour. "We need to slow down," he said.

"The dual-phase engines work most efficiently when supersonic," Samkamka replied. "Mach 3 is best."

"That's great and all, but none of the things we have strapped to the craft have been flight tested for those speeds. The laser designator, especially, wasn't designed to be flown in-atmosphere and isn't aerodynamic in the slightest. If you put too much of a load on it, you're going to tear it off, and then where will we be?"

Samkamka grumbled a little, but then he called the lead aircraft and got them to slow down. Even at that speed, though, they passed over the mechanized columns in just over a minute and reached the contact point, fifty kilometers south of the J'Stull town, after a few minutes more. Behind the small town sat the mountain range, and in the valley directly behind the town, Bowden could see the antenna strung from one mountain to another. It seemed surreal to actually see it in person after all the target study and preparation. *Especially since I never planned to be here.*

"Cookie, this is Bluebird, over," a voice said on the radio.

"Who is that?" Samkamka asked.

"That's Byrd calling the ground troops," Bowden replied.

"Cookie, this is Bluebird, over," Byrd repeated.

"Where do you suppose the ground team is?" Samkamka asked. "Do you think they got captured?"

Bowden shrugged. "No idea. I hope they didn't get caught. Maybe their radio is bad."

Byrd tried one more time, but the soldiers on the ground still didn't reply.

"Hornet, Bluebird."

"Go ahead, Bluebird," Bowden replied.

"I don't know if you heard, but we've got negative comms with Cookie."

"We heard."

"We have the fuel to hold here and give them a chance to check in. Looks like two blimps in the target area. We're going to thin them out while we wait."

"Roger," Bowden said as the other craft peeled off. "Good hunting."

Ferenc shoved the throttles to the firewall, and Byrd looked at the pilot as the craft leaped forward.

Ferenc smiled. "You said speed is life. So, more is better, yes?"

Byrd nodded. "The worst place to be is low, slow, and out of ideas." He nodded toward the target area. "Let's go for the one on the left; it's a little closer."

The pilot nudged the thrusters back gently and moved the nose of the craft toward the intended target.

"Master arm is on," Byrd said, throwing the switch that energized the weapons system. "Sidewinder is selected."

A veteran of numerous dogfights over Vietnam, Byrd knew what to expect. The adrenaline boost as the craft rocketed forward into the fight. The dilation of time. The sharpened focus. What he wasn't prepared for was the relative difference in their target's speed. Every other fight he'd been in, the MiGs had been going as fast—or faster—than his craft. Compared to the interface craft, now approaching the speed of sound, the blimp was at a standstill, and it expanded in the front canopy faster than any target he'd ever seen. Without his radar, he had to guess the distance, but with a closing velocity of more than a mile every six seconds, it swelled quickly.

But it was also starting to drop a little lower on the windscreen. "Nose down a little," he coached. "We have to be aimed at the gondola." Ferenc dropped the nose of the craft until it was boresighted on the gondola.

"Fire!" Byrd yelled when they reached what he thought was five miles. Nothing. "Fire! Now!"

Still nothing.

"Shit!" Byrd exclaimed, figuring Ferenc had forgotten what he was supposed to do. It happened in combat, sometimes, where newer pilots lost track of what they were supposed to do next on their checklists. Byrd slapped the missile launch button on his console, and the missile roared off the left wing. "Break left!" he yelled. The blimp almost filled the windscreen.

They continued heading straight at it. Byrd risked a glance over at the pilot.

Ferenc was staring at the blimp, his eyes wide and mouth open as he watched the missile race toward the floating oval. "*Shit!*" Byrd had heard of crews that had gotten target fixation and augured in—and had even had to yell at a pilot once to break him out of it—but as a backseater, he'd never seen the corresponding look on a pilot's face. Until now.

The lights were on, but Ferenc had left the cockpit.

Byrd grabbed the control stick and ripped it to the left. He had a glimpse of one of the crewmen jumping off the blimp—the image of which now blocked any view of the sky—then the missile impacted the gondola, followed immediately by the right wing of Byrd's interface craft.

Bowden watched in horror as the interface craft clipped the blimp at more than 800 kilometers an hour. The impact sheared the gondola from the airship, while simultaneously ripping the right wing from the interface craft.

Free of the weight of the gondola and with massive holes torn in the underside of the envelope, the blimp deflated like a balloon that had been blown up and then let go. It traced a lazy rising spiral as the plane went down and to the left, crashing just short of the antenna complex. Some of the debris may have ended up on the antenna's panels, but nothing that couldn't be easily and quickly cleaned off.

Bowden's life—and Byrd's friendly face—flitted past his mind's eye as he saw the interface craft's fuselage to roll to a stop. *There's no one left to destroy the antenna; it's all on me.*

"What just happened?" Samkamka asked. "Why did they do that?"

The remains of the blimp, deflated, floated down between the J'Stull town and the fireball that marked the end of the interface craft. In Bowden's mind, the corpses of little kids bounced up and down on the gas bag as if it were a trampoline.

"What happened?" Samkamka asked again. The SpinDog's voice was indistinct and came from somewhere far away. The little kids on the trampoline had all become girls with holes in their stomachs, and blood sprayed out as they bounced, streaking their bright white dresses.

"*What happened?*" Samkamka roared. He grabbed Bowden's arm and tugged fiercely.

Bowden pulled his arm away, but the spell was broken. He shook his head and looked back at the crash site. The children were gone; all that remained was the pyre of a Marine aviator who'd given his life a long, long way from home.

"I don't know," Bowden said, trying to put himself in Byrd's place. "It looks like they got too close to the blimp and flew into it. No way to know. They were going pretty fast, though. Maybe they just couldn't pull out in time." He shrugged. "Maybe they fixated on the target, too. They always tell you not to watch the missile come off the rails."

"So, what do we do now?" Samkamka asked with a healthy amount of fear in his voice.

"We destroy the antenna," Bowden said, and his voice dropped to little more than a whisper. "It's all on us now."

Dork's stomach groaned as the squad came to a halt unexpectedly. He put his hands on his knees, trying desperately to keep everything inside where it belonged, but the pressure was building up, and if he didn't get a rest stop soon, there *were* going to be issues. Explosive, nasty ones.

"Hey, Sublete," Sergeant Cook said. "Have you heard anything from the aviators yet?"

"No," the radioman replied. "I may not, either, as long as we're down in this ass-crack."

"According to the map, we've got about a mile to go, and then we'll be at the target. We'll pop up when we get there. No sense giving ourselves away early."

Aliza looked at her watch. "According to what I was told and where we are, we should be hearing something very soon."

As if she'd called it into being, the ground rumbled slightly. Seconds later, a *Boom!* rolled over them.

"What was that?" Aliza asked. "Are they bombing already?"

"I've been bombed before," Sergeant Cook said. "That didn't sound like a bomb, but something definitely blew up."

"We had better hurry then," Aliza said.

"Can I get a couple of minutes for a rest stop?" Dork asked. "I think I got some bad jerky or something. My insides are tied up in a knot, and I'm about to explode. I need to stop."

"Seriously, Dork?" Cook said. "We're almost there and you need to take a crap? *Now?*"

"I can't run with confidence," Dork replied. "I'm having to squeeze my cheeks together, *hard*, just to walk."

"Oh, for fuck's sake," Cook said. "We don't have time for this. Take your crap and catch up to us." He looked at his map. "There's only one fork in front of us. When you get there, go right."

"I'll be right with you," Dork said, stepping aside as everyone went past. No matter how badly he had to go, he couldn't do it with the woman watching. That wouldn't be right. Once she was out of sight, though, he couldn't get his trousers down fast enough.

Chapter Seventy-Seven

R'BAK

"Blow up the antenna?" Samkamka asked. "All by ourselves? How?"

"Well, first we're going to have to blow up that last blimp, then we're going to have to self-designate the control station for the antenna and bomb the shit out of it."

"But I thought we needed to drop the transmitter facility, too."

Bowden shrugged. "It would be nice if we could, but we don't have a chance in hell of doing it. In my Hornet, back home? Sure, I could do that. With all this jury-rigged shit? I'll be happy to just take the control station out. Even so, the columns being led by Moorefield and Tapper will probably still have to roll in here hard and hit this thing again. If they can push through, that is. Our intel on ground defenses was incomplete to start with, and we haven't had an update in forty-eight hours. But at least the satraps won't get a message off today or any time for the next week or two."

"I think we should abort the mission," Samkamka said. "We no longer have the other aircraft to ensure success."

"No, we don't," Bowden said, "but this mission was planned all along as something one aircraft could do, it if had to." *It just wasn't supposed to be mine!* "We had three airborne so that two could make it to the target and at least one would have weapons that worked and could hit the array." He shook his head. "No. We press on."

"I am the pilot of this craft. If I say we go back, then we go back."

"Sure you are, Samkamka, and if that's what you decide, I can't stop you, but let's look at what's already been invested in this attack. One aircraft with its gear ripped off is back at the airfield. That plane will fly again—maybe—but not for a while. The one Ferenc and Byrd were in is *gone*. And we're *never* going to have the opportunity that we do now.

"What's worse, though, is that the J'Stull are almost ready to transmit. If we don't stop them—now, today—then they're going to get a message off to Kulsis. I'm not going to be the one who could have stopped it but didn't. If we go back without hitting the target, *you're* the one who's going to have to explain it to the Primus. You'll have to explain why you chickened out and decided not to attack the target when we were within visual range with a full bomb load and only one blimp in our way."

Samkamka shied away at the mention of the Primus, and Bowden knew he had him.

"So, what's it going to be?" Bowden asked. "Are we going to do this, or are we going to go back to base with our tails between our legs?"

"I do not have a tail," Samkamka muttered stubbornly. Bowden continued to glare at him, and the pilot finally sighed. "Yes, we will do this, but I do not want to fly into the blimp."

"Neither do I," Bowden said. *Nor do I want to do the rest of this crap, but there's no one else who can.* He set his shoulders and looked out the front windscreen. "Let's keep the airspeed at about 700 kilometers per hour. That will be fast enough to make us hard to hit, but slow enough to get things done."

"What do I do?"

"You fly this thing straight at the blimp, and I'll fire the missile. We'll take out the blimp, then come back around to drop bombs on the control station. Sound good?"

"No."

"What's wrong?"

"You left out, 'Then we fly home and get drunk with the local women.'"

Bowden smiled. "Okay, after we drop our bombs and flatten the control station, we fly home and get drunk with the local women."

Samkamka laughed long and hard. "Now that, my friend, is a plan I can embrace. Let us do precisely that."

Dork cleaned up the best he could, pulled his pants up, and grabbed the designator pack. It had taken a little longer than he'd wanted, but now he knew he could jog; he would catch up to the squad in no time.

Two minutes later, he came to the fork in the crevice and stopped, unable to remember which way Sergeant Cook had said to go. The ground was hard, and there were no boot prints he could use to indicate the correct direction of travel.

"I think he said to go right," Dork said. In fact, he was pretty sure the sergeant had said to go right, but the longer he looked at the two passages, the more he doubted his memory and sense of direction.

"Right is always right," he said, "but I'm always wrong, so I'm going to go left."

His mind made up, he hustled down the left-hand cleft in the surrounding rock formations.

Samkamka pointed the nose of the craft at the blimp in the distance and advanced the throttles.

"Not too fast," Bowden warned. "And don't watch the missile when it launches."

"Just perform your tasks and allow me to fly the craft." Samkamka's voice was testy, but his statement sounded like it was still half-request.

"Sure." Bowden said. Getting into a pissing match inbound to the target wasn't the best way to score hits.

Bowden risked a glance at the ground in front of them. The town extended for several kilometers, almost to where two fingers stuck out from the mountain range behind it. The massive dish sat in the little valley between the two projections, with some sort of militia or army base in front of it.

He could see a number of vehicles, tents, and small figures running around as they approached. The men wouldn't be much of a factor this time, as they didn't have to fly over the base, but they'd have to fly over all of them on the bombing run. *That's going to suck.*

His eyes snapped back up to find the blimp growing in the windscreen. It really was a monster, its lifting bag more than a hundred meters from end to end and held together by a latticework of heavy ropes, like a coarse fishing net. Hanging beneath the envelope was a long, enclosed gondola with two propellers mounted amidships and an exhaust stack projecting to its starboard.

And now they were almost co-altitude with it. "Master arm is on," Bowden said, throwing the switch. "Port Sidewinder selected."

He looked back up in time to see several tracers arc up in front of them. He pointed them out to Samkamka "Tracers. Every fifth or tenth bullet is one of those, so the guys on the ground can tell where they're aiming."

"Shit!" Samkamka exclaimed as he jerked the craft away from the tracer streams. "There are more bullets than the ones I can see?"

Bowden chuckled. "Yeah, lots. Bring us back onto the target."

Samkamka gingerly pushed the nose back toward the dirigible. "How can we fly through them? There are so many!"

"Big sky, little airplane," Bowden said, chanting the mantra from back home. Except he wasn't in a little, agile plane anymore; he was in a big, fat, 120-foot-long interface craft that was never meant to dodge ground fire. Or soak it up, if the truth were known.

"If it makes you feel better, move the plane around in three dimensions to make their targeting harder," Bowden suggested. "Just try to keep our nose close to the blimp."

They were only a minute from firing range, and the blimp continued to grow. "Fifteen kilometers," Bowden guessed. "We'll fire when it's at eight."

"Thirteen klicks. Twelve, eleven ..." Bowden's held his finger poised over the release button. "Ten…nine…steady now…"

A stream of tracers flashed in front of the craft, and Samkamka jerked the stick back and right, flinching from the fire as Bowden hit the missile release. The Sidewinder leaped from the rail and roared off into the sky, arcing high over the blimp. Bowden knew there was no chance the seeker would acquire the blimp.

"D'jeq!" Samkamka cursed, trying to push the nose of the plane back down toward the blimp.

"No, no, no!" Bowden exclaimed. "Break right and get us out of here. You're going to run into the blimp!"

Almost too late, Samkamka saw the airship right in front of them, and, at the last instant, yanked the stick back up and right, narrowly averting another mid-air collision.

"What do I do?" Samkamka asked.

"Take us out to fifteen klicks," Bowden said, internally seething but keeping his voice level. "We'll turn back in and set up for the shot again."

Samkamka continued the turn away from the target, and Bowden looked down to turn off the armament switches.

Ptink! Something struck the cockpit blister. The plane seemed to wiggle once, then rolled wings-level; Bowden looked over at Samkamka.

"Big sky, little airplane" was something aviators said to steel their nerves; however, they all knew it was a lie. Never had that been more clear than now. A bullet had pierced the starboard canopy at an angle and gone through Samkamka' neck. Blood painted the back of his seat and the firewall behind as it sprayed out.

Bowden started to unstrap to go to Samkamka' aid, then caught sight of the mountain toward which they were now flying. At high speed.

Chapter Seventy-Eight

R'BAK

Bowden dove back into his seat, slammed the throttles forward, and pulled back and right as hard as he could, continuing the turn they were in before Samkamka was shot. The climbing turn helped him miss the promontory sticking up, but Bowden knew it hadn't been by much. He came back to wings-level in time to see motion out of the right corner of his eye.

A handheld missile plumed up toward him, clearly having acquired lock.

"Shit!" Bowden exclaimed, pushing forward on the stick. He'd climbed so sharply that he'd highlighted himself against the clear sky. He pulled toward the missile in a diving turn, taking the engines out of the missile's field of view, and watched as the missile went ballistic, unable to keep track of him.

Luckily, the weapon had been an early-model IR missile. A more advanced model, something like an SA-18, wouldn't have been fooled as easily. He breathed a sigh of relief.

However, the close call answered the question of whether or not the satrap's forces had missiles. *Great. One more thing to watch for.*

He pulled out of the dive at about 100 feet and retarded the throttles to keep from over-speeding his ordnance. A quick glance showed Samkamka not only dead but ghostly pale; the bullet had clipped his carotid artery.

One more investment in the success of this mission. Having talked Samkamka into staying, he owed it to the man to successfully complete it.

Bowden took a deep, steadying breath and turned back toward the blimp. Samkamka's death actually simplified things; now he was flying his own aircraft again, and it was just like being back in his Hornet. Except it was about two and a half times as big and about as graceful as a giant pig in a concrete hang-glider. Aside from that, it was just like flying over Somalia again—*No, don't think about Somalia. Focus on the mission.*

He steadied up with his nose on the target, descended to about fifty feet, and pushed the throttles forward again as he raced toward the target. At least there weren't any power lines here to worry about. Hell, if B-52s could fly this low, he could, too. *Too bad I don't have their terrain-following gear.*

Bowden glanced at the jury-rigged armament panel, selected the other Sidewinder, then turned the master armament switch on. Not having to deal with Samkamka meant he could run the attack exactly how he wanted, and he focused on the long, enclosed gondola. A thin haze trailed behind the exhaust stack projecting to its starboard. *Perfect.* The dirigible's power plant was on and operational. He wasn't concerned with the two propellers on the midships rail; they weren't hot enough for the improvised missile to see.

He gently tapped the thruster that functioned like the rudder in his old F/A-18 Hornet and brought the craft into alignment with the blimp. He pulled back slightly so the nose of the missile was pointed at the gondola, which—by staying low—he had highlighted on the open sky behind it. He noticed the tracers reaching up for him out of his peripheral vision, but he was too low and fast for them to hit him—he hoped—and he wasn't going to mess up the shot by yanking the plane away from his target.

Easy...nice and easy...gotcha, bitch!

He slapped the launch button, and the Sidewinder leaped from the wing and raced toward the blimp. The airship yawed to its port, trying to follow his craft so the men inside could shoot at him—but even though the interface craft was a pig, it was far more maneuverable than a blimp, and he was away from it and turning outbound before its crew had a shot at him.

Bowden chuckled. *Not like you have a chance in hell of hitting me.*

Still, Bowden put the craft into a right-hand 360 that took him to the other side of the J'Stull town. Whether the missile worked or not, he wasn't going to play chicken with a craft that was as big as a football field. He was parallel to it when the missile hit.

The left rear of gondola blasted outward in a spray of planks and struts and fire leaped forward from the impact point, several of the burning flares from the warhead punching upward into the gas bag. The center of the envelope turned into a sun as the gas caught fire, and Bowden flinched away from the flash. When he looked again, the center of the blimp had crumpled, and the gondola's weight was pulling the front and back of the airship together as it fell from the sky.

Flames roared across the lifting bag and the gondola, and several figures fell from the structure. Bowden winced but understood. Given the choice between dying from the impact at the bottom of the fall and being burned alive, Bowden reflected he would have jumped, too. Hell, for all he knew, the jump might even be survivable.

He wrapped the turn up harder to get around as quickly as possible; the way to the target was now clear. He eased the interface craft back to 200 feet and turned toward the massive dish on the other side of the town.

Bowden selected two of the Skipper stations, turned on the laser designator, then swore when the "Ready" light didn't illuminate on the panel. Worse, the TV screen that should have shown him a view of where the laser was pointing stayed black, rather than bringing up an image. He cycled the switch again. Nothing.

Damn it! He leaned forward then looked out the window to where the laser package was mounted. He could just see the device…and several wires flapping in the wind, having come undone, just like he'd warned the SpinDogs would happen.

Whether something had hit them or they hadn't been able to withstand the speeds at which the craft had traveled didn't matter. The designator wasn't fixable in flight, and his worst fear was confirmed.

He was screwed.

As screwed as screwed gets.

"Has anyone seen Dork yet?" Aliza asked as they came to the end of the crevice and crawled up to the top to look around.

"Want me to send someone back to look for him?" Cook asked when the rest of the squad replied in the negative.

Aliza shook her head. "There's no time." She looked out over the plain and pointed. "Look—there are several big fires. The planes have already come and gone, and the antenna is still standing."

"And it will remain standing," a voice from behind her said.

Aliza spun to find twenty men along the edge of the crevice—in good cover—pointing rifles at the squad.

"Put your hands up," the man commanded, "and no one has to die. As you can see from the fireballs out there, your mission has failed."

Chapter Seventy-Nine

R'BAK

Bowden did a right 180 and headed outbound while he tried to think. He took a deep breath. He wasn't *totally* screwed—the mission was still salvageable if he could get a hold of the ground team. Maybe they were in position.

"Cookie, this is Hornet," he transmitted. "You there? I say again, Cookie, this is Hornet. Come in if you can hear me. Over."

Nothing.

He tried it again but didn't get any response.

Well, fuck.

The bombs he was carrying were less than useless without a laser designator. The rocket motors were hard-wired to fire when they were droppcd, so he couldn't drop them as dumb bombs; they would race off in search of a laser spot. Where would they hit? There was no way to tell. Way beyond the target.

I'm not launching them just to kill another child.

The bombs were out. He didn't have any missiles. He had to complete the mission, *now*. If there'd been time, he could have gone back to the base and gotten the other laser designator or reconnected the wires on the one he had. But that meant another takeoff, and he wasn't sure the SpinDogs had any more pilots with enough in-atmosphere experience. Perhaps Burg Hrensku had survived the wreck earlier, but if not, they'd have to bring someone down from orbit.

And there wasn't time for any of that.

A flashing light from the instrument panel caught his eye. Low fuel. He looked out the window and could see a line of holes across the wing. Fuel was wicking faintly out of them. Unfortunately, it was also probably pouring out of the matching set on the underside of the wing.

The gauge read just over one quarter full but was noticeably dropping.

He had enough for one run, maybe two, then he'd be bingo fuel.

But, he realized with a sudden, cool calm, with no way to target the bombs, there wouldn't be any need for a second run. The only weapon he had was the interface craft itself. And crashing it would be enough to take out the suspended antenna, which would set the satraps back months, if not years.

He sighed, his mind made up. When he'd signed his commissioning papers, he'd known that one day he might have to give his life on a foreign shore. He hadn't realized it would be one *so far* away from home, but if it were, so be it. It was the only way he could buy the rest of the Lost Soldiers the time they needed to set up their base. And maybe this would—in some small way—make up for Somalia. Make up for the death of that little girl.

He began a climbing turn back inbound to the target and pushed the throttles forward. Speed was better on this run—he only needed to keep the missiles away from him for a few seconds; after that, they could chase him down and add to the destruction. A fitting pyre for him and the rest of those lost on the most screwed up mission he had ever flown. Murphy's Law, indeed.

The antenna was easy to find. He pointed the nose of the craft at it and leveled off. His airspeed continued to build as he raced to his doom.

"Guys?" Dork called, running as fast as he could with the pack on his back. "This ain't funny! Where'd y'all go?"

He'd about come to the conclusion that he'd gone the wrong way at the intersection when he got to the dead end. There was no way forward. The sides of the crevice were worse than sheer—they leaned inward—and they were about five meters high and too far apart to use one to climb up the other. He tried to climb it a couple of times but couldn't find adequate hand- and foot-holds.

His stomach sank; he'd gone the wrong way, and he wouldn't have time to catch up with the rest of the squad before the planes arrived. He could hear distant gunfire, and then—with a roar—one of the craft raced overhead with a white plume coming from its right wing. They were already here and in combat! The quick flash he'd seen of the plane had shown it still had all its bombs attached—*the pilots had counted on him, and he had failed!*

Slowly, he slid down the side of the crevice, tears wetting his cheeks for a moment before the heat dried them into itchy, salt-crusted lines. It was just like Vietnam all over again. He'd been separated from his squad and, when they'd needed the machinegun he'd been carrying, he'd gotten lost. He'd heard the fighting, but by the time he found the squad, they'd all been killed. A man in sunglasses had shown up, and then he'd woken up here—only to repeat the process all over again.

They were right—all of them—to call him dumb, clumsy, and stupid. He *was* a dork. The tears fell, and he was unable to stop them.

Sniff! Grunt!

He looked up at the unexpected noise and saw one of the whinnies looking down at him. It looked like Scout, but Dork didn't have enough time around the creatures to know for sure. The whinnie stared down at him with its head cocked to the side, grunted again, then flipped his head in a motion that looked like, "Come on up."

Dork held up his hands. "I'd love to come up, boy, but I can't make it."

The whinnie looked down the crevice, then sprang into it with him. The passage widened at the end, and there was enough room for the whinnie—barely—though he scraped Dork's side getting into it. The whinnie then knelt and looked back over his shoulder at Dork expectantly.

"You can get us out of here?" Dork asked. He clambered up and onto the whinnie. The creature looked back at Dork as it stood, then looked at the wall of the crevice.

"Got it. You want me to hold on," Dork said. He grabbed the neck of the big lizard, clenched his legs hard against its flanks, and the whinnie sprang forward. As it reached the end of the passageway, it sprang up and to the left, bounced once, twisting as it did so, to land on the ground above the crevice.

Dork hit the ground like a sack of potatoes, having lost his grip when the whinnie twisted, *but he was out!* Better yet, he'd protected the box in his pack, at the cost of some lacerations on his back and what felt like a few cracked ribs.

"Thank you!" he exclaimed as he struggled to his feet. His back was on fire and breathing hurt, but he ignored it, knowing he had only seconds left before the plane came back—if it made it back at all. He snapped out the tripod's legs and turned the box on.

He scanned the surroundings, and his eyes widened—not only was Scout there, but it looked like the whole pack of whinnies had followed them. The group stood around as if waiting to be told what to do next.

"We'll go find my friends in just a minute," he said, "but first I have to do something."

Although he could see the antenna—it was impossible to miss—he couldn't see the control station because a series of low hills intervened. He ran up the side of one hill with the mule, *and there it was!* It was a long designate at about 2,500 meters, but it was within the pre-briefed range.

A quick glance to the south showed the plane was already inbound and appeared to be moving faster than what he'd thought the pilot had said he'd be doing. *He only had seconds!*

He dialed in the code—1555—for the control station, found it in the viewfinder, and turned on the laser, hoping—and praying—that this time he wasn't too late.

Chapter Eighty

R'BAK

Tracers arced lazily into the air, but they hadn't anticipated the interface craft's new speed, and they fell behind him. Bowden saw movement as a missile launched parallel with his right wing, but he was in his final dive and gaining speed. There was no way the missile would catch him in time. Even if it guided on him, it was a tricky aspect angle.

His eyes returned to the transmitter facility suspended over the antenna bowl, and he smiled. His life had a purpose again. Take out the transmitter and give the rest of the Lost Soldiers the thing they needed most, time.

A flash of yellow caught his eye, and he glanced at his left panel. *Laser Acquired* and *Code Verified* were illuminated on the Skipper receiver. He'd forgotten to turn off the master arm switch, and the weapons were still armed and ready! And—even though the soldiers weren't talking to him—the missiles were receiving a laser designate!

He was close—maybe too close to the target, but he slapped the release button, and the Skipper roared off the port wing. He glanced right in time to see the other bomb fall away, its rockets failing to ignite.

He dove for the deck and turned toward where the missile had been launched, but a flash of fire caught his eye—the second Skipper's rockets had finally ignited. He started to cheer, but then the surface-to-air missile flashed by and detonated on the bomb. It was tumbling harmlessly when he lost sight of it.

He dipped a wing as he headed outbound, and his eyes found the target as the remaining thousand-pound bomb dove into it and detonated. The building erupted into a fireball that spewed out a rough sphere of metal hail—a million pieces-worth.

Bowden grinned as he looped around the town situated in front of the base. After several passes, it now appeared every satrap flunky who had a weapon was standing on their roofs shooting at him. The only thing he had going for him was that it had been almost ninety years since anyone down there had ever seen an aircraft going as fast as his. They had no idea how far they had to lead him.

Still, some marksman was more intuitive—or lucky—than the others: rounds spattered into the fuselage next to him, stitching upward. He reflexively ducked as the side canopy next to his head starred, but the bullets didn't make it through. Then he was past the jumble of civilian roofs and inbound toward the target.

With only one aircraft remaining, this would be a harder run, and he quickly dialed the codes into his two remaining bombs as he pulled back the throttles.

A red light flashed on the instrument panel. *Emergency—Fuel Low.* The attack run would be even harder if he ran out of gas.

Cook glanced at Aliza, and she shook her head. "Don't," she warned. "There are too many of them."

Cook's shoulders slumped, but even he understood the odds weren't in their favor.

"Place your weapons on the ground," the J'Stull leader said, and all the soldiers—and Aliza—complied.

The radio Sublete was carrying finally came to life. "Cookie, this is Hornet. You there? I say again, Cookie this is Hornet. Come in if you can hear me. Over."

The enemy leader motioned some of his men forward. While several collected the Lost Soldiers' weapons, one grabbed the radio from Sublete and slammed it to the ground, then fired his rifle into it once for good measure.

The leader chuckled. "I'll bet you thought you could just sneak in and blow up our antenna, didn't you? We figured you might try something like that, so we've been watching the crevice on the chance you would. The satrap would *love* to talk to you and find out where your base is so we can get rid of you once and for all. We will have everything well in hand by the time our friends arrive. Some of you may even survive long enough to be questioned by them, too."

"I'll bet you'd love us to talk," Cook said. "But we ain't."

The man slung his rifle over his shoulder and stepped forward. "Oh, I think you will. We have plenty of ways to loosen tongues…" He ran a finger up Aliza's side. "And other things, too."

The soldiers bristled, but Aliza waved them down. "I can take care of myself."

"I am sure you can," the man said, "but—"

The building housing the antenna control station 1,000 meters away exploded in a massive fireball. Most of the men and Aliza threw themselves to the ground.

When nothing else exploded, they climbed back to their feet.

"Failed?" Cook asked. "If that's failure, I can't wait to see what success looks like."

The leader walked over to Cook, drew his pistol, and placed the barrel to Cook's forehead. "You won't see anything because you'll be dead."

Dork whooped with glee and pumped his fist as the antenna control station disintegrated in a sudden blast, and the aircraft screamed past him. Whatever had been coming out of the wing had stopped, but whether that was a good thing or not, he had no idea.

The aircraft still had two bombs under its wings, though, and Dork hastened to type the new code—1666—into the designator. As he flipped the last digit, a whinnie that looked like Athena came running up from the north. It whistled at Scout, and the whinnie took hold of Dork's sleeve and tried to pull him away from the designator.

"What?" Dork asked.

Scout and the rest of the herd ran a few steps in the direction Athena had appeared from. The way Scout looked at him reminded him of an old Lassie movie he'd seen at the drive-in right before he'd left on his fateful deployment to Vietnam.

"You want me to follow you? You know where the rest of the squad is?"

The whinnies pranced a little farther.

"I will, but I have one more thing to do."

The aircraft was coming back, and it looked like every gun on the planet was firing at it. Tracers reached up from everywhere in the city and from the military units camped outside the city. At least two missiles launched.

Dork could see the aircraft was a little slower, and he understood what the pilot was doing. He was going to try to launch one bomb and then the other. They'd talked about such an attack when they were contingency planning but had decided it was impractical because they didn't know if the weapons would work.

He took a deep breath—the pilot wouldn't know there was only one designator down here; he would be expecting two. Dork would have to be perfect. He squared his shoulders, leaned into the designator, and lased the spot where the closest cable was tied into the mountain.

Chapter Eighty-One

R'BAK

Surface-to-air missiles lifted off from all sides as *Laser Acquired* and *Code Verified* illuminated on the Skipper receiver. Bowden realized he was out of time, and he fired the selected Skipper. He then selected the remaining bomb, dialed in the new code, and fired it off in the same direction as the first without waiting for the lights.

Both bombs roared off, and he yanked the craft around, pushing the throttles to the stops. The first bomb hit somewhere—he couldn't tell where because he was dodging missiles—then the craft shuddered as a missile hit the craft, followed a heartbeat later by a second.

The tiny handheld missiles weren't big enough to knock the massive interface craft from the sky, but they were plenty big enough to kill an engine, and a multitude of warning and caution lights illuminated as the starboard motor died.

He pushed the nose down, trying to get below where the enemy forces could see—and shoot at—him as he roared back across the J'Stull town. He started trying to jink, but as soon as he did, the port motor coughed twice, so he settled for straight and level flight to try and get as much distance between him and the town as he could before the engine died from fuel starvation. That was probably better, too, because the large craft hadn't responded correctly to the control input; the thrusters had obviously been hit, as well.

A couple missiles arced over him, and he chuckled. At some point—*right around the time the control station building blew up,* he thought—he'd rediscovered his will to live, and the missiles flying by him impotently gave him a longer lease on life. He'd been prepared to die, but now—for the first time in 133 years—he was finally prepared to live.

A few rifle rounds hit the plane, and he crouched lower in the seat. There was no fuel left in any of the tanks and not much else to blow up; all he had left to protect was himself.

The motor started chugging again as he cleared the city, and he started a gentle climb. Although he hadn't had long to learn the systems of the interface craft, he knew the fuel fed from the aft portion of the tank, and he tried to get every drop he could into the engine.

The port motor lasted about 30 seconds more, and then he became a glider pilot as it cut out and everything in the cockpit died. The sounds of silence quickly overwhelmed him as he searched for an emergency power source. He finally found what he was looking for and pulled the RAT handle. The ram air turbine—nothing more than a small motor that converted his airspeed into electricity by means of a fan blade—extended from the wing, started spinning, and power returned to the cockpit.

The RAT also gave him limited hydraulic power, and he was able to gently turn the craft toward the largest patch of sand he could find. The interface craft had all the glider characteristics of a rock, though, and it was apparent as he descended through 1,000 meters altitude that he wouldn't reach it.

Scout came back to stand over Dork's shoulder and grunted another time.

"I know," Dork said. "You want me to come. We have to finish this." He placed the designator where the first steel cable on the closest mountain tied into the support that had been erected there. The box turned off.

"What the hell?" he exclaimed. He realized immediately what had happened and grabbed his pack to get the other battery. Scout grumbled again, louder.

"I know!" Dork exclaimed. "You're not helping!"

Scout blew out a breath and stepped back as Dork snapped the new battery in and powered the mule back up. He verified the code was still correct, re-centered the cable in his view, and turned on the laser.

He'd only thought every gun had been firing at the aircraft before; now it sounded like World War III as the aircraft approached again, and everyone in the city opened up on it. He could see the first bomb launch from the plane and did his best to hold the laser steady.

Fire blossomed in his view, and he pulled back, set in the third code—1777—and leaned forward into the viewfinder. He frantically steered the viewer up and long, and hit the designate button when he was on-target. He didn't have long to wait; the bomb burst ten seconds later.

"*Damn it!*" As the smoke cleared, he could see the wire was still attached. The platform swayed, though, and he pulled back the view and saw the first bomb had been a success; the first cable had been severed and was hanging limply from the platform. Movement caught his eye, and he zoomed back in on the second cable. It frayed under the additional weight as he watched, and finally separated.

The transmitter arm fell, shattering the giant dish beneath it in a crash that shook the ground underfoot. *We've done it!*

Boom!

He looked up as a missile hit the aircraft, then a second missile that blew off a chunk of the starboard wing. The plane was still flying, though, and it made it past the town before it was lost to sight, although the smoke it was trailing gave a pretty good indication which way it was headed.

Scout grunted again, emphatically.

"Yes," Dork said with a smile. "*Now* we can go."

Chapter Eighty-Two

R'BAK

"That right there!" Cook crowed as the antenna transmitter arm fell 150 meters and crashed into the dish below it. "That's what success looks like *right there!*"

"Halt!" the J'Stull leader called. The squad had been marching toward the military facility through a series of low hills when the plane had come back and fired its last two bombs toward the antenna.

The leader walked up to Cook and pistol whipped him across the temple. Cook collapsed to the ground.

"Bastard!" Aliza said, bending over to help him.

Cook looked up groggily. "That the best you got?" he asked. "You hit like…a sissy."

The leader leaned over and stuck his pistol in Cook's face.

"Go ahead and do it. Won't change the facts, though. You still hit like a little girl."

The leader drew back to strike Cook again but then relaxed and smiled. "I see what you're doing."

"Winning, mostly," Cook said, nodding to the cloud of dust rising from the antenna.

"No, you're trying to make me lose my temper and kill you." The man nodded. "But I won't. I will take you back, and then I will smile while they torture the answers from you."

"Hopefully, they have someone…stronger than you, then," Cook muttered. "Or we'll be at it…all day."

"Don't taunt him anymore," Aliza said quietly. "Save your strength." She looked up suddenly as a whistle sounded.

"What is that?" the leader asked. "Are there more—"

A gun fired, and the man's head exploded.

The satrap soldiers turned to find the source of the shot and didn't see the herd of whinnies pour quietly over the hill behind them. More shots rang out from the unknown gunman, then the whinnies were on them. The giant lizards' assault rolled over the satrap's forces, and the creatures leaped into the air to tackle the opposing soldiers. Wet crunching noises ensued as the lizards bit through skulls and tore out throats.

It was over before the Lost Soldiers could even throw themselves out of harm's way. Some of them picked up scratches from the creatures' horny hides as they raced past, but no one was seriously injured.

Athena stomped one of the soldiers' heads and came over to nuzzle Aliza's shoulder as Dork stood and walked down the hill toward them.

"What?" Aliza asked, looking at the twenty-some whinnies. "How? Where'd these whinnies come from?"

Dork shrugged. "I don't know. I got lost, but then Scout came and found me, along with our whinnies and some others that the big one we met must have rounded up. I designated the targets for the aircraft, but then the whinnies wanted to come and save you, so we set up an ambush." He shrugged again. "Worked pretty well, I think. Those buggers are *smart*."

"That's a hell of a job, Private Dorkhouse," Sergeant Cook said.

"Yes," Aliza added, shaking her head in disbelief. "Well done."

The other men clustered around to pat him on the back.

"Thanks, y'all, but I was just trying to do what I could to make up for my mistake. If I hadn't gotten lost—"

"We might very well have all been captured," Aliza said. "But you *did* get lost, and then you successfully completed the mission, and you saved us from the J'Stull. That's a pretty good day for anyone to have."

"It's not over yet," Dork said.

"Yeah," Cook said. "We need to get the hell out of here before the satrap's forces come looking for us."

"That's not what I was talking about."

Cook's eyebrow rose. "No?"

"No," Dork said. "We've still got an aviator to go save. I think his plane must have crashed on the other side of the city. But there's just one thing…"

"What's that?" Aliza asked.

"I got kinda turned around in the attack," Dork said. "Can someone else lead?"

Bowden woke to a tapping sound. He opened his right eye—the left one didn't seem to be working very well—but then realized his right eye didn't work very well, either. All he could see was yellow. The second thing he noticed was that he was hanging forward in his straps, and the third thing was he hurt all over.

The crash came back to him as he rubbed the dried blood off his left eye and was able to finally open it. The nose gear had collapsed in the crash. The interface craft made a terrible glider, and it had stalled and gone in nose-first. When the gear collapsed, the nose had buried itself in the sand, all the way to the cockpit. At least he'd been out of fuel, so the craft hadn't gone up in a spectacular fireball.

The sudden stop had been painful, though, and he was pretty sure he'd hit his head on the instrument panel. As he focused, he saw a clump of hair on the altimeter. The knob to set the atmospheric pressure was bent to one side. He had a corresponding indentation a couple of inches long above his eyebrow.

The knocking continued, and he realized it was coming from the side window. He turned his head slowly—he didn't think his neck was broken, but it was a definite possibility and he didn't want to take any chances. Dork's happy face was just outside, and he was waving for Bowden to get out of the craft.

Bowden nodded, braced himself on the instrument panel, and unstrapped. He turned to exit the cockpit, saw Samkamka, and more of the flight came back to him. The other craft with Byrd in it was gone. Samkamka was gone, and, judging from the smell, had been dead a little while.

He sighed and continued working to extricate himself. The collapse of the nose gear meant the craft was at about a 30-

degree angle, and it was difficult for him to climb up the cockpit floor to the access door, especially in the shape he was in. Eventually, he figured out how to use the seat as a brace and made it up and out.

Thankfully, the skin of the craft hadn't crumpled, and he was able to unlock the door. It flipped to the side—a gravity assist—and he looked out to see the ground team all mounted on their whinnies.

"Did we win?" Bowden asked. "Because I feel like I was in a plane crash."

"Yes, sir, we did!" Dork exclaimed. He came over and helped Bowden down, although he winced as he did so. "The control building is in a bazillion pieces, and the transmitter got knocked down and wrecked the antenna dish. We did it!"

"Yeah, you did it," Sergeant Cook said. "And, believe it or not, you pissed off about 10,000 J'Stull, who are now on their way to capture us and ask us a lot of painful questions." He pointed to the north, where a cloud of dust could be seen. A larger, fainter one was rising behind it. "That said, I think the attack columns being led by Captain Moorefield and Lieutenant Tapper might cut that process pretty short. But unless we want to find ourselves as the hostages in a very tense situation, I'm thinking we want to be someplace else, right now. Unless we want to experience more of the J'Stull's tender mercies, that is. So, all due respect, sir…but let's get the hell out of here."

"Where are we headed?"

"Home, suh," Dork said as he helped Bowden down. "We're going home."

Chapter Eighty-Three

SPIN ONE

Murphy stared at the final page of the final after-action report. It stared back at him from the computer screen, as if defying him to contradict it…if he dared.

But it *was* hard to believe. Transmitter destroyed. The J'Stull defenders and their regional allies crushed and scattered by Moorefield's and Tapper's mechanized columns. Dozens of fuel-cell APCs captured not just intact, but in perfect condition. Hundreds of serviceable long arms thrown down by the impressed locals. Hundreds of said locals were now eager-to-please POWs ready to spill their guts about what their "enslavers" had said, planned, feared.

The loss of Bowden's flight was a brutal reminder of the grim costs paid for thc victory—but if there was any consolation to be had, the results were certainly an enduring testimony to those who had made the ultimate sacrifice achieving them. Murphy sighed; that kind of rhetoric didn't make him feel any less responsible, any less guilty, for the men lost, but that didn't mean that he wouldn't compose a few memorial words to be spoken at some time and place when all the Lost Soldiers could be gathered together. Wherever and whenever the hell that might be.

He checked his G-shock. Only ten minutes until the Acclamation began. The invitation had been so solemn that he dared not be late, fashionably or otherwise. Just why the SpinDogs called a victory celebration an "Acclamation" was a bit of a mystery, but he'd certainly have the answer by the end of the evening. Or rather, as soon as he could politely extract himself from the event. He leaned forward to turn off the computer…and the screen blanked momentarily. Just before it re-illuminated with a familiar message:

"If alone in a secure environment, enter assigned access code.
N & N."

Murphy realized he had stopped breathing. He exhaled slowly, entered his code, and waited.

Numbers started scrolling across his screen, appearing in clusters and groups. He frowned, wondered at the pattern…and then realized what they were: coordinates. He copied them down, swiped to the next screen.

A long list of entries—labels and descriptions—began scrolling past.

Murphy leaned forward, paused on one, and read greedily. He allowed himself the luxury of a small, hopeful smile as he did.

Max Messina didn't enter the large almost cavernous room in which the Acclamation was being held, although the SpinDogs used the verb "convened." Which had Murphy thinking, for the first time, that maybe something a little more formal was needed to fill the gap between cheap local mufti and duty uniform. But the Ktor hadn't been thoughtful enough to pack a lot in the way of wardrobe options when they had kidnapped him.

Being in that frame of mind, he started when the bay doors opened and revealed a scene that was anything but staid or formal. Well, there was formality in the dress, but it included a lot of variation by Family, age, and personal taste. He had read somewhere that, in Venice of the early 17th century, if you entered a party of the upper classes, you could tell almost everyone's job and social station just by reading the obvious or subtle differences and cues present in their dress and adornment. In point of fact, the prostitutes were every bit as well-marked as the priests.

To the best of Murphy's knowledge, SpinDog society had neither holy men nor whores, but the Venetian paradigm seemed applicable—if only he'd known what the differences in outfits and ornaments signified. Skylights let in the night-cycle twilight of the hydroponic farms that dominated the inner surface of *Spin One*, the various crops reaching toward the axis of rotation where luminous filaments ran the length of the hollow asteroid. The dance floor—such as it was—seemed to be more a central space for interpretive athletic display than anything else.

Max leaned toward Murphy. "Boss, stay where I can see you, okay?"

Murphy shook his head. "Can't promise that, Sergeant. I've got to go where the diplomatic currents carry me tonight."

Max may have cursed under his breath before replying. "Yeah, I get it. Okay. Look, if I go in there, I can't be sure I won't get mobbed up when you need me."

"Then hang back here, Max, and do the best you can."

"You really have to go into that viper pit, sir?"

"C'mon, Max, they're not *all* vipers."

"Yeah, I'm sure there are some rattlers in there, too." But the big man smiled.

Murphy returned the grin, slipped into the room…

And was accosted/greeted before he got three yards in. "Major Murphy!" shouted a person he'd never seen before, wearing the colors of the Otlethes Family. "We are honored that you have come! Acclaim and be Acclaimed." He handed Murphy what looked like a miniature mace and dashed off into the crowd.

Murphy held the mace out at arm's length and looked at it. He looked back at Max. Who shrugged. Murphy returned the shrug and pushed deeper into the room.

Two steps in and the purpose of the mace became clear. Two women, garbed similarly, caught sight of each other, rushed together, and as if they were play-fighting at swords, clashed their maces. The dull *clank* was quite loud and almost everyone in earshot shouted. The shout didn't sound like a word because it wasn't, it was just a distracted roar of approval. Kind of like ardent fans rooting for their favorite team.

Which seemed to be relatively close kin to this mace banging ritual, which always occurred between two individuals who had some similarities in their markings: insignias that identified them as military or security personnel or some equivalent thereof. So: banging maces was apparently about "warriors meeting and letting the world know it."

By the time Murphy caught sight of Anseker Otlethes, he'd grown used to the din, and was able to hear the Primus' shout to join his party. Somehow, without being alerted, the attendees obstructing the path between them melted back to the margins.

Murphy arrived with a small bow which was returned by the half-dozen people with the Primus, including Guild-mother Shumrir and Naliryiz. Anseker looked disappointed. "Major! Will you not use your *fethshern*?"

Murphy followed Anseker's eyes to the mace. "You mean…this?"

"Yes! Of course! It will be an insult for you not to be magnanimous in sharing your glory."

If the reference to a *fethshern* had confused him, encouragement that he "share his glory" was utterly baffling.

Before Anseker could frown, Naliryiz intervened. "The *fethshern* is how warriors greet each other after a great victory, which is what we celebrate at an Acclamation. The clash of a leader's *fethshern* is much sought after by those of lesser renown and rank. You are one of the great victors of this day. Sharing clashes with your *fethshern* is a great honor."

"Ah," said Murphy.

Anseker frowned anyway. "False modesty so profound as yours could be mistaken as a sign of arrogance."

Murphy was now totally flummoxed. "Sorry, come again?"

Shumrir seemed to understand Murphy's confusion. "In our culture, the very proud might affect an unwillingness to clash *fethsherns* out of 'concern' for making the lesser warrior look ridiculous in comparison to the greater one."

Murphy had to spend several seconds figuring that out. "Wow," he murmured.

Anseker caught the surprised sound. "Clearly this is unfamiliar to you."

"It takes arroga—uh, pride to a whole new level, Primus. In my experience, I mean. In my culture, one congratulates or one shuns. There's really nothing much in between. Some might exaggerate their congratulations as a form of mockery, but that's the closest any of our interactions come to what Shumrir just described."

Shumrir looked oddly satisfied. "The directness you describe could be quite refreshing."

Murphy had his balance again. "Besides, Primus, I didn't do any of the fighting. Not one bit of it. For me to claim any honor…well, it would be like trying to make their deeds mine. I just gave orders."

Anseker looked genuinely shocked. "This is true? A war leader's capability and cunning is not deemed as worthy of honor as valor upon the battlefield?"

Murphy wasn't sure how to answer that without leaping into a potential minefield…so he just shrugged.

Anseker stared then shook his head. "I see no dissembling in you, so I can only presume you speak the truth. If so, it is a strange truth…at least, one very unlike our own."

"I hope to mend my ignorance of your ways," Murphy put in, seeing an opportunity to score some points and get away from thc dicey intercultural slalom in the same act.

"I am sure you shall, Major. Now, even if you take no share in the honors of your victory, I would hear of the next steps in your campaign."

Whew, back on safe ground...I think. "Firstly, I ask your forbearance if any of my synopsis repeats information you have already heard."

"He apologizes so much," a rather frail woman murmured too loudly to Naliryiz. "Was he elevated from a lower class?"

"At any rate," Murphy went on, suppressing the urge to grit his teeth, "today's destruction of the transmitter achieves more than preventing a message from reaching Kulsis. It signifies an enormous strategic reversal in that part of R'Bak, specifically the Hamain and the Ashbands immediately to its northwest.

"Twenty-five percent of the satraps that provide support and survey and gathering services for the Harvesters in their most profitable region are now on the deep defensive. This also means that, at least in this region, there is no reason not to establish more routine planetary interface.

"The short-horizon CONOPS…" Murphy saw blank stares. "Um, our immediate concept of operations is to continue to recruit from the local tribes, overrun the towns of the smaller satraps, isolate the larger ones, and cut off and eliminate any columns or patrols they send further than bowshot."

"That will take many warriors," Anseker observed sagely.

"It certainly will," Murphy agreed. "Fortunately, the satraps have not only oppressed but occasionally hunted the local tribes, even when the Harvesters are not present to 'cull' them. Those tribes are eager to repay the favor." *Too eager, in fact.* "Frankly, we have more volunteers than we can organize. The task of turning indig warriors into half-trained soldiers is going to require as many of my men as our combat operations." *More, actually, but no reason to add that detail here.*

Anseker nodded slowly. "I hope the tribes stay by your side when the Searing grows and they know the Kulsians are approaching. Whatever loyalty they feel toward you is unlikely to be as great as their fear of the Harvesters."

Murphy nodded. "However, they might stand with us if, when the Searing comes, the Harvesters still have not arrived to collect the plants they prize or cull the R'Baku they find objectionable."

"As we hope. But there are still no clear plans for ensuring that the Kulsians will not return to this system as they always do."

"Well," Murphy murmured, "I didn't say they wouldn't come to this system…just that they'd never make it down to the surface of R'Bak."

There were a few knowing looks, but mostly startled eyes. A military type without any insignia of rank or unit nodded. "That would sway many *if* it could be made to happen. Only the satraps and their chosen lackeys have any love for the present order."

Another in the circle observed, "You speak as if you intend to expand your operations on R'Bak."

Murphy nodded. "As much as I hate to say it, I don't see an alternative. Dolkar Kormak was correct in at least one of his assertions: this was never going to end with a return to the status quo. Unless the Kulsians discover evidence of a global disaster, they are going to know that something in this system *selectively* annihilated their bush-beaters…er, 'coursers.' And given what I've been told, the enemy Overlords will not stop investigating until they know what that was."

The group was atypically silent and somber before Anseker drew himself up and asked, "Clearly, you have a plan to defeat or deter them. But I cannot foresee how we might fend off the Kulsian fleet when they arrive."

Murphy nodded. "I appreciate the Primus' directness. I am sure he does not wish me to address specifics during these festivities, but, very generally, let me posit a scenario. Let us suppose that the second group of intruders from Kulsis arrives as expected—the surveyors, I think you call them?"

"Yes," Naliryiz answered, "they are responsible for arranging to buy the desired exoflora from the satraps, prospecting more themselves, and organizing the transport that will convey these goods to the downports from which they will be sent to orbit."

Murphy nodded. "So, let us make a safe conjecture: that they are given the additional task of discovering what happened to the coursers. However, upon arriving, they not only fail to find any sign of the coursers' ships but cannot contact any of the raiders on the planet, either. When the surveyors finally venture dirtside, they discover R'Bak almost entirely unchanged, except for the Ashbands north of the Hamain. There, new satraps hold power, who apparently replaced the old ones, recently toppled by a wave of war bands from the wastes. What do the surveyors do then?"

The frail woman—a Breedmistress, judging from her cloudy eyes—answered. "As you suggest, they would begin to investigate more closely, both there on the planet and here in space."

"And how long do you think their investigation would last, particularly if it produced no ready evidence or answers, and their work as surveyors was falling far behind because of all the personnel tied up in solving the mystery of the missing coursers?"

Smiles sprang up. "I doubt they could afford to spend a whole year on it," Naliryiz mused. "The surveyors are not numerous enough to conduct an exhaustive search of the system. And the Harvester fleet does not have the time to seek, identify, and collect what it means to carry back to Kulsis; that is what the surveyors must complete before it arrives."

Murphy nodded. "And so, a year after their arrival, but as much as a year before the Harvester fleet arrives, the surveyors will have to turn their attention to their primary job in this system. And, in rushing to complete those tasks in only half the usual time, they are likely to grow inattentive to anything else. *Very* inattentive."

Anseker's eyes had become sharp, hawklike. "And how would you take advantage of that interval of 'inattentiveness,' Major Murphy?"

"I would launch a surprise attack upon the surveyors' ships."

Confused faces ringed him. "Attack them where?" one goggled. "On the ground? Where they almost never go?"

"No," Murphy replied. "In space."

Anseker was clearly struggling against incredulousness. "But…we do not have the warships needed for such an attack."

Murphy smiled. "You do not have the warships *yet*," he emphasized. "Nor do you have access to the Kulsian secure codes, since monitoring their communications is another necessary asset to ensure the success of such an operation."

Anseker's eyes were narrowed, careful, assessing. "And yet again, you believe that lack can be corrected."

Murphy bowed slightly. "Primus Otlethes, I am sure of it. Now, if you will excuse me, I would take this opportunity to dance with Naliryiz."

He caught up her hand and, without waiting for a response, drew her on to the dance floor. She said something in a Family-specific argot to the group they'd left behind as she trailed him at arm's length.

He drew her to the middle of the floor, where the crowd was thickest. She smiled expectantly…but frowned when she realized Murphy had only stopped long enough to make sure that Anseker's social cluster could no longer see them. He resumed towing her gently to the opposite side of the room.

"Major Murphy, where are we going?" she asked over his shoulder.

"Captain Lee tells me you can pilot a spaceship. Is that correct?"

"Yes, but—?"

"And given your family rank, my research strongly suggests you could requisition one at a moment's notice if you needed to."

"That is a distressingly accurate conjecture. But I do not understa—"

Murphy stopped just before they cleared the far side of the dance floor, turned, and looked her straight in the eyes. "I need you to pilot me somewhere. It will take about a day each way. I wouldn't ask if there was any other way to do it. And you're the only one I trust. Will you take me there?"

Naliryiz blinked at the rapid-fire requests and revelations. Then she nodded. "Yes. I will."

Murphy sighed in relief, smiled. "Good. Let's go."

Chapter Eighty-Four

55 TAURI B
DEEP SPACE

The SpinDog craft was approaching the coordinates that had appeared on Murphy's computer screen. It was moving so slowly that the star field appeared frozen, unchanging.

Naliryiz sighed. "But there is nothing here, Major Murphy. The scanners are still empty."

He nodded, but coaxed, "Give it another minute. Continue to approach."

And sure enough, at that moment, the scanners lit up with a hard contact only 127 meters ahead.

Naliryiz started back from the controls. "That is not possible. Nothing, not even an object so small as these instruments show, could remain unseen by multispectral scanners within the last one hundred kilometers."

Murphy smiled, looked sideways at her. "You need to spend some time with the Dornaani."

"You mean your mysterious allies and benefactors? What is their role in this?"

"I'll tell you some time," he answered as he unstrapped and guided himself slowly over the back of his acceleration couch and into the after compartment.

"Where are you going?" she asked.

"To put my helmet on so I can go out and get that thing."

"Are you sure it is safe?" She sounded worried.

Murphy turned and smiled at her. "Trust me, if we were in any danger from that object, we'd have been dead long before now. Do me a favor and keep track of my vitals. I'll be back soon."

Naliryiz was waiting for Murphy just beyond the inner airlock hatch. "Well," she asked, "what is it?" She stared at the nondescript ovoid in his hands; it wasn't much bigger than one of the propane containers his Dad had used to fire up the grill back home.

"I think it's a buoy of some kind, with a small payload compartment attached here at the bottom. But I can't be sure of that without trying to open it."

"Well, do so," Naliryiz said. She sounded testy. Or anxious. Maybe both.

Murphy looked at her. "There's no reason to be scared."

Naliryiz's face was stern. "I am fearful, but not for me. That is an alien object. And you mean to bring it back to *Spin One*. You may not do so until I have tested it for alien pathogens and other harmful anomalies. If you do not allow me to do so, you shall not bring it on the station."

Murphy shrugged, uncoupled the container, and removed the radio-sized device he had expected to find within. "Knock yourself out," he said.

"You wish me to do myself harm?" she asked, horrified amazement in her voice.

Murphy laughed. "God no, that's just an expression." He smiled gently when he noticed her hands were clenched and bone-white. "Run all your tests. I don't have to be on R'Bak for a few days, so no rush. We've got plenty of time."

R'BAK

The collected cadre of the Lost Soldiers was silent for a moment, enjoying the scene of a desert tableau dominated by their forces. Two Hueys *thup-thup-thupped* in the distance as three dust plumes continued to disappear over different parts of the horizon. An interface shuttle—probably Murphy's—passed overhead, thrusters rotating into vertical mode as it descended toward the small FOB behind them.

Moorefield returned his gaze to the horizon. "I like that view."

"Sir," Chalmers started, "you mean that? You like seeing our guys heading *away*?"

Bo smiled at him. "When they're moving out to surround the satraps in their towns and make their lives narrow and miserable before we come and roll over them? Hell, yes, Chief."

"And the longer they live in fear and uncertainty," Bowden added, "the more likely someone inside those walls will cut a deal with us. Maybe even 'depose' their satrap."

Bruce rested back on her elbows. "Gonna be extra stressful for them, living blind and deaf to what's happening out in the Ashbands. With all the Hueys coming online in the next month, they won't be putting up many balloons to keep watch for anything coming over the horizon. Or, if they do, they'll have just that many fewer balloons."

"Owning the skies is a wonderful thing," Harry Tapper mused philosophically. "Particularly since that gives us the opportunity to see when they're planning to send out a caravan, or a patrol, or a convoy. All for us to cut off and seize."

Jackson looked around the group. "All you officers seem to be forgetting how much training we'll be doing throughout all that."

Moorefield shook his head and laughed. "Oh, I haven't forgotten a bit of that, Sergeant. I'm just trying not to *think* of it."

Tapper nodded. "So many of our people are going to be tied up with training that we won't be able to reserve more than a squad or two for absolutely crucial missions."

Chalmers raised an eyebrow. "It's going to be that bad?"

Tapper shrugged. "Look, the good news is that we're getting recruits faster than we can organize them. But the bad news is that, well, we're getting recruits faster than we can organize them. And because the Ashbanders speak some weird dialect that's half debased Ktor and half something else, we've got a language gap down here. So, we're going to need local trainers."

Moorefield nodded. “They’re the first guinea pigs who’ll go through our training python. And then they’ll have to turn right around and help train more indigs.”

Bruce frowned. “And don’t forget the message we got from Pistol Pete yesterday: that we’re all getting ‘O bumps.’” She glanced apologetically at Chalmers and Jackson. “‘E’ and ‘S’ bumps, too, as I understand it.”

Jackson checked the faces around the group. “Someone want to clue me in, since Chalmers doesn’t bother to share the memos with me.”

Bruce shrugged. “Murphy is leveling out ranks and titles. He says it’s confusing to the locals that some our titles and ‘O’ ranks aren’t consistent. For instance, as an Air Force captain, I’m an O3. But in the Navy—” she nodded at Bowden, who nodded back “—an O3 is a lieutenant.”

Tapper grinned. “So, does that mean I get to call myself a captain, now?”

Moorefield shrugged. “Or we become commanders and lieutenant commanders. No word on the scheme Murphy’s going to use. Although you ask me, I think Makarov is behind this.”

“Yeah,” agreed Bowden, “he’s a smart guy, but he’s got an extra measure of starch in his boxers.”

“Still,” Chalmers drawled, “couldn’t be happening if Murphy didn’t approve it. Like we have the time for that kind of pogue bullshit.” He smiled darkly. “It’s just another way for him to impress us by swinging his bureaucratic dick in our faces—since he doesn’t have an actual one.” When nobody laughed or even grinned, he checked the faces around him, noticed that most were looking away, or over his shoulder. Chalmers sighed. “He’s standing right behind me, isn’t he?”

No one said anything.

“Yup,” Chalmers acknowledged with a nod. “He’s right behind me.”

“There’s probably a crude come-back about that being your favorite position,” Murphy’s voice speculated, “but as an officer and a gentleman, I would never indulge in that kind of humor.”

A few surprised grins sprang up, even a tentative one on Chalmers' face. Jackson was trying very hard not to laugh.

Murphy walked around to stand in front of the view they'd all been enjoying. "Frankly, I'd probably feel the way you do. Like mushrooms: left in the dark and fed shit. So, I don't expect any different when it comes to your opinion of me. I put you in a shit situation, gave you shit missions, and had shit support for you."

He glanced at the scene behind him. "And yet, here you are: king of this hill and every other for hundreds of klicks in all directions." He smiled. "So much for Murphy's Law. You beat it. Every one of you."

Jackson shook his head. "Ya ask me, sir, Murphy's Law never had a *chance* of applying to us." He looked sideways at Chalmers. "'Specially since *some* people here are a whole lot better at breaking laws than following them."

Chalmers shifted uncomfortably. "Well, Jacks, it's like the major says: we were *supposed* to break Murphy's Law."

"So, I guess that makes us Murphy's Law*less*," Bruce quipped through a bubbling laugh.

Harry grinned. "Murphy's Lawless. I like that."

Moorefield nodded. "Yeah, I've heard worse nicknames for a unit."

Bowden hung his head. "And I was going to use that phrase for nose-art. Once I get a ride worthy of the paint."

Chalmers cracked a lopsided grin. "So, what new shit missions with shit support are you here to dole out today, Major?"

Murphy was all business, again. "For a while, none. Right now, the objective is the same for almost all of you: squeeze and smother the satraps and take control of their turf, leaving the largest towns for last. After that…well, we're getting ready for when we finally see inbound ships. Which we'll detect long before they get to this system, thanks to the Dornaani microsats."

Bowden nodded. "And when those ships pop up on those scanners?"

"We start putting the next major attack in motion. Until then, we gather intelligence for the operations we'll activate when they arrive. You'll get the intel priority list in a day or two. Other than that, you've got a lot of Ashbanders to train and units to stand up."

"Gonna take these locals a long time to be anything more than an armed rabble," Jackson observed cautiously.

"Very true, Sergeant, but if we can get just a few companies of modestly trained soldiers on the line, they can function as the tip of the spear. With their new weapons, the tribal warbands can rush in through whatever gaps those companies cut in our enemy's defenses."

"C'mon, Major," Bruce leered sardonically, "training our guys and hunting down occasional satrap troopers? That's it? Sounds like a vacation compared to what we've been doing."

Murphy nodded. "I suppose it does. But I doubt it will work out that way. Still, if the present 'do it yesterday' tempo does ease off, well, that could be a good time to catch up on sleep. Get some R&R. Learn local customs. Make a life." His look settled on Lee. "Wouldn't you say, Captain?"

Upon him uttering the words "make a life," her smile shifted from ironic to almost grateful. "I completely concur, Major."

But Moorefield was frowning. "Something you haven't covered, Major. Let's say everything works out like we want and we're in control of a bunch of satrap towns. How do we occupy, or at least control, them? That's tricky duty for the best-trained soldiers. For the Ashbanders?" Bo shook his head. "There's too much bad blood to leave them in charge. Almost all of them have lost relatives to satrap forces within the last few years alone."

Murphy nodded. "There's no way to control all of that, Bo. But in addition to having a stick—allowing the Ashbanders to 'restore order'—we also have a carrot: anyone in the towns who cooperates with us will almost certainly get rich."

"Where's that money going to come from, sir?"

"The work of their own hands."

Moorefield squinted skeptically. "You never struck me as a wild-eyed optimist. Sir."

"That's because I'm not, Bo. I just got a surprise package of new schematics that Nephew and Nuncle left behind. Those who cooperate get access; those who don't, don't."

Bowden's laugh was sardonic. "And how are the pre-industrial R'Baku going to make any use of replication schematics?"

"They're not, because most of them are not replication schematics, and they're not for military gear. These are plans for simple devices that most village craftsmen could make. Some—like crystal sets for radio reception—would require the better artisans in the bigger towns. But no matter the size of the community, you'll be armed with information that will allow the locals to not only sell new products but will up their technology baseline in a big way. Not to our way of thinking, perhaps, but it will improve their lives—and give us a source of better basic tools."

Bowden still sounded doubtful. "Such as?"

"Drill improvements, easy lighting solutions, time pieces, wagon designs, basic lathes and looms designed for hook up to basic mechanical power sources, smoother and modular gearing for both water- and windmills. All the stuff that apparently hasn't changed in centuries here because, between oppressive and secretive guilds, a Searing which knocks over industry and the knowledge base every century, and Harvesters who raze any progress they consider threatening, the R'Baku can't achieve anything like true industrialization." His gaze swept the sere horizon. "Not that this place makes it easy to begin with."

"Yeah, well," Jackson muttered, "woulda been nice if your bosses had shared all that out at the start."

Murphy surprised everyone by nodding. "It would have been, but it would have also been too big a risk." When frowns sprang up around the group, Murphy expanded. "Look, let's say they shared it at the start. Then let's say that we—all of us Lost Soldiers—got plowed under by the SpinDogs—"

"Damn near happened," Bowden muttered with a glance up in the very general direction of the Spins.

"—or that someone ratted us out to the Kulsians, or they were early arriving and caught us while we were trying to achieve all this." He waved a hand at the horizon behind him. "If any of them got their hands on this basic tech compendium, that would have been like sending them an outline of our—and our bosses'—strategy and ultimate goal—"

"To take the whole planet," Tapper said through an exhale. "And they'd have started to craft their own ambush to spring on *Olsloov*. Because by distributing those basic tech plans, your bosses would have sent a clear message that they actually *do* intend to return, to use R'Bak as some kind of base or staging area."

"So," Bruce asked in a quiet voice, "are the SpinDogs with us on all this?"

Murphy shrugged. "Everything that I've told them about. I'm still working out some details. The biggest problem is time."

"You mean, how soon you can bring the SpinDogs around?"

"No, Bruce: how soon the next group of Kulsians—the surveyors—will show up."

"I thought we had about two years," Bowden muttered.

Murphy shrugged. "Except that timing is based on the operational status quo. But this time, their coursers disappeared after signaling that they were about to investigate an anomaly."

Bowden nodded. "Yeah, the Kulsians are going to accelerate their operational timetable. Probably add some stiffening elements to the usual surveyor TOO."

"So," summarized Moorefield with a sigh, "the clock is still ticking."

Murphy's nod was slow, regretful. "Never stopped, Bo."

"Now *there's* the R'Bak I know and hate," Jackson snarled softly as he started to rise. "Well, I guess it's about time to get back to work."

Chapter Eighty-Five

SPIN ONE

Murphy had just thrown his duffle on his bunk when the door paged. Knowing that Max had already seen and approved whoever it was, he shouted. "It's open."

Naliryiz strode in. Without preamble, she declared, "Our trip has put me in a difficult position. I need to tell Anseker and the Family council something about why we traveled into deep space and what we did there. And I cannot lie."

Murphy made a gentle wave for her to sit. She looked at the chair but did not use it. He shrugged and fell into his own. "There's no problem with that, Naliryiz. I understand. I felt the same way when Bru—er, Captain Lee started spending more time with your Family than she did with us. A commander—a *Bo'Skelm* of whatever rank—needs to know what his subordinates do when they spend time alone with someone from a rival power…or even an ally."

"So, you will tell me what was in the buoy you retrieved?"

He nodded. "More schematics than you would—than I *can*—believe. And from a lot of different sources."

"You mean the different cultures of your planet?"

"Well, that too, but I was talking about different species. Some of the stuff is pretty amazing, the simple solutions other races came up with long ago for problems that we kept bouncing our head into. I suspect they'd feel the same about some of our solutions, but the bottom line is they're all right at our fingertips, now." He considered. "There are some more advanced designs that could be of use to SpinDogs and RockHounds, but it's mostly basic tools and devices that can be built by any metal-working culture, and they'll improve everything from communications to mining to transport. Hell, the list is endless."

She sat. "So, this compendium was compiled for the benefit of the R'Baku, more than us."

"It looks that way, yes."

She nodded. "Thank you." She fidgeted.

Murphy smiled. "I get the feeling we are not done."

She tried to smile back. "I am not sure. Logically, the data would have been stored inside the buoy itself. But the device you removed from the container that was attached to it did not resemble a data storage device. And its manufacture, the shape of the device, did not look the same as that which was used to construct the buoy."

Murphy shrugged. "I won't deny that."

Naliryiz squared her shoulders. "I am of Family Otlethes. Its full trust has been conferred upon me as its most accomplished Healer. I already suspected the purpose of that device was not data storage, and so, am honor-bound to ascertain if I am correct and if its actual purpose and capabilities might bear upon the security of my Family."

Murphy considered. "How it bears upon their security or their strategic considerations?"

Naliryiz frowned. "How are those even different?"

"As I mean them, security concerns would be limited to ascertaining if the device poses a threat to your people. Strategic considerations would include acquiring and relaying all the information you could gather on it, even if your Family had no way to use it and was not threatened by it."

"In short, you are asking if I am just trying to protect my people or am acting as a spy."

"Well, you're not being deceitful, so I wouldn't call you a spy. But an intelligence-gathering asset? Yes, if you are obligated to learn and share every detail that you can."

Naliryiz frowned. "It is an interesting question that has never arisen before. Our relations with other Families and factions have been more clearly and rigidly defined."

Murphy just kept looking at her.

"I can make you no promises, Major," she concluded. "If I am called upon to give an exhaustive accounting of everything I did and saw while with you, then I would be honor-bound to comply."

"And if you weren't *explicitly* ordered to do so?"

"Then I would not feel compelled to add unnecessary details to my report unless my assessment and conscience told me that what you reveal *does* negatively impact the welfare of Family Otlethes."

"Well, then, I'll tell you…because unless Family Otlethes decides to attack us, there's no way this device would reasonably figure in their security considerations." He smiled. "And if Family Otlethes *does* decide to attack us, this little toy probably wouldn't matter much at all. If you decide to, er, 'eliminate' us, we Lost Soldiers would just be a speed bump."

"A what?"

"An almost unnoticeable obstacle." Murphy shrugged. "The device is a translator."

"You mean, such as your leaders used to teach your men our language—well, Old Ktor?"

Murphy cocked his head. "Not as advanced as that. This one is from a less advanced alien species called the Arat Kur."

Naliryiz shook her head. "Then I do not understand how that is of any strategic significance at all. To anyone."

Murphy smiled. "It's a really sophisticated, compact computer. Consider what it's designed to do. Starting with just bits and pieces of a language, it listens to more of that language being spoken in response to statements and questions conveyed in a different, already known language. The more equivalences and vocabulary it learns, the faster its progress in mastering the rest."

She frowned silently for five seconds. Then: "So does that mean it can be used to decrypt coded communications?"

Murphy managed not to start in surprise. *Damn, she is smart;* really *smart.* "Correct. It's not actually designed for that purpose, so it's a 'low-end' substitute, at best.

"But then again, no one in this system uses anything but the most basic computing technology. You have spreadsheets and calculators and word processors and basic image-capturing, but nothing that aids or performs analysis. Which is basically how and why computers can produce—and can crack—really complex cyphers. So, *your* cyphers, while pretty robust against human codebreakers, wouldn't stand a chance against this translator."

Naliryiz nodded. "So, this is what you meant at the Acclamation when you spoke of having access to the Kulsian secure codes and monitoring their communications." She smiled. "But you're not going to tell me where you plan on finding the warships you promised, are you?"

Murphy smiled back. "A guy has to have *some* secrets."

At the word "secrets," her glance flickered toward his left hand. Suddenly, neither one of them were smiling.

"It seems wrong," she said slowly, "that you are the only one who is sharing secrets."

Murphy shrugged. "I am pretty sure that if I asked about any of the ones I'd like answers to, that would be considered rude, threatening, or both."

Naliryiz shared a wan smile. "Most…but not all."

Talk about bait trailed in water. Murphy decided to bite. "Such as?"

"Such as why our Matriarch Kelrevis was down on R'Bak at all; why she placed herself at such risk. Surely, you have wondered. Captain Lee has intimated as much."

Murphy frowned. "I wondered, yes. But I never felt it urgent to discover the answer. I presumed it was a private matter concerning your Family. And I learned a long time ago that nine-tenths of human wisdom is knowing when to mind your own business."

Her smiled widened. "That is indeed wisdom. And Kelrevis's visit was partly a Family decision, but it was one that concerned you, as well."

"Well, if it has to do with the welfare of the Lost Soldiers, then I—"

"No, I mean it concerned *you*, Major Rodger Murphy."

Oh. Well, in that case... "I would be grateful for whatever you feel it proper and prudent to share, Doct—*Healer* Naliryiz."

She seemed to flinch at his use of her formal honorific, but she pressed on. "Matriarch Kelrevis was not just a Breedmistress and our Guild-mother. She was a healer. One of our greatest." Naliryiz paused, as if that revelation alone would be meaningful to Murphy.

He shrugged. "Yes. And so…?"

"So, she saw the signs in you. The first time you came aboard one of our habitats with your two Terran leaders, to meet with us after the space battle."

"The signs?"

Naliryiz glanced at his left hand again.

Murphy nodded. "I see."

"I'm not sure you do. She understood that you were to become the only link between us and your leaders. I believe they revealed to her that there were some secrets—and some resources—they would share only with you. That they could not answer for what the Lost Soldiers might do, or with whom they might ally, if you died. No matter the cause."

"And that's why you trusted Maximilliano Messina with so much information, so quickly?"

Naliryiz shrugged. "It was better that your bodyguard should be one of your own. It was far better that ours remain distant."

"Wait, *you* had a bodyguard watching me?"

She nodded. "How could we take the risk of *not* protecting you, when so much was at stake? And that is also why the Matriarch traveled to the surface of R'Bak: to try to find a cure for your condition."

"I'm sorry to keep correcting you, but I don't have—"

"You have a disease called—" she stopped as she took care to utter the unfamiliar words in English "—multiple sclerosis. Our term for it translates roughly as 'coated neurons.'"

Murphy's body felt like it was being dipped in ice water. He discovered that he was staring at her. "How did you learn that term? How did you learn about the disease at all? I thought it was unknown among—"

"It is unknown amongst both Dogs and Hounds. But on the planet, its precursors occasionally manifest in the young, aged between eight and twelve of your years."

"What precursors? The…the unsteadiness?"

"No, that is a symptom of the active form of the disease. Here, the most common precursor reaction appears years before. Specifically, on R'Bak, there is a food that some children cannot stomach. All those who will one day have this…this 'multiple sclerosis' will find that food not merely unpalatable, but unbearable. It is similar to what you call anaphylactic shock. They are given oral infusions of a root extract, and the disease you call 'multiple sclerosis' never occurs."

"But in an older person like me—"

Naliryiz shook her head. "It is unknown. There are old tales that indicate it might have been an affliction of adults, many centuries past. Mentions of a cure are more the stuff of legend and myth than proven knowledge. But R'Baku alchemists still have records of it."

"And how was it that Matriarch Kelrevis had knowledge of such obscure information?"

Naliryiz smiled slowly. "You have not guessed, yet? In her youth, she too was a liaison. She knew the ways of the communities of the poles. As a healer, she exchanged knowledge with the alchemists. That is why she had to travel to the planet personally. To speak to them and to ensure…"

"…to ensure that her questions could not be intercepted or reported by anyone else. Because the disease is so unknown among your kind that the Hardliners would have deduced that it must have been seen among us. And if the inquiry came from your Family's Matriarch, that implied it had been detected in a person you and the Expansionists deemed essential to the success of our joint plans."

Naliryiz nodded. "There were other considerations. It had been two decades since Kelrevis had been in communication with the villages among which she had traveled as a liaison. She first had to ascertain who among her useful contacts was left alive and remained mentally competent.

"Unfortunately, fate prevented her from making any significant inquiries. Consequently, we remain almost wholly ignorant. We have only what she committed to notes that were shared with me after her death. Those records seem to indicate that for the root extract to be beneficial for adults, it must be exposed to the rays of the true Searing. If harvested earlier, it is too weak to reverse the disease process that has already spent years building in an adult body."

Murphy frowned, refused to allow his hopes to rise and then be dashed by giving any credence to information that owed more to folktales than fact. "Exposed to the rays of the Searing? What does that mean?"

She sighed. "It means that the root is only found reliably in the desert beyond the Ashbands and must be harvested soon after the Searing has begun."

He shrugged. "Well, even if there's some truth behind these legends, it sounds pretty moot. We'll almost certainly have visitors from Kulsis before then."

"Yes, but you say you will have the means of preventing their return."

It was Murphy's turn to sigh. "Military campaigns and courses of disease treatment have at least one thing in common: uncertainty of outcome. In the case of the Harvesters, we have plans, we have growing resources, and we've preserved the advantage of surprise. But from what little we've been able to learn about Kulsis, they have all the other advantages and powerful motivations to keep coming here and getting the exoflora that they seem to value more than gold."

"That is not an exaggeration: they do value it more than gold. Perhaps more than anything."

Murphy raised an eyebrow but kept on the topic. "Which means that Kormak was right when he warned us that we are embarked upon a journey that essentially means jumping from the fire, into the frying pan, and then straight down the nozzle of a blowtorch. Yes, I've got a plan, but I don't know if all the pieces will fall into place, or how well it will work. Hell, we have almost no intelligence on the Overlords of Kulsis and no way to impact their ability to project force into this system."

"Then perhaps you should acquire those capabilities."

Murphy was ready to dismiss her reply as hopelessly ingenuous until he noticed the measured, serious look in her eyes. He nodded. "That is part of the plan, but it depends upon me convincing enough of you SpinDogs to work together. And not just with us, but each other. *Really* work together." He smiled. "Perhaps you could be a good-will ambassador to the Families, encourage that spirit of cooperation?"

She smiled back. "Perhaps I could. However, I cannot hope to convince anyone with mere assurances. I would need to know some specifics of your plan."

"I figured as much. I'll share what I can as soon as I've worked out more of the details."

"And I shall keep you apprised of anything more we might learn about finding a treatment for your multiple sclerosis."

He shrugged. "I wouldn't want anyone taking those kinds of risks on the basis of a half-forgotten myth."

"I understand." She rose. "But you will understand that you have no say in what risks I—*we*—are willing to take to ensure your survival." She nodded. "I suspect we shall talk again soon, Major Murphy."

A moment after she exited, he experienced a sudden regret that he hadn't stolen a few moments to dance with her at the Acclamation…

That thought seemed to set his left hand tremoring. Violently. He closed his eyes, tried willing it to stop, to put it out of his mind.

But the moment he controlled that part of his mind, another part reiterated what he had been feeling for weeks now: *There are too many clocks ticking down.*

And one of them is inside me.

ABOUT THE AUTHOR

Dr. Charles E. Gannon's Caine Riordan hard sf novels (Baen Books) have all been national best-sellers and include four finalists for the Nebula, two for the Dragon Award, and a Compton Crook winner. In 2020, the "Caineverse" expanded into an exclusive imprint, Beyond Terra Press, under the aegis of Chris Kennedy Publishing. It has already brought the essential side series *Murphy's Lawless* to readers, has a second "season" in process, and is also reissuing the anthology *Lost Signals of the Terran Republic.*

Gannon's epic fantasy series, *The Vortex of Worlds*, debuts in 2021. He collaborates w/Eric Flint in the NYT/WSJ bestselling Ring of Fire series, has written two solo novels in John Ringo's Black Tide Rising world, and co-authored three volumes in the Starfire series. He's also worked in the Honorverse, Man-Kzin, and War World universes. His other writing credits include lots of short fiction, table-top roleplaying games (Traveller, 2300 AD, Twilight: 2000, Dark Conspiracy) and years of work as a scriptwriter/producer in NYC.

As a Distinguished Professor of English, Gannon received five Fulbrights. His book *Rumors of War & Infernal Machines* won the 2006 ALA Choice Award for Outstanding Book. He is a frequent subject matter expert for national media venues (NPR, Discovery, etc.) and for various intelligence and defense agencies. He resides in Annapolis, Maryland, with his wife and four living children.

The Caine Riordan Universe

The Caine Riordan series and Terran Republic universe deliver gritty yet doggedly optimistic hard scifi in a world that is a believable and embattled successor to our own. For those who are not familiar with the series' hallmark blend of exploration, alien encounters, intrigue, and action, you can find them all right here:

The **Caine Riordan** series
(Baen Books)

Fire with Fire
Trial by Fire
Raising Caine
Caine's Mutiny
Marque of Caine
Endangered Species (forthcoming)
Protected Species (forthcoming)
Triage (forthcoming, with Eric Flint)

The **Murphy's Lawless** series

Shakes
Obligations
Man-Eater
Promises
Pearl
Waveoff

Other works in the **Terran Republic** universe

Lost Signals (Re-release January 29, 2021)

Since that list includes a winner of the Compton Crook Award, four Nebula finalists, and two Dragon finalists, they're not hard to find. Just go wherever books are sold. Want to learn more about the Caine Riordan series? Easy. Contact any of the publishers, or you can reach out to me at contact@charleseganon.com.

Want to see more of what's going on in the Terran Republic universe? Check out http://www.charlesegannon.com for exclusive written and visual content.

And if you decide you don't want to miss a single new release or announcement, then go to http://charlesegannon.com/wp/sign-up/ to join the all-inclusive mailing list for sneak peeks, special offers, and features you won't see anywhere else.

And most important of all…welcome aboard; we're glad you're here!

The following is an
Excerpt from Book One of the Revelations Cycle:

Cartwright's Cavaliers

Mark Wandrey

Available Now from Seventh Seal Press

eBook, Paperback, and Audio Book

Excerpt from "Cartwright's Cavaliers:"

The last two operational tanks were trapped on their chosen path. Faced with destroyed vehicles front and back, they cut sideways to the edge of the dry river bed they'd been moving along and found several large boulders to maneuver around that allowed them to present a hull-down defensive position. Their troopers rallied on that position. It was starting to look like they'd dig in when Phoenix 1 screamed over and strafed them with dual streams of railgun rounds. A split second later, Phoenix 2 followed on a parallel path. Jim was just cheering the air attack when he saw it. The sixth damned tank, and it was a heavy.

"I got that last tank," Jim said over the command net.

"Observe and stand by," Murdock said.

"We'll have these in hand shortly," Buddha agreed, his transmission interspersed with the thudding of his CASPer firing its magnet accelerator. "We can be there in a few minutes."

Jim examined his battlespace. The tank was massive. It had to be one of the fusion-powered beasts he'd read about. Which meant shields and energy weapons. It was heading down the same gap the APC had taken, so it was heading toward Second Squad, and fast.

"Shit," he said.

"Jim," Hargrave said, "we're in position. What are you doing?"

"Leading," Jim said as he jumped out from the rock wall.

* * * * *

* * * * *

The following is an
Excerpt from Book One of the Salvage Title Trilogy:

Salvage Title

Kevin Steverson

Available Now from Theogony Books

eBook, Paperback, and Audio Book

Excerpt from “Salvage Title:”

The first thing Clip did was get power to the door and the access panel. Two of his power cells did the trick once he had them wired to the container. He then pulled out his slate and connected it. It lit up, and his fingers flew across it. It took him a few minutes to establish a link, then he programmed it to search for the combination to the access panel.

“Is it from a human ship?” Harmon asked, curious.

“I don’t think so, but it doesn’t matter; ones and zeros are still ones and zeros when it comes to computers. It’s universal. I mean, there are some things you have to know to get other races’ computers to run right, but it’s not that hard,” Clip said.

Harmon shook his head. *Riiigghht,* he thought. He knew better. Clip’s intelligence test results were completely off the charts. Clip opted to go to work at Rinto’s right after secondary school because there was nothing for him to learn at the colleges and universities on either Tretra or Joth. He could have received academic scholarships for advanced degrees on a number of nearby systems. He could have even gone all the way to Earth and attended the University of Georgia if he wanted. The problem was getting there. The schools would have provided free tuition if he could just have paid to get there.

Secondary school had been rough on Clip. He was a small guy that made excellent grades without trying. It would have been worse if Harmon hadn’t let everyone know that Clip was his brother. They lived in the same foster center, so it was mostly true. The first day of school, Harmon had laid down the law—if you messed with Clip, you messed up.

At the age of fourteen, he beat three seniors senseless for attempting to put Clip in a trash container. One of them was a Yalteen, a member of a race of large humanoids from two systems over. It wasn’t a fair fight—they should have brought more people with them. Harmon hated bullies.

After the suspension ended, the school’s Warball coach came to see him. He started that season as a freshman and worked on using it to earn a scholarship to the academy. By the time he graduated, he was six feet two inches with two hundred and twenty pounds of muscle. He got the scholarship and a shot at going into space. It was the longest time he'd ever spent away from his foster brother, but he couldn't turn it down.

Clip stayed on Joth and went to work for Rinto. He figured it was a job that would get him access to all kinds of technical stuff, servos, motors, and maybe even some alien computers. The first week he was there, he tweaked the equipment and increased the plant's recycled steel production by 12 percent. Rinto was eternally grateful, as it put him solidly into the profit column instead of toeing the line between profit and loss. When Harmon came back to the planet after the academy, Rinto hired him on the spot on Clip's recommendation. After he saw Harmon operate the grappler and got to know him, he was glad he did.

A steady beeping brought Harmon back to the present. Clip's program had succeeded in unlocking the container. "Right on!" Clip exclaimed. He was always using expressions hundreds or more years out of style. "Let's see what we have; I hope this one isn't empty, too." Last month they'd come across a smaller vault, but it had been empty.

Harmon stepped up and wedged his hands into the small opening the door had made when it disengaged the locks. There wasn't enough power in the small cells Clip used to open it any further. He put his weight into it, and the door opened enough for them to get inside. Before they went in, Harmon placed a piece of pipe in the doorway so it couldn't close and lock on them, baking them alive before anyone realized they were missing.

Daylight shone in through the doorway, and they both froze in place; the weapons vault was full.

* * * * *

* * * * *

Made in United States
Orlando, FL
07 March 2022

15487625R00426